"PROMETHEUS?" MRS. LISLE ASKED AGAIN.

"Yes, ma'am. I know your late husband wrote under that name—I must offer my condolences, belated, I fear. A sad loss to the nation!"

"And to his family," the widow said with quietly sorrowful dignity.

"Of course. I ... er ... You are aware, I daresay, that someone else is now employing Mr. Lisle's pseudonym?"

"Certainly. The person concerned very properly requested my permission."

"Then you know who he is?" Lord Selworth enquired eagerly.

"I regret that I am not at liberty to divulge the name."

His lordship's face fell, but he rallied. "Perhaps I can change your mind, ma'am, when you hear why I wish to approach the gentleman."

Mrs. Lisle's mouth twitched, and she cast a quizzical glance at her elder daughter. For an anxious moment, Pippa feared her mother would be unable to repress the chuckle quivering on her lips.

However, with assumed gravity she replied, "I doubt it, Lord Selworth, but you are at liberty to try."

BOOK YOUR PLACE ON OUR WEBSITE AND MAKE THE READING CONNECTION!

We've created a customized website just for our very special readers, where you can get the inside scoop on everything that's going on with Zebra, Pinnacle and Kensington books.

When you come online, you'll have the exciting opportunity to:

- View covers of upcoming books
- Read sample chapters
- Learn about our future publishing schedule (listed by publication month *and author*)
- Find out when your favorite authors will be visiting a city near you
- Search for and order backlist books from our online catalog
- Check out author bios and background information
- Send e-mail to your favorite authors
- Meet the Kensington staff online
- Join us in weekly chats with authors, readers and other guests
- Get writing guidelines
- AND MUCH MORE!

Visit our website at
http://www.zebrabooks.com

CROSSED QUILLS

Carola Dunn

Zebra Books
Kensington Publishing Corp.

http://www.zebrabooks.com

ZEBRA BOOKS are published by

Kensington Publishing Corp.
850 Third Avenue
New York, NY 10022

First Printing: October, 1998
10 9 8 7 6 5 4 3 2 1

Printed in the United States of America

CHAPTER 1

"Brilliant!" sighed Wynn, tossing the *Political Register* onto the table at his elbow. He leaned back in his chair and reached for his glass of brandy, a superb pre-Revolution vintage. "I'd give my right arm to write like that."

"If you gave your right arm," pointed out the Honorable Gilbert Chubb, "you wouldn't be able to write at all."

Wynn grinned, shaking his head at Chubby's invincible literalism. "My left arm, then. Don't you agree that Prometheus is brilliant? His arguments are well-reasoned yet pithy, both incisive and persuasive. Whereas Cobbett's language is far too incendiary to be taken seriously by anyone but rabble-rousers and the starving masses. Just listen to this bit here."

Chubby groaned as Wynn picked up the *Register* again, the shilling edition. He no longer had to be satisfied with the twopenny pamphlet edition, reduced in size from the newspaper to avoid the stamp tax which put it beyond the reach of the poor.

"No, please!" Chubby begged. "I don't mind listening to your speeches, old chap, but I'll be damned if I'll sit still for any more Prometheus, however pithy."

"My efforts only make you laugh." Wynn kicked gloomily at the nearest of the sheets of close-written foolscap scattered on the hearthrug.

"I didn't laugh."

"You sniggered. I heard you. I don't blame you, mind. There's no denying that the style I developed to write those wretched Gothic romances is as unsuitable for a maiden speech to the House of Lords as a nightshirt in a ballroom. Somehow I just can't seem to keep out the melodrama and bombast."

"Seems to me," said Chubby judiciously, "you were a devilish sight happier writing your romances than you have been since your great-uncle popped off and made you Viscount Selworth."

Wynn glanced around the cosy library, walled with calf-bound books; the solid, old-fashioned oak, beech, and cherrywood furniture gleaming in the light of a dozen wax candles; the fire blazing on the hearth. How could he regret inheriting Kymford? His books—exciting, amusing, and distinctly bawdy—though popular had never afforded more than a meagre supplement to his stepfather's meagre benefice.

Yet he and his family had never been without food or clothes or a roof over their heads. They had even scraped up enough to give his eldest sister a Season on the fringes of Society. In spite of gowns turned, made over, and retrimmed, Albinia had married well, into an ancient if untitled family.

In fact, they had fared splendidly compared to a large proportion of Britain's people, workless and hungry since the end of the war. Now, having inherited a seat in Parliament along with the Selworth title and fortune, Wynn was eager to do his best for his fellow-countrymen.

"Happy or not," he said, "I shan't have a hope of a serious career in politics if anyone gets wind of my authorship of such lamentably unserious tales."

"*I* shan't tell," Chubby assured him.

"No one else knows—except my publisher, naturally—but I can't risk writing any more. The last romance by Valentine

Dred will appear in a month or so. It was fun while it lasted, but it's speeches for me from now on.''

Wearily, he bent down to gather up his latest literary effort. He crumpled the sheets together and tossed them on the fire. The words he had struggled over flared up. Black cinders floated up the chimney.

''Tell you what,'' said Chubby, looking pleased with himself, ''you want to get Prometheus to help you with that speech. I daresay the fellow could turn it out in a trice, just the way you want it.''

''Prometheus is dead.''

''Dammit, he can't be!'' Chubby protested. ''The stuff you read me was all about the universal suffrage petitions and Prinny getting shot at in the Mall. That happened only last week, the twenty-eighth of January, you said. A fine state of affairs when people make excuses for people firing at the Prince Regent!''

''You were listening?'' Wynn said in mock surprise. ''You're right, of course, but so am I.''

''Now you're talking in riddles,'' his friend complained. ''What the deuce do you mean? Either a chap's dead or he ain't.''

''Not Prometheus. He's chained to a rock for eternity with an eagle eating his liver, as punishment for giving fire to mankind.''

''A load of rot, those Greek stories. Stands to reason, he'd die.''

''But he didn't.''

''Cut line, Wynn, do. Maybe that Prometheus is still alive chained to a rock somewhere, but you're not telling me he writes articles for William Cobbett's 'twopenny trash'!''

Wynn laughed. ''All right. 'Prometheus' was commonly known to be the pen-name of Benjamin Lisle, the Radical M.P. Lisle died last year, but Prometheus continues to write—as you pointed out—on current events. No one knows who has taken on the pseudonym. Therefore, I can't approach the gentleman in question to beg his assistance with this devilish speech.''

* * *

The speech lay in abeyance for the following fortnight as Wynn set himself to entertain Chubby, his first guest at Kymford. New to the dignities and responsibilities of a noble landowner, he enjoyed showing off his farms, orchards, woods, and coverts.

He was also glad of the opportunity to consult his friend. Mr. Chubb, heir to a baron, had been brought up to understand the management of a large estate. Though by no means the brightest star in the firmament, he had an almost instinctive grasp of such esoteric (to Wynn) subjects as drainage and crop rotation. He knew almost as much about sheep and cattle as about horses.

"M'father's more of a country squire, you know, than a member of the Ton," he said apologetically, as they halted their mounts by a gate, to gaze out over a field striped with green shoots of winter wheat. "He'd rather spend his blunt on a new breed of milch-cow than on Weston's tailoring—for himself or for me."

Wynn glanced from Chubby's neat but modest brown riding coat, buckskin breeches, and serviceable riding boots, to his own shabby version of the same. He laughed ruefully.

"I've been far too busy moving the family from the rectory to Kymford, exploring the place, and working on my speech to spare a thought for new clothes. I daresay I shall have to dress up to address the House of Lords, if I'm ever satisfied enough with the damn thing to present it."

"You'll have to fig yourself out decently anyway, if your sister's to make her curtsy to Society this spring."

"Millicent won't need me to squire her about. Mama will stay here to look after my stepfather and the children, but Albinia's taking on the whole business, bless her. Debenham is all the escort they will need. My part is just to frank her, which I can afford to do in style now."

"Don't you believe it," Chubby warned. "Mrs. Debenham

and Miss Warren will expect you to do the pretty, too, take my word for it. Thank heaven I haven't any sisters.''

"If you had, you might not find yourself so tongue-tied around young females, old fellow. Though, Lord knows, Millicent seldom lets anyone get a word in edgewise. What a chatterbox!''

"That's all right. It means I don't have to try to come up with something to say to her.''

"Well, I'll be damned if I'm going to dance attendance on the chit, though I'll keep an eye on her until she finds her feet. I'll be too busy with Parliament. Balls and routs and Venetian breakfasts—what a waste of time! Let's ride on. So the land looks to you to be in good heart? You think my bailiff is competent?''

They returned to topics more interesting than clothes and come-outs. Wynn's great-uncle had been an old-fashioned but conscientious landlord. Something of a recluse, long outliving the rest of his immediate family, he had plowed the profits from his rents back into the soil. The farms belonging to Kymford were prosperous, the lesser tenants well housed, and there were funds in Consols besides.

The late Viscount Selworth had kept the early Jacobean manor house in good condition, without attempting to turn it into a mansion. Not wasting his money on building fine porticos or changing casements to sash windows, he had instead installed modern conveniences such as water closets and a closed stove in the kitchen. Comfortable if not smart, to a large family from a small rectory the house seemed the height of luxury.

All in all it was an inheritance to be proud of. Wynn was duly proud, and grateful.

Gratitude to Providence for his good fortune made him all the more anxious to help those less fortunate. His tenants' lot might be improved by the cautious and gradual introduction of the up-to-date agricultural methods Chubby suggested, but they were not in dire need.

"But half the population is destitute," he explained to Albinia some two weeks later.

He had brought Millicent up to London to prepare for her first Season. Persuaded, somewhat against her will, that she was tired from the journey, she had been bundled off to bed for a rest before dinner, leaving her elders to a comfortable cose. George Debenham was out on business, so Wynn was closeted with his favorite sister.

Albinia was, in fact, his only full sister, the rest of his siblings being the offspring of his mother and the Reverend Ernest Warren. Six years Wynn's junior, Mrs. Debenham was a pretty, lively young matron of four-and-twenty summers, with fair hair, blue eyes, and a round, rosy-cheeked face. She had left her two little boys in the country, with their paternal grandparents, to come up to Town and present her half-sister to the Polite World.

Now she looked in dismay at her brother and said, "You are not going to make speeches at me, are you, Wynn dear? I know there is a great deal of poverty, and George and I do what we can to relieve the paupers in our part of the country, I assure you. George says, the need is too great for private charity to suffice."

"Exactly," Wynn exclaimed, jumping up and striding the length of the elegant drawing room. "Nothing will suffice as long as the laws remain unchanged. The Government must be persuaded to act, to lower taxes on necessities and—"

"Wynn, you are speechifying!"

He turned back towards her with a sheepish grin. "Sorry, Bina." Running his hand through hair as fair as hers, he dropped back onto the sofa beside her. "The thing is, I'm a member of the House of Lords now."

"Heavens, so you are! You mean to take your seat?"

"Of course. It's my duty to involve myself in politics since I believe those in power are—"

"Speech!" Albinia protested yet again.

"Speech is the trouble. If I'm to have any influence at all, it's very important that my maiden speech should be well received. And I just can't seem to get the knack of it."

"Of making a speech? Pray do not practice on me."

"Of writing one, to start with. Dash it, if only Benjamin Lisle were still alive!"

"The Member of Parliament? Why?"

Wynn explained about Prometheus. "Lisle's articles used to be a trifle too inflammatory for my taste, but whoever is using his pen-name writes just the sort of thing I want to say, just the way I want to say it. Only no one knows who he is."

"Why not ask his family?" Albinia suggested. "They must surely have given permission for his pen-name to be used."

"I can't very well intrude upon his widow. She don't know me from the Sheik of Araby."

Albinia smiled. "Perhaps not, but she knows me, and her daughter is a friend of mine."

"Bina, you're gammoning me!"

"I am not. Pippa—Philippa—Lisle came out the same year I did, and in much the same circumstances, the difference being that I was lucky and found George. We were both older than most girls in their first Season, neither of us had *entrée* to the inner circles of the *beau monde,* and we both had to make do and mend. We even used to exchange gowns with each other to enlarge our wardrobes."

"You must have been very good friends," Wynn remarked thoughtfully.

"We were, and we have kept in touch with regular letters ever since. You would have met her if you had deigned to put in an appearance at my aunt's house during my Season."

"Can you imagine how things would have gone at home if Papa had been left alone with the children? Besides, you may have had to make do and mend, my dear, but it was out of the question for me to squander the ready on togging myself out to make a decent appearance in Town."

"At a guess," said Albinia, looking him up and down with amusement, "clothes have not precisely been a priority with

you since you *have* been able to afford the proper attire for
your new station in life. You will have to acquire a new wardrobe before Millie is ready to go about.''

''Oh no, I'm not escorting that little bagpipe to balls and
such!''

''Oh yes, you are,'' Albinia calmly contradicted him, ''and
as a reward, I shall give you a letter to deliver to Pippa, as an
excuse for calling.''

''*Lord* Selworth and Mr. Chubb, madam.'' Sukey, the plump,
middle-aged maid, beamed with delight. After a few visits of
condolence on the demise of Mr. Lisle, the nobility had ceased
to call at Sweetbriar Cottage.

As conversation stilled in the small parlor, crowded with
afternoon callers, Pippa looked round in surprise. Selworth?
His lordship must be related to Albinia—which did not explain
his presence here in this out-of-the-way Buckinghamshire village.

Yes, that flyaway flaxen hair was the image of Bina's. A
close relative, then, perhaps the elder brother she used to talk
about in such worshipful tones. She had mentioned a title in a
distant part of the family. The two must have somehow come
together.

Lord Selworth was slim, and not much above middling
height, shorter than his companion, who was tall and lanky,
with an incongruously round face. Both wore riding dress, with
mud-splashed boots. Mr. Chubb, after a quick, nervous glance
about the room, appeared to find a peculiar fascination in the
toes of those boots.

Bashful, poor fellow, Pippa diagnosed. Prematurely thinning
hair doubtless added to his diffidence.

While these thoughts sped through her mind, her mother had
risen to greet the unexpected visitors with her usual placid
friendliness.

''Forgive our intrusion, ma'am,'' Lord Selworth responded

with an attractive smile, "and our dirt. We happened to be passing nearby and I was commissioned by my sister, Mrs. Debenham, to carry a letter to your daughter. Miss Lisle is a friend of long-standing, I collect."

"Yes, indeed. Pippa, my love."

Passing nearby? Whence and whither, Pippa wondered as she rose to make her curtsy. The village was well off any beaten track, lost in beechwoods at the back of beyond. And she had received a letter from Bina only a fortnight since, she recalled.

"And this is our vicar, Mr. Postlethwaite, Lord Selworth," Mrs. Lisle continued, then turned away to say, "Mr. Chubb, do let me make you known to my younger daughter, Kitty."

Lord Selworth bowed to Pippa and exchanged bows with Mr. Postlethwaite. The vicar looked decidedly discomposed. A perennial suitor of Pippa's, he was a pleasant, worthy gentleman she occasionally considered accepting. Never for long, though. He would be shocked to the core should she ever dare reveal her unorthodox views on the Established Church.

However, he clearly looked upon Lord Selworth as a rival. Ridiculous, when Pippa had so far exchanged no more than a how-do-you-do with Bina's brother, who would doubtless be on his way after a polite five minutes, never to be seen again.

A pity, she thought wistfully. While he was not precisely handsome, at close quarters his lordship's smile was simply devastating. Pippa could not help returning it.

"You have a letter for me, Lord Selworth?"

"Oh, yes." He felt in the pocket of his dark brown riding coat—on the verge of fraying at the cuffs, she noted. His title must have descended to him without a fortune. "Dash it, where did I put the thing?" He felt in the opposite pocket, then in the inside breast pocket. "Ah, here it is."

Taking the folded missive, Pippa set it aside for later perusal. Odd that he should have had to fumble for it, when it was his sole reason for calling. "Mrs. Debenham is well, I trust, sir?" she said.

"In fine fettle, Miss Lisle. She is looking forward to the coming Season."

"She is to bring out your sister, is she not? She mentioned Miss Millicent Warren's come-out in her last letter. Has she gone up to London already?"

How awkward it was to make polite conversation standing up in the cramped parlor! Pippa's eyes were on a level with his chin—a strong, determined chin—and she was too close to glance up without appearing arch. On the other hand, not raising her gaze must make her look timidly demure, equally at odds with her character. She wished she might invite him to sit down, but the vicar clung tenaciously to her side and there were not seats enough for all.

Ah, the Misses Bradshaw were half-reluctantly taking their leave. The news of Lord Selworth's visit would be all over the village within the half hour.

"Excuse me, my lord, I must see Miss Bradshaw and Miss Dorothy out." Pippa did not want the old dears to feel slighted by her paying more attention to a nobleman, a fleeting acquaintance, than to her neighbors. Daughters of the previous vicar, they lived in greatly reduced circumstances.

Several minutes passed in the presentation of a jar of strawberry jam and effusive thanks therefor. Returning from the front door across the tiny hall, Pippa paused on the parlor's threshold.

His lordship and his friend had taken the Misses Bradshaws' chairs. The speechless Mr. Chubb sat next to Kitty. She was being kind to him in between making arrangements with her friend Mary, Squire Ruddock's daughter, to visit the Hall to play duets upon the new pianoforte.

Across from them, gazing fixedly at Kitty, Mary's brother John appeared to be suffering from an acute attack of indigestion. He had recently taken to attempting to ape Lord Byron's romantically brooding manner, without much success to date. Kitty was worth gazing upon, though, thought her partial sister. The amber shade of her high-waisted kerseymere gown complemented her dark curls beautifully, and her rosy cheeks never looked sallow.

Lord Selworth, seated next to Mrs. Lisle, conversed courteously with his hostess and Mrs. Stockton, the apothecary's stout wife. He smiled again at Pippa, who was hesitating in the doorway. Her heart did a most peculiar flip-flop.

Drat the man, did he realize how disturbing his smile was? Could he not keep a straight face? Still, he would be leaving any minute. He and Mr. Chubb had no doubt awaited her return to the parlor to make their farewells, to avoid adding to the crush in the minuscule entry. If Pippa returned to her seat beside the vicar, which she was most unwilling to do, she would only have to pop up again to say goodbye.

But, though the gentlemen rose politely when she failed to sit down at once, Lord Selworth showed no sign of departing. Rather than keep them on their feet, Pippa subsided perforce.

She was forced to listen to a low-voiced soliloquy from Mr. Postlethwaite, on the subject of Town Bucks and their extravagant, self-indulgent habits. Never had she had less patience with that good man.

Mary completed her business with Kitty and dragged her brother away to escort her home. Mrs. and Miss Welladay and Miss Jane Welladay, wife and daughters of a yeoman farmer, stopped by on their way home from market, to show off some French merino bought at a bargain. Leaving, they bore off Mrs. Stockton with them. Lord Selworth and Mr. Chubb stayed and stayed. So, determinedly, did the vicar.

Conversation becoming general, the weather for the past three months was discussed in excruciating detail. Pippa was nearly ready to scream when the maidservant from the vicarage arrived with a message from Mrs. Postlethwaite, desiring her son's presence at home.

"I shall be glad to set you in the right way, my lord," said Mr. Postlethwaite in a last-ditch effort to outflank his enemy. "The lanes hereabouts are lamentably confusing to the uninitiated."

"I thank you, sir," Lord Selworth replied cordially, "but Chubb and I are in no hurry. That is, we don't object to going a little astray, seeing something more of the fine countryside in this part of the world."

The vicar left, disgruntled.

Pippa's suspicions redoubled. To be sure, the country was beautiful—in June. Now, at the end of February, it was a study in sodden, muddy sepias and duns. No flush of green yet tipped the beech trees' boughs; thorny hedgerows dripped, honeysuckle and dog-rose a distant dream; the bottoms were mired ankle-deep. Walking abroad was a penance, riding no pleasure. What was Lord Selworth up to?

She soon found out. He turned to her mother and said coaxingly, "Mrs. Lisle, I must confess to being here under false pretences. I have come to speak to you about Prometheus."

Her head whirling, Pippa gripped her hands tightly in her lap. Had the Government sent him? Surely William Cobbett had not given away Prometheus' true identity. However much trouble he was in, blamed for civil disorders all over the nation, the publisher, editor, and chief contributor to the *Political Register* would not betray his friends.

Cobbett was a true and generous friend, who paid liberally for Prometheus' articles despite his own financial woes. Without that income, the Lisles would be in sore straits—and the income would cease if the world discovered who had taken over Benjamin Lisle's pen-name.

Cobbett could not afford to go on publishing articles the world did not take seriously. How much influence would they exert if it became known that the author was a mere female?

And a youthful female, at that!

CHAPTER 2

"Prometheus?" said Mrs. Lisle cautiously. Avoiding Lord Selworth's eye, she tucked a graying curl under her lilac-ribboned cap.

Pippa regarded her mother with affection. Mama's calm nature, especially in contrast to Papa's quicksilver intellect, led some to consider her slow-witted. Not so her elder daughter.

Mr. Lisle's political career had been founded on the bedrock of his wife's common sense and exceptional ability to hold household. Too principled to accept the perquisites of his seat in the House of Commons, the sinecures and outright bribes offered for his support, he had relied on her to contrive on their small income. She had succeeded to admiration. Their home was a modest but comfortable haven whither he retreated every weekend during the Parliamentary sessions.

She had taught their daughters herself, not only the house-wifely arts, but such ladylike accomplishments as music, fine needlework, watercolors, and dancing. It was not Mama's fault that Pippa had not "taken" during her one scrimped and saved-for London Season.

Skinny and dark when the fashion was for well-rounded blondes, more interested in politics and rhetoric than fashion and gossip, Pippa herself was to blame. For Mama's sake, she had done her best to conform, and Mama had never reproached her for failing to catch a husband. Papa was pleased, since, escaping with relief back to Sweetbriar Cottage, his daughter resumed the making of fair copies of his speeches and articles.

As his health deteriorated, Pippa had taken more and more responsibility for the content and phrasing of his work. When he went to his reward in the Afterlife in which he disbelieved, what more natural than that she should take on the mantle of Prometheus?

Mama would never give away the secret, neither on purpose nor inadvertently. Nor would Kitty, as practical and common-sensical as their mother in spite of being the prettiest girl in the entire neighborhood.

Pippa glanced at her young sister. Kitty's sparkling brown eyes met hers in a look brimming with merriment. At the same time, she continued to tell Mr. Chubb quite seriously about the poultry which were her especial care. The bashful young man seemed interested, and even ventured a question. Dear Kitty had quickly set him at his ease.

Lord Selworth, to the contrary, had lost his appearance of ease. Under Mama's questioning gaze, he ran his hand through his hair with an air of harassed uncertainty. He opened his mouth, but no words issued forth.

"Prometheus?" Mrs. Lisle asked again.

"Yes, ma'am. I know your late husband wrote under that name—I must offer my condolences, belated, I fear. A sad loss to the nation!"

"And to his family," the widow said with quietly sorrowful dignity.

"Of course. I . . . er . . . You are aware, I daresay, that someone else is now employing Mr. Lisle's pseudonym?"

"Certainly. The person concerned very properly requested my permission."

"Then you know who he is?" Lord Selworth enquired eagerly.

"I regret that I am not at liberty to divulge the name."

His lordship's face fell, but he rallied. "Perhaps I can change your mind, ma'am, when you hear why I wish to approach the gentleman."

Mrs. Lisle's mouth twitched, and she cast a quizzical glance at her elder daughter. For an anxious moment, Pippa feared her mother would be unable to repress the chuckle quivering on her lips.

However, with assumed gravity she replied, "I doubt it, Lord Selworth, but you are at liberty to try."

He smiled at her. "You are laughing at me, I see. I expect more persuasive men than I have badgered you in vain. But perhaps their reasons were less . . . altruistic. I hope you will consider my aims altruistic."

"Tell me."

Once more his lordship ran his hand through his hair, increasing its likeness to an ill-made hayrick. As if suddenly recalling its unfortunate tendency to go its own way, he then hastily smoothed it down, with a rueful sidelong peek at Pippa. It was her turn to try not to chuckle.

"May I enlist you on my side, Miss Lisle?" he begged.

"It is not my place to enlighten you as to Prometheus' identity, sir," she said, adding frankly, "I cannot imagine any circumstances which would change that, but I own I should be glad to hear what you have to say."

"Very well. First, I must tell you that I have unexpectedly and very recently inherited the viscountcy, from a distant relative with whom my immediate family had lost touch. I had no idea I was so close in line to the succession."

"Indeed!" said Mrs. Lisle skeptically.

"Albinia certainly never knew, Mama. Lord Selworth's father died many years ago, did he not, sir?"

"Near twenty, ma'am. My eldest half-sister is eighteen. My mother has too large a second family to keep track of her first husband's relatives, and my stepfather is a rather unworldly clergyman. I knew, of course, that my great-grandfather was titled, but the connection was too distant to be of pressing interest.''

Mrs. Lisle was still disbelieving. ''You never wondered?''

''Mama, pray do not catechise Lord Selworth!'' said Pippa, laughing.

''No, no, Miss Lisle, I have no objection. Convincing you of my credentials must include explaining why I have no inbred sympathy with the landowning classes. To tell the truth, I had little time to fret over my noble relatives, and no inclination to apply to them for assistance.'' A flush stained his fair skin. ''Since I attained years of discretion, I have been busy helping to support my family.''

''Too proud to ask for help, yet ashamed of working for a living,'' Mrs. Lisle observed dryly.

''Not at all!'' exclaimed Lord Selworth with considerable indignation, his color still further heightened.

Though her mother appeared satisfied, Pippa wondered if it was the kind of work the viscount had done which embarrassed him, rather than the fact of working. If he were a character in one of the Gothic romances that she found an agreeable change from polemics, he would have taken to the highways as a Gentleman of the Road.

With regret, she decided a career as a highwayman was sadly improbable. Perhaps he had been employed by one of those middlemen or jobbers whom Papa and Mr. Cobbett regarded as abominable parasites.

Maybe that was the only work he could find, she thought charitably.

''Anyway, that is all in the past,'' his lordship said hurriedly. ''Now I am a peer; I have a seat in the House of Lords. I want to do what I can to help the poor, but I cannot expect to wield any influence unless I make an impression with my maiden speech. I have tried to compose a suitable oration,'' he confessed, ''but I made a mull of it.''

"So you wish to consult Prometheus?" Pippa guessed.

"I have long admired his writings. I hope he will realize that, quite apart from the injury to my *pride*"—he gave Mrs. Lisle a wry look—"it will do the cause no good if I stand up and make a cake of myself."

"Speaking of cake," Kitty put in, "do you wish me to make tea, Mama?"

"Pray do, my love. You will drink tea, gentlemen?"

"Thank you, ma'am, we shall be delighted."

Mr. Chubb mumbled something indistinguishable, turned crimson, and muttered semiaudibly, "Give you a hand, Miss Catherine."

Kitty smiled at him and said, "How kind of you, sir."

A besotted look on his face, he followed her out. Pippa swallowed a sigh. Her sister had made another instant conquest.

Lord Selworth frowned after his friend, but quickly returned to business. "I am sorely in need of Prometheus' advice, Mrs. Lisle. Naturally I expect to pay for his assistance."

"No matter how much you are willing to pay, sir," Mrs. Lisle warned him, "Prometheus would never write or help to write anything not wholeheartedly in accord with my husband's principles."

"Nor would I ask it of him, ma'am. I fancy my aims agree with those of the late Mr. Lisle and the gentleman who has stepped into his shoes, or picked up his quill, I should say."

Mrs. Lisle nodded approvingly. "I am delighted to hear it. The poor and voteless have too few champions in the House of Lords."

"Mama!" Pippa exclaimed in alarm. "I think it most unlikely that Prometheus will be willing to unmask, even in so *noble* a cause." Drat, she should not have risked the pun. Being clever might arouse the viscount's suspicions. She must strive to seem feather-witted—yet she could not let Mama make unredeemable promises. "Did not Mr. Cobbett's letter say those horrid Tories are threatening him with imprisonment again?"

"I assure you, Miss Lisle, I should do nothing to endanger Prometheus. His secret would be safe with me. Besides, he is no vitriolic insurrectionist, as Cobbett frequently appears to be. Cobbett's prejudices too often get the better of his common sense, and even drive him to be careless with facts, whereas Prometheus is known for his brilliant use of reasoned argument."

Pippa felt herself blushing at this fervent compliment. "I beg your pardon, sir," she said hastily, hoping he would ascribe her pink face to embarrassment for having misjudged him. "I did not mean to suggest that you would betray Prometheus on purpose."

"Your concern for the gentleman's safety does you credit, Miss Lisle." The viscount's warm smile did nothing to cool her cheeks. "He is a close friend of the family, I collect, or a relative, perhaps?"

To Pippa's relief, her mother drew his lordship's attention. "I have no sons, Lord Selworth," she said, with severity belied by the twinkle in her eye, "nor brothers, nor nephews."

Perfectly true, and perfectly irrelevant.

"I did not intend to probe, ma'am. Or perhaps I did—my apologies. However, it is clear that you are personally acquainted with Prometheus. All I ask is that you set my proposal fairly before him."

"A reasonable request, is it not, Pippa? If you will leave your direction, sir, I shall see that you are notified of the outcome, one way or the other."

"If you think you might have an answer for me by tomorrow, we shall put up at the inn in the village."

"The Jolly Bodger is not known for its comfort, sir," Pippa advised him, trying to discourage him from remaining in the vicinity. "It is little more than a tavern."

"The Jolly Bodger?" Kitty asked cheerfully as she ushered in Mr. Chubb bearing a laden tea-tray. "Are you staying there tonight? Set it down here, if you please, sir. Shall I pour, Mama?"

On receiving an affirmative, she busied herself with cups and saucers, allotting the only two remaining matching sets to the gentlemen.

"Are we staying, Wynn?" Mr. Chubb enquired, passing tea and honey cake. Pippa thought he sounded hopeful.

"The inn is shockingly uncomfortable," she restressed, "and I have heard horrid tales of their dinners."

"You are welcome to dine with us, Lord Selworth, Mr. Chubb," Mrs. Lisle offered, "if you care to dare the other discomforts. We have not room to put you up, alas."

Pippa stared at her mother in dismay. She was positively encouraging the viscount! Surely she did not suppose Pippa was prepared to disclose her secret to him?

He would be incredulous at first. Once convinced of the truth, he would cease to admire and start to wonder at her. Like Dr. Samuel Johnson, he would say, doubtless to himself, being a courteous gentleman, "A woman preaching is like a dog's walking on his hind legs. It is not done well: but you are surprised to find it done at all."

Even if she could trust him to hold his tongue, of which she was by no means certain, to have him regard her as a nine days' wonder would be painful, she acknowledged. Not that he showed any signs of admiring her for herself. She had no reason to expect it. Nor did she consider him anything out of the common way for a personable gentleman—

Until he smiled, and he was smiling at her now, the dastard!

"You are thoughtful, Miss Lisle," he said in an undertone. Mama was occupied in listening to Mr. Chubb's long, inarticulate utterance of gratitude for her invitation, which Pippa gathered had been accepted while she reflected. "I trust," Lord Selworth continued, "that the presence of two extra mouths at dinner will cause no difficulties?"

Pippa was about to inform him waspishly of her ignorance of such housekeeping details. Realizing he might well enquire as to how she occupied her time if not in womanly domestic tasks, she drowned the words in a gulp of tea.

Her face must have reflected her annoyance, however, for he suggested tentatively, "Shall we cry off? Be honest with me."

It was considerate of him to ask, she told herself sheepishly. Most men would not think twice about the awkwardness of feeding unexpected guests. "I am sure Mama would not have invited you were there any difficulty, sir," she said, her tone cool.

"I fear you are still not persuaded of my innocuous intentions towards your friend. I give you my word, Miss Lisle, no harm shall come to him through me. He has only to refuse my request and not another word shall be said—I shall cease to seek him out. But pray don't deny him the chance to decide for himself."

Pippa had already decided. She wished she could say so without further ado. Since that was impossible, she sighed and promised, "I shall not try to keep Mama from discussing your offer with Prometheus."

Standing at the parlor window, Pippa watched the gentlemen in their top hats and greatcoats tramping down the garden path in the dusk, on the way to take rooms at the Jolly Bodger. Their tethered horses' ears stuck up above the beech hedge, still thickly hung with dead brown leaves.

The dead leaves depressed her. So did the muddy flower beds on each side of the path, though snowdrops bravely strove to raise their heads, battered and splattered by the recent rains, among green spikes of daffodil and papery crocus buds. In spite of their promise of spring, she felt winter would go on forever.

Much as she loved Mama and Kitty, the spice had gone out of life when Papa died.

Her writing—the emotions aroused by the injustices she wrote about—were a palliative, not a remedy. When she laid down her quill and posted the result to Mr. Cobbett, the emptiness returned.

What frightened her was that she saw no end to the desert. Kitty would marry, whether John Ruddock or some other love-struck swain, and go away. Pippa might surrender her hand to Mr. Postlethwaite, but her heart was untouched. Worse, she would have to give up the work which, she sometimes fancied, was all that kept her from running mad.

Would children compensate? She found it impossible to imagine indulging with the vicar in those intimacies necessary to create a family.

The click of the gate latch returned her to the present. She swung back to the lamp-lit room.

"Mama, this is the outside of enough. You know I dare not reveal my authorship."

"It would have looked very singular, my love, had we declined to convey Lord Selworth's proposal. He might have attempted to approach Prometheus in some other way over which we had less control. At the very least his curiosity would be aroused, and by conjecture he might arrive at the truth. He struck me as an intelligent and determined young man."

"Pigheaded! As though a hundred others could not help him equally well—a dozen, at any rate. You are right, of course, but I wish you had insisted on writing with the answer instead of encouraging him to stay by inviting him to dinner!"

Her mother laughed. "I had no choice in the matter once you had abused the Bodger's fare."

"Perhaps that was a mistake," Pippa admitted with a wry grimace. "You will just have to tell him tomorrow that you have spoken to Prometheus, who desired you to convey a refusal."

Mrs. Lisle had opened her workbox as soon as the gentlemen left. She was darning a stocking heel, and her needle flashed back and forth twice before she responded, "Are you so sure you ought to refuse, Pippa?"

"Yes," Pippa said promptly. Lord Selworth had succeeded in shaking her composure without even trying. To work with him would be to endure a constant state of uncomfortable ferment. "Even if I agreed, I expect he would change his mind as soon as he discovered Prometheus is a female. And though he may be *willing* to keep the secret, who can guess whether he is capable of it? Should he let slip only to Mr. Chubb—''

''No fear of Mr. Chubb letting the cat out of the bag,'' said Kitty, giggling as she glanced up from her hemming. ''It was a struggle to extract a single word from him. He is woefully shy.''

''With ladies, certainly,'' Pippa said, ''but I daresay he is on easier terms among gentlemen.''

''Do you think so?'' Kitty enquired with interest. ''I hope you are right, for he is quite amiable. He was interested in my chickens, or at least kind enough to seem so, and he helped with the tea-tray, though I fancy he had never before set foot in a kitchen! I hate to picture him going through life with his tongue tied in knots.''

''He had more to say for himself than John Ruddock,'' Mrs. Lisle pointed out tartly. ''What a mooncalf the boy is!''

''A veritable nodcock,'' Pippa agreed, ''but we are straying from the point, Mama. I cannot risk telling Lord Selworth that I write the articles, so I must refuse him.''

''I suppose so, my love. It is a great pity, for if William Cobbett is imprisoned again and forced to stop publishing the *Register* for a while, the money from Lord Selworth would come in handy.''

''I doubt he could pay much. Title and fortune do not always coincide. Did you not notice how shabby his clothes are?''

''Yes,'' said her mother thoughtfully, needle poised in mid-air. ''It is the more admirable that he wishes to spend part of what he has to ensure a serious reception of his ideas for the relief of the truly poor.''

''The viscount may indeed be all that is admirable. The situation remains unchanged. He will have to contrive without my assistance.''

''Pippa,'' said Kitty, ''I do not perfectly understand why you cannot help Lord Selworth without his knowing who you are. That you are Prometheus, I mean. He will be in London, after all, and you here, so you will have to write back and forth. You have only to tell him Prometheus chooses to communicate through you, rather than directly.''

''He might believe it,'' Pippa said doubtfully, ''given the present threat to Mr. Cobbett.'' Her resistance began to crumble. With Lord Selworth at a distance, there was no danger to her peace of mind.

''I wonder.'' Mrs. Lisle's gaze was fixed on an invisible scene. A smile curved her lips. ''Yes, it could work. A clever notion, Kitty love, and I see no reason why it should not work even if we were in London.''

''Mama!'' cried her daughters as one. Kitty's eyes sparkled with excited hope. ''We are going to London?'' she asked.

''Impossible,'' Pippa objected. ''Lord Selworth would be bound to discover our whereabouts.''

''We shall not try to keep it from him. What is important is to give him the impression that *Prometheus* remains in the country.''

''Corresponding with his lordship, through me?'' Pippa felt a peculiar twist of anticipation. Alarmed, she protested, ''But, Mama, he might expect to deal with me in person if we were in Town.''

''Very likely, my love.''

''I cannot!''

''Mama,'' Kitty burst out, ''can we truly go to London? Is it not horridly expensive?''

''I have been saving, thanks to your sister's contributions. Pippa had her Season, and I have always intended that you should, too. I had thought to wait until next spring—you will be nineteen by then, but better another twelvemonth and another few pounds put by. However . . .'' Mrs. Lisle paused dramatically.

''With what Lord Selworth will pay Pippa, we shall have enough?''

''We do not know what he will pay,'' Pippa reminded her, ''and it is not likely to be a great deal.''

"I have a better notion." With the air of a fairground conjurer pulling a gold watch from a yokel's hatband, Mrs. Lisle continued. "We shall not ask Lord Selworth for money. We shall tell him Prometheus is so kind a friend of ours that he wishes to be paid with introductions for you girls into the best Society!"

Kitty's face was ecstatic. Pippa could not bear to disappoint her little sister.

Resigning herself to working with the disturbing Lord Selworth, she merely demurred, "Not for me, Mama. My first Season was a disaster, and I do not care to repeat the experience at my advanced age, especially before an audience as critical as the *haut ton.*"

"My love, you are much improved in both looks and address since then, and hardly at your last prayers! Still, I do not mean to carp at you. It is for you decide."

Kitty protested, "But it will be horridly unfair, Pippa, if you must work to pay for my pleasure."

"I enjoy wrestling with ideas and words, dearest," Pippa assured her, with a smile, "much more than dancing. And *very* much more than sewing. If you will engage to spare me the wielding of a needle, I shall gladly wield the pen to enable you to take the Ton by storm."

CHAPTER 3

"She is as kind as she is pretty," Chubby enthused as they turned their horses' heads back towards the village.

"Kind!" Wynn exclaimed. "I hardly think so. She was not at all pleased when her mama invited us to dinner, and her warnings about the inn were obviously designed to drive us away. But as for 'as kind as she is pretty,' I daresay you are right, for no one could call Miss Lisle pretty."

"Oh, Miss Lisle! It's Miss Kitty I mean. Didn't you notice how she went on talking to me even though I couldn't think of any clever compliments? Not prattling on about hats and gowns, either. She has some very sound ideas on poultry management."

Wynn grinned. "Does she, indeed?"

"And she let me help her with the tea, too, though most young ladies would be ashamed to admit they hadn't enough servants."

"Is Miss Kitty to cook our dinner?" Wynn demanded in mock alarm.

"I expect she is capable of it, but Sukey, their maid, does

that. They have just the one maid, and her husband who is gardener and handyman, and a woman who comes in to do floors and laundry and such.''

''My dear fellow, you disappoint me,'' Wynn teased. ''I was ready to allot the laundry to Mrs. Lisle and the digging and wood-chopping to Miss Lisle.''

''Are Mrs. Lisle's hands rough and red?'' Chubby asked seriously. ''I did not notice that Miss Lisle's face is weathered at all. You say she is not pretty, but I did not think her ill-favored.''

''Lord no, she is no antidote. When animated, her face is quite fetching if rather pale, and that simple style of knotting back her hair suits her, but she would not do as the heroine of a romance, you know.''

''Oh, your heroines must all be diamonds of the first water, though clad in rags!''

''One must have rags. How is the hero to discern her beauty—or beauties—if not through the holes?''

''I think,'' said Chubby doggedly, ''a neat, plain dress don't hide a girl's beauty. Miss Kitty looked very well in that yellow woollen thing she was wearing, without laces or furbelows *or* holes.''

''I cry pax, old chap. Pax!'' Wynn begged, laughing. ''Let us stipulate that Miss Catherine Lisle is a very pretty chit, and have done. Here is our inn.''

The Jolly Bodger was long and low, built of red brick mellowed by age to a rosy hue, crisscrossed by ancient, crooked beams. In the deepening dusk of the cloudy evening, lamplight shone from small, diamond-paned casement windows. A lantern suspended above the inn sign illuminated a faded picture of a man with an axe over his shoulder. A foaming tankard in his other hand presumably represented jollity, as well as advertising the inn's wares. His expression was indistinguishable.

''What's a bodger?'' Chubby asked, dismounting.

''I've not the least notion, except that his trade requires an axe. A headsman, no doubt.''

"An executioner? Hang it all, Wynn, what a grim name for an inn!"

"As well call it the Happy Hangman or the Gay Gibbet," Wynn agreed, smothering a smile as he hitched his hired mount to a post. "By Miss Lisle's description, it sounds like a grim place. Still, I don't know that that's what a bodger is," he added, taking pity on his easily gulled friend. "No doubt Miss Lisle will know. I'll ask her this evening."

"I'll ask the landlord tonight," said Chubby, "before we take rooms. Be damned if I'll be able to sleep with an executioner hanging outside my window!"

He pushed open the creaking door, over which was written *Prop. Chas. Bucket.* Wynn followed him, stepping directly into the taproom.

It was a cosy place, despite walls and ceiling blackened by centuries of tobacco and wood-fire smoke. A cheerful fire burned in the grate, its ruddy gleam reflecting from the well-polished pewter tankards in the callused hands of the occupants. The tiny windows which would make the room gloomy in summer now kept out the chill February night.

"It doesn't look bad," Wynn observed, the more convinced that Miss Lisle had done her best to drive him away.

"Ho, landlord!" cried Chubby.

A small, spare man in an apron came through a door at the back of the room. "Chas Bucket at your service, sir," he said genially.

"What's a bodger?"

"A bodger, sir?" Mr. Bucket asked in surprise. "Why, bless your heart, sir, a bodger's a chap what goes out in the beech woods to shape the wood rough-hewn, afore it's took to the cabinetmakers for a-making of chairs and the like."

Listening, Wynn wondered why he had proposed to ask Miss Lisle, in particular, for the information. Unaware that it was a local term for a local craftsman, for some reason he had assumed she would know the answer. He could not recall anything she had said to make him suppose her to be both intelligent and well-informed, yet that was the impression he had of her.

A false impression, possibly. What he could be certain of was her antagonism. She did not want him to work with Prometheus. In fact, she distrusted him and did not want him to discover the writer's identity.

She was downright protective of Prometheus. Could the fellow be a suitor she was in love with? Not the vicar, heaven forbid! Surely she could do better than that prosy bore, even if she was not a diamond of the first water.

With an odd sense of relief, Wynn realized that whatever Prometheus was, his writings proved him no prosy bore. He didn't like to think of her tied to Postlethwaite for life.

If Miss Lisle loved Prometheus, no wonder she was reluctant to entrust his safety to a stranger. Wynn had done his best to reassure her. Though she had surrendered, she had remained deucedly cool, not to say frosty. Best avoid the touchy topic at dinner. What he wanted was a nice, neutral subject.

Bodgers, for instance. Of course, in hindsight, that must be why he had offered to ask her rather than anyone else.

The landlord was waving at a settle in the inglenook. "Tom Bowyer, there, he's a bodger, sir. Mayhap he'll tell you more."

Chubby started towards the inglenook. Wynn reached out and hauled him back.

"All you need to know is that his trade isn't going to give you nightmares."

"I'm interested," Chubby said indignantly, "and my father will be too, if you let me find out. We don't have bodgers in our part of the world, though a fair bit of our timber goes to the furniture workshops."

"My humble apologies! I didn't realize you were in pursuit of enlightenment. Off with you, then, and I'll sort out our accommodations."

"Accommodations, sir?" Chas Bucket sounded distinctly dubious.

"Yes, we'll need a couple of chambers for the night."

"Well, sir, being as how this here do be an inn, not a hedge tavern, I'm bound by law to offer accommodations to any as seeks 'em. But the fac' is, we've only got the one chamber, sir, and it ain't fitting for gentlemen. It's gen'rally carters and drovers what stops here, sir, and that's the truth."

So Miss Lisle had not been cozening him, though it did not mean she had not been anxious to be rid of him. "Let me see it," Wynn said cautiously.

"I'll call the missus."

Mrs. Bucket was a stout, red-faced woman beneath whom the narrow stairs squawked alarmingly. She panted to the top and flung open the nearest door, standing back to let Wynn see.

The chamber was just big enough to contain a vast bed, into which four or five drovers or carters might be fitted nose to toes, and a chest. The ceiling sloped down to a window even tinier than those below. Though not tall, Wynn could only stand upright just inside the door—not that it mattered, since that was the only unoccupied bit of floor.

" 'Tis a good featherbed," wheezed Mrs. Bucket behind him, "and I s'll put on clean sheets for your worships."

Wynn had no desire to ride on several miles to find a better hostelry, then ride back and forth again for dinner, in the dark, on unfamiliar roads, and under a sky threatening rain. He could always send word to Mrs. Lisle that he and Chubby would be unable to accept her invitation after all. Yet he found he very much wanted to dine with the Lisles, to talk to Miss Lisle about matters which would not arouse her protective instincts.

At least the chamber looked reasonably clean, whatever the state of the sheets beneath the counterpane. But . . . "No wash-stand?"

"There do be the pump out back," the landlady advised him.

Wynn shivered. "Sixpence for a basin of hot water in the kitchen," he bargained. "And another sixpence to press our evening clothes."

''Lor' save you, your worship, you don't need to dress up for scrag end o' mutton and cold pease pudden fried up.''

Wynn shuddered as a long-forgotten nursery rhyme returned to haunt him:

> Pease pudding hot,
> Pease pudding cold,
> Pease pudding in the pot
> Nine days old.

''Thank you, ma'am, but we are to dine with Mrs. Lisle,'' he said with relief; then another horrid thought struck him. ''And we'll pay extra to have the bed to ourselves.''

Mrs. Bucket chuckled, her vast bosom billowing. ''Lor' save you, sir,'' she said again, ''I knows better'n to put mucky workingmen in wi' gentry. We've had gentlemen stay afore, when poor Mr. Lisle was alive. 'Tis late in the day for carters or drovers, but any comes by, there's allus the hayloft.''

Coming to an agreement on terms, Wynn followed his hostess down to see the horses stabled, and to retrieve the saddlebags and his friend.

Shivering in her shift, Pippa doubtfully regarded her reflection in the mirror. She had hoped the curls Kitty had labored over with a hot iron would make her look less intellectual than her usual severe coiffure. They just made her look like someone else, not herself at all.

''Very pretty, my love,'' said her mother, coming into the small chamber, already dressed in her Sunday-best gray silk.

''I am not trying to look pretty,'' Pippa said crossly. ''I just want Lord Selworth to believe I am more concerned about my appearance than my mind. But the curl is already coming out.''

''Perhaps just one more turn,'' said Kitty, reaching for the iron leaning on the grate, where glowing embers battled the draft from the ill-fitting window.

"No, my hair is incurably straight and that is all there is to it. Thank you for your efforts, Kitty dear. I should have known it was useless. I shall just pin it up, as usual."

"Thread a ribbon through the braid before you knot it," Mrs. Lisle suggested. "Which gown are you going to wear?"

"The green Circassian cloth, I suppose. I refuse to freeze for Lord Selworth's sake."

"Enough of this nonsense!" her mother said sharply. "That gown does very well when we are alone, but whatever your opinion of the viscount, you will dress nicely for guests, my girl. There is a good fire in the dining parlor, and you may wear a shawl. Let me see." She crossed to the old beechwood wardrobe.

"Oh, the apricot poplin." Pippa did not own so many dresses as to make the choice difficult. "I have a bit of ribbon to match. I beg your pardon, Mama, for being prickly. Lord Selworth's interest in Prometheus has ruffled me a trifle."

Mrs. Lisle gave her a loving smile. "I know, dearest, but truly I believe all will work out for the best. Lord Selworth seems to me too much the gentleman to give away your secret, should he guess it, and Papa would be very proud of your labor on behalf of the unfortunate. Kitty, go and dress now. I shall finish off your sister's hair, then come to help with your fastenings."

While Mama's nimble fingers braided the satin ribbon into her hair and pinned the plait into her usual topknot, Pippa pondered what she had said.

Was Lord Selworth too gentlemanly to betray her? He was a gentleman by rank, though recently risen to the peerage—what *had* been his profession before?—but Papa had often pointed out the frequent gap between rank and behavior. His daughters were not to be taken in by a title. Still, the viscount's concern for the poor argued in his favor, and it was not just talk or he would not have sought out Prometheus.

Unless he was a Government spy.

Surely not! That smile which sent shivers down her spine

had warmed his blue eyes in a way no spy could feign. Pippa dismissed the possibility with a shake of her head.

"Ouch!"

"Hold still, child, or I shall jab you again, and the whole will come down before I have pinned it securely."

"Yes, Mama," Pippa said meekly.

Her thoughts continued to wander. Assuming Lord Selworth's stated aims were genuine, Papa would wish her to help him. She had taken up the mantle of Prometheus chiefly in tribute to her dearly loved, much admired, and greatly missed parent. Also, she acknowledged, because she was proud of her ability and enjoyed the work.

It went without saying that she believed in Papa's ideals, but she was afraid the plight of the voteless masses had had less influence on her decision than it ought. Without the other spurs to write for Mr. Cobbett, she might have satisfied her charitable instincts with carrying soup to sick cottagers. *Not* sewing for the poor-basket.

"I fear I am sadly selfish, Mama," she said, chagrined.

"How can you say so, my love?" After pushing in a last hairpin, her mother enveloped her in a warm embrace. "Your concern about giving away the identity of Prometheus is perfectly understandable, though, I trust, unnecessary. There is perhaps some little risk, but I consider it justified in view of the opportunity for your sister. And the good you may do in helping Lord Selworth, of course."

Her disgust with herself lightened by Mama's order of priority, Pippa warned, "Lord Selworth may not be willing to pay with an introduction into Society."

"We can but ask," Mrs. Lisle said serenely.

"Not until tomorrow, remember. We have not had time to 'consult Prometheus.' "

"Darling," said Mrs. Lisle, a twinkle in her eye, "though you are the acknowledged intellectual of the family, I hope I am neither feather-witted nor in my dotage!"

With that she swept out, leaving her abashed daughter to dress.

The apricot poplin, a silk and worsted weave, was actually quite warm, as well as pretty enough to make up, almost, for the lack of curls and Pippa's pale complexion. Mama and Kitty were skillful dressmakers. The high neckline and the cuffs of the long sleeves were trimmed with Honiton lace. Another strip of lace circled the hem of the skirt, between two rows of satin ribbon a shade darker than the poplin, a leftover length of which was braided into Pippa's hair. The same ribbon circled the high waist, tying just below her bosom in a bow with long, fluttering ends.

Her bosom drew her scrutiny. All too aware of her scrawny figure, Pippa rarely bothered to use the looking glass except to make sure she was tidy—and that not as often as Mama would wish. She had been known to greet callers with a spot of ink on her chin or sleeve.

Now she discovered she *did* have a bosom! Mama was right: her looks had improved while she was not watching. Her clavicles no longer ridged the bodice, nor did her hipbones protrude when she smoothed down her skirt. Turning, she peered over her shoulder and saw no sign of jutting shoulder blades.

She swung back to study her face. Not only had her chin no inkspot, it was not pointed like an imp's, but gently rounded, as were her once sharp cheekbones. Even her nose was less like a beak.

Pippa realized she had not really noticed herself in years, merely seeing a fleeting image she vaguely recognized as herself. She would never be as pretty as Kitty, she thought, but neither was she woefully plain. Perhaps Mr. Postlethwaite was not so utterly lacking in taste as she had supposed!

Perhaps Lord Selworth might . . . She cut off the wistful thought before it completed itself in her mind, and started again. Perhaps she could make Lord Selworth believe she was a commonplace young lady too concerned with her appearance to have room in her head for politics. She opened a drawer and took out the carved ivory rose pendant and earrings Papa had given her for her eighteenth birthday.

"And do you share your father's political opinions, Miss Lisle?" Lord Selworth enquired politely, passing the bowl of leek soup Mama had ladled from the tureen.

"La, sir," Pippa trilled, with an attempt at a simper, "is it not a daughter's duty to embrace her father's principles, whether or not she understands them?"

Lord Selworth blinked. Had she laid it on rather too rare and thick?

Accepting his own bowl of soup, the viscount said, "I regret to see anyone espouse views she, or he, doesn't understand. Do you not agree, ma'am?" he asked Mrs. Lisle.

"In general," she said, "but where understanding fails, it is surely preferable for a daughter to be guided by a father she respects."

"Gentlemen know best," Pippa said inanely, then immediately wished she had not voiced a dogma so at odds with her own beliefs, even for the sake of misleading Lord Selworth.

He took her to task at once. "Desolated as I am to contradict a lady, gentlemen as a class cannot possibly know best, or they would all agree, which is very far from the truth!"

Pippa had to laugh. "As my father's daughter, I cannot fail to be aware of that truth. Papa throve on controversy. I find it conceivable that some of his stated views, if not his principles, were founded upon a desire to contradict."

"Hardly an example one would wish to hold up to one's daughters," said Mrs. Lisle dryly, with a warning glance. "You have more than one younger sister, I collect, Lord Selworth, besides Mrs. Debenham?"

"Three half-sisters, ma'am, and four half-brothers. I own, the spirit of contradiction needs no reinforcement in them, boys or girls," he said with a rueful smile.

"Your mother has her hands full!"

"She has been too much occupied with the youngest, and with keeping house, to check them, and my stepfather is too gentle. Fortunately, I'm now able to provide a governess for the girls and to send the older boys to school."

"You do not care to have your brothers at home?" Pippa asked reproachfully.

"Oh, I shouldn't mind it now that I have a house and grounds extensive enough to contain their energies. You cannot imagine the turmoil created by a large and lively family in a small rectory. Nine children, remember, including Bina and me. Not two sedate young ladies like you and Miss Kitty."

Pippa was not sure she appreciated being called sedate, but she admitted, "I can imagine one might come to long for peace and quiet."

Lord Selworth grinned. "To say the least! Not that I would have you suppose my brothers and sisters are really mischievous. They are likeable enough, only in need of discipline."

"Can you not provide it? If the eldest Miss Warren is to make her début this spring, you must be much older than the others."

"A veritable graybeard, in fact!" He took pity on her confusion. "You are right. I'm ten years older than Millie. But while I have some influence over my siblings, it would be unconscionable of me to usurp my stepfather's place."

"Whatever your opinion of his tutelage, or lack thereof. Yes, I do see your difficulty."

"So I feel school is the best place for my brothers. I went to school," Lord Selworth said cheerfully. "It was my father's wish, and he left just funds enough for the purpose. Not Eton or Harrow or Winchester, but a respectable academy. I'm sending the boys there, and I doubt they'll suffer for it. Chubby, did attending Tuke House blight your life?"

Mr. Chubb had fallen silent, having, in response to Kitty's query about the inn, regaled her with every scrap of information he had gathered on the subject of bodgers. He looked up from his soup and said, "Blight? No. Dashed good soup, ma'am. Leeks from your own garden?"

"Yes. The receipt is one collected by Kitty. Whenever we eat anything particularly good at someone else's house, she makes a point of requesting the receipt."

"Dashed good notion. Don't suppose you'd let me have it for my mother's cook, Miss Kitty?" Mr. Chubb turned bright red. "The leek soup, not the whole collection," he clarified in a hurried mumble. "Don't want to impose."

"I shall be happy to copy it out for you, sir," Kitty said soothingly.

"Dashed kind. Leeks grow well at home. No blight."

"Are you interested in gardening, Mr. Chubb?" Kitty asked as Sukey removed the soup plates. "Sukey's husband takes care of the kitchen garden, but Pippa and I grow flowers."

Pippa seized upon the subject, which could not possibly lead Lord Selworth to see her as intellectual. Though Mr. Chubb was more conversant with edible crops than flowers, the three found common ground in a discussion of blights, insect pests, and weeds.

As they ate fricasseed chicken with carrots and parsnips, the talk moved on to the depredations of rabbits and wood pigeons.

"Shoot 'em," said Mr. Chubb.

"It is the only way to keep them down," Kitty agreed.

"Pigeon pie."

"Rabbit stew. I have an excellent receipt. It is a nuisance digging out the shot, though."

Pippa, while she enjoyed pigeon pie and rabbit stew, not only had no interest in cookery, but did not like to think of the poor creatures having to be shot first. She would have dropped out of the conversation, but Mama and Lord Selworth were discussing Papa's career. If she listened more closely to them, she would be tempted to put her oar in, at the risk of revealing her knowledge of politics.

Instead, she said to Mr. Chubb, "Do you marl your soil? Ours is so chalky, it is not necessary."

His response led to other soil amendments. Pippa sought a polite circumlocution—suitable for the dinner table—for manure, only to have Kitty and Mr. Chubb argue unabashedly over the relative merits of fowl droppings and cattle muck.

Conscious of Lord Selworth lending an amused ear, Pippa wished her mother would call Kitty to order. Trying to conceal her intellectual abilities was one thing; joining in a debate on the grosser aspects of rural economy was quite another. However, either Mrs. Lisle did not hear her younger daughter, or she chose not to reprove her for fear of embarrassing Mr. Chubb, who was guilty of the same fault.

Pippa had to acknowledge that the bashful gentleman might well be driven back into his shell, never to reemerge.

Mrs. Lisle started to reminisce about her husband's first election. Since Pippa had been an infant at the time, she felt safe in transferring her attention to the familiar story. Mr. Lisle had lost, but he had fought hard and his efforts had drawn the notice of the wealthy patrons who made future wins possible.

With a struggle, Pippa managed not to inveigh against the corrupt electoral system. Lord Selworth said it for her.

"Wealth ought not to be necessary. As long as the present system holds sway, the poor will never be properly represented in Parliament, their grievances will never be heard by—"

"Here, old chap," Mr. Chubb intervened, "spare us the speeches at the dinner table. There's a good fellow. Preaching to the converted, dash it. I say, ma'am, I've been telling Miss Kitty she ought to get a milch-cow."

Indulgently, Mrs. Lisle encouraged him to give his reasons.

Pippa turned to Lord Selworth. "Have you considered, sir, that as well as taking your own seat in the Lords, you might help a like-minded commoner into Parliament?"

"Why no, I hadn't."

His arrested look, surprised and interested, made her flush. Wishing she had not spoken, she added hastily, "I don't wish to presume. Of course, I know nothing of your means, and you have a large family to support. Seven younger children, you said? What are their names?''

He followed her lead, and she dared to hope she had distracted him. It was a temporary reprieve, however. She had given her assent to Mama's plan, but how on earth was she to help Lord Selworth write his speech without giving herself away?

CHAPTER 4

"Dashed pleasant evening!" said Chubby as they hurried back along the dark lane to the Jolly Bodger, through a chilly drizzle. "I don't know when I've enjoyed myself more."

"I don't know when I've heard you talk so much," Wynn teased, "at least not among womenfolk."

"Did I talk too much?" his friend asked anxiously.

"Lord, no! Two whole sentences would amount to more than usual."

"It's just that Miss Kitty is dashed easy to talk to. She's interested in the same sort of things I am."

Wynn wondered if Kitty Lisle was not more polite and kind than interested, but he would not dream of saying so. "It was a delightful evening," he agreed. "Singing glees is one free amusement my family often indulges in—with mixed results, I confess. I didn't know you sang."

"Used to sing in the church choir," Chubby confessed. "Miss Kitty has a capital voice, and she plays the spinet devilish neatly, don't she?"

"Miss Lisle sings well, too, even if she did refuse to play

on the grounds that no criminal can be forced to give evidence against himself! She puzzles me.''

''Miss Lisle? Nice girl. No, nice young lady. Mrs. Debenham's age, ain't she? Practically on the shelf, poor thing.''

''Hardly,'' said Wynn with some asperity. ''Didn't you see the vicar casting sheep's eyes at her this afternoon?''

''Did he? Well, but a vicar, you know. I daresay he's looking for a housekeeper and someone to help with parish work. Nothing puzzling about that. Stands to reason, a girl wouldn't take a parson if she could catch anything better.''

Amused as much by Chubby's tortuous thought process as by his conclusions, Wynn said lightly, ''I can't agree with that, you know. My mother and my stepfather are quite devoted to each other.''

The lantern over the inn sign illuminated Chubby's pink, horrified face. ''I say, old chap, forgive me! Quite forgot Mr. Warren's in orders.''

''My dear fellow, I shan't call you out. Don't give it another thought. I just wanted to set you straight.'' He pushed open the door. ''Let's have a nightcap, and a game of piquet if Bucket can provide cards.''

A greasy pack with no seven of diamonds amused them for an hour or so. Until they lay in bed, a scrawny feather bolster between them, and Chubby snuffed the candle, Wynn did not spare another thought for Miss Lisle. Then he reverted to his puzzlement.

Most of the time, she seemed much like any other young lady of his acquaintance. True, she had not set her cap at him, a practice he had grown used to in the few months since his accession to the viscountcy had made him a matrimonial prize. But though pursued by damsels from miles around Kymford, he was not so set up in his own conceit as to expect every female of marriageable—or near marriageable—age to swoon at his feet. It was possible, just barely possible, that Miss Lisle preferred Mr. Postlethwaite, though more likely that Prometheus was her beloved.

However, it was not her preference in suitors which puzzled Wynn. It was the surprisingly penetrating remarks she made from time to time. Coming from an otherwise unremarkable young woman, these flashes of erudition stood out like pearls of wisdom in a bucketful of oyster shells.

No doubt she was merely repeating parrot-fashion what she had learnt from her father, Wynn thought sleepily. Mrs. Lisle said Pippa used to copy out his scribbling in a fair hand, so she could have absorbed and repeated his ideas without truly understanding. That must be the answer.

She understood enough to make appropriate use of what she had learnt, though. And enough to be aware of the danger to Radical writers in the present political climate.

Wynn hoped he had convinced her he was to be trusted. Not through him would her lover come to harm, if he decided to help. Mrs. Lisle had told Wynn on parting that Prometheus had been informed of his request. A response should be forthcoming by midday tomorrow.

Satisfied with his efforts to ensure the success of his speech, Wynn drifted off to sleep, in spite of the unconscionably lumpy mattress. His last thought was that Miss Lisle, whatever her motives, had told the truth about the Jolly Bodger.

"Was thinking I might stroll up to the Hall this morning," said Chubby, unconvincingly casual, "and pay my respects to Miss Ruddock. You coming?"

Pushing aside his plate of rock-hard eggs and leathery bacon, Wynn regarded his friend with suspicion. "Miss Ruddock? Who the deuce is Miss Ruddock?"

"The squire's daughter. I made her acquaintance yesterday. That was her talking to Miss Kitty, and her great oaf of a brother gaping at her like a . . . like a . . ."

"Like the ravening maw of a sea monster?"

"Lord, no. Like a village idiot."

"Why on earth would he gape at his sister like a village idiot, unless he is one?"

"Gaping at Miss Kitty, old chap. Stands to reason even a jobbernowl like that wouldn't go around gaping at his sister, however pretty she was."

"Miss Ruddock's pretty?" Wynn could not remember noticing her in particular.

"Nothing out of the ordinary."

"Then why . . . ? Chubby, don't tell me you have come upon *two* young females you find conversable in the same village?"

Chubby shook his head. "There's only one Miss Kitty," he said simply.

"My dear fellow, you can't be head over ears on such a brief acquaintance!"

"Why not? Bedamned if your dashed heroes and heroines don't fall in love at first sight, every last one of 'em. Why shouldn't I?"

"But . . ." The only reason Wynn could think of was that his books were fiction and this was real life. It seemed inadequate. "All right, if you are so besotted with Kitty Lisle, why call upon Miss Ruddock? Are you hoping she will put in a good word for you with her friend?"

"I'm not besotted. I love her. And she's going to the Hall this morning to play duets on the pianoforte. Got a new one. The Ruddocks, that is. Heard 'em talking about it. I know a slowtop like me hasn't a chance with her, but I thought maybe she wouldn't mind if I went to listen."

"Why shouldn't you have a chance with her? You're heir to a barony, and plump in the pocket besides. She may not know it, and you can't very well puff off your own consequence, but I can easily drop a tactful mention in passing. You'd be a splendid match for a purse-pinched girl stuck here in the country with a village idiot for her only suitor."

"If Ruddock were the only one . . ." Chubby said gloomily. "But there are bound to be others about the place, and worse still, she told me her mama has saved up to give her a Season in London. She'll have all the eligibles on the Town flocking after her.''

Wynn doubted it, but to say so not only might raise unwarranted hopes in Chubby's breast, but would cast aspersions on his beloved. While he wondered what to say, Mrs. Bucket heaved into sight.

"Off your grub, your worship?" she enquired sympathetically.

"I'm afraid I'm not very hungry," Wynn agreed.

" 'Spect Mistress Wynn set a good feed afore you yestre'en. Ah well, the pig'll eat it." Picking up his plate and Chubby's empty one, she waddled out.

The empty plate almost made Wynn take his friend's sentiments seriously. Gilbert Chubb was usually quite particular about what he ate. To consume his breakfast without noticing that it was virtually inedible was the equivalent in him of the traditional lovesick swain's loss of appetite.

On the other hand, Chubby had reached the advanced age of eight-and-twenty without ever suffering the pangs of calf love. Very likely that was all that ailed him now, the more painful for being a belated case. If so, the more he saw of the object of his infatuation, the sooner he'd be cured. Miss Kitty could not possibly be the paragon he believed.

"I'll come up to the Hall with you," Wynn decided. "Mrs. Lisle isn't expecting me till noon. Let's hope she will invite us to eat a nuncheon!"

Miss Kitty and Miss Ruddock were nothing loath to have an audience of gentlemen for their duets. However, Mary Ruddock's pleasure in entertaining a lord clearly far outweighed Kitty Lisle's in Chubby's attendance. She greeted him with friendly equanimity and paid him no more attention than she did Wynn, or her friend Mary.

With Mary present, Chubby lapsed into taciturnity, his few utterances brief and incoherent. His manners were too good to allow him to sit and stare at Kitty like a booby, but he was incapable of doing anything to advance himself in her affections.

Just as well, Wynn thought. He did not want his best friend to marry and retire to the country to raise a family just when his own political ambitions were going to fix him in London for a good part of the year.

He was further reassured by Miss Kitty's tranquil farewells. She was to spend all day at the Hall. Wynn had to depart at midday to call upon her mother, and Chubby could not properly prolong his visit.

When they took their leave, Kitty smiled and said gaily, "I did not forget the leek soup, Mr. Chubb. I copied out the receipt, but I left it at home for you since I did not expect to see you again. Ask my sister. She knows where I put it." Brushing aside Chubby's stammered thanks, she turned to Wynn, a mischievous look in her eyes. "I do hope you come to an agreement with Prometheus, sir. I am excessively fond of Prometheus."

Chubby groaned as they walked down the carriage drive towards the village. "She's in love with that damned fellow Prometheus. I thought he was an old man."

"I fancy not," Wynn said hesitantly.

"You found out that much about him, did you?"

"Not exactly. I suspect he's a youngish man because I believe Miss Lisle's in love with him, too. Why else should she be so protective of him?"

"Good gad, the fellow's a regular Turk!"

"This is England. Console yourself. He can't have 'em both."

"Perhaps not," Chubby gloomed, his round, usually cheerful face set in lines of despondency, "but he'll choose Miss Kitty. Stands to reason. She's younger and ten times prettier."

"Not ten times," Wynn protested.

"To me she is," Chubby maintained stoutly. "Prettiest thing I ever saw. And the kindest heart in the kingdom."

"Spare me your raptures, old chap. I must collect my arguments in case this rural Lothario needs further persuasion."

As they walked on in silence, Chubby picked up a stick and cut viciously at the nettles in the ditch as if each one represented the rural Lothario's neck.

No persuasive arguments came to Wynn. Instead, he found himself considering what would happen if Prometheus agreed to help. Would he come up to London or, horrid thought, might he expect Wynn to stay on at the appalling Jolly Bodger while consulting him?

Miss Lisle would surely go to stay in Town with her mother and sister, if Chubby had correctly understood their plans. No doubt Prometheus would choose to go, too, to be near his sweetheart. Which of the young ladies did he prefer? Or was he making up to both, the blackguard?

Mrs. Lisle seemed utterly unsuspecting of the villain she regarded as an intimate friend of the family. *Intimate,* ha! Ought Wynn to warn her?

Suddenly recognizing his ruminations as the beginning of a Gothic plot, Wynn laughed aloud. However he started out, everything turned to melodrama, which was precisely why he needed Prometheus' assistance. Doubtless the fellow was perfectly inoffensive, and it made no difference to Wynn which of the Lisle sisters he preferred.

"All very well for you to laugh," Chubby said accusingly. "You ain't in love."

"Thank heaven!" said Wynn.

Sweetbriar Cottage came into sight just as a pale wash of sunlight slithered between the clouds. In the beech hedge, still hung with last year's sere leaves, glossy brown buds swelled with promise. A wren, already nest-building, chattered in noisy annoyance as the gentlemen approached. Pushing open the white gate, Wynn saw that several bright yellow crocuses had burst into bloom overnight.

"Cheer up," he said, "Spring is on its way. At least once Miss Kitty's in London, you'll be able to see her."

Chubby brightened. "That's right. I couldn't very well keep

popping down here, could I? I'll make sure to get their direction in Town before we leave.''

The maid ushered them into the small parlor. By daylight, without a crowd of people, Wynn saw how shabby it was. Polished wood gleamed, but the upholstery stuffs, once patterned, had faded to a nearly uniform murky rose. A colorful hooked rug on the floor all too obviously hid a worn spot in the threadbare carpet.

All in all, it reminded him of the rectory where he grew up. He himself had been quite a dab at hooking a rug.

Mrs. Lisle looked up from her needlework with a smile, a greeting, and an invitation to be seated. Bowing, Wynn looked questioningly at Miss Lisle, who stood by the window as if she had been watching for their arrival.

Reluctance in every line of her slender figure, she came forward and sat down, thus allowing the gentlemen to take their seats.

''Has Prometheus reached a decision, ma'am?'' Wynn asked Mrs. Lisle eagerly.

''Yes, I have a decision to pass on to you. I hope you will not take it amiss.''

His spirits sinking, Wynn glanced around the room, though he knew quite well no stranger was there. ''He is not here. It is a negative I suppose.''

''On the contrary. Prometheus is willing to help you.''

''He is coming?'' Wynn started up. ''Or does he wish me to go to him? How I look forward to meeting him!''

''I fear you will be disappointed. I am not permitted to introduce you. Prometheus wishes to remain incognito and to work with you, as with Mr. Cobbett, entirely through my daughter.'' Mrs. Lisle smiled slightly at Wynn's astonishment. ''Pippa was used to help her papa, you know. She is quite competent to . . . to act as an intermediary, let us say.''

Wynn turned to Pippa. ''Miss Lisle, far be it from me to doubt your competence. I hate to be instrumental in placing

such a burden on your shoulders. You must have better things
to do with your time.''

"No." She shook her head, a hint of irony in the quirk of
her lips. "What could be better than helping to forward Papa's
favorite causes? But before you rejoice, wait until you have
heard what further conditions Prometheus has set, what payment is to be exacted.''

"I am willing to pay any reasonable sum, ma'am," Wynn
assured Mrs. Lisle, "but . . . conditions?"

For the first time in their admittedly brief acquaintance, the
widow looked a trifle discomposed. "The payment is not in
money," she said with an air of dogged determination. "You
must understand, Prometheus was my husband's pupil and intimate associate, and remains closely concerned with the family.
The recompense required for assisting you is that you provide
an entrée into the best Society for Kitty and Pippa.''

If Wynn was startled, so was Miss Lisle, who cried in obvious
dismay, "But, Mama—"

"For both my daughters," Mrs. Lisle cut her off firmly.
"Pippa has already made her come-out, but that is no reason
for her to miss the pleasures of the Season.''

"No indeed, ma'am," Wynn agreed, with a glance of pitying
sympathy for Pippa. If Prometheus wanted her introduced into
the Marriage Mart that was the London Season, he certainly
could have no urgent desire to make her his bride, poor girl.
Nor Kitty neither, apparently. An Adonis, perhaps, rather than
a Lothario—the pursued, not the pursuer.

Pippa was furious. She was annoyed with her mother, who
had said she could decide for herself about venturing upon
a second Season, and she bitterly resented Lord Selworth's
condescending pity.

Who was he to make it obvious he expected her to repeat
her failure? She and Mama must both be mistaken in believing
her looks had improved. Mama was partial, but how could
Pippa, with her vaunted intelligence, have so misled herself?

She was as plain and as gauche as ever, and an ape-leader to boot, she thought miserably.

"You cannot do it, can you?" she said sharply to Lord Selworth, who had lapsed into a reflective silence. "I daresay your credit would not survive foisting such an unfashionable family upon the Ton."

He gave her a smile of such dazzling sweetness that her anger evaporated like dew in the sun. "Not at all, Miss Lisle. The sad fact is that I am too new come to the title to *have* any credit with the *haut ton*. I cannot suppose my sponsorship would do you any good."

"Need a lady anyway," Chubby blurted out. He crimsoned but plowed on gamely. "Gentleman can't sponsor ladies, old fellow, with the best credit and the best will in the world."

Lord Selworth turned his smile on his friend. "Just what I was thinking, my dear chap. Fortunately, there is a lady waiting in the wings, and one who already knows Miss Lisle. Please convey to Prometheus, ma'am, that I accede to his requests so far as is in my power. Now all depends on my sister. And, to tell the truth, I shall be mightily surprised if Bina refuses her aid."

Recalling Albinia's worship of her brother, and considering her steadfast friendship, Pippa rather doubted it, too.

CHAPTER 5

"Of *course* I had Mrs. Debenham in mind, dearest," said Mrs. Lisle complacently, when the gentlemen, after a neat nuncheon, had departed for London. "Most implausible for Prometheus, however, so I could not mention her without making it apparent that I had a hand in the proposal, which would *not* serve."

"Gracious no!" Pippa shuddered. "I pray he never finds out. From Prometheus it is a generous notion; from us, the beneficiaries, both encroaching and shockingly self-serving."

"Far from it, my love! Your sister is the beneficiary, and it was not her notion. She is worth a little roundaboutation, is she not?"

"I agreed to do it, did I not? But talking of roundaboutation, Mama, you said I was to decide for myself whether to take part in the Season's entertainments. Now Lord Selworth expects me to go to balls and parties and I shall be the most d-dreadful f-failure again!" Ending on a wail, Pippa felt for her handkerchief.

"You will not!" her mother said adamantly. "Have a little

faith in yourself, Pippa. Actually, what I meant was that it was your decision whether to agree to the whole scheme.''

"That is not what it sounded like," Pippa sniffed.

"No, it was carefully worded."

"Mama, I do believe you grow quite hardened in deceit!"

"I trust you noticed," Mrs. Lisle said with pride, "I did not once refer to Prometheus as 'he' or 'him.' ''

Pippa had to smile. "Yes, I noticed. But that does not change the fact that you told Lord Selworth I shall take part in the Season."

"Think, dearest! I had to. Mrs. Debenham is *your* friend. Even I have not the sheer effrontery to ask her to sponsor Kitty alone. I hope you will go to one or two dances at least, to see how you go on, but if you hate it, my love, you know I shall not force you to continue."

Dropping to the floor, Pippa rested her cheek against her mother's knee. "Oh Mama, I dread it so."

"I know, Pippa love, but give it a chance." Mrs. Lisle stroked her hair. "I cannot bear for you to wither away into an old maid, or worse, to become Mrs. Postlethwaite! Not that I mean to say the vicar is not a worthy man, and kind in his way."

"It was kind in Lord Selworth, was it not, to offer to find us a place to stay in London?"

"Yes indeed. I do not know how we should contrive without his assistance. Most houses will be taken already at this late date, and I cannot afford to pay enough to give us much choice at the best of times. I hope Kitty will not be disappointed to be living in an unfashionable district."

"She will learn to know her true friends by whether they consider themselves too grand to call," Pippa said tartly. "Dearest Mama, how can she, or I, be disappointed when we have the best mama in the world?"

Mrs. Lisle smiled. "I trust you will one day discover," she said softly, "that what a mother does for her children she does to please herself. Well then, I hope we shall not all be disappointed. It is by no means certain Mrs. Debenham will

choose to support her brother. For all we know, she disapproves
of his Radical views.''

"Wynn, the most vexatious thing!" Millicent jumped up
and ran to meet her brother at the drawing-room door. Hanging
on his arm, she prattled on, "Some horrid busybody has persuaded Mama that Bina is too young to be a proper chaperon
for me. Mama says she will come to lend us countenance, but
Bina says we must not tear her away from the children and
Papa, and the only other person who will do is George's horrid
Aunt Prendergast. Wynn, I cannot bear—"

"Hush, chatterbox! And pray don't let me hear you speaking
ill of George's relatives." Detaching her from his sleeve, over
her blond head he gave his brother-in-law a wry nod. "Especially in his presence! Apologize, Millie."

"Well, I'm sorry, George, but it was you who told me—"

"It's all too true," George Debenham interrupted, having
already learnt the necessity if one was to make oneself heard in
his young sister-in-law's presence. A tall, dark, rather saturnine
gentleman, he moved forward and shook Wynn's hand. "I
wouldn't wish my aunt on anyone, and poor Bina is in despair."

"But there is no one else, Wynn," Millie moaned. "Neither
George nor Mama and Papa have any relatives both suitable
and available. I do think Mama could leave the children now
that there are servants to take care of them and Papa, but Bina
says—"

"Bina says," said that lady as Wynn bent to kiss her cheek,
noting that she looked more determined than despairing,
"Mama hates to be away from the young ones and Papa, and
she hates London. I recall all too well how she pined when she
brought me up for my Season. I will *not* be responsible for
putting her through the misery again."

"Quite right," Wynn seconded her. Her unruffled firmness
reminded him strongly of Mrs. Lisle. A splendid notion struck
him. "Hush, infant," he ordered, raising his hand as Millie

started to babble again. "If you will only let me think, I may have the answer."

In a pregnant silence, he sat down, absently accepting the glass of Madeira Debenham inserted into his hand.

Mrs. Lisle lacked connections in the *beau monde,* but she was perfectly respectable. Bina had the connections, through her husband, but lacked an older lady to lend her countenance as a chaperon. She was acquainted with Mrs. Lisle, and she was Pippa Lisle's friend.

On the other hand, Debenham had at most a fleeting acquaintance with the Lisles, several years ago. Was it too much to ask him to take into his house three females of whom he knew next to nothing? Was it too much to ask of Millie, to share her Season fully with Kitty Lisle rather than just having Bina invite the Lisles to a few parties?

He looked at Millicent, sitting on the edge of her chair with her eager gaze fixed on her brother. Her mouth opened, but closed again at his frown. Apart from the ever-wagging tongue, she was amiable enough, a pretty chit in her new, modish morning gown, with blue eyes and the fair hair inherited from their mother, but no conceited beauty. The contrast with Kitty's darkness would be a charming sight for connoisseurs of feminine pulchritude.

And Kitty's availability as a listener might do much to spare Albinia from the ever-wagging tongue.

"Wynn, what is it?" Millie's muteness had reached its outer limit. "What is the answer? Have you remembered another aunt? It does not matter if she is quite decrepit, for all she need do is live here and be respectably elderly while Bina takes me to parties and—"

"Not an aunt, and not in the least decrepit. But—forgive me, Millie, and you, too, Debenham—this is something I must discuss privately with Bina. If she mislikes the idea, it need go no further. Otherwise, nothing shall be done without the assent of both of you."

"I should hope not," Debenham growled with a mock fero-cious glance at Albinia.

"Nothing shall be done without your consent, husband mine," she said tranquilly.

"And mine," Millie insisted. "Wynn said I have to agree as well, don't forget. Who is she, Wynn? Is it someone I shall like? Is she—"

"Come along, Millicent," said Debenham. "Come to my den and tell me all about your presentation gown. Again." With a martyred face, he swept her ruthlessly from the room.

"Deuced lucky you are, my dear," said Wynn, "to catch a capital fellow like George."

"Pray never tell him so, Wynn. He is under the impression he caught me. Now, what is all this mystification about?"

"The Lisles."

"You have been to see them already? How is my dear Pippa?"

"Very well," Wynn said impatiently. "At least, she seemed in the pink of health and no one mentioned any dread disease. She sent her best regards, or whatever it is females send each other."

"Thank you for conveying her greeting so elegantly! What of your mission? Were they able to introduce you to Proteus?"

"Prometheus, Bina, Prometheus. Yes and no."

Bina laughed. "My dear brother, this shilly-shallying will never do if you wish to make a good impression with your speech. Come, let us have a round tale."

"You started all that nonsense about Miss Lisle's health!" Wynn grumbled. "She, incidentally, was most reluctant even to put my case to Prometheus. Her mother persuaded her to allow the gentleman to make up his own mind."

"And he said 'yes and no'?"

"He said yes, but as payment he wishes me to introduce the younger Lisle girl to the Ton. Both girls, actually, only Miss Lisle was not merely reluctant but strongly averse to a second Season."

"Poor Pippa had a miserable time of her first, I fear. But, Wynn, a gentleman cannot sponsor ladies. Do I, by any chance, see where this is leading?"

"I expect so," Wynn admitted. "I would never make the mistake of regarding you as a widgeon just because you don't know Prometheus from Proteus. Will you do it, Bina?"

"Let me make sure I comprehend the full depths of your deviousness," Albinia said cautiously. "You wish me to sponsor Kitty Lisle. No difficulty there. Invitations to a few parties, introductions to a few hostesses, easily done. Is she pretty?"

Wynn grinned. "Ask Chubby. He's heels over head for the chit."

"Mr. Chubb went with you?" She held up her hands. "No, no more red herrings, I beg of you! If I am not mistaken, you believe Mrs. Lisle would be an acceptable substitute for Aunt Prendergast."

"Would she not? I cannot imagine anyone disliking her, but no doubt you saw more of her during Miss Lisle's Season than I did in two short days."

"Oh, as to that, I liked her very well. She was very kind to me when Mama could not cope. But it is a question of whether the world, the starchiest part of the world, will regard her as a suitable . . . chaperon's chaperon!" Bina's smooth forehead wrinkled in thought. Her brother held his breath. "A respectable, well-bred widow of a certain age . . . Wynn, I cannot see why she should not be acceptable."

Wynn breathed again. "To you, to the world, what of George? He is not acquainted with the Lisles, is he? Mrs. Lisle would have to live in the house to be of any use to you."

"George will be only too delighted to welcome anyone who obviates the need to receive his aunt," Bina said dryly. "When I tell him she was kind to me, he will greet her with raptures. Or if he does not, I shall want to know why. But Pippa and Miss Kitty will have to stay, too, of course. I hope Millie's nose will not be put out of joint. Is Kitty pretty? Your opinion, now, not Mr. Chubb's."

"Very pretty," said Wynn, pausing before he added, "and
as dark as her sister."

"Aha! Millie will be glad to hear it. And is she as amiable
as Pippa?"

"Much more so. I don't wish to malign your friend, Bina,
but I should say she can be prickly upon occasion."

Bina smiled, a reminiscent smile. "Yes, Pippa was never a
commonplace, compliant sort of girl. I shall have to make sure
she has an agreeable experience this time. Pray invite them,
Wynn, and leave George and Millicent to me. This is going to
be such fun!"

This is going to be simply dreadful, Pippa thought, gazing
unhappily out of the carriage window. As well as suffering
through at least a few balls and routs for Mama's sake, she
was going to have to struggle to keep her alter ego secret from
Lord Selworth while helping him with his speech. If he resided
with the Debenhams in Town, it would be a doomed struggle.

Even the pleasant prospect of seeing Albinia again was
marred by a sense of obligation. However kindly she tried to
convey her need of Mama's chaperonage, her offer of accommodation was the height of generosity. As for her husband, he
must be very fond indeed to allow three strangers in his home
for a stay of several months, and to go so far as to send this
comfortable carriage to fetch them.

"Mama, I cannot believe we ought to have accepted the
Debenhams' invitation," Pippa said for the dozenth time.

Mrs. Lisle shook her head, smiling. "I should not have
dreamt of angling for such hospitality, still less of making it a
part of Prometheus' conditions. However, as it was freely
offered, I have no hesitation in accepting. With no rent to pay,
there will be much more money to dress you two properly. Not
to mention the advantages of having an address in the best part
of Town."

"I think it is simply splendid of Mrs. Debenham," said

Kitty, "but Miss Warren does seem to believe Mama's presence is necessary to them. And she is happy to share her Season with me, as far as I can make out!" She took from her reticule the crossed and recrossed letter Millicent Warren had sent along with her sister's invitation.

While Kitty and Mrs. Lisle pored again over the indecipherable scribble, Pippa reflected upon the disadvantages of living with two practical optimists. Mama and her sister simply did not understand Pippa's concerns. Though capable of dealing with adversity, both accepted good fortune without a second thought, never fretting about the dark cloud behind every silver lining.

Put thus, it sounded ridiculous, Pippa admonished herself. She really must learn to take the smooth with the rough, not to cross her bridges before she came to them—while continuing not to count her chickens before they hatched. And to avoid clichés like the plague.

Her chief worry, she realized, was lest she fail Lord Selworth. A speech was very different from an article, Papa had taught her, but he had always written his own. By the time she took over the greater part of the labor of writing his articles, he was too ill to make speeches. Suppose, after all Lord Selworth's and his sister's kindness, she proved incompetent to improve on his own efforts?

Cross that bridge if and when you come to it, she reminded herself.

"Mama," cried Kitty, "do look at those celandines. How they shine in the sun. I should like a ball gown that color."

"White and pastels, my love, for a girl making her début, though perhaps a satin underdress would be acceptable. Mrs. Debenham will know. But Pippa would look very well in a bright shade of yellow, I fancy. What do you think, Pippa?"

Pippa glanced out at the hedge bank, golden-yellow with the shiny little flowers. "Perhaps, Mama," she said cautiously, but a surge of hope took her by surprise.

She had forgotten she was no longer condemned to the pale

colors which suited her so ill—made her look ill, in fact. In vivid shades, and without the need to skimp quite so much on fabrics, maybe she could show Lord Selworth she was not altogether an antidote.

Rouge? she pondered. If she was practically on the shelf, surely she was old enough to try rouge, just a little bit, carefully applied. She must consult Bina.

Kitty tapped her arm. "You are lost in a brown study again," she said with a smile. "I asked you what Mr. Debenham is like. Mama has no more than the haziest recollection of him, but you were Mrs. Debenham's best friend, so you must recall the gentleman she married."

"I did not see a great deal of him. For the most part he moved in circles we did not aspire to. The Debenhams are a very old and well-respected Kent family, I collect, connected to the nobility by marriage, though not titled. Once Bina had caught his eye, she was invited to the houses of the best hostesses."

"But what was he *like?*"

"Tall, dark, and handsome, like the hero of a romance."

"Oh, handsome! I do not care about his looks, only his character. He sent his carriage and is to let us stay at his house, so he is kind and generous, but so is Mr. Postlethwaite."

Pippa laughed. "As like as cheese and chalk—both can be cut and crumbled! Generous he may be, but I suspect his kindness has more in it of indulgence for his wife. As I recall, he impressed me as being decidedly high in the instep, frequently satirical, and not a little cynical."

"Then he must positively dote on Mrs. Debenham," Kitty marvelled. "He must have fallen *desperately* in love with her to marry her before her brother became a lord. And she has reformed his character. Oh, excessively romantic!"

"Such high flights," Mrs. Lisle reproved with a smile. "I daresay desperation had nothing to do with it, simply that they found they should suit, a far sounder basis for marriage."

"I expect Bina does suit him very well," Pippa concurred.

"Like the two of you, she is calm and cheerful, and no doubt bears with his crotchets to admiration. However, I may be slandering him! Remember, I did not know him well."

"You are too prosaic, I vow," Kitty exclaimed. "I am sure it is a love match. Never fear, though, Mama, I shall not require a tall, dark, handsome gentleman who loves me desperately. I shall be quite satisfied to find someone who *suits.*"

"As long as he indulges your every whim?" Pippa teased.

"Kitty is by far too sensible to take odd whims into her head," said their mother. "Yet I would not have you suppose suitability precludes love. My dearest wish is for each of you to find a gentleman with whom you can be as happy as I was with your dear papa."

Pippa vowed to do everything within her power to make sure her sister found happiness. For herself she had no such hope.

She could never be contented with a husband who did not respect and appreciate her talents, nor with one who did not share her beliefs. Where was she to find another paragon like Papa?

Lord Selworth—no. Though his political philosophy was in harmony with hers, she had every reason to assume he shared the world's view of clever females. That one of the Lisle ladies might be Prometheus had not so much as crossed his mind, because the sole purpose for the existence of females was to look decorative.

And to bear children, whispered a small voice in Pippa's head. Feeling a warmth stealing up her cheeks, she turned her face to the window.

Country born and bred, Pippa was not entirely ignorant of the significance of the marriage bed. Would the intimacies which seemed so distasteful when considered in connection with Mr. Postlethwaite appear less so with respect to Lord Selworth?

Pippa put her hands to her hot cheeks. That was a subject she ought not—must not—did not wish to pursue.

Fortunately, her leisure for reflection was at an end, their journey nearly so. Kitty had a thousand questions as the carriage passed the Tyburn turnpike and continued along Oxford Street. She gazed all agog at the busy shops, their lamp-lit windows displaying china, silks, watches, fans, pyramids of fruit, or crystal flasks of different colored spirits. Pedestrians thronged the broad, flagged pavements; along the center of the street stood a row of carriages which yet left space enough for two coaches to pass on either side.

"Is it not splendid?" cried Kitty. "Shall we shop here, Mama?"

"Sometimes, I expect. It is less expensive than Bond Street or Pall Mall. The cheapest places are further east, however. We shall have no shillings to waste."

Kitty's face fell. "No, I know, but may I visit these shops, just to look?"

"Of course, my love. And you need not fear that lower cost necessarily means lower quality. Shops in fashionable districts charge more because their customers can afford it and do not mind paying for the convenience."

"And because their rents are higher," Pippa pointed out, to be fair. As the carriage turned right into Davies Street, she continued, "Now this is Mayfair, is it not, Mama?"

Kitty once more glued her nose to the window. "The houses are quite smart," she said doubtfully, "and tall, but so very narrow. I cannot see how Mrs. Debenham will fit us all in."

"Let us hope the Debenhams' is one of the larger houses," Mrs. Lisle said, "though if we have to sleep in the garrets, I, for one, shall not complain."

"Nor I," said Pippa, "but the servants may if they are driven out to bed down on the kitchen floor."

The carriage rolled on down the southwest side of Berkley Square, where the houses were grand enough to impress Kitty. At the bottom of the square they turned right into Charles Street, and pulled up before the largest house on the north side.

Kitty breathed an ecstatic sigh and exclaimed, "Oh, splendid!

I should not mind sleeping on the kitchen floor, I vow! Their kitchen must be grander than my bedchamber at home.''

Pippa smiled, but absently. The elegance of pillars and pilasters, pediments and cornices, elaborate fanlight and ornate wrought iron, dismayed her. Though aware that her friend had married well, she had continued to think of her in the setting where she had known her.

Albinia's letters, full of the dry, yet gently tolerant humor which had attracted Pippa to her, had not reflected her altered circumstances. She had become a wealthy, fashionable wife and mother, whereas Pippa remained an impecunious, unimportant spinster, now verging on old-maidship.

Bina must surely have changed to suit her new position. The easy friendship between them was in the past, and Pippa could only resolve sadly not to presume upon it.

CHAPTER 6

The starchy butler, pink and black marble-floored hall, and handsome staircase further increased Kitty's rapture, and Pippa's misgivings.

"I know I shall enjoy myself excessively," Kitty whispered as they followed the butler and their mother up the stairs. "Dearest Pippa, thank you again for consenting to—"

"Hush, not a word. Pray recollect, it is Mama and our good friend Prometheus who have provided this opportunity."

"I shall not say a word," Kitty promised, "even if Miss Warren and I become as close friends as you and Mrs. Debenham. You have not told her?"

Pippa shook her head, her finger to her lips. The butler opened a door and announced, "Mrs. Lisle, Miss Lisle, Miss Catherine Lisle, madam."

He stepped aside. Mrs. Lisle glanced back at her daughters with a smile, then moved forward into the room. Peering past her, Pippa held her breath. Would Albinia greet them with condescension, and make it plain that she had invited them for her brother's sake? Would she stare at their shabby clothes, forgetting she had once scraped and saved?

How Pippa wished she had not come! It was not being an object of disdain she minded, it was the loss of the precious friendship, nurtured in absence, withering in the harsh light of reality.

"Mrs. Lisle, how utterly delightful to see you again!" Albinia Debenham swept forward with a rustle of silks, and took both Mrs. Lisle's hands in hers. "And how very kind of you to agree to lend us countenance, my sister and me. Allow me to present Millicent."

As Miss Warren made her curtsy and enthusiastically seconded her sister's gratitude, Albinia turned to Pippa and without further ado enveloped her in a hug.

"Dear, dear Pippa, how I have longed for this moment. What times we shall have together, just wait and see." Blue eyes sparkling, holding Pippa's hand, she turned to Kitty. "And you are Miss Catherine, of course. Yes, I see the resemblance. Welcome, my dear."

Pippa did not hear Kitty's response. She was overwhelmed with shame for having misjudged Bina. If only she were like Mama and Kitty, always expecting the best of people. Though they might sometimes be disappointed, they suffered neither anxiety before, nor pangs of guilt afterwards.

"Struck dumb, Pippa?" Bina said. Glancing at Miss Warren, she raised her eyes to heaven with a look of comical despair. Her sister was still chattering away to Mrs. Lisle about someone called Aunt Prendergast. "I cannot blame you," Bina continued. "You will soon learn to interrupt. Millie, pray come and make the acquaintance of Miss Lisle and Miss Catherine."

"Kitty, please, Mrs. Debenham. How do you do, Miss Warren?" Kitty's eyes sparkled with amusement as the full force of Millicent's verbiage flooded over her.

"Do call me Millie. We are going to be the greatest friends. It is above anything that you are come to stay! Coming out with a friend will be much more fun, do you not agree? And so very lucky you are dark and I am fair. We shall make quite a sensation, I am sure, though we must be careful to coordinate our colors. My favorite color is blue, but Bina says we shall have to wear white for grand balls because—''

''My mother told me the same,'' Kitty interrupted firmly, ''and pale colors in general.''

''Come up to my chamber and I shall show you the gowns I already have. Bina says she and Miss Lisle used to—''

''Bina says, first show Miss Lisle and Miss Kitty to their chamber, if you please. They will want to put off their bonnets and pelisses. Pippa, Miss Kitty, I hope you will not mind sharing a chamber.''

Pippa found her tongue at last. ''Not in the least.''

''When I first saw the size of London houses,'' Kitty said gaily, ''I quite expected we should have to sleep in the garrets, if not on the kitchen floor.''

''Not quite so bad,'' Bina said with a smile, ''though even the best Town houses are wretchedly small compared to the country. Mrs. Lisle, will you come with me?''

They all went up another pair of stairs, then Bina led Mrs. Lisle to the back of the house while Pippa and Kitty followed Millicent to the front. Millie chattered the whole way.

''At the rectory I shared a chamber with Bina until she grew up and married. Then my next sister moved in with me, but when Wynn's great-uncle died and we removed to Kymford, we each got a chamber of our own. I asked Bina if you might share with me now, only she thought you would like to be with your sister. She said I would never get a wink of sleep if I had someone to talk to all night, and nor would you. I know I talk a lot, and it is not the least use telling me to stop, because once I have started I cannot, but you must just interrupt when you feel like it. Everyone does. Miss Lisle, pray interrupt when you will. Here is your chamber and mine is next door, so as soon as you have put off your bonnet—''

''I shall come to see your new gowns, Miss Warren,'' Kitty promised.

"Oh, 'Miss Warren'! You really must call me Millie. Let me see, yes, here is hot water for you already, and this is my maid, Nan," she continued as a smiling, round-faced girl in a gray stuff dress and white apron bobbed a curtsy. "Imagine, an abigail of my own! Nan will unpack for you and you must tell her what else you wish her to do. Nan, this is Miss Lisle, and Miss Catherine. I shall wait for you in my chamber, Kitty. I have all the latest fashion magazines, too. Do not be too long!"

As Millicent whisked out, seemingly afraid she would be tempted to stay if she did not remove herself quickly, Pippa surveyed the room. It was decorated in white and pale rose pink, with curtains and counterpanes patterned with wild roses. Larger than her and Kitty's chambers at home combined, it was more than spacious enough for the two beds, two washstands, a dressing table, and a huge clothes press. Banked coals glowed in the tiled fireplace.

"What luxury," Kitty marvelled, untying her bonnet ribbons. "Which bed would you like, Pippa? I am glad we are together. I like Millie, but—" She paused as Pippa glanced warningly at the maid. "But you and I know each other's ways."

When Nan had carried off their pelisses to be brushed, Pippa said, "We shall have to grow accustomed to having servants about and taking care what we say."

"Yes, thank you for stopping me." Kitty giggled. "In any case I am quite certain you can guess exactly what I was going to say."

"I daresay Nan guessed, too," Pippa said dryly.

"The trouble is, some of what Millie says is worth hearing, so one must listen all the time so as not to miss anything."

"She seems good-natured and well-intentioned, so do try to bear with her prattle."

"I mean to, but how fortunate that she is not offended by interruptions, or I might lose my voice through disuse!"

They washed faces and hands in the rose-sprigged china basins. Kitty tidied her hair at the dressing-table mirror and

went off happily to examine Millicent's gowns. Pippa sat down
at the dressing table. Her hair needed little attention, the advantage of straight tresses and a severe style. She wondered what
to do next.

Someone tapped on the chamber door. Servants bringing up
their boxes, she thought. Nan would want to unpack, so she
had best get out of the way.

"Come in."

Albinia appeared. "Pippa, are you comfortable? Is all as it
should be? You will have to accustom yourself to asking the
servants for whatever you need. All too easy, I promise you.
It took me no time at all to grow spoiled."

"No doubt," Pippa said, laughing. It was impossible to feel
awkward with Bina. "You are certainly doing your best to
spoil us. This room is charming, and very comfortable."

"Good. Millicent's maid will help you two, and my dresser
will take care of your mama. She is shockingly toplofty—
Bister, I mean, not Mrs. Lisle—and I was quite terrified of her
when George's mother made me hire her, but your mama had
her eating out of her hand in no time."

"Mama is equal to anything."

"As I know very well. I meant to stay only to make her
comfortable, but we started to reminisce, or I should not have
left you so long. She is lying down now, in preparation for a
strenuous day reconnoitering the shops tomorrow. Come down
to my sitting room where we shall have peace for a private
cose, a rarity in this house, I fear!"

"Your sister is very friendly," Pippa said diplomatically,
following her hostess from the room. "She has made Kitty feel
quite at home already."

"But one does need an occasional respite. Before we go
down, let me just show you . . ." Bina opened the door next
to Mrs. Lisle's chamber. "I have fitted the nursery up as a
sitting room for you and Mrs. Lisle and the girls. I thought
you would like that better than a separate bedchamber."

"Oh yes, I truly do not mind sharing with Kitty."

"If you look down, you can see our garden, though you will scarcely think so tiny a plot worthy of the name."

"There is a garden in here." Pippa glanced around the room, all flowered chintzes and green dimity, with vases of daffodils here and there. She noted the writing table between the windows. It would be perfect for her work. "Thank you, Bina. I cannot judge whether or not you have grown spoiled, but I see you have grown into a first-rate hostess."

"My mama-in-law taught me the way of it. We entertain a good deal in the country. I only wish you had been one of our guests, long since," Bina said seriously as they started down the stairs. "At first I was caught up in adjusting to my new life, and then when I was settled enough to invite you, you wrote about your father's illness."

"I could not have left Papa. Nor Mama afterwards."

"I know. And then, when you were out of mourning, Wynn asked me to present Millie—our mama is *not* equal to anything, as you are aware. I had not thought to expose you to my dearly loved but loquacious sister . . . Here is my sitting room, next to our bedchamber, with George's dressing room beyond, and the drawing room opposite, as you saw."

She opened a door and ushered Pippa into a cosy room, all blue and cream, which someone more pretentious might have dubbed a boudoir. It contained not only comfortable chairs, a small sofa, and a walnut rolltop bureau, but a wardrobe and dressing table. A branch of candles was already lit, for the room faced north and the March evening was already drawing in.

"As I was saying," Bina continued when she had rung for tea and they were seated on either side of a flickering fire, "I had intended to postpone your invitation until the summer. Then Wynn told me about Prometheus and his price, and at the same time I found the threat of George's Aunt Prendergast dangling overhead like the sword of Damascus."

"Damocles," Pippa murmured. "Mr. Debenham's Aunt Prendergast was to be your dragon, I take it."

Bina nodded ruefully. "Someone persuaded Mama I am not old enough to chaperon Millie on my own. Aunt P. is indeed a dragon." She giggled. "Privately George calls her Aunt Prenderghastly, deplorable . . ."

"But clever."

"And appropriate. So you can guess how delighted I was to be able to wave Mrs. Lisle in her face, so to speak. Also, there will be four of us to share Millie's chatter, though I fear Miss Kitty will likely bear the brunt," she said guiltily.

"Kitty is like Mama," Pippa told her, "equal to anything."

"So, you see, I am shockingly selfish and prodigious grateful to Prometheus. Who is this mysterious gentleman who is so solicitous of your family, Pippa? Do tell!"

Pippa was tempted. She trusted Albinia not to broadcast her secret to the world. However, she was certain her friend would be vastly diverted by Lord Selworth's ignorance of who was really helping him, and she was incapable of hiding her amusement. Laughing eyes and a half-concealed smile at the wrong moment could easily lead her brother to the truth.

"Forgive me, Bina, I must not."

"No, of course it is not your secret. I shall not press you, though I assure you I am very safe. Why, Wynn does not even know that I know . . . But that is *his* secret." Her eyes sparkled with glee, just as Pippa had imagined in her own case. "Ah, here is our tea."

While one footman set up a small table in front of the fireplace and the other unloaded his tray onto it, Pippa wondered about the skeleton in Lord Selworth's closet. Unless he had more than one, his sister must have found out how he helped support his family before he inherited the viscountcy.

Bina obviously did not regard it as disgraceful. No doubt it was something dull and unromantic in the way of trade, anathema to the Ton, but perfectly acceptable to ordinary people. Pippa felt slightly hurt that he had not trusted her family not to despise him for it.

"Do you still take your tea without milk?" Bina asked.

"Yes, please. Lemon! What a treat!"

"You see, I remember. And gingersnaps, but do not eat too many. I have ordered all your favorites for dinner, the things we only had at parties: salmon in aspic, escalopes of veal, apricot-almond tarts—do you recall how we sent our partners back for more?"

"Oh yes!" said Pippa, blinking back tears. How could she have doubted her welcome?

"And," said Bina triumphantly, "from George's father's succession houses—a pineapple!"

They looked at each other and burst out laughing.

Into this scene of merriment intruded Lord Selworth. He was wearing evening dress, and despite the tears of mirth in her eyes Pippa noticed the pristine newness of his black coat, fawn Inexpressibles, white marcella waistcoat, and neat cravat.

"Excuse me, ladies," he said with a grin, "I did knock but I daresay you didn't hear. May I share the joke?"

Bina dabbed at her eyes with a tiny lace-edged handkerchief. "You are early, Wynn. Come in, do, and ring for another cup if you would like tea. As for the joke, whether we share it is Pippa's choice."

Pippa hesitated, suddenly shy of this elegant stranger. She and Bina had laughed at the absurd figures they had cut on that evening four years ago. She was not at all sure she wanted Lord Selworth to see her in so ridiculous a light.

Then he smiled at her, and it was the same heart-stopping smile as when he had been a shabby stranger. "Have mercy, Miss Lisle," he said. "You must know the agonies suffered by those who hear laughter and are not permitted to know the cause."

After all, if he thought her a ninnyhammer, he would be the less likely to guess she was Prometheus. "Bina told me she has provided a pineapple for dinner, sir, which reminded us of an occasion on which we both made cakes of ourselves. Pineapple was served at a supper at a ball we both attended."

"Neither of us had ever eaten it before," Bina put in. "We were sitting together, and our partners each brought us a slice."

"I had been chewing away for some time at the little round piece in the middle," Pippa went on, "when I looked up and saw Bina sawing away at hers with her knife. Our escorts were too embarrassed to tell us the core was too tough to be edible."

"They never stood up with us again."

"At least you were able to abandon yours. I had to swallow mine whole!"

Lord Selworth chuckled. "That reminds me of the first time I was served an artichoke, and choked half to death trying to eat the whole leaf. No ladies present, fortunately, or I'd never have been able to face them again."

"No artichokes tonight," said Bina. "Wynn, dinner is at eight, as usual. You are much too early. Pippa and I have not changed yet, and George has not even come home. You will have to entertain yourself."

"I had hoped for a word with Miss Lisle. Can you spare me a few minutes, Miss Lisle, before you dress?"

Pippa consulted the pretty china clock on the mantelpiece. Not yet seven. She supposed some ladies might take over an hour to change their dress for dinner. However, twenty minutes would be more than enough for her, and his artichoke confession had made her feel quite at ease with him again.

"By all means, Lord Selworth."

"Shall we step across to the drawing room? Our business is of no interest to Bina. I don't want to deprive you of your tea, though. Let me pour you another cup, and I'll carry it for you."

Preceding him into the drawing room, Pippa looked around, as she had not had leisure to do on her arrival earlier. She did not know a great deal about furniture, but she thought the prevalent style was slightly old-fashioned. The house belonged to George Debenham's parents, she remembered. Clearly they had no interest in keeping up with the latest rage in decoration. The walls were plain cream, the chairs covered with moss green brocade figured in saffron yellow, and the curtains cream brocade with a saffron design. The effect was at once gracious, soothing, and comfortable.

Pippa took a seat on a sofa by the fire and held out her hands to the flames, a little nervous at finding herself alone with Lord Selworth. He had left the door open, she noted, and reminded herself that this was a business meeting.

"Are you still chilled after your carriage ride?" he asked abruptly, standing over her. "Are you fatigued from the journey? There is no real need for such haste on my part."

She smiled up at him. "No, I am neither cold nor tired, sir. It was but half a day's journey and Mr. Debenham's carriage is quite the most luxurious I have ever been in."

"I'm glad I thought to suggest that he send it for you."

"It was your notion? Thank you!"

"Oh, don't thank me," he said wryly. "It was entirely for my own benefit. I have not my own travelling chaise with me—which is in any case an antiquated and dilapidated vehicle—and I feared Prometheus would dislike your travelling on the Mail or the common stage. You must know it is an object with me to keep that gentleman happy."

Though she murmured assent, Pippa still thought it was considerate of him, even if he had made use of his brother-in-law's carriage for the kind gesture! Few gentlemen would have troubled to spare them the discomfort and expense of a journey by public coach.

"Will you not be seated, Lord Selworth?"

"Just a moment." He went over to a small table in a corner and retrieved a sheaf of papers, then returned to sit opposite her, holding them on his knee. "Before I show you what I have here, I fear I bear bad news."

"Bad news?" With Mama and Kitty abovestairs and in good health, Pippa could not imagine what he meant.

"Bad news for Prometheus, I should say, though I expect you also will be sorry to hear it. I heard rumors that William Cobbett was to be arrested, so I went to see him."

"Oh no, has he been imprisoned at Newgate again?" Pippa asked in dismay.

"No, but he feels it necessary to flee the country. Friends are helping him to evade arrest and take ship for America. He is on his way already."

"I am so glad, but I hope he will be safe in America. Papa told me he was prosecuted there, too, for his writings when last he went into exile."

"I believe so." Lord Selworth shook his head with an air of amused disapproval not unmixed with admiration. "Perhaps he will go to a different state, since each has its own laws, I understand. Be that as it may, he entrusted me with what he owes to Prometheus, a foolish gesture, perhaps, since he is badly in debt."

"Mr. Cobbett is an honest man," Pippa flared up, "if sometimes foolish and prejudiced in his enthusiasm."

Lord Selworth gave her a curious look. "I did not intend to cast doubt upon his honesty."

"I beg your pardon, sir, only Papa used to grow quite heated when people failed to appreciate Mr. Cobbett's many excellent qualities." Which was quite true, but Pippa also hoped the viscount would assume she had been merely quoting her father rather than expressing her own view.

She *must* keep a closer guard on her tongue.

"Cobbett deserves respect for his dedication to principle even at risk of his own safety," Lord Selworth said pacifically, adding with a rueful smile, "I share many of his opinions, and those of your father and Prometheus, as you know, but I'm not sure I'm willing to go to prison to defend them. Let us hope it will not come to that! Nor do I wish to be jailed for embezzlement—here is the money for you to convey to Prometheus."

Standing, he took from his pocket a small cloth purse, which clinked as he placed it in Pippa's hand. He sat down again, at her side now, and riffled through the sheaf of papers.

"I have here two versions of my speech. One is the full text, my latest effort, and the other the same stripped of all the flowery stuff.'' He dropped them in his lap, leant back, and ran his hand through his hair, his expression frustrated and mortified. ''You see, it's the figures of speech and illustrative examples and that sort of thing which defeat me, yet one needs something if one is not to put one's audience to sleep.''

''Nothing so dull as undiluted facts and figures. As Papa was wont to say!'' Pippa added hastily.

''Precisely. Since you were used to make fair copies for Mr. Lisle, perhaps you would not mind skimming through and deciding which will be most useful for Prometheus to work on?''

Pippa could scarcely believe her luck. He had handed her the perfect excuse for knowing the contents of his speech. Moreover, without seeming to suspect the truth, he trusted her judgment as his go-between with Prometheus, making it much easier to pretend to interpret that mythical figure's pronouncements.

Besides being flattering.

''I shall be happy to read them,'' she said primly. ''Do you wish me to inform you which I have picked before I send it to Prometheus? You are staying here?''

''Just send your choice, or both, if you think it best. I shall refund the postal charges, naturally. No, I'm not putting up here.''

''Oh dear, have we driven you out?'' Pippa asked in dismay. ''I am so sorry!''

He smiled. ''Come now, Miss Lisle, you must recollect that you are doing me a favor, not the reverse. I have perfectly comfortable lodgings, I promise you. A friend of Chubb's and mine has sublet his rooms in Albany to us for the Season, as neither of us has a family house in Town. Chubb's parents are as averse to London as was my great-uncle.''

''Does Mr. Chubb mean to do the Season? How brave!'' Pippa said without thinking, then clapped a horrified hand to her mouth.

To her relief, Lord Selworth's blue eyes twinkled. ''Brave

indeed. Perhaps I should warn you that he is rather taken with your sister. I hope she will continue forbearing.''

''As long as he does not start to *brood* at her like John Ruddock,'' said Pippa tartly. ''Heavens, look at the time. I must change for dinner.''

On her way upstairs, she reflected with consternation on how easy she found it to talk to Lord Selworth. She was indeed fortunate that he was not residing with his sister! So much propinquity would certainly have led her into indiscretion.

Yet she could not deny that it would have been pleasant to spend some time with him other than over the Prometheus business. Pippa sighed.

CHAPTER 7

Pippa giggled, then hastily glanced around the sitting room to make certain she was still alone.

The original image was striking: the Government as a castle on a hill, impressively dominant from a distance, a dangerous ruin close to. What had possessed Lord Selworth to elaborate his metaphor?

The common people figured as ghosts rattling their chains in the castle's dank dungeons, while their rulers held a ghostly banquet among tottering towers above. The noble peers would die of laughter. How fortunate that the viscount recognized his own limitations and had turned to Prometheus.

Lord Selworth must read the same Gothic romances Pippa borrowed from the subscription library in High Wycombe, she thought.

She read on, approving the sentiments and a few of the minor embellishments, chuckling over the wilder flights of fancy. The style reminded her of one particular author. She liked Valentine Dred's novels because there was always an undertone of amusement beneath the horrors of headless horsemen and mad monks.

One smiled even as one shuddered. They must be Lord Selworth's favorites, too, to have so influenced him.

It was something else she and his lordship had in common. Something else she must take care not to reveal, for Mr. Dred's stories were not only thrilling and funny, they were distinctly bawdy. Not at all proper reading for an unmarried young lady!

Besides, a serious aspiring politician was bound to be distressed if informed that his style resembled that of a writer of racy fiction.

"Pippa!" Kitty came in, a spring in her step. Pippa quickly covered the manuscript with a large blotter, before she realized her sister was alone. "Still poring over those moldy old papers?"

"Neither old nor moldy," Pippa said with a smile, "and I find them interesting. And come to think of it, I don't need to hide them yet, since Lord Selworth asked me to read them. It is an automatic reaction! You are back early."

"Not at all. It is nearly one o'clock."

"Heavens, is it really?"

The speech was taking longer to read than she had supposed. How long ought a maiden speech in the House of Lords to last? According to Papa, for maximum impact a speech should be neither long enough to send listeners to sleep, nor so short it was easily overlooked among scores of others.

But at first reading Pippa was not sure whether Lord Selworth's was actually too long. She had paused to ponder phrases and paragraphs. It had taken a while to learn to decipher his large, sprawling hand, so different from Papa's and her own neat, small writing—which also made the number of pages misleading.

"You have not heard a word I've said!" Kitty protested.

"You have been to hundreds of shops, each one more splendid than the one before. Yet somehow you are still full of energy!"

"It was such fun. Dozens, not hundreds—at least a score—and all much larger and finer than anything at home. Mama has decided which we are to patronize, so this afternoon you are not excused. You must come to choose which materials you like so that Mama and I can begin to make up our gowns.''

''I am perfectly willing to trust your judgment, Kitty. Well, yours and Mama's! I must finish reading this. Lord Selworth wishes me to decide which version to 'send to Prometheus.' ''

''But you don't have to send it anywhere,'' Kitty pointed out, ''so there is no hurry.''

''Sshh!'' Pippa glanced at the door. ''Remember we are not at home. Anyone might come in.''

''There is no hurry,'' Kitty repeated in an exaggerated whisper.

Pippa frowned. ''I forgot to ask Lord Selworth when he expects to give the speech. I wonder whether the date is set?''

''It cannot be soon, or he would have asked Prometheus to make haste. Darling Pippa, Mama says you must come, and I am sure Lord Selworth would not encourage you to disobey her for his sake.''

Outside the sitting-room door, Wynn paused with his hand raised to knock. Miss Lisle to disobey her mother for his sake? What on earth was the girl talking about? Anyone would think he had tried to persuade her to elope!

He knocked. A pause ensued before Miss Lisle called, ''Come in.''

''Good morning, Miss Lisle, Miss Kitty.''

''Oh, it is you,'' said Miss Lisle with relief. ''I just shoved your papers into the drawer in case—'' She stopped, her cheeks tinged with pink, and fished the manuscript out of the desk drawer.

Wynn pulled a face. ''Is it so awful that I shall be utterly mortified should anyone else read it?''

''Not at all!'' she disclaimed, then bit her lip, her changeable hazel eyes dancing.

She had most expressive eyes, Wynn noted, even as he said with a rueful shake of his head, ''I see my *rough* draft amuses you.''

"I am sorry," she said guiltily.

"Don't apologize! Chubb's reaction was exactly the same."

"I beg your pardon," Miss Kitty put in, "but if you two mean to discuss the speech, I shall leave you to it. Remember, Pippa, Mama expects you to go with us this afternoon." She tripped out, closing the door behind her.

Wynn hesitated, undecided whether to open the door again for propriety's sake. Everyone knew he and Miss Lisle had business together; everyone knew there was no more intimate association between them; and it would look so pointed. He left the door closed, pulled up a chair, and sat down beside the writing table.

"I'm afraid I have kept you from some outing this morning."

"One I gladly missed, but I must go with Mama and Kitty to the shops after luncheon, to buy dress materials. It will not delay things much, though I have not quite finished reading."

"My dear Miss Lisle, I realize the Season is far more important to you than my affairs can possibly be." He paused, with an enquiring look, as she opened her mouth. However, she closed it again firmly, rather tight-lipped. "Believe me, I intend no irony. I am eternally grateful for your help."

Sensitive lips relaxed in a quirk. "You too! Bina tries to make me believe we are doing her a favor, when it must be plain to the meanest intelligence how deeply indebted to her we are."

"I'm sure she will be as relieved as I if you will agree to cry quits! My bargain with Prometheus requires that you enjoy a Season, and believe me I don't wish to deprive you of any of its pleasures, shopping included. Besides, there's no knowing when I may be able to give the speech," he added with a smile.

She looked down, long, dark lashes veiling her eyes in apparent discomposure, to Wynn's puzzlement. In another female he might suspect coyness, but Miss Lisle seemed a stranger to the art of coquetry.

"No date has been set?" she said. "I forgot to ask."

"I haven't yet approached Lord Eldon, the Lord Chancellor,

not being sure when I shall be prepared. So you may tell Prometheus I am in no great haste, though I hope this session of Parliament will be possible.''

"With Mr. Cobbett gone to America, there will be no articles to write. Though other matters may intervene,'' she added hurriedly. ''There should be plenty of time before the end of this session, but I can give you no assurances as to how long it will take.''

"It depends upon how busy Prometheus is, of course, and upon how much work there is to do." Wynn gestured at the pile of papers and made a show of bracing himself. "Be honest, is it truly dreadful?''

"By no means. Your points are well ordered and well argued—insofar as I may presume to judge.''

"It's the embellishments, isn't it? Meretricious metaphors and fanciful figures of speech, that's where my troubles lie. So you will send Prometheus the unadorned version, to be ornamented with genuine pearls in place of my artificial roses.''

Deliberately sought, her laugh delighted him. "Your roses are not all artificial. Rather, they are rosebushes, sadly in need of pruning. I am sure Prometheus will agree. It will be much better to take your bushes as a starting point and keep what blooms can be saved.''

"Watered with my tears! I own I should be glad to preserve a few.''

"I daresay you will deliver the speech with more conviction if at least some of the imagery is your own. Papa said he could always tell in the House when a man had had his words written for him. The spark of enthusiasm would be missing.''

"A fate I wish to avoid! Pray use your influence with Prometheus.'' Wynn observed her closely as he spoke, hoping for a hint as to how much influence she expected to have.

Again she lowered her lashes, and her porcelain-pale skin flooded with a rosy blush as she nodded.

Damn! he thought. She does love him. But as to whether

she fancied Prometheus returned her love, Wynn was none the wiser.

"Prometheus has had a first consultation with Lord Selworth, I hear," said Mrs. Lisle, as the Debenhams' landau rolled along Charles Street. "How did it go?"

The landau's hoods were up against a fine rain, so the Lisles were able to talk freely without fear of the coachman overhearing. Mrs. Lisle had refused to take a footman, who would draw too much attention in the districts they were bound for.

"I rubbed through unscathed," Pippa said doubtfully, "I think."

"Was he troublesome? I should not have expected it of him. Still, gentlemen become amazingly defensive when their competence is called into question, even when they have already admitted to being in difficulties."

"No, he took criticism like a lamb. And I trust he still has no notion that I am Prometheus."

Yet he had studied her face when he mentioned her influence with Prometheus, and she had felt her face grow stupidly hot. With luck he would put the blush down to his scrutiny—especially as she had still more stupidly flushed when he smiled. But no doubt he was accustomed to young ladies swooning when he smiled, she told herself tartly. She must hope to grow sufficiently accustomed to his smile for it to cease to ruffle her.

"Pippa, he did not attempt any familiarities? It was unwise of Kitty to leave you alone together!"

"He did not even try to flirt, Mama. I am quite sure my only attraction for him is as his conduit to Prometheus. At my age, I have no need of a chaperon when we are discussing business in his sister's house." Nor at any other time or place, she thought, a trifle wistful.

"Let us have no more of this nonsense about your age, my love. No man of sense thinks the worse of a woman for being beyond the first foolishness of youth."

''Do you mean that I am foolish, Mama,'' Kitty cried, laughing, ''and must marry a fool? I shall defy you and marry a man of genius.''

Mrs. Lisle smiled. ''You are a sensible girl for your age, Kitty, but remember that a fool is sometimes easier to deal with than a man of genius. Not that I wish you to choose your husband by his intellectual attainments. However, when you fall in love, as no doubt you will, ask yourself whether you can imagine the gentleman in question as a friend as well as a lover.''

Pippa recalled receiving the same advice before her first Season. It had undoubtedly prevented her making a cake of herself over more than one beau of handsome face or insinuating charm. She had been quite unable to picture them taking a vigorous country walk with her, or talking politics at the breakfast table.

The longest, most vigorous of country walks would have exhausted her less than their afternoon of shopping. Muslins and shawls from Waithman's at Ludgate Hill; Irish linen from Newton's in Leicester Square; poplins from Layton and Shear at Bedford House; all these and the silk merchants and haberdashers of Cheapside blurred in Pippa's mind.

''Thank heaven for Bina's carriage,'' she said, leaving the shelter of a shop assistant's umbrella to climb into the landau for what she hoped was the last time today. ''If we had had to traipse about in hackneys, I doubt I should have survived.''

''Cranbourne Alley next, for bonnets,'' Kitty proposed, lively as ever, ''now that we have the colors to be matched.''

Pippa groaned.

''Not now,'' said her mother, to her relief. ''Ladies do not frequent Cranbourne Alley so late in the day, and after we inspect our purchases this evening we shall have a better idea of what we need. As much as possible we must make one bonnet do for several gowns.''

''I like trimming hats,'' said Kitty. ''One or two plain bonnets and a variety of trimmings will be plenty.''

"But consider, my love, when you change your dress you will not have time to be altering the trimmings of your bonnets."

They continued to discuss hats, while Pippa's mind drifted. Why did ladies only frequent Cranbourne Alley in the morning? Since Mama gave no reason, it was probably not a proper subject for young ladies. Unmarried young ladies, at least. Bina might know. Why were unmarried young ladies supposed to be kept in ignorance of so much that was going on in the world? Surely the more they knew the better they could deal with life.

If women were properly educated, they would want to run their own lives. Men would have to give up their authority—which was the answer to her question. They set the rules, and in their determination to keep hold of the reins, they dictated what respectable young ladies should or should not know.

Hence the need to keep the identity of Prometheus secret. However much men admired "his" articles, if they discovered a woman wrote them they would somehow convince themselves they were unworthy of serious consideration.

If Lord Selworth found out, he might believe himself justified in reneging on his agreement with Prometheus. The secret *must* be kept, or Kitty's Season would be ruined.

"It is a great pity styles have become so elaborate," Mrs. Lisle bemoaned. "Silks are more expensive than muslins, to start with. Then the wider skirts take more material, and there is endless trimming to be done."

A trifle enviously, Kitty asked, "Have you seen Millie's Presentation gown, Mama? The train alone uses yards and yards of lace, and the bodice is embroidered with seed pearls. And hoops are still *de rigueur* at Court, just like in the old days, so the skirt is enormous, and the petticoat also." She giggled. "I should feel such a figure of fun wearing hoops!"

"I am glad, dearest, because I cannot manage such an expense, though if it were possible I daresay Mrs. Debenham would be kind enough to present you."

"In any case," Pippa flared up, "it would go against all Papa's principles to make obeisance to the monarchy."

"In any case," Kitty pointed out pacifically, "the poor Queen is not well and Millie's Court dress may very well go to waste!"

"In any case," said Mrs. Lisle, "we shall be hard-pressed to make all the gowns we really need. I hope you will have time to help with the sewing, Pippa."

Pippa groaned again. "Pray do not expect me to cut out, Mama. You know I am terrified of making expensive mistakes. Give me the simplest seams and hems, and I shall contrive to do my part."

"We shall see. I do not wish you to tire your eyes with stitchery if you have a great deal of reading and writing to do."

"Think how tired the eyes of seamstresses must get."

"And they have not even the pleasure of sewing for themselves," Kitty agreed.

"They are paid for their labor," Mrs. Lisle said, "when many would be glad of any work."

"How lucky I am," cried Kitty, "not to have to work for my living, thanks to my dear family."

"And how lucky I am," said Pippa, "to be paid to do what I should very likely choose to do even without pay! It is a pity, though, that Mr. Cobbett has gone abroad. We shall have less money than you expected, Mama, and I have less excuse to avoid sewing."

The landau turned into Charles Street, passed the Running Footman public house at the corner of Hay's Mews, and stopped in front of the Debenhams' house. A boy ran up to hold the horses' heads while the coachman clambered down from his perch to come and let down the step.

Kitty glanced around and said, "We shall have to make several trips to carry in all these parcels."

"The footmen will fetch them," Mrs. Lisle told her. "It will never do for the Debenhams' guests to be seen trotting up the front steps laden with packages. We have done very nicely, girls, and there is more yet to be sent round by the shops." With satisfaction she shook her purse, which jingled. "Stuffed full when we started out but not empty yet—very nicely indeed!"

Pippa was shocked to realize how much they had bought. Why, Mama must have spent enough to keep a poor family for years! Papa's principles had fallen by the wayside without a word of protest from his elder daughter.

Yet she had had her Season, for all the good it did her, and it was not for her to spoil Kitty's. She said nothing now, but resolved to ask Mama later how Papa had felt about the expenditure on the earlier foray into the marriage market.

As they entered the hall, the butler informed them stiffly that Mrs. Debenham and Miss Warren were entertaining callers in the drawing room.

"We shall not disturb them," said Mrs. Lisle, smiling slightly at the butler's involuntary look of relief. "Have our purchases taken up to the little sitting room, if you please."

"At once, madam."

On the way upstairs, Mrs. Lisle observed complacently, "We are most fortunate that Mr. and Mrs. Debenham senior entertain a good deal at their country home. Although Mrs. George Debenham has only visited Town briefly since her marriage, she is already acquainted with a great many people, I collect."

"I believe so," Pippa agreed.

"For the present we shall concentrate on making up morning gowns and walking dresses so as to be able to join in morning calls. Time enough for evening gowns when we have met hostesses who are likely to invite us to evening parties."

"The primrose and white cloud muslin first," Kitty decided, bouncing up the second flight of stairs, "then the green sprig. Which do you want for your first gown, Pippa?"

After a moment's thought, Pippa confessed, "I fear I cannot for the life of me remember what I chose."

Her mother and sister laughingly scolded her. Kitty went on to remind her of deep rose mull muslin and violet jaconet muslin, willow green Circassian cloth, and celestial blue lustring.

"You will have to tell me which is suitable for which kind of dress," Pippa told her as they doffed bonnets and pelisses in their chamber. "I bought at your direction."

They hurried to the sitting room, where Mrs. Lisle joined them a moment later.

"This table is perfect for laying out and cutting patterns," she said, going over to a large table Pippa had scarcely noticed. "I daresay that is why Mrs. Debenham had it put in here. She attends to our needs with the greatest delicacy, never commenting on the difference in our situations. You could not have made a better friend, Pippa."

"I know it." Pippa drifted towards the little writing table. "Mama, pray excuse me for the moment. I should like to finish reading this speech while Bina and Millicent are otherwise occupied. Kitty may choose which dress I am to have first, and once it is cut out and pinned, I shall struggle with the seams."

Even as she spoke, she sat down at the desk. One of the drawers had had a key in it, and in this she had locked the manuscript, putting the key on a ribbon around her neck. She unlocked the drawer. Soon she was so absorbed she scarcely noticed the arrival of two laden footmen, the rustle of paper, Mama and Kitty's soft chatter, the snick of scissors. When a cup of tea miraculously appeared in front of her, she drank thirstily without sparing a thought for its provenance.

Coming to the end of Lord Selworth's speech, Pippa pondered the necessary alterations. She was almost sure it was going to be too long, even with the overfanciful passages cut down to size. He wanted to solve all the world's evils at once.

"Pippa," Kitty said gaily, "unless you wish this gown to be merely *nearly* the right size, you must come now and have pins stuck into you."

"Is it not enough that I shall soon be sticking needles into myself?" Pippa grumbled, but she locked away the speech and mustered her patience for the fitting.

* * *

Altogether weary of clothes, Pippa changed quickly for dinner. Leaving Kitty to share Nan's ministrations with Millicent, she went to her mother's chamber.

"May I come in, Mama? I want to talk to you."

"Of course, my love. Bister has done everything but put my cap on for me, so we shall not be disturbed." Mrs. Lisle, sitting at her dressing table, picked up her best cap and set it on her head. Tying the ribbons, she went on, "You are a little dismayed, are you not, by the number of gowns I propose to make for you? I have promised not to force you to go to parties if you attend a few and find you still dislike such affairs excessively."

"It is not so much that, Mama, as the cost."

"Are you afraid I shall fall into debt? You may be easy, dearest. You know your papa's opinion of those who buy luxuries upon credit and then deprive honest shopkeepers of their due."

"Papa held no high opinion of those who waste good money on luxuries when others want for necessities," Pippa pointed out. "I never wondered before, but seeing all we purchased today—Was he not distressed by the expenditure on my Season?"

"He realized the need. When I pointed out to him that in the circumscribed society at home you had little chance of meeting a man you could love, he had no objection to our repairing to Town. Or rather, his only objection was that he did not wish to lose you. He loved you dearly."

"I miss him dreadfully, still."

"And I, my love. But Papa knew you would one day want a home of your own. He was a sensible man, as well as an idealist, and he recognized his duty to his family as well as to humanity."

"Lord Selworth is the same, I think," Pippa said slowly.

"Eager as he is to change the world, his first consideration upon attaining the viscountcy was to provide for his family."

"Very true."

"I believe he is very fond of them, but the sad truth is, if he gave away all his worldly wealth except enough to keep them from poverty, his influence would be greatly lessened." Becoming aware of her mother's intent scrutiny, Pippa grimaced. "He confuses me."

"My darling, I hope I have not imperilled your heart with my clever scheme! I should never forgive myself. You have had little contact with personable gentlemen; it is not surprising that his attentiveness should disturb you. Remind yourself that he seeks your company because of Prometheus."

"As *I* told *you*," Pippa concurred. "I know it well." She gave her anxious mother a reassuring smile, yet she could not have sworn that her heart was not in peril.

CHAPTER 8

George Debenham dined at his club that evening. "He knows I shall require his escort once we begin to go about in company," Bina explained as the ladies went in to dinner. "He is making the most of a brief freedom before he is expected to dance attendance upon us."

"Shepherding five females about will keep him busy," Mrs. Lisle agreed with a smile.

A rooster with a flock of hens, Pippa thought. Or, as Lord Selworth would doubtless dramatically have it, a Turkish sultan with his harem. She wondered whether the viscount would occasionally condescend to escort his sisters. His presence would do much to reconcile her to frequenting the entertainments of the Season.

"So we shall have a comfortable domestic evening," Bina said. "Millicent and I request permission to display our needlework skills. Dare I hope you will trust us not to spoil your new gowns?"

"Oh no," said Mrs. Lisle, for once visibly flustered. "That is, of course we should trust you, but you cannot wish—"

"Indeed we do," Millicent burst out "For until you have fashionable gowns, Kitty cannot go about with me and that is what I want above anything, and we are both quite good at sewing. At least, Bina has done nothing but fine work for years and years, ever since she married, but I helped to make all the family clothes, shirts and chemises and trousers and aprons and—"

"A complete catalogue is unnecessary," Bina cut her off with a smile.

"And everything else right up until Wynn became suddenly rich, which was just a few months ago, so you see we can certainly be of assistance. And I am simply dying to see what you have bought and to learn where you found bargains, because the prices in the Bond Street shops are outrageous and those in Oxford Street not much lower, and when you have been accustomed all your life to counting pennies, it goes against the grain to see them squandered, I assure you," Millicent said earnestly, "though what grain has to do with anything, I cannot guess."

Here Kitty interrupted to explain to her that the grain concerned was wood, not corn. Mrs. Lisle seized the opportunity to gratefully accept Bina's offer of assistance, so the ladies spent a cosy evening with their needles.

At least, Pippa spent part of the evening with a needle. The third time she pricked her finger, she spotted a delicate India muslin. After the bustle attendant upon swift removal of the bloodstain, she was invited to read to the workers from one of Mr. Scott's novels.

This had the added advantage of curbing Millie's tongue. Somehow she managed to confine herself to comments upon the story and necessary questions about the sewing.

All in all, it was a pleasant and productive evening, ending with a gown for each of the Lisles finished to the last knot of ribbon.

"We shall do it again," Bina vowed, "for, you know, Mrs. Lisle, in this I am as self-interested as Millie. Until *you* are able to go about, I must not accept invitations to evening parties, and until *Pippa* can, I shall not wish to.''

Pippa marked the place in the book and set it aside, and the others folded their work. As Mrs. Lisle, Kitty, and Millicent left the room, Bina held Pippa back, closing the door behind the others.

''Stay a moment. Pippa, the last thing I wish is to offend, but I see no reason why you and I should not share gowns again, as we used to.''

''Oh Bina, how can you call yourself selfish or self-interested? You are quite the most generous of friends, but it will not do.''

''Why not? Just because I had the good fortune to meet George four years ago, and you were not lucky enough to meet the right gentleman? It would save both labor and your mother's purse. Change a few ribbons and no one will recognize the dresses. You are as dark as ever, and I as fair, and we were always much of a size.''

''I skinny and you slender,'' Pippa reminded her. ''The fact is, I shall need few gowns, as I do not mean to go about much. Just one or two parties to satisfy Mama.''

''What nonsense, my dear! If you were skinny and I slender, now you are slender while my figure, I fear, is rapidly tending towards the matronly. With proper clothes and the wisdom of four more years—indeed, I cannot think why girls are thrown so young and ignorant into the world!—there is no reason why you should not enjoy yourself thoroughly this time.''

''But I—''

Bina ruthlessly interrupted. ''Besides, I shall not let you disappoint my brother.''

''Lord Selworth?'' Had he told his sister he looked forward to escorting Pippa to parties, perhaps even to dancing with her at balls? For a heart-stopping moment Pippa wondered, before the brief dream was swept away by the chilly wind of reality.

''Wynn promised Prometheus to introduce you to Society,'' Bina reminded her unnecessarily. ''He will not feel he has

carried out his end of the bargain if you merely attend a ball
or two. So that is settled. We shall go through my wardrobe
tomorrow and see what will suit you best.''

Pippa surrendered, at least temporarily. Kissing Bina, she
said, ''How can I thank you, my dearest friend?''

''Pray do not! So tedious,'' Bina said with a smile, opening
the door. ''George gives me a simply enormous dress allow-
ance, you must know. Now, let us set a time. What are your
mama's plans for tomorrow morning?''

''We are to go to Cranbourne Alley to choose hats. That
reminds me, why do ladies shop in Cranbourne Alley only
in the mornings?'' Pippa asked, following Bina out into the
passage.

''Because it is an insalubrious district with a great many
bawdy houses, and—'' At the sound of a gasp behind them,
she stopped and turned. ''Yes, Reuben?''

One of the footmen had come out from the backstairs in
time to hear his mistress's remark. Crimson to the ears, he
stammered, ''Was you wanting me to snuff the candles and
bank the fire, madam?''

''Yes, thank you, we are finished in there.'' As the footman
disappeared into the sitting room, Bina continued in a lower
tone but without much concern, ''Oh dear, I trust the Running
Footman will not be all abuzz with tales of how we were caught
discussing houses of ill repute! As I was saying, in the afternoon
and evening, caps and bonnets are not the only wares displayed
in Cranbourne Alley. Or so I have heard.''

''I did not suppose you had gone to see for yourself!'' Pippa
assured her, laughing.

They parted, to retire for the night. In bed, Pippa and Kitty
talked for a little while about the experiences of the day, but
Kitty soon fell asleep in the middle of a sentence. Pippa lay
wakeful, her thoughts returning to Lord Selworth's speech.

Perhaps she should suggest he stuck to one topic rather than
trying to cram in all the ills he wished to combat. The talk of
bawdy houses reminded her of Papa's descriptions of the dread-

ful lives of women, some no more than young girls, forced into prostitution by pimps and abbesses, or by simple poverty. Pippa had laughed at Bina's comment, but their plight was no laughing matter. Lord Selworth might be willing to take up their cause.

But Pippa could never bring herself to broach the subject with him, even if he believed the notion came from Prometheus. She had best just work with what he had given her.

She slept. In her dreams, she was back in the sitting room, trying on half-made clothes. As she stood in her shift, Lord Selworth came in without knocking. Failing to notice her deshabille, he swept her into a dance, but everyone else in the ballroom started to point at her and whisper to each other. Angrily, Lord Selworth accused her of displaying her wares.

Half-waking, Pippa muttered, "At least you have realized at last that I have wares to display!" She turned over and went back to sleep.

"I thought I might drop in to see Miss Lisle this morning," Wynn said casually, picking up knife and fork to tackle a rather meagre beefsteak.

Chubby looked at him in surprise over the rim of his coffee cup. "Gurgle?" he said.

"Don't speak with your mouth full," Wynn reproved him. "Just to find out if she's forwarded my speech to Prometheus yet."

"Wouldn't plague her about it, if I was you. Don't want to vex her."

"I shouldn't dream of plaguing her," Wynn said with dignity. "A man may call on his sister, may he not? And being there, it's only polite to exchange a word or two with her guests. And if Miss Lisle has sent it off, what more likely than that she'll mention it?"

"Ah." Chubby chewed on this proposal and a mouthful of beef, swallowed both, and brightened. "In that case, I could come, too. I've met Mrs. Debenham. Met Miss Lisle, come to that, and Mrs. Lisle.''

''Not to mention Miss Kitty.''

Chubby pinkened. ''Not the thing for a single gentleman to call on an unmarried young lady uninvited, but I can go with you to visit your sister.''

''And being there,'' Wynn teasingly quoted himself, ''it's only polite to exchange a word or two with her guests.''

''If I can think of anything to say,'' Chubby fretted.

''Come now, you and Miss Kitty got on swimmingly.''

''That was in the country. We're in Town now,'' said Chubby inarguably. ''It's different. Not the thing to talk about cows and chickens in Town.''

''I shouldn't worry, if I were you, old fellow,'' Wynn advised him. ''The chances are, with Millicent there, neither of us will need or have the opportunity to open our mouths.'' He opened his newspaper to the political news.

As usual, the doings of Lord Liverpool and his myrmidons infuriated Wynn. The Prime Minister was still fighting the introduction of a sliding scale to the Corn Law to allow more grain imports. As well as his Tories, many Whig landowners of an otherwise Reformist bent supported him. Wynn itched to discuss this betrayal of the hungry poor with Miss Lisle.

Whoa! He was confusing Pippa Lisle with her father and Prometheus. Just because she seemed quite a clever young woman, he must not forget that she was a woman. Though she had clearly learnt from Benjamin Lisle something of the art of politics, Wynn would have to be careful not to discomfit her by stretching the limits of her understanding.

Tempted, he told himself severely that it would be most ungentlemanly to put her deliberately to the blush only because she was dashed pretty with roses in her cheeks.

''Do put that damn newspaper away and eat your breakfast,'' Chubby said impatiently. ''If we don't get on, the ladies will have gone out.''

Solely for his friend's sake, Wynn obliged. He, after all, was in no particular hurry to see Miss Lisle. Whether she had already sent off the manuscript or not, she would be unable to tell him what Prometheus thought of it for at least several days.

Breakfast dispatched, the gentlemen abandoned dressing gowns and carpet slippers in favor of morning coats and Hussar boots. Donning hats and gloves, they sallied forth un-topcoated, for the sun shone and spring was in the air.

Had he been striding across the fields at home, Wynn would have whistled. In Piccadilly, he managed to restrain himself insofar as the whistle was concerned, though his gait had nothing in common with the saunter of a Bond Street Beau. As he walked, he looked about him with interest at the shops, the passersby, the vehicles in the street. He ought to have a carriage of his own. Curricle, phaeton, or gig, he pondered. Not a phaeton; one type was too impractical, the other too staid.

At his side Chubby, also country born and bred, kept pace. Not for several minutes did Wynn notice that his silent companion's gaze was fixed on his feet.

"It won't do," said Chubby at that moment, shaking his head.

"The boots? Dammit, I know we decided not to pay Hoby's exorbitant prices, but the fellow we patronized did a perfectly good job."

"Nothing wrong with the boots themselves—it's the polish. They ain't got the shine they had two days ago."

"We've been wearing 'em," Wynn pointed out as they turned up Berkley Street. "You can't expect them to look new forever."

"Not forever," Chubby admitted, "but for a while yet. If I had a proper valet . . . No, m' father would think I'd run mad."

"Miss Kitty won't care if your boots look two days old. The Lisles aren't so finical."

"Maybe not, but I wouldn't want Miss Kitty to think I don't hold her in high enough esteem to take the trouble. Besides," Chubby said doggedly, "whatever you say, Mrs. Debenham's going to expect you to do the pretty. Can't leave it all to

Debenham, five females to squire about. Daresay he won't
mind if I lend a hand, too.''

To his surprise, Wynn discovered balls and routs and breakfasts no longer sounded like an utter waste of time, though he
would not admit it aloud. His mother would expect him to
accompany his sisters now and then, and he did not want to
disgrace them.

Glancing down at his boots, he could not help but note the
dullness of the blacking. ''Come to think of it, I shan't make
much of an impression in the Lords if I'm not turned out bang
up to the mark. And you're right. The fellow who does for us
hasn't time for a thorough job with half a dozen others to take
care of. I'll hire us a valet, or better, a chap who don't hold
himself too high to cook us a decent breakfast, too.''

''I say, didn't mean to hint—''

''You can pay what you're paying now, so that Lord Chubb
won't know the difference. Look, there's the Sign of the Pot
and Pineapple. Do you suppose Miss Lisle . . . the ladies would
like some of Gunter's kickshaws?''

''You're the one with sisters.''

''So I am. Come along, then.''

They cut across the corner of Berkley Square to Number
Seven, the premises of Gunter's, Confectioner, Pastrycook, and
Caterer. Outside, a notice board announced the receipt of a
cargo of ice from the Greenland seas; patrons were advised
that cream fruit ices were once again available.

Wynn and Chubby were in pursuit of more durable prey.
They emerged from the shop a few minutes later, each bearing
a pasteboard box full of vanilla, apricot, cinnamon and orange
flower pastilles; candied ginger; and Gunter's famous cedrati
and bergamot chips.

''Shall we treat them to an ice this afternoon?'' suggested
Chubby.

''Not today. With all these bonbons as well, they'd make
themselves sick,'' said Wynn with the ruthless practicality of
the possessor of many small siblings.

"Miss Kitty wouldn't!"

"She might. Don't suppose she's used to a lot of sweets. Miss Lisle wouldn't, nor her mother or my sister," Wynn conceded, "but I wouldn't put it past Millicent, and it would ruin the party."

Chubby blenched. "Yes, rather. I'll just dash back in and see how long they expect the ice to hold out."

He returned to report that Gunter's expected, barring shipwreck, to be able to serve ices well into the summer months. "So that's all right. Bring 'em round any time. You know what, old chap, I'm almost looking forward to the Season!"

"Your father doesn't object to your frittering away your time in Town?" Wynn asked as they turned the corner into Charles Street.

"Been at me for years to get a bit of Town bronze before I settle down. He and my mother hope I'll find a wife, of course, but I never expected I'd find a girl I'd really want to marry."

"Hold hard, Chubby, you can't be serious about the chit! You hardly know her."

"I know what I want," Chubby said stubbornly. "And I know I haven't much chance with such a wonderful girl."

Wynn still suspected calf love, in which case time would cure his friend if allowed to do its business. Whereas, should Kitty be offered and grasp an immediate opportunity to wed a future title and comfortable fortune, Chubby might find himself repenting at leisure.

"You don't mean to throw the handkerchief right away, I hope," he said, stopping on his sister's doorstep.

"Lord no. It wouldn't be fair. She's bound to have dozens of offers. If she hasn't accepted someone better by the end of the Season, I'll try my luck."

Satisfied, Wynn gave a brisk *rat-tat* with the brass lion's-head knocker on the green front door.

The first footman opened the door. The butler would have been on hand to usher callers up to the drawing room if Mrs. Debenham were receiving, but after all Wynn was her brother.

"M'sisters in, Reuben?" he asked.

"Mrs. Debenham and Miss Warren are not at home, my lord."

"You mean they have gone out, or they're just 'not at home'?"

"Gone out, my lord," the footman clarified apologetically.

"What about the Lisles?"

"Not at home, my lord."

"Dash it all, man, are they in or not?" Wynn bethought himself too late that he had no right to intrude upon the Lisles—as opposed to his sister—if they were euphemistically "out" rather than really out.

Looking a trifle bemused, Reuben said, "Mrs. Lisle, Miss Lisle, and Miss Catherine *left the house* with Mrs. Debenham and Miss Warren."

"Blast. Where did they go, do you know?"

"To pay calls, I understand, my lord."

"No hope of catching up with them, then," said Wynn, disappointed.

"Miss Lisle did express the hope of stopping at Hookham's Library in Bond Street."

"Hookham's, eh? Splendid. I'll leave a note for Miss . . . for Mrs. Debenham."

"Mr. Debenham is at home, my lord. That is, he is in the house. Whether he is 'at home'—"

Wynn held up his hand. "Enough! We don't want to see Debenham."

"Always happy to see Debenham," Chubby corrected with punctilious politeness.

The gentleman in question burst out of his den at that moment. "What the deuce . . . ? Oh, it's you, Selworth. Good morning, Chubb. Is something amiss, Selworth?"

"Only the inability of the English upper classes and their servants to say what they mean. Not Reuben's fault," Wynn added quickly as Debenham cocked an eyebrow at his footman.

"A minor misunderstanding. Sorry to disturb you. I just dropped in to see Albinia."

"All the ladies have gone out to pay morning calls on prospective hostesses and Almack's patronesses."

"So I gather. I'll leave Bina a note."

"Come into my den," said Debenham resignedly, ushering them into a pleasant, book-lined room. "May I offer you a glass of Madeira?"

"Thanks, but we've just breakfasted and we don't want to keep you from your business." Wynn waved at the papers on the desk. "I've been meaning to say, Debenham, it's dashed good of you to put up the Lisles, especially as I know you disagree with my political opinions."

"My dear Selworth, you must know by now your sister can twist me around her little finger. As it turns out, they are a charming family and I'm happy to have them. Moreover, it leaves you with no excuse to avoid your share of escorting the ladies about."

"Naturally I'll do my share," said Wynn, his tone as hurt as if he had never contemplated leaving the whole affair to his brother-in-law. "In fact, I was going to offer our services, mine and Chubb's, to squire the ladies to the Park this afternoon."

Debenham pushed a sheet of paper, pen, and inkstand across the desk to him. "I'm sure they will be delighted to accept. I'm much obliged to you, Chubb, for lending your support."

"Not at all, not at all," Chubby muttered, blushing. "Do what I can. A pleasure."

"Allow me to include you in the standing invitation to my brother-in-law to take your mutton with us whenever it won't upset my wife's numbers for a dinner party."

"I say, dashed kind!"

Wynn blotted and folded his note, and he and Chubby took their leave, entrusting the sweetmeats to the footman. On reaching the street, Wynn turned left towards Bond Street.

"Where are we going?" Chubby asked.

"To Hookham's Library."

Chubby stopped dead. "I wondered why you were so pleased to hear Miss Lisle wanted to go to Hookham's."

"It's a good place to wait until they turn up."

"They may have gone there first. It strikes me you're even wilder to see Miss Lisle than I am to see Miss Kitty."

"Not at all," Wynn said defensively. "I simply want to find out about my speech."

"Well, you may not mind spending hours and hours in a library on the off chance, but I can think of better things to do with my time." He turned and started in the opposite direction, saying over his shoulder, "I'm off to Tattersall's to look for a carriage horse or pair. My father said I should buy myself a gig that's useful both in Town and in the country. I'll be able to take up Miss Kitty—or any of the ladies."

Wynn caught up with him. "All right, Tatt's it is. I was thinking of a tilbury gig."

As they strolled on, arguing the relative merits of various light carriages, Wynn wondered whether Chubby could possibly be right. Was he wilder—as wild—almost as wild to see Miss Lisle as his friend was to see Miss Kitty?

Impossible!

CHAPTER 9

"The Misses Pendrell?" exclaimed Lord Selworth and Mr. Chubb with identical looks of horror. Pippa was hard put to it not to laugh aloud

"We made their acquaintance at Lady Castlereagh's," Millicent rattled on, "and they asked us to walk with them in St. James's Park this afternoon and we—"

"Who are the Misses Pendrell?" Lord Selworth demanded with an ominous frown.

"They are some sort of relatives of Lady Castlereagh, Wynn, so we could not say no without offending her and she is one of the patronesses of Almack's, and besides, they are nice girls, are they not, Kitty? How were we to know you wished to go to Hyde Park with us? You need not come to St. James's Park if you do not—"

"I didn't bargain for swarms of unknown females. I'm happy to escort Miss Lisle and Miss Kitty, and I don't mind squiring you, Millie, but I draw the line at wholesale husband-hunting misses, however nice."

"I'll come," Mr. Chubb put in with a stoic air, then blushed and said pleadingly to Kitty, "if you don't mind."

"Of course not, but you must not feel obliged, sir. Lieutenant Pendrell promised to accompany his sisters, so we shall not be without male protection."

"I'll come," Mr. Chubb repeated, this time with determination.

Lord Selworth sighed. "I daresay I had best go, too, in case you need protection against this lieutenant chap. Females tend to fall for a dashing scarlet coat without considering what sort of scoundrel is wearing it."

"Lieutenant Pendrell wears Rifle green," Pippa informed him, "and he seems an inoffensive gentleman, not especially dashing."

"Ha! the better to humbug you," Lord Selworth said with a grin. "Do you go, Mrs. Lisle, Bina?"

"Not if you will be there to guard the lambs against the wolf in rifleman's clothing," said Bina. "Mrs. Lisle and I have plans to make."

The Pendrells arrived shortly, the young ladies in a smart barouche, their brother riding. On horseback, though his uniform was green, not scarlet, the lieutenant had a dashing air absent in the drawing room.

His sisters were delighted to find two more gentlemen were to join their party, especially when they heard one was a lord. They fluttered their eyelashes at Lord Selworth, but accepted his utter lack of interest philosophically.

As Millicent said, the Misses Pendrell were nice girls. There was not a great deal more to say about them, Pippa reflected, greeting them as Lord Selworth handed her into the carriage to join them. At least on first acquaintance, she corrected herself charitably.

Respectively eighteen and seventeen years of age, Miss Pendrell and Miss Vanessa both had light brown hair, with rather vapid but not unattractive faces. Their clothes were smart, though with a tendency towards overadornment. They had an inexhaustible fund of chatter on clothes, the weather, entertainments, and the latest *on-dit,* without in any way rivalling Millicent. Millie, in her good-natured way, had already assured them that they might interrupt her without offence. Of this permission they availed themselves unstintingly.

As the barouche rolled towards St. James's Park, Pippa, feeling ancient, was free to marvel at the dullness of the conversation without needing to join in. Miss Pendrell, seated beside her facing forward, occasionally turned to her politely as if to solicit her opinion. Luckily she was satisfied with an "Indeed," or a "Good gracious."

Kitty appeared to be enjoying herself. When she glanced across at Pippa, it was with a sort of conspiratorial amusement. She could chatter away with the best of them, her eyes said, but was it not absurd?

At first the narrow streets, and then the busy traffic of Piccadilly, prevented the gentlemen's riding alongside. When the barouche turned down Constitution Hill, between Green Park and the tree-hidden gardens of Buckingham House, Lord Selworth and the lieutenant at once moved forward on either side.

"I hope the talk of walking was not a fudge," Pippa said to the viscount in a low voice, though there was little fear of being overheard over Millicent's prattle. "I am sorely in need of exercise after sitting in carriages and drawing rooms all day."

"Do you ride?" he asked, ignoring Miss Vanessa Pendrell's attempts to catch his attention. "What a great deal I don't know about you!"

"How should you? No, I have never had a chance to learn to ride. I should have liked to learn, but I suppose I am too old now."

"Old! Don't let Bina hear you saying such a thing. I'd be glad to teach you—but London is no place to learn," he added hastily. "I'm thinking of buying a tilbury. I shall be able to take you driving, then. Chubb's set on a stanhope gig—says it's more practical."

"Why?"

"It has a larger boot. Some tilburies don't have a boot at all."

"The stanhope does sound more useful," Pippa said, looking around for Mr. Chubb.

"But a tilbury is more sporting," Lord Selworth argued.

"If you want to be sporting, why not get a curricle? If you ever wish to use it for longer journeys, two horses are more practical than one. Oh, poor Mr. Chubb!"

On the other side of the barouche, Lieutenant Pendrell had positioned his mount so as to monopolize Kitty. Mr. Chubb lurked beyond, scarcely able to see her, far less to exchange a word. He looked downcast but resigned, as if the situation was just what he had expected.

Kitty was laughing merrily at something the officer had said to her. Pippa hoped her sister was too sensible to be swept off her feet by the glamor of a uniform.

"Chubby's no dashing blade, just a thoroughly good sort," said Lord Selworth.

"I do think you ought not to call him Chubby," Pippa suggested tentatively. "I realize it comes from his name, but it cannot be comfortable having such a nickname. Whether it would be worse if he were actually chubby rather than thin as a rake, I cannot guess."

He stared down at her, eyebrows raised, a thoughtful look in his eyes. "You have a point there, Miss Lisle. It dates from our schooldays, of course. Boys are not the most sensitive of creatures, I fear, and the habit stuck without ever being consciously considered."

"It is really none of my business," Pippa said in some confusion. "I beg your pardon."

"No, no, I'm glad you mentioned it. You have not only a kind heart, but a perceptive mind."

Though pleased he should think her kind, Pippa did not at all wish him to see her as perceptive. To her relief, they came to the beginning of the Mall and Miss Pendrell called to the coachman to stop. They all got down to walk, the gentlemen leaving their horses with the coachman.

Lieutenant Pendrell at once offered Kitty his arm and strolled off towards the lake. Mr. Chubb turned towards Pippa, but Lord Selworth had already determinedly appropriated her, positively seizing her hand and laying it on his arm.

"I'm sorry to throw Chubb to the wolves," he whispered, "but I'll be dashed if I'll sacrifice myself for him."

"You are far better able to hold your own," she reproved him, though she could not but be flattered by his preference for her company.

With an apprehensive glance at the three remaining young ladies, Mr. Chubb decided to choose the devil he knew. "M-miss Warren," he stammered with an uncertain gesture of his right hand.

Without a pause in the flow of words, Millicent smiled at him and took his arm. The Misses Pendrell cast hopeful looks at Lord Selworth, but he promptly adopted a Napoleonic pose with his free hand thrust between his coat buttons, and bent his head to speak to Pippa.

"Tell me when it's safe to look up," he hissed.

"You are a coxcomb, sir," she responded, trying hard not to laugh.

Miss Pendrell hastened to take possession of Mr. Chubb's left arm, leaving Miss Vanessa to walk beside her. Bringing up the rear, Pippa saw Miss Pendrell address several questions to Mr. Chubb. After a series of incoherent monosyllables in answer, she gave up and followed Millicent's lead in talking past him as if he were not there.

"As long as he's not expected to speak, he'll live through it," said the callous viscount. "Speaking of speech, I don't suppose you have had a chance to finish reading mine. Bina said you were all sewing away last night to finish your new gowns. Which are very becoming!" he added quickly, with a sidelong inspection which swept Pippa from yellow-ribboned bonnet past shawl of Norwich silk to the frill round the hem of her buttercup muslin gown.

"I am persuaded, sir, that in spite of your sister's mention of the sewing, you have not until this very moment spared the product so much as a glance."

"Untrue, ma'am! At least," he said with a rueful grin, "even if I failed to pin down the cause, I was—am—aware of your being in particularly good looks today."

"Fine feathers make fine birds," Pippa said tartly, but she was pleased with the compliment—only because the more he believed her concerned with her looks, the less he would suspect her secret. "Bina kindly did *not* mention that I was dismissed as a seamstress for bleeding onto my work."

"Bleeding! You were hurt?"

"I did not mean to alarm you. I merely pricked my finger. Repeatedly. When it comes to needles I am all thumbs, I fear. However, my incompetence did allow me to finish reading your speech. Prometheus will soon be studying it."

"You have sent it off to him already? Thank you. Can you tell me how much I owe him for postage? I don't wish to leave him out of pocket for longer than need be."

His request put Pippa in something of a quandary. She could not charge him for what had not been spent.

"I was not sure whether Prometheus would have sufficient funds at hand to pay postage for so many sheets," she said. "Sending a packet by the stage, paying half in advance, is much cheaper, and you did say there was no real need for haste. It will be easier to reckon up the total at the end, when the work is all finished." And she would have time to think up a reason not to accept any money.

He nodded. "As you wish. But you must promise to let me know at once if the delay in payment causes any difficulties. Tell me, when you said you are in need of exercise, is this what you had in mind?"

"Heavens no. I would not call this a walk, scarcely even a saunter."

"A mere dawdle," Lord Selwor~ agreed. "Let us see which way the others turn to circle the lake, and we shall go the opposite way."

"I ought to chaperon the girls," Pippa said reluctantly.

"Chaperon? My dear Miss Lisle, if Albinia, married with two children, is too young to assume that weighty mantle without aid, you are unquestionably ineligible. Besides, I believe Millicent, Chubb, and two sisters are watchdogs enough for the lieutenant. You don't mean to hint that Chubb is a threat to Millie and the Misses Pendrell, I take it?"

Laughing, Pippa shook her head. Reaching the lake, Kitty and Lieutenant Pendrell turned south, so Pippa and the viscount took the path along the north bank, walking at a brisk pace. Not until then did it dawn on her to ask herself whether it was quite proper for her to be alone with Lord Selworth.

He seemed to see nothing amiss, and his conduct was not remotely loverlike—not that she had for a moment expected it. Their relationship was not of that sort. Chiding herself for missishness, she nonetheless removed her hand from his arm to point to the flock of white pelicans on the lake, and failed to replace it.

Lord Selworth was interested in the pelicans and the other waterbirds swimming or resting on the grass under the willows and plane trees. Pippa knew no more than he about the rarer varieties, but they both vowed to look for an illustrated book and try to identify them. The spring flowers were easier: crocuses, daffodils, narcissus, cheeky-faced pansies, and bright-hued polyanthus.

Though Pippa had spent only a few months in London, Lord Selworth had spent less. She was able to point out to him, through gaps in the trees, the backs of St. James' Palace and Carlton House.

Unfortunately, the sight of Carlton House brought to the viscount's mind the Prince Regent's debts and the rest of his iniquities. Pippa forced herself to murmur agreement to his strictures without adding her own ideas on the subject. Before temptation grew too great to be resisted, they came to the end of the lake.

Before them the wide open space of the Parade Ground spread to the impressive buildings of the Horse Guards and the Admiralty. A crowd was gathering as a military band in scarlet, white and gold uttered a few preliminary toots on their gleaming brass instruments.

"Oh, may we stay and listen?" Pippa cried.

"Why not?" Lord Selworth turned to gaze back along the lake. "For a while, at least. The others will not catch up with us for a good five or ten minutes, and then we shall have as long again to catch up with them on the way back if they don't wish to listen."

"Yes, much better than to dawdle back or to have to wait at the barouche for them. This sounds familiar," Pippa said as the band struck up a rousing tune.

"A march."

"By Handel, I fancy. Kitty plays it upon the spinet, and I have been known to attempt it. How splendid it sounds with trumpets and horns and drums!"

"Perhaps you would have more success with a trumpet than a spinet," Lord Selworth proposed when the march ended.

"What a sensation that would create," Pippa exclaimed, smiling up at him, "a female playing the trumpet! However, I think I should prefer the clarinet. I once heard a concerto for clarinet by Mozart. Is there not something wonderfully mellow about the clarinet?"

Lord Selworth, it turned out, was unfamiliar with the clarinet, had, indeed, never attended a concert of the Philharmonic Society. Pippa, who had delighted in her one experience of orchestral music, advised him to purchase a ticket for the next performance.

"I am sure you will find it agreeable," she said.

"If you will go with me and explain which parts I must particularly admire. We shall make up a party, of course," he added hastily. "Your sister is musical; she will like to go, too."

The others came up then. "You are prodigious energetic, I vow, Miss Lisle!" said Miss Pendrell languidly. "We saw you striding along at a great rate. I am quite fatigued after walking so far."

"Yet I wager you think nothing of dancing all night," Lord Selworth drawled with a touch of sarcasm.

Lieutenant Pendrell laughed heartily. "He has you there, Lyddy. If you are so tired, you had best wait here while the rest of us go back and bring the barouche to fetch you. You are not tired, are you, Miss Catherine?"

"After so short a stroll?" said Kitty. "Heavens, no, though I do believe walking slowly is more tiring than walking fast. But there was such a great deal to admire. Pippa, did you ever see such a variety of fowl? And some of them very pretty. I wish we had brought bread crusts to feed them."

The Misses Pendrell stared, and even their brother, though clearly much prepossessed with Kitty, looked taken aback. Miss Vanessa murmured something to her sister; Pippa thought she caught the word "hoydens."

Mr. Chubb sprang to the rescue. "Splendid notion, Miss Kitty. We'll come back with bread, a loaf, two loaves. Drive you myself, soon as I've bought my carriage."

"I shall look forward to it, sir," Kitty said with a serene smile, not at all distressed by the Pendrells' disdain. "Do you suppose it might be possible to obtain eggs or ducklings of the rarer birds for my poultry yard?"

Pippa envied her sister's equable temperament. The jibe about her "striding" had hurt, though Lord Selworth's prompt retort soothed the wound. She resolved not to let petty snubs daunt her as they had in her first Season, not to allow others to dictate her behavior. This time she came without any expectation of attracting a husband, so what did it matter what people thought of her?

Lieutenant Pendrell did not long permit Mr. Chubb to enjoy Kitty's attention, Pippa saw. He won her back with an outrageous plan to enlist his fellow officers in a plot to ducknap her chosen waterfowl from the park one dark night. His sisters, too, abandoned their supercilious airs to join in the laughter.

Mr. Chubb was left to listen in philosophical silence to Millicent's monologue, which began with the misdeeds of a rooster at the Rectory and drifted into uncharted byways.

"Millie, Chubb," Lord Selworth interrupted, "Miss Lisle and I will listen to the band for a while, then catch you up."

"Come back to fetch you," Mr. Chubb suggested, "and Miss Pendrell."

"I fancy Miss Pendrell has forgotten her exhaustion," said Pippa dryly, waving at the others, who had already set out around the north side of the lake. "And I have not yet had as much exercise as I would wish."

"We shall stay and listen, too," said Millicent. "I do not mind walking fast, and I shall like to hear the music. I like a military band of all things, such a splendid sight in their scarlet—"

"Oh no," said Lord Selworth, "we shan't hear a note if you stay. Take her away, Chubb, there's a good fellow."

Millie pulled a face at her brother, but obediently went off. She and Mr. Chubb might suit each other very well, Pippa decided. The lady would never be interrupted, and the gentleman would never have to struggle in vain for words to fill a silence.

Pippa and Lord Selworth stayed a few more minutes, then walked back along the southern path, talking of music. They joined the others at the barouche all too soon for Pippa. She was sure she had never passed a pleasanter afternoon, in spite of an odd contretemps or two, minor in retrospect.

It was wonderful to find a variety of subjects she could discuss sensibly with Lord Selworth. As long as they avoided politics, she felt no need to guard her tongue.

The trouble was, they both found politics so absorbing it was an excessively difficult subject to avoid.

CHAPTER 10

"If skirts get any wider," grumbled George Debenham, seated between his wife and Mrs. Lisle, "we shall have to take two carriages."

"I hardly think it likely, dear," Albinia said placidly, tucking a white kid-gloved hand beneath his arm. "No one would choose to return to those ridiculous hooped skirts of the last century. It is bad enough having to wear them at Court."

"I am glad I never had to manage a hoop," said Pippa, sitting opposite her. She smoothed her ball gown with nervous fingers.

The claret red crepe, trimmed with full-blown white satin roses and worn over a white satin slip of Bina's, was quite the most beautiful dress she had ever owned. It was wasted on her. Even Bina's superior dresser had given up trying to put a fashionable curl in Pippa's hair, and pinned it up into a topknot as severe as her usual style. Her cheeks were so pale with trepidation, the least touch of rouge made her look like an actress, so that, too, had to be abandoned.

"I found the train of an evening dress difficult enough, remember, Bina?" she continued.

"I recall one or two stumbles," Bina admitted.

"Thank heaven they are no longer worn. As for a hoop, I would surely have made a shocking mull of it and disgraced myself."

"Must I be presented, Bina?" Millicent asked plaintively. "Everyone says it is a dreadful ordeal. You were not until you married, and Kitty does not have to. I should prefer just to go to balls without having to worry about it. I am sure we could alter my Presentation gown to make it into another ball gown. I wish I had thought of it sooner; then I could have worn it tonight, for our first ball."

"You are the sister of a peer now," said Bina, "which I was not then. It is proper for you to make your curtsy to the Queen, if she is well enough."

"She is *excessively* old," said Millicent, with a note of hope which drew instant censure from her elder sister.

Unrepressed, Millie chattered on. Pippa ceased to listen, concentrating on trying to still the flutters in her stomach. At her age, she ought to have outgrown such foolish apprehensions, yet she felt just as she had four years earlier on the way to a ball. Worse, even, since tonight she would be thrust into the heart of the *beau monde* instead of flitting about on the outskirts.

It was some comfort that Lord Selworth would be there. Indeed, he had already requested a country dance of each of the ladies, as had Mr. Chubb, so Pippa would not be a wallflower the entire evening.

After dining at the Debenhams', the two of them were coming together in Lord Selworth's brand-new curricle. The viscount had confessed to Pippa that he was in not much less of a quake than his friend when it came to their first venture into Polite Society.

"Far more frightening than speaking before the entire House of Lords," he had said. "From all I hear, the ladies of the *haut ton* are a thousand times more critical."

Though she had not said so, Pippa thought she, too, had rather face the House of Lords, speech in hand.

Lord Selworth had promised Bina to be there. He would not break his promise, nor fail to attend his younger sister at her first ball, would he? Surely he and Mr. Chubb would not sheer off at the last minute!

Pippa longed to let down the window and peer out into the lamp-lit night at the row of carriages they had just joined. Millicent, with the same notion, nearly put it into practice.

"I wonder if Wynn is in front of us or close behind?" As she jumped up and reached for the strap, Mrs. Lisle caught her hand just in time.

"We shall get there no faster for fidgeting," she pointed out.

"May we not get down and walk, ma'am?" Millie begged. "I cannot sit still while we crawl along like this. We should arrive much sooner walking, and I daresay—"

"I fear etiquette requires us to arrive by carriage, my dear," Mrs. Lisle said sympathetically.

"What a goosecap you are, Millie," said Kitty. "You cannot wish to soil your slippers in the dirty street!"

"No indeed, I did not think. Miss Vanessa Pendrell says there is generally a carpet laid across the pavement to the front door to keep the ladies' feet clean, and if it looks like rain the first-rate hostesses have an awning set up over the carpet. Would it not be dreadful to arrive soaked to the skin at one's first ball? Silk spots so shockingly and—Oh, look, there is Wynn!" She pointed at the window on Pippa's side.

About to knock, Lord Selworth lowered his hand as Bina reached across to let down the window.

"We were held up," he said, raising his top hat in salute. "We're a long way back in the line. We didn't want you to think we had abandoned you, so we left the curricle with my groom and walked on."

"What!" Pippa exclaimed. "You entrusted your new carriage to a mere groom?"

He grinned at her, walking alongside as the Debenham carriage moved up a place. "I'd be happier standing guard over

it all night, but then I might as well not have come at all. The
fellow knows his head is on the block if there is a single scratch
or nick in the paintwork.''

"You settled on black picked out in gold?"

"Yes, or yellow, rather. Gold seemed unnecessarily extravagant. The seat is black leather."

"It sounds prodigious smart, Wynn," said Millicent. "You
will be quite one of the swells. Will you take me for a drive
in it? I should like it above anything. Only think—"

"If you promise not to frighten the horses with your prattle.
I decided against maroon—your choice, Bina—in case I find
myself driving a lady dressed in a conflicting color."

By the dim light within the carriage, Pippa saw Bina raise
her eyebrows. "Did you indeed, brother mine! Are we all to
be honored with invitations, then?"

"Certainly, starting with Miss Lisle, since it is on her advice
I purchased a curricle instead of a tilbury."

"I only said two horses were better than one for longer
journeys," Pippa protested.

"A very material point, Miss Lisle. I shall be able to leave
the chaise for my mother's use while I gad about the countryside. Will you drive with me in the Park tomorrow afternoon?"

"I am honored, sir, and I shall be delighted to accept if my
mother has no need of me. And if the weather continues fine.
I should hate to be the cause of rain spots on your paintwork
and the seat leather!"

"Your true concern is for your best bonnet, confess! For the
weather I cannot answer. I shall beg Mrs. Lisle on bended knee
to spare you—as soon as we are inside, for here we are at the
door at last."

He opened the door, and would have let down the step but
that their host's footman forestalled him. However, the servant
then stood back and permitted Lord Selworth to hand down
first his sister and then Pippa.

George Debenham emerged next and turned to assist Mrs.
Lisle. Mr. Chubb, who had been lurking behind Lord Selworth,

moved forward to hand out Kitty, and Millicent, exclaiming over the red carpet, also accepted his help.

The footman signalled to the coachman to drive on. Another carriage pulled up as Mr. Debenham offered one arm to Mrs. Lisle and the other to his wife. By then, Pippa and Lord Selworth had moved as far as the doorstep to make room. The press of people behind forced them to continue into the house together.

Once they were inside the hall, the crush was much worse. Pippa gave up her shawl reluctantly, for between décolleté neckline and high waist, the bodice of her gown was alarmingly brief.

Lord Selworth did not appear to see anything amiss. "Dash it," he whispered in Pippa's ear, though he might as well have shouted for the babble of voices, "I don't want to go first. It's for Debenham to lead the way."

"I am sure Bina intended you to take in Millicent," Pippa hissed back.

"In that case, by all means let us forge ahead. I had ten thousand times rather face the lions with you at my side than my sister! I trust you are acquainted with our hostess, for I certainly am not."

"I have been presented to her, but she will not remember me." Pippa glanced back at Bina, who gave her an encouraging smile. Hemmed in as they were, and constantly inching forward, they could not exchange a word, far less places.

Thus Pippa made a grand entry into the Fashionable World on the arm of one of its most eligible bachelors. That Viscount Selworth was little known to Society only increased the general interest in the young lady accompanying him. To this as much as to the Debenhams' sponsorship Pippa attributed her success.

For it was a success. She was not the Belle of the Ball. There were diamonds of the first water present, eligible maidens with large fortunes and blue bloodlines and fathomless funds of inconsequential chatter. Even Kitty and Millicent gathered larger crowds of would-be partners. Yet to one accustomed and expecting to sit out a great many dances, simply to stand up for nearly every set was triumph beyond her wildest dreams.

Mama was right. Pippa had gained in address in the past few years, if address was the ability to make small talk—and listen to it without obvious impatience. She found herself more tolerant of other people's foibles.

It helped that she no longer felt the pressure to catch a husband, experienced by every girl in her first Season. She did not study every gentleman she met wondering whether she could bear to be his wife, if ever he happened to show the slightest interest in her.

It helped also that she was one of hundreds in a huge ball-room, not one of a couple of dozen in two rooms thrown together with the carpet rolled back. She did not feel her looks, her clothes, her every move under constant scrutiny.

It helped to have three sets taken in advance, by Lord Selworth, Mr. Debenham, and Mr. Chubb. Knowing one would not be an utterly unredeemed wallflower gave one self-confidence. Pippa recalled entire evenings spent examining her toes. Tonight she looked about her, admiring the glitter of the chandeliers' lustres in the light of a thousand wax candles, and the scarcely less glittering throng swirling and spinning beneath.

She expressed some of these thoughts to her mother, when a partner delivered her back to Mrs. Lisle, where she sat at the side of the room chatting to the other chaperons.

"As I expected, my love," said Mrs. Lisle. "I am prodigious glad you are enjoying yourself. Dear Albinia would be most disappointed if all her efforts to that end were in vain, and she has been so kind I should hate to disappoint her."

"She is a darling. And Lord Selworth—" Pippa stopped in some confusion as that gentleman appeared at her elbow.

Eyebrows raised, he grinned. "Do go on, Miss Lisle. Dare I hope I am to receive the supreme accolade of being named a darling?"

"Certainly not," Pippa said crossly.

"They do say eavesdroppers seldom hear good of themselves," he acknowledged with a mournful sigh.

Goaded, Pippa told him, "I was going to say you have been *almost* as kind as your sister, but you are by far too great a tease for me to risk setting you up in your own conceit."

"Alas! I was about to beg you to be kind to me. You see, Bina has just warned me that whoever I take in to supper is bound to arouse a good deal of speculation." He glanced over his shoulder and continued in an exaggerated whisper, "And there is a young lady throwing out strong hints."

"Millicent—"

"Millie, I'm delighted to report, is already bespoken. By a gentleman of the strong, silent, saturnine sort who appears to find her amusing. Dare I hope, Miss Lisle, that you are still free for the supper dance?" He scanned her dance card. "Will you not come to the rescue? Persuade her, ma'am," he begged Mrs. Lisle.

"Lord Selworth has done his duty, I fancy, Pippa. I have not seen him sit out a single dance. He is not to blame for any young ladies left partnerless."

"There, you see, I deserve your kindness. Have pity on me."

"If you wish, just to save you from speculation. Everyone will believe you are simply being kind to your sister's guest, not realizing it is I who am doing you the favor."

Writing his name on the card, he laughed and was about to retort when a large matron clad in plum-colored satin and superb rubies swooped upon Mrs. Lisle.

"Anna Burdick, as I live!"

"Eva Gore?" said Mrs. Lisle, a note of doubt in her voice as she stood up.

The matron chuckled merrily and patted her plump cheeks. "Yes, inside this is Eva Gore, now Marchioness of Stanborough, believe it or not. And you?"

"Mrs. Lisle. How delightful to see you again after so many years, Lady Stanborough. May I present my daughter, Philippa?"

Pippa made her curtsy, and Mrs. Lisle introduced Lord Selworth to the marchioness. "And here comes my younger daughter, Catherine," she added as the viscount bowed.

"Two out at once? I have a boy around here somewhere, my second son, Edward." Lady Stanborough craned her double-chinned neck and made an imperious summoning gesture. "A young man, I should say. He would be furious to hear me calling him a boy."

Kitty arrived on the arm of her partner, unknown to Pippa, and was presented to the friend of her mother's youth. Then Lord Edward came up. He was a plain young man, already running to plumpness. His high shirtpoints, waistcoat embroidered with pink and blue butterflies, and multitude of fobs suggested a fondness for foppery. His air of self-consequence might charitably be ascribed to the golden-haired beauty of the young lady at his side.

Once the introductions were completed, Lord Edward turned back to Lady Stanborough and said, "I am glad to see you have both your earrings, Mother. I've heard a ruby earring was found on the floor somewhere."

The marchioness felt the drops at her ears. "Yes, both there, thank heaven. The rubies are a family heirloom," she explained. "Stanborough would have been most distressed if I had lost one."

"They are very beautiful, ma'am," said Kitty, "just like enormous red currants."

Lady Stanborough looked decidedly taken aback by this rural metaphor. Her son, his partner, and Kitty's partner all looked shocked. Pippa racked her brains for something to say in support of her sister, but Mr. Chubb, arriving unnoticed in his silent way, beat her to it.

"Very true, Miss Kitty," he said resolutely. "The rubies glow just like red currants in the sun. Nothing prettier. And what's more, you can eat currants."

The shock was transferred to him. As he blushed, Lord Selworth hastily presented him to Lady Stanborough.

"My good friend, the *Honorable* Gilbert Chubb."

"Lord Chubb's heir?" asked Lady Stanborough with interest. "I knew your father once, but he never comes up to Town now."

Mr. Chubb, his flash in the pan extinguished, mumbled something about life in the country. He missed Kitty's grateful look since by then—Pippa noted with sympathy—he was examining his toes.

"I have not been up to Town in years," said Mrs. Lisle. "We are staying with the Debenhams."

"The Kent Debenhams?" Lady Stanborough enquired, clearly impressed.

"Philippa is a particular friend of Mrs. George Debenham."

Lord Edward turned to Pippa, claiming acquaintance with George Debenham. To her surprise, he solicited the honor of a dance and inscribed his name on her card for one of the sets after supper. Pippa's next partner came to fetch her just then, so she heard no more. However, as she danced, she saw her mother and the marchioness with their heads together, so she assumed Kitty's *faux pas* had been smoothed over.

Poor Kitty! Of course red currants looked like rubies, and vice versa. Why should she be considered gauche for mentioning the resemblance? Not that she appeared to be repining. Pippa saw her in the next set, smiling up at a startlingly handsome gentleman as they turned arm in arm.

Lord Selworth, promenading in another set with a sadly branfaced young lady, caught Pippa's eye. He nodded towards Kitty, smiled, and winked.

The next country dance was the one preceding supper. When Lord Selworth came to lead Pippa onto the floor, she said to him innocently, "What were those extraordinary grimaces you directed at me a few minutes ago, sir?"

"Why, did you not guess . . . ? Ah, Miss Lisle, you are quizzing me, and you call *me* a tease! If you wish to be taken seriously, you must strive to suppress the gleam in your eyes."

"Do they glow like red currants?"

"They may tomorrow, if you dance until dawn and then rise too early!" He gazed down into her eyes, and shook his head. "No, like opals, always changing."

Lowering her gaze, Pippa hoped her cheeks were not glowing like red currants. "You are gallant, Lord Selworth. I do believe that is the prettiest thing anyone has ever said to me." Thoughtfully she cooled her hot cheeks with her fan, then looked up at him through her lashes. "Tonight, at least."

He burst out laughing. "Minx! Is it permissible to address a lady of your mature years as 'minx'?"

"No mature lady objects to being regarded as younger than she is. Though why anyone should wish to return to the agonizing awkwardness of extreme youth, I cannot conceive," she added candidly. "Still, not all girls are as easily mortified as I was. Kitty scarcely turned a hair just now."

"As I was attempting to draw to your attention with my 'extraordinary grimaces,' ma'am!"

"So I guessed," said Pippa, laughing.

She thoroughly enjoyed their dance, and the supper that followed. Lord Selworth set himself to entertain her, succeeding with such charm that she was sure every young lady he had danced with must be at least half in love with him.

Including herself?

She had been half in love with Wynn Selworth before the evening started. She must not allow herself to fall any deeper. He was kind, charming, amusing, attentive, and she knew him to be a man of principle. But that final quality nullified the one before: he was attentive because he had promised Prometheus to smooth the Lisles' path in Society.

To Lord Selworth, Pippa was a means to an end—a noble end, to be sure, but that did not change the basic fact. She *must* not forget it.

In the early hours of the morning, Wynn drove back to Albany through the dark streets. He could feel Chubby—no,

Gil—at his side bursting to talk about the ball, but the presence of the groom on his perch behind them inhibited any but the most impersonal comment.

Clark, their shared gentleman's gentleman, was waiting up for them, determined to do his duty despite their instructions to the contrary. Unused to Town hours as they were, by the time he had stripped them of their evening finery they were both half-asleep, fit only to pull on nightshirts and tumble into their respective beds. Confidences had to wait until the morning.

The habit of early rising was not easily abridged by a single night's gallivanting. By half-past eight, Wynn and Gil were seated at the breakfast table in the sunny window of their parlor. The table also served Wynn as a desk—the friend who had sublet the rooms was never known to pick up a pen if he could help it, so needed no bureau.

Clark served them with fine rashers of gammon topped with sizzling eggs, and hot muffins with lashings of butter and honey. Pouring coffee, he left the pot to keep hot over a spirit lamp and went off to put a final polish on their boots.

Wynn swallowed a tender bite of gammon and said, "How did we manage without him? The fellow's a treasure."

"Deuced lucky to get him," Gil Chubb agreed. "I must say I'd never have thought of looking for an ex-Navy man."

"A captain's servant has to do a bit of everything, from making salt beef and biscuit edible to keeping a dress uniform smart, and few half-pay captains can afford to keep servants. The way the Navy has been reduced since the war, I was sure there must be some in need of work. It's disgraceful the way the soldiers and sailors who beat Boney are neglected now."

Gil waved a fork at him. "No speeches! I say, Wynn, are you taking Miss Lisle for a drive in the Park today?"

"Yes," said Wynn contentedly, "but not till this afternoon, at the fashionable hour. No hurry."

"I know that. Do you think Miss Kitty might drive with me?"

"Ask her. You should have invited her last night. They are

bound to have dozens of callers this morning, and she had swarms of beaux flocking around at the ball.''

"I know." Gil heaved a dispirited sigh. "It's no more than I expected, but it's enough to drive a fellow to drink. D'you think she minded what I said about red currants and rubies?''

"Minded? Gad no! I'm sure she was devilish grateful for your gallant defence against those toplofty prigs. I didn't know you had it in you, old chap.''

"You'll understand if you ever fall in love," said Gil with dignity.

Wynn's heart did an odd sort of flip-flop. He set down his knife and fork and said in a peculiar voice, "I think I am. I do believe I must be.''

"Good Lord, you, too? With one of the girls you met last night?''

"Those featherheads? Not an ounce of brain between the lot of them!''

"Not Miss Lisle?''

"Philippa," said Wynn dreamily. "Pippa. Do you feel you really wouldn't object to spending the rest of your life with Kitty? Even seeing her at breakfast every morning? No, that's not right. It's more that you can't imagine waking up every morning and her not being there. It wouldn't be worth waking up.''

Gil nodded. "That's it all right; only the chances are I'll have to," he moped. "All very well for you, but I haven't much hope of winning Kitty. Are you going to pop the question this afternoon?''

"N-no. It's too soon," Wynn declared in a sudden excess of panic. Suppose he was mistaken? Suppose this was the calf love he suspected in his friend's case? He had never imagined himself seriously in love before, nothing beyond an infatuation with an apple-cheeked dairymaid three years his senior and unreal fantasies about the squire's coquettish daughter. "No," he repeated. "What if she refused me? She wouldn't wish to go on working with me, and I'd lose Prometheus' help.''

"Of course she won't refuse you. You're a viscount, full of juice, not bad-looking, clever, and conversable. No girl in her right mind would refuse you."

"Miss Lisle might. She wouldn't marry for title or money. It'd be against her father's principles. And what's more, though she pays lip service to her father's opinions, it's my belief she's got ideas of her own. I can't count on her behaving like any other husband-hungry damsel, even if she doesn't love Prometheus. No," Wynn repeated, "I can't risk an offer until I've finished with Prometheus. A political career will be the only thing to make life worth living if she turns me down."

CHAPTER 11

"Almack's!" squealed Millie, bursting into the ladies' sitting room. "Pippa, we have vouchers for Almack's! All of us."

Hastily slipping Lord Selworth's papers into the desk drawer, Pippa swung round as Kitty followed Millicent. Bina and Mrs. Lisle came in after them.

"It is quite true," Bina confirmed. "Maria Sefton, Emily Cowper, and Silence managed to overcome the scruples of the high-in-the-instep set."

"Silence?" Pippa asked vaguely, striving to disentangle her mind from the starving children of out-of-work weavers in the Midlands.

"Sally Jersey," Bina explained, "whose tongue runs on almost as much as Millicent's."

"Fortunately Lord Jersey is a Whig," said Mrs. Lisle, "and, though hardly a Radical, he was quite well acquainted with your father."

"Pippa, did you know Lord and Lady Jersey were married at Gretna Green?" Millicent asked. "Is it not romantic? And only think, her mama eloped to Scotland, too! She was a banker's daughter, and she ran off with the Earl of Westmorland, though he wasn't the earl yet, which is—"

"Millie!" protested her sister. "Pippa is not at all interested in such vulgar gossip, and I trust you do not mean to rattle on about Lady Jersey in company. She is one of the most important hostesses, besides being a patroness of Almack's. Her history is no secret, but if she were to learn you had been raking up the past, I daresay we should find our Almack's vouchers withdrawn."

"I shan't say another word," cried Millicent, horrified. "Miss Pendrell told me, so I did not—"

"Come and take off your bonnet, Millie," said Kitty, pulling on her friend's hand. "At the musicale last night, at least five gentlemen begged permission to call today."

"You sang charmingly," said Bina, "and the sort of songs gentlemen appreciate, not Italian arias like the rest."

"It is fortunate that they like country airs," Kitty said frankly, "for I do not know any Italian arias."

"Only two of the gentlemen left cards while we were out," Millicent reminded her, "so the other three may turn up at any moment. Let us hurry."

The girls went off. Bina sank into a chair.

"What energy the young have!" she sighed. "Do sit down, ma'am. They can manage without a chaperon for a few minutes, however many gallants arrive. Kitty is vastly popular, and Millicent profits from her friendship."

"Kitty does seem to have a great many admirers," said Mrs. Lisle with quiet satisfaction, "though how many are willing to take a wife without a portion remains to be seen. But there are those who prefer Millicent."

"One or two of those who have nothing to say for themselves," Bina agreed with a laugh, "though the most silent of all, Mr. Chubb, languishes after Kitty. I wonder if it is his doing that Wynn is so assiduous at doing his duty. I must confess I doubted he would attend more than the bare minimum of parties to launch Millie, but he goes with us everywhere." She gave Pippa a sly glance.

Pretending not to notice, Pippa reminded her, "Lord Selworth is anxious to turn us up sweet—us Lisles, that is—for fear of giving offence to Prometheus."

"He has done all Prometheus required," said Mrs. Lisle, "and more. I am sure Lord Selworth's chief aim is to promote the comfort of his sisters."

"He has always accepted responsibility for the family's well-being," Bina conceded. "I do believe, though, that he has not found the Season the ordeal he expected. It will be interesting to see if he fights shy of Almack's, which is, in its way, the distilled essence of the Season. Today being Thursday, he has a whole week to screw his courage to the sticking place."

"I had much rather not go," said Pippa. "Its only purpose appears to be to exclude half of those who wish to go so that the rest may regard themselves as superior."

"The exclusivity is precisely why young ladies may be certain of meeting unexceptionable gentlemen," Bina argued, "many of them with marriage in mind."

"But I am not on the catch for a husband."

"Even so, I hope you will go with us, my love," Mrs. Lisle said. "Obtaining vouchers is more of a triumph than I ever expected. You are at liberty not to regard yourself as superior, but it cannot hurt for others to think you so."

Bina and Pippa both laughed; then Bina heaved herself to her feet with an exaggerated effort, saying, "I shall leave you to persuade her, ma'am. I had best go and see what the girls are doing."

Mrs. Lisle eyed her elder daughter consideringly. "I thought you had been enjoying yourself, dearest," she said. "If not, you have put on a brilliant show. Was it just so as not to appear ungrateful to Albinia?"

"Oh no, Mama, I have enjoyed myself much more than I supposed possible, much more than I ought when people all over the country are in desperate straits."

"I fear your absence from Almack's will not help to feed the hungry, my love. Indeed, who knows but what you will make some acquaintance there whom you may later influence for the general good."

"Now there is an original reason for attending an assembly!" Pippa teased. "I should do better to spend the time working on Lord Selworth's speech."

"How do you go on?"

"I can no longer postpone the evil day. When we meet at the theatre this evening, I shall tell him I have his manuscript and Prometheus wishes me to discuss the suggested alterations with him."

"Evil day?" asked Mrs. Lisle with raised eyebrows. "I have never known you reluctant to express your views!"

"On the contrary, I am constantly at great pains to hold back."

"Do you dislike the prospect of consulting with Lord Selworth? I was under the impression you took pleasure in his company."

"I do," Pippa confessed, turning away and hiding her face in her hands, "too much. Oh Mama, I know his only interest is in the connection to Prometheus, but I dread his finding out who Prometheus really is and turning from me in disgust."

Her mother came over and put an arm about her shoulders. "My poor darling, have you conceived a *tendre* for the viscount? It is my fault. I ought to have foreseen the possibility."

"It is only a slight attachment." Pippa strove to convince herself as much as Mama. "I shall be quite content to be his friend, truly. But I should hate to lose his friendship, and I doubt my ability to conceal the truth once I cannot avoid the subject of politics altogether."

"I suppose there is no chance . . . No, your papa was one in a million, and you being his daughter he had cause for pride in your intellectual achievements. You will just have to do your best to keep Lord Selworth in the dark, my love."

Pippa summoned up a smile. "So it is fortunate that I am

not wildly enamored,'' she said wryly. ''To be forced to with-hold one's complete confidence from one's beloved cannot be considered desirable.''

''The quality of mercy is not strain'd,'' quoth Portia. ''It droppeth as the gentle rain from heaven upon the place beneath. It is twice blest: it blesseth him that gives and him that receives.''

Lord Selworth leant forward to whisper in Pippa's ear, ''Would that I might lift this speech entire!''

''Hush!'' Pippa was entranced by *The Merchant of Venice*, often read, never before seen on the stage. Edmund Kean made Shylock come alive, no bogle but a tormented man struggling for his rights in an unsympathetic society.

Jews ought to have the vote, she thought, as well as Catholics, Nonconformists, and the property-less masses. Not to mention women. Had not Portia faced a court full of men and outargued them all? Three hundred years ago, with the example of his accomplished queen before him, Shakespeare had recognized the talents of women. Pippa was not unique in her abilities, merely rare in being encouraged to develop them.

Music brought her attention back to the stage. She had always found the final scene clever and amusing; now, with Lord Selworth close behind her, its bawdy innuendos made her blush. She fanned her face, glad that the heat of a thousand bodies and as many candles in the theatre was reason enough for pink cheeks.

The curtain descended for the last time. In the noise and bustle of departure, Pippa found it no easier than before or during the play to speak privately with Lord Selworth.

As he handed her into the Debenhams' carriage, she said, ''I must talk to you. Are you free tomorrow morning?''

His face lit up. ''You have heard from—'' Glancing over his shoulder at the crush of playgoers close behind him, waiting for their carriages, he lowered his voice. "News from my mentor? Splendid! Will eleven be too early?"

"No, I shall expect you then." Sadly Pippa took her seat in the carriage. His delight at the conclusion he had so quickly jumped to, when she asked him to call, confirmed that his only interest in her was the connection to Prometheus.

As the carriage rolled towards Charles Street, Bina interrupted Millicent's interminable review of the play. "Poor Shylock, losing his only daughter. It has made me realize how much I miss my boys. Mrs. Lisle, I have a great favor to beg of you. Now that you have met a great many people, would you mind chaperoning Pippa and the girls alone for a few days while I go down to Kent?"

"Not a bit, my dear," said Mrs. Lisle cheerfully. "You will return in good time for Almack's on Wednesday, no doubt, and we do not entertain formally before then, do we? For the rest, just make sure I know what invitations we have accepted each day, and I shall make your excuses to our hostesses."

"No dinner parties, as I recall, so my absence will not upset anyone's numbers."

"May I hope you can spare me also, ma'am?" George Debenham asked Mrs. Lisle. "There are one or two matters of business on which I should like to consult my father in person. If you don't care to be without male protection, I daresay Selworth will agree to stand in for me."

"I cannot think we shall need protection," Pippa protested. If Lord Selworth were to move into the house, she would be unable to work on his speech without fear of his catching her at it.

"We have had large numbers of gentlemen callers recently," Bina pointed out, "though I hardly fancy any of them are likely to trouble you."

"There is safety in numbers." Pippa did *not* want Wynn Selworth constantly at hand, disturbing her peace of mind.

"Besides," said Kitty, a laugh in her voice, "I have noticed that Mr. Debenham takes great care to leave for his club well before our swarms of beaux begin to arrive. Whereas Lord Selworth or Mr. Chubb or both almost always turn up. I am sure we can rely upon Mr. Chubb as much as Lord Selworth if Lieutenant Pendrell starts to wave his sword or Lord Fenimore's invitations to a masked ball at the Pantheon become too pressing.''

''Oh dear,'' said Mrs. Lisle, ''has he asked you again, Kitty? Still, a butler and three stout footmen are surely sufficient to eject him should it become advisable!''

''I shall direct my butler to station two footmen within earshot whenever Lord Fenimore is admitted,'' George Debenham promised dryly.

Next morning, the Debenhams departed for Kent shortly before Lord Selworth arrived. Pippa had advised her mother of her appointment with the viscount. Mrs. Lisle and Kitty had no difficulty enticing Millicent out to the shops to look for matching ribbons and buttons and such fal-lals. Nor was Millie surprised that Pippa stayed at home. Her lack of interest in fashions and fripperies had long since ceased to arouse comment.

Millicent had been told originally that her brother had business with a friend of the Lisles. The nature of the business was kept from her, in view of her lack of discretion, and she appeared to have forgotten all about it. Everyone agreed that the longer she could be kept in ignorance, the better.

So Pippa awaited Lord Selworth alone in the ladies' sitting room. She ruffled through the sheets of manuscript, noting with dismay the proliferation of red ink.

Had she made too many changes? He might be offended by such lavish criticism, or so discouraged he decided to give up.

Through the open window came the chime of church clocks striking eleven. Though she expected him and had left the door ajar, Lord Selworth's knock made Pippa start.

''I beg your pardon, Miss Lisle.'' He stood on the threshold, a trim figure in a blue morning coat, fawn Unmentionables, blue and gray striped waistcoat, and neatly tied cravat. Only the unmanageable flyaway hair had not been spruced up since their first meeting. Pippa was glad he had not taken to pomading it into submission. "I did not mean to startle you," he continued. "I ought to have sent a footman to announce me, perhaps. I have grown accustomed to treating my sister's house as my own, but she has gone off to Kent, I am told, and in her absence—"

"Oh no, Lord Selworth, I am sure Mama would not wish you to feel less at home because Bina is away. Do come in and be seated. It was idiotish of me to be taken by surprise when you arrived exactly on time."

He moved a chair alongside the desk and sat down. "Your thoughts were far away. I fear you were wondering how to convey Prometheus' verdict without driving me to despair."

His guess was too close to the truth. Mutely Pippa pushed the pile of papers across to him.

Ruffling through the sheets as she had just done, Lord Selworth groaned. "A sea of red ink! I daresay I ought to be grateful it isn't the red ink of debts. Have you read his comments, Miss Lisle? Can you tell me if it is salvageable, or shall I take up agriculture instead of politics? Has Prometheus pruned, as you suggested, or has he uprooted my roses and consigned them to the bonfire?"

"By no means. Your rootstock is sound. That is, Prometheus has no quarrel with what you wish to say, only it might be put more persuasively. At least . . ." Pippa hesitated.

"Pray let me know the worst."

"I . . . Prometheus is inclined to believe you are attempting to cover too many disparate subjects in a single speech. It might be more effective if you concentrate on a few closely related topics rather than putting all your convictions in one basket."

Lord Selworth looked much struck. "That is precisely what I was doing," he admitted with a rueful grimace. "Now I come to think of it, I suppose I tried to include the whole batch for fear of never having the opportunity to make a second speech!''

"But if the first is good enough, you will make many more,'' Pippa encouraged him. "I am not sure how long a maiden speech in the House of Lords is expected to last, but Papa used to say if your listeners are bored by the end, they will forget the beginning.''

"And everything in between, no doubt. So Prometheus says it is too long, as well as too complex and too verbose?''

"It is hard to tell without reading it aloud.''

"Which would be a waste of time until it is whipped roughly into shape. I had best take this home to study.'' He tapped the manuscript on the writing table to straighten the sheets. "Then, when I comprehend what Prometheus approves and what he condemns, I shall make a fresh start. Miss Lisle, may I ask a very great favor of you?''

"Of course,'' Pippa said cautiously.

"It is perfectly clear to me that you understand and agree with the criticisms Prometheus has written here. Will you be so good as to advise me as I go along, so that I shall not humiliate myself by sending him another thoroughly bungled effort?''

With what she hoped was a becoming degree of hesitant modesty, Pippa acquiesced. In fact she was delighted. She would be able to express her own opinions openly, without having to constantly filter them through "Prometheus suggests . . .'' and "I believe Prometheus means . . .''

She must be careful not to venture far afield from the comments already attributed to her alter ego. Fortunately, she had dissected Lord Selworth's first effort with ruthless thoroughness. His second was unlikely to present new difficulties unsolvable by the same methods. On the whole, Pippa was inclined to believe she had a good chance of scraping through with her secret preserved.

* * *

Wynn spent the afternoon poring over his annotated speech. On the whole he had to agree with the extensive deletions. What remained was more forceful for being leaner, though it hurt to lose the intricate embellishments he had labored over so lovingly.

Perhaps some of the purple prose could be used in his next Gothic novel, he thought. Then he recalled that he must write no more romances. The risk of his authorship coming to light was too great.

Sighing, he returned to the manuscript. At least the germs of his metaphors had been preserved, thanks to Miss Lisle, no doubt. Here and there, Prometheus had even written in praise of a particularly strong image. There were one or two comments Wynn did not quite understand. Perhaps Miss Lisle would be able to elucidate, so that he did not have to trouble Prometheus about minor details. He did not wish to look more of a sapskull than he need.

Somehow he didn't mind Pippa Lisle seeing his blunders. He knew he had her sympathy and her approval of his aims.

That his speech had too many aims was obvious, now that she—or rather Prometheus—had pointed it out. Like a scatter of birdshot compared to a rifle bullet, his speech might hit with every ball, yet to little effect. Though he had succeeded in weaving his plethora of opinions into a coherent sequence of ideas, the central theme was weak.

Reading through again, he could not make up his mind where to concentrate his efforts. Prometheus had made no suggestions. Wynn decided to consult Pippa.

He set about abstracting from his manuscript a list of topics ranging from the Seditious Meetings Bill to the use of spring guns and mantraps against poachers: a regular stew, all excellent ingredients but losing their individual flavours in the mixture.

What he wanted was roast beef with a few complementary

side dishes. In fact, he was deucedly hungry. Glancing at the clock on the mantel, he saw he had missed tea with the Lisles and escorting them to the Park. It was nearly time to change for dinner.

He and Gil Chubb had arranged to dine with friends at Boodle's Club, he remembered with annoyance. They were to meet the Lisles and Millicent at some party afterwards, but that was no time or place to present his list to Miss Lisle and request her advice.

Was it too much to ask of her? She had not wanted to come to London for the Season, but Wynn had noticed that she seemed to be enjoying herself. It didn't seem quite fair to expect her to spend her time on politics, a subject she usually tried to avoid, in common with the majority of females. Of course she could have refused to help directly, to air her own opinions as opposed to conveying messages from Prometheus. However, Wynn suspected a sense of duty to her father's ideals had driven her to give her hesitant consent.

He was not really sure why he believed she was competent to advise him. Copying Benjamin Lisle's work was a far cry from producing original work. Still, if consulting her proved profitless, he could always take his minor difficulties directly to Prometheus.

And meanwhile he had a perfect excuse for spending a great deal of time with Miss Philippa Lisle.

"I have a confession to make," Wynn told Miss Lisle on Tuesday morning, laying down his pen and leaning back in his chair. "Promise you won't take snuff?"

"How can I?" she retorted. "Until I know what your offense is, I cannot guess whether it will offend me. However, I hope I can safely promise not to hit you on the head with the poker."

"You have my permission to haul me over the coals." He went over to the grate, where flickering sea-coals strove to disperse the chill of the drizzling day, and poked up the fire. "Come and warm your hands, Miss Lisle."

"Procrastinating, Lord Selworth?" With a smile, she came over and held out her hands to the flames he had stirred up.

"Not at all. It isn't the sort of confession which must be made for fear of being found out. My fingers are cold and cramped from writing, and you have done just as much writing as I have, if not more."

"Not this morning. I have been dictating to you. I trust you do not mean to confess to finding me shockingly dictatorial when all you wished for was a few gentle hints?" she asked anxiously.

"You are the gentlest of dictators. And you *have* been writing—if I had not watched, I should have guessed by the smudge of ink on your forehead." Such a broad, clear, intelligent forehead, with beautifully curved brows, set off by two wings of dark, smooth, glossy hair. "Have I ever told you how much I like the way you wear your hair?"

Blood tinting her pellucid cheeks, Pippa raised a hand to touch the hair at her temple. "Thank you, but I must say I should like to be able to coax it into curls in the evenings."

"Oh no, then it would be just like every other young lady's. You look distinguished, and elegant, and . . . intelligent. Which brings me back to my confession. When I asked you to help me, I had the gravest doubts of your ability to do so. There, it is said." Wynn laughed as her expression changed. "May I offer you the poker?"

"I have done very little." She bit her lip. "No more than . . . than giving a few suggestions as to how to set your ideas in order."

"You have done quite as much as I ever expected of Prometheus."

The color fled from her cheeks, and she shook her head violently. "Impossible!"

"I mean it. I wager he comes to you for—Good gad!" Wynn struck himself on the forehead with the heel of his hand. "How can I have been so blind? You *are* Prometheus!"

Miss Lisle swooned.

CHAPTER 12

As the room ceased to whirl about Pippa's head, she became aware of a frantic voice.

"Miss Lisle! Pippa! Oh Lord!"

Through clearing mists, she saw Lord Selworth's appalled face. She was lying on the floor with her head in his lap. "I am . . ." She faltered and tried to sit up. Nausea rose in her throat.

"No, you aren't. You're pale as rice pudding. Lie still, or you will go off again. Good gad, Miss Lisle, you gave me a frightful shock!"

"Nothing to the . . . shock I gave myself. Did I . . . faint?" she asked, eyes closed.

"Went down like an elm in a gale. I just caught you before you whacked your head on the fender. No," he mused, "more like a wilting lily."

"You are too kind!"

"At any rate, I'd say it must have been a swoon, a faint if you prefer. I've no experience."

"Nor have I," Pippa said indignantly, opening her eyes,

then hastily shutting them again as she met his blue gaze mere inches above her. "I have never fainted before in my life."

"I'm afraid it was my fault." Lord Selworth squeezed her hand, which she had not realized he was clasping. She was still far too weak to withdraw it, she told herself, as he went on, "I gave you the first shock. I should not have accused you so abruptly."

Now she recalled in dismay why she had fainted. "It is not true," she cried, suddenly finding the strength to pull her hand from his and once more trying to sit up.

"Be still," he commanded, pressing her back with a hand to her shoulder. "Doing it rather too brown, my girl. Of course it's true. Why else should you have crumpled like an unstarched neckcloth?"

"You grow more and more complimentary, I vow! I want to get up."

He frowned down at her. "You are still awfully pale."

"I am naturally pale."

"True, but pearly pale, not pasty. Still, the floor cannot be comfortable."

Refusing to admit she was perfectly comfortable, Pippa said, "And suppose someone comes in?"

Lord Selworth cast an alarmed glance at the door, left ajar as propriety demanded. Without warning, he swept her up in strong arms, and before she had time for more than a gasp of surprise, he deposited her full-length on the nearest sofa.

She started to swing her feet to the floor.

"Please, lie still! If you collapse again, I shall have to call your maid, since Mrs. Lisle is out. We cannot explain what happened, and what she'll guess doesn't bear imagining."

Pippa blushed, imagining all too clearly that Nan would assume Lord Selworth had attempted improper familiarities. Then, though she had briefly suppressed the awareness, she once again remembered what had in fact caused her to swoon.

"You know," she said faintly.

"That you are Prometheus?" He pulled up a chair. "Now

I look back, it's quite obvious the family friend was a fiction, but then, everything is always clear in hindsight.''

"It was Mama's notion to ask for a Season in payment, not mine."

"You would have refused me outright, would you not? To safeguard your secret. You are afraid of being sent to prison?"

"A little." Pippa shuddered. "You know how easy it is to be condemned for sedition now that *Habeas corpus* is suspended. Have you read of the appalling conditions of women in Newgate Gaol?"

"No, as you might guess since I'd have tried to fit it into my speech," he said ruefully.

Pippa managed to smile. "No doubt. I was less concerned about prison, though, than about not being taken seriously. Who will pay the least heed to my articles if they know them to be written by a woman?"

"I will!"

"You are kind to say so. However, you cannot persuade me you would have asked Prometheus to assist you if you had known then."

Lord Selworth frowned. "You may be right," he admitted. "So is it not fortunate that I remained in the dark until I had discovered your abilities for myself?"

"But now you will wish to find another mentor," Pippa said sadly. "No gentleman wishes to take advice from a female, especially one younger than himself."

"Come now, I am no Methuselah, Miss Lisle! And speaking of mythical figures—your wide acquaintance with Greek and Latin myth was one thing which gave you away—do you know who the original Mentor was?"

"Something to do with Odysseus." She was a trifle impatient with the irrelevant question when her future was at stake. "Adviser to his wife and son, Penelope and Telemachus, was he not? A man."

"Ah, but at some point in the story his place was taken by Athena in disguise. A female!" he said triumphantly.

"A goddess!"

His blue eyes gleamed. "If it weren't the sort of flummery tossed about by honey-tongued coxcombs, I might call you a goddess. Be that as it may, I most certainly wish you to continue to play the part of Athena, Mentor, or Prometheus. All three if you will! Surely you cannot find it in your heart to abandon me in the middle of this thicket of half-pruned rosebushes?"

"If you truly wish me to continue, I shall." Pippa sighed. "But once everyone finds out that I am Prometheus . . ."

"Everyone finds out? Why the dev—deuce should anyone find out?" Lord Selworth drew himself up and addressed her sternly. "Miss Lisle, do you mean to insinuate that *I* might give you away?"

"Not on purpose!"

"Then you must be confusing me with Millicent."

"Oh no!" Relieved to see a twinkle in his eye, Pippa giggled. "Impossible."

"I am delighted to hear it. I shan't confide in her, believe me."

"Nor anyone else."

"Nor anyone else, I give you my word. Perhaps it will set your mind at ease if I give you a means of retaliation as well. I, too, have a secret I should hate to see bandied about the world."

"Tell me," Pippa breathed, burning with curiosity.

Lord Selworth turned rather pink. "You may recall I told your mama I worked to help support my family?"

"Yes, and you were so reticent about it I immediately thought the worst."

"Did you, indeed! Well, I don't know what your worst is, and I don't want to know, but it was nothing so very dreadful. I was neither pirate nor slaver, I assure you. The trouble is, public exposure would blight my political career, if not wither it entirely. Like you, I should not be taken seriously."

"Exposure of your consulting *me* would very likely be as

bad for you," Pippa felt bound to point out. "I shall consider that surety enough, if you like. You need not tell me."

"Generously spoken, when I can see you are all agog. I would not be so cruel." Lord Selworth took a deep breath. "The fact of the matter is, I used to write quite successful Gothic romances. Like you, under a pseudonym."

"Valentine Dred!" cried Pippa.

"How did you know?" he asked, startled.

"I recognized your style, turns of phrase, in your speech."

"Oh Lord, is it so evident?"

"I never dreamt you had written the books, only that you had read and enjoyed them."

"Dare I hope you enjoyed them?"

Pippa was about to assure him that she loved his books, when she recalled the ribaldry which went with the tongue-in-cheek adventures. Lord Selworth had written those bawdy tales? Shocked, her face aflame, she looked away—and saw her ankles exposed to his view. Swinging her limbs down from the sofa, she primly smoothed her apricot mull muslin skirt over her knees, her gaze fixed on her fingers.

"Sir, your books are not at all proper for young ladies to read."

Lord Selworth roared with laughter, the wretch! "My dear girl, if you have read enough of them to recognize my style, you have no possible excuse for denouncing them."

Bowing her head, Pippa wished she could sink through the floor. "I . . . I have read them all," she confessed in a constricted voice, "and I like them very much. *Not* because of the . . . the improper bits, but because you seem not to take your characters and their exploits and misadventures very seriously. I hope I am not mistaken?" she asked, looking up as interest overcame embarrassment.

"No indeed. I'm glad you realized it. Not all my reviewers have been equally perceptive!" he told her wryly. "But you understand why I fear I shall not be taken any more seriously than I take my stories if I'm discovered to be the author."

"Yes. I suppose you will not write any more now? What a pity!"

"There is one more due to come out shortly, *The Masked Marauder.*"

"A splendid title," Pippa exclaimed.

"Perhaps I ought to have stopped publication when my great-uncle died, but the bookseller pleaded with me to let it go forward. To tell the truth, having written the dashed thing, I should be sorry not to see it in print."

"I can imagine. I feel much the same about my articles, and a novel is a far greater undertaking. How did you come to begin writing them?"

"I started by scribbling down the scary stories I used to tell Albinia, when she was still in the nursery."

"Oh, that must be why she guessed."

Lord Selworth looked stunned and alarmed. "Bina guessed?"

"So I would assume. She told me she knew a secret of yours and had kept it so well even you were unaware that she knew. It is safe with her. She refused to tell me. Does no one else know?"

"The bookseller, of course, and Gil Chubb. Who knows about Prometheus?"

"Mr. Cobbett, Mama, and Kitty. And now you."

"Don't faint again, I beg of you!"

"I cannot think how I came to do anything so totty-headed," Pippa said candidly. "It must have been because you took me by surprise. I am perfectly well now. Shall we go back to work?" She started to rise.

He put out a hand to stop her. "No, we have done enough for today."

"Do you know yet when you will be able to speak?"

"No, but these last few days I have grown confident enough of having a speech worth giving to have a word with Lord Grey and Lord Holland. They promise to approach Lord Eldon in my behalf. The Chancellor is an intransigent Tory, however, who will be in no hurry to fit a Reformist speech into the agenda, far less one they suspect of being Radical. We have time enough.''

''Nonetheless, I should like to—''

''Not now,'' he said commandingly, his gaze searching. ''You must not overtire yourself with poring over my papers.''

''I am not tired,'' Pippa protested. ''We are already agreed that my complexion is naturally pale.''

Lord Selworth grinned. ''Then let us put roses in your cheeks with a walk to Green Park, and on the way back I shall treat you to an ice at Gunter's. Not a word of politics the entire time! Go and put on your bonnet—and wash that ink off your face!''

''Yes, my lord. At once, my lord,'' Pippa said tartly, and whisked off to obey.

Changing into walking shoes, she donned her straw-colored, plumed bonnet and the matching *gros de Naples* spencer which went with almost everything. Lord Selworth awaited her downstairs in the front hall. He turned from studying with disfavor a portrait of George Debenham's great-grandparents.

''Deuced odd clothes people used to wear.'' He regarded Pippa with a slight frown. ''Will you be warm enough? The sun is shining, for a wonder, but there is a nippy breeze.''

''Do you have a dawdling stroll in mind? I had hoped for a brisk, warming walk.''

''How unfashionable!'' he bantered. ''And what a relief. Like Miss Kitty, I find a saunter far more tiring than a stride.''

They went out into Charles Street. Lord Selworth did not suggest taking a maid or footman—not that Pippa had any intention of doing so, but it went to show that he considered her past the age of needing a chaperon. Past the age of romance and marriage, she thought sadly, recalling the notably youthful heroines of his novels.

''Tell me about writing your books,'' she said. ''It must be quite different from writing a speech.''

''As I discovered, to my dismay!''

"Where do you begin? Do you plan the story beforehand, or just plunge in?"

Lord Selworth was delighted to be able to talk freely about his literary achievements, and scrupulous to avoid all mention of the naughty parts. He kept Pippa amused and fascinated all the way around Green Park and back to Berkley Square, where he turned towards Gunter's.

"Should we not come back later with Millicent and Kitty?" Pippa suggested. "They would consider it a great treat."

"As you do not?" he queried mournfully.

"Of course I do!"

"I shall bring them some other time. This is *our* morning. My heart is set upon a raspberry cream ice, and you shall order whatever elaborate and expensive concoction you please to compensate for the shock I gave you earlier."

"I had forgotten it."

"Then I beg your pardon for reminding you."

"Unnecessary, since you offer amends. Tell me," she teased, "in other circumstances would you balk at standing the nonsense for whatever elaborate and expensive confection I might choose?"

"To say no were ungallant, yet to say yes is to court bankruptcy, at Gunter's prices! Besides which, I should have to do the same for your sister and mine."

Pippa laughed. "Then this would be no special treat. However, a raspberry cream ice sounds perfect to me."

The ices, served with crisp wafers, were delicious. Lord Selworth insisted on ordering a pot of tea as well. Pippa accepted graciously, though her thrifty soul cavilled at the extra expense when they were scarcely two minutes' walk from the Debenhams' house.

Returning to the house, they found the others wondering where Pippa had disappeared to.

"Not that I was upon the fret, my love," said Mrs. Lisle, drawing Pippa aside, "but I wish you will leave a note or inform one of the staff if you go out unexpectedly."

"I am sorry, Mama. I did not think."

"And you ought to take Nan or one of the footmen."

"I know I must not go out alone in London. I was with Lord Selworth."

Mrs. Lisle glanced at the other end of the drawing room, where the viscount was teasing the girls with a panegyrical description of Gunter's ices. "The more reason for taking a servant."

"Lord Selworth behaved with perfect propriety."

"I should expect nothing less of him, but propriety is in the eye of the beholder. I know you believe yourself too old to need a chaperon, dearest, but that is utter nonsense. Anyone seeing you escorted only by a personable young man would have good reason to be shocked."

"I shall not do it again, Mama," Pippa promised. He was most unlikely ever to invite her again. "I fear I had had something of a shock myself and was not thinking straight." Looking to make sure Millicent was still beyond earshot, she continued softly, "He has guessed."

"That you are Prometheus? Oh, my love, what a horrid shock indeed! Perhaps I was wrong to propose this masquerade . . . yet you are still on friendly terms with Lord Selworth. Never say he is willing to accept assistance from a female?"

"So he claims, though he may yet change his mind. Maybe he said so only to comfort me, and he will find some excuse to cry off. He has scarcely had time enough to consider the possible consequences."

"There need be none if he can hold his tongue," Mrs. Lisle pointed out, "and if you are more careful. You left his papers out on the desk."

"Oh no, did I? My mind was more disordered than I had supposed."

"And his, too. I put the speech in the drawer, but you have the key. You had best lock it before luncheon."

"I shall go up at once. Did Millicent see it?"

"Saw, but did not read. She made some comment about how you are forever scribbling. Do take care, my love."

"I shall, Mama."

Pippa kissed her mother's cheek and ran upstairs to lock the drawer and put off her bonnet.

Sitting at the dressing table to tidy her hair, she stared at herself in the looking glass. He had said he liked her hair, unrelentingly straight as it was. He said she looked distinguished, elegant, intelligent. That was before he guessed she was Prometheus. When had he called her "my dear girl," before or after? Her head had been in such a whirl, she could not remember.

It must have been before. Though the phrase had no great significance, a gentleman surely would not use it to one he had accepted as his mentor. She would always be Athena to him now, never Aphrodite.

Not that she had ever dreamt of aspiring to the beauty of the Goddess of Love, she thought with a sigh, regarding her cheeks, still pale despite the brisk walk. It was definitely after she fainted that he had compared her to a wilted lily, an unstarched neckcloth, a rice pudding! Admittedly Lord Selworth was given to exotic metaphor, yet surely even he would not so disparage a lady in whom he had the least romantic interest.

Still, he had described her usual paleness as pearly, Pippa recalled, a little cheered.

More important, he respected her intelligence and had not promptly refused her continued help, as she had feared. And she still had his friendship. Their walk and the visit to Gunter's testified to that.

She had much to be thankful for. Doing her best to persuade herself she was satisfied, Pippa went down to luncheon.

* * *

"You will be quite the prettiest girl at Almack's, I vow," said Pippa, fastening the last hooks in her sister's gown. "Turn around now and let me look."

Kitty twirled and curtsied, the primrose satin slip and silver Urling's net overdress swirling about her ankles. "I am in a dreadful quake," she said with no visible diminution in her usual placidity. "Suppose I say something shockingly bucolic and give the Patronesses a disgust of me?"

"Anything you say, Mr. Chubb will turn off as wit or wisdom. Keep him at your side whenever you are not dancing. It should not prove difficult."

"He is a dear, is he not? I cannot think why he is so speechless in general, for he always has plenty to say to me. Not nonsensical compliments, either, but sensible talk about things which matter."

"Do you favor him, Kitty? He would be an excellent *parti.*"

"Oh, I don't mean to favor anyone for ages yet. I am enjoying myself far too much. To tell the truth," she admitted, laughing, "I find the nonsensical compliments most agreeable!"

"I am not at all surprised. What girl would not delight in collecting such a court of admiring beaux as you have?"

Kitty flung her arms about her sister. "It is all thanks to you, darling Pippa."

"Not to mention Mama! Careful. Do not crush your gown, dearest. You must have noticed how I profit by your court. As soon as your admirers notice that we are on excellent terms, they spare no effort to stay in my good books. I do not expect to sit out a single dance tonight."

"Of course not, but it is nothing to do with their admiring *me,* goosecap. Come, let me help you put on your dress."

Pippa's gown for the all-important assembly was of emerald crepe, scalloped to expose a sarcenet slip the pale green of new leaves, the same color as the brief bodice. The hems of over- and under-skirts were ornamented with silk vine leaves in the contrasting shade. Bina had wanted to lend her emeralds to go with it, but Pippa regretfully refused—clothes were one thing, jewelry another. She wore her gold locket with a twist of Papa's hair, the twin of Kitty's.

Going downstairs, Pippa wished Lord Selworth was to dine with them. He had been bidden to dinner at Holland House, an invitation he could not refuse, for Lady Holland was one of the two great Whig hostesses of the day and her husband was a leader of the party.

Lord Selworth had promised to meet the Debenhams and the Lisles at Almack's. However, Holland House was a few miles out of town, in Kensington. If he were to become involved in political discussions, he could very well arrive too late in King Street. The Lady Patronesses were as adamant about closing the doors at eleven o'clock as they were about gentlemen having to wear knee breeches.

Though Pippa had gained vastly in confidence since the first ball of the Season, Lord Selworth's presence was a prop on which she had come to depend. She did not want to face the most select circles of the Ton without him nearby.

CHAPTER 13

"Five to eleven," Bina muttered in Pippa's ear as the figures of a country dance brought them together. "I shall give him a fine trimming if he misses Millie's first appearance at Almack's."

"She is doing very well without him," Pippa defended the viscount, glancing over at Millicent, who was chattering away to her partner while they danced up the next set.

"It is a matter of principle. It is his duty to support his sister," Bina insisted, pronouncing the last word over her shoulder as she tripped away to meet her partner.

Then it was Pippa's turn to take George Debenham's hand and follow. She liked dancing with her friend's husband. His saturnine manner belied a very real kindness, generosity, and patience, and she appreciated his decidedly dry wit.

"Bina fears Lord Selworth is not going to turn up in time," she told him. "She is preparing to read him a dreadful scold."

He laughed. "One of Albinia's scolds would not cow a scullery maid, far less her brother, but he will not have to suffer it. I saw him come in a few minutes ago. He is with Mrs. Lisle."

"How fortunate!" Pippa suppressed an urgent desire to turn her head and peer back in the most ill-bred fashion at the spot where her mother sat, on the far side of the room.

Mr. Debenham apparently read her mind. "You would have to grow several inches to see them," he said with a smile. "I assure you it is really he. And he looks none the worse for having dined at Holland House."

"Why should he?" Pippa enquired, intrigued.

"One hears stories—but I have never been invited to that hotbed of Whiggery. You must ask Selworth."

"I shall."

At last the dance ended, with a fine flourish from Gow's Band in the balcony. By the time Pippa and Mr. Debenham made their way to Mrs. Lisle, Millicent and Kitty had already rejoined her. Lord Selworth stood talking to them, a slim, elegant figure in black coat, white cravat and waistcoat, and black knee breeches and stockings. Pippa thought he looked pleased and excited, his blue eyes alight with jubilation, not at all as if dinner with the Hollands had caused him any distress.

He had promised to stand up first with his younger sister, then with Kitty. "And may I hope for the honor of the dance after that with you, Miss Lisle?" he requested, adding in a lower voice, "I must talk to you."

Pippa pretended to consult her card, though she had taken care not to engage herself much in advance so as to be free in case Lord Selworth asked her. "I believe I might squeeze you in, sir," she said, writing down his name.

"Don't mention squeezing, I beg of you!" With that mystifying plea, he allowed Millie to drag him away.

When the time came for their dance, Lord Selworth asked Pippa if she would object to sitting it out. "A country dance makes sustained conversation impossible, at least, for anyone but Millicent," he said, watching his prattling sister go off on Mr. Chubb's arm, "and I have a great deal to tell you while it is fresh in my mind."

"I want to hear all about the Hollands' dinner party. Besides,

I shall be glad of a rest. My last partner stepped on my toes twice.''

"Splendid!''

"Sir!'' Pippa exclaimed in mock affront.

He grinned. ''My apologies to your toes, and my sympathies. Mrs. Lisle, may we join you, ma'am? I have one or two messages for you from colleagues of your late husband.'' He handed Pippa to a chair next but one to her mother and seated himself between them. ''First, ladies,'' he said portentously, ''my news: the Lord High Chancellor has set a date for my speech!''

"Already?'' said Pippa. ''When?''

"Three weeks from tomorrow. That is time enough, is it not?''

"Oh yes, plenty. I was afraid you were going to say tomorrow. As Lord Eldon is a dyed-in-the-Woolsack Tory, he might have tried to catch you unprepared.''

"He might, though I doubt he expects my speech to have much effect. True, I am a dark horse, but he has hedged his bets by—'' Taking in the ladies' blank expressions, Lord Selworth paused.

"A dark horse?'' asked Mrs. Lisle, bemused.

"I beg your pardon, ma'am, a metaphor from the Turf— horse racing. Not that I would have you suppose I make a habit of throwing away my blunt on the races, but I picked up some of the lingo when I was looking for cattle at Tattersall's. A dark horse is one about which little is known.''

"Like your ability as an orator,'' Pippa said. ''Hedging one's bets is wagering both for and against, to avoid losing badly, is it not? I have seen it used metaphorically.''

"Are you accusing me of unoriginality, Miss Lisle?''

"Never! On the contrary, Lord Selworth, you know I have been at some pains to restrain your excessive originality. What has the Chancellor done?''

"Put me last on his schedule for the day, after a debate on whether or not to raise the duty on tea by a farthing.''

"A subject so profoundly uninteresting to the wealthy

Lords," said Pippa, "that everyone will have fallen asleep or gone home by the time you stand up."

"Precisely."

"What a shame!" said Mrs. Lisle sympathetically. "Nonetheless, you must both do your best. Make it rousing enough and some of them will wake up and take note."

"We shall try, ma'am, I promise you, shall we not, Miss Lisle? Now, let me see, Mr. Thomas Creevey, Mr. Henry Grey Bennet, and Mr. Henry Brougham asked me to convey their respects. Oh, and Sir Francis Burdett." He passed on brief messages from those gentlemen encountered at the Hollands'. "I took the liberty of telling them you are residing at my sister's. Creevey will call without delay, and the other three as soon as their duties in the Commons allow."

"Mr. Bennet is a true reformer, is he not, in spite of being a son of Lord Tankerville?" Pippa asked.

"I'd go so far as to call him a Radical. It is a pity he is not heir to the earldom. I made the acquaintance of all sorts of interesting people at Holland House, and the conversation was fascinating." Lord Selworth described the people he had met and repeated some of the talk. "But I cannot do it justice. I wish you had been there."

"So do I," said Pippa, "except that Mr. Debenham expressed surprise on seeing you none the worse for the experience. Nor have you explained your abhorrence of the word 'squeeze.' "

"Squeeze!" He laughed. "Lady Holland is noted for always inviting more people than will comfortably fit at her table. I am told she once ordered Luttrell to make room for some late arrival, whereupon he replied, 'It certainly must be made, because it doesn't exist!' "

"If you were jammed elbow to elbow, Lord Selworth," said Mrs. Lisle, "I hope you had enough to eat, for the refreshments here are shocking. Nothing but bread and butter and cake, and the cake I had was quite stale."

"There was plenty of food, ma'am, though eating was not easy! Lady Holland is a splendid hostess, in spite of a tendency to be imperious. She doesn't take snuff at a witty retort, however. When she commanded Sydney Smith to ring the bell for her, he asked if she wanted him to sweep the floor, too, yet afterwards she was perfectly affable to him. And though she likes to rule the conversation, the result is so excellent one cannot object.''

So different, Pippa thought, from the tittle-tattle which passed as conversation elsewhere. With the Season scarcely under way, she was already growing tired of gossip, scandal, fashion, and sport. Although this Season was by no means the nightmare her first had been, she would just have soon have been back at Sweetbriar Cottage—if it were not for Lord Selworth and his need for help with his speech.

''Even if I end up addressing an empty House at midnight,'' he said softly, turning from Mrs. Lisle to Pippa with a smile, as Kitty and Millicent and their partners approached, ''I know it will be a good speech, because I have Prometheus to help me.''

By the time Pippa saw Lord Selworth next afternoon, his mood of elation had worn off and he was less sanguine. After making his bow to Bina and Mrs. Lisle and briefly greeting some other callers, he came straight to Pippa.

''Is there any point in working so hard,'' he grumbled in a disgruntled undertone, slumping beside her on a sofa in the drawing room, ''when I may have no audience? I tried to put pen to paper this morning and not a thought came into my head.''

''You were dancing until three,'' she pointed out. ''Mama has forbidden us to rise before noon when we are out so late, which is why she told you not to call this morning. I am sure you are no less in need of sleep because you are a gentleman.''

''Very likely,'' he said ruefully. ''I shall lose my mind, and the roses in my cheeks.''

''Mama threatened Kitty and Millicent with losing their roses,'' said Pippa, chuckling, ''and me with losing my mind. I cannot spare it, for I do not mean to let you give up. Papa made many a speech which was little heeded, but he always put just as much effort into the next.''

"I stand rebuked." He sighed. "You are right, of course. Politics requires perseverance above all else, particularly in a member of the Opposition.''

"And a minority within the Opposition. Let us take a holiday today, though. Three weeks is more than enough time to finish. We shall do better tomorrow after you have slept your fill.''

"An excellent idea. I don't wish to overwork Prometheus and lose 'his' assistance.''

Millicent came up then, having just bid some visiting young ladies farewell. She was obviously bursting with news.

"Wynn, did you know," she began in a conspiratorial whisper, "Lady Gwendolyn just told me, when I mentioned that you dined at Holland House yesterday, and I promise I shan't repeat it in company because it is just like Lady Jersey only worse and Bina was so angry when I talked about Lady Jersey, so even though Lady Holland is not a Patroness, I don't mean to tell anyone but you and Pippa. Kitty was with me, so she heard.''

"Heard what?" her brother demanded impatiently. "What is this about Lady Jersey?''

"Oh, you were not there, were you? Lord Jersey, too, really, only he was not yet earl, I think." Millicent frowned in doubt, then her face cleared. "Anyway it is always the female who is blamed. They ran away together, and so did Lord and Lady Holland, only she was already married to *someone else!* She is *divorced!*''

"Good Lord, Millie, this is ancient history. Bina is quite correct. You are going to land in the suds—land us all in the suds—if you start to rake up old scandals about important people. Leave it to the tabbies who have nothing better to do and don't care whom they offend.''

"Lady Gwendolyn told us," Millicent said with an injured pout. "I *said* I shall not say a word to anyone but you.''

"See that you don't," commanded Lord Selworth, "for I won't put up with a scandalmonger in the family."

Thus castigated by her adored brother, Millicent was for once downcast, but only momentarily. A new group of callers was announced, and she went off to greet them with a flood of blithe chatter.

"Seed sown upon stony ground, I fear," Lord Selworth said wryly.

"She will not repeat the story of Lady Holland," Pippa said, "but there is no guessing what gossip she may pick up next, and without a specific prohibition . . . She does not deliberately disobey, you know. When she opens her mouth, she truly seems to have little control over what comes out, as if there is some sort of filter missing in her brain. Fortunately she is most good-natured, never actuated by spite, and she is more interested in the latest modes than anything else."

"Thank heaven for small mercies. If she favored political gossip, I'd be sitting constantly upon thorns!"

Wynn found himself too busy to worry about Millicent's rattling tongue. He worked on his speech with Pippa. He attended debates in the House of Lords, both to learn what was going on and to listen to how his peers framed their speeches—many of them deadly dull as well as misguided, he decided. He hobnobbed with Radical and Reformist members of the House of Commons, which gave him new ideas. Pippa had to be ruthless to make him stick to the points they had decided on for his own speech.

Missing the frequent exercise of a country life, he made sure to ride every day and often walked with Pippa and the girls in the parks. A friend introduced him to Gentleman Jackson, in whose boxing saloon Wynn began to study the noble art of pugilism, one of the few subjects in which Pippa expressed no interest whatsoever. Indeed, she positively forbade him to mention it!

The ballrooms of Mayfair and St. James's also provided a good deal of exercise. Though Millicent was well and truly launched, no longer in need of her brother's support, Wynn continued to escort his sisters and the Lisles to dances, routs, Venetian breakfasts, soirées, musicales, plays, and the Opera. Card parties he considered above and beyond the call of duty. Cards were for amusing the children in the long, dark evenings of a country winter. Bad enough that politeness occasionally forced him to play at Boodle's.

He found himself dining more rarely in Charles Street, more frequently with his new political cronies, at Boodle's or Brooks's or private houses. At the latter, women were usually present, though less often heard. Wynn wished he had Pippa beside him, with her firm grasp of principles and her cleverness with words.

Life without her would be flat indeed. He was tempted to propose to her at once, but the prospect of adding the complications of a betrothal to his already overfull days deterred him.

After he had given his maiden speech, he would have time to do the thing properly. That day was almost upon him.

"Tomorrow, ain't it?" asked Gil Chubb on Tuesday morning at breakfast, spearing a piece of sausage. "The great day?"

"Thursday, you clunch."

"Ah, lucky I asked. I'll be there in the gallery, all right and tight."

"You may be the only person there," Wynn said gloomily, "or the only one awake, assuming you manage to stay awake."

"I'll keep pinching myself," Gil promised. "Wouldn't miss it for anything, but I'm glad I shan't have to miss Almack's tomorrow. Lady Jersey gave Miss Kitty leave to waltz last week, and she promised to save me a waltz. She always stands up with me at every ball, you know. Deuced kind of her when there's so many clamoring for the honour."

"She is popular, but her lack of fortune is bound to knock out lots of your competitors as suitors," Wynn encouraged him. "Ah, here's the post."

''My lord.'' Clark proffered a silver salver with two piles of letters and cards. Wynn scooped up the nearest and leafed through as Gil accepted his pile.

''A letter from Mama and one from my bailiff. Might be trouble, I'll read 'em later. Invitations—one, two, three—Lord, at least half a dozen. Hallo, what's this?''

The folded sheet bore the impressive imprint of the Lord High Chancellor of England. Wynn carefully slit the seal, with a twinge of misgiving. It must be confirmation of the date and time, but he had not expected . . .

''Devil take it, they've postponed it! Another three weeks,'' he groaned, jumping up and taking a rapid turn about the room to relieve his feelings. ''Another three weeks on tenterhooks, and the damned speech growing stale.''

''Stale?'' said Gil uncomprehendingly. ''Do sit down, there's a good chap. You'll ruin my digestion, and your own.''

Wynn subsided into his chair. ''I had just got to the point where I could deliver it practically verbatim. Miss Lisle says if one practices too much it begins to sound mechanical. Blast Eldon!''

''Daresay Miss Lisle will know what to do.''

''Yes.'' Wynn jumped up again. ''I'm off to Charles Street to tell her.''

''Hold hard, old fellow! Too early by half.''

Consulting the clock, Wynn said, ''Half an hour. By the time I've finished dressing and walked over to Charles Street—''

''Finish your breakfast first,'' Gil urged. ''Can't make good decisions on an empty belly.''

That reminded Wynn of Pippa's advice to get enough sleep. He gobbled down sausages and muffins before setting off for his sister's house.

As always, he asked for Bina. She had pointed out long since that for a highly eligible viscount to constantly seek out an obscure spinster was bound to arouse undesirable speculation, not to mention jealousy. Fortunately he had the excuse of Pippa's being his sister's guest, but that façade must be maintained.

At balls he was careful always to dance with Millicent first, and with Kitty whenever he could pry her away from her admirers. He took Bina or Mrs. Lisle in to supper as often as he did Pippa. The servants knew, of course, that he spent a good deal of time closeted with Pippa, but he hoped they believed it was because she was frequently the only one at home when he called.

"Is my sister in?" he said, he and the first footman having reached a mutual accommodation in the matter of euphemisms.

"The ladies have gone out, my lord."

"*All* of them?"

"*All* of them, my lord," Reuben confirmed.

Today of all days! Wynn groaned silently. "Do you know where they went?"

"To a ladies' luncheon, I understand, my lord. The younger ladies are to practice for their Presentation to the Queen, God bless her."

"*All* of them?" He had thought the Misses Lisle were not to be presented.

"All the young ladies present, I should say, my lord. Mrs. Debenham took Miss Warren. Mrs. Lisle and the Misses Lisle went to the shops, I believe. Miss Catherine spoke of bugle beads and Miss Lisle of books."

"Books?"

"I rather think Miss mentioned Hatchard's Booksellers, my lord. Or was it Hookham's Library?"

Wynn had a disorientating sense of *déjà vu:* the confusion with the footman, followed by the news that Miss Lisle was at Hookham's—he doubted she had blunt enough to patronize a bookseller. The difference was, Gil Chubb was not with him this time. He set off for Bond Street.

The circulating library was full of patrons reading newspapers and periodicals at the long tables or browsing the bookshelves. Scanning the hushed room, Wynn damned the bonnets which hid the ladies' hair and faces from the side and rear. Yet when he caught sight of Pippa, moving away from him between two rows of shelves, he recognized her figure instantly. He hurried after her.

"Miss Lisle!" he hissed.

She swung round, her hand to her heart. "Lord Selworth, how you startled me! What is wrong?" she whispered with a frown after one look at him.

"Dash it all, does my face inform the world I'm in the briars?"

"Not the world, I daresay, but me. However, it does not go into particulars."

"Eldon has postponed my speech. For three weeks!"

"What a nuisance."

"Nuisance! It—"

"It is annoying, to be sure, but there is no need to fly off the hook," she said soothingly. "Three weeks? I should have thought the Chancellor might find an earlier time, if he tried."

"But what shall we do? I cannot—"

"Really, Lord Selworth, this is not the place to discuss it."

"Then come back to Charles Street. Allow me to escort you. You are not here alone, are you?" Wynn asked disapprovingly.

Her lips quirked and she spoke soothingly again. "Mama and Kitty are somewhere about. I expect they have found what they want, but I have not. There is no need for haste. We have three weeks in hand."

"I didn't mean to rush you," Wynn said, abashed, noting for the first time the five volumes cradled in her arm. "Let me carry those for you. How many more are you looking for?"

"Oh, half a dozen or so," she said, laughing as she handed him the stack. "I believe people buy books by the yard to fill their library shelves, but *borrowing* by quantities is an altogether new notion!"

"All my own," he said with a grin. "Do you think it will become the rage?"

Her calm reception of his news had entirely allayed his agitation. He should have trusted her to know how to deal with the delay.

The speech they had toiled over was neither abandoned, forcing Wynn to learn a new one, nor kept as it stood, losing its freshness. Instead, they made a few major changes and several smaller ones. As the new date approached, Wynn decided it was better than ever, and once again he was confident of his ability to deliver it without too many references to his notes.

Then another letter arrived from the Lord Chancellor.

"Dammit!" he yelled. "Three weeks' postponement again. What is the man about?"

"Three weeks again? Sounds fishy to me," agreed Gil, neatly dissecting a succulent kipper.

Wynn forsook his kipper and rushed around to Charles Street. The ladies had not come down yet. When he said he would wait, Wynn was ushered into the dining room, where he found George Debenham at breakfast.

Though not involved in politics—except at elections—or government, Debenham had Tory sympathies. He was a member of White's, and his family's considerable influence in their constituency always supported the Tory candidate. Laboring under a strong sense of ill-usage, Wynn poured out the story of his shabby treatment at the hands of the arch-Tory Lord Eldon.

"I had heard there was to be another delay," Debenham admitted.

"What? It's bandied about at White's?"

"One hears rumors. Look, I'll be frank with you. I gather Liverpool and the others have learnt you are hand-and-glove with Prometheus. Don't look daggers at me. I have not breathed a word to a soul, upon my honor! It pains me to divulge to you," Debenham continued, at his most sardonic, "that the Government is shaking in its shoes for fear of the power of Prometheus' rhetoric."

CHAPTER 14

"They don't know who Prometheus is?" Pippa asked apprehensively, clasping her hands tight in her lap to stop her fingers twisting.

Lord Selworth shook his head. "No sign of that. You ought to be flattered, you have the Government's collective teeth chattering with terror."

"But who told them? You are sure it was not Mr. Debenham?"

"I have his word as a gentleman. It's possible—in fact I strongly suspect—he has guessed you are Prometheus, but I trust his discretion absolutely."

"As I trust Bina's—I am certain she knows—to say nothing of Mama's and Kitty's. But who, then? Not Mr. Chubb!"

"No." Lord Selworth turned to the window and gazed unseeing at the gray drizzle which dripped relentlessly on the back garden. In a voice as leaden as the rain, he said, "Millicent."

"Millie? I am quite sure Bina did not tell her. It would have been sheer folly, if you will excuse my speaking so of your sister."

"It could be no one else. She must have overheard something."

"Perhaps." Pippa thought hard. "When she told us about Lady Holland, do you recall? When she came up to us, I believe you were saying something about not losing Prometheus' help through overwork. No doubt there were other times, too."

"I'll kill her," Lord Selworth said through gritted teeth.

"I hardly think that would be advisable! Being hanged for murder is not the way to win influence for your opinions."

He turned, with a wry smile. "True. I had best limit retribution to cutting out her tongue while administering a thorough tongue-lashing."

"Scolding will not help. Very likely she would not recollect having said anything. I daresay it just slipped out in a flood of words without her even noticing She would not realize the significance and did not know it was a secret. It is our fault for being so careless as to let her find out."

"My dear girl, you are far too lenient! Consider the damage she has done! Suppose Eldon never lets me speak?"

"Is that not impossible? You are by right a member of the House of Lords."

"I'm not sure," he said with a frown. "Even if he cannot stop me joining in a debate, he can continue indefinitely to postpone my maiden speech—my best hope to make my mark—which amounts to preventing it. No, Millie has a great deal to answer for."

"At least she does not know, or has not told, that I am Prometheus. If you rake up the subject, she will have it on her mind and may put overheard oddments together to work that out next."

"I surrender! Millie shall keep her life and her tongue. When you argue against me, instead of for me, I perfectly understand the Government's misgivings."

"Well, I do not." Pippa shook her head doubtfully. "It is prodigious hard to credit that all those powerful lords are afraid of what I might say!"

"You don't look dangerous," said Lord Selworth, contemplating her with a curious glint in his eye, "but if I could have you beside me in the House, to put the words in my mouth, I'd gladly make do with the extempore speech of a debate. Failing that, what are we to do?"

"You must give me time to think. We shall contrive," said Pippa, with more confidence than she felt.

Pippa spent most of the day reading over all the notes she had made in the course of the past few weeks, hoping for inspiration. None came. Simply rewriting the speech to concentrate on different topics would not help. It was not any specific opinion the Tory Lords objected to, but Lord Selworth's entire philosophy—and that of his mentor.

That evening she assured him that she had the seed of an idea, but did not want to discuss it until it had time to germinate. Since he had not the least notion how to proceed, he was forced to be content.

When Pippa retired to bed, she lay long awake with thoughts running aimlessly around in her head. There *must* be some way to outmaneuver Eldon, Liverpool, Castlereagh, and the rest. Lord Selworth trusted her. She could not bear to let him down. How despairing he had been that morning, before she promised to find a solution!

Drowsily, she recalled their conversation. He had called her "my dear girl" again—but only in exasperation at her defence of Millicent. He had looked at her with what might conceivably have been an appreciative light in his eye—but all he said was that she did not look dangerous. Then he had said he wanted her beside him—but only in the House of Lords, during a debate, when the Chancellor could not stop him speaking.

It was no use. She could not persuade herself he admired anything but her mind. On that unhappy thought, at last she fell asleep . . .

. . . And half-awoke at dawn with the germ of an idea. A

debate, when the Chancellor could not stop him speaking, that was the key.

She did not wake again until Nan came in with the morning chocolate and drew back the curtains on a sunny day. The sunshine made Pippa feel cheerful even before she remembered that she had come up with the beginnings of an answer to Lord Selworth's difficulties.

Yesterday the heavens wept for him, today they smiled. "The pathetic fallacy," she said aloud.

"What is that?" asked Kitty, sitting up and sipping her chocolate.

"Imputing human emotions to inanimate objects. The sky is blue in sympathy with my cheerful mood."

Kitty laughed. "More likely you are cheerful because the sky is blue. Yesterday's rain was horridly depressing. I had rather have a brief downpour than drizzle. In Town, at least. Drizzle is better for crops, if it does not go on too long. A storm tends to beat them down."

"Do you miss the country?"

"Oh yes. The Season is fun, but I could not bear to spend every spring in London. When I think what I am missing, the wildflowers, the lambs and calves and chicks . . . I hope my chicks are all right without me."

"I am sure Sukey is taking excellent care of them."

"Mr. Chubb has discovered a place where I might buy the chicks of a new breed of fowl from Cochin China, and Musk Ducks from Africa. But there is no point getting them now. I should want to be at home to make sure they settle well and to find out how best to help them thrive."

"Perhaps you can send for some next year," Pippa said absently. *Debate,* she thought, as Kitty obligingly fell silent, recognizing her sister's cogitative expression.

Debates concentrated on a single subject. She and Lord Selworth must find a subject which was to be debated in the not too far distant future. It must be something about which he had strong feelings, yet which would not threaten the status quo in such a way as to make the Government take fright. Their aim was to prove his ability as an orator, not to reform the country radically in one fell swoop.

That could come later, gradually, once he had the respect of his peers.

Two problems remained to be solved before Pippa could settle down to writing a new speech. First, she must find a suitable debate. Second, she must persuade Lord Selworth to limit himself to a single topic. The second, she suspected, might be the more difficult.

She half-expected him to be awaiting her at table when she went down, as he had the day before. However, discretion had apparently mastered impatience—he had, after all, no open invitation to breakfast at his sister's house.

Mr. Debenham, with a satirical air, handed Pippa the *Morning Chronicle,* as was his habit. Lord Selworth was probably right, she realized. His brother-in-law had surely worked out by now that she was Prometheus. Fortunately Millicent had no interest whatsoever in periodicals without fashion plates. Since she had no idea that the *Chronicle* was full of Parliamentary news, she did not wonder why Pippa read it.

After a thorough search of every page, Pippa was no nearer choosing a suitable subject. She had hoped to present the viscount with a *fait accompli,* or at least a specific proposal to show him what she meant.

"But everything was either inconsequential," she told him when he called that afternoon, "like the farthing duty on tea, which they still have not settled, or too consequential, like the Seditious Meetings Act and the suspension of *Habeas corpus.*"

"I could talk forever on *Habeas corpus,*" Lord Selworth grumbled. "Why not?"

"Because a great many other people will talk about it, too. If you have prepared a speech, you are likely to find half of what you have to say already said. What we want is something few members of the Lords have thought about seriously or in depth. We must keep looking. Something is bound to come up soon.''

''I hope so! I should hate the Tories to prevail to the extent of shutting me out of an entire session.''

''You have only been a peer for a few months,'' Pippa consoled him. ''Some only appear in Parliament for state occasions.''

''They say Lord Melbourne has only made one speech in his entire life,'' Lord Selworth agreed. ''His wife is a more active Whig than he is. I'd best go and talk to someone else now. If you and I are seen *tête-à-tête* too often now it's known that I'm consulting Prometheus, someone may add two and two.''

Pippa had to agree. After all, there was no chance anyone would come to the conclusion that the eligible Lord Selworth was courting so undistinguished a female.

The drawing room was somewhat thin of company. The morning sun had given way to wind and rain, inducing many ladies to curtail their usual routine of calls for fear of damage to slippers and bonnets. However, the flock of young gentlemen around Kitty and Millicent was undiminished. Millicent was silent at present, listening with the rest to an ode a youthful poet had written to a curl on Kitty's brow.

Mr. Chubb came over to Pippa when he saw Lord Selworth leave her. ''Such balderdash!'' he snorted. ''A crow's wing on a snowy field! Crows are vermin, and what's a wing doing in the middle of a field, anyway, without the rest of the bird? I wish I could write such stuff,'' he added wistfully.

''You would not if you heard Kitty and Millicent giggling about Mr. Darlington's poems when he is gone.''

''Truly?'' His round face brightened, then fell again. ''But I daresay she laughs at me, too, though I know you are too kind to tell me so.''

''If she did, I would not tell you, to be sure, but she does not, and I would not lie to you. Only this morning she was talking of your discovery of a place selling rare poultry and

her regret that she could not buy any this year as she is not at
home to tend them. She hopes to try next spring.''

"I shall send her some," Mr. Chubb said eagerly, "or better
still, bring her the chicks myself, to be sure they are well cared
for on the road." Again despondency overcame him. "But by
next spring she will be long married, to someone else."

Pippa wished she was able to assure him that he had an
excellent chance of winning Kitty's hand. She thought the two
extremely well suited, and she liked Gilbert Chubb very well
now that he had overcome his bashfulness with her. But Kitty
showed no disposition to favor him—or anyone else, for that
matter. She had already turned down two suitors. As far as
Pippa could see, her sister's heart was whole.

Kitty apparently knew none of the doubts and fears which
kept Pippa awake at night, nor the rush of light-headed joy she
felt whenever Wynn Selworth came into a room—the joy which
must be hidden, the light-headedness which must be overcome
before she was able to concentrate on ideas and words. How
Kitty would stare if she knew her intellectual sister quivered
inside when her hand accidentally brushed Wynn Selworth's,
went weak at the knees when she placed her hand on his arm,
melted from top to toe at his smile.

Somehow she had hidden her love from Kitty, and from
Lord Selworth. If he knew, he would surely relinquish his
mentor rather than risk encouraging by his constant presence
the passion to which he was indifferent.

Sometimes Pippa wondered whether Mama or Bina had
guessed. If so, unable to encourage her to hope, they were too
kind to add to her heartache by pointing out the unlikelihood
of his ever returning her feelings.

Mr. Chubb had a better chance with Kitty, Pippa thought.
"Kitty's affections are as yet unengaged," she said, "and you
and she have a good deal in common. You must not give up."

"I shan't," he promised.

* * *

By the fourth day of searching the newspapers in vain, Pippa was ready to give up. It seemed the Lords had nothing quite suitable on their agenda this session. Lord Selworth would just have to wait and hope that Lord Eldon might relent.

She persevered, however, and the very next day was rewarded by finding precisely what she was looking for.

"Climbing boys?" said Lord Selworth dubiously.

"The children chimney sweeps send up chimneys. There is a society trying to abolish the practice, and they are to present a petition to Parliament. It is perfect, Lord Selworth! The petition will arouse interest, but it is not a matter which will make the Government fear you are striking at the very roots of society."

"I don't know much about climbing boys."

"They are shockingly badly treated, and quite unnecessarily, for a machine has been invented—a sort of elongated brush—which does the job just as thoroughly. The sweeps prefer to use little boys because it is easier and less labor for themselves. All they need do is stick pins in the child's feet, or light a straw fire, to force them to climb."

"Good Lord! Do they really?" exclaimed the viscount, shocked.

"You see? Few people know what happens, because naturally they leave the house when the sweep comes to do his messy business."

"Yes, but bad as it is, even you can't make a whole speech out of pins and a small fire."

"Of course not," Pippa agreed. "We need to find out more, only I am not sure how. The master sweeps certainly will not tell us anything useful."

"I'll go and talk to the society who are getting up the petition," Lord Selworth proposed. "They must know the worst or they wouldn't be up in arms."

"Oh yes, why did I not think of that?"

"Are you sure you didn't?" he asked suspiciously. "You are not just trying to cheer me up by allowing me a small contribution to your plan?"

"Heavens no. I honestly never considered consulting the society, perhaps because I have always had to work from published reports. I shall go with you."

"No."

"Why not?" Pippa demanded indignantly. "Because it is your idea?"

"Don't be a widgeon. For the same reason you have always worked from published reports, only more so. If I go and make enquiries with a view to airing the matter in Parliament, and you go with me, you might as well stand on the rooftops and proclaim yourself Prometheus. Well, nearly."

"Oh. I daresay it would be rash," she conceded.

"You could go on your own account," Lord Selworth offered, "as a philanthropist considering signing the petition, but wanting to know more first. They might tell you things they hesitated to tell me."

"I cannot think what, but thank you for allowing me a part in the venture!"

He gave her a straight look. "If I had forbidden your approaching them, would you have heeded the prohibition?"

"Not unless I saw good reason for it," Pippa said promptly, "and no good reason to go against it."

"*Not* a compliant female," he said, his tone reproachful, with a sigh and a shake of the head.

Pippa was glad to see a twinkle in his eye. If she had had the least chance of winning his affections, proving herself far from submissive was likely to dish it. As it was, she said pertly, "No compliant female could possibly have directed your efforts these past two months. I should like to call upon the Society for the Abolition of Climbing Boys, or whatever they call themselves, but I do not know their direction."

"They cannot circulate a petition without coming out into the open. I'll find 'em. And I'll let you know when I do."

"Noble of you!" Pippa exclaimed, and he laughed.

When she danced with him that evening, he had not yet tracked down the society, but when they met next day he passed her a slip of paper with their direction.

"I have something else for you," he said. "Come for a drive in the Park."

"You said we should not be seen together," Pippa demurred.

"Not too often, I said. I drove Millicent yesterday, Bina the day before, and your mama the day before that—there's no getting near your sister. Be compliant for once: go put on your bonnet."

Pippa complied, her curiosity aroused. What did he have to give her that he chose not to give openly, in company? Not a betrothal ring, alas. In such an unlikely event he must have spoken first to Mama, and Mama would certainly have informed her of such a momentous occurrence.

Instead, she informed Mrs. Lisle that she was going out with Lord Selworth, and went upstairs to fetch bonnet and gloves.

The viscount's curricle was waiting at the door. He handed Pippa up, took the reins from his groom, and joined her. The groom scrambled up to his perch behind as the horses, a stalwart pair of blacks to match the carriage, set off along Charles Street.

Pippa with difficulty restrained herself from asking about her mysterious gift. Conscious of the groom's ears close behind, she made an innocuous remark about the weather. This led— the servant's presence soon forgotten—to a discussion of the prospects for a good harvest, leading to the relief of hunger across the country and its effects on politics.

The afternoon was warm for May, with a thin haze of cloud obscuring the sky but letting the sun shine through. In the narrow streets, the heat reflected uncomfortably from cobbles and brick walls, but they soon reached the Chesterfield Gate and entered Hyde Park.

The grass was bright with buttercups, daisies, and dandelions,

reminding Pippa of the wide variety of wildflowers now bloom-
ing in the country. The woods would be carpeted with bluebells,
the hillsides with cowslips, the water meadows with lady's
smock. Much as she enjoyed them when at home, she reflected,
she did not miss them as Kitty did. To her, the fascination of
politics made up for spending spring in Town.

Pulling up just inside the gates, Lord Selworth told the groom
to wait nearby for their return. Then he headed south, but he
turned off towards the Serpentine before they reached Rotten
Row.

Though there were a good many people about, it was too
early for the crowds of fashionable carriages, riders, and pedestrians who would flock to the Park later for the daily Grand
Promenade. When the curricle pulled up in the shade of a tall
elm, they were quite private.

Lord Selworth reached under the seat and pulled out a rectan-
gular parcel wrapped in brown paper and tied with string.
"Here," he said, thrusting it into Pippa's hands, and at once
looking away with an air of unconcern, apparently watching a
pair of riders cantering across the grass.

Books? The size and weight were right, though several layers
of paper obscured details of the shape. Pippa struggled with
the knotted string, in vain. In vain she felt in her reticule for
scissors. "Have you a pocketknife, Lord Selworth?"

"What? Oh, sorry." For some reason he flushed as he handed
her his penknife.

Comprehension dawning, Pippa abandoned any attempt to
save useful lengths of string. She sliced through it, unfolded
the paper, and found three calf-bound, gold-lettered volumes.
"The Masked Marauder! Oh, splendid!"

"I thought you might like a copy of your own," said Lord
Selworth, looking pleased at her pleasure.

"Thank you, Mr. Valentine Dred. I shall treasure it. I did
not know it was out already."

"In the bookshops tomorrow, the libraries the day after. The
publisher says a great many copies were sold beforehand," he

said modestly. "You had best keep yours well hidden, as I have inscribed each volume to you."

"Assuming it is similar to your previous works, I should in any case hide it away. It is not at all proper for Kitty or Millicent to read."

Almost reluctantly, Pippa opened the first volume to the title page, wishing his inscription might say: "To darling Pippa, with all my love, Wynn." Naturally it did not. But nor was it a formal "To Miss Lisle, from your obedient servant, Selworth."

For my dear Prometheus, she read, *this, with humble gratitude and devoted admiration, Valentine.*

Pippa laughed. "I shall keep them *very* well hidden," she promised. Devoted admiration? For Prometheus, of course.

Whatever Pippa's views on the propriety of Kitty and Millicent reading *The Masked Marauder,* within the week all Society was talking about it. Demure damsels whispered and giggled behind their fans; mature matrons told each other, "My dear, I positively blushed when . . . ;" Corinthians and Tulips alike vowed to each other they had laughed till they cried; serious gentlemen condemned the book as trivial, indecent nonsense, but it was to be noted that not one had failed to peruse all three volumes.

And all Society asked with a single voice, "Who wrote it? Who is Valentine Dred?"

CHAPTER 15

"Who is Valentine Dred?" asked Millicent, as she and Kitty strolled down Piccadilly, their abigail a pace behind.

It was certainly a rhetorical question, for not only did she not expect an answer, she failed to pause to allow her friend to provide one had she been able.

"No one talks of anything else, I vow," she continued without taking a breath. "It is becoming a shocking bore. Who do you think he can be, Kitty? At least, Valentine is generally a man's name, is it not? But as it is only a pen-name—everyone seems to agree it is a pen-name—it could just as well be a woman. Do you think it might be Lady Caroline Lamb? She wrote *Glenarvon* last year, after all."

"I have not read *Glenarvon*," Kitty deftly inserted into the stream, practice having made her expert, "nor met Lady Caroline, but I have heard that she has no sense of humor."

"Then it cannot be her, for everyone is laughing over *The Masked Marauder*. I wish Bina and your mama had not forbidden us to read it," Millicent mourned. "The Pendrell girls have read it. Vanessa says it is very shocking, to be sure, but funny and thrilling, too. The hero is quite the most dashing gentleman you can conceive, and the heroine's plight most pitiable.''

''I do not believe I should care to be married to too dashing a gentleman. Suppose he were to make a habit of dashing off whenever one needed him?''

''You are laughing at me again,'' Millicent said resignedly. ''It is true that in real life a dashing husband may not be altogether comfortable, but it is only a book after all. I think it very hard that we may not read it when the whole world talks of nothing else.''

''Not having read it does not stop *you* talking of it, Millie dear,'' said Kitty, laughing aloud. ''We have heard so much about it, we scarcely need to read it ourselves. Here is the haberdasher's I told you about. Let us hope they can match your ribbon.''

Millicent dropped the subject of *The Masked Marauder* for quite half an hour. Unfortunately, they then happened to encounter two young gentlemen of their acquaintance who had just been to Hatchard's to purchase a copy—without luck, as the entire stock was sold out.

On parting from the disconsolate pair, Kitty said to Millicent, ''I never thought to see Mr. Carlin or Sir Anthony looking to purchase a whole book! The perusal of a single page in a newspaper is a great labor to them.''

''Oh, but a novel is quite different. Only think, Kitty, what a great labor it must be to *write* a whole book! My wrist positively aches at the very thought, I declare. Yet Pippa is always scribbling away with never a complaint of fatigue. I wonder what it is she writes, that she always hides it when one enters the room.'' Her mouth dropped open as a notion struck her momentarily dumb. ''Kitty, do you suppose *Pippa* is Valentine Dred?''

''Good gracious, no!'' cried Kitty in horror.

''Well then, what is it she writes so busily? I am sure it cannot be letters, for there are pages and pages and it would cost a fortune to post them all. You must know, Kitty. You are her sister. If it is not a book, what is it?''

"I cannot tell you, Millie, so be a dear and do not press me. I repeat, Pippa is *not* Valentine Dred. Oh, Millie, do but look at the signs in the window of this shop! 'Guineas taken with delight; Shillings quite welcome; Halfpence will not be refused.' ''

" 'Half sovereigns taken with avidity,' '' Millie read, " 'Crowns hailed with pleasure; Farthings rather than nothing.' It quite makes one want to go in and buy something, only I cannot see anything I need. That beaded reticule is quite pretty, but I have spent nearly all my pin money for the week.''

Fashion regained its usual preeminence in her chatter. Kitty was able to persuade herself that the nonsensical notion of Pippa having written naughty romances had flown from her companion's head as swiftly as it had entered.

Meanwhile, Wynn and Miss Lisle had each called upon the leaders of the society circulating the petition against the employment of climbing boys to clean chimneys. By prior arrangement, they met in Charles Street in the ladies' sitting room to discuss their findings.

Before he knocked on the open door, Wynn paused on the threshold. His beloved sat at the writing table, one slender, shapely hand reaching out to dip her quill in the inkpot, her delicate profile framed against the window. In the north light her pale skin was translucent, her dark, smooth hair sleek. Wynn had a sudden, almost irresistible desire to pull out all her hairpins and see her cloaked in those silken tresses.

Had he really once told Gil Chubb she was plain?

As if she felt his gaze, she turned, her face lighting in a smile which at once gave way to anguish. "Oh, it is perfectly horrible!'' she cried, casting down her pen.

"I ought not to have let you go,'' Wynn said grimly, striding forward to take her hands in his. Not pretty? She was beautiful in her passion! Finding his mind drifting to how her face would look under the influence of a different sort of passion, he sternly called himself to order. "I had not imagined such painful stories, I confess."

"How could anyone imagine such inhumanity? Those little boys driven up chimneys, often so narrow they can barely pass, sometimes hot enough to burn, at best scraping and bruising themselves, and suffocated by falling soot. And then, if they come down alive—which they do not always—forced to carry heavy bags of soot, and beaten; never washed and frequently not fed . . ."

"Small wonder many turn to begging and some to stealing, but that some people believe the solution is to send them to Sunday school is incredible!"

"Is it not? If they do not die of burns, or suffocation, or beatings, they may cough and choke and wheeze as they please provided their morals are good, and live on stunted and deformed."

"To die later of chimney-sweeps' cancer."

"Such *little* boys, Wynn," she said, tears in her eyes, "as young as four!"

He yearned to kiss away the tears. For the first time, she had called him Wynn, but he must not read too much into the mark of intimacy. It had probably slipped out unintentionally. After all, she constantly heard his sisters calling him by his Christian name.

Letting go of her hands, he sat down. "The official minimum age is eight, but as long as the law is not enforced, destitute parents will sell younger children to the master sweeps for a guinea or two."

"Some sweeps send their own children up the chimneys," Pippa said with incredulous abhorrence.

"And some buy boys kidnapped for the purpose. Did Mr. Montgomery tell you about the child rescued by a Yorkshire family?"

"The Stricklands? Yes." She gestured at the papers on the

desk. "I have been trying to work out the best way to make that story the centerpiece of your speech. Surely any responsible, loving parent hearing it must instantly wish to free all climbing boys, if only for fear of their own sons suffering a like fate! But I have not enough information. I should like to question the Stricklands, to meet the child if possible, only Mama would never let me travel so far. Lord Selworth, do you suppose you . . . ?"

"I do." To see the hope in her hazel eyes turn to warm approval, Wynn would have traveled a great deal farther than to Yorkshire—if it were not that he must leave her behind. "Montgomery gave me their direction in case I wished to correspond, but you are right, a personal interview will be much more useful."

"I believe so."

"What we want is details, is it not, to flesh out the story. How they happened to rescue him, what made them suspect he came from an affluent home, anything he recalls of his abduction?"

"Exactly. Doubtless you will have a better idea of just what to ask once you have spoken to them."

"I shall leave in the morning." *Will you miss me?*

"I wish I might go, too. How long do you think you will be away?"

"Two or three days each way. Say three: Kymford is not far off the Great North Road, so I may as well spend a night at home in each direction. It will not delay me much."

"Oh yes, you should take the opportunity to see your family. Two, perhaps three days in Yorkshire. Ten days in all, or less, not so *very* long." Pippa's sigh, though slight, did not go unnoticed, but she returned at once to business. "While you are gone I shall put my notes in order—you brought yours?"

"Yes, here, I copied them from my pocketbook for you." Wynn retrieved the papers from his pocket and handed them over.

"Thank you. I should be able to bring the speech into some

sort of shape, ready to insert the child's story. I do believe this
will be a truly splendid speech. I only wish such horrors did
not exist for you to speak about.''

"We are doing what we can to put a stop to them," Wynn
consoled her, "but if brooding over the misery throws you into
the dismals, you must let the speech wait until I come back to
cheer you up. Promise?''

"I promise not to fall into a decline," she said with a faint
smile.

It was two days after Lord Selworth's departure that Pippa
first noticed the cold looks. Mrs. Drummond Burrell, haughtiest
of Almack's patronesses and usually distantly condescending
towards the Lisles, actually turned her back when they entered
a room.

Then, in the course of a single evening, Pippa was invited
to dance by three gentlemen of decidedly rakish reputation who
had never before noticed her existence. All three made sly
remarks she could only interpret as improper. One actually
suggested that they should retire together to a small salon near
the ballroom where he knew they would not be disturbed. When
Pippa frostily refused, he muttered something about "whited
sepulchres," but to her relief he did not persist.

Rather than repeat the unpleasant experience, she told her
mama she was a little tired and would sit out the rest of the
evening. She need not have troubled. Not one of Kitty's court,
her usual partners, asked her to stand up.

In fact, their numbers were considerably diminished, and
Kitty herself sat out three sets for the first time since their
arrival in Town.

The next morning, Bina asked Pippa to join her in her sitting
room. When Pippa arrived, her friend thrust a pile of notes into
her hands. "Read these."

Every one was from a hostess requesting that Mrs. Debenham
not bring the Lisles with her to her entertainment.

"What is going on?" Bina asked, troubled.

"I have not the least notion." Pippa described the insulting behaviour of her partners last night. "Surely discovery of my political interests would not lead to that particular form of disrespect," she said helplessly. "I cannot imagine what I have done to earn it."

"Nothing!" Bina was furious. "Some scandalmonger has invented a story about you for want of anything better to do. Now that Princess Charlotte is safely married, people can no longer employ themselves in wondering whether she will shy off at the eleventh hour! Believe me, if you are not welcome at these parties, you may be sure *I* shall not attend."

"But you must, Bina. It is not fair that Millicent's Season should be ruined because someone is slandering me. Poor Kitty! Perhaps if I go home to Buckinghamshire, people will forget and accept her again."

"No, I shall not let you run away, if only for Wynn's sake. It might be just as well, though," Bina said thoughtfully, "if I continue to take Millie about so as to have the opportunity to try and find out what is being said. One cannot fight a rumor one has not heard. For a start, we shall call on every notable gossip in Town."

But one notable gossip called on the Lisles while Bina and Millicent were out. Lady Jersey, an elegant and influential lady of about thirty years, came straight to the point.

"I fear you are sailing in troubled waters, ma'am," she said bluntly to Mrs. Lisle. "I regret to say that, in view of Jersey's association with your late husband, I have been deputed by my fellow-Patronesses to request that you no longer attend Almack's."

Kitty gasped. Aching for her, Pippa took her hand.

"Why?" asked Mrs. Lisle, matching Lady Jersey's bluntness.

Her ladyship's delicate eyebrows rose. "Surely you can guess."

"Indeed I cannot! To my knowledge, neither I nor my daughters has done anything to deserve the way we are being treated."

"Can it be, ma'am, you are unaware of your elder daughter's authorship?"

Pippa felt cold inside. Was it indeed her writing which had brought down disgrace upon her family? She had expected to be laughed at if it became known, not spurned.

Kitty was frowning. Mrs. Lisle, visibly disturbed, demanded, "Authorship? What exactly is Philippa accused of writing, Lady Jersey?"

"Why, *The Masked Marauder,* of course," said the countess with a tinkling laugh. "A delicious book, certainly, but far too titillating for its author to lay any claim to the innocence Society demands of young ladies."

Stunned, Pippa burst out, "But I am not its author! I assure you, ma'am, I did not write *The Masked Marauder,* nor anything remotely similar."

"My daughter is not a novelist," Mrs. Lisle supported her. "She could not possibly have concealed it from me in our small cottage. I beg of you, ma'am, do what you can to contradict this calumny. It is utterly without foundation."

Lady Jersey looked from Mrs. Lisle to Pippa and back, her gaze shrewd and not unkindly. "Well, well, I believe you, and I will do what I can."

"Thank you, Lady Jersey!"

"However, I must warn you that many will refuse to credit the word of Miss Lisle and her family—it is only what you might be expected to say, after all. I fear the book's popularity makes the *on-dit* too toothsome a morsel to be easily abandoned. Your best hope is that the real author will come forward."

"He surely cannot like to see someone else credited with his work," said Kitty hopefully.

"So we will hope, Miss Catherine. In the meantime, I must advise you all not to appear at Almack's. I should hate to see you suffer the same sort of reception as Lord Byron's last year."

With that bitter remark, Lady Jersey took her leave

"What happened to Lord Byron?" Kitty enquired.

"Ask Albinia," her mother advised absently. "I am very much afraid Lady Jersey is correct, and no denials from us will bear any weight."

"Mama, if I went home—" Pippa said.

"Certainly not! Your papa would never permit you to concede defeat. I shall go up to the sitting room at once and write to Lady Stanborough and one or two others of those I have come to regard—perhaps mistakenly—as friends." She went out.

"I am sorry, Kitty," Pippa said miserably.

Kitty flung her arms around her and gave her a hug. "Pippa darling, it is not *your* fault. I have a very good notion whose fault it is, only I am not perfectly sure what to do about it."

Pippa scarcely heard her. It was Lord Selworth's fault, of course, for writing those shocking books. Why could he not have been satisfied with stories which were thrilling and funny, without also making them *titillating?*

Lady Jersey thought only exposure of the real author would save the Lisles' reputation. Pippa could expose him, but—if she was believed—his political career would be nipped in the bud. Even if she could bring herself to do that to him, what of all the good he might be expected to do in the future to right the miseries of the world?

"I have the headache, Kitty. I believe I shall go and lie down for a little while."

"Let me make you a tisane!"

"No, it is not bad," said Pippa, wanting nothing so much as to be alone with her megrims. "You had best stay here in case anyone is brave enough to call. Send for me or Mama if any gentleman comes."

Left alone, Kitty crossed to the window and stood, half-hidden by the brocade curtains, gazing down into the street. Normally at this time of day the phaetons, curricles, and gigs of her admirers would be thronging there, joined by the barouches and landaus of visiting ladies.

It was some slight comfort that Millicent also would undoubtedly suffer from the dearth. How could she do this to Pippa?

A barouche approached along Charles Street, a gentleman riding alongside. Kitty recognized the Pendrells. Her heart leapt: at least some friends did not believe the slander, and would not let the censure of the rest of the Ton influence their conduct!

The barouche rolled on without slowing, the Misses Pendrell pointing out the Debenhams' house to the two unknown young ladies in the carriage with them. Vanessa Pendrell said something to her brother, and he laughed.

Chagrined, Kitty turned from the window and dropped onto a nearby sofa. They were all the same. She did not care if she never again saw any of the so-called gentlemen who claimed to adore her. All she wanted was to go home to Buckinghamshire and live the rest of her life peacefully in the cottage with Mama and Pippa—but what about Pippa?

Pippa must be vindicated, if only Kitty could work out how to do it.

"Mr. Chubb, miss."

Startled, Kitty jumped up.

"Didn't mean to take you by surprise, Miss Kitty," Mr. Chubb apologized, bowing.

"Do you not know that we are in disgrace?" she demanded bitterly.

"Yes. That is, heard stories. Wouldn't have credited them anyway, of course, but as it happens I know the truth."

"It hardly matters, sir. We are proclaimed outcasts by Society, and if you go against Society's—You *what?*"

"As if anything Society dictates could make me stay away from you!" said Mr. Chubb with scorn, adding eagerly, "You do believe me, don't you?"

"Yes, yes, but what do you mean, you know the truth? You know Millicent dreamt up the whole thing out of thin air?"

Mr. Chubb looked bewildered. "Miss Warren? What has she to say to the matter?"

"That is the trouble. She has something to say to every m-matter!" To her own astonishment and dismay, Kitty burst into tears. "I n-never cry!" she sobbed.

After a moment of startled alarm, Mr. Chubb sat down on the sofa beside her, thrust his handkerchief into her hand, and patted her shoulder soothingly. "There there," he murmured. "I daresay it will all turn out to be a tempest in a teapot, though how even the smallest tempest can blow up in a teapot I have always failed to comprehend."

Kitty gave a watery giggle, blew her nose heartily, looked up at his sympathetic, concerned face, and came to a decision. "You are quite the nicest, kindest, most sensible gentleman I know," she said encouragingly.

Mr. Chubb turned pink. "D-dashed kind in you to say so," he stuttered, "but the others, the rest of your beaux, you know, I'm sure it's just a temporary misunderstanding. What is it Miss Warren's been saying to distress you?"

"I am certain it is her doing," said Kitty, with an internal sigh.

Was she going to have to do the proposing? Give the poor, diffident dear a bit more time to come to terms with the fact that she was available to him, she decided. Besides, she did not want him to imagine she was pursuing him because of the defection of the rest of her suitors. If she was, it was only in a roundabout way, his loyalty being the deciding factor when she was already predisposed in his favour.

"Miss Warren has been spreading the *on-dit* about Miss Lisle being Valentine Dred?" he asked in surprise. "What makes you think so?"

"She put two and two together and came up with five. She knows Pippa does a lot of writing. I *told* her it is nothing to do with novels, and I hoped she had forgot the notion. I ought to have made sure she was convinced."

"Now don't start blaming yourself, Kit . . . Miss Kitty. Whatever Miss Warren believes," Mr. Chubb said severely, "it was very unkind—indeed, downright wrong—to talk of it."

Kitty shook her head. "Millicent is very good-natured. I am sure she did not realize the damage it would do. In fact, I doubt she intended to mention her guess at all, but she talks such a great deal things slip out inadvertently. I should not like to carry tales to her brother or sister, yet unless the source of the story is known, who will believe our denials? I cannot bear to see Pippa pilloried. What should I do?"

"I've no qualms about telling Wynn his sister started it. Ought to know. Pity he's out of town."

"It might not help anyway. Lady Jersey said our best hope is that the real author reveal himself. By the way, do you know what happened to Lord Byron at Almack's last year?"

"What?" Mr. Chubb appeared to be wrestling with a knotty problem. "George Gordon? What I heard was that his behavior was so shocking his wife deserted him and he was ostracized. Lady Jersey and some others gave a party for him to try to bring him back into Society, but everyone left the room when he arrived."

"Poor man!" Kitty glanced around the empty drawing room. "I can imagine how he felt."

"Yes, well, he really is a pretty shocking fellow, you know. Don't ask," he added hastily. "Not the sort of thing to tell a young lady. Besides, your case is quite different. Miss Lisle *didn't* write *The Masked Marauder*. I know who did."

"You do?" Kitty cried. "Then you can tell people and they will know it was not Pippa."

"That's the trouble." Mr. Chubb looked so harassed and miserable Kitty's heart went out to him. "You know I'd do almost anything for you, but this would be betraying a friend's trust."

"The author is a friend of yours? Can you not persuade him to come forward?"

"I'd do my best, believe me, only he's out of town at present."

Kitty stared at him. "Not *Lord Selworth?*"

Mr. Chubb nodded unhappily. "If people knew, they would never take him seriously as a politician."

"I shall not tell." Her promise was reluctant, but she suspected Pippa would not wish to save herself by ruining Lord Selworth's career, which she was trying so hard to get off to a good start.

Kitty chewed her lip, recollecting the warmth in the viscount's eyes when his gaze fell upon her sister. Pippa would not sacrifice Lord Selworth to save herself, but he . . . ? "I think he ought to be told as soon as possible what has happened. He will be horrified to hear Pippa is being vilified, and I am sure he will not wish to let it continue a moment longer than it need. Do you know where he went?"

"To Yorkshire. He said he was going to put up at the Black Swan in York."

"Could you . . . Oh, Mr. Chubb, it is a great deal to ask, but could you possibly go after him?"

"I'll leave at once," said her cavalier gallantly, rising to his feet.

"No, wait a moment, let me think. You are sure his career would be badly damaged if he was known to be the author of *The Masked Marauder?*"

"Positive."

"Then it would not be fair to ask him to give himself away if other means might suffice. Let us wait until tomorrow and see whether Lady Jersey and my mother and Mrs. Debenham can quash the rumors. Perhaps the morning will bring new invitations."

"All right," said the obliging Mr. Chubb. "Send me word after you know what's in the morning post, and I'll leave right away."

"In the meantime, pray do not tell anyone I asked you to go, or about Millie or anything."

"Shouldn't dream of it."

"Bless you!" said Kitty fondly.

CHAPTER 16

"Pippa, I am so dreadfully sorry!" wailed Millicent, rushing into the drawing room. "Bina says it is all my fault, but indeed I told people you are *not* Valentine Dred, not that you are, and only my most particular friends, laughing at myself, you see, for making such a harebrained guess just because you are always scribbling away. Forgive me, pray say you forgive me, or I declare I shall go into a decline and—"

"Of course I forgive you, Millie," said Pippa in bewilderment.

She had come downstairs a few minutes earlier, Nan having woken her from a semidrowse to tell her Reuben said Miss Catherine was alone with Mr. Chubb. The abigail had not wanted to "peach" on Miss to her mama.

"You may be sure I have rung a thorough peal over Millie's head," said Bina grimly, following her sister into the room at a more decorous pace. "But I thought it best she should not try to explain the mistake to people for fear of confusing matters still further."

"If anyone is confused, I am," Pippa declared, her arm about a weeping Millicent.

Bina sank into a chair, untying the ribbons of her bonnet. "As soon as we returned to the carriage after discovering— oh, but you do not yet know the cause of our difficulties."

"Yes, we do," said Kitty. Mr. Chubb had quietly departed, Pippa noted with a pang. No doubt he had only now learnt what was being said about her. He was just another rat deserting a sinking ship.

"Then you will have gathered," said Bina, waving at her watering-pot sister, "that this little bagpipe is responsible. When we heard of the wretched *on-dit,* Millicent confessed to me that she had suspected Pippa of writing *The Masked Marauder.*"

"I'm *sorry!*" sobbed Millie.

"But when Kitty set her straight she told her friends it was not true. Since she had never confided her suspicion in the first place, I suppose it is possible some of them genuinely misunderstood, though one cannot but wonder whether malice . . . Less fortunate girls are bound to be jealous when Kitty is so very popular."

"*Was,*" Kitty corrected her sadly.

"Mr. Chubb was your only caller?"

"No," Pippa said, "Lady Jersey came to inform us that we are no longer welcome at Almack's. I do think she believed us. At least, she promised to contradict the rumors."

"She may," Bina said pessimistically, "but her denials may be as useless as mine. Though no one was impolite enough to say to my face that they did not believe me, I could see they thought I felt obliged to defend my guests."

"But we are not Lady Jersey's guests," Pippa pointed out. "Why should not people believe her?"

"For a start, the other Patronesses might well suppose she was trying to exculpate herself for persuading them to grant you vouchers. Then, others—especially those who *wish* to credit your guilt—could simply say you have pulled the wool over her eyes, and mine."

There seemed no answer to that. Mrs. Lisle came down with

the several notes she had written, and Bina agreed that sending them could do no harm. She held out little hope of their having much effect, however. Very few people, she pointed out, were brave enough to stand up against the weight of the entire Ton's condemnation.

Bina was in two minds whether to cry off the dinner party she and George were engaged to attend that evening. Her husband persuaded her nothing was to be gained by lowering the flag, so she went off, promising to continue her efforts in the Lisles' behalf. Mrs. Lisle, Kitty, and Millicent spent a dreary evening sewing gowns which might never be needed. Pippa immersed herself in the chimney-sweep speech, which might prove equally futile should Lord Selworth's Gothic proclivities become widely known.

For herself, she would gladly keep his secret and retire to Sweetbriar Cottage, to write her articles for Mr. Cobbett and perhaps to help the viscount a little with future speeches. She could always hope he might occasionally feel the need to consult her in person.

But Kitty deserved better. If she wanted one of the craven wretches who had so meekly deserted her at the dictate of Society, she must have the chance to win him.

So Lord Selworth had to be persuaded to confess his authorship to the world.

Yet, which was more important, Kitty's happiness or the services Lord Selworth might render to the oppressed poor? Not to mention *his* happiness. That night, Pippa tossed and turned for hours, unable to make up her mind. She needed to discuss it with him. She had come to depend on debating issues with him, she realized, on sharing ideas and insights and reaching a deeper understanding together.

He would return to Town in a few days, but by then the Fashionable World might have grown so accustomed to shunning the Lisles that no rehabilitation was possible. If only he had not gone to Yorkshire just now!

The morning brought no new counsel but several more withdrawn invitations. The afternoon brought not a single caller. Pippa had hoped Mr. Chubb's apparent desertion yesterday was due to embarrassment over the to-do with Millicent, but it seemed her first guess was right. He wanted no part of the Lisles' downfall.

Kitty valiantly showed no dismay at the defection of her last remaining suitor.

Bina returned from another round of calls no more optimistic than the day before. "No one was actually rude," she said to Pippa in her private sitting room. "George's parents have consequence enough to prevent that. But I was met everywhere with indulgent disbelief. I am so very sorry, Pippa. I confess, I do not know what else can be done until Wynn comes back."

Pippa recalled Bina's claim to have guessed a secret of her brother's. "You know, do you not?" she asked. "You know Wynn—Lord Selworth—is . . ." She hesitated. Suppose Bina knew some other secret?

"He's Valentine Dred, yes. Absurd name! He used to tell me stories just like the novels, only without the naughty bits which are causing all the trouble. He was the best big brother anyone could possibly have, especially when our father died and Mama remarried. I simply cannot betray him, Pippa, not even for your sake. Can you forgive me?" she pleaded.

"Of course." Pippa hugged her friend. "I find I cannot betray him myself, so how should you?"

Bina took both her hands and looked at her seriously. "I have sometimes wondered . . . No, this is not the time. I know Wynn will do the honorable thing, but it must be his decision. We shall have to wait until he returns."

"I am just afraid people will grow so used to shunning us that their attitudes will become carved in stone. Not that I care, but for Kitty . . . ! I wish I could go after him and tell him what has happened," Pippa cried, not because she had worked out a useful plan; she simply longed to see him and to lay her dilemma before him. She came down to earth. "However, hiring a post chaise is far too expensive, and on the stage I could not stop to make enquiries.''

"As though I should let you! You must take the landau, and one of the maids, with John Coachman to drive you, if you truly believe chasing after Wynn will help.''

Pippa tried to think. The prospect of taking action—any action—was tempting. If she found Lord Selworth still in York, he could hurry back to London. If she found him already on the way, he could postpone his visit to his family at Kymford and at least arrive back in Town a little sooner.

Very likely it would make no difference, but she had to try. "I shall go,'' she said resolutely.

Wynn was rather pleased with himself. As he tooled the curricle down Hampstead Hill, he wondered whether he would have time to tell Pippa all about little Henry before dinner.

No, alas. The sun was setting over the smoky city, and as he reached the foot of the hill, church clocks struck eight. In Charles Street they would be sitting down to dine. He was too late to join them, even had he not been grimed with a long day's road dirt.

Fortunately today was Wednesday, so he knew where to find them this evening. He would drive straight to Albany, have a wash and a bite to eat, don knee breeches, and repair to Almack's. There he could at least tell Pippa he had thoroughly fulfilled her request for all possible details of the child's abduction and subsequent fate.

A note awaited from the Chancellor. His speech had been entered into the House of Lords' calendar. Wynn nearly rushed straight round to Charles Street, but contrived to restrain himself.

Some two hours later, clean, fed, and a trifle puzzled to have learned that Gil Chubb had left town in haste and without explanation, Wynn presented himself at the King Street rooms. His reception puzzled him still more.

Mrs. Drummond Burrell and Countess Lieven, on duty in the anteroom, greeted him graciously enough, but with odd looks. As he moved on, he was conscious of their putting their heads together and whispering behind his back. One or two gentlemen spoke to him overheartily, asking if he had been out of town. Entering the ballroom, he felt himself the cynosure of every eye, the subject of a hundred low-voiced murmurs.

Had he forgotten his stockings, to display hairy shins to the world? No, all present and correct. His neckcloth? He raised a nervous hand, felt the starched folds where they ought to be. To comb his hair? His hair went its own way, always, but was scarcely noticeable among the Windswept and Brutus coiffures of Dandy and Corinthian.

Whatever was wrong, it did not stop the determined advance upon him of a horde of hopeful matrons with marriageable daughters in tow.

Lady Jersey nipped in front and appropriated his arm. "They see you for once unprotected by your sisters," she said tartly, leading him to a pair of chairs in a semisequestered nook.

"Albinia is not here, ma'am?" he asked, disappointed. "They usually arrive early."

"I understand Mrs. Debenham and Miss Warren will not be coming tonight." Lady Jersey gave him a curious look. "Out of sympathy for the Lisles."

Wynn rose in alarm. "They are ill?"

"No, no." The countess tugged him back down by the sleeve. "You have just returned to Town, I collect?"

"An hour since. What has happened? What is amiss?"

"The gabble-grinders have been tearing Miss Lisle to shreds. I have an open mind on the subject, but there is no denying nine-tenths of the world believes she wrote *The Masked Marauder*."

"*What?*" Wynn laughed wildly. "I must be dreaming. Philippa Lisle as Valentine Dred?"

"That is the *on-dit*." Lady Jersey's inquisitive eyes gleamed.

"Naturally, certain of the qualities which have made the book such a success are enough to damn a young lady author, to destroy her reputation forever."

On the instant, Wynn's slightly hysterical amusement turned to cold fury. "Miss Lisle damned on a rumor? 'Fore gad, ma'am," he snarled, "someone shall suffer for this."

"Hush, everyone is staring."

"Let them stare," said Wynn in a ringing voice, standing again and facing the room, "for they are staring at the real Valentine Dred!"

Everyone within earshot fell silent, and those who were not already agape turned to stare. Then they put their heads together, shook them skeptically, muttered, and snickered.

Lady Jersey stood up and put her hand on Wynn's arm. "Come now, Lord Selworth, you are only giving food for further scandal. Everyone knows you are close to the Lisles, that they are your sister's guests. Of course you are honor-bound to do what you can to defend Miss Lisle's reputation."

She had given Wynn time to think. "It should not be necessary to defend her, ma'am," he said reasonably, "if only people would give the matter a little thought."

"Indeed?"

"Consider: The first of Valentine Dred's romances was published eight years ago, when I was still up at Oxford. Miss Lisle is Albinia's age. Eight years ago she was a schoolroom miss of sixteen! Can anyone seriously credit that a mere chit of sixteen, living secluded in a country village, could write such a book?"

Much struck, Lady Jersey nodded. "Which one was that?" she asked.

"The Heart and the Dagger." Wynn grinned. "I hope my titles improved with practice."

"I remember it well. You are right. None but a complete nodcock could believe a schoolroom chit wrote that gory farce. Much more like the work of an undergraduate—the stories, if not the titles, have certainly improved with practice. So you are the author!''

''I am,'' said Wynn wryly, recalling the pains he had taken to protect his anonymity.

With a raised hand and an imperious gaze, Lady Jersey collected several of her cronies. The work of reestablishing Pippa's good name began.

By the end of the evening, Wynn felt he had convinced enough people that he was Valentine Dred to be sure the news would quickly spread. The few who held out were those who preferred a juicy bit of scandal to the truth, at any cost. The new Viscount Selworth's authorship did not make half so piquant a story as a young lady's disgrace.

Piquant enough, though, to wreck his Parliamentary hopes. Lady Castlereagh had made that quite plain.

Tapping his arm with her fan, the plump, dowdy wife of the Foreign Secretary said amiably, ''So you are the naughty man we have all been racking our brains to discover! Castlereagh will be excessively relieved to hear it. He and Lord Liverpool have been quite concerned about you, I collect, and all for nothing!''

Wynn returned to Albany torn between elation at having saved his beloved from public ignominy, and depression at having ruined his prospects of public service.

After spending all day on the road and half the night at Almack's, Wynn slept late the next morning. Having forgotten to tell Clark to wake him, he was annoyed with himself, for he had intended to go early to Charles Street to tell the Lisles the end of their ostracism was in sight.

He ate a quick breakfast and hurried round to his sister's house.

Opening the door to him, the first footman exclaimed, ''My lord!'' and peered past him into the street. The result of his peering appeared to disappoint him.

Puzzled, Wynn glanced back. A knife-grinder was receding down the street, and a groom held a pair of horses outside one of the houses opposite. What had the footman hoped or expected to see?

"The ladies at home, Reuben?"

"In the drawing room, my lord."

Wynn took the stairs two at a time. As he entered the room, Bina, Millicent, Kitty, even Mrs. Lisle surged to their feet and advanced upon him, all talking at once. The only word he could make out was Pippa's name. They, too, seemed to be looking behind him and to be disappointed by what they did not see.

Indeed, Mrs. Lisle was half-distraught, an alarming sight in a lady usually so serene.

Holding up his hands to still the clamor, he went to her and urged her to sit down on the nearest sofa. He seated himself beside her, took both her hands in his, and said soothingly, "You may be easy, ma'am. I have already refuted the rumors about Miss Lisle, at Almack's last night, and all is in train to set matters to rights. I'm heartily sorry she, and you, landed in the suds on my account."

"On your account?" said Millicent. "But—"

"*I* am Valentine Dred," said Wynn, "as half the *haut ton* knows by now, and the other half will by nightfall."

"You! But—"

"Does Pippa know?" asked Mrs. Lisle eagerly.

"Yes."

"Then at least that explains it!"

"Where is she, ma'am? I must make my apologies to— Explains what?"

"Why she went off to find you, hoping you might be able to alleviate our troubles."

"She what?" Wynn cried, springing to his feet. "When? How?"

"It is my fault," Bina said penitently, "at least in part. She spoke of going by stagecoach to search for you. I could not let her do that, so I offered the landau and John Coachman and a maid. I wish I had not, for she might have realized the impossibility and stayed at home to wait for you."

"But you are back, Lord Selworth," said Kitty, "and Pippa is not. You must have missed each other on the road."

Bina frowned. "She was going to enquire for you along the way, though, Wynn. She must surely have been told you were on your way south, yet you arrived last night in time to go to Almack's and she has not come home."

"Where can she be?" moaned Mrs. Lisle. "How could she go off alone like that?"

"My dear ma'am, she has the Debenhams' coachman and a maid with her." Wynn forced himself to sound calm. "I'm sure she is quite safe and will turn up at any moment, but if she is not here very shortly I shall go and look for her. When did she leave?"

"The day before yesterday," Kitty told him. She took a deep breath, apparently steeling herself to continue: "And the day before that, Mr.—" She stopped, staring at the door. "Pippa!"

Wynn swung round. There she stood, tired, tousled, begrimed, and absolutely the most beautiful sight he had ever seen.

And behind her stood Gilbert Chubb.

"Pippa, my dearest!" Mrs. Lisle rushed to embrace her errant daughter. "Thank heaven you are safe. Where have you been? What happened?"

Pippa kissed her. "Pray let me sit down, Mama. I am quite exhausted. Though Mr. Chubb's gig is excellently sprung" —she smiled over her shoulder at Gil, firing a dart of pure jealousy through Wynn's chest—"a gig is not the vehicle I should choose for a long journey!"

She sank into a chair. Gil, exposed to everyone's gaze, bleated, "Accident!"

"What do you mean, accident?" Wynn demanded. "Where do you come into this?"

Gil turned bright red and threw a pleading glance at Kitty.

"I asked Mr. Chubb to try to find you," she said defiantly. "He told me the author was a friend of his, and I guessed it must be you. I could not bear Pippa to be under a cloud a day longer than need be.''

Mrs. Lisle gave her a penetrating look.

"Wynn has already told people he wrote that book, Pippa," Millie said. "He went to Almack's last night and—"

While his sister chattered, Wynn met Pippa's eyes, full of gratitude and regret. "It was the only way," he said softly, knowing she understood what it cost him to protect her.

"But what is this about an accident, my love?" Mrs. Lisle interrupted Millicent, "and why have you been traveling with Mr. Chubb?"

"The landau went into a ditch in the dusk in a narrow lane, after we turned off the Great North Road to go to Kymford."

"That's where we missed each other," Wynn said. "I didn't stop at Kymford on the return journey. I was in a hurry to get back. You were not hurt?"

"Not at all. The wheel of the landau broke, I fear, Bina, and we were some distance from a village where it could be repaired. I cannot tell you how delighted I was when Mr. Chubb turned up and offered to drive me back to London!"

"Couldn't leave you beside the road," Gil exclaimed.

"I am not sure where Kymford is," said Mrs. Lisle. "How long were the two of you traveling together?"

"Since Tuesday evening, Mama. We owe Mr. Chubb for two nights' lodging on the way."

"Oh dear!" Her mother shook her head in dismay. "As I feared. You are hopelessly compromised, Pippa dearest. Mr. Chubb, I know I can rely upon you to do the gentlemanly thing. Come, Kitty."

Somehow, without being quite aware how it had happened, Wynn found himself swept out of the drawing room with the others, leaving Gil and Pippa alone there.

"I shall order refreshments," said Bina. "Wynn, will you take tea or would you prefer Madeira? Or shall I send for champagne, Mrs. Lisle?"

His best friend was proposing marriage to his love, and his

sister offered him tea or Madeira! Champagne? Pah! ''Hemlock,'' he growled inaudibly.

Turning on his heel, he sprang down the stairs and strode away from the house, his heart in his boots, bleeding with every step.

CHAPTER 17

Pippa gaped after her mother, too taken aback to believe she had heard correctly. But there she was, alone in the drawing room with Mr. Chubb.

Who stood with his mouth agape, looking utterly terrified.

"It is quite all right, sir," Pippa said kindly. "I shall not accept, you know."

Hope flared in his eyes. "You won't?"

"No. I do not intend ever to marry. I shall keep Mama company when Kitty is married."

"M-miss Kitty m-married?"

"She is bound to be, you know. Her suitors will flock back now that Lord Selworth has exonerated me. Kitty is not the sort to hold a grudge."

"Not at all," spluttered Mr. Chubb. "Sweetest temper, kindest, most—"

"Exactly," Pippa cut short his paean, "and very pretty, too, so she is certain to marry, even though she has no portion."

"Money! Who cares about money?"

"Well, if one has none . . ."

"Got plenty. M'father's no Chronos—that the fellow I mean?"

"Chronos was a Titan who swallowed his children. I expect you mean Croesus," Pippa suggested, fighting to keep a straight face. "The richest man in the world."

"That's the chap. M'father ain't one, but he's not short of the blunt and he's no nipfarthing. When I marry—"

"Mr. Chubb, you do not need to tell me all this. I promise you, I do not expect an offer."

"B-but Mrs. Lisle relies on me," he said, distressed and uncertain. "Said so."

"Very well, then, make your proposal, and I promise you I shall refuse you."

Awkwardly, Gil Chubb went down on one knee before her. "Miss Lisle," he said earnestly, "it would be a great honor if you would give me your hand. And I mean it, even if I know you won't."

"I am honored by your offer, sir," Pippa said, as gentle as she could be when she wanted to burst into tears, "but I cannot marry where my heart is not given. And nor should you."

"No." He sighed, then heaved himself to his feet with a thoughtful look. "Dashed if you ain't right, ma'am. Dashed if I won't try my luck."

"I cannot say whether Kitty will have you," Pippa warned, "but I shall send her to you." She sped from the room.

A couple of sniffs restored her control of her emotions. She went up to the sitting room, where she found her mother, Bina, and Millicent, but no Kitty.

Millie rushed to meet her. "Are you betrothed? I am so glad everything has worked out so well. I think it is excessively romantic, Mr. Chubb coming to the rescue when you were stranded, but Kitty is quite overset for fear you are forced into a distasteful marriage, though I am sure the heir to a baron must be considered an excellent match and Mr. Chubb is not so very ill-favoured, only a little shy, so I daresay you may be as happy with him as with—"

"I am *not* betrothed, Millie," Pippa said firmly.

"But you are compromised! Mrs. Lisle said so."

"I do not care if I am, but Mama gave us no opportunity to explain. We stayed at small, out-of-the-way inns, where I had a chambermaid sleep in my chamber each night, and we kept off the turnpike, so no one saw us together. I see no need to marry Mr. Chubb. Mama, what were you thinking of to put me in such a position?"

"I had my reasons, dearest." Mrs. Lisle was her usual serene self once more. "I did not for a moment suppose you would accept Mr. Chubb, though I fear Kitty was not so certain."

"Where is she? I told Mr. Chubb I would fetch her to him."

Her mama and Bina exchanged a congratulatory glance. "Locked in your chamber, weeping her heart out," said Bina. "If I am not mistaken, the position your mother put you in forced her to examine her own feelings."

"Mama! I have had reason before now to accuse you of being hardened in deceit, have I not?" Pippa protested, half-cross and half-laughing. "I shall go and tell her he is waiting for her."

Kitty felt as if the world had crashed about her ears. Pippa was to marry Gil Chubb! And all because he had so gallantly agreed to go off on a wild-goose chase, at Kitty's request, to spare her and her family a day or two of infamy.

He was not as dashing as Lieutenant Pendrell, not as romantic as Lord Fenimore, not as handsome as Mr. Carson, as witty as Lord Bellamy, as smart as Lord Edward Stanborough, nor as good a dancer as Mr. George Tarrington. But Kitty could not imagine spending the rest of her life with any of those attractive and eligible gentlemen—even if they had not abandoned her in the time of trouble.

Gil was kind and constant. He was clever and knowledgeable about the things which interested Kitty. Above all, she was always comfortable with him.

And he was to marry Pippa! Tears flowed afresh.

"Kitty, I must speak to you," came her sister's urgent voice through the door.

"C-coming." Kitty blotted her eyes, blew her nose, and tried to prepare herself to offer sincere-sounding felicitations. It was not Pippa's fault she had stolen Gil away. She did not even know Kitty loved him, for she had been at pains to show no preference amongst her suitors.

She unlocked the door, opened it, and was enveloped in a hug before she had time to attempt a smile.

"I am *not* going to marry Mr. Chubb," Pippa said at once. "He is waiting for you in the drawing room, and Mama says you may see him alone—if you wish."

"I wish!" The world sparkling about her, Kitty floated down the stairs, her heart as light as her feet.

Mr. Chubb was standing by the window, fiddling aimlessly with the catch. He turned as Kitty entered the room.

"You came!" he said in some surprise.

"Of course."

He came towards her. "You have been crying," he accused her. "Did your mama make you come down? Is my suit so distasteful? I wouldn't for anything make you cry."

"I was crying because I thought you were going to marry Pippa," she said with a tremulous smile.

His face lit. "Then you won't refuse me?"

"You have not asked me yet," Kitty pointed out demurely.

But the diffident Mr. Chubb enfolded her in a passionate embrace, and it was some time before he actually got around to offering his hand and his heart.

Which Kitty gladly accepted, giving her own in return.

Wynn felt as if the world had crashed about his ears. He had given up his career to save Pippa from ignomiy, and she was to wed his best friend!

Of course, had he known in advance that she was lost to

him, for her sake he would still have broadcast his authorship.
But how was he to face the future without even the prospect
of a useful career in Parliament to console him?

Retreat to Kymford to tend his acres was all that was left to
him, he supposed. He wouldn't have minded with Pippa at his
side. They could have discussed politics at least. She would
have helped him decide which Parliamentary debates he should
go up to Town for, to add his twopennyworth for whatever
good it could do. She might have let him help her with her
articles. But all that was over.

Betrothed to Gil—Wynn recalled all the bustle and turmoil
attendant upon Bina's betrothal—why should Pippa even go
on helping him with his speech, when it had more prospect of
being laughed out of the House than of doing any good?

If only he had not been in Yorkshire just when she needed
him most! She had been right to send him, though. Speaking
to the child himself, and to the compassionate family who had
rescued him, had ignited a fire in Wynn to fight for the thousands
of little boys who had not escaped.

Dammit, he *would* fight! Between what he had learnt in
Yorkshire and what work Pippa had already completed, he
would cobble together a speech good enough for the few listeners who were likely to turn up. If all he achieved was to awaken
one or two consciences, so be it.

His agitated strides had taken him across Berkley Square
and down Bruton Street to Bond Street. He turned south towards
Albany.

Bond Street was the wrong place for a notorious gentleman
in a hurry to seek the solace of solitude and hard work. Every
three paces he was stopped by strolling friends and acquaintances. Carriages halted in the street to allow their occupants
to call to him. Shoppers dashed out of shops at the sight of
him passing the windows.

The same question was on every tongue: "Is it true you are
Valentine Dred?"

"I was."

Dowagers scolded indulgently. Matrons decried his announced intention to write no more. Damsels blushed and giggled. And gentlemen quizzed him, laughing.

As Wynn had expected, he would never again be taken seriously. Somehow he managed to reach Burlington Gardens without losing his temper. Turning off Bond Street, he almost ran to the shelter of his lodgings.

Gil Chubb was not there. A last, unacknowledged seed of hope—that in spite of being compromised Pippa would refuse him—shrivelled. Rejected, he would surely have come home. Accepted, he had stayed in Charles Street to celebrate and make plans.

Wynn sat down at the table in the window, pulling from his pockets the sheaf of Yorkshire notes he had taken to give Pippa. "Damn!" he muttered. He had forgotten he hadn't got her notes for the speech. How long would it be before he could bear to face her and ask for them? He'd send a message through Gil, he decided, if he could ever bear to speak to his friend again.

Running footsteps sounded on the stairs and Gil burst into the room. "Congratulate me!" he cried jubilantly. "She loves me!"

The shrivelled seed died. "I thought you loved Kitty," Wynn said sourly.

Gil blinked. "I do. She is the dearest, sweetest girl in the world!"

"Then why should I congratulate you for being engaged to marry Miss Lisle?"

"You shouldn't. I'm not. We aren't. She won't. It's not Miss Lisle I'm going to marry—it's Miss Kitty."

Somewhere within the seemingly dead seed, life must have lurked, for in a fraction of a second it sprouted, budded, put forth leaves, and burst into bloom. "Not Pippa?"

"Not Pippa," Gil confirmed. "Had to propose to her. Honor of a gentleman, don't you know. Mrs. Lisle said I ought. But Miss Lisle said she don't mind being compromised, ain't planning to marry anyway. She sent Kitty down to me, and I had the whole thing all settled in a trice," he said proudly.

"Congratulations, old fellow!" Wynn said with fervor, jumping up to give him a hearty handshake. "I'm sure Lord and Lady Chubb will be delighted."

"D'you think so?"

"I do. Miss Kitty is amiable, and pretty, and enters fully into all your country concerns. I have never seen two people so well suited."

"Well, I have. You and Miss Lisle. Going to propose to her now?"

Wynn hesitated. "Not yet, I think," he said reluctantly, remembering again the fuss and bother when Bina was betrothed to Debenham. "I have too much on my mind at present—we both do. There is this business of making sure everyone knows she is not Valentine Dred, and dealing with everyone knowing I *am*, and my speech is only ten days away."

Only ten days! With all her own troubles, Pippa might not have been able to put her mind to the troubles of sweeps' boys. If he was going to make the speech at all, he might as well make it as good as possible.

Swinging round, Wynn swept up his papers and stuffed them back into his pocket. "I'm off!" he announced unnecessarily, bolting through the door and down the stairs.

A few minutes later, the first footman opened the Debenhams' door to him for the second time that day.

"Miss . . . m'sister in, Reuben?"

"Mrs. Debenham is in her sitting room, I believe, my lord." The footman looked even more impassive than usual, so much so that Wynn fleetingly wondered what the servants were making of the recent goings-on.

He hurried upstairs. Having asked for Bina, he supposed he had best, for the sake of appearances, at least stick his head into her sitting room to say hello. He knocked on her door.

"Who is it?"

"Wynn."

"Oh, good. Come in. I was just going to write you a note."

"Saying what?" Wynn advanced into the room, where Bina sat at her bureau. "I know Gil and Kitty are engaged."

Bina beamed at him. "Is it not splendid? They are perfect for each other. That was one thing I had to say, though I was sure Mr. Chubb must have told you by now."

"What else?" Wynn asked, a trifle impatiently. He wanted to go to Pippa, and he was just afraid that if he lingered his sister might want to know why he had rushed off in such a hurry when Gil was about to offer for Pippa.

"Well, I have already given the order—request, rather, for one cannot precisely order such a thing—but it can easily be rescinded if you do not like it."

"You sound like Millicent. Cut line, Bina!"

"Millicent is another . . . Do sit down, Wynn, instead of hovering over me like a buzzard."

"What order?" he demanded, sitting.

"Request. No, suggestion. I suggested to my housekeeper that she should delicately pass the word to the staff that it would be no bad thing if they should gossip to other people's servants about you having written *The Masked Marauder*."

Wynn sighed. "I daresay it's as good as any way to spread the word fast. Your butler and footmen frequent the Running Footman, no doubt, as it is just up the road."

"Yes, and George's valet, too. All the best people's menservants go there, I collect. And the worst scandalmongers seem to place the most credence in what they learn from their servants. You are not angry?"

"No." He shook his head. "If the Ton is busy ripping my dignity to shreds, why shouldn't the servants have their share? What were you going to say about Millie?"

"I thought it might help if she confessed—to a select few— that she started the *on-dit* about Pippa."

"She *what?*" Springing to his feet and starting for the door, Wynn shouted, "I'll wring her neck!"

"Wynn, come back! I phrased that badly. Do come back

and calm down. It was all a mistake." Bina explained what their sister had done. "It would not surprise me if someone deliberately twisted her words, someone envious of Kitty's success perhaps."

"If I ever find out who—"

"Unlikely. In any case, now that she is to marry Mr. Chubb, her other suitors will have attention to spare for her rivals, so the jealous cats will have no reason to try to drag her family's name in the mud. So, do you think it will serve to have Millicent explain the origin of the rumors?"

"No, best not. It would undoubtedly embarrass her, which would be fitting punishment, but it would also draw further attention to Pippa's . . . Miss Lisle's writing. Someone might guess the truth."

"You are quite right, best not to have Millie publish to the world that she suspected Pippa because she is forever scribbling."

"Where is she?" Wynn asked, reminded of his speech.

"Wait a minute. Two more points."

"You said you were writing me a note, not a four-page screed."

"Two more points," Bina said firmly. "First, you and I will drive with Pippa and Mrs. Lisle in the Park this afternoon."

"We haven't the time to spare, Miss Lisle and I. My speech is in not much more than a week!"

"You will have to make the time, and for more than that. If we are to reestablish Pippa, she must be seen about as much as possible for the next week or so at least."

Wynn groaned. "If you say so."

"And what is more, you must be nearby, to deflect any attacks. Starting with the *soirée* I am giving tomorrow. It is very short notice, to be sure, but that means if people do not come—and some are certain not to—I can tell Pippa they must be already engaged elsewhere, so she will not be hurt."

"Bless you, Bina." Wynn kissed his sister's smooth brow.

''I shall be there. But that makes it the more urgent to get to work. Where is she?''

''Up in the ladies' sitting room, with her mama, writing invitations. Millicent and Kitty are in the drawing room at the same task, as am I now, since I do not have to write to you. I am inviting practically everyone I have ever met, so as to be sure of a good crowd. It will be an informal betrothal party for Kitty and Mr. Chubb. We shall hold a formal one for family and close friends as soon as Lord and Lady Chubb can come up to Town.''

''Kitty is not family,'' Wynn pointed out, purely in the spirit of accuracy, since he had no objection whatsoever to the Debenhams giving a party for her.

''Almost,'' said Bina cryptically.

As he left, Wynn wondered just what the deuce she had meant by that.

Pippa was progressing with utmost sloth through her share of the invitations to be written. She kept catching herself gazing out of the window.

Not that there was anything of particular interest out there, just the usual view of the mews, and the backs of the houses in Hill Street, and roofs and chimneypots beyond. She would have had to stand up to look down to the patch of garden below, but in any case she did not see what lay before her eyes. Her mind was elsewhere.

Delighted as she was for Kitty and Mr. Chubb, she could not help wondering whether Mama had also intended her ploy to bring Pippa and Lord Selworth together. If so, it was a dismal failure. He had not even waited to discover the outcome of his friend's proposal to her. Obviously he did not care in the least whom she married.

His noble gesture in relinquishing his political prospects to save her from disgrace was not a sign of his feelings for her, but purely impersonal gallantry. For just a moment, when Millie told her he had revealed his alter ego at Almack's, she had fancied he must have done it for love.

Sheer folly, she sighed, dipping her pen and returning to the list of names and addresses, only to find her attention wandering again a moment later. Would he give up his speech, robbing her of those precious hours together?

Came a tap on the door, and Mrs. Lisle, seated at the large table, called, "Come in."

Lord Selworth entered, looking distinctly harassed. "Mrs. Lisle, Miss Lisle." He bowed slightly. "Will you excuse me, ma'am, if I beg Miss Lisle to give me her assistance at once? Time grows short."

"Of course, Lord Selworth," Mrs. Lisle said cordially, with a smile. "Just allow me to thank you for your promptness in disabusing the Ton of their mistaken apprehensions."

"It was nothing, ma'am. Honor demanded it. A gentleman could do no less."

Not even a generous gesture, Pippa thought. Merely a moral obligation.

"Still, we are vastly grateful," her mother maintained. "Pippa, you had best give me your list. I have nearly finished mine."

"I have not got very far," Pippa said guiltily.

"No matter, my love. You have more important things to do."

With the smile that turned Pippa to jelly, Lord Selworth took her list from her hand and passed it to her mother. Taking some papers from his pocket, he set them before her on the writing table.

Anxious to avoid talking about anything remotely personal, Pippa said eagerly, "Your Yorkshire notes? You mean to proceed with the speech?"

"Yes. I've decided anything I can do to alleviate the lot of those miserable children is worth a try. At worst, no one will come to listen, or only those who come to scoff."

"They may go to scoff, but surely when they hear the horrors you have to tell, they will stay to weep?'' Seeing his doubts in his face, Pippa hurried on. ''I shall study your notes later. Tell me what you learnt from the Stricklands.''

''It seems they were visiting neighbors when a tiny boy, about four years old, came crashing down the chimney and was seriously bruised. They took him home, the master sweep being glad to rid himself of a bungling encumbrance. When he was cleaned up, he turned out to be a handsome little fellow—I met him, by the way, and can vouch for his looks. Whether the Stricklands would have taken such an interest in an ill-favored child, I cannot tell.''

''Perhaps not,'' Pippa said soberly, ''but let us allow them the benefit of the doubt. What is his name?''

''Henry. He's well-spoken, too, clearly from a prosperous family, as the Stricklands guessed when he saw a silver fork and cried out in delight that his papa had such forks. Other things also were 'just like Papa's.' He knows the Lord's Prayer and will not get into bed without repeating it, but unfortunately he is too young to know his surname—or was when he was stolen away.''

''He was abducted, then?''

Lord Selworth nodded. ''The Stricklands pieced the story together. His mother died and his father went abroad, 'across the sea,' leaving him with his uncle, of whom he was very fond. He was picking flowers in Uncle George's garden one day. A woman came by, asked if he liked riding, took him up on her horse, and carried him off.''

Pippa shuddered. ''So easily! Enough to give any parent nightmares. And the House of Lords is made up of parents. The Stricklands could not find his family?''

''He comes from southern England, to judge by his accent. He says he and the woman sailed to Yorkshire by ship.''

''I daresay he thought he was going to join his papa.''

''Very likely,'' Lord Selworth agreed. ''According to the master sweep, it was in Yorkshire that the woman sold him the child. The Stricklands advertised in southern newspapers, without success.''

''I am very sorry for the poor little boy, but, you know, from the point of view of your speech, it is better that he will never see his family again. Or rather, that they will never see him. Too happy an ending would lessen the impact on all those noble fathers and grandfathers. What is to become of Henry?''

''A friend of the Stricklands will adopt him and educate him,'' said Lord Selworth with satisfaction.

''I am so glad, but I believe we shall leave his fate up in the air. Let us hope his story helps to alleviate the lot of all those other unhappy mites. It will fit perfectly into what I have already prepared.''

''You have contrived to work on my speech in spite of . . . your recent difficulties?''

''Oh yes,'' Pippa said dryly, ''I have had all the time in the world with no parties to go to, scarcely daring to leave the house for fear of being snubbed. It is not a pleasant sensation.'' She shivered. ''I must confess, grateful as I am to Bina, I positively dread tomorrow's *soirée.*''

CHAPTER 18

Pippa dressed with the utmost care next evening. She wore her emerald green crape, remade to open down the front over a white satin underdress, the set-on ivy leaves replaced with white silk roses. Instead of the fashionably brief pale green bodice, it now had a white one with a rather higher neckline, trimmed with emerald ribbons. For tonight, modesty was the watchword, but it must not be so blatant it became an obvious attempt to belie the immodesty attributed to her.

Fastening her locket about her neck, Pippa prayed that all the efforts to restore her to favor would not be in vain. The stitchery; the writing of invitations and running of footmen to deliver them; the magnificent refreshments provided by Gunter's at a moment's notice; George Debenham's noble sacrifice of the best wines in his cellar; all would go for naught if the Ton refused to accept her innocence.

Mama and Kitty would be devastated. Perhaps Lord Chubb would make his son break off the engagement. The Lisles would have to retreat to the country to lick their wounds in obscurity, leaving the Debenhams no choice but to repudiate their guests in order to regain their own position.

As Pippa descended the stairs with Kitty and Millicent, Lord Selworth and Mr. Chubb were admitted to the house. Mr. Chubb had flowers for Kitty, the viscount two nosegays, for Pippa and his younger sister.

"You look particularly lovely this evening," he said to Pippa, presenting a posy of white rosebuds.

She scarcely heard him. Her looks were irrelevant tonight. "Thank you," she said automatically, then voiced the only thought her mind was at present capable of accommodating: "What if no one comes?"

But everyone came. Had everyone come at once, Mrs. George Debenham's party would have been not a "dreadful squeeze," an accolade, but an unbearable crush. However, most people had prior engagements, so they came before, or after, or in between.

Those who apologised for giving credence to false rumor could be counted on the fingers of one hand. Some, like Mrs. Drummond Burrell, brazened it out as if they had never given the Lisles the cut direct. Some, like the Pendrells, were shame-faced and would not quite meet Pippa's eye. Some, like Lady Stanborough, were overeffusive when they complimented Mrs. Lisle on her younger daughter's splendid match.

To Pippa's relief, though few guests were so embarrassed as to avoid her altogether, Kitty was the focus of attention. Less satisfactory was the attention Lord Selworth received.

He stayed near her all evening, ready to spring to her defence if necessary, so she could not but notice the way the gentlemen chaffed him about his books. In spite of his prophecies of disaster, she had hoped he might still be taken seriously as a politician. Dismayed, she realized it was now highly unlikely his unconventional views would receive a respectful hearing.

As he said, all they could do was to make his speech as brilliant as possible, regardless of the probable outcome.

* * *

Delighted as he was to see his love no longer an outcast, Wynn wished her sister's disappointed suitors would leave her alone. Whether they wanted to make reparation for having snubbed the family, or, no longer blinded by Kitty's more obvious attractions, they had discovered Pippa's quiet charm, they flocked about her.

"She was engaged in advance for every single dance last night," Wynn grumbled to Gil one morning.

"Eh? What's that?" Gil went around in a revoltingly blissful daze these days.

"I said, Miss Lisle didn't stand up with me even once last night."

"You should ask her the day before. Or better still, pop the question. There's nothing like it, old chap, simply nothing like it. You can dance with her all night and no one gets in a pother."

Wynn grunted. He was not ready yet to propose. In fact, though he loved her more each day, he was less ready than ever, in spite of his jealousy of her new admirers.

They were part of the problem. Whereas before he had at least been able to tell himself that he had little competition, now he had a lot. This one was richer than Wynn, that one handsomer, one of higher rank, another the very image of elegance, another the height of *savoir faire*.

What Wynn had hoped to offer Pippa was the opportunity to support and share in a political career devoted to the principles they held in common. He might as well ask her to buy a gold mine in Peru as beg her to enter upon a betrothal without knowing whether he had a career before him or not.

Suppose no one came to hear him? Or suppose the peers were kind enough to attend despite his notoriety as a trifling creator of frivolous fictions—and he made a mull of her brilliant speech?

In spite of her new popularity, Pippa found time to work

hard with him on the speech, and that it was brilliant he had
no doubt. She played every note of pathos, every sharp of terror,
every flat of despair, with a sure ear, never overornamenting the
tune as he was still wont to do.

If Wynn did it justice, the House of Lords ought to end up
weeping bucketfuls. He was just afraid that, while they might
howl into their handkerchiefs, it would be with laughter, not
tears.

He pushed away his breakfast half-finished and turned once
more to conning his speech.

The day after tomorrow . . .

The petition to abolish the employment of climbing boys
was presented to the House of Commons that afternoon. Despite
its thousands of signatures, it aroused little interest among
gentlemen more concerned with putting down the uprisings of
desperate men across the country. The harvest promised well,
but would it be enough to make up for last year's deficit?
Would the mills start rolling again in time to prevent revolution?

The torment of several hundred, even thousands, of small
boys was of little importance in comparison with the torment
of a nation.

The Commons found time, however, to crowd into the Upper
House that evening to listen to the maiden speech of a new
member of that august body. Viscount Selworth was an author
of novels; more, an author of Gothic romances which were
ribald as well as funny and thrilling, said those who had read
them. His speech should be worth hearing.

The noble lords were apparently of the same opinion, for
every seat on the red leather benches was filled. To Wynn,
rising to his feet upon the invitation of the Lord Chancellor,
the room was a sea of heads, an ocean of pale faces all agog.

He took a deep breath and launched his words, Pippa's words,
upon that sea, fragile lifeboats to save yet more fragile children
from drowning in misery.

"My lords, gentlemen, . . . "

Thanks to Pippa, he had no need to resort to his notes, yet he had not studied so much as to render the matter stale. He spoke with fire and passion, the horrors of a climbing boy's life vivid in his mind as the periods rolled from his tongue. Lords and Commons alike, they hung upon his words. A collective gasp went up when he spoke of little Henry, torn from the wealthy family he would see no more.

Not so short as to seem unimportant, not so long as to bore the audience—and then, closing with a final plea to end the unnecessary suffering, it was over. With a slight bow, Wynn dropped exhausted to his seat.

The Whig lords crowded round, shaking his hand, slapping him on the back, congratulating him, lauding his eloquence. As they eventually began to drift away, some of the Tory lords took their place. Even the Prime Minister and the Lord High Chancellor approached Wynn to present their stiff, cool compliments.

"How soon can a bill be presented?" Wynn asked eagerly.

"Oh, as to that," said Liverpool, "the agenda is already overfull, is it not, Eldon?"

The Chancellor agreed. "No knowing when we shall be able to prorogue," he said testily.

"After all," put in Lord Lauderdale, "affecting as was your tale of the child Henry, there are only one or two cases of the sort. I for one am not acquainted with anyone who has had a child abducted, are you, my lords?"

The rest of the noble gentlemen nearby shook their heads.

"As for the rest," Lauderdale continued, "they are guttersnipes who if they were not engaged in an honest trade would be out on the streets a-begging—or picking our pockets!"

Amid laughter, the group broke up.

Furious, Wynn strode out to the lobby. Half an hour had passed since his speech ended, and the Commons had long since returned to their chamber. No doubt by now they had forgotten all about him.

A page boy stopped him. "Lord Selworth? Mr. Bennet, m'lord, he told me to beg you to wait a while till he can have a word with your lordship. The gallery's that way, my lord, if you was to wish to go up."

Wynn hesitated. He was in no mood to be polite, nor to lounge about waiting. He wanted to hurry back to Charles Street to acquaint Pippa with his success and his failure. On the other hand, he did not want the Radical Commoners to think him too top-lofty to care for their opinions of the speech.

He turned to head for the stairs to the gallery, just as the doors of the Commons chamber opened and Henry Grey Bennet came out. With him were Brougham and Burdett and two or three others.

Bennet saw Wynn. "Selworth! Well met. I was just coming to look for you. Any luck with the Lords?"

"None," Wynn fumed. "Oh, they liked the speech."

"Damn good speech," put in Brougham. "I'd be hard put to it to do better myself, and I'm not sure I wouldn't bet on you against Orator Hunt, if you weren't on the same side, more or less."

"Thank you," Wynn said, "but what's the use of speaking well if you can't persuade anyone to take action? They don't care a rap for the agonies of mere guttersnipes."

"They may not," said Burdett, "but we do. And what's more, you have talked enough Members into caring to pass a vote to set up a Select Committee to study the question. Congratulations!"

As the others added their congratulations, Wynn's spirits soared.

"It's a small first step," Bennet warned, "but I'm to be chairman of the committee, and I'll see its findings don't gather dust in a corner. Come, let's go and drink to your achievement and the abolition of climbing boys! Tell me, is it true you had Prometheus' help in drafting the speech? There are others who could do with his help."

Parrying questions about Prometheus, Wynn accompanied his friends to the Blue Boar to celebrate.

Pippa was on tenterhooks. She knew exactly how long Wynn took to deliver his oration. He ought to have finished an hour ago, but he did not come.

She made allowances for a late start. Perhaps it would take him a while to escape afterwards if everyone wanted to talk to him, to congratulate him. He did not come.

As time passed, she grew more and more certain that the speech had been an abject failure. Wynn was reluctant to face her and tell her he had made a mull of it. Or he had delivered it perfectly, but what had seemed so clever in the sitting room in Charles Street turned out to be hopelessly inappropriate for the House of Lords. He did not want to tell her she had wrecked his chances.

It was time to change for dinner, and still he did not come. Pippa was in two minds: Should she go and hide in her chamber lest he arrive with a tale of disaster? Could she bear to be in the middle of dressing and thus unavailable if he turned up in need of comfort?

Her mother chased her upstairs. "My love, your sitting and moping will not alter matters for better or worse," she pointed out. "I daresay he will come in time for dinner. Your papa was wont to say nothing gave him such an appetite as making a speech."

As soon as she was upstairs, Pippa knew she wanted to be downstairs. Not waiting for Nan's help, she flung on the first evening gown which came to hand, though she had decided days ago that the azure crepe, made over from one of Bina's, did not become her. She unpinned her hair, swiftly ran a comb through it, and hurriedly pinned it up again.

"That is a mess," said Kitty. "It is going to fall down any moment. Let me do it for you."

"No, it does not matter. We are staying at home this evening and not expecting visitors."

"Except Gil and Lord Selworth," Kitty reminded her unnecessarily as she departed.

If he came. Where was he?

Pippa went down to the drawing room. At least she would not have to go out and dance, nor even stay in and try to help entertain guests. Mama and Bina had decided a quiet evening at home was a good idea after all the gallivanting of the past ten days, besides giving Lord Selworth a chance to tell them all about his speech.

If he came. Pippa went over to the window and looked out, just in time to see Gil Chubb arriving. Alone.

She heard Gil's knock on the door, his voice as he spoke to the butler, his feet on the stairs. Turning from the window, she was moving towards the door when he came in.

He glanced swiftly around the room. Seeing no one else there, he said, "Congratulations, Miss Lisle!"

"Congrat—? It went well?"

"Brilliantly. Almost had me in tears. I was up in the gallery, of course. Could have heard a pin drop while Wynn was talking—well, almost." He frowned dubiously. "Don't know if you could have heard a pin drop while he was actually talking."

"But they listened? Were many there?"

"Place was full to bursting. All the Commons came in, too. A good half of 'em, anyway. You should have seen 'em crowding round him afterwards—the Lords—patting his back and shaking his hand. A grand success." Puzzled, he added, "He hasn't come to tell you?"

"No," said Pippa bluntly. "You have not seen him since?"

"Missed him somehow at Westminster Hall, what with all the people swarming about. He'll be here any minute, I expect."

Kitty came in then and distracted Gil's attention. Pippa went on hoping Lord Selworth would arrive at any moment right until they all went in to dinner.

Then she began to grow angry.

Rearranging the food on her plate to pretend she was eating, she let Millie's chatter wash over her unheard as she racked her brains to think why he should stay away. Only one answer came to mind. Now that his speech had proved a triumph, he did not want to acknowledge her part in writing it. He wanted all the glory for himself.

Pippa neither expected nor desired any public glory. She did not want Lord Selworth's gratitude—she had worked for herself and for the climbing boys as much as for him. But she did want to know he appreciated her help and recognized its value. Here, where all but Millicent knew she was Prometheus, he would have to share the honors.

So he did not come.

At long last dinner ended. The ladies arose to leave George Debenham and Gil Chubb to an undoubtedly brief session with their port. Pippa was telling the truth when she murmured to her mother that she had the headache.

"Go to bed, my love, and I shall bring a tisane."

"It is not bad enough to need rest, only quiet. I shall go up to the sitting room."

Mama nodded understandingly. "I am certain there is an explanation," she said.

Indeed there was, and Pippa had guessed it. By now he had probably persuaded himself it was all his own doing. After all, when it came to politics, what had a mere female to offer?

The others went into the drawing room. Pippa continued up the stairs to the sitting room, where she slumped into an easy chair. Tears pricked her eyelids, but she refused to let them flow. Crying would only worsen her headache, and he was not worth it.

How could she have believed he was different from all the rest, that he respected her talents and was glad to see her make use of them? No doubt all along—or at least since he guessed she was Prometheus—he had told himself he was humoring her while he did all the real work. He was deluding himself, as he would discover when he tried without her, but nine hundred and ninety-nine men out of a thousand contrived to delude themselves that they were superior beings.

Only Papa was different. Even Mr. Cobbett had not liked to admit that a woman was capable of taking on the mantle of Prometheus. Only his friendship for Benjamin Lisle had persuaded him to consider Pippa's articles, though once convinced of their value he remained a staunch friend.

A letter from him, from America, had arrived yesterday, when Pippa was too busy putting the final touches to the dastardly viscount's speech to pay much attention. Now she needed something to distract her thoughts.

She went to sit at the desk, unlocked the drawer, and took out Mr. Cobbett's letter. Holding it so as to catch the fast fading light from the window, she reread it. He intended to resume publication of the *Political Register,* writing from America, and he wanted Pippa to start writing articles again. What should she write about? Her mind was still full of chimney sweeps.

Chimney sweeps and Wynn Selworth. Again she felt the prickling of tears, tears of anger, not of heartache, she told herself.

She concentrated on the view. Chimneypots silhouetted against a dusky pink sky, so many chimneypots, every one needing to be swept, every one an instrument of torture to a small, terrified child. She would start an article with that view, and lead on from climbing boys to other injustices equally capable of solution by men of goodwill.

Men like Wynn Selworth. How could someone of such generous principles prove so perfidious? And having betrayed her, would he next betray his principles?

Pippa sat musing unhappily, the twilight deepening about her. When she heard the door open behind her and a soft glow suffused the room, she assumed Mama or Bina had sent a footman up with a branch of candles.

"Thank you," she said without turning.

"Wrong way round," said a slurred voice. "I've come to thank *you.*"

"Wynn!" Pippa swung round. "Lord Selworth, I mean."

"Wynn'll do nicely." He stood leaning against the doorpost, his flaxen hair in wild disarray, cravat loosened, candelabra in hand.

"I thought you were a footman," she said inanely.

"Met him on the stair. Said I'd bring you this." Beaming, Lord Selworth gestured with the candelabra. As candles wobbled and flames flickered and flared, Pippa sprang to rescue it. "Sorry. A trifle bosky—just a trifle, mind!"

"You had best sit down." She took the candelabra to the desk and set it down.

He was close behind her. "Come and sit with me," he begged, taking her hand and tugging her over to a sofa. "Got a lot to say to you. Lots and lots."

The hours of anxiety burst forth. "Then why did you not come sooner?" Pippa demanded angrily, withdrawing her hand from his clasp.

"Tried. Tried and tried and tried. Every time I got to the door, someone else came in, same thing all over again. Congrat—you know, drink to your success—my success, that is, only *your* success, too. Pro-me-the-us," he said with great care. "All his doing. Yours. Had a deuce of a time answering all their questions."

"You did not tell them who I am? Who Prometheus is?"

"Not *that* bosky. Anyway, wouldn't give you away if I was drunk as a wheelbarrow. Want to keep you. All for myself."

He recaptured her hand. However bosky he was, his smile was the same as ever, and had the same effect on Pippa.

"Wh-what do you mean?" she faltered.

Lord Selworth looked surprised. "Marry you," he said. "Marry me. Pippa, do say you'll marry me. Be a viscountess, and it's the only way I'll be sure of an endless supply of brilliant speeches. Do say you will."

It was exactly what she wanted, was it not? A gentleman who truly appreciated her abilities and was not reluctant to admit it. So why the sinking feeling, as if her heart were heavy

enough to plunge all the way to the tips of her blue kid slippers?
Why the catch in the throat, making it impossible to speak, to
accept Lord Selworth's flattering offer?

"Dash it, I nearly forgot." He slid from the sofa and thumped
to his knees before her. "I adore you, you know. Life won't
be worth living if you won't marry me. I've loved you for ages
and ages and ages . . ."

Gazing into his hopeful, slightly bloodshot blue eyes, Pippa
knew he spoke the truth. Touching his lips with her finger to
stop the string of "ages," she murmured, "Oh Wynn, I have
loved you for simply ages, too," and she kissed him.

HISTORICAL NOTE

Henry Grey Bennett's Select Committee produced a bill to abolish the use of climbing boys, but there was no time for a hearing that session. The following year, 1818, the bill passed the Commons. In the Lords, Lord Lauderdale made a funny speech which killed it.

Though the practice gradually decreased, little boys continued to be forced up chimneys until it was at last banned in 1875.

CULTURE SMART!

ITALY

Barry Tomalin

·K·U·P·E·R·A·R·D·

ISBN 978 1 85733 830 0

British Library Cataloguing in Publication Data
A CIP catalogue entry for this book is available from the
British Library

First published in Great Britain
by Kuperard, an imprint of Bravo Ltd
59 Hutton Grove, London N12 8DS
Tel: +44 (0) 20 8446 2440   Fax: +44 (0) 20 8446 2441
www.culturesmart.co.uk
Inquiries: sales@kuperard.co.uk

Series Editor Geoffrey Chesler
Design Bobby Birchall

Printed in India

About the Author

BARRY TOMALIN, M.A., is Senior Lecturer in International Communication and Cultural Awareness at the London Academy of Diplomacy, and Director of the Business Cultural Trainer's Certificate course at International House, London. After graduating with a B.A. (Hons) in Anthropology and Linguistics from the School of Oriental and African Studies, University of London, he gained an M.A. in International Liaison and Communication at the University of Westminster. He has taught at Link University in Rome, and run training programs in Milan, Rome, Genoa, and Naples. He has traveled extensively in Italy and brings firsthand experience and professional insight to the country and its people.

contents

Map of Italy	7
Introduction	8
Key Facts	10

Chapter 1: LAND AND PEOPLE | 12
• Geography	12
• Climate and Weather	13
• Population	14
• Regions and Cities	16
• A Brief History	22
• Postwar Italy	39
• Government	43
• Politics	43
• Economic Life	44

Chapter 2: VALUES AND ATTITUDES | 46
• Family First	46
• Feelings and Emotions	47
• The Church	48
• Tolerance	49
• *Bella Figura*	50
• Loudness	51
• Order and Hierarchy	52
• *Garbo*	53
• Relationships	54
• *Campanilismo* and the Piazza	54
• Bureaucracy–The Fourth Estate	56
• Being *Furbo*	57
• Conclusion	58

Chapter 3: FESTIVALS AND TRADITIONS | 60
• Main Italian Public Holidays	61
• The Festive Year	61
• Annual Vacations	65
• Local Holidays	66
• *Carnevale*	66
• The *Palio*	67
• Name-Days	68

- Saints 69
- Behavior in Church 70
- Superstition 71
- Conclusion 73

Chapter 4: MAKING FRIENDS 74
- *Esterofilia* 74
- Close-Knit Circles 75
- Commitments 77
- Jealousy 78
- Power 78
- Invitations 79
- Gift Giving 79
- Social Clubs 79
- Bars and Nightlife 80
- Conclusion 81

Chapter 5: DAILY LIFE 82
- Housing 82
- Shopping 84
- Education 87
- Military Service and the Armed Forces 88
- Finding a Job 88
- Marriage 89
- Birth 90
- Money and Banking 90
- Keeping Healthy 93

Chapter 6: TIME OUT 96
- Eating and Drinking 96
- Dress 103
- Outdoor Life 104
- Football as a Way of Life 105
- Seeing the Sights 106
- Festivals 107
- Museums and Art Galleries 107
- Monuments 108
- Music and Theater 110
- Cinema 111

contents

Chapter 7: GETTING AROUND   112
- Air Travel and Entry to Italy   113
- Police Registration   113
- The Ubiquitous *Bollo*   114
- Residency   114
- Public and Private Transport   115

Chapter 8: BUSINESS BRIEFING   128
- Business in Italy   128
- Company Structure and Organization   130
- Company Finance and Corporate Governance   131
- Labor Relations   132
- Planning   133
- Leadership   133
- Decision-Making   136
- Teamworking   137
- Motivation   138
- The Overall Language of Management   139
- Feedback and Managing Disagreement   139
- Communication Styles   140
- Making Contact   141
- Business Hours   142
- Preparing For Your Visit   143
- The First Meeting   144
- Making a Presentation   145
- Meetings and Negotiating Skills   146
- Business Entertaining   148

Chapter 9: COMMUNICATING   150
- Language Skills   150
- The Media   151
- Telephones   156
- The Postal Service   158
- *Conversazione*   160
- Gender Issues   162
- Conclusion   163

Further Reading   165
Index   166
Acknowledgments   168

Map of Italy

introduction

It is impossible to be bored in Italy. To excite, delight, and stimulate you there is the beauty of the land, the elegance and charm of its people, the variety of its regional cultures, the richness of its food and wine, the quality and dash of its design and engineering, the reputation of its artists, sculptors, writers, musicians, and filmmakers and, above all, the glory of its monuments and architecture. There is the sensuous pleasure of the Italian language, everyday as well as operatic; and the way Italians use diminutives and nicknames to create familiarity and intimacy with those around them. There is the whiff of intrigue and even scandal as well as tragedy in its history and politics, from the time of the ancient Romans, through the Renaissance right up to the present day.

Like all the *Culture Smart!* guides, this book focuses on the people. How do they behave, and what makes them tick? What is the best way to get on good terms with them? For that is the real way to enjoy Italy.

Above all other European nations, the Italians epitomize style. *Fare bella figura*—"to look good, to make the right impression"—is a social imperative, not a fashionable option. Some people have commented dryly that Italy represents a "triumph of style over substance." As this book shows, style is part of the substance—it helps explain the success of Italian design and fashion worldwide.

Like the other titles in this series, *Culture Smart! Italy* shows you as a foreigner how to get the best out of being in Italy and meeting and working with Italians. It tells you what you need to know about its history and culture and gives you a platform for further investigation of this fascinating country. It shows you how the Italians go about their daily lives, and highlights some of their passions and preoccupations. It introduces their festivals and traditions. It suggests how to have a good time in the Italian way, and gives tips on how to travel around. It offers a guide to communications, in particular to communicating successfully with Italians in a business situation.

Italian culture has been exported all over the world. What is it like at home? The Italians are the most European-minded of nations, emerging as they do from a long history of regional fragmentation, with some ancient battles still fought out on the football fields of Italy every week in season. This is your chance to get to know them better.

Key Facts

Official Name	Repubblica Italiana (Republic of Italy)	
Population	61.5 million (2013)	
Capital City	Rome (population 3.5 million)	
Other Main Cities	Milan (pop. 2.9 million); Turin (pop. 1.6 million); Genoa (pop. 607,000); Bologna (pop. 384,000); Florence (pop. 374,000); Venice (incl. mainland, pop. 270,000); Naples (pop. 2.27 million); Palermo (pop. 872,000)	
Area	116,310 sq. miles (301,245 sq. km)	
Climate	Mediterranean	
Currency	Euro (previously Italian lira)	
Ethnic Makeup	85% Italian national	
Language	Italian. Many distinct regional dialects	German is spoken in Trento and Alto Adige. French is spoken in the Valle d'Aosta. Slovene is spoken in parts of Trieste and Gorizia.
Religion	No official religion	Roman Catholicism is the main religion.
Government	Italy is a multiparty democracy with a president as head of state and a prime minister as head of government.	Elections are held every five years.

Media	Regional press with national distribution. Main newspapers: *Corriere della Sera* (Milan); *Il Messaggero* (Rome); *Repubblica* (Rome); *L'Osservatore Romano* (Vatican); *L'Unità* (Rome; formerly Communist, now more centrist); *La Stampa* (Turin)	Rai is the state broadcasting station with three TV channels (Rai 1, 2, and 3) and three radio channels (Radio 1, 2, and 3). There are also numerous commercial channels.
Media: English Language	The *International New York Times* has an Italy Daily section covering Italian news. *Wanted in Rome* is an English-language news and listings magazine that comes out every two weeks. *L'Osservatore Romano* has a weekly English-language edition.	
Electricity	220 volts, 50 Hz AC, but check if older hotels still have 125 volts.	Standard continental plugs
Video/TV	PAL 625 lines	
Internet Domain	.it	
Telephone	Italy's country code is 39.	Always put 0 before the local area code, even if dialing from within Italy (and even within the same town). To dial out, dial 00 plus country code.
Time	One hour ahead of Greenwich Mean Time (GMT + 1)	Six hours ahead of US Eastern Standard Time (EST + 6)

LAND & PEOPLE

GEOGRAPHY

Bordered on the north and west by Switzerland and France, and to the northeast by Austria and Slovenia, Italy's landmass extends south into the Mediterranean, between the Ligurian and Tyrrhenian seas in the west and the Adriatic and Ionian seas in the east. Italy is first and foremost a Mediterranean country and the Italians share characteristics with other Latin nations—spontaneity, and a relationship-based and not particularly time-conscious society. Of the three main islands off its coast, Sicily and Sardinia are Italian, while Corsica—birthplace of Napoleon Bonaparte—is French. The capital, Rome, lies more or less in the center.

Italy is shaped like a boot, reaching down from central southern Europe with its toe, Sicily, in the Mediterranean and its heel, the town of Brindisi, in the Ionian Sea. From top to toe it is about 1,000 miles (1,600 km) by the national expressway (*autostrada*) network. The Brenner Pass in the north is on the same latitude as Berne in Switzerland, whereas the toe of southern Sicily is on the same latitude as Tripoli in Libya. Only a quarter of the country is arable lowland, watered

by rivers such as the Po, Adige, Arno, and Tiber. The whole of the northern frontier region is fringed by the Alps, including the jagged peaks of the Dolomites, while the Apennine Mountains run like a backbone down the peninsula from the Gulf of Genoa to the Straits of Messina, with snow-covered peaks until early summer.

CLIMATE AND WEATHER

Italy's climate is Mediterranean, but northern Italy is on average four degrees cooler than the south because the country extends over ten degrees of latitude. The inhabitants of Milan, in the great northern plain of the River Po, endure winters as cold as Copenhagen in Denmark (40°F/5°C in January), whereas their summers are almost as hot as in Naples in the south (88°F/31°C in July)—but without the refreshing sea breezes. Turin, at the foot of the Alps, is even colder in winter (39°F/4°C in January) but has less torrid summers (75°F/24°C in July).

All the coastal areas are hot and dry in summer but subject also to violent thunderstorms, which can cause sudden flash floods. Inland cities such as Florence and Rome can be delightful early in the year (68°F/20°C in April), but unpleasantly heavy and sticky in July and August (88°F/31°C).

Spring and early summer and fall are the best times to visit, though in Easter week Italian town centers are full of tourists, and in April and May they are packed with crowds of Italian schoolchildren on excursions. September and early October, when hotel rates and plane fares are cheaper, are often especially beautiful with clear fresh sunny days at the time of the grape harvest. October and November, the months of the olive harvest, have the heaviest rainfall of the year, but the winter months can also be wet, so take a waterproof coat and a good comfortable pair of walking shoes. (Naples has a higher average annual rainfall than London!) This is the time for the opera-goer, and the winter sports enthusiast, or to enjoy crowd-free shopping in Milan, Rome, or Venice. But before February is out, the pink almond is already blossoming in the South.

POPULATION

Italy's population is about 61 million, in spite of having one of Europe's lowest birth rates and the greatest gaps between births and deaths. The population has fallen 3.7 percent since 2009. The greatest decline, according to the Italian Statistics Office ISTAT is in the northeast and the islands.

Changes in the population are due to three factors; lower birth rates, greater emigration, and a longer-lived population. Italy now has one of the oldest populations in Europe, second only to Germany, and the level of population has been boosted by immigration. According to statistics, 4.9 million foreigners now have Italian citizenship.

One reason for this is smaller families as more and more women seek their own careers, even though women still make up only a relatively small percentage of the professional and technical workforce. While 88 percent of all Italian women have one child, over half decide not to have another. Interestingly, the life expectancy of Italian women has doubled in fifty years to an average age of eighty-two.

According to UN estimates, some 300,000 immigrant workers a year will be needed to maintain Italy's workforce. There has been a steady stream of migrants from North Africa and the Far East, but the majority now come from central and southeastern Europe. Although Italy has made some attempts to curb immigration, these foreign workers are also regarded as "useful invaders." For decades, Italy was a land of emigration (principally to the USA and Latin America, and later Australia). The presence of immigrants in Italy's cities is a relatively new phenomenon and many Italians are still coming to terms with it.

A noted issue in recent Italian politics has been the influx of refugees from southeastern Europe and the war-torn areas of Syria, Libya, and the Sahel, many via Istanbul.

Stories of refugees crossing the Mediterranean in ageing hulks of boats, trafficked by criminals, often abandoned and left to drift toward the Italian shores maybe to be rescued by Italian coastguards, was one of the recurring tragedies in international news in 2014–15 and one which the inadequately resourced EU Mediterranean fleet could not successfully resolve.

The Italian navy said it could no longer resource the rescue operations at the level needed, and at the end of 2014 EU backers were also announcing cutbacks in their support.

REGIONS AND CITIES

Italy contains two mini-states, the Republic of

San Marino and the Vatican. San Marino covers just 24 square miles (61 sq. km), and is the world's oldest (and second smallest) republic, dating from the fourth century CE. The Vatican City, a tiny enclave in the heart of Rome, is the seat of the Pope, head of the Roman Catholic Church.

The Vatican City (*Stato della Città del Vaticano*)
Measuring 109 acres (0.4 sq. km), less than a third of the size of Monaco, the Vatican is a sovereign

REGION	CAPITAL
Valle d'Aosta	Aosta
Piemonte (Piedmont)	Torino (Turin)
Lombardia (Lombardy)	Milano (Milan)
Trentino-Alto Adige	Trento
Veneto	Venezia (Venice)
Friuli-Venezia Giulia	Trieste
Liguria	Genova (Genoa)
Emilia-Romagna	Bologna
Toscana (Tuscany)	Firenze (Florence)
Umbria	Perugia
Marche	Ancona
Lazio	Roma (Rome)
Abruzzi	L'Aquila
Molise	Campobasso
Campania	Napoli (Naples)
Puglia	Bari
Basilicata	Potenza
Calabria	Catanzaro
Sicilia (Sicily)	Palermo
Sardegna (Sardinia)	Cagliari

state on the west bank of the Tiber. This tiny area is what remains of the Papal States, which were created by Pope Innocent II (1198–1216) by playing off rival candidates for the title of Holy Roman Emperor. Before their conquest by the Piedmontese in the 1860s, the Papal States stretched from the Tyrrhenian Sea in the west to the Adriatic in the east, and had a population of three million souls. Today the Vatican is the world's smallest state, with an army of Swiss Guards (actually mainly Italians on temporary posting), and a population of about a thousand. Most of the workers in the Vatican City live outside and commute in every working day. As a state, it has all it needs: a post office, a railway station, a helipad, a TV and radio station broadcasting in forty-five languages, a bank, a hospital, refectories, drugstores, and gas stations.

The authority of the Vatican was established in 380 CE when the primacy of the Holy See—the jurisdiction of the Bishop of Rome—was officially recognized by the Western Church. As a result Rome is the "Eternal City" to 1.2 billion Roman Catholics worldwide. Paradoxically, in 1985 a Concordat was signed under which Catholicism ceased to be Italy's state religion.

The glories of the Vatican City are its museum, which houses the Sistine Chapel and countless works of art, and St. Peter's Basilica. This can seat a 60,000-member congregation and is 611 feet (186 meters) long, 462 feet (140 meters) wide, and 393 feet (120 meters) high. Built between 1506 and 1615, its magnificent dome and the square Greek-cross plan were designed by Michelangelo, who worked on it "for the love of God and piety"—in other words, without pay! St. Peter's houses Michelangelo's *Pietà* (the statue of the seated Virgin holding the limp body of the dead Christ), and Bernini's bronze canopy (*baldacchino*) over the high altar.

At the head of the Vatican administration is the Pope, aided by his state secretariat under the Secretary of State. There are ten congregations, or departments, dealing with clerical matters, each headed by a cardinal. The most important is the Congregation for the Doctrine of the Faith, formerly the Inquisition. All Catholic bishops are enjoined to go to Rome at least once every five years to see the Pope "at the threshold of the Apostles."

The leading sacred establishment in the Vatican is the Curia, or College of Cardinals, which comprises 226 members, of which 124 are entitled to elect the new Pope. After the death of a Pope the electors meet in conclave and are locked into the Sistine Chapel until a new Pope is elected. After each vote, the ballots are burned and black smoke drifts up from the Sistine Chapel chimney. When a new Pope has been elected, a chemical is added to the ballot papers to turn the smoke white, and the new Pope in his papal regalia appears to the public in the piazza. He is crowned the following day in St. Peters.

Rome

Rome is Italy's capital and the seat of government
and has a population of 3.5 million. Though
situated in the center of Italy, Rome is regarded as
a "Southern" city in its style and general outlook.

Milan

With a population of 2.9 million and situated in
the northern region of Lombardy, Milan is Italy's
"New York." Sometimes described by its citizens
as the real capital, Milan is the industrial center of
Italy and home to two of its most famous football
teams, Inter Milan and AC Milan. It is also the
seat of Italy's *Borsa*, or Stock Exchange.

Naples

One of the busiest ports in Italy and the "capital"
of the South, Naples has a population of over two
million. It is the jumping off point for visits to the

towns of Pompeii and Herculaneum, preserved
by the lava that buried them after the eruption
of Mount Vesuvius in 79 CE, and for visits to
the islands of Capri and Ischia.

Turin
The capital of Piedmont, Turin (pop. 1.6 million)
is the gateway to the Italian Alps and a major
industrial center and transportation junction.

Palermo
Founded by the Phoenicians in the eighth century
BC, Palermo (pop. 872,000) is the capital and chief
seaport of Sicily.

Bologna
This industrial city and ancient university town
(pop. 384,000) is the capital of Emilia-Romagna.
It is famous for the quality of its food and is also
a transportation center and agricultural market.

Genoa
Genoa (pop. 607,000), the capital of Liguria in
the northwest, is Italy's largest port and a leading
industrial and commercial center.

Florence
The capital of Tuscany, Florence (pop. 374,000) is
famous for its architectural and artistic treasures,
dating from its heyday as the leading architectural
city of the Italian Renaissance under the Medici.
Today it is also a fashion center and a major
commercial, transportation, and industrial hub.

Venice
Capital of the Veneto
region, Venice (pop.
270,000, including the
mainland) is the other
great Renaissance center.
The old city is built on
piles on islands in a
saltwater lagoon, and is
famous for its canals
and bridges. It is both
a leading cultural and
architectural attraction
and a major port.

A BRIEF HISTORY

Italy is renowned for its magnificent art treasures
and breathtaking scenery. Two of its greatest
admirers were the nineteenth-century Romantic
poets Percy Bysshe Shelley and Lord Byron, both
of whom lived there. Shelley, who was drowned in
a storm in a small boat off the coast, near La Spezia,
described Italy as "Thou paradise of exiles" (*Julian
and Maddolo*, 1819), and Byron in a letter to
Annabella Milbanke on April 28, 1814, wrote
"Italy is my magnet." Almost a century later,
Henry James wrote to Edith Wharton, "How
incomparably the old coquine of an Italy
is the most beautiful country in the world—of a
beauty (and an interest and complexity of beauty)
so far beyond any other that none other is worth
talking about."

Interestingly, Italians, from the late medieval poets Boccaccio and Dante onward, describe their country very differently. Over the centuries Italy has been depicted as a whore, a fallen woman, or even a brothel. Many of Italy's contemporary problems derive from its history as a land of separate, warring city-states, later ruled by other European powers. Italy was not unified until 1861 and in a sense still has the feeling of a "young" country, despite its antiquity.

Prehistory

In the Bronze Age, from about 2000 BCE, Italy was settled by Indo-European Italic tribes from the Danube basin. The first indigenous sophisticated civilization was that of the Etruscans, which developed in the city-states of Tuscany. In 650 BCE Etruscan civilization expanded into central and northern Italy, setting an early example of urban living. The Etruscans controlled the seas on either side of the peninsula, and for a while provided the ruling dynasties in neighboring Latium, the lowlands in the central part of Italy's western coast. Etruscan ambitions were eventually checked by the Greeks at Cumae near Naples in 524 BCE, and the Etruscan navy was defeated by the Greeks in a sea battle off Cumae in 474 BCE.

At about this time, Greek colonies in Southern Italy were introducing the olive, the vine, and the written alphabet. Greek civilization would, of course, have a major influence on the future Roman Empire.

The Rise of Rome

During the fourth and third centuries BCE Rome, the leading city-state of Latium, rose to prominence and united the Italian peninsula under its rule. Legend has it that Rome was founded by Romulus and Remus, twin sons of the god Mars and the King of Alba Longa's daughter. Left to die near the River Tiber, the abandoned babes were suckled by a she-wolf until they were discovered by a shepherd, who brought them up. Eventually Romulus founded Rome in 753 BCE on the Palatine Hill above the banks of the Tiber where the wolf had rescued them. He was to become the first in a line of seven kings.

Following the expulsion of its last Etruscan king, Rome became a republic in 510 BCE. Its political dominance was underpinned by its remarkably stable constitutional development, and eventually all of Italy gained full Roman citizenship. The defeat of foreign enemies and rivals led first to the establishment of protectorates and then the outright annexation of territories beyond Italy.

The Roman Empire

The Republic's victorious march across the known world continued despite political upheavals and civil war, culminating in the murder of Julius Caesar in 44 BCE and the establishment of the Roman Empire under Augustus and his successors. Thereafter Rome flourished. Augustus famously "found Rome in brick and left it in marble." The city was burned down in 64 CE during the reign of the Emperor Nero, who, to deflect the blame, initiated a period of persecutions of Christians. It is around this time that Saints Peter and Paul were executed. Peter was crucified upside down, whereas Paul—a Roman citizen by birth—was beheaded.

The Roman Empire lasted until the fifth century CE, and at its peak extended from Britain in the west to Mesopotamia and the Caspian Sea in the east. The Mediterranean effectively became an inland lake—*mare nostrum*, "our sea." The civilization of ancient Rome and Italy took root and had a profound influence on the development of the whole of Western Europe through the Middle Ages, the Renaissance, and beyond—in art and architecture, literature, law, and engineering, and through the international use of its language, Latin, by scholars and at the great courts of Europe.

The Fall of the Empire and the Rise of the Church

In 330 CE Constantine, the first Christian emperor, moved his capital to Byzantium (renamed Constantinople—modern-day Istanbul), and Rome declined in importance. In 395 the Empire was divided into eastern and western parts, each ruled by its own emperor. There was continuous pressure along the borders as barbarian tribes probed the overstretched imperial defenses. In 410 Rome was sacked by Visigoths from Thrace, led by Alaric. Further incursions into Italy were made by the Huns under Attila in 452, and the Vandals who sacked Rome in 455. In 476 the last western Emperor, Romulus Augustus, was deposed, and in 568 Italy was invaded by the Lombards, who occupied Lombardy and central Italy.

With the collapse of the Roman Empire in the west, the Church in Rome became the sole heir and transmitter of imperial culture and legitimacy, and the power of the papacy grew. Pope Gregory I (590–604) built four of the city's basilicas and also sent missionaries to convert pagans to Christianity (including St. Augustine to Britain). On Christmas Day 800, at a ceremony in Rome, Pope Leo III (795–816) crowned the champion of Christendom, the Frankish king Charlemagne, Emperor of the Romans, and Italy was briefly united with Germany in a new Christian Roman Empire. From then until 1250, relations between the papacy and the Holy Roman Empire, at first friendly but later hostile, were the main issue in Italian history.

The City-States

In the twelfth and thirteenth centuries Western Christendom's spiritual and temporal powers, the papacy and the Holy Roman Empire, competed for supremacy. During this struggle the Italian cities seized the opportunity to become self-governing republics. Supported by the papacy, the Northern cities formed the Lombard League to resist the Emperors' claims of sovereignty. Papal power and influence reached their peak under Pope Innocent III (1198–1216).

Italy became a jigsaw of kingdoms, duchies, and city-states running from the Alps to Sicily. Centuries of war and trade barriers fanned animosity between neighboring Italians and reinforced local loyalties. With the exception of the territory of Rome, ruled by the Pope, most of these states succumbed to foreign rule. Each preserved its own distinct government and

customs and vernacular. Italian history was
marked less by political achievements than by
achievements in the human sphere. The great
cities and medieval centers of learning were
founded in this period—the University of
Bologna, founded in the twelfth century, is
Europe's oldest.

The Italian Renaissance

The fourteenth century saw the beginnings of the
Italian Renaissance, the great cultural explosion
that found sublime expression in learning and
the arts. In the move from a religious to a more
secular worldview, Humanism—the "new
learning" of the age—rediscovered the civilization
of classical antiquity; it explored the physical
universe and placed the individual at its center.
Boccaccio and Petrarch wrote major works
in Italian rather than Latin. In painting and

sculpture, the quest for knowledge led to greater naturalism and interest in anatomy and perspective, recorded in the treatises of the artist-philosopher Leon Battista Alberti.

During this period the arts were sponsored by Italy's wealthy ruling families such as the Medici in Florence, the Sforzas in Milan, and the Borgias in Rome. This was the age of the "universal man"—polymaths and artistic geniuses such as Leonardo da Vinci, whose studies included painting, architecture, science, and engineering, and  Michelangelo, who was not only a sculptor and painter, but also an architect and a poet. Other great artists were Raphael and Titian. Architects such as Brunelleschi and Bramante studied the buildings of ancient Rome to achieve balance, clarity, and proportion in their works. Andrea Palladio adapted the principles of classical architecture to the requirements of the age, creating the Palladian style.

Andreas Vesalius, who made dissection of the human body an essential part of medical studies, taught anatomy at Italian universities. The composer Giovanni Palestrina was the master of Renaissance counterpoint, at a time when Italy was the source culture of European music. Galileo Galilei produced seminal work in physics and

astronomy before being arrested by the Inquisition in 1616 and obliged to recant his advocacy of the Copernican view of the solar system in 1633.

The invention of printing and the geographical voyages of discovery gave further impetus to the Renaissance spirit of inquiry and scepticism. In its bid to halt the spread of Protestantism and heterodoxy, however, the Counter-Reformation almost extinguished intellectual freedom in sixteenth-century Italy.

Foreign Invasions

In the fifteenth century most of Italy was ruled by five rival states—the city-republics of Milan, Florence, and Venice in the north; the Papal Sates in the center; and the southern Kingdom of the Two Sicilies (Sicily and Naples having been united in 1442). Their wars and rivalries laid them open to invasions from France and Spain. In 1494 Charles VIII of France invaded Italy to claim the Neapolitan crown. He was forced to withdraw by a coalition of Milan, Venice, Spain, and the Holy Roman Empire.

In the sixteenth and seventeenth centuries Italy became an arena for the dynastic struggles of the ruling families of France, Austria, and Spain. After the defeat of France by Spain at Pavia, the Pope hastily put together an alliance against the Spaniards. The Habsburg Emperor Charles V defeated him and in 1527 his German mercenaries sacked Rome and stabled their horses in the Vatican. For some modern historians this act symbolizes the end of the Renaissance in Italy.

Spain was the new world power in the sixteenth century, and the Spanish Habsburgs dominated Italy. Charles V, who was both King of Spain and Archduke of Austria, ruled Naples and Sicily. In the seventeenth century Italy was effectively part of the Spanish Empire, and went into economic and cultural decline. After the Treaty of Utrecht in 1713, Austria replaced Spain as the dominant power, though the Kingdom of Naples came under Spanish Bourbon rule in 1735, leaving a profound influence on the culture of the South.

French Rule

The old order was swept aside by the French revolutionary wars. In the years 1796–1814 Napoleon Bonaparte conquered Italy, setting up satellite states and introducing the principles of the French Revolution. At first he divided Italy into a number of puppet republics. Later, after his rise to absolute power in France, he gave the former Kingdom of the Two Sicilies to his brother

Joseph, who became King of Naples. (This later passed to his brother-in-law Joachim Murat.) The Northern territories of Milan and Lombardy were incorporated into a new Kingdom of Italy, with Napoleon as King and his stepson Eugène Beauharnais ruling as Viceroy.

Italians under direct French rule were subject to the jurisdiction of the Code Napoleon, and became accustomed to a modern, centralized state and an individualistic society. In the Kingdom of Naples feudal privileges were abolished, and ideas of democracy and social equality were implanted. So although the period of French rule in Italy was short-lived, its legacy was a taste for political liberty and social equality, and a new-found sense of national patriotism.

In creating the Kingdom of Italy, Napoleon brought together for the first time most of the independent city-states in the northern and central parts of the peninsula, and stimulated the desire for a united Italy. At the same time, in the South there arose the revolutionary secret society of the *Carbonari* ("Charcoal-burners"), which aimed to free Italy from foreign control and secure constitutional government.

The Unification of Italy

After Napoleon's fall in 1815, the victorious Allies sought to restore the balance of power in Europe. Italy was again divided between Austria (Lombardy-Venetia), the Pope, the kingdoms of Sardinia and Naples, and four smaller duchies. However, the genie was out of the bottle.

Nationalist and democratic ideals remained alive and found expression in the movement for Italian unity and independence called the *Risorgimento* ("Resurrection"). In 1831 the utopian radical Giuseppe Mazzini founded a movement called "Young Italy," which campaigned widely for a unified republic. His most celebrated disciple was the flamboyant Giuseppe Garibaldi, who had started his long revolutionary career in South America. The chief architect of the *Risorgimento*, however, was Count Camillo Cavour, the liberal Prime Minister of the Kingdom of Sardinia.

The repressive regimes imposed on Italy inspired revolts in Naples and Piedmont in 1820–21, in the Papal States, Parma, and Modena in 1831, and throughout the peninsula in 1848–49. These were suppressed everywhere except in the constitutional monarchy of Sardinia, which became the champion of Italian nationalism. Cavour's patient and skillful diplomacy won over British and French support for the struggle against absolutism. With the help of Napoleon III, Victor Emmanuel II of Sardinia expelled the Austrians from Lombardy in 1859. The following year, Garibaldi and his army of  1,000 volunteers (known as "*I Mille,*" the Thousand in Italian, or the Red Shirts) landed in

Sicily. Welcomed as liberators by the people, they swept aside the despotic Bourbon dynasty and made their way north up the peninsula.

Victor Emmanuel then entered the Papal States and the two victorious armies met at Naples, where Garibaldi handed over the command of his troops to his monarch. On March 17, 1861, Victor Emmanuel was proclaimed King of Italy at Turin. Venice and part of Venetia were secured by another war with Austria in 1866, and in 1870 Italian forces occupied Rome, in defiance of the Pope, thus completing the unification of Italy. The spiritual autonomy of the Pope was recognized by the Law of Guarantees, which also gave him the status of a reigning monarch over a certain number of buildings in Rome. The Vatican became a self-governing state within Italy.

With the passing of the heroes of the *Risorgimento*, the national government in Rome

became associated with corruption and inefficiency. A sense that Italy's unity had been made possible largely by its enemy's enemies (France and Prussia) and real economic hardship led to demoralization and serious unrest. There were bread riots in Milan in 1898, followed by crackdowns on socialist movements. Against this backdrop, in 1900 King Umberto I was assassinated by an anarchist.

Italy now entered the arena of European power politics and started to entertain colonial ambitions. Thwarted by France in Tunis, Italy joined Germany and Austria in the Triple Alliance in 1882 and occupied Eritrea, making it a colony in 1889. An attempt to seize Abyssinia (Ethiopia) was decisively defeated at Adowa in 1896. However, war with Turkey in 1911–12 brought Libya and the Dodecanese islands in the Aegean, and dreams of the rebirth of a glorious overseas Roman Empire. On the outbreak of the First World War, Italy denounced the Triple Alliance and remained neutral, but in 1915 entered on the side of the Allies. The treaties of 1919, however, awarded Italy far less than it demanded—Trieste, the Trentino, and South Tyrol, but, importantly, very little in the colonial sphere. This humiliation would rankle for years to come.

The postwar period in Italy saw intense political and social unrest, which the universally despised governments were too weak to subdue. Patriotic disappointment with the outcome of the war was swelled by the existence of large numbers of ex-servicemen. In 1919 the nationalist poet and aviator Gabriele D'Annunzio led an unofficial army to seize the Croatian port of Fiume, awarded to Yugoslavia under the Treaty of Versailles. Although the coup collapsed after three months, it proved to be a dress rehearsal for the Fascist takeover four years later.

The March on Rome

In the following years inflation, unemployment, riots, and crime were rife. Workers' soviets were set up in factories. Socialists and Communists marched through the streets. Against this background, the "clean sweep" offered by Benito Mussolini's right-wing populist Fascist movement appealed widely to the threatened middle classes, industrialists, and landowners, and to patriots of all classes. Its insignia was the ancient Roman symbol of authority, the *fasces*— an ax surrounded by rods tightly bound together for strength and security. Electoral gains in 1921 led to growing arrogance and violence, and squads of armed Fascists attacked and terrorized their enemies in the big towns.

In October 1922 the fiery young Mussolini addressed thousands of black-shirted followers at a rally in Naples demanding the handover of government; the crowd responded with chants of "*Roma, Roma, Roma.*" The Fascist militias mobilized. Luigi Facta, the last constitutional Prime Minister, resigned, and thousands of

Blackshirts, or "*Camicie Nere,*" marched on Rome unopposed. King Victor Emmanuel III appointed Mussolini Prime Minister, and Italy entered a dangerous new era.

The Fascist Years

Mussolini moved quickly to secure the loyalty of the army. Critically, he reconciled the Italian state with the estranged Vatican, signing a solemn Concordat with the Pope in 1929 that conferred authority on his government. Although technically still a constitutional monarchy, Italy was now a dictatorship. The Fascist regime brutally destroyed all opposition, and exerted almost complete control over every facet of Italian life. In the early years, despite the suppression of individual liberties, it won wide acceptance by improving the administration, stabilizing the economy, improving workers' conditions, and inaugurating a program of public works. Italy's man of destiny, *il Duce* ("the Leader"), was idolized and came to embody the corporate state. There are obvious parallels with Adolf Hitler's regime in Germany. Unlike the

Nazis, however, Fascist doctrine did not include a theory of racial purity. Anti-Semitic measures were introduced only in 1938, probably under German pressure, and were never followed through in anything like the German manner.

Mussolini saw himself as heir to the Roman emperors, and aggressively set about building an empire. The well-equipped Italian army sent to conquer Ethiopia in 1935–36 used poison gas and bombed Red Cross hospitals. When threatened with sanctions, Italy joined Nazi Germany in the Axis alliance of 1936. In April 1939 Italy invaded Albania, whose king fled, after which Victor Emmanuel was proclaimed King of Italy and Albania, and Emperor of Ethiopia. Naturally supportive of fellow dictators, Mussolini intervened on the side of General Franco's nationalist forces in the Spanish Civil War (1936–39), and entered the Second World War as an ally of Germany.

The war did not go well for Italy. Defeats in North Africa and Greece, the Allied invasion of Sicily, and discontent at home destroyed Mussolini's prestige. He was forced to resign by his own Fascist Council in 1943. The new Italian government under Marshal Badoglio surrendered to the Allies and declared war on Germany. Rescued by German parachutists, Mussolini established a breakaway government in northern Italy. The Germans occupied northern and central Italy, and until its final liberation in 1945 the country was a battlefield. Mussolini and his mistress, Clara Petacci, were captured by Italian partisans at Lake Como while trying to flee the country, and shot. Their bodies were hung upside down in a public square in Milan.

POSTWAR ITALY

In 1946 Victor Emmanuel abdicated in favor of his son, Umberto II, who reigned for thirty-four days. In a referendum in June, Italians voted (by 12 million to 10 million) to abolish the monarchy, and Italy became a republic. It was stripped of its colonies in 1947. A new constitution came into force the following year, and the Christian Democrats emerged as the party of government.

The new monarch abdicated and, with all members of the house of Savoy, was forbidden to reenter the country. (In May 2003 the Senate voted by 235 to 19 to allow the royal family, the Savoia, to return to Italy.)

In attempting to weld the peninsula's separate entities into a single unified kingdom, Italy's early leaders had created a highly bureaucratic state that was tailor-made for Mussolini to manipulate fifty years later. This overcentralized system, run from Rome, survived the downfall of Fascism and the end of the discredited monarchy, but it landed the fledgling republic with a huge and costly bureaucracy and antiquated mechanisms for decision-making.

For most of the second half of the twentieth century, Italy was governed by an increasingly corrupt Christian Democrat–Liberal–Socialist coalition. Endless power struggles within the coalition caused governments to collapse and reconstitute themselves with notorious regularity, but the regime was assumed to be a fixture. Since it was a powerful source of patronage, its excesses remained unchecked until the early 1990s, when scandalous revelations of graft at all levels of politics and big business caused the Christian Democrat majority to wither away overnight. For the Italians, this was almost as momentous an event as the end of the Soviet Empire.

The darkest period in Italy's postwar history, echoes of which can be heard even today, were the *anni di piombo*, or "Years of Lead." During what one Italian journalist described as a low-intensity civil war in the 1960s, there were 15,000 terrorist attacks in which 491 Italians were killed, including leading politicians such as the Christian Democrat leader Aldo Moro. The *anni di piombo* lasted right up to the early 1980s and spawned a number of notorious groups such as the Red Brigades (*Brigate Rosse*), and atrocities by left-wing activists such as the explosion in Piazza Fontana in Milan in 1969. In this period Italy was plagued by crime from both left and right.

The Mafia, the traditional source of organized crime in Italy, originating in Sicily, controlled local politicians and businesses, often with considerable internal violence, and assassinated judges and politicians who resisted them. (In Sicily the Mafia is known as the Cosa Nostra; its Neapolitan counterpart is the Camorra.)

The *Mani Pulite* Campaign

The 1990s saw the *Mani Pulite*, or "Clean Hands," anticorruption campaign to clean up public life. Although there is a degree of cynicism about the results, the campaign marked a break with the violent extremist politics of the '60s and '70s and the emergence of a more mainstream government. After major electoral reforms, the 1996 elections were a fight between the old-established opposition parties and a cluster of newcomers, the ex-Communists and their allies versus a hastily assembled right-wing coalition consisting of the reformed neo-Fascists, a rapidly growing Northern separatist party (the Lega Nord, also known just as the Lega), and Forza Italia, led by the media tycoon (and one of the world's richest men) Silvio Berlusconi. For fifty years after the Second World War, Italy had succeeded in keeping its two extremes, Fascism and Communism, out of national government. The Communists were the second-largest and best-organized party in Italy but were excluded due to the Cold War fear of Marxism. The neo-Fascists were still seen as too closely associated with memories of the rule of Mussolini.

Now the old antagonists have changed their images and today both right and left are trying to present themselves as "mainstream." The ex-Communists (rebaptized Partito Democratico della Sinistra, or PDS) were the leading players in the center-left coalition that led the country after 1996 and presided over the stringent fiscal reforms that enabled Italy to join the European Monetary Union in January 1999.

The Age of Berlusconi

In the 2001 elections, Silvio Berlusconi, head of Mediaset and a range of other international and national business interests, and leader of the Forza Italia coalition in the Italian Parliament, became prime minister. The following year, Italy held the presidency of the European Union.

Berlusconi was the longest serving prime minister in Italian history but stood down in 2011 following his failure to achieve an outright majority in Parliament and on a budget vote and faced with an increasing number of scandals in his own private life.

Faced with a leaderless coalition, the President appointed a former economics professor, Mario Monti, as head of a "government of technocrats" with the remit to initiate reforms aimed at putting the faltering Italian economy back on its feet. Monti's style was completely the opposite of Berlusconi's. He introduced a series of austerity measures aimed at rebalancing the Italian economy, notably cutting politicians' "perks," reviewing the early and generous state employees' pension scheme, and investigating and attacking tax evasion.

Monti's government coalition fell after two years, in 2013, following the withdrawal of Berlusconi's Forza Italia party. The Chamber of Deputies appointed a new prime minister, Enrico Letta in 2013, replacing him with Matteo

Renzi in 2015. Since 2011, therefore Italy has had three prime ministers but no general election.

GOVERNMENT

Under its constitution, Italy is a multiparty republic with an elected president as Head of State and a prime minister as Head of Government. There are two legislative bodies, a 325-seat Senate and a 633-seat Chamber of Deputies. Elections are held every five years. The prime minister is the leader of the party or coalition that wins the election. The country is divided administratively into twenty regions that reflect to a considerable degree its traditional regional customs and character.

POLITICS

Politics in Italy is confrontational, and at street level has sometimes been murderous, but in the end it is always about the art of accommodation.

Some Italian cities such as Bologna are famous for their left-wing politics, and the large and prosperous center-north "red" regions of Tuscany, Emilia-Romagna, and Marche have a long Communist tradition. Over the years, however, Italian politics has become more centrist,

and the country is settling into an alternation of center-left and center-right coalitions.

Apart from competing ideologies, when two strong personalities within a political party clash, the loser often starts another party, which then becomes part of one of the major coalitions.

Today in Italian politics, television is king and the center-right bloc is still dominated by Silvio Berlusconi, whose Mediaset conglomerate owns half of Italy's TV and publishing industry and a top football team, AC Milan. Despite (or perhaps because of) extensive charges of corruption and tax scams, this self-made billionaire, calling for tax cuts and deregulation, is the hero of many of Italy's small businessmen and entrepreneurs, not to mention soccer fans and TV addicts.

ECONOMIC LIFE

Fifty years ago, Italy was a largely agrarian society. It is now the eighth-biggest world economy by GDP according to the World Bank (2013 figures). Even today, though, it is characterized by great disparities of income. Pockets of wealth and industry, such as Milan, are in marked contrast to areas with a far lower standard of living, particularly in the South (known as the *Mezzogiorno*), where patron/client relationships are still common. Lombardy alone accounts for 20 percent of Italy's GDP.

Although visited for its historic art treasures, Italy strikes the visitor as a modern nation in a continuing state of evolution. It is a relatively young nation, too. This is often reflected in a "get rich quick" mentality of unrestrained commercialism. Many areas of natural beauty have been ruined by indiscriminate property development, particularly along the coasts.

Italian business life is riven with contradictions. It is dominated by small enterprises with small staff, driven by the wish to avoid taxation and labor laws. But it is also led by international companies of great drive, flair, and ingenuity. As former editor of the *Economist* magazine, Bill Emmott, points out in *Good Italy, Bad Italy*, Italian companies do well when they internationalize. Italy leads the world in fashion, automobiles, food, and luxury goods, with brands such as Prada, Ferrari, and Nutella, whose founder and president Michele Ferrero, Italy's richest man, died in 2015 at the age of eighty-nine.

chapter two

VALUES & ATTITUDES

Italy's geographical structure and historical divisions have produced a country of distinct regions, each with its own dialect, politics, and culture. For this reason one feature dominates Italian life—the family.

FAMILY FIRST

The importance of family in Italian life cannot be overestimated. Your family are the people you can trust, the people you work for, the people you do favors for or who do favors for you. The most

extreme example of "family first" is probably the Sicilian Mafia, whose code of honor permits vendettas or revenge killings between families lasting generations and whose loyalty is based entirely on the family.

At an everyday level, the Italians love talking about families and regard the family as giving you roots and a stake in society. It is always useful to carry photos of your family with you (if you don't have one, invent one!) to show around and discuss. It is one of the best ways of creating links with Italians.

Business in Italy is still dominated by family firms, with the sons or daughters of the founder frequently taking over and running the business. The Italians take family seriously and if they have known you since they were young, then you too are part of their family. When one foreign company ended its agency contract with its Italian distributor after years of unsuccessful performance, the distraught head of the Italian firm protested, "But I've known you since I was four! I sat on my father's knee while he negotiated with you." The implication was, "How could you do this to a member of your family?"

FEELINGS AND EMOTIONS

Italians are "feeling" people. They readily accept and exchange information, but ultimately decisions are made on gut feeling, with family and regional considerations also playing an important role. This means that the way they look at things tends to be particular and subjective. Rather than apply universal rules, an Italian will look at the details of each situation and decide each one on its (or your) merits. That is why, whatever the rule, there is always an exception if you can make a case for it.

This is not to say that facts have no place in Italian life, but they will always be considered in relation to the people concerned. This attitude may even bind people together who are poles apart politically. It is perfectly possible to have extreme left-wing and extreme right-wing views within the same family but this does not prevent communication. What characterizes Italian society, as American author Terri Morrison points out in *Kiss, Bow or Shake Hands*, is a strong capacity for social and cultural resilience and continuity.

THE CHURCH

Although Italy is not officially a Catholic country, the Catholic Church still has an important role in providing a structure to Italian life. Whether in opposition to it or in sympathy with it, the Church provides a focus for values and attitudes, and has shaped Italian culture. Religion is still a part of everyday life for large numbers of Italians.

The authority of the Catholic Church rests upon the apostolic succession—the belief that Christ ordained St. Peter, his successor on earth, who became the first Bishop of Rome. The Pope's word, when spoken *ex cathedra* (from his throne), is considered to be God's law.

It is impossible to overestimate the importance of the Catholic tradition in people's daily lives, whether or not they are believers or are practicing Christians. Life in Italy is to a degree influenced by your belief in or opposition to the Catholic hierarchy. Catholicism is an autocratic, top-down religion, with a hierarchy of authority extending from the Pope, down through the cardinals, archbishops, and bishops to the local parish priest. This hierarchical approach is reflected in society in the authority of the father, the structure of Italian business, the artistic culture of the people, and the church bells summoning the faithful to mass.

TOLERANCE

On the other hand, the Italians are remarkably tolerant of moral lapses that the Catholic Church finds unacceptable. So petty crime, fraud, and sexual infidelity are, if not accepted, recognized as examples of human frailty and overlooked. After all, who has not sinned at some time? The important thing is to keep up appearances at all times and at all costs. This means that Italians can be astonishingly flexible and understanding in difficult situations. A foreign middleman once drew up a contract incorrectly. Afraid of being sued by both sides, he asked his Italian counterpart if it would be possible to draw up a new one. "No problem," said the Italian. "Just give me the new contract, I'll sign it and tear up the old one. After all, we all make mistakes."

BELLA FIGURA

In Britain it's humor, in France it's ideas, in Germany it's respectability, and in Italy it's appearances that make the world go round. It's true that in Italy how you dress and act speaks volumes about you and it's important to dress and act correctly. "When in Rome, do as the Romans do," goes the popular saying, and the Romans, like all Italians, set great store by making a *bella figura*.

In a country with so many fine fashion houses, and where individuals can seem very assertive, looking good and making the right impression is paramount. The Italians, especially women, spend a small fortune on clothes and place importance on the right designer labels. So a cyclist dresses like a champion and dress rivalry starts in nursery school.

Italians claim they can spot foreigners from a mile off not only by what they wear but by how they wear it—if you protest that this is a victory of style over substance, Italians will retort that their style is part of the substance. So cutting a *bella figura* is important for visitor and businessperson alike.

This means that many problems in Italy are seen as less a matter of corruption or poor management than as poor presentation. *Fare una brutta figura* is to make a bad impression. To make a *good* impression, it is important to show off. People admire *ricchezza* (wealth) and *bellezza* (beauty). Putting on a good face to disguise a bad performance is admired. So much of Italy is a beautiful presentation, rather like a swan gliding across the surface of the water while its legs paddle furiously beneath.

LOUDNESS

Italy is traditionally noisy. Life is lived much more in public than in Britain or the USA, and private conversations can be easily overheard in the piazzas and streets. Added to this is the incessant roar of the cars and the hooting of the mopeds (*motorini*). The noise of conversation or shouted commands mingling with the sound of traffic takes some getting used to, but as English author Tobias Jones notes in *The Dark Heart of Italy,* "After a while, other countries begin to seem eerily quiet, even dull."

A characteristic of Italy is the verbal jousting as people exchange lively opinions and even criticisms in earthy, uninhibited language. It feels as if reserve and reticence have fallen away and been replaced by vivacity and sensuousness, a quality that the English writer D. H. Lawrence termed "blood knowledge."

ORDER AND HIERARCHY

Italy's strong sense of hierarchy and formality, as Tobias Jones found, is reflected in the language. "*Ciao*," the ubiquitous way of saying "Hi" and "Good-bye," is derived from *schiavo*, meaning "slave." If you go into a shop in Venice, the shopkeeper will say, "*Comandi*," or "Command me." To do all kinds of things in Italy you need to obtain permission, "*chiedere il permesso*," either informally or by the grant of a *permesso* (permit), and a situation often needs to be *sistemato* (systematized, or sorted out). *Tutto a posto*, "everything in its place," is not perhaps what you naturally expect to be an Italian ideal.

One aspect of hierarchy is the deference paid to Italy's first families, *il salotto buono*, who run the country's key industries and who have a huge influence on politics as well as business. Following the Italian penchant for nicknames, all have their pet public titles: Gianni Agnelli, the owner of Fiat, was known as *l'Avvocato* (the Lawyer), Carlo de Benedetti, media mogul and owner of *Repubblica*, is known as *l'Ingegnere* (the Engineer), and Silvio Berlusconi, former Prime Minister and owner of Mediaset, was known variously as *il Cavaliere* (the Cavalier) and *Sua Emittenza* (His Emittance, in an ironic combination of a Cardinal's title, His Eminence, with the idea of a mass-media tycoon whose stations emit broadcasts).

The Italian way is top-down, authoritarian. As an Italian associate of an international legal firm explained, "The senior partner is God. He takes all the decisions. I am there to obey." This sense of hierarchy emanates from Church and state and bureaucracy and influences both family and social life. It is made acceptable by *garbo*, and by a sense of responsibility for personal lives, and also by a tolerance of human foibles and mistakes.

GARBO

This search for order is systematized in *garbo*, which can be translated as graciousness, courtesy, politeness, good manners. It describes the ability to calm or smooth over difficult situations, usually by the use of elaborate language.

Derived from the Arabic greeting, "*Salaam Aleikum*," the *salamelecco* is the ability to use obsequious, even groveling language to obtain something from officials. To the Americans and the British, who are used to being more concise, this can be a challenge. By comparison, the Italians tend to see the British and the Americans as rather brutal and to-the-point. The expressive, courteous way of communicating in Italian means it can be very difficult to get to the point of a conversation; and it may also mean that the real issues are hidden or confused.

RELATIONSHIPS

In Italian business and social life everything depends on relationships and who you know. (More on this in Chapter 8, Business Briefing.) At any level, the way to get things done is to be introduced by a common friend, associate, or acquaintance. This *raccomandazione*, or recommendation, is vital to both business and social life. It will not necessarily ensure acceptance—that will depend on your own personal qualities—but a *raccomandazione* will ensure that you make the initial contact and are treated with consideration.

The other side of the coin is that your Italian colleagues will expect regular contact, consideration, and participation from you. Friendship needs to be worked at—contacting someone only when you need support or have something to offer is simply not enough. Once you have an Italian friend or associate it is a lifelong family relationship, not just an arm's-length cordial agreement. To be a friend of an Italian means being welcomed not just into their family but also into their community.

CAMPANILISMO AND THE PIAZZA

The Italians are local people and devoted to their community. The piazza is the symbolic center of a town and the seat of civic pride. It is close to a similar concept, *campanilismo* (literally, affection for one's own bell tower), or local patriotism. The Italians identify much more readily with their

job for life. Although civil-service jobs are now awarded on merit rather than on contacts, getting as far as the selection board may require the help of a *raccomandazione* from an important family.

Bureaucracy looms so large in the lives of Italians that an entire profession is devoted to smoothing one's way through the red tape. A *faccendiere*, or "fixer," will get you the forms, show you how to fill them in, and stand in line on your behalf. Any Italian will tell you that although most problems can be managed, a little cunning goes a long way. It pays to be *furbo*.

BEING *FURBO*

A perennial Italian preoccupation is how to beat the system: that can only be done by noncompliance until the last moment, trying to find ways of getting around laws and edicts, and generally being *furbo,* or cunning. This is the exact opposite of people who stick by the rules or play it by the book, and can cause frustration and even anger in foreigners. For an Italian, *ingenuità* doesn't mean being ingenuous but being gullible. Personal wrongdoing may be excused by comparison with the corruption that is evident at all levels of government, in the legal system, and even in the Church itself.

Being *furbo* means looking out for yourself and your family and friends, which helps to explain the Italians' cavalier attitude to traffic lights, jaywalking, pedestrian crossings, no smoking signs, speed limits, and even the wearing of seatbelts in cars. (When Italy first made seatbelts compulsory, Naples developed a thriving trade in T-shirts with a seatbelt printed across them!) Only the rules for dining and dress seem to be rigidly observed.

CONCLUSION

The key values that can be said to distinguish Italians are their adherence to personal loyalty and friendship over any commitment to universal, state-instituted laws and regulations, and their strong commitment to the local community over and even against the state. As we have seen, Italians may be Italians to foreigners, but to other Italians they are Florentines, Venetians, Milanese, Romans, Neapolitans, or Sicilians. By upholding local customs, institutions, and traditions, they create the astonishingly rich and varied tapestry of Italian life that allows the foreigner to enjoy the distinctiveness of Venice and Rome, and to appreciate the artistic creations of both the Florentine and the Venetian schools of the Italian Renaissance, and so much more besides. The Italians themselves value their local culture and traditions, whether it be in food, wine, art and architecture, music, or drama.

Italy is above all a country of contrasts. That being said, many Italians recognize the need for change—from being an inward-looking, relationship-based society, based to a large extent on patronage and privilege, to a more egalitarian society allowing greater access to jobs and the reform of labor laws and taxation to allow this. However, what no Italian wishes to lose is the quality of life, the generosity and openness of local communities, in what is still in many respects, "*il bel paese*" (the beautiful country).

FESTIVALS & TRADITIONS

Italy is predominantly a Catholic nation. Although church attendance has declined dramatically in recent years, surveys show that 80 percent of the population believe in God, and *Famiglia Cristiana* (*The Christian Family*) is still a widely read magazine in Italy. Catholic attitudes, stressing the importance of the family, still count enormously.

The power of local bishops and of the Vatican, although not overt, is immense and even if people adopt an anticlerical stance, they are still very aware of the influence of "the Church" in a way that Protestants find difficult to understand.

However, the puritanism that accompanies belief in some other Christian countries is absent from Italy. "We are all sinners," say the Italians, so peccadilloes such as tax evasion (estimated to account for up to 25 percent of GDP), and the millions of illegal dwellings built in defiance of government regulations, as well as extramarital affairs, are all unofficially recognized as part of Italian life.

Italy enjoys Christian as well as lay public holidays, although fewer than in many other Latin countries. With its strong local and regional

MAIN ITALIAN PUBLIC HOLIDAYS

DATE	FESTIVAL
January 1	New Year's Day
January 6	Epiphany
March/April	Easter Day
	Easter Monday
April 25	Liberation Day
May 1	Labor Day
June 2	Republic Day
August 15	*Ferragosto* (Assumption Day)
November 1	All Saints' Day
December 8	Immaculate Conception
December 25	Christmas Day
December 26	Santo Stefano

traditions, it also enjoys holidays associated with local areas. Every town or village has its patron saint, and on the saint's day there may well be a celebration and a day off work. Check the mayor's office or the local tourist information bureau before visiting. When a holiday falls in the middle of the week, Italians tend to "make a bridge" (*fare un ponte*) and take the extra day or two off leading into the weekend.

THE FESTIVE YEAR
Christmas
The birth of Christ is one of the two major festivals of the Christian liturgical calendar and is celebrated at home. Pine trees are erected in

the main piazzas and hung with red ribbons and other decorations, shepherds from the Abruzzi mountains play their bagpipes in the streets of Rome, and Naples' historic center swarms with people buying the traditional figurines for their Christmas cribs. It is the perfect time to visit towns that are usually clogged by tourists, such as Rome, Florence, and Venice. Although Italians tend to leave the big cities to spend Christmas with their families, the tradition of eating out continues, so you can share the atmosphere of a real family Christmas meal. One warning: book first, otherwise you won't get in.

If you are in Rome over Christmas, High Mass on Christmas Day at the Vatican is a great event. After the Pope has presided over the mass, assisted by his cardinals, he addresses the faithful in the piazza in front of St. Peter's, flanked by a phalanx of *carabinieri* and the Vatican's own Swiss Guards.

New Year's Day and Epiphany
While Christmas is spent at home with the family, New Year's Eve is the time to party with friends. For the Italians (as for the Spanish), another important festival is Twelfth Night, or Epiphany, the day the three Wise Men, or the Three Kings, visited Christ's crib in Bethlehem.

It is a custom on New Year's Eve to get rid of unwanted objects. New Year's Day is a great time to salvage good-quality discarded possessions— you may find anything from a slightly battered leather sofa to last-season's Gucci handbag.

As well as Father Christmas (known as *Babbo Natale* in Italian), Italy has the *Befana*, a little old lady, ugly but wise, who stuffs socks with sweets as presents on Epiphany.

Easter

The second-biggest festival in the Catholic Church is Easter, which celebrates the death and resurrection of Christ. Although Christmas is more widely celebrated by the general public, from a religious point of view Easter is more important.

Although Easter Day (Sunday) and Easter Monday are the official public holidays, many Italians will also take off the whole of Holy Week, or *Settimana Santa*. All over Italy there are processions and passion plays. One of the oldest is at Chieti in Abruzzo. In Taranto in Puglia on Holy Thursday, there is a procession of the Addolorata, and on Good Friday statues displaying the Passion of Christ are carried around town. At Piana degli Albanesi, near Palermo in Sicily, Easter is celebrated according to Byzantine rites and women in fifteenth-century costumes give out Easter eggs.

On Good Friday, the *Via Crucis* ("Stations of the Cross") service is held, and all votive statues and paintings in the churches are covered in black, to mark the beginning of the feast of Easter. Many practicing Catholics will have given something up for Lent (sweets, cigarettes, eating meat on Fridays). Easter Saturday is a "normal" day—the real celebration takes place on Easter Sunday, when the statues are uncovered, the churches are filled with flowers, and the church bells ring out. Easter Day is celebrated with a huge family meal, which leaves Easter Monday as a day to recover.

Liberation Day (April 25)

This celebrates the end of the German occupation in 1945. It is marked by processions through the streets and the laying of wreaths on Italian war memorials.

Labor Day (May 1)

The international day of the worker is celebrated in some Italian towns with processions organized by trade unions and political parties.

Republic Day (June 2)

This commemorates the founding of the Republic of Italy in 1946.

All Saints (November 1)

All Saints Day venerates the love and courage of all the Christian saints and martyrs. The day after (All

Souls) is traditionally the day of the dead, when people go to the cemeteries to lay wreaths on family graves.

Immaculate Conception (December 8)
The festival of the Immaculate Conception, like the Assumption, demonstrates the great reverence in which the Virgin Mary is held by the Catholic Church. The feast celebrates the purity of the Virgin, who gave birth to the Son of God through divine conception, and is marked by church services and processions.

ANNUAL VACATIONS

Italians take a month's vacation every year and this tends to be in August, when most family firms close down completely—except for those in the tourist trade, which tend to take their vacations over Christmas and the New Year, so if you are visiting major cities at that time, don't be surprised if some of your guidebook's recommendations are closed. Although August is the official vacation month, things tend to slow down in July in preparation for the holiday, and are slow in picking up again in September.

A particularly popular vacation time for the Italians is the week around August 15 (the feast of the Assumption of the Virgin Mary), known as *Ferragosto*. Many shops and restaurants close from then until early September, giving Italian cities a strangely deserted air.

LOCAL HOLIDAYS

One of the unexpected results of *campanilismo* (the strong sense of local identity) is that local saint's days often become unofficial local holidays. In Parma, for example, January 13 is the feast of St. Hilary, the town's patron saint, and no one in Parma works on that day.

In the capital, Rome, additional local holidays are: April 21 (which celebrates the founding of the city by Romulus), and June 29 (the days celebrating St. Peter and St. Paul, the city's patron saints).

Italy has far too many local festivals to mention here, but two of the best-known internationally are *Carnevale* and Siena's *Palio*.

CARNEVALE

In the ten days or so before Ash Wednesday, many towns put on carnivals as one last blow-out before Lent, the six-week period of fasting and abstinence leading to Easter. The most famous is in Venice, with its masked balls and gondola processions and invitation to general licentiousness. Many celebrations in Italy hark back to the Middle Ages and are commemorated with revivals of medieval fairs, horseback sports, and costumes.

The day before Ash Wednesday is known as *Martedì Grasso* (Mardi Gras), when Venetians and visitors alike don the *bautta* (a hood and cape) and the *tabarro* (a cloak), with a tricorn hat and a white decorated mask. This allows people to

go around incognito. Not everyone dresses up, but Venice is full of boutiques ready and able to sell you the gear, and you'll have a lot more fun if you join in.

THE *PALIO*

One of the most famous of the medieval throwbacks is Siena's *Palio* (literally, banner), in which members of the different quarters of the town ride bareback in a horse race around the central piazza. The event includes a parade in which their supporters in medieval costume go before them. The *Palio* takes place twice a year, on July 2 and August 16, and is the climax of five days of rehearsals and months of preparation.

In the Middle Ages, each of Siena's seventeen *contrade*, or districts, provided a local militia to defend the city against Florence. Over the years their administrative role waned but their social

influence grew. The *contrada* registers baptisms, marriages, and deaths; and many Sienese men and women are reluctant to marry outside it. The original purpose of the *Palio* was to give thanks to the Madonna, but it is really a competition between the *contrade*, each team with its own colors and flag. The race itself lasts barely ninety seconds, but is preceded by some three hours of pageantry and parades. The winning *contrada* is presented with the banner (the *palio*), which is the prize, and each team then retires to its own neighborhood for a celebratory meal, with long tables laid out in the back streets and alleys.

NAME-DAYS

Italians often celebrate their name-days. A name-day (*onomastico*) is the feast day of the particular saint after whom someone is named. So Antonio will celebrate the day dedicated to St. Anthony of Padua, and Francesca will celebrate the day dedicated to St. Francis of Assisi, perhaps even taking the day off work and enjoying a celebratory meal with friends and family.

This is not to say that Italians don't work hard or appreciate hard work in others. But it is hard work for a specific purpose, or to get a specific job done on time to the required standard. Workaholics are not appreciated!

SAINTS

A person who is recognized as having lived a holy life, or who is notable for the manner of their death (martyrdom in defense of the Faith, for example), may become a saint in the Catholic Church. The candidate's life and background are subjected to exhaustive examination—reported miracles must be scientifically authenticated—and, if accepted, this leads, first, to beatification and then to canonization by the Pope.

Padre Pio

One of the most important candidates for sainthood in Italy in recent times was Padre Pio (1887–1968), a parish priest in San Giovanni Rotondo in the Gargano mountains of the southern region of Puglia. This is now Italy's most visited tourist spot, with 6 million visitors a year (even more popular than Lourdes in France). His fame derives from the fact that in 1918 he became the only Catholic priest to receive the stigmata, the appearance of the bleeding wounds of Christ's crucifixion in his hands and feet. During his life and after his death, numerous unexplained events are alleged to have occurred. Padre Pio was beatified in 1999 and was canonized as a saint by Pope John Paul II in 2002.

BEHAVIOR IN CHURCH

Because many festivals are celebrated in church, which is also where the most magnificent art, architecture, and sculpture are to be found, it is important to be aware of the correct way to behave in a Catholic church. Clothing, first: in many churches, it is seen as disrespectful for a woman to enter wearing shorts and a low-cut top, although it is no longer necessary to cover one's head (and men should not wear a hat). So do not wander in and out of churches in shorts, sun tops, and baseball caps. You will see older women with shawls over their heads as a mark of respect.

In a Catholic church, God is always present in the host, kept in the tabernacle on the high altar or in one of the side chapels. It is denoted by a small red oil lamp left burning. You will find that many worshipers genuflect at the entrance to the nave that leads up to the altar, or when crossing in front of the altar. As you enter the church, there is always a bowl set into the wall by the door, containing holy water. Practicing Catholics will dip their fingers into it on entering and leaving the church, and make the sign of the cross.

It is important to remember that a church is a place of worship (in popular tourist sites, one area may be roped off for prayer), so a quiet, low-voiced, and respectful demeanor is appropriate.

SUPERSTITION

Where there is devotion, there is also superstition. "Italy is a land full of ancient cults, rich in natural and supernatural powers," said the Italian film director Federico Fellini, "and so everyone feels its influence. After all, whoever seeks God, finds him ... wherever he wants."

Italians are addicted to superstition. Fortune-tellers are given space on national TV, and astrologers and diviners are ubiquitous. Superstitions are often specific to particular regions, arising as they do from local peasant myths and beliefs. (They are particularly strong in the South.) What they have in common is a belief in good and bad luck, and the presence of spirits.

GOOD AND BAD LUCK

For a religious country like Italy, it may be surprising that it is considered unlucky to see a nun, and Italians may touch iron (their equivalent of touching wood for luck) to ward off the bad luck.

- To hear a cat sneeze is considered lucky, but to have a bird in the house is unlucky.
- Peacock feathers may be banned from the home because the big circular eye in the feather looks like "the evil eye."
- Chrysanthemums in Italy are only for graves, and they are always associated with funerals—don't take them as a present for your hostess!
- Italy's unlucky number (not strictly observed) is 17 because it is the sum of the Latin letters VIXI, which can be read as "I have lived," or "I'm now dead"! Thirteen, unlucky in most Western cultures, is considered lucky in Italy. However, 13 is still an unlucky number to have around a table, and 4 is also associated with death.
- *Gnocchi* are small round potato dumplings. Eating them on September 29 brings good luck.

Malocchio (pronounced "malockio;" the evil eye) is an important element in Italian superstition. Extending your little and index fingers, while keeping the others folded down, is supposed to ward off the evil spirit that someone has put on you. Some people wear a necklace or bracelet with a horn-shaped charm (*corno*) to ward off the evil eye.

Even a compliment may invoke the evil spirit. If someone praises your small son or daughter, for example, you may fear this has attracted the evil eye. Parents may make the sign of the horn over a child to protect it. One way of telling whether someone has put the evil eye on you is to pour oil into holy water—if the oil spreads, it's a good sign, but if it coagulates, you're in trouble!

A number of superstitions surround death and burial. For example, taking a coffin to the cemetery by one route and returning by another is meant to confuse the dead and avoid them returning. Putting salt under a person's head in the coffin was done for the same reason. It was common to place the deceased's favorite personal effects in the coffin and, if something was forgotten, to include it in the next burial as it could be safely assumed that both the dead would meet up in heaven.

CONCLUSION

Italy does not just have historical and religious festivals but some of Europe's most important music, drama, and film festivals as well. More about those in Chapter 6, Time Out.

chapter four

MAKING FRIENDS

The Italians are used to foreigners. Pilgrims, poets, merchants, artists, tourists, and invading armies have all made their way through the country. In the eighteenth and early nineteenth centuries no young English nobleman's education was complete without the "Grand Tour" of Europe, taking in the famous sights that tourists still flock to today. Venice, for example, has about 270,000 inhabitants, but 9.8 million visitors a year!

ESTEROFILIA

By and large, Italians are friendly people who are "*esterofiliac.*" This describes a liking for all things foreign; it is manifested in the wide use of foreign words, particularly English words in broadcasting and sports. This is not a linguistic failure of Italian but a delight in incorporating buzzwords from other languages and Italianizing them. A football manager is "*il mister,*" for example, and the terms *corner*, *dribblando* (dribbling), and *offside* are common in football commentary.

CLOSE-KNIT CIRCLES

Forming close links with Italians can be more difficult, however. The Italians are essentially local people with strong and extensive family and regional links. Their close friendships are formed when they are young and remain a tight circle all their lives. They often feel no need to reach outside it, and have difficulty understanding how anyone else doesn't have their own network.

Outside the big international cities it can be hard to break into the local community. When the English author Tim Parks and his Italian wife, Rosa, moved to a small village on the outskirts of Verona, they found it a slow and gradual process. He describes this with humor and insight in his book, *Italian Neighbours*.

Even before Tim got to know his neighbors, he paid a visit to the village *bar/pasticceria*, a habit he considers essential for anyone wishing to integrate into Italian life. Timing, he stresses, is important. Everything has its right time, and the measure of how well you've integrated is that you know when to order your *cappuccino* (before 10:30 a.m.) and your *digestivo*, or Prosecco. Pick up the local newspaper (which all bars are legally obliged to provide) to get a sense of what's going on.

Gradually, you advance and are recognized. Someone nods to you. Once they know you are a native English-speaker, you may be asked to help with a short translation. In time you will get to know your neighbors. The initial contact may be formal, but polite and kind; while Italians recognize the importance of hospitality, they prefer to retain a degree of formality at first.

Doing a service or being useful to the people in your building can help build up good relations, but remember, the Italian sense of privacy can be just as strong as that of the British. As Tim Parks observes, "If the Englishman's home is his castle, an Italian's is his bunker."

When talking to Italians, an obsession with health and doctors is a common subject. Blood pressure, visits to the doctor, and tests are all exhaustively discussed, quite often on very slight acquaintance. The superiority of all things Italian is taken as a matter of course by Italians, although they will show a polite interest in life abroad.

The initial reserve toward outsiders applies equally to Italians from "out of town." Rosa Parks' greetings of "*Buon giorno, Signore,*" or "*Buona sera, Signora,*" were met with embarrassment and silence until, eventually, nods of acknowledgment were accompanied by a return greeting.

The breakthrough, Tim found, came when his wife became pregnant. Suddenly the couple weren't fly-by-nights but people with a recognized role in society. A family distinguishes you as a "serious person," someone who can take responsibility. That is why in Italy business colleagues will inquire about your family. A family means you have something to lose, a network of support, a sense of responsibility. This gives a sense of belonging that is in no way reflected in modern British or American society.

COMMITMENT

As befits a land with close, long-standing networks of relationships and trust, friends are always in contact with each other. This provides a tremendous sense of security, but for people used to their own space it can all prove rather intense! Your new Italian friends will shower you with invitations so that every weekend there is something to do. The downside is that whenever invited to weddings, birthdays, and funerals, you will be expected to go. The only respite is to leave the country. Unlike the British and the Americans, who, once a connection is made, are able to pick up a conversation several months later, the Italians expect you to maintain constant contact.

The political philosopher Antonio Gramsci wrote: "Rather than joining political parties and trade unions, Italians prefer joining organizations of a different type, like cliques, gangs, *camorras*, and mafias." Circles of friends are just such a clique—supportive, but sometimes a bit stifling.

For an Italian, a relationship implies responsibilities. You don't just drop in or out of a friendship when it pleases you. You are either on the inside or on the outside.

JEALOUSY

June Collins, an attractive single teacher living
and working in Italy, discovered another aspect
of Italian friendship, based on gender. As Luigi
Barzini says in *The Italians*, Italy is a crypto-
matriarchy. Men run Italy but women run men.
The way they run them is to seduce them. The
Italian woman is beautifully turned-out, and, on
the surface, quite subservient to men, especially in
public. To a young Scot like June, eager to make
women friends like those at home in Edinburgh,
it was upsetting to find that the other women
teachers were wary of her. June was used to
holding her own in men's company, and she was
surprised to see that Italian women appeared to
be more submissive when in a mixed group.

POWER

The secret of any Italian structure, says Barzini,
is who holds the power: the ultimate source
of power is the family. "Family loyalty," he
writes, "is the Italians' true patriotism." This
explains why an Italian may behave formally
to you in the office but be informal at home. In
the home you are part of a different network.
Foreigners find the contrast contradictory and
even disillusioning. The Italians see no such
contradiction. The two worlds are entirely
different domains. Any foreign territory is hostile
until proven friendly or harmless. If you can't
ignore it or adopt it, then you deceive or suborn
it in whatever way you can.

INVITATIONS

Invitations home are therefore an important step in the development of a relationship, as are invitations to family events such as birthdays, name-days, weddings, and funerals. If a family invites you to church, do go—even if you aren't Catholic. As the Protestant Henry of Navarre is supposed to have said when invited to be King of France, on condition he converted to Catholicism, "Paris is worth a mass."

GIFT GIVING

Gift giving in some cultures can be a minefield. Common sense will get you through. If invited to an Italian home, gift-wrapped chocolates, pastries, or flowers are acceptable. Italy is an "odd number" country, so do not give an even number of flowers. Also avoid taking chrysanthemums, which are laid on graves at funerals and on November 2, All Souls Day (known as *il Giorno dei Morti*). Brooches, handkerchiefs, and knives all suggest sadness or loss so these should be avoided.

SOCIAL CLUBS

Most major Italian cities have expatriate sports and social clubs and organizations that cater to all nationalities. The American Women's Club, the

Rotary Club, Anglo-Italian clubs, and Lion Clubs all have branches in Italy. These can be a real point of contact for visitors as they offer a wide range of activities, and short-term membership is often available. Many organize Italian classes as well. Clubs are a good way to meet people (check the local tourist office for details).

BARS AND NIGHTLIFE

On the whole, it's not difficult to meet Italians. They are outdoorsy and outgoing. Social life revolves around the piazzas, with their bars and cafés, many with live music in the evening. There are even Irish pubs in northern Italy.

For young Italians, there is a lively clubbing culture. Discos are often huge and spread over many floors; they charge a high entrance fee (the price usually includes your first drink). They open around 11:30 p.m. Ask your hotel, or look in the local paper, for the best "in" place of the moment.

If you enjoy gambling and fancy a small wager, you'll need your passport to enter a casino. Italians are not allowed in unless they can prove they are employed. Evening wear is obligatory. Opening hours are from 2:00 or 3:00 p.m. to around 4:30 a.m. Be careful not to confuse the word *casinò* (with the stress on the last syllable), which means casino, with the Italian *casino* (stress on the second syllable), which means brothel!

CONCLUSION

Friendship is a gift and the Italians are famous for it. No people could be warmer or more hospitable, but they realize that friendship must be worked at—it is a contact sport. Regular contact and, where possible, face-to-face meetings, are what count. The building of opportunities to help each other in an inhospitable world is an important part of that. Chapter 5 shows how that belief translates into everyday life.

chapter five

DAILY LIFE

Italian life is rooted in the family and the
network of close family friends. As we have seen,
they are the ones who can always be relied on.
This attitude has led to a realistic and slightly
pessimistic view of life.

HOUSING

In the cities, most Italians live in rented
apartments, but in the suburbs and small towns
and villages, families own their own houses.

Housing is extremely
hard to come by in
Italy, and many people
wait years before
moving into their
own home. Italian
apartments can be
quite small. Three-
bedroom apartments
are rare but two
bathrooms are
common. The Italians
take great pride in
decoration and design

and spare no expense to make their homes beautiful. The use of marble, wood, and stone is common. Italy is famous for its ceramics, which can be found in bathrooms and in kitchens. Bathrooms will normally have a toilet and a bidet, and the washing machine is often placed in the bathroom rather than the kitchen.

When Italians move they take everything with them except, literally, the kitchen sink and perhaps the bath. All furnishings, including fixtures and fittings, have to be installed, usually by a local artisan/carpenter. Every Italian has his or her "special" person whom they will recommend. Italian floors are usually tiled rather than carpeted. Parquet flooring is expensive and tends to be reserved for the "master" bedroom.

One interesting feature of many Italian houses is the top-floor balcony, which is open to the elements and called a *loggia*. Another is the basement *taverna*. This is a sort of playroom or rumpus room for grownups, which is used for parties and barbecues. It may have a fireplace, wines, rustic-style furniture. Found in newer houses, the *taverna* is a throwback to the old Italian hunting lodge and may be where the *condominio* inhabitants join up with friends on the mid-August bank holiday of *Ferragosto*, or on Liberation Day on April 25.

Some experts say that if you intend to stay in Italy for less than five years it is more economical to rent than to buy, but beyond that it is worth considering buying. Some foreigners buy into a *condominio*, a group of apartments around a garden and perhaps a swimming pool, in which utilities and general upkeep are shared between the owners. If you do this, always make sure that your contract allows you full use of the facilities.

Experts also suggest that, even if you eventually intend to buy, it is better to rent for the first six to nine months, and to do so in the worst part of the year weather-wise. Many foreigners have bought in the balmy spring and autumn and repented at leisure in the steaming hot summer or damp freezing winter.

The Italian rental market is strong, with houses and apartments available in all categories. Rentals are usually unfurnished (*non ammobiliato*), and long-term furnished rentals (*ammobiliato*) are rare. Some properties are rented semi-furnished, in which case they are like a self-catering apartment. For detailed advice on renting or buying accommodation in Italy, consult Graeme Chesters' *Living and Working in Italy* (see Further Reading). One piece of advice he gives is that the worst time to look for apartments or houses is September/October. That is when the Italians are back from vacation and their wanderlust translates into the search for a new home.

SHOPPING

The Italians like to buy their food fresh, and going to the market is an important part of daily life. Italy works on the metric system, and items are bought in kilos (kilograms), half-kilos, or grams (usually measured in hundreds). There are

permanent indoor markets, street markets, and traveling markets, which are usually cheaper than stores (depending on your bargaining skills). As well as fresh local produce you can buy all kinds of manufactured products, including clothes.

Supermarkets are not as ubiquitous as in North America or Britain and account for about six percent of the Italian food market. Small grocery stores and open-air markets are still the preferred way of shopping, but the major supermarkets are Coop Italia, Interdis, Conad, and SPAR. Italians

take their own bags to the supermarket (plastic bags are usually charged for and there is no "bagging and carry-out" policy).

Milan and Rome are the centers of Italy's department stores, of which the most famous is La Rinascente (www.rinascente.it) as well as Metro, Standa, and Upim. Department stores have international facilities, take credit cards, usually have English speakers, and may well be easier for foreign shoppers than small local stores.

The *saldi* (sales) take place in January, and in July and August before the summer holidays, but even then prices can seem high. (Italian "cheap" is often British or American "expensive.") Sportswear and sports equipment, children's clothing, and toys are also expensive, even in the children's wear chain, Prenatal.

If you are taking children to Italy it is worth making sure you have supplies of their favorite food. It may not be available locally as children's diets in Italy are somewhat different to those in the US and the UK.

Items that can be hard to find, or are expensive, are electric kettles, duvets, and bayonet light bulbs (only screw-type bulbs are sold in Italy).

Italy works on the standard two-prong round pin at 220 volts and 50 hertz, so although British appliances work perfectly, American ones will need an adaptor. Phone adaptors for modem connection may be different, and you may wish to buy one of the multiadaptor packs available at airport duty-free stores.

Shopping Hours

Shops normally open from about 8:30 a.m. and close around 6:00, 7:00, or 8:00 p.m. Many shops, especially in the South, take a *pausa* (long lunch break) and close between 1:00 p.m. and 3:00 or 4:00 p.m. It is always worth checking opening times. To compensate for Saturday working, many shops close on a weekday afternoon: this varies from city to city. Once again, the advantage of most department stores and supermarkets is that they are open all day.

EDUCATION

The school year runs from September to June. The state education system is supplemented by private schools, all following the national curriculum. Education starts at an early age: compulsory schooling is from six to fifteen years old, but a child may go to infant school (*scuola dell'infanzia*) as early as four. From six to eleven, children attend primary school (*scuola primaria*). At age eleven, they take the *licenza elementare* before attending middle school (*scuola media*) from eleven to fourteen. At fourteen, they take the *diploma di licenza media*, a year before the end of compulsory schooling.

Between fourteen and eighteen, children have a considerable amount of choice. They might opt for a *liceo classico* (which specializes in a traditional humanistic education), a *liceo scientifico* (scientific studies), a *liceo linguistico* (languages), a *liceo tecnico* (technical studies), or an *istituto commerciale* (commerce). Or they might prefer an arts education in a *liceo artistico*, *istituto d'arte*, *conservatorio* (musical studies), *accademia di danza*, or *accademia drammatica*. If they want to start teacher training, they will attend an *istituto magistrale* or *scuola magistrale*.

The type of school does not mean that basic subjects are excluded, but that extra hours are devoted to the disciplines in which the school specializes. The *maturità* exam at eighteen allows access to university and the *diploma di laurea* (bachelor's degree).

MILITARY SERVICE AND THE ARMED FORCES

Military service in Italy for men only was only phased out at the end of 2004.

Women can join the armed forces and since 2000 can serve in any post, including the *carabinieri*.

FINDING A JOB

Italy has relatively high unemployment with 12.9 percent of the working age population unemployed, largely due to the slow economy. Of the unemployed in 2014, 42 percent were under twenty-five years old. Youth unemployment is a major issue in Italy, resulting in increasing migration from the South to the

North, and migration from Italy to other countries in Europe in search of work. For well qualified students this may result in longer periods at university in search of further qualifications due to the lack of employment in the jobs market.

There are practically no unemployment benefits in Italy and getting on the employment ladder can be hard, even for graduates. Many go from university into vocational courses to learn a trade. One of the main employers is the family firm, where, as we have seen, sons and daughters frequently take over when their father retires. Although Italy has traditionally had the best long-term employment conditions in Europe, more than a quarter of the workforce is now on short-term contracts.

As in Britain, one of the fastest-growing sectors of the Italian economy is the service and leisure industry. On the other hand, a widespread ambition is to become a *statale* (civil servant), which offers security of employment, regular hours, and early retirement on a state pension.

MARRIAGE

Most Italians live at home until they get married. It is not uncommon to find thirty-year-olds still living with their parents, and indeed for married couples to live with parents-in-law while waiting to find a suitable house or apartment to rent or buy. Italian children therefore leave home much later than their British, American, or Australian counterparts.

BIRTH

In Italy the birth of a child is an important event, not just for the family but for the whole neighborhood. Unlike Britain, where traditionally children are "seen but not heard," in Italy children are celebrated. An Italian father's first job is to buy a rosette, blue for a boy, pink for a girl, and stick it the front door. The second is to register the birth within seven days, in the place of birth, and with two witnesses. As we have seen, Italians are born into, live by, and die by bureaucracy.

In 2014 the Italian birth rate continued to be low, at 8.9 births per 1,000 population, a condition affected not just by the difficulties of the Italian economy and changing lifestyles but also by a fall in religious conviction. The Pope himself has encouraged Italians to breed more. What has stopped the Italian population falling more rapidly is immigration, although Italy now has the second-oldest population in Europe after Germany. There are signs that from an all-time low of 1.18 children per woman in 1995, it is creeping up in the richer north and central areas of Italy.

MONEY AND BANKING

Italy is part of the Eurozone, and since 2002 the lira has no longer been legal tender. There is a strong cash economy, especially outside the major cities. Credit cards may not be accepted everywhere and it is worth checking this in restaurants and shops in smaller towns, and definitely in villages. The strength of the black market in Italy also encourages cash transactions. The important thing is not to rely on one source of funds: take both cash and credit. Always have your passport as ID and be careful of personal security. Travelers' checks are the safest form of currency, but they are not directly cashable in most hotels and restaurants.

ATM outlets, called Bancomats, are available via the CIRRUS and NYCE networks, but they often run out of money or are not in working order, so if you need weekend cash, get there in good time. Most Italian banks don't accept checks drawn on foreign banks, but travelers' checks and foreign currency can be exchanged at banks and at international stations and airports.

It is worth shopping around as rates of exchange can differ markedly. Airports and change machines offer the worst exchange rates and the highest handling charges. Banks offer the best exchange rates and post offices the lowest charges, but to American and British visitors, banks can be quite intimidating, with revolving security doors and armed guards.

Banking hours vary according to the city, but in general are from 8:30 a.m. to 1:00 p.m. They may open for a further hour from 3.00 to 4.00 p.m. in the afternoon. They are closed on Saturdays and Sundays and on public holidays and, in the case of pubic holidays, may also close on the Friday afternoon. It is important to check in advance. Major hotels can change money and advise you where the nearest ATM is.

Credit Cards

The main credit cards accepted in Italy are Mastercard, Visa, and Carta Sì. Credit cards are less popular than debit cards, but as a foreigner your credit card can be very helpful.

Opening a Bank Account

You will need to open a bank account if you're living in Italy for any length of time. However, it isn't that easy. The majority of banks will only permit foreigners to open an account if they are in possession of a residence certificate (*certificato di residenza*). It might make life easier if you approached an Italian bank with overseas branches (*filiali*), like the Banca di Roma, before departure. Other people feel the personal approach works best, so when in Italy, try to go with a friend who is known to the bank.

> To open an account as a foreigner, you'll need the following:
> - Valid passport
> - Valid residence certificate
> - Proof of address in Italy, e.g. telephone or electricity bill, rental contract

Other useful facts about Italian banking are that bounced checks are illegal, overdrafts are very expensive, postdating checks is also illegal, and checks can be cleared on the day of writing regardless of the date. You can only stop a check if it has been lost or stolen, in which case you must report it to the police or the *carabinieri*.

KEEPING HEALTHY

A recent survey showed that Italians are among the healthiest and longest-lived people in Europe—due, it is said, to red wine, olive oil, and a Mediterranean diet. According to UN figures, men tend to live to seventy-six and women to eighty-two.

Italian health care expenditure is low, about six percent of GDP, and the standard of hospitals, especially in the South, varies widely. However, Italian doctors and medical staff are among the best-trained in the world, and Italy has the highest number of doctors per capita of any country (1 per 160 inhabitants). Many speak English. There is also a medical service for tourists with English-speaking staff (*guardia medica turistica*), and it is worth asking your embassy or consulate for a list of local English-speaking doctors.

Although Italy has a national health service (the *servizio sanitario nazionale*, or SSN, established in 1978), some Italians buy private health insurance. If you are living in Italy for any length of time, it is worth your doing so too. For Britons, who are members of the EU, an E111 form from the local British post office confirms your right to low-cost or free medical treatment on the Italian national health service, which provides free emergency health care to visitors, regardless of nationality.

If you are ill you can attend a family doctor (*medico generico*) or a health clinic (*azienda sanità locale*, or ASL) or you can go to the emergency department (*pronto soccorso*) of the local hospital (*ospedale*). Hospitals are marked with a white H on a blue background. Make sure you have the relevant insurance card as you will be required to pay before you receive treatment. If you are in Rome, try the Salvator Mundi International Hospital or the Rome American Hospital, or in Milan, the Milan Clinic, where English-speaking staff are available.

If a local doctor prescribes medicine for you, it will be dispensed in a *farmacia*. Note that the word *droga* is reserved exclusively for narcotics. Homeopathic medicines are popular in Italy and are often prescribed by doctors and stocked by all chemists. You will normally see a green sign, saying *Omeopatia*.

Always get your teeth attended to before you go to Italy. There are few dentists per capita, fewer still speak English, and charges are very high. Although it is possible to be seen by an optician on the national health service in Italy, it is simpler to get things checked before you go. Remember to take a spare pair of glasses with you and a copy of your eyeglasses prescription in case of emergency.

Other items that you might expect to find at a chemist or pharmacy in Britain or the States are sold in general stores or boutiques. Pharmacies in Italy are reserved for medicine. For natural toiletries and cosmetics, one British store that is well represented in Italy is the Bodyshop.

If you need more supplies of a regular medicine, take a packet with you as, although the brand may

be different, the pharmacist will be able to
recognize the ingredients. Italian pharmacists
often have the knowledge and authority to advise
on a wider range of medicine and treatments for
ailments than may be the case in the UK.

Spas

One of the pleasures of Italy is the *terme*, or spas,
offering not just immersion in spa waters but
hydrotherapy and beauty treatments. Health
care tourism is big business in Italy, and millions
of Italians go to the country's more than one
hundred spas every year. Spas can be found in the
north near Milan, in Tuscany (Montecatini is one
of the most famous), and also on the island of
Ischia in the south. Costs are not excessive and
it is a pleasant way to detox and chill out.

chapter six

TIME OUT

EATING AND DRINKING

One of the great pleasures of Italy is eating and drinking. Each region has its individual cooking style and ingredients. In the north black pepper, butter, and rice are the staples. In the south it's hot red pepper, olive oil, and pasta. In Piedmont scented truffle may be grated over your risotto, Liguria has a pasta sauce of crushed basil and pine nuts called *pesto*, in Tuscany you may eat fresh-caught hare and tomato, or wild-boar sausages, and in Sicily you will be offered the most delicious sardines. Many of these ingredients will have been prepared that day, bought fresh from the market.

Italy's rich diversity and localism explains why there are over two thousand names for the huge variety of pasta shapes, and more wine labels—at least four thousand—than anywhere else in the world. Italy has many food festivals, called *sagre*, where local food is on display for tasting. Wine and truffle festivals are very popular. The Italian state tourist office, ENIT, publishes a booklet on the local festivals called *An Italian Year*.

Meal Culture

In Italy breakfast (*prima colazione*) is normally around 8:00 a.m. and consists of biscuits or croissants, accompanied by strong coffee or perhaps tea. The main meal of the day is often lunch (*pranzo*), which starts anywhere between 1:00 and 2:00 p.m. and may last up to three hours (depending on the region), although office workers will usually eat and leave faster. If a heavy lunch has been eaten, the evening meal may consist of a light snack.

Dinner (*cena*) is usually around 8:00 p.m., but may be as late as 10:00 p.m. If the breadwinner cannot get back for lunch, dinner becomes the main meal. Children tend to stay up late, with no fixed bedtimes. Bread without butter is served and there is usually wine and water. When the family has guests, the head of the household pours the first round of wine and may propose a toast (*brindisi*) and then everyone serves themselves. "Cheers" in Italian is "*Salute.*"

A full-scale Italian meal is substantial, and so varied that it bears out the adage, *l'appetito vien mangiando* (the appetite grows with eating). Two main courses are preceded by a starter and followed by cheese, a dessert, and/or fruit. The starter, or *antipasto*, is often a selection of cold meats and marinated vegetables. Parma ham and melon are popular *antipasti*.

The first main dish, the *primo*, is usually pasta or risotto or perhaps a soup (*minestra*). *Minestrone* is a vegetable soup. The second main course, or *secondo*, will be meat or fish plus a cooked vegetable, often served separately as a side dish (*contorno*). The *contorni* (including potatoes) often follow the second dish as they are seen as palette cleansers rather than as an accompaniment to the meat or fish. Pasta is almost never eaten as a meal in itself, except for lasagne, and if you feel a whole portion of pasta as a first course is too much for you, it is acceptable to ask for a *mezza porzione* (half portion).

This may be followed by cheese and fruit, then dessert (*dolce*) and coffee. It is absolutely normal for Italians to drink wine with their meal, even in working hours. Tap water (*acqua semplice*) is free, but most Italians will ask for mineral water (*acqua minerale*), either sparkling (*gassata*) or still (*non-gassata*).

The bill (*conto*) will include Value Added Tax (IVA in Italian), and either a cover charge for *pane e coperto* ("bread and cover") or a service charge (*servizio*) of around 12 percent. This does not go to your waiter so you may wish to add an extra few euros for him or her. Because of the prevalence of tax evasion in Italy, all shops, restaurants, and bars are required by law to issue customers with a *scontrino* (receipt). If they do not do so, they can be fined heavily.

Tipping is entirely at your discretion. Many restaurants have a service charge. The Italians are not generous tippers. If tipping for good service, they generally round up the bill to the nearest euro. A small gratuity is normally left for hotel porters and doormen and also chambermaids. Taxi fares may be rounded up, and if you buy a drink at the bar a small coin for the barman is often left along with the tab for your drink.

A TIME TO RELAX

No one is in a hurry when eating out in Italy. The interval between the *secondo piatto* and the cheese and fruit, followed by dessert and coffee, is the time for leisurely conversation and may easily add an hour to your meal.

Italians eat out a great deal and there is a wide range of establishments, all clearly identified. A *ristorante* (restaurant) is usually the most expensive option. A *trattoria* is a small local restaurant, usually family-run and mid-priced, offering a limited menu, but sometimes with excellent food. A *taverna* or *osteria* is simpler

and less pretentious. However, always check the menu first as the type of restaurant isn't always an indication of price.

Italians tend not to frequent burger joints, unless they have children. A pizzeria with a wood-burning stove is very popular, as is a *gelateria*, or ice-cream parlor. For quick meals, a *rosticceria* does spit-roasted meats and precooked chicken dishes. A *tavola calda* is a modest hot food bar. An *enoteca* (wine shop) may serve basic meals to accompany the usually excellent wines. Look for signs saying "*Cucina casalinga*": this means the food is home-cooked, simple, unfussy, but satisfying. Avoid the *menu turistico* or *menu a prezzo fisso* (set-price meal) unless you want to eat quickly and cheaply, as the standard is often poor.

Drinking

In Italy it is common to drink an *aperitivo* (aperitif) before meals. This may be a light white wine such as a Verdicchio or a Prosecco. Or you may be offered a *spumante* (sparkling wine). White and red wine (*vino bianco* and *vino rosso*) will be served during the meal. Wine can be ordered by the carafe (*caraffa*), quarter-liter (*quartino*), half-liter (*mezzo litro*), or liter (*litro*). Most Italians opt for the house wine (*vino della casa*), usually red. The meal may be followed by a *digestivo* (digestive), such as a cognac, a *grappa*

(Italian brandy), or an *amaro* (a vermouth-type liqueur).

Like many Latins, Italians are not heavy drinkers and prefer to drink with food. Monsignor Della Casa in the *Galateo*, a manual of etiquette published in 1555, writes, "I thank God that for all the many other plagues that have come to us from beyond the Alps, this most pernicious custom of making game of drunkenness, and even admiring it, has not reached as far as this."

Stand or Sit?

If you are in a hurry and just want a quick coffee, or a refreshing drink, go into a bar and drink standing up at the counter (*al banco*). It is up to three times cheaper than sitting at a table inside or out on the terrace. Why? Because when you sit down, you have paid not just for a drink but for a "pitch" where you can talk, write, read, or watch the world go by. There will be no pressure to move on, although the waiter will ask if he/she can get you another drink.

Although Italian alcohol consumption is among the highest in Europe, it is spread evenly across the population and most people probably drink little more than a couple of glasses of wine a day. The idea of drinking to get drunk is foreign to the Italians. They may have a glass of *grappa* with their morning coffee, but alcohol is really seen as an accompaniment to food.

Beer Culture

Although Italy is famous for its wines, beer is also popular. Moretti, Frost, and Peroni are popular local brands, served *alla spina* (draught), *piccola* (20 cl), *media* (40 cl), and *grande* (66 cl). For soft drinks, try *granita*, an iced summer drink made with lemon, orange, mint, strawberry, or coffee.

Coffee and Tea

Few people in Britain or North America need educating about Italian coffee culture. Listed below are the most frequently ordered types. (Note that if

you ask for *un caffè*, this means a small black *espresso*.)

If you want a decaffeinated coffee, ask for *un decaffeinato* or *un caffè Hag*. This isn't drunk much in Italy. If you ask for tea, you will be brought hot water with a tea bag . By law, Italian bars and cafés must serve you a glass of water free of charge regardless of whether you buy anything.

Coffee

Espresso: small strong black coffee (*doppio espresso* is double-size).

Caffè lungo: small and black, but weaker than *espresso*.

Caffè corretto: black with a shot of *grappa* (or some other liqueur).

Caffè macchiato: black with a dash of milk.

Caffelatte: a large coffee with lots of milk.

Cappuccino: coffee with a thick layer of frothy milk and a scattering of chocolate on top (only drunk by Italians with breakfast and up to mid-morning).

DRESS

Italy is an extremely fashion-conscious culture, and Italian women, in particular, expect to spend a large percentage of their disposable income on clothes and accessories. You are how you dress, and clothes are a badge of success. Women wear quiet, well-cut, expensive and elegant clothes, and men's ties and suits should also be fashionable and well-tailored. Even casual clothes are smart and chic. Remember that Italy, especially Milan, is a center of European fashion. Dress codes are relaxed, but Italian women do not normally wear shorts in the cities. In churches, as we have seen, you may be forbidden to enter if you are wearing shorts or a sleeveless top.

OUTDOOR LIFE

One of the great delights of Italy is how much of life is lived outdoors, at least in the warmer months of the year. All large towns have more or less permanent outdoor markets and every village has a lively market day.

Sunday at the beach is a family ritual. After hours of preparation, the family emerges in public on the beach, the mother leading her flock to the chosen spot. As Tim Parks commented, in Italy, despite its individualism, people tend to do the same thing at the same time, whether it be tending a grave or going to the beach on June 18 after the end of the school year.

A characteristic of Southern life in particular is the *passeggiata*, a ritual more unmissable than Sunday mass. Young people gather in the hour or so before dinner and whole families put on their best clothes and walk arm-in-arm through the streets to see and be seen.

The Italians also enjoy camping, and Italy has over two thousand campsites, mostly open from April through September. They are graded according to facilities, from one to four stars; the best may have their own supermarkets, swimming pools, and cinemas. You may need an international camping ticket book: this can usually be bought at the campsite.

Tip for Campers

If you're heading for a campsite, aim to arrive by 11:00 a.m. If you wait until after lunch, all the spaces may have gone.

FOOTBALL AS A WAY OF LIFE

Some observers have called football (soccer) Italy's real religion. In Italy football is an art and is described as such by commentators and spectators alike. Watching the local team on a Sunday is an important event, and a national team's success will be celebrated in banner headlines. The top teams such as Juventus (Turin), AC Milan, Inter Milan, and Lazio (Rome) are owned by leading business and political figures and are as much symbols of Italian pride as Benetton, Ferrari, Fiat, Armani, or Versace.

With the verbal felicity for which Italians are famed, footballers are given nicknames. Marco van Basten is called "the swan," for example, and the Brazilian, Cafu, is "the little pendulum."

In some ways, the rivalry between Italian clubs reflects the ancient rivalry between the medieval city-states; the drama is played out in stadiums across the country every week in season. Sit in any café (called *bar* in Italian) with its big screen and enjoy the exhilaration when the home team scores and share the misery when they lose a match. Strategy and tactics are discussed endlessly and with passion.

SEEING THE SIGHTS

There is so much for the visitor to see in Italy, but where to start? A good idea is to visit the local office of the national tourist board, ENIT (*Ente Nazionale Italiano di Turismo*). They have offices in London and New York as well as at most of Italy's border posts and airports. The state travel

agency, CIT or CIT Italia (*Sestante-Compagnia Italiana di Turismo*), also provides information, and has a train-booking service. Each of Italy's twenty provincial capitals has a local tourist office, called EPT (*Ente Provinciale di Turismo*) or APT (*Azienda di Promozione Turistica*). IAT (*Ufficio Informazione e Accoglienza Turistica*) and AAST (*Azienda Autonoma di Soggiorno e Turismo*) all provide maps, local information, public transport details, and opening times of the main sights in the area. Opening times are usually 8:30 a.m. to 7:00 p.m., Monday to Friday.

A National Call Center for English-speaking tourists is available on 800-117 700. It provides information in English on health care, safety, museums, accommodation, events, and shows.

FESTIVALS

As we have seen, the annual *festa* in an Italian town is an important event and can last several days. It may be a religious celebration, and it may also date back to Renaissance or medieval times: examples are the *Palio* horseback races in Siena (July 2 and August 16), the *Regata* in Venice (the first Sunday in September), and the *Scoppio del Carro* ("Firing of the Cart") at Easter in Florence. On three days in June, one of which is always June 24, Florence is the venue for the sixteenth-century costume parade (*Calcio Storico Fiorentino*). There is also the lively sweet and toy fair from Christmas to January 5 in Rome's Piazza Navona.

MUSEUMS AND ART GALLERIES

There are some seventy state-run museums in Italy, and one estimate says that the country is home to half the world's great art treasures. Part of the reason is the extraordinary flowering of art and sculpture in Renaissance Italy, the legacy of which is visible in churches, palaces, and museums throughout the land. Almost every church seems to have its masterpiece—and almost every church wants to charge you 3 euros to enter and find it! Museums often close on Mondays, to compensate for being open on the weekend, and are usually open Tuesday through Saturday from 9:00 a.m. to 1:00 or 2:00 p.m. (later in big cities), and on Sundays from 9:00 a.m. to 1:00 p.m.

Some of the sites are so famous that you might think they are overrated: don't be put off! The lines in the Vatican City may try your patience, but the soaring roof of the Sistine Chapel, once you squeeze through its narrow door, is breathtaking. The Villa Borghese in Rome is a gem, as are the Accademia and the Peggy Guggenheim Museum of Modern Art in Venice, and the Uffizi in Florence. Although Venice, Florence, and Rome draw the crowds, it is well worth visiting Naples, Palermo, and smaller towns such as Padua, Siena, and Pisa.

Some galleries such as the Villa Borghese require prior booking. Churches have a dress code. No bare shoulders or shorts, and visitors are asked not to wander around when a service is in progress.

MONUMENTS

Some of the best-preserved monuments of ancient Greek civilization are found in southern Italy, known as Magna Graecia (Greater Greece) when it was a Greek colony. The most impressive temples are at Paestum (south of Naples), and at Selinunte, Agrigento, and Segesta in Sicily. The theater at Syracuse is the largest in the world.

One of the most memorable ways to gain a sense of Italy's multilayered civilizations is to visit the church of San Clemente in Rome, overseen by Irish Dominicans. The eleventh-century upper church contains a magnificent Romanesque mosaic, but also Renaissance wall paintings and lavish Baroque decor. Under its floor you can visit a fourth-century church containing fragments of frescos, one of them with the oldest description in Italian. Descending even further, some 100 feet (30 meters) below street level, you find yourself in a narrow alley in ancient Rome leading to a first-century patrician house and a Mithraic temple.

For the glory that was Roman Italy, you must go to Pompeii and Herculaneum (Ercolano). Both were buried by the volcanic eruption of Mount Vesuvius, in 79 CE, and the site was not excavated until 1750. And, yes, if you're in Naples, it's worth the trip. Pompeii is open from 8:00 a.m. to 7:30 p.m., Monday through Saturdays, and you need three or four hours to take it all in.

MUSIC AND THEATER

The country of Verdi and Puccini is not short
of opera houses and theaters. Italy hosts many
world-renowned opera performances, and, if you
speak Italian, you can see plays by names such as
Pirandello and Dario Fo. The opera season runs
from December to June, but there are summer
festivals in open-air theaters.

One of the greatest outdoor concert venues is
Verona's huge first-century amphitheater, known
as the "Arena," which can seat an audience of up to
25,000. Large as it is, the Arena is dwarfed by Rome's
Colosseum, which, in its day, could hold 50,000
spectators. The most famous opera house is La Scala
in Milan; you can book ahead on www.musica.it.

If you stroll around the piazza in front of the
Doge's Palace in Venice, sellers in eighteenth-
century costume will give you fliers for baroque
music in the Venetian style, performed in concert
halls in the center of the city. Tourist trap though
it may be, the music is usually enjoyable and

respectably played. You'll enjoy your late evening *grappa* in the famous Caffè Florian even more.

Music festivals are also popular in Italy. One of the most famous is the Festival of Two Worlds in Spoleto in June and July. The Sanremo Italian popular song festival (Festival della Canzone Italiana) in February is the equivalent of the Grammy or the Brit awards.

Apart from open-air festivals, all the opera houses and theaters, as well as the majority of cinemas, shut their doors in the summer. Entertainment moves outside with feasting, dancing, and music in the courtyards of old palazzos, and opera in city parks and amphitheaters. This is also the season for a thousand local *festas*, or festivals.

CINEMA

In Italy, almost all foreign films are dubbed. Italian cinema has a great tradition, however. Fellini's old home in Via Marghera in Rome has a commemorative plaque outside, and Rome's Cinecittà film studios were home to Sergio Leone's "spaghetti westerns," which made Clint Eastwood famous. In the major cities you will find at least one cinema showing English-language films in the original. The Venice Film Festival in August and September is the world's oldest film festival (founded in 1932) and a major event in the international calendar. Venice's Golden Lion is one of international cinema's most prestigious awards.

chapter seven

GETTING AROUND

"Who has been to Italy," proclaimed the Russian author Nicolai Gogol to his friend Zhukovsky, "can forget all other regions…Europe compared to Italy is like a gloomy day compared to a day of sunshine." Admiring Italy is one thing. Getting around it may be another matter.

In the eighteenth century, when traveling around Europe on the "Grand Tour" was *de rigueur* for young noblemen, Italy was where they learned to become "perfect gentlemen." A trip to Venice, Florence, Rome, and Naples was an essential part of a man's education. The compiler of Britain's first English dictionary, Dr. Samuel Johnson, wrote, "A man who has not been to Italy is always conscious of an inferiority, for his not having seen what a man is expected to see."

So much for what to see, but what about how to get there? The good news is that things have improved since the days of the Grand Tour. Brigands no longer haunt the mountain passes, and the advice given to tourists by Murray's *Guide to Southern Italy* in 1858 to " . . . make their bargains with the landlords on their first arrival," is no longer necessary. However, all of Italy's transport systems, can be uncertain and the great quality you need—as always in Italy—is a degree of flexibility.

AIR TRAVEL AND ENTRY TO ITALY

Since Italy is a member of the European Union and the Eurozone, any EU citizen can enter freely. North Americans need a passport, but not a visa.

The main points of entry are Rome's Leonardo da Vinci (also known as Fiumicino) and Ciampino airports, and Milan's Malpensa and Linate airports.

Alitalia and ATI are the Italian international and domestic carriers. The best way to book an internal flight is through a recognized travel agency, and a wide range of discounted fares are available on both national and international flights. (It's important to ask for these discounts; they are rarely offered automatically.) To contact Alitalia or ATI by Internet, go to www.alitalia.it.

POLICE REGISTRATION

By law, non-EU visitors staying more than three days in Italy are required to register with the police. A hotel will do this for you automatically, but if you are staying with friends you need to go to the local *Questura*, or *Commissariato*, or *Stazione dei Carabinieri*. Because, as we have seen, Italy can be extremely bureaucratic, it is worth taking an Italian friend with you to see that everything goes smoothly.

If you are a non-EU citizen and are staying for longer than ninety days, you need to get a *permesso di soggiorno* (residence permit) within eight days of arrival. These are issued by the *Ufficio Stranieri* (foreign department) or *Questura* of the police, and you need an official letter stamped with the *bollo* (state stamp).

THE UBIQUITOUS *BOLLO*

An important part of anyone's life in Italy is the *bollo*, a special type of state postage stamp, affixed to official documents and requests, which attests that the relevant administration fee has been paid. *Bolli* are sold at *tabacchi* (tobacco

kiosks), as indeed is the special legal paper on which you must write your formal request. This is called *carta uso bollo*, or *carta bollata*.

The complexity and time-wasting of much of Italy's bureaucracy has led to the creation of large numbers of agencies (*agenzie*) that specialize in getting your documents for you, obtaining the necessary stamps, and standing in the inevitable lines. Many people find the convenience and expertise of this service worth the extra cost.

RESIDENCY

Where an *agenzia* may seem a blessing is in getting a residency certificate (*certificato di residenza*) and a tax code (*codice fiscale*). If you are settling in Italy for any length of time, the *certificato di residenza* is essential: you will need it when buying a car or when getting utilities such as gas and the phone connected. The *codice fiscale* is useful as an ID, and may be demanded for anything such as joining a club or opening a bank account.

To get a *certificato di residenza*, take your *permesso di soggiorno* and your ID to the *Ufficio Anagrafe* and apply to be registered with the local *comune*. Buy some *bolli* and take them with you so that the official can affix them to the document.

For the *codice fiscale*, you take your passport and ID card to the provincial tax office, the *Ufficio Imposte Dirette*, which will issue the card.

With the number of documents the average Italian has to carry, is it any wonder that Italy pioneered the fashion handbag for men?

PUBLIC AND PRIVATE TRANSPORT

Italy's public transport system is reasonably priced by European standards, but chaotic because it is plagued by strikes. Italy has both a public and a private transport system. The latter operates on a local basis in towns and outlying villages. The train system is mainly state-owned and can be inefficient, unpunctual, and strike-ridden, although the modern trains are extremely comfortable.

Trains

The rail system in Italy is extensive and comfortable and there is a system of high speed *frecciarossa* trains with regular services linking major cities. Train strikes are not uncommon and it is worth checking in advance and also reserving seats when you buy your ticket. Strikes (*scopieri*) are usually announced reasonably well ahead, and you can contact the national rail operator at www.trenitalia.com. Their home page is in English.

The state railway is called the *ferrovia statale*. The timetable is available on www.trenitalia.com. Nonresidents can buy an Italy Rail Card, which gives unlimited travel for up to thirty days. There is also an Italy Flexi-card for four, eight, or twelve days up to one month. This is available from ticket offices at railway stations and from travel agencies.

There is a range of different types of train service, all with different prices.

The ETR 450 Pendolino is a first-class high-speed train, equivalent to France's TGV. These run mainly from the southern region of Puglia, through Rome to Milan, and seats need to be reserved in advance. The Eurostar (Italia), like the Pendolino, needs advance reservation. The *espresso* and the *diretto* cover local distances but stop at main stations only. The *locale* is the slow local train, which stops for long periods at stations—fun to travel on if you have the time.

There is a huge range of discounts and special tickets and it is worth asking at a booking agency what is available. If you buy your ticket on the train, there is a surcharge of 20 percent, and if reserved seats are not occupied as the train leaves, other passengers have the right to occupy them. One important point: you must "validate" your ticket before you travel by punching it into a machine on the platform: if you fail to do so, you will be charged a hefty fine.

The *Metropolitana*

Milan, Genoa, Rome, Naples, and Palermo all have subway systems, although the network does not cover the whole city. Transport is cheap and there is usually an overall flat fee for bus or tram. Since the ticket is valid for more than an hour (for example, seventy-five minutes in Milan and Rome, ninety minutes in Genoa), it can be used for more than one journey. Except in Rome, this also applies to transfers between bus and metro.

Tickets can be confusing. Metro stations have no ticket offices, and so tickets must be bought at newsstands along main routes or near the metro stations. Look for a big sign that says T for *tabacchi* (tobacconist). Tickets can be bought singly or in a book of ten. Day and weekly tickets are also available.

Buses and Coaches

You should get on a bus or tram at the back, through the doors marked *Salita* (entry). The middle doors are used for getting off, and are marked *Uscita* (exit). Validate your ticket by pressing it into the yellow or orange machine just inside the door. Don't automatically expect a seat. Buses and trams are crowded and children do not normally get up if an adult is standing. Watch out for pickpockets in a crowd and be prepared to shout "*Permesso!*" (Excuse me) or "*Scendo!*" (I'm getting off!) when you reach your stop.

Coach services between cities are popular and inexpensive. Coach companies also offer guided tours, including several major cities. For example, it is possible to do Venice, Padua, and Florence in one day or, in the South, Rome, Naples, Pompeii, and Sorrento. Round the City tours are a good way of getting to know the lay of the land when you have just arrived; they are a little like the Gray Line tours of American cities.

Taxis

Travel by taxi is common in Italy, but you can't usually flag one down in the street. There are taxi stands in piazzas and at stations, but the best way is to phone from a hotel, restaurant, or bar. Fares are

Standing in Line

This is not an Italian custom. Be prepared to use your elbows a bit or be carried along with the crowd, particularly in the South. Until the recent introduction of a numbered waiting system, in most public buildings one would have to try to catch the employee's eye. He or she would decide whom to serve first. Even today, a degree of assertiveness is necessary.

shown on the meter, but there is an extra charge if you have luggage, are traveling after 10:00 p.m. on Sundays or public holidays, or are taking a long-distance trip out of town or to an airport. If you want to tip, round up the fare to the nearest euro.

Driving

And so we come to cars. Italian traffic is a nightmare. People drive fast, and park in very narrow spaces with little regard for other cars,

animals, or pedestrians. Pedestrian crossings are rarely respected, and an Italian saying goes that "Red traffic lights are only a suggestion!" Added to which, the confusion of cars, buses, and mopeds all jostle through narrow city streets. To walk around Rome's *centro storico* (historic center), where cars cannot easily get through, is a pleasure, and Venice is traffic-free bliss. Other places where motorists must leave their cars outside the city limits are the hill towns of Umbria and Tuscany, and of course Venice itself. Even though all towns now have traffic-free zones in their historic centers, this increases congestion outside.

Drivers entering Italy from the relative peace of France and Switzerland can be dazed by the intensity and apparent chaos of the traffic. Italy has the second-highest percentage of car ownership in the world after the USA and since most people live in high-rise buildings their parked cars block the roads and pavements. *Automobile* (with the stress on the third syllable) is the word for car in Italian, but most Italians say *macchina* (stress on the first syllable; the machine).

Florence and Naples are two of the worst cities for traffic congestion. Fortunately, if you need to get around by other means than on foot, there are alternatives.

Rent a Scooter
That's what the natives do, and not just the young ones. You don't need a driver's license for a *motorino*, and although the law demands a crash helmet, many spurn it as a degrading curb on their

freedom. Scooter drivers often go around the city in packs.

Rent a Bike
Dangerous in the big towns, but cycling is a popular weekend sport. The place to do this is in the flat lands of the lower Po Valley, in quiet provincial towns like Mantua or Ferrara.

Rent a Car
There are car-rental offices at major stations and airports. The regulations stipulate that you must be at least nineteen years old, and there is actually a law that says that unless you have held a license for more than three years you cannot drive a car with more than 93 mph (150 kph) speed capacity.

Driving a Car
Italians may be fast and rule-breaking but they are quite safety conscious. They are often

excellent drivers, and the Italian accident rate is by no means the highest in Europe. Italian drivers may be assertive, but they are also careful not to damage their paintwork. They do, however, ignore speed limits unless they spot a speed control or a motor cycle policeman. "Me first" is the rule, and over-courteous foreign drivers can actually cause accidents.

Expressways: 130 kph (81 mph)

Urban stretches: 90 kph (55 mph)

Dual highways: 110 kph (68 mph)

Outside built-up areas: 110 kph (68 mph)

Built-up areas: 50 kph (30 mph)

The *carabinieri* (police) and *polizia stradale* (traffic police) can give you an on-the-spot fine for speeding, and will also fine you for not having your traffic documents or internationally required equipment such as a fluorescent life jacket or red warning triangle in case of breakdown. The police may ask for your *patente* (driver's license), *libretto* (registration document/logbook), *assicurazione* (insurance), and *carta verde* (green card). It is worth obtaining an international driver's license before you leave home as it will facilitate matters if you get into trouble.

Gasoline (Benzina)
Two types are available, leaded (*piombo*) and unleaded (*verde*—green). Except on expressways,

service stations tend to keep to shop hours (see Chapter 5, Daily Life) and to close on Sundays. To plug the gap, self-service pumps are available in larger towns. Most gas stations are not automated, but tipping the attendant is not expected. Diesel pumps are marked *gasolio*.

Breakdown
In this case, you need the *autosoccorso* (breakdown service) and *autoservizio* (repairs garage). Telephone the ACI (*Automobile Club d'Italia*) for help. The emergency number for police, doctor, or ambulance is 113.

Parking
It has been estimated that an Italian motorist spends seven years of his or her life in a car, two of them looking for a parking space. In cities it is best to park wherever you can and proceed on foot or by public transport. A tow-away zone is marked by pictures and the legend *Zona Rimozione* or *Rimozione forzata*. Reclaiming your car is expensive.

Be careful if you park in a street: if it is scheduled for cleaning that night, and your car is causing an obstruction, it will be towed away. Avoid parking where there are no other cars: other people may know something you don't. Streets are cleaned once a week, and every street affected has a sign giving the dates and times.

Finally, a parked car is an invitation to thieves. Never leave anything visible inside your car.

COMMON ITALIAN ROADSIGNS

Pericolo	Danger
Alt/Avanti	Stop/Go
Entrata/Uscita	Entry/Exit
Rallentare	Slow down
Senso unico	One way
Deviazione	Deviation
Lavori in corso	Roadworks
Limite di velocità	Speed limit
Divieto di sorpasso	No passing
Divieto di sosta	No parking
Parcheggio	Parking

Expressways
There are over 3,700 miles (6,000 km) of
expressways in Italy, most of them toll roads. A
green sign with a white A marks the *autostrada*,
followed by the number. You take a ticket as you
enter and pay as you leave. If you want to pay by
card, a *Viacard* or *Telepass* is available from toll
booths and expressway services.

Autoclubs
The Italian automobile club is called *Automobile
Club d'Italia* (ACI). It offers a breakdown service
that can be accessed by dialing 116.

Road Rules
Driving is on the right, and you give way to
traffic from the right at traffic circles and
crossroads. You are required by law to have a

warning triangle in the trunk of your car and to carry your road documents (license and car registration) at all times. It is also necessary to have a basic first-aid package and spare warning lights.

Traffic crossings are often ignored, but the police will fine you on the spot if a child between the ages of four and twelve is not wearing a seat belt. Children under four must be in a child safety seat, or an on-the-spot fine will be issued. Drivers commonly plead innocence in an attempt to reduce the amount; if you can't pay immediately, you have a sixty-day grace period.

Buying a Car

To buy a car you need your *codice fiscale*, and to be registered as a local resident. To complete the transactions, you accompany the seller to the local ACI (*Automobile Club d'Italia*). The transfer of ownership is known as a *trapasso*. Your primary car operating costs are insurance and road tax. An MOT (called *revisione*) is necessary for cars over three years old, and every two years afterward. They receive a *bollino blu* to show they are clean.

Driving Your Own Car in Italy

Within the EU, foreigners can drive their own car for up to twelve months. British-registered cars with GB plates can only be driven for up to six months. It may be cheaper and less time-consuming to buy a car locally. Importing your own vehicle is both expensive and complicated.

Licenses

If you have an EU driving license you can use it in Italy for an unlimited period. If you decide to live in Italy, you can still use your EU license but you must get it stamped at your local motor registry or ACI office to show you are resident. If you have a larger vehicle than Class B, then you need to reapply for an Italian license.

If you are a non-EU citizen you can drive for up to a year on your driver's license (although you should have a translation into Italian). However, to avoid taking an Italian driving test, you must apply for the Italian license before the year is up or before you get a residence permit.

Many international drivers buy an international driver's license every year rather than go through the process of getting an Italian driver's license, which can be lengthy and time-consuming. Driver's licenses are obtained through the *comune* or *municipio* (town hall). Armed with an Italian translation of your driver's license, you fill in a special form on *carta uso bollo* with the appropriate number of *bolli*. This needs to be stamped at the *pretura* (magistrate's court) and taken to the *comune* with three passport-size photos. One of your photos should be authenticated by the *comune*.

You also need a *certificato medico* (medical certificate). This starts with a medical report form and a blank medical certificate. The medical report is signed by your family doctor; and the certificate, plus *bollo*, plus photo, is taken to the *unità sanitaria locale* (USL) for an eye test and a signature on the certificate.

All this finally goes to the local *motorizazzione civile* with your driver's license, a photocopy of it, and a postal order and another *bollo*. In all, you will need to obtain five documents to acquire an Italian driver's license. Thankfully, today everything can be done through the ACI.

Ferries

Some of the glories of Italy are its islands and lakes. There are some 4,650 miles (7,500 km) of coastline and the ferry services are good. Two of the most popular excursions are from Naples to Capri and Ischia. Naples to Sicily by hydrofoil (*aliscafo*) is five and a half hours.

chapter eight

BUSINESS BRIEFING

Italy's manufacturers, middlemen, and entrepreneurs are very able producers, promoters, and salespeople, and experienced at thinking internationally. "*Il made in Italy*" is a mark of high-quality design and function in fashion, in cars, in food and drink, and in white goods. The "Economic Miracle" of the 1950s transformed much of Italian business, in particular the go-ahead family firm.

By the end of the 1980s, Italy claimed to be the fifth-largest economy in the world after Germany, France, Japan, and the USA. However, it may be bigger—an estimated one third of the economy is dominated by what is called the black or "gray" economy, unreported in statistics or tax returns.

BUSINESS IN ITALY

The three sectors of the Italian economy are the state, the conglomerates, and small- and medium-sized enterprises.

The State Sector

The Italian government still has a strong indirect role in business, despite the privatization of public corporations over the last twenty years, and government spending as a proportion of GDP is the highest in  the EU. One in five employees works for the public sector, which accounts for the majority of business funding.

Privately Owned Conglomerates

The private sector is dominated by a small number of key families that control major industries and have cross-interests— Berlusconi, Agnelli, Pirelli, De Benedetti (the *salotto buono*). Their conglomerates include international household names such as Fiat, Benetton, Versace, Armani, and Olivetti. These are large corporations but, with the retirement and death of their founders, their interests are diminishing, and new companies with professional management, such as Bulgari, are following in their footsteps.

Small Business

The majority of businesses, especially in the North, are small- and medium-sized family-owned firms, in which the son or daughter takes over on the retirement of the father. Their productivity is higher than in the state sector. They tend to pay cash, employ family and friends, and outsource work to avoid banks, unions, and taxes. These enterprises now face stiff competition from the conglomerates, both national and international, with their higher output, lower costs, and resources to spend on technological innovation. Other obstacles to competitiveness are low investment in research and development and the inefficiency of public institutions. Ninety percent of all Italian companies are SMGs with fewer than fifteen employees.

The *Mezzogiorno* (South) begins just south of Rome (some say it includes Rome!). Northerners are widely seen as more interested in money, Southerners as more concerned with power and the good life. Unemployment is 5 percent in the North and 22 percent in the South. Northerners criticize Southerners for grabbing state subsidies and handouts. The Southerners criticize the Northerners for exploiting labor and diverting savings into their factories.

COMPANY STRUCTURE AND ORGANIZATION

An Italian company is managed by a board of directors (*consiglio d'amministrazione*) under a president (*presidente*). The managing director (*amministratore delegato*) is responsible for company operations, with department heads (*direttori*) reporting to him or her. Italy is a

country where decisions are made at the top.
You need to speak to a director or the president
to get your business done, and finding the right
decision-maker in a large organization with many
branches can be difficult and time-consuming.
Coporate flow charts and directories are mostly
for show and do not necessarily reflect true
responsibilities or even reporting lines.

True hierarchies are based on networks of
people who have built up personal alliances
across the organization. Different departments
will have different management styles, depending
on the boss. The primary attributes of a manager
are flexibility and pragmatism. This means
that Italian managers will focus on getting the
essentials done without overreliance on protocol,
rules, and procedures, which may be ignored.

COMPANY FINANCE AND CORPORATE GOVERNANCE

Banking investment in start-ups
tends to be minimal, and key
investment funding generally
comes from other sources.
Banks cannot own commercial
companies. Those providing
short-term financing or bank product sales
cannot make medium-term loans. These are the
domain of specialized medium- and long-term
credit institutions. Apart from the Banca d'Italia,
which is the national regulatory bank, there are
several nationwide banks with branches across

the country, as well as many local banks specific to a town or region. Italy boasts the highest personal savings rate in Europe.

In the country that created accountancy in the fifteenth century, auditors tend to prepare reports that do not always correspond to the book value of the company. In due diligence proceedings, an independent auditor is advisable.

LABOR RELATIONS

Italian businesspeople work long and flexible working hours when under pressure. Executives arrive early and often stay late.

Any company in Italy with more than fifteen employees has a works committee (*consiglio di fabbrica*), with the right to monitor investment plans and working conditions.

An estimated 40 percent of the workforce is unionized, along political rather than craft lines. The main unions are Christian Democrat,

Communist, and Social Democrat—known respectively as CISL, CGIL, and UIL—but there are smaller unions and workers' councils that are responsible for a large number of strikes in the public sector. It has been estimated that 25 percent of the Italian labor market is unregulated.

PLANNING

Italian companies thrive on opportunity and risk, not on planning. They will identify and exploit a niche without long-term analysis. This means that long-term joint-venture agreements will be difficult to achieve. There is a bias against long-term strategy. Italians look for short-term consistent profit.

LEADERSHIP

In most countries a key criterion for leadership is the ability to make decisions. In Italy, the key criterion is power, expressed as *autorità* (authority), *autorevolezza* (authoritativeness), and *autoritarismo* (authoritarianism). Impersonal organizational mechanisms have low validity. This means that authority resides in whomever the boss trusts. Irrespective of whether a manager is technically qualified, he or she *is* someone the boss can work with.

The Role of the Boss

"He is the boss, I am his slave," was the view of one Italian associate of the senior partner in a Milan law firm. As befits an economy in which the family-run firm is the basic model, the management style is both authoritative and authoritarian. Decisions are made by senior people and passed down for implementation.

Although the boss (or bosses) have sole responsibility for policies and decisions, they are expected to take a human interest in their staff. They should also be *simpatico*, charismatic, and creative, and to cut a *bella figura*, while being consistent and reliable.

Italian bosses are expected to lead and to exact deference. Employees give loyalty not just because it is in their contract, but because they personally support the boss. In general, employees are suspicious of authority, and will challenge any way of working with which they do not agree.

An important part of leadership in Italy is implementation and control. Instructions and procedures are not enough. You need to get a consensus and obtain agreement. Persuasion, insistence, and follow-up are essential. This will yield flair, creativity, and hard work. But it requires intense personal input.

The first thing to do when dealing with an Italian company is to study the leadership structure, bearing in mind that the formal system may not reflect the true situation regarding power and decision making. Power may be operated by clans based on family, marriage, or wealth. The best way to find out who is important is to be prepared to mix, to socialize, and at all times to display your human side. Doing favors for people, being charming, and staying flexible are vital.

Stiffness, coldness, and bureaucracy do not go down well. Neither does doing everything by the book. The recognition that everyone has their little foibles means that an Italian manager will avoid speaking sharply or delivering moral lectures. Although there may be pressure to focus on core business, recognizing that everybody has fingers in different pies means that being involved in peripheral business may lead to greater things.

As a boss, it is important to tread a careful line between being sympathetic and accessible, and getting too close to your staff. A boss will delegate to trusted individuals, but not in terms of formal goals. Appraisals and job descriptions are rarely implemented. The key indicators monitored are cash flow, turnover, and gross profit.

The Role of the Manager

A manager's job is to display charisma to obtain a personal commitment from the workforce to the project at hand, and the drive and technical competence to implement it. Without this the project will fail. Procedures and action plans alone will achieve little.

Multinational companies with internationally trained managers conduct business according to international procedures. In family businesses, particularly in Tuscany and Emilia-Romagna, which are run by fathers and sons and daughters, negotiation will be on a much more personal basis. The hierarchies are built less on clear responsibilities and reporting lines and more on personal alliances. Italian managers will routinely ignore procedure and rules, putting their confidence in the competence and reliability of the people they have chosen to work with, and in close personal supervision of the task.

Strategic planning is rare in Italian companies. Directors know where they want to go and broadly how to get there. If there is a plan it is not made public. The key ability of Italian managers is to spot opportunities and go for them.

The implications of this strategy for joint venture planning are obvious. Deep-rooted personal confidence is necessary to a successful business relationship, which will last only so long as it is profitable. This is what the networking and close personal contact are designed to achieve. Managers from non-Italian companies need to learn to live with it and to enjoy the ride.

DECISION-MAKING

In such a personalized management system it is obvious that delegation by department or by designated subordinate is unlikely. Delegation is to trusted individuals, wherever they are in the organization. Feedback and appraisal will be personal. That is the only environment in which personal criticism is accepted. Formal appraisals can be difficult to conduct in an Italian company. Achievement of objectives will be judged by contribution to turnover, cash flow, and profits.

The Italians feel they are good at making intuitive decisions and will back up their instincts by consulting widely. Initial decisions are often taken quite quickly but are then subjected to discussion and may change. Personal connections and personal feelings will always be part of the decision-making process.

Foreign managers should know that basing decisions purely on the figures and the business plan, or regarding decisions as "black and white" is not the Italian way. A multiplicity of factors, political, economic, and personal, come into play.

TEAMWORKING

Teams operate on the same principle as the decision-making process—top down in a family-type structure. Words like family, mutual obligation, and mutual dependence are actually used in describing team members. Teams are made up of specialists under a team leader, selected on the basis of seniority and experience, who must enjoy the personal respect of the group.

Hierarchies are respected within teams and it can be difficult for a new young team leader to make his or her presence felt. Once again, the family model comes to the rescue. The elder team members become "godfathers" to the young team leader and offer advice on procedure. If that does not happen, and the team's commitment is not achieved, then the opposite can occur. Older or more senior colleagues will do everything they can to undermine the younger team leader, using procedural and other devices. In this case, the only solution is to pay off and release the troublemakers.

The pace of teamwork tends to be steady and teams are happy to work together, with frequent meetings and interaction. Hours are not fixed and activities are not over-structured as this would reduce motivation. The onus is on each team member to maintain good relationships with colleagues. Showing enthusiasm for the work, and being sensitive in one's dealings with others, is important. So are socializing with other team members, remaining good-humored, and developing a positive attitude. Loyalty is a high priority. Teams may welcome support in planning and in progress chasing. Although deadlines are regarded as fixed, slippage may occur.

MOTIVATION

Enough has been said to suggest that good social relations are of above average importance for a team motivator, especially in the South. Team loyalty and appeals to the emotions are common. If, as a manager, you can provide a goal that contributes to the success of the group while helping individuals achieve their own personal goals, you will have succeeded.

THE OVERALL LANGUAGE OF MANAGEMENT

Fluency of expression is very important in Italian management. Managers will normally be good talkers. Although authoritarian in style, the tone is usually friendly and can be quite indirect, and foreigners can easily misinterpret the subtlety with which statements are made. Italians themselves frequently find the language of their British and American counterparts to be crude and overly direct by comparison.

FEEDBACK AND MANAGING DISAGREEMENT

Italians are not on the whole confrontational, but may well hit back with everything they've got if criticized directly. They are especially sensitive to accusations of volatility or disorganization.

Feedback may be given in writing in the North, but is much more likely to be oral in the South. A key feature of giving and receiving feedback is to be able to ask about and express personal feelings. So a face-to-face meeting is important in the case of disagreement. The Italians believe that any difficulty can be resolved as long as there is goodwill. Italian managers will ask you to help them on a personal basis, will show an eagerness to find solutions, and will provide you with most of the information you require. Flexibility and openness to other people's feelings are important.

COMMUNICATION STYLES

The Italians are adept at exchanging verbal information. They are less good at writing or reading memos, e-mails, and documents. In communicating with an Italian counterpart, you are far better off telephoning than writing. Many executives even telephone to say that they will be writing or that they have written. On the whole, written communication should not be allowed to stand on its own; it needs verbal backup. The further south you go in Italy, the truer this is.

Italians are also speechifiers, long on rhetoric and ideas but often short on facts. They can also be very assertive and direct and this can be seen as abrupt or dismissive. Where an Italian is at his or her most polite is in saying "No." It is important to keep the door open for other possibilities.

Good speaking skills are important and body language is used to emphasize one's point. The Italians can use intense, emotive language and be quite imaginative in their way of expressing themselves. Words like "definitely," "fantastic," and "absolutely" will be used frequently to emphasize a positive point of view.

Conversational overlap, or "ping pong" conversation, is frequent and the volume may be quite loud. Talking about yourself, your family, and your success, and revealing your emotions is accepted as a way of building good relations. Lively argument and debate are appreciated. Italians may criticize their own company in front of others and make jokes about intentions or proposals. Open disagreement and agreement is common, although it is usually done politely. Dissent is rarely final. There is always a way of resolving difficulties. Italians apologize frequently, even for small things. It is seen as part of courtesy.

Revealing oneself as human is the key to successful face-to-face communication with Italians in a business situation. Being responsive, smiling, and showing interest is important. Helping people with their problems, and telling them your own once you have established a relationship, is valued. So is making eye contact and adopting a confiding tone. Ask questions to maintain attention levels, and note any personal information. Aim to get close to people in private.

The Italians often find the British and the Americans cold and distant. Use relaxed body language and try to smile. Establishing a personal relationship will be more appreciated than a focus on economic advantage and profit. Don't be overassertive, overfrank, and too direct, as this may be considered uncultured. Avoid giving too detailed instructions and boasting, although being confident and positive is important. It is also important to avoid criticizing Italy—Italians may be critical of their country, but you shouldn't be.

MAKING CONTACT

The Italians prefer to deal with people they know. They are more open than, say, the French to "cold contact," but they need to feel that a new contact is *raccomandato*, i.e. recommended by a known or recognized office or individual. This may be a client, a chamber of commerce, or an embassy, or personal contact through a trade fair. The initial contact may be by means of a formal letter, but this will need to be followed up by telephone calls and a personal visit. Even if you write to an Italian firm in English, small- and medium-sized companies will often reply in Italian. You may need the services of a translation agency as commercial and bureaucratic Italian has its own terminology. To avoid unnecessary delay, it is better to write your first letter in Italian.

Italian bosses, particularly in family-run firms, may not speak a foreign language, and the English-speaker in the company may be fairly low down in the chain. A senior Italian negotiator will often bring an interpreter, usually an assistant, who speaks English reasonably fluently. If so, remember to direct your conversation to your Italian counterpart, not to the assistant.

Remember that holidays are important in Italy, and that from mid-July to the end of August everything slows down. Although Italy has fewer public holidays than many Latin countries, every city celebrates its own patron saint and has its own local festival, when things close down.

BUSINESS HOURS

There is a difference between the North and the South. Northern business hours are 8:30 a.m. until 12:45 p.m., and 3:00 p.m. to 6 or 6:30 p.m., Monday to Friday. In Central and Southern Italy, because of the heat, business hours are 8:30 a.m. to 12:45 p.m., and 4:30 or 5:00 p.m. to 7:30 or 8:00 p.m. Many businesses are open on Saturday morning from 8:30 to 12:45 p.m. Many Italians live within easy commuting distance of where they work, and go home for lunch.

PREPARING FOR YOUR VISIT

Business has a strong social and presentational aspect in Italy. Making a *bella figura* is important. Ensure the clothes you take are conservative but stylish, and that your shoes are of good quality. To Italians, smart clothes are indicative of business success and even casual clothes are fashionable and chic. Trousers are fine for women, but once again should be well-cut and stylish. Make sure your briefcase and watch are smart. A good ballpoint will be noticed, a scruffy ballpoint even more! Take some family photos as well as the business documents you need. Make sure the documents are in tidy folders. This is all part of creating the right stylish impression.

Italian business cards are usually printed in plain black on a white background; as a rule, the less information they give, the more important the person.

Gift Giving

It is quite common to give a small present to any staff member who has been particularly helpful, so think about taking some modest corporate gifts—travel alarm clocks, pens, silver key fobs, diaries, or calculators. (Make sure they are name brands, but be careful that this is not seen as a crass way of highlighting your company logo.)

Any "company" gift you receive is likely to be elegant and discreet. Some Italian companies have privately published, top-quality coffee-table books and products. It is very important not to turn these down, no matter how heavy or inconvenient they may be to carry home!

THE FIRST MEETING

Small talk is important for Italians. People will want to ask you about your family and your background. This is partly a discreet way of establishing roots and confirming that you have a stake in making the business work because you have your own social responsibilities.

If you arrive in the evening and your hosts are meeting you, they may invite you for a meal. No matter how tired you are, you should accept. It will be enjoyable and relaxing, and to refuse will cause offense, and start your negotiations off on the wrong footing.

Don't be informal. The Italians are quite formal in the office and may address people by titles such as *Dottore* or *Dottoressa* for a professor or doctor, and even *Avvocato* (lawyer) or *Ingegnere* (engineer). Male and female endings are used, so the feminine of *Avoccato* is *Avvocata*, and of *Ingegnere* is *Ingegnera*, etc. The Italians also prefer to use surnames in the office, so that the person who calls one Charles at home may call one Smith in the office. In societies like Britain and North

America, which tend to see the use of surnames as distancing, this form of address, often without the Mr. or Mrs., can feel quite rude. In fact, it is just a misplaced translation of an Italian practice. Younger international managers slip quite easily into first names.

As the guest, you will normally be introduced first, and the senior or eldest person present will be shown deference. Shake hands with everyone in the room on arriving, and again on leaving.

Your first meeting may not go into too much detail. Your Italian opposite number will be interested in your company and in your personal background and will tell you about his or hers. As we have seen, Italy is all about relationship-building, and this stage may be followed by lunch or at least a *panino* (bread-roll snack).

In the South it is important to allow more time for business visits. You will do twice as much in Milan as you will do in the same time in Rome or Naples. In Milan allow for, say, three meetings a day and an evening engagement. In Rome, allow for two meetings and an evening engagement and in Naples or Palermo, depending on who you are visiting, allow for two meetings in the day. Breakfast meetings have not yet caught on in Italy.

MAKING A PRESENTATION

In Italy a lecture or formal presentation should last about thirty minutes, with time for questions and discussion afterward. Audiences expect to be persuaded and appreciate a moderate to hard sell of ideas and products. The success of the presentation depends largely on the skills of the speaker, and good-quality materials matter. Formal language should be used to begin with, but informal language can also be used later. Visual aids such as films or photographs are appreciated, and should be aesthetically pleasing as well as informative. Strong eye contact is necessary, and your pace should be brisk.

Italian listeners are interested in the personality and style of the speaker. Standing stock-still during a presentation is less appreciated than the use of body language. People may interrupt your speech for clarification, but save questions and comments for the end.

When presenting your company and your product, find out what your audience is interested in, listen for any personal details, and incorporate these into your presentation. Show an interest in them and they will reciprocate.

MEETINGS AND NEGOTIATING SKILLS

The main object of most meetings is either to communicate decisions or to discuss matters and examine issues. Some discussions may be aimed at achieving good personal relations in the interest of a long-term partnership. The Italians look for long-term profit rather than short-term gain. Meetings will often begin with a few minutes of small talk (in the South these preliminaries may last anything from twenty to thirty minutes).

Meetings rarely have a formal structure. The idea is that everyone should have the opportunity to express their point of view. People may all talk at once, or even conduct mini-conversations or take telephone calls in the room. This is not considered rude. Work around it; don't get upset.

Even if there is an agenda, it is not considered necessary to take each point in order and people happily return to items raised previously. Agendas, action points, time frames, next steps, and even minutes are not considered seriously in most Italian companies, as the decision will be made by people who may not even be present.

Negotiations can be finalized quite quickly, but Italian negotiators are also very patient, can go into great detail, and may take time to achieve their aims. Their approach can be quite subtle. The Italians like win-win outcomes, and may take a piece of secondary business if they cannot get the main contract they were after. Establishing a contractual relationship is the way to a longer and more fulfilling relationship.

The Italians may move quickly to apparent agreement but then take quite a long time to discuss the details, which may substantially change the nature of the contract. Discussion, though intense, is conducted in a pleasant way and Italians can be very accommodating, especially if personal considerations are involved.

A word of caution: while it is important to express optimism and not to knock your negotiating partner's enthusiasm, try to separate facts from speculation and check that your Italian counterparts are not promising more than they can deliver. A good way to do this is to take notes that you can check later. It may also be useful to periodically summarize what has been agreed to.

Always listen carefully to advice from your Italian partners and respect their know-how. They understand Italy much better than you do and they are also very experienced in world markets.

BUSINESS ENTERTAINING

The Italians like to get to know their partners, and this takes place over long and leisurely meals. On the whole, they do not like to conclude business without lunch, dinner, or at least a *panino* to "set the seal" on the relationship, and they are very good at choosing the right restaurant, food, and wine. Entertaining is usually semiformal, or formal, in a good restaurant with excellent wine and food. Dress is either smart or casual, but always elegant, with matching accessories. The conversation may be about business in general, but will very often turn to art, history, or regional culture. Avoid topics such as the Second World War, politics, corruption, and the Mafia. It is normal to keep your hands on the table when not eating, and you should be on your best and most charming behavior.

Remember that when meeting for the first time in a business setting, people will introduce themselves by their surname, not by their company or their job, which would be considered gauche or even rude. Do not go to first names until you are invited to do so. On the whole, guests leave when they are ready; it is considered rude for the host to end the meal. In the South, the host often arranges transport home for guests.

If going to someone's home, the same rules apply. You are expected to bring a gift (perhaps flowers, or gift-wrapped chocolates), but be careful about giving wine unless it is of high quality, as many Italians are connoisseurs and may even have their own vineyards. Liqueurs, delicacies, and craft items from your own country are all suitable gifts; whiskeys and liqueurs are usually appreciated.

The Italian genius for entertaining can pose a problem if you are returning the favor. If you are inviting a business acquaintance while you are in Italy, it is a good idea to ask his or her secretary to recommend a favorite restaurant, and to defer to your guest in the choice of food and wine. This will be taken as a compliment.

Even if you are entertaining in your own country, you will find that most Italians prefer eating Italian food, so look for the most authentic Italian restaurant available. Your guest may also know of a wonderful restaurant (perhaps owned by a relative) that you have never heard of but that serves food to die for. All you need do is pay the bill.

chapter nine

COMMUNICATING

LANGUAGE SKILLS
Italy is a country of communicators, but not
always successfully in English. Although
English is taught in primary school, many
Italians (especially the older generation) are not
particularly confident English-speakers. For
those who are, their English is often quite heavily
accented, with the vowels strung out musically,
extending the length of words and sentences. It is
important not to expect everyone to understand
English. There are two ways of dealing with this:
one is to make allowances with your English,
and the other is to learn some Italian. Both
approaches should be adopted.

Using English
Speaking English clearly isn't a matter of slowing
down, it's a matter of leaving pauses so that your
interlocutor can catch up. So speak a little more
slowly and clearly than you would normally, but
leave a short gap (a mere beat will do) between
sentences or phrases to allow the conversation
to breathe.

Secondly, avoid idioms and slang. And if you use initials or acronyms, spell them out the first time you use them as they will probably be different in Italian.

Finally, it's clearer if you use shorter sentences and make them active ("I do it") rather than passive ("it is done") if possible.

Learn Some Italian

Many universities and private language schools in Italy offer short courses in Italian for foreigners from two weeks' to three months' duration. Courses cover both Italian language and culture, ranging from Etruscan history to contemporary Italian literature and art. Florence has some twenty-five foreign language schools teaching Italian, and there are two state-funded organizations, the *Università Italiana per Stranieri* in Perugia, and the *Scuola Lingue e Cultura per Stranieri* in Siena. Study grants may be available and it is worth inquiring at the Italian Consulate or Italian Cultural Institute. Perugia and Siena run courses year-round, as do private language schools. Universities usually only offer courses during the summer vacation.

THE MEDIA
Newspapers and Magazines

Italians aren't such avid newspaper readers as the British or the North Americans, and readership is greater in the North than in the South. Newspapers are published regionally, but some have national circulation. All newspapers have political leanings and it is useful to know about these.

Italy's best-selling newspapers are *Repubblica*, published in Rome and holding center-left views; the Milan-based *Corriere della Sera*, which holds center-right views and includes an English section; and *Italy Daily*, which is more centrist. *L'Unità*, Italy's Communist newspaper, is also influential although less widely read. A number of regional newspapers are also important, such as *La Nazione* (Florence), *La Stampa* (Turin), *Il Tempo* and *Il Messaggero* (Rome), *Il Secolo XIX* (Genoa), and *La Sicilia* (Catania). The main Italian news magazine is *L'Espresso*.

Italy doesn't have downscale tabloid newspapers, but the specialist sports papers *Corriere dello Sport* and *La Gazzetta dello Sport* have a wide readership. Gossip magazines like *Oggi* (Today) and *Gente* (People) are very popular. This is where you'll find the paparazzi pictures.

Several English-language magazines are available in the big cities. You can ask for *Time Out Rome* (monthly), *Where Rome* (monthly), or *A Guest in Milan* (monthly) at your hotel, though they usually run out early in the day.

Newsdealers are uncommon in Italy. Instead there are state-run kiosks (*edicole*) all over the cities. They are where Italians buy the popular weekly part-work magazines with CD-Roms or videos on any number of subjects.

The international press is well represented in Italy. The *International New York Times* is one of the most popular papers. The weekly news magazine *The Economist* is also widely read.

Radio and TV

The first thing to know about Italian TV is that it works on the PAL system and may not be compatible with systems outside Europe. The second is that Italian TV went digital in 2012, massively increasing the number of free to air terrestrial TV channels. The third thing is that most broadcasts are in Italian. English-language access channels are hard to come by. The state television and radio network is RAI, but the private Mediaset (Rete 4, Canale 5, and Italia 1) network, owned by former Prime Minister, Silvio Berlusconi, is extremely powerful.

If you live or own property in Italy and have a TV or radio you have to pay a TV and Radio license tax (*canone rai*), even if you don't access domestic broadcasts. Even if you are in a furnished flat, if it has TV, you have to pay the license fee. Get the form from the Italian Post Office and you will need a tax code (*codice fiscale*) to apply. The RAI Web site has details in English (www.rai.it). For Italian and international music commercial stations, try Radio Italia, Radio Globo, or Radio DJ.

For English-language radio and TV the BBC World Service is the world's largest international broadcaster with services in English and twenty-seven languages. It also operates the satellite subscription service BBC World TV. To find program schedules for BBC World Service radio visit www.bbc.co.uk/worldservice.

Other international services may also be available, notably Eurosport, CNN, France 24, Russia Today, and the US stations CBS, NBC, and Bloomberg, depending on availability through your hotel or satellite network.

If you have access to satellite TV in Italy, you can receive BBC 1, 2, 3, and 4, and also Radio Canada, Radio Australia, and Voice of America. To access BBC programs online, go to www.bbc.co.uk.

Television

After the Portuguese and the British, Italians watch more TV than any other European nation (on average, about four hours per day). Surveys suggest that 90 percent of Italians watch some TV every day and that most receive their news from the television.

There is little or no cable TV in Italy, but wide use of satellite TV (see next page) from the Astra satellite. Imported programs are dubbed into Italian. Violent or sexually explicit programs cannot be shown between 7:00 a.m. and 10:30 p.m.—it was the Italians who pioneered the "violence chip" that filters out violent programs when children are watching.

Until 1976 all TV was state-owned and censored by the Church. Since deregulation, however, Italy has acquired six main stations and hundreds of local ones. Of the six main terrestrial stations, three are run by the state: Rai 1, Rai 2, and Rai 3. The state channels command about half of the regular viewing audience.

The main commercial stations—Italia 1, Rete 4, and Canale 5—are owned by Silvio Berlusconi through his Mediaset company and command about 50 percent of the viewing audience.

The remaining 10 percent of the audience watch programs put out by the approximately nine hundred local TV stations.

Italian TV is not noted for the quality of its programing. The key issue, however, is that in a country where TV is the main opinion-former, the entire private sector has been owned by one person, who is also the leader of a political party.

Satellite TV

Pay TV is very popular in Italy, with over a million subscribers. The advantage of pay TV and satellite TV is that they offer much wider access to English-language programs. The *doppio* audio track allows you to bring up the original English-language soundtrack. You can also receive BBC World TV and other English-language stations such as CNN.

TV Systems

Standard PAL, NTSC, and SECAM videos won't work in Italy, which uses the PAL-BG system. It's best not to import a TV or video into Italy, but to buy a multi-standard system locally. Italy is a Zone 2 DVD area, so US Zone 1 DVDs can only be viewed on a multi-standard DVD player.

TELEPHONES

The Italian state telephone company is Telecom Italia but, like Britain and the USA, other suppliers are now in the market, notably Tiscali and Wind. All major towns have a Telecom Italia office, which is responsible for the installation and maintenance of phone lines. Telecom Italia is the first port of call if you are getting a new phone line installed or changing the subscriber name, but the phone itself may be provided by another company.

Dialing Codes

In most countries area codes begin with a (0), and when you dial from abroad you omit the zero. In Italy you don't. So if you are dialing a number in Florence, for example, which is 00 39 (0)55…, you should dial 00 39 055 followed by the subscriber number. If you forget, a recorded message will remind you, but in Italian only.

All calls, even local ones within the area you are calling from, require the area code to be entered. Dialing out is much simpler: simply 00 and the country code.

Many Italians now have mobile devices. To call someone on their cell phone, you must always dial the area code before the number, even if you are in the area.

Answering the Phone

Italian has a universal greeting for answering the phone: "*Pronto.*" If you hear an answering machine message, it will probably be something like "We are momentarily absent." No Italian will let you know that they have gone away for three weeks as it would be considered tantamount to an invitation to burglars.

Using Public Telephones

This can be tricky as public pay phones are frequently out of order. You will need to buy a phone card (*carta/scheda/tessera telefonica*) from a *tabacchi* (tear off the marked corner first).

If you need a landline, go to one of the numerous telephone centers that have sprung up in the cities. In the countryside, bars or restaurants may still have a *telefono a scatti* (points telephone), which records the number of units of each call. The barman switches on the phone for you and you pay him for the units used.

In the countryside, some houses display a telephone symbol that means they are authorized as public phone-service providers.

Finding a Phone Number

Telecom Italia publishes directories in two formats, *Pagine Bianche* (White Pages) for personal numbers, and *Pagine Gialle* (Yellow Pages) for business. You can also access them on the Internet at www.paginegialle.it and www.paginebianche.it.

An English Yellow Pages service is available for major cities at www.englishyellowpages.it.

Directory inquiries in Italy are accessed by dialing 12, but the procedure is automated and you have to hold for a human voice. There is no English directory inquiries service.

Emergencies

Italy's general emergency number is 113. Local operators speak only Italian but a translation service into English is available on 170.

THE POSTAL SERVICE

The PT (*Poste e Telecomunicazioni*) is a limited company with a 75 percent government holding. Traditionally, the postal service in Italy is considered extremely unreliable and most Italians prefer to use registered post (*posta raccomandata*) or a private courier service for anything important. The most reliable postal service is from the Vatican in Rome, which sends all its international mail from Switzerland, so you get interesting Vatican stamps and safe delivery too! All the major courier services have offices in the main cities. US Mailboxes Inc. now has several franchisees in Italy.

Italy has an ordinary postal service (*posta ordinaria*) and a priority service (*posta prioritaria*). *Posta prioritaria* guarantees delivery within Italy on the next working-day, and in three to four days within the EU. You need a gold priority stamp and an airmail sticker for foreign destinations. There's also a

Postacelere express service available in main post offices. For anything important make sure you obtain proof of posting.

Postcards and letters (if they arrive) will take three to seven days within Italy, and four to ten days within Europe. Allow at least a week for airmail letters to North America; for Australia and New Zealand, two weeks.

The best place to buy stamps is in a *tabacchi* (marked with a black T sign). Stamps (*francobolli*) are sold loose, not in booklets. The official identification color of the post office is red, although documentation is often done in blue. There is usually only one collection per day.

Post offices get very busy and have different windows for different services, so make sure you are in the right line. Post offices deal with telegrams, faxes, telex, foreign currency exchange, cash transfers, utility bills, road tax, and TV licenses. You can buy the *bollo* for the car in the post office. They also pay state pensions and deal in lottery tickets. Unless your business specifically needs a post office or you have plenty of time, you are better off buying stamps in a *tabacchi* and posting in a mailbox. Main post offices are open all day during the week but close at 1:00 p.m. on Saturdays.

Sending Mail to Italy
Italian addresses have a five-digit postcode, or CAP (*codice di avviamento postale*). It is important to get this right to ensure delivery. You can find postcode details at www.poste.it.

Here is the normal way of writing an Italian address:

Maggiore Paolo
(surname followed by first name)
Via Marghera, 2
1-10234 Torino
Italy

CONVERSAZIONE
The communication that really matters to Italians is face-to-face. *Conversazione* originally meant associating with others, and it is here that the Italians excel. They will go to great lengths to draw you in to conversation, and every town has its piazza, which is essentially a space for conversation. *Stare insieme* (being together) is important for Italians as it gives a chance to air grievances, express feelings, and defuse flare-ups. Even on the beach, where the British and the Americans will walk miles to find a lonely

cove, the Italians will crowd deck chair to deck chair in a good-neighborly fashion.

A new venue for *conversazione* is provided by the TV talk shows, which are exceptionally popular and go on for hours.

Body Language

An amusing way of passing time is to sit in a café and watch Italians talking. They talk with their hands, and their gestures can be very expressive, particularly in Naples and the South.

A person who is expressing disagreement may stroke their fingers upward under their chin, palm down, and then thrust them forward.

At a football match, you may see people pointing their hands at the referee with the "pinky" and forefinger out and the other fingers and thumb turned in, palm down. This means that the spectators disagree with the referee. If the palm is turned upward in the same gesture, then you know that they are saying something obscene to the referee.

Greetings and Forms of Address

Despite its charm and openness, Italy is quite a formal society. Italian has the formal "you" (*Lei*) and the informal "you" (*tu*). You should remain on formal terms until invited to use first names, though this doesn't apply when you are with children, teenagers, or young adults, or in an informal environment. As a guest you will always be introduced first.

Shaking hands is a physical affair. Hands will be shaken warmly and your arm may be grasped with the other hand. Friends and male relatives will often embrace or slap each other on the back in greeting, and women (and sometimes men) will kiss on both cheeks. At a large gathering, it is considered acceptable to go up to someone, shake hands, and introduce yourself.

Topics of Conversation

Most Italians are highly cultured people, and will be happy to talk about art, architecture, and monuments, particularly in their local area. Local food and wine are popular subjects, and sports are very important. Don't treat soccer lightly—it is taken seriously by many Italians. Family, local scenery, holidays, and movies are other favorite topics of conversation.

As mentioned previously, although Italians are often critical of things in their country, they do not appreciate it when foreigners criticize them. Religion, politics, and the Second World War are off-limits, and sexually explicit jokes are not usually exchanged in mixed company.

GENDER ISSUES

The downside of "romantic Italy" has always been the impression that foreign women are "fair game." In fact, Italian women are on the whole strictly brought up, and Italian men live at home longer than their counterparts in the US or UK.

In the North, it is acceptable (though still unusual) for a single woman to eat alone in a restaurant. In the South, however, people are less accustomed to this idea, and you may attract unwanted attention. One way to show that you do not wish to be bothered is to keep work or reading matter on your table.

CONCLUSION

Italy, as we have seen, is a land of contradictions, combining conformity and anarchy, bureaucracy and evasion, extreme riches and great poverty, scandal and religion. One writer has compared Italy's shining surface with its "dark heart."

And yet what keeps Italy and the Italians going is the conviction that the one loyalty that matters is family and close friends, and that with time and understanding everything can be worked out. It is only a matter of finding the way. This fluidity makes life in Italy exceptionally attractive, even seductive, for foreigners, although for residents and business people it can be frustrating.

Modern Italy faces unemployment, immigration (particularly from the Balkans), environmental pollution, rising housing costs and crime, and the social fallout from economic reform. However, it has overcome political extremism and achieved a degree of government stability, and is one of the main upholders and beneficiaries of the EU and the euro.

Italy has one of the largest economies in the world, and is a powerhouse of manufacturing ingenuity and creativity in food, fashion design, and the automotive industry. The Italians are a vital, warmhearted, and inventive people whose contribution to Western civilization cannot be overestimated, and who have contributed hugely to the gaiety of nations.

Further Reading

History, Politics, and Society

Barzini, Luigi. *The Italians*. London: Penguin Books, 1983.

Emmott, Bill. *Good Italy, Bad Italy. Why Italy Must Conquer its Demons to Face the Future*. New Haven, Connecticut: Yale University Press, 2012.

Gilmore, David. *The Pursuit of Italy. A History of a Land, its Regions and their Peoples*. London: Penguin Books, 2011.

Ginsborg, Paul. *Italy and its Discontents*. London: Penguin Books, 2003.

Jones, Tobias. *The Dark Heart of Italy*. London: Faber and Faber, 3rd edition, 2013.

Lintner, Valerio. *A Traveller's History of Italy*. London: Windrush Press/ Cassell, 2001.

Severgnini, Beppe. *La Bella Figura: An Insider's Guide to the Italian Mind*. London: Hodder & Stoughton, 2007.

Guides

Belford, Ros, *et al.The Rough Guide to Italy*. London: Rough Guides, 2003.

Simonis, D., and F. Adams, M. Roddis, S. Webb, and N. Williams. *Lonely Planet Italy*. London: Lonely Planet, 2003.

Streiffert, Anna. *Eyewitness Guide to Italy*. London: Dorling Kindersley, 2003.

Living in Italy

Chesters, Graeme (ed). *Living and Working in Italy*. London: Survival Books, 2003.

Hinton, Amanda. *Living and Working in Italy*. Oxford: How To Books, 2003.

Morrison, Terri, and Wayne A. Conaway and George A. Borden. *Kiss, Bow, or Shake Hands: How to Do Business in Sixty Countries*. Avon, Massachusetts: Adams Media Corporation, 1994.

Parks, Tim. *An Italian Education*. London: Vintage Books, 2000.

– – –. *Italian Neighbours*. London: Vintage Books, 2001.

– – –. *A Season with Verona*. London: Vintage Books, 2003.

Language

In-Flight Italian. New York: Living Language, 2001.

Fodor's Italian for Travelers (CD Package). New York: Living Language, 2005.

culture smart! italy

Index

air travel 113
All Saints Day 61,
    64–65
Alps 13, 21
Alto Adige 10
annual vacations 65
Apennines 13
appearances 50–51
art galleries 108

banking, money and
    90–93, 131–132
bars and nightlife
    80–81
bella figura 50–51
Berlusconi, Silvio 41,
    42, 44, 52, 129,
    153, 155
birth 90
body language 140,
    141, 161
bolli (state postage
    stamps) 114, 126,
    127, 159
Bologna 10, 21, 43
    University of 28
Borsa (Stock
    Exchange) 20
Brindisi 12
bureaucracy 56–57
buses 118
business cards 143
business entertaining
    148–149
business hours
    142–143

campanilismo (local
    patriotism) 54–56,
    66
camping 105
Capri 21, 127
Carnevale 66–67
cars *see* driving
Catholicism 10, 18,
    49, 60
Christmas 61–62

church, behavior
    in 70–71, 104,
    108
cinema 111
cities 10, 20–22
civil service 56–57
climate 10, 13–14
close-knit circles
    75–76
coaches 118
commitment 77
communication skills
    140–141
Communism 36,
    41, 43
companies
    finance and
    corporate
    governance
    131–132
    structure and
    organization
    130–131
conglomerates,
    privately owned
    129
Congregation for the
    Doctrine of the
    Faith 19
conversazione 160–162
    body language 140,
    141, 161
    greetings and forms
    of address 161–162
    topics of
    conversation 162
Corsica 12
credit cards 90–91, 92
Curia (College of
    Cardinals) 19
currency 10, 90, 91
cycling 121

decision-making
    136–137
disagreement,
    managing 139

Dodecanese islands
    35
Dolomites 13
dress 70, 81, 103–104,
    108, 148
drinks 100–101
driving 119–127

Easter 61, 63–64
eating and drinking
    96–103
    business entertaining
    148–149
    drinking 100–103
    meal culture 97–100
    stand or sit? 101–102
economy 44–45, 128,
    163, 164
education 87–88
electricity 11, 86
emigration 15, 89
Emilia-Romagna
    21, 43
employment 89
Epiphany 61, 62, 63
Eritrea 35
esterofilia 74
Ethiopia 35, 38
ethnic makeup 10
European Monetary
    Union 42
European Union (EU)
    16, 113, 129, 163
Eurozone 90, 113
expressway
    (*autostrada*)
    network 12, 124
eye contact 141

family 46–47, 76–77
    businesses 135–136
Fascism 36, 37–39,
    41
feedback 136, 139
feelings and emotions
    47–48
Fellini, Federico 71

Ferragosto
(Assumption Day)
61, 65, 83
ferries 127
festivals 60–65, 107,
144
Fiume, Croatia 36
Florence (Firenze) 14,
21, 67, 107, 108,
120
food *see* eating and
drinking
football 29, 74, 105–
106, 162
forms of address 161
Forza Italia 41
funerals 73
furbo (cunning) 57–58

gambling 81
garbo (graciousness)
53
gender issues 162–163
Genoa 10, 21
geography 12–13
gift giving 56, 79, 149
Gorizia 10
government 10, 43,
163
Gramsci, Antonio 77
greetings 161–162

health 76, 93–95
Herculaneum 21, 109
history 22–39
prehistory 23
rise of Rome 24
Roman Empire
24–25
fall of the Empire
and rise of the
Church 25–27
city-states 27–28
Italian Renaissance
28–30
foreign invasions
30–31

French rule 31–32
unification of Italy
32–36
march on Rome
36–37
Fascist years 37–39
postwar Italy 39–43
housing 82–84, 163

Immaculate
Conception 61, 65
immigration 15, 90,
163
Inquisition 19
internet 11
invitations 77, 79
Ischia 21, 95, 127

jealousy 78

Labor Day 61, 64
labor relations
132–133
language 8, 10, 74,
150–151
of management 139
leadership 133–136
Lega Nord 41
Levi, Carlo 55
Liberation Day 61,
64
Libya 35
Liguria 21, 96
local community
75–77
local holidays 66–68
Lombardy 26, 32,
33, 44
loudness 51–52

Mafia 40, 47, 148
making contact
141–142
Mani Pulite campaign
41–42
Marche 43
marriage 89

media 11, 151–156
meetings 81, 138, 139
first 145
Metropolitana 117–118
Mezzogiorno 44, 130
Milan 10, 13, 14, 20,
32, 35, 40, 44, 86,
103
military service 88
Modena 33
money and banking
90–93
monuments 108–109
motivation 138
Mount Vesuvius 21,
109
museums 107–108
music and theater
110–111

name-days 68–69
Naples 10, 13, 14,
30–34, 62, 108, 120
negotiating skills
147–148
New Year's Day 61, 62
newspapers and
magazines 11,
151–153
nicknames 52

order and hierarchy
52–53
outdoor life 104–105

Padua 108
Palermo 10, 21, 108
Palio 67, 107
Parma 33
passeggiata 105
passports 81, 91, 92,
113, 115
piazza, the 54, 80
Piedmont 21, 33, 96
Pio, Padre 70
Pisa 108
planning 133, 136

police 122
  registration 113–114
politics 43–44, 162
Pompeii 21, 109
Pope, the 16–19, 27, 31, 32, 34, 37, 48, 49, 62, 69, 70, 90
population 10, 14–16, 90
postal service 158–160
power 78, 133, 134
prehistory 23
presentations 145–146
privacy 76
public holidays 61, 142
public sector 129

radio 11, 153–154
recommendation (raccomandato) 54, 57, 141–142
refugees 15–16
regions/regional capitals 16–22
relationships 54
religion 10, 18, 162
Republic Day 61, 64
residency 114–115
Roman Catholic Church 16, 26–27, 48–49, 53, 57, 63, 65, 69, 155
Roman Empire 23, 24–25, 26
Rome 10, 12, 14, 18, 20, 24–25, 34, 62, 66, 86, 107, 108

St Peter's Basilica, Rome 18, 19, 62
saints 69
  saints' days 66, 68
salamelecco 53
San Marino, Republic of 16
Santo Stefano 61
Sardinia 12, 32, 33
Savoia 39
scooter 120–121
Second World War 38, 162
shaking hands 162
shopping 84–87
Sicily 12, 21, 30, 31, 34, 38, 40, 55, 96
Siena 67–68, 107, 108
Sistine Chapel, Vatican 18, 19, 108
small business 129–130
soccer see football
social clubs 79–80
South Tyrol 35
spas 95
state sector 129
style 8–9, 51
superstition 71–73
Swiss Guards 17–18, 62

taxis 118–119
teamworking 137–138
telephone 11, 156–158
television 11, 153–156
timing 75

tipping 99
tolerance 49–50
tourism 14, 62, 74, 95, 106–107
trains 115–118
travelers' checks 91
Trentino 35
Trento 10
Trieste 10, 35
Turin 10, 13, 21, 34
Tuscany 21, 23, 43, 96, 120

Umbria 120
unemployment 36, 88–89, 163

Vatican 16–19, 34, 60, 62, 108
Venetia 32, 34
Veneto 22
Venice (Venezia) 10, 14, 22, 34, 66, 67, 107, 108, 120

women
  in armed forces 88
  gender issues 162–163

Acknowledgments

The author would like to acknowledge the contributions of Hugh Shankland, Professor of Italian at the University of Durham.

Whatever it take

"We need those records Todd said.

"Are you insane?" Serena asked. There seemed to be a pattern evolving here. She'd already asked him this question twice in the brief time she'd known him.

"The doctor is dead," he said unrepentantly. "We need a look."

"You're serious." They'd been through this routine before. How could the Colby Agency send her someone prepared to break the law?

"Dead serious. Think about it, Serena. If playing by the rules would give you the answers you wanted, the police would have found them. Whatever happened to your friend, it wasn't executed by the rules. We can either keep butting the same brick wall or we can go around it. The choice is yours."

He was right. She turned away from him. Struggled with her age-old problem: Be a good girl and do this the right way or take a chance—and do whatever it takes.

DEBRA WEBB

INVESTIGATING 101

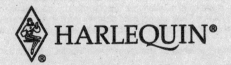

HARLEQUIN®

TORONTO • NEW YORK • LONDON
AMSTERDAM • PARIS • SYDNEY • HAMBURG
STOCKHOLM • ATHENS • TOKYO • MILAN • MADRID
PRAGUE • WARSAW • BUDAPEST • AUCKLAND

Our children are our future. There is
no more precious resource on the planet.
This book is dedicated to all those
who take the time to mentor a child. Your work
is an investment in our future. I salute you!

ISBN 0-373-22909-7

INVESTIGATING 101

Copyright © 2006 by Debra Webb

www.eHarlequin.com

Printed in U.S.A.

ABOUT THE AUTHOR

Debra Webb was born in Scottsboro, Alabama, to parents who taught her that anything is possible if you want it bad enough. When her husband joined the military, they moved to Berlin, Germany, and Debra became a secretary in the commanding general's office. By 1985 they were back in the States, and finally moved to Tennessee, to a small town where everyone knows everyone else. With the support of her husband and two beautiful daughters, Debra took up writing again, looking to mystery and movies for inspiration. In 1998, her dream of writing for Harlequin came true. You can write to Debra with your comments at P.O. Box 64, Huntland, Tennessee 37345 or visit her Web site at http://www.debrawebb.com to find out exciting news about her next book.

Books by Debra Webb

HARLEQUIN INTRIGUE

583—SAFE BY HIS SIDE*
597—THE BODYGUARD'S BABY*
610—PROTECTIVE CUSTODY*
634—SPECIAL ASSIGNMENT: BABY
646—SOLITARY SOLDIER*
659—PERSONAL PROTECTOR*
671—PHYSICAL EVIDENCE*
683—CONTRACT BRIDE*
693—UNDERCOVER WIFE**
697—HER HIDDEN TRUTH**

701—GUARDIAN OF THE NIGHT**
718—HER SECRET ALIBI*
732—KEEPING BABY SAFE*
747—CRIES IN THE NIGHT*
768—AGENT COWBOY*
801—SITUATION: OUT OF CONTROL†
807—PRIORITY: FULL EXPOSURE†
837—JOHN DOE ON HER DOORSTEP††
843—EXECUTIVE BODYGUARD††
849—MAN OF HER DREAMS††
864—URBAN SENSATION
891—PERSON OF INTEREST
909—INVESTIGATING 101‡

*Colby Agency
‡Colby Agency: New Recruits
**The Specialists
†Colby Agency: Internal Affairs
††The Enforcers

CAST OF CHARACTERS

Todd Thompson—The Colby Agency's new recruit. Todd is exactly the kind of raw talent the Colby Agency is looking for. Will his natural talent override his lack of experience? There's only one way to find out.

Serena Black—She is young but dead serious about her work and finding her friend. But just when she is certain she knows who's responsible for her friend's abduction, a new clue gets tossed into the mix and points her in an entirely different direction. The only thing Serena can be sure of is her growing attraction to one sexy new recruit.

Dr. Charles Landon—A pioneer in his field, could he really murder his wife and unborn child? Everything he has worked for is about to see fruition, but how much is he willing to pay to reach that pinnacle?

Molly Landon—The only things she ever wanted were her husband's love and to have the family she'd always dreamed of. Is it too late for that now?

Delia Neely—Was her affair with Charles Landon the reason his wife is missing?

Arthur Miles—He has every reason to be jealous of his colleague Charles Landon. How far would he go to see him fall?

Nolan Fairbanks—He knows plenty of secrets... The question is can Serena trust him?

A. J. Braddock—Colby Agency investigator. A.J. is supposed to keep Todd Thompson on the straight and narrow during his first assignment, but that may prove an impossible task—even for an ex-marine.

Chapter One

Victoria Colby-Camp sat at her desk and stared at the neat pile of manila folders Mildred had placed in the exact middle of her clean blotter pad.

It was the same each Monday morning. Mildred gathered the assignment and status reports from each investigator and brought the bundle to Victoria at nine sharp for her perusal. At ten, a standard staff meeting would take place in the conference room. New assignments would be dissected and doled out, old business would be discussed. The work week would continue from there.

The routine never varied.

Victoria sighed, the sound echoing softly in her empty office.

She had no right to feel this way. Life had been extremely good to her for months now. She certainly could not complain....

And yet, she felt...bored.

Her brow furrowed deeply in denial of her last thought. Perhaps bored was not the proper word. She and Lucas had celebrated their first wedding anniversary a few months ago with a long weekend in the Cayman Islands. Her son was happily married and anticipating the arrival of the first Colby grandchild.

What else could she ask for from her personal life?

The Colby Agency continued to thrive. The cases that walked through reception's doors included the most intriguing and challenging from right here in Chicago as well as all across the nation—ones that no other agency seemed able to solve in addition to those of longtime, loyal clients.

Still, Victoria felt restless.

She pushed up from her chair and walked across the room to look out at the city she loved. A city pulsing with life, filled with magnificent and innovative architecture. A place rich with colorful and turbulent political history as well as vibrant cultural venues.

There was no other city in the country quite like it. No other place she'd rather be.

Dozens of memories filtered through her mind, warming her heart. It seemed so long ago now that she and James, her first husband and the father of her only son, had started this agency. She had known even then that the Colby Agency would be something very special. How could it be anything else? James Colby had orchestrated its creation.

But now, more than twenty years later, something was missing. She concentrated hard in an effort to pinpoint the motivation for the fleeting sensation.

This odd emptiness had started almost one month ago. At first she'd considered that, with her highly trained and efficient staff, maybe she was bored with her level of participation in the business of private investigations. Her right-hand personnel oversaw most of the day-to-day operations. Though she came to the office each and every day and reviewed all activities, she was not personally involved with the execution of assignments.

But her role had always been in oversight rather than execution. Why would she suddenly feel unsettled in that role now? Admittedly, change could be a good thing. With that in mind, and much to the dismay of her staff, she'd launched a complete overhaul of the agency's decor. A smile tilted one corner of her mouth. Unquestionably the renovations were a nuisance, but she'd hoped that the transformations would fulfill this sense of lacking she suffered.

The distraction had not worked.

Victoria turned to view her elegantly decorated office. Though the new gold and red tones were quite exquisite, as were the rich jewel tones of the rest of the offices, the relief she'd hoped for had not come.

Nor had the carpet. Her gaze dropped to the beige carpeting on the floor. The contractor had apologized repeatedly for the error. The wrong color had been ordered and, of course, returned, leaving the floor rather bland amid the rest of the opulent decor.

Her attention moved back to her desk and the stack of files. She really should get on with her Monday morning review, but the usual anticipation proved glaringly absent.

There was always the chance that her lackadaisical attitude wasn't work-related at all.

She'd toyed with the idea of a personal makeover. Nothing elaborate. A new hairstyle perhaps, and possibly a color. Victoria smoothed her hand over her firmly coiled French twist. Never one to bother with such trivialities, she'd worn her hair the same way for half a lifetime, never bothering with touching up the multiplying silver strands that gave away her true age.

Was it time for a personal change?

Lucas appeared more than happy with her hair just as it was. She traced the tiny lines accentuating her eyes and wondered why she'd never worried about those, either. Most women her age and of her social standing had undergone at least one facelift by now.

No, she decided, that wasn't the problem.

As simple as it would be to pretend a new wardrobe and a visit to a salon would cure her restless feelings, she knew deep down that it wouldn't help.

Her working life lacked the edge and excitement of the past. Though it was certainly true that the Colby Agency worked many, many intriguing and exciting cases, that wasn't what she meant.

When she and James had first started the agency, everything had been new, including the investigators they hired. One or two had had previous experience in the field, but most learned from the master, James Colby himself. Time and experience had honed this agency to a gleaming, precious jewel among its competition.

No more rough edges, no more raw exhilaration.

Affection tugged at her lips when she thought of Trevor Sloan and his untamed surliness. He'd been a man with more rough edges than most, and yet the best damned investigator any agency could hope to retain. He'd been young and so had Victoria.

On the heels of that thought came an epiphany.

That was the missing ingredient that had her out of sorts.

Youth.

It wasn't that she resented growing older. On the contrary—her life was everything she wanted it to be and more. This was strictly business.

And no one knew better about the business of private investigations than she.

Victoria stepped over to the phone on her desk and pressed the intercom button.

"Mildred, find the date and location of that job fair we talked about last week. I'm considering participating." Anticipation surged in Victoria's veins. She was on to something here. She could feel it all the way to the pads of her feet.

"I have it right here, Victoria," Mildred said as she shuffled through her calendar. "Embassy Suites downtown, this weekend."

Perfect. "Sign the agency up ASAP. I don't want just a booth, I want a conference room. Get it in tomorrow's edition of the *Tribune*."

"It may be too late to sign up," Mildred warned.

Victoria grinned. "Talk to Lyle Vandiver at the Chamber of Commerce. He'll get us in. Pull out all the stops, Mildred. I want to make a big splash."

"The usual employment requirements?" her secretary asked.

There was no need to mull over the question; Victoria knew what she wanted. "No. This is going to be different. No experience necessary. Drop the age requirement to twenty."

"Pardon? Did you say *twenty?*"

"Twenty," Victoria repeated. That was a far cry from the twenty-five guideline the agency generally used. It had been a very long time since she had considered an applicant too young to have any real job experience. And there was no time like the present to see what she'd been missing.

Still sounding befuddled, Mildred assured, "I'll get right on it."

Victoria sat at her desk and began to review the case files with a new sense of purpose.

That was what she'd been missing—just exactly

what this agency needed—new blood. Young blood. Raw talent.

The unexpected.

AT 10:00 A.M. on the dot that morning Victoria moved to the conference room where all not on assignment waited.

Ian Michaels and Simon Ruhl sat on either side of her vacant chair at the head of the long polished mahogany table. Ian's wife, Nicole, as well as Ric Martinez, Ryan Braxton, Pierce Maxwell, Ethan Delaney, Doug Cooper-Smith, Daniel Marks and A. J. Braddock, one of the agency's newest investigators, were present. Patrick O'Brien, the other new member on Victoria's staff, was currently on assignment, as were three other investigators.

As Victoria took her place at the table, Elaine Younger, the agency receptionist, poked her head through the door.

"Victoria, the gentlemen are here to install the carpet."

A litany of groans and sighs went around the room. Elaine looked worried, as if she feared she'd somehow done the wrong thing by making the announcement no one in the room—other than Victoria—wanted to hear.

"Excellent," Victoria said with a nod of approval in Elaine's direction. "Let them know they can start in my office."

Elaine nodded eagerly and quickly closed the door to carry out her orders.

"Victoria."

Victoria turned to Simon and waited for him to proceed.

"Mildred mentioned that you had decided to join in this weekend's job fair."

He didn't have to say the rest; Victoria read the question in his eyes. Why on earth had she lowered the usual standards for hopeful applicants?

"That's correct." She surveyed the table. Judging by the expression on each face, all present had heard the news. "I felt the need to venture into new territory." She clasped her hands and placed them on the table in front of her. "I'd like to sample the raw talent out there," she added bluntly. "Any questions?"

Victoria didn't miss the smile that flirted with Ian's lips. "You have someone in mind for heading up the event?"

Leave it to Ian to cut to the chase. "Actually," Victoria said, "I do." She turned her attention to the right. "I hoped Nicole would be free to handle the job fair."

Nicole Reed-Michaels was former FBI. She had the incredible beauty of the women gracing the covers of fashion magazines. Sleek blond hair and breathtaking blue eyes. But anyone who let her appearance fool them was in for a big surprise. Nicole was not only highly intelligent, she was downright lethal. No one got in her way.

"I'd be happy to, Victoria," Nicole volunteered without hesitation. She shifted those assessing blue eyes to her husband. "You won't mind watching the kids, will you, Ian?"

A moment of loaded silence passed as every man in the room struggled to restrain a grin or a chuckle. Victoria didn't bother holding back. Her lips spread wide with amusement. She loved the power Nicole had over the enigmatic Ian.

"Of course not," he said to his wife before turning back to Victoria. "Shall we move on?"

The status of each ongoing case was reported and new ones assigned. Victoria observed the well-educated, refined members of her outstanding staff. Only the best. The Colby Agency employed the most outstanding in their respective fields...the cream of the crop from many walks of life, including the military as well as other government agencies and law enforcement. Victoria had always prided herself on ferreting out those who had excelled in their former careers. Men and women who were highly trained and well experienced.

But that was about to change.

She needed an infusion of the unknown...of raw, edgy talent.

Excitement. That was what the Colby Agency needed.

Pure T-type adrenaline. Young blood, ready to do anything to prove him or herself.

Just like in the old days.

Chapter Two

It wasn't every day a guy got the goods on a cheating, backstabbing employee. Especially one who was in line for the job said guy wanted.

Todd Thompson grinned.

He'd gotten the evidence.

Pictures didn't lie.

He tapped the nine-by-twelve envelope on the passenger seat of his car. Oh, yeah, today was going to be a very good day. Less than one year out of college and he would make senior associate at the agency.

He'd gotten a callback on his résumé even before graduating. Todd had never believed in waiting until the last minute. He'd liked being prepared, knowing what his future held. So he'd sent out résumés six weeks before graduation. The Wellsly Agency of private investigations had contacted him immediately.

It wasn't every day a student with a major in psychology and a minor in criminology knocked on their door.

The way he saw it, his choice of studies gave him an edge as an investigator. That was exactly how he'd known that his colleague was up to no good. He had a knack for reading people.

Todd parked his beat-up Volvo in the only vacant slot in the parking lot of the building his agency called home. Six months on staff and he was up for promotion already. The only problem was, there was only one senior associate position available and both he and his colleague Janelle Dryer wanted it. Janelle had two months on him at the agency. She also had a killer pair of legs.

But she'd made one fatal mistake. She hadn't covered her tracks well enough.

The agency had suspected for a while now that someone amid their ranks was leaking information to the attorneys of certain high-profile targets. At least two incidents had led to this conclusion, but no one had been able to nail the culprit.

Until now.

Todd had decided to do a little extra investigating himself. The fact that his nemesis was the leak just made victory all the more sweet. When he'd set out to do this he'd merely hoped the move would get him the attention he wanted, and, of course, the promotion. He'd never expected to knock the competition completely out of the running in the same blow. Janelle was guilty. No question in his mind. Why else would she be sleeping with one of the attorneys involved? No reason he could think of. At the very least, this infraction made her un-reliable and put him at the top of the food chain.

He felt a prick of guilt, might even have felt some remorse if Dryer hadn't backstabbed him three times already in the past six months. She'd taken every op-portunity to make him look bad. Had accomplished her mission once. But this wasn't about revenge—this was about survival of the fittest. The best man should get the job and all that jazz.

He was the best man.

He hustled through the front door and straight up to the bank of elevators a full thirty minutes before his workday actually began. His immediate supervisor, Chet Syler, was waiting. Todd had called him at home last night and informed him that he had evidence as to the identity of the leak. His supervisor had insisted that the information be kept between the two of them until whatever evidence Todd possessed could be confirmed. Todd didn't have a problem with that. It was hard to dispute Dryer and the attorney rolling between the sheets when he had a whole roll of prints to back up his asser-tion.

He stabbed the button for the seventh floor and leaned against the back wall of the elevator. He held the envelope firmly in one hand. It wasn't that he enjoyed ratting people out, but this was business. Dryer would have done the same to him. It didn't take a degree in psychology to know that. And he had one.

On the seventh floor he said hello to the reception-ist already at her post then strode confidently to Syler's office. He didn't particularly care that the receptionist didn't bother returning his greeting. Maybe she was distracted. Whatever. He had bigger things on his mind. Such as his first promotion.

Feeling triumphant and utterly satisfied, Todd took one last deep breath before knocking on the door.

Oh, yeah, today was definitely going to be a stellar day.

Syler glanced up but didn't bother standing as Todd entered his office. Funny thing was, his superior didn't look the least bit happy. Without so much as a good morning, Syler reached for the envelope. Confusion elbowing out his victorious afterglow, Todd placed the envelope in his boss's hand. He didn't sit since he hadn't been invited to. The whole situation suddenly felt off kilter somehow.

Syler shuffled through the glossy eight-by-tens, his expression never changing. Somehow Todd hadn't expected this kind of reaction. Anger, disappointment, jealousy maybe, but not this total lack of emotion.

The older man shoved the pictures back into the envelope and turned his full attention on Todd. Todd had the uneasy feeling that he'd just walked into a trap.

"Did you know that Ms. Dryer had been married and divorced?" Syler asked, his voice flat as he deliv-ered the seemingly irrelevant question. "Her maiden name is Syler."

Todd blinked as the relevance hit him square between the eyes. "No, sir," he admitted before swallowing hard to force down the massive lump of crow in his
throat. "I didn't know that." But he knew exactly what
it meant. "She's your daughter?"

The blush of fury started at his superior's crisp white
collar. "That's right." He snatched up the incriminating
envelope and shoved it into his middle desk drawer.
"I've suspected for some time that one of the senior
partners was the leak. I asked Ms. Dryer to find the
truth." His jaw flexed twice with rage. "She was to do
whatever necessary to accomplish her mission. Today
she will announce her findings in a closed briefing to
the senior partners."

The whole scenario suddenly made perfect sense to
Todd. Syler was a partner, but not a senior partner. If he
could prove one of the senior partners was the leak, he
would be in line for a promotion, as would his lovely
daughter. The information she had obtained would
cinch both moves.

Oh, man. "I can assure you, sir," Todd put in quickly,
"no one will hear about her methods from me."

"The problem is, Mr. Thompson—" Syler rose from
his chair as he said this "—I don't like you. My daughter
doesn't like you. Let's just leave it at that. When you've
cleared out your desk, you can pick up your severance
pay from the receptionist."

There was nothing else to say. Todd knew a brick

wall when he hit one and he'd damned sure rammed headfirst into this one.

Todd cleared out his desk and picked up his severance pay as instructed. All under the careful watch of a security guard. As hard as he'd tried to be out before the staff started to arrive, he ran into Dryer in the lobby. She smirked and gave him a universal hand signal that stated her position quite clearly.

She'd won. The promotion was hers and he was out of a job.

He tossed the box of odds and ends into the backseat of his car and then dropped behind the wheel. At least it was Friday. He'd have time to look over the classifieds and update his résumé before hitting the streets on Monday.

The severance pay would cover the coming month's rent.

He swore as he twisted the key in the ignition. Maybe he should have gone to grad school. His folks had said he'd regret not pursuing a higher degree. But no, he'd been too on fire to get out there and dive into the world of investigations. It had been his dream since he was a kid.

It should be simple. He was good. Just ask any of his professors. Hell, he'd even lived a double life for three whole months to write a thesis like no other. The plan had backfired a little, but he'd come out all right. His advisor had secretly told him he'd never read a thesis so compelling. So what if Todd had pretended to be someone he wasn't to make it happen. No harm had been done, except to a few egos.

Oh, well. Chicago was a big city. There had to be an agency that would appreciate his particular skills.

He pulled over to the curb in front of the diner where he usually grabbed breakfast on Saturdays. Might as well eat and maybe scan today's paper. Anything was better than going back to his studio apartment and walking the floors.

He couldn't call his parents. They would only plead with him to come back home to Alabama. What was a small-town boy like him doing in a big city? That was his folks' way of looking at the situation. He couldn't explain to them that there was a great deal more to life than being the star football player on the high school team and going on to teach at the same school as his father had. No offense. Todd loved and admired his father. But that life just wasn't for him.

He wanted—yearned for—excitement. The kind he wouldn't find in Birmingham, Alabama. Chicago was the place to be. And even if Wellsly wasn't the very top agency in this city, it had been a damn good starting place.

But he'd blown that opportunity by being overzealous.

Who the hell else would give him a shot without any real experience? Listing Wellsly as a previous employer might not be the best way to get his foot in the door someplace else, considering he'd just been fired.

"Morning, Todd." Anna, the waitress who took his order every Saturday morning, greeted him from behind the counter. "You want the usual this morning?"

He dredged up a friendly smile. "You got it, pretty lady." He winked and the older woman blushed. She reminded him of his mother. Gray hair tucked into a practical bun. Conservative uniform concealing every inch of her from the knees up and shiny pink lip gloss making her smile sparkle. A genuinely nice lady.

Todd slid onto a bar stool and listened to Anna chatter about late April's sudden cool snap as she poured him a cup of coffee.

"Winter's determined to hang on this year," she said knowingly, then shivered visibly. "It's almost May, it ought to be warmer than this." She sat the carafe back onto the warming plate and snagged the nearest news-paper. "Here you go." She studied him a moment, her expression suddenly serious. "Looks like you could do with something to occupy your mind this morning."

Yep, just like his mother. A mind reader.

"Thanks." Todd took the paper and turned the page without even surveying the front headlines. It wasn't that he didn't care about current events but he had his own problems today. Such as finding a job and pretend-ing that his ego wasn't stinging like hell.

His gaze snagged on a large advertisement for this weekend's job fair. He scanned the staffing agencies and firms participating, his hopes faltering with each name he read. The dead-last one had him sitting up a little straighter.

The Colby Agency.

He steadied his runaway imagination and reminded himself that he'd looked at their requirements once before. Minimum age was twenty-five with at least two years of pertinent experience. And, as good as he was at pretending to be someone or something he wasn't, lying wasn't going to work with the premier investigative agency. A firm like the Colby Agency would surely do an extensive background search.

Just when he would have moved on, his eyes encountered three seemingly innocuous words that sent a broad smile stretching across his lips and a burst of adrenaline-driven anticipation through his veins.

No experience necessary.

"Well, I'll be damned," he muttered. Maybe he'd done something right lately, after all. Whatever had gained him the favor of the gods, he hoped it was enough to see him through the screening process.

"Here you go, son," Anna announced as she set the plate laden with eggs, bacon and toast in front of him. "Clean your plate, you'll feel like a new man."

"Yes, ma'am." Todd dug in. He would need every ounce of energy he could summon for today's performance. And that was all any job interview was. The opportunity for a prospective employer to watch candidates perform to whatever music they played.

And no one was better at that dance than Todd. He had every intention of dazzling whoever was in charge. It was what he did best.

He could charm or talk his way out of practically anything, anywhere, anytime.

Well, except for this morning. But then he hadn't known he was taking pictures of his boss's daughter. Even he wasn't that good.

Chapter Three

When the elevator stopped, Todd hesitated before stepping into the lobby of the Colby Agency.

This was definitely the floor on which security had instructed him to alight. But this wasn't at all what he'd expected.

The furnishings, chairs and tables, including what was clearly the receptionist's desk, sat in one corner while three men worked quickly to install new carpeting starting at the opposite wall.

"Mr. Thompson?"

Todd's gaze turned to the woman who'd said his name. "That's me." The smile he saved for charming the ladies pushed automatically into place. "And you are?"

The pretty lady's cheeks turned pink, but she managed a shaky smile of her own. "Elaine. The receptionist." She glanced around the spacious lobby. "Sorry about the mess. They were supposed to have finished last week, except something went wrong and…" She shrugged. "May I get you a cup of coffee?"

After leaving the job fair, Todd had spent the entire weekend walking the floor of his one-room apartment. The call from Victoria Colby herself this morning had dragged him from the closest thing to sleep he'd gotten since. A quick shower and about a dozen cups of strong black coffee had followed that much anticipated call. He definitely did not need any more caffeine.

"No, thanks." Somehow he managed to keep his smile in place. The receptionist's blush deepened and for a moment she seemed completely flustered.

"This way, Mr. Thompson," she said finally, with a gesture toward the corridor to the left of where her desk likely sat under normal circumstances.

"Call me Todd," he insisted as he followed Elaine to what he presumed would be Victoria Colby's office.

His guide took him to the far end of the long corridor and another, smaller lobby. This one had already been dressed in the new, no doubt expensive gold carpeting. He wasn't that knowledgeable about decor, but even he was impressed with the lush ambience he'd encountered so far. But then, this was *the* Colby Agency, the very top of the tip top of the private investigations heap. He expected nothing less.

"Mildred, this is Mr. Todd Thompson," Elaine announced to the older woman behind the desk. "Victoria is expecting him."

Elaine flashed him a shy smile then headed back to her own domain. Todd watched her for a second longer than he should have, but she had a nice walk. In fact, she was very, very nice. He liked this place already.

"This way, Mr. Thompson."

The stern tone tugged him back to attention. Though he felt confident the gesture was wasted, he gifted the lady—Mildred Parker, according to the name plate on her desk—with a flash of pearly whites that generally charmed most of her gender. As he suspected, she wasn't buying it. Despite the firm expression, she had a pleasant face and looked to be well into her fifties. This, he decided, was a woman on whose good side he definitely needed to stay. She might not be the boss, but she was damned close.

"Mrs. Colby-Camp is ready to see you now."

"Yes, ma'am." Taking note of the addition tacked onto Victoria Colby's name, Todd followed the all-business Mildred through a set of double doors and into a lavish office that made him think of royalty.

"Good morning, Mr. Thompson."

Victoria Colby-Camp stood near a small conference table to the left of her impressive desk. She looked exactly as he had expected, extremely classy and completely unreadable.

"Thank you, Mildred," she said, her tone soft, polite and yet commanding somehow.

Todd took the hand Victoria offered and shook it

firmly. Behind him he heard the door close with Mildred's exit.

"It's a pleasure to meet you, Mrs. Colby-Camp." He wondered if she had any idea just how sincere those words were. He wasn't entirely sure it was possible to relay with a mere sentence how much it meant for him to be here.

Victoria indicated the chair closest to him. "Let's sit and talk, Mr. Thompson."

"Todd," he suggested as he waited for her to take her seat first. She acknowledged his suggestion with a nod and settled into the chair at the head of the oval table. He pulled out his own chair and got comfortable. At least as comfortable as he could with his whole future hanging in the balance. He wasn't generally a guy who got nervous about much of anything but this was the most important moment of his life—he had to make this happen.

"Nicole and I reviewed the video of your interview and considered the results at length."

Todd wasn't surprised that the interview had been videoed. Agencies this high profile didn't leave anything to chance. If he was hired it would likely be by committee.

"I assume your conclusion was favorable," he offered. His confidence level rose significantly. He'd known he had impressed Nicole Reed-Michaels. Unlike this lady, Nicole had been somewhat easier to read. And gorgeous. Was everyone who worked here beautiful? Whatever Victoria's age, she was still an attractive woman.

Life at the Colby Agency would certainly be easy on the eyes, at least if the rest of the female staff lived up to what he'd seen so far. Beautiful, intelligent. Very cool.

He'd been somewhat surprised that Nicole had conducted the interviews alone. He'd expected at least three interviewers and that a minimum of two would be male. But the Colby Agency appeared to know exactly what they'd been looking for. He'd watched with interest as Nicole had weeded out literally hundreds of applicants. Only twenty had moved on to the written exam. A mere twelve had survived that portion of the extensive interview. Less than half of those had remained once the intense one-on-one portion concluded. Nicole Reed-Michaels was a hell of a looker, but that hadn't kept her from being as hard as nails. She was one tough lady.

But not nearly as tough as the one analyzing him just now.

"Favorable yet cautious," Victoria allowed. "This is the Colby Agency, Todd. We don't take chances with our reputation."

He experienced a glimmer of worry, but he didn't flinch. "Understandable."

She assessed his response for three seconds. "Of the five recruits Nicole selected, only three received a call this morning," Victoria informed him, her eyes still gauging his response.

Todd held his ground, didn't let her see him sweat. "I'm flattered to be among those three."

"Considering the number of applicants, you very well should be." That dark gaze that gave away nothing remained pinned to his, waiting, watching for him to make his first mistake…for him to falter.

The next ten seconds ticked by with excruciating slowness. He gave himself a mental pat on the back when he managed not to squirm.

"You did extraordinarily well on the written exam," she said eventually, tossing out that bone with scarcely any inflection in her tone.

"Thank you." He'd known he'd aced the test. He was particularly good at giving the answers people wanted—which weren't even always the correct ones. Because folks had certain expectations of success as well as failure and he'd met each one as if he'd designed the test himself. No one was better in that arena. Every professor whose class he'd taken at the University of Alabama had said the same: Todd had his own personal guardian angel when it came to test taking…either that or he was the luckiest bastard on the planet.

"My single hesitation, Todd," Victoria went on, instantly snapping him back to the present and putting him on edge, "is with your somewhat overlarge ego."

Uncertainty streaked through him. For the first time in his life he wasn't sure how to respond. Though he felt confident Victoria wasn't the first to think as much, she was definitely the first to say so.

"Not that there is no place in this line of work for a

healthy ego," she allowed. "To the contrary." The knowing expression she kept aimed in his direction did nothing to alleviate his mounting uneasiness. "It takes courage and confidence to be the kind of investigator this agency seeks out."

"I agree," he said, seeing no reason to deny what she obviously understood about him. "You'll find that I have no shortage of either. But I also know how and when to keep the latter in check."

A smile gave him a moment's reprieve. "I'm certain you know exactly how to conduct yourself in any given situation." She leaned back into her chair, adopting a more relaxed posture. "Let me be frank, Todd."

He didn't relax, couldn't have if his life had depended upon it. That fleeting reprieve he'd experienced had just vanished. This was the moment. Whatever she said next would determine where he went from here. Every minute of every hour of his adult life so far had been leading up to this.

"This agency is constantly inundated with applicants more than qualified," she explained. "We choose carefully, and only the very best."

And then he knew why he was here. He didn't have to see it in those closely guarded eyes or to hear it in her voice. He understood exactly why a lady who could command this prestigious agency even bothered to talk to him, a guy who lacked any semblance of the qualifications of which she spoke.

"Mrs. Colby-Camp," he said, that cocky attitude he was known for taking precedence and showing, probably a little more than it should. "I don't have that experience you speak of with such reverence, but I do have a couple of assets you might find every bit as admirable."

She inclined her head slightly to the right and waited for him to continue.

"Ambition. Determination. You give me this opportunity and I guarantee you won't be disappointed." He leaned forward, anticipation burning through him like flames licking a path through a dry field. "I will do whatever it takes to ensure you're impressed."

The intensity in those dark eyes cranked up a notch. "Make no mistake, Todd, I am already duly impressed, otherwise you would not be here."

With considerable effort, he reclined into his chair, barely resisting the urge to jump up and do a little victory dance. "What happens next?"

That smile that had toyed with her lips moments ago reappeared full-force. "Now you have to impress the rest of my staff. Do that, and you've earned yourself a permanent position here."

It was his turn to smile. Oh, yes, he was in. "Just tell me what you want me to do and consider it done."

"You're certain about this, Victoria?"

She turned from the view outside her office window

to face her second-in-command. "Yes, Ian, I'm absolutely certain."

He nodded once. "How would you like to begin?"

Victoria considered his question for a moment. The
three new recruits were currently in the conference
room with a member of human resources. There were
numerous forms to be filled out. Benefits to be discussed. All of which would buy Victoria time for this
final phase of the plan.

"Let's start with Mr. Thompson." There hadn't
actually been any question in her mind. He was the one
who stood out to her. The other two, both female, were
excellent candidates, but neither possessed the level of
in-your-face self-assurance young Mr. Thompson did.

"He's a cocky one," Ian offered.

Victoria had to smile. "Yes, he is."

"You reviewed the background details in Simon's
report?"

"Yes." Victoria knew of which detail in particular he
spoke. Todd Thompson had decided that for his final
thesis he would write about taking on a new identity and
how easy it would be to fool people. In his opinion, most
people wanted to believe what they were told, and he
proved as much by living a double life for a short period
and fooling all those around him. No actual harm had
been done, but the small community where he'd played
out his little hypothesis had been less than pleased to
learn they'd been deceived by the young man they had

presumed to be a traveling missionary from another country.

"He'll require close supervision," Ian countered as he considered the four case files in his hands.

"Without a doubt," Victoria agreed. "I was thinking A.J. would be an excellent mentor."

Ian nodded. "Perfect choice."

Though A. J. Braddock was fairly new to the agency, his record spoke for itself. A former marine who'd turned Homeland Security agent, A.J. had worked through a number of domestic crises that required an innate ability to maintain calm in the worst possible situations. Not to mention that as a marine, he'd been one of the first assigned to Iraq when that deadly dictator had been brought down. A.J. would know just how to take the roughest edges off Mr. Thompson.

"The Serena Blake case is my top priority." Victoria considered, remembering the young woman's desperation. "I think Mr. Thompson's unique skill would be an excellent match."

"Might I recommend that we put these new recruits in the field one at a time?"

Ian's concern was first and foremost for the agency and its clients. He was absolutely right to make such an assertion. Victoria had already decided as much.

"Agreed." Victoria took a deep breath. "Shall we brief A.J. first?"

TODD WAITED as patiently as he could for the next step. The other two recruits, Gabrielle Hanson and Michelle Robb, had gone to lunch with Nicole Reed-Michaels.

He wasn't worried that his being left behind was a bad sign. Nope. He figured he had been chosen for another meeting with the boss.

Or maybe they'd found out about his thesis. There was a good chance he might never live down "Charmed and Dangerous." He'd shown quite literally that fooling others was a simple matter of determination versus skill. Anyone could do it and anyone could be conned. It was simply easier to believe what one was told. Most folks did just that. And none wanted to learn they'd been wrong. As cynical as some parts of American society had become, folks still preferred the uncomplicated. Believing was far simpler than overanalyzing.

Would Victoria change her mind about him in light of his college exploits?

She'd said she was impressed. Maybe she'd changed her mind since learning a few more details.

The door opened and the woman herself appeared as if he'd somehow summoned her with his troubled musings.

"Mr. Thompson."

He stood. "Todd," he reminded her.

"Todd," she allowed, "this is A. J. Braddock."

A big guy, definitely former military, Todd decided,

considering his bearing and the high and tight haircut, followed Victoria into the conference room. The big guy closed the door behind him and thrust out his hand.

"Mr. Thompson," he said as he grabbed Todd's hand, "I've heard a lot about you this morning."

The guy looked sincere and quite friendly. He had to be six-three if he was an inch, close to two hundred pounds. Even the nice suit jacket couldn't disguise what were likely bulging biceps to go along with those extra-wide shoulders.

"Call me Todd." He looked from Braddock to Victoria, determined not to be dismissed without an opportunity to prove his worth in the field. "Is this the part where you see if I can play nice with the other kiddies?"

Apparently his humor wasn't appreciated.

"This," Braddock said with an edge no doubt prompted by his total lack of a sense of humor, "is the part where we see if you can hold your own with the big boys."

Todd grinned. "Touché."

Victoria took a seat at the conference table. Braddock joined her. Todd did the same.

She opened a manila folder and viewed the contents for a moment before she began. "Serena Blake is a lab assistant at Milestone Laboratories."

Todd wasn't familiar with Milestone Laboratories so he sat quietly and listened.

A. J. Braddock took the ball. "Serena's immediate supervisor is a research scientist named Charles Landon. He is also the heaviest investor at Milestone as well as the most renowned scientist on staff."

Now there was a name Todd recognized. "His pregnant wife went missing a few weeks ago." Every local channel, and some national, had carried the story for weeks. In the past two or three, the hype had appeared to dwindle, but as far as Todd knew, the woman hadn't been found.

Victoria nodded. "She was seven months pregnant and simply disappeared. The police have excluded Dr. Landon as a suspect. They believe he is innocent of any wrongdoing and that, in fact, there may not be any foul play involved at all. According to my sources at Chicago P.D., the unanimous conclusion, considering certain details, is that Mrs. Landon left of her own volition. Since the police have no evidence to the contrary and there has been no ransom demand, the case is being treated more like a missing-person case rather than a kidnapping."

"What kind of details?" Todd wanted to know.

With approval in her eyes, Victoria answered, "A large withdrawal made by Mrs. Landon the day before and a missing photo album from her childhood."

Todd chalked one up in his favor. His new boss liked that he asked questions. He quickly reviewed what he'd watched about the case on the news and read about in the papers. He'd never heard the name Serena Blake. "So what does Miss Blake have to do with this?"

"She," Victoria explained, "believes that foul play is definitely involved."

"She has no evidence," Braddock put in quickly. "This is more her gut feelings. Apparently she and Mrs. Landon were friends."

Todd thought about that for a second. "Does Mrs. Landon have any other friends who support this scenario?"

Victoria sighed. "This is part of the problem. Mrs. Landon had no real friends. She had acquaintances of her social standing with whom she attended parties and sat on various charity committees, but she didn't have a single true friend that we know of. Even her relationship with Miss Blake had been kept secret from her husband. Miss Blake insists he can't know about it now."

"We haven't confirmed this part as of yet," Braddock added. "We only have her word."

"There is always the possibility that Miss Blake is hoping to damage her boss's career," Victoria suggested. Before Todd could ask questions along those lines, she went on. "From what we've discovered since she came to us four days ago, there is some tension between her and Dr. Landon. Apparently he has passed her over for promotion once and he requires long hours without additional pay more often than not. I get the impression that he takes advantage of her any way he can. The consensus is that as far as his work goes, he's quite ruthless."

Todd shrugged. "Then why take the case?" Seemed like a no-brainer to him. The police didn't think the guy had anything to hide. Why believe his assistant who, apparently, had reason to want to hurt him?

"First," Victoria said with a bluntness that told Todd she didn't like being second-guessed, "Miss Blake was willing to drain her savings to put up the required retainer fee."

So she was willing to give her life's savings to get this done. Todd didn't see where that let her off the hook. Anyone with a little ambition would have done the same and would have considered it an investment in the future.

"Second," Victoria continued, "if there is even a remote chance that this man had something to do with his pregnant wife's disappearance, we have an obligation to take the case. As a private agency there are steps we can take that the police cannot."

Todd knew the statistics; when wives went missing or were found dead, more often than not the husband was responsible. Landon certainly had the kind of money required to get rid of a wife he no longer wanted without sullying his hands. But did that make him guilty?

"Of course, we must tread carefully," Braddock suggested. "We have to approach this in a way that gives us access without allowing damage to the doctor or his reputation, since he could very well be innocent."

In other words, they had to pretend to be someone they weren't. Now he got the picture. This was his specialty.

"Who do we need to be?" he asked with the same bluntness Victoria had used.

"I have a dear friend in nonfiction publishing," she explained, "who is very interested in genetics, which is one of the main fields of research at Milestone. This friend will allow one of my investigators to open a line of dialogue with Dr. Landon in pursuit of a book about him and his research. Since my friend is genuinely interested, our investigation will set things in motion along that avenue while allowing us to get close enough to make our own conclusions about the good doctor."

"And if all goes well," Todd concluded, "Dr. Landon will get a book deal and we'll have our answers. Miss Blake will simply have to come to terms with her friend's disappearance."

"This case is too high-profile to approach it any other way," Braddock put in, apparently annoyed by Todd's elementary assessment.

"A.J. is new at the agency as well as in Chicago, making him the logical choice," Victoria interjected. "There's little possibility that anyone, including Landon, would recognize him."

"How do I fit into this scenario?" Todd liked doing things his own way, but he had a feeling that wasn't going to happen this go-around.

"You'll be introduced as A.J.'s research assistant," Victoria told him. "This will be your trial run, Mr. Thompson," she added, her tone direct and to the point. "If we like what we see on this assignment, you'll stay on. If not…"

She didn't have to clarify. "When do we start?" Todd didn't see the need to waste any additional time. He intended to prove himself beyond a shadow of a doubt. Now was as good a time as any.

Victoria stood. She stopped him when Todd would have done the same. "I'll leave you and A.J. to work out the finer points. An initial appointment with Landon has been arranged for nine tomorrow morning. I'll expect you to let me know if you decide to withdraw, Mr. Thompson."

With that ominous statement, she left the conference room. Why in the world would he withdraw?

"There are a few details we'll need to iron out, Thompson," Braddock said, calling Todd's attention back to him.

"Shoot."

The look in the other man's eyes had Todd wishing he'd used some other terminology.

"During the course of this investigation, you will answer to me," Braddock stated flatly. "You will do exactly what I say when I say. No exceptions. Period. There will be no second chances. Do we understand each other?"

Todd wondered briefly how much of his military time Mr. Braddock had spent as a drill sergeant. "Perfectly."

Braddock pushed in Todd's direction what on first glance gave the impression of a simple typed report. "This is your cover profile. Study it. Preparation is the key. I'll pick you up at eight in the morning. If you've changed your mind, you will notify Victoria prior to that time and save us both the unnecessary trouble."

Why the hell was everyone so concerned with whether or not he would change his mind?

"Don't worry, Braddock," Todd replied without reservation, dropping the "mister" as the older man had done when addressing him. "I won't change my mind."

The hint of a smile cracked the man's no-nonsense exterior. "Maybe you'd better read the profile before you make that decision."

The big guy pushed out of his seat. "Take the rest of the afternoon off, Thompson. Consider long and hard whether you're cut out for this line of work. The Colby Agency employs only the best. Ask yourself one defining question. Can you, no matter the circumstances or personal sacrifice, be the best?"

Todd didn't get up. He just watched the other man leave. Then he picked up the single page that outlined his cover for this assignment.

"Might as well see what all the fuss is about."

Nothing Victoria or Braddock could have said would have properly prepared him for the blow to his ego.

Chapter Four

Her heart pounding, Serena Blake waited in the corridor until Dr. Landon had gone into the conference room. Even then she waited a few seconds more. If he caught her going through his office…

She closed her eyes, took a deep breath and blocked the fear. Finding the truth had to be paramount, but if she was fired—or worse—she certainly couldn't help Molly then. Obviously the police weren't going to get the job done.

Decision made, Serena moved toward her destination. She had maybe thirty minutes, but couldn't afford to waste even one precious second. Although she was thankful the Colby Agency had taken her case and had, apparently, arrived, she couldn't let down her guard. She had to do her part, as well. Molly was counting on her.

Victoria Colby-Camp had warned Serena to be very, very careful. To do only what she felt comfortable attempting and nothing more. Now that Investigator Braddock and his assistant were in place Serena could breathe easier. Still, she had access to places the Colby Agency wouldn't be able to reach—not legally, anyway. For that very reason she needed to take exceptional precautions.

Two other Milestone Lab employees, both wearing the requisite white lab coats, exited one of the doors on the right up ahead and started in her direction. Serena managed a smile and a brisk "Good morning" as she passed her colleagues.

With her blood roaring in her ears, she scarcely heard their responses, vague good-mornings. Thankfully they didn't slow down but kept walking. Probably headed for the nearest coffeepot.

Serena took a right onto an intersecting corridor and walked as quickly as she dared to Dr. Charles Landon's private office. Her much smaller office was right next door. It would take less than five seconds to move from one to the other...all she needed to know was when he left the conference room. She could set the monitor on his desk to observe the goings-on in the conference room, but there was a chance he might notice. A tiny red light came on whenever the viewing cameras were activated.

Did she dare risk it?

Maybe not.

She glanced at her watch again. Dr. Landon had been

in the conference room for seven minutes. Surely she could count on at least twenty if not the thirty she'd originally estimated the meeting would take.

No more hesitating.

Serena glanced in both directions. All clear. She pulled her badge from her lapel, swiped it for clearance then opened the door in one smooth, swift motion that startled even her.

No more second thoughts. She had to do this.

She eased inside, squeezed her eyes shut and cringed as the door closed behind her with a succinct click of the heavy-duty lock.

It was done.

She was in.

She opened her eyes and her breath promptly evacuated her lungs.

Intense blue eyes stared directly at her.

Male.

Tall.

Longish brown hair.

No white lab coat.

Who was this man? How did he get in here?

She started to scream but he was around the desk and had his hand over her mouth before the sound her brain commanded her to issue left her throat.

"Don't do that," he growled.

Deep, husky.

Panic clawed at her as if her frantically racing heart

had suddenly sprouted talons and wanted to rip its way from her chest.

He grabbed her right wrist with one hand while the other stayed firmly planted over her mouth, ultimately keeping her pinned to the closed door. He pulled her hand up and studied the badge.

"Serena Blake?" The recognition that flared in his blue eyes did nothing to relieve her rising terror. "Don't scream, okay?" he urged.

Her head moved up and down, though she wasn't entirely sure if her brain had actually ordered the move or if it was mere survival instinct.

"I'm Todd Thompson from the Colby Agency," he explained quickly, his voice whisper-soft but still rough as if he, too, was scared half out of his mind. As he told her this, his hand loosened somewhat but didn't move completely away from her trembling lips.

Serena inhaled an unsteady breath. "I'd like to see some ID." Good thinking. Though she couldn't imagine how anyone could know she'd contacted the Colby Agency. He had to be telling the truth. But she had to be absolutely certain. Victoria had called her and told her that Mr. Braddock and a Mr. Thompson would be working on her case, but she hadn't met either man. Victoria had wanted to set up a meeting last night except Serena hadn't been able to get out of a prior commitment to work late without appearing suspicious. Dr. Landon didn't like what he called slackers.

She hadn't really worried about it. To her way of thinking it might be better if she met the men for the first time when Dr. Landon did. He was so good at reading her, she hadn't wanted to take any chances. Who would have guessed that he'd have her running reports downstairs for him this morning? When she'd returned to the sixth floor at five after nine she had assumed that both representatives of the Colby Agency were in the meeting with Dr. Landon.

The man standing far too close for her comfort finally removed his hand from her mouth and reached for his wallet. He flashed his driver's license, which backed up his assertion as to his identity.

"Why aren't you in the conference room?" She was certain Dr. Landon would not have left anyone, much less a stranger, in his private office.

"Braddock doesn't need me right now," he said, but Serena wasn't sure she believed him.

Her gaze narrowed. "How did you get in here?"

He shoved his wallet into his back pocket. "We're wasting time."

He was right about that, but his response didn't answer her question.

She planted her hands on her hips, mainly to camouflage their shaking, and demanded, "I want to know how you got in here, Mr. Thompson. It's my understanding that the Colby Agency is one of the most prestigious private investigations firms in the country. This doesn't feel right." Mostly she was just flustered and she hated feeling that way. That he could fluster her so easily annoyed her unreasonably.

He stared at her, his mouth set in a grim line. She tried not to notice the fact that he was really cute...but he was.

"All right," he relented, but the tick in his stubbled jaw announced loudly that he didn't like having to answer to her or anyone else.

They were wasting valuable time. She glanced at Dr. Landon's desk. She wanted to look at his computer files, view anyone he'd contacted recently. The police claimed to have done all that, but she needed to be sure they hadn't missed anything. And the truth was, they'd ruled out Landon almost immediately. He had an airtight alibi. He'd been here at work when his wife went missing.

"I thought I'd do a little off-the-record browsing while Braddock has Landon preoccupied," Thompson admitted.

Well, at least they thought along the same lines.

"Do you know what you're looking for?" she asked bluntly. Though she was certain he knew what he was doing, something about him went against the grain. He just wasn't what she'd expected.

Irritation flickered in his eyes, turning the pale blue to a deeper sapphire. "Are we going to stand around here all morning or are we going to do this?"

"Move out of my way." Serena wasn't sure where the

courage to make the demand had come from but she couldn't very well get anything done with him looming over her like this.

To her surprise, he stepped aside and let her pass. She bit back a smile. Wow, that felt good.

She hurried around Landon's desk and skimmed the top for his calendar. She quickly flipped through the pages since April seventh. Nothing unusual, not that she expected anything to be there. Landon was too smart for that. She dropped into his chair, entered his password— the one he didn't know she had—and scanned his computer log. Thank God, Landon was one of those overconfident men who didn't delete his electronic trail very often.

"Anything out of the ordinary?"

She shivered at the unexpected question, refused to look at the man crouched next to her. How could she have forgotten he was so close? "Not yet."

She didn't have to look at the clock to know the minutes were ticking by. She gritted her teeth to hold back a curse when she reached the date in Landon's log two weeks prior to Molly's disappearance.

"Nothing."

"What about his files?" Thompson stood and moved toward the first of half a dozen file cabinets.

Serena swiftly scanned the rest of the log, desperation gnawing at her. "No. I'm responsible for those files," she said to Thompson. "There's nothing in there that I haven't seen." It was his computer that she'd hoped to find something on. He never, ever allowed her in his office when he wasn't present. She'd been certain she would find a clue in this log. Hope deflated as she viewed the last entry. Maybe Landon was better at covering his tracks than she'd realized.

Thompson surveyed the office. "Any place else we can look?"

She shrugged. "His cell phone or maybe his Palm Pilot."

Thompson turned to her, a wicked grin on his face. "I think I can arrange that."

Despite her annoyance at his cockiness, she felt her lips shifting into a smile. "Are you really that good, Mr. Thompson?" He looked so young…maybe the same age as her.

"Call me Todd."

A sharp rap on the door sent the oxygen out of Serena's chest once more and Todd Thompson wheeling in the direction of the sound.

Their gazes collided with the second knock.

It couldn't be Landon: he would simply walk in.

Todd pointed to her and then at the file cabinets.

Before she could fathom what he meant, he'd moved around behind her and was ushering her away from the desk. As she moved toward the file cabinets, he crouched behind the desk to conceal his presence.

Okay, she got it.

She swiped her badge along the channel of the cabinet's electronic lock and dragged a file drawer open, then grabbed a handful of manila folders. With a deep, bolstering breath, she opened the door. "Yes?"

It was Nolan Fairbanks, the mail clerk and a distant cousin of Arthur Miles, the CEO of Milestone. Nolan, since he didn't have anything beyond a high school education, was working his way up in the business. Dr. Miles couldn't very well turn away blood, no matter how far removed.

"What's up, Serena?" Nolan winked and walked far enough into the room to toss a handful of mail onto Landon's desk.

Serena glanced at the desk and forced herself to appear calm. "Just doing the dirty work," she said, incredibly without her voice wobbling.

"Hey." Nolan moved in close, the smell of his new favorite cologne preceding him.

Every female on the staff knew what a flirt he was, occasionally to the point of being a nuisance. But he was only twenty, with the maturity level of a teenager, and basically, he was harmless. Right now, it behooved Serena to let him play out his little game.

"You busy for lunch? You owe me a rain check, you know."

He was right. She did and she wasn't busy for lunch. She thought about Todd Thompson under Landon's desk but resisted the impulse to look that way. She tacked on a wide smile. "I'd love to have lunch with you, Nolan. Twelve okay?"

He nodded, his face beaming as if the hottest new actress on his favorite weekly sitcom had just said yes to his proposal. "The cafeteria?"

She managed an affirmative movement with her head. Going out for lunch was generally too much trouble with Milestone Labs so far out of the city.

Nolan winked one last time and backed out of the door as if he had to keep his eyes on her until the door closed for fear that he'd imagined the whole scene.

Serena shoved the folders back into the drawer and spun around at the same time that Thompson moved around the desk. She shook herself, banished the thought of how fluidly he moved. Where was her mind? She'd just been caught in her boss's office. If Nolan mentioned it...

"We should get out of here," Thompson suggested.

She glanced around, made sure all was as it had been. The calendar. The file drawer. "Push the chair in," she said past the giant lump in her throat.

Thompson did as she told him then gestured to the door. "Do you want me to go first?"

That definitely wasn't a good idea. She glanced at the clock—9:20. How could all that have happened in twelve minutes?

"I'll go first. If it's clear, I'll keep going."

"Gotcha."

He moved up close behind her when she hesitated at the door. "Don't be afraid," he murmured.

She squeezed her eyes shut. He was standing so close she could swear she'd felt his lips against her hair when he spoke.

She wiped her palm against her lab coat, then reached for the knob. Now or never. She turned it and pulled the door open. Her jaw was set so hard her teeth felt ready to crack as she moved into the corridor. Forcing her gaze first right then left, she let go of the door and started walking toward the conference room.

Before she'd taken three steps, Todd Thompson moved up alongside her. Only then did she notice his visitor's badge. Had he been wearing it before?

The cell phone in her pocket vibrated, making her jump. To her chagrin, Thompson noticed.

She dragged the phone from the pocket of her lab coat. Landon. She swore softly, guiltily. "Serena Blake."

"Serena, would you come to the conference room?" Landon asked in that too pleasant voice he used whenever he had company that he wanted to impress.

"Yes, sir."

"Oh, and, Serena, there's a young man waiting in my office, Todd Thompson. Bring him, as well."

Serena dropped the phone back into her pocket and turned to the man next to her. "He left you in his office?"

Todd shrugged. "I had to make a call."

Now she was plain old PO'd. Landon blew a fuse if

she went into his office without him present. And yet he left a total stranger there? "Then why hide when the mail clerk popped in?" she demanded.

He gave her a hopeful look. "Felt like the right thing to do. I knew it wouldn't be Landon and anyone else was more likely to speak openly to you if my presence was unknown." He smirked. "Was that your boyfriend?"

A new slash of irritation whipped through her. "That's none of your business." How could Landon trust a total stranger in his office when he didn't trust his own assistant?

Realization struck. The files were locked. So was his computer unless you knew his password, which she did. His desk was always locked and she still didn't have a key. Of course he wouldn't mind leaving Thompson in there. Not to mention that the act of trust would look good on Landon's part. He had an ulterior motive for everything he did.

The idea made her all the angrier. Bastard.

At the conference room door Thompson laid a hand on her arm, stalling her when she would have gone inside without pause.

She glared at him.

"We good?"

She feigned a smile. "We're great, Mr. Thompson."

She opened the door and stepped inside. Landon, pretending to be a gentleman, stood. The other man, Mr. Braddock she presumed, did, as well.

"Serena, this is A. J. Braddock from Sun Publishing." He gestured to the man who had come to a stop near the table next to Serena. "And his research assistant, Todd Thompson."

Serena extended her hand to Braddock. "Serena Blake."

"It's a pleasure, Miss Blake," the broad-shouldered man assured her. "Dr. Landon told me how indispensable you are."

Serena choked on a laugh. "Thank you."

"Miss Blake." Todd Thompson offered his hand next. "We didn't make it official."

Hard as she tried, Serena couldn't help hesitating before taking his hand. "Mr. Thomp…Thompson," she said, stumbling over his name.

"Serena," Landon said, calling her attention back to him. "Sun Publishing is interested in my work in the field of stem cell research."

Serena kept that artificial smile in place. "That's amazing." She turned to Braddock. "The work he has done is nothing short of incredible. All that's stopping him from going the full distance is full private funding." She pressed a hand to her chest, mostly in an attempt to slow the fluttering in her heart. "Then I'm sure you know that otherwise you wouldn't be here." Landon's work was unparalleled. She had to give credit where credit was due.

Braddock smiled, a gesture that somehow calmed

her. "Absolutely, Miss Blake. The study of genetics is the key to mankind's future. Dr. Landon's work has bestseller written all over it. He's a pioneer."

For the first time in weeks Serena knew she wasn't in this alone. Something about Mr. Braddock made her feel safe and secure. Whether it was his massive size or the strength she saw in his eyes, she couldn't say. But she instinctively knew that he had the situation under control. He was exactly what she had expected from the Colby Agency. Todd Thompson was not.

As Landon and Braddock moved back into a dialogue about Landon's achievements, Serena stole a glance at Thompson. There was no doubt in her mind that this guy would do whatever he had to, to accomplish his mission, but she didn't get the same safe, secure feeling from him that she got from Braddock. Oh, no. Thompson gave off a different vibe altogether.

She would have to watch her step with Todd Thompson. He was impulsive.... And far too cocky for his own good, much less hers.

"Serena?"

Her head snapped up. Landon had said something to her. "I'm sorry, sir." She shook her head. "I guess my mind was on that report that's overdue."

"What did I tell you, Mr. Braddock? She's a dedicated one." Landon's attention came back to rest on Serena and she didn't miss the irritation in his expression. "So much so, I'm not sure what I'd do without her."

Serena's heart lurched at the look in his eyes. There was a warning there…one she didn't quite understand.

"…are hard to find."

She missed whatever Braddock had said.

"Serena," Landon said, dragging her full regard back to him, "I'd like you to assist Mr. Thompson in any way he requires. He'll be doing the legwork for Mr. Braddock."

"Certainly, Dr. Landon." Serena glanced in Thompson's direction. Strangely, he didn't look any happier about the situation than she did. She almost frowned. What was up with that? She was a paying client, he shouldn't have a problem doing whatever he had to.

Another epiphany hit with entirely too much force. Maybe he didn't like her. Before she could stop herself, she'd smoothed her hand over her somewhat less than fashionable hairdo. She felt certain she wasn't exactly the type guys like Thompson went for. Her clothes were too conservative. Her whole personality was too conservative. Truth was, Nolan was the only man who had flirted with her in so long she couldn't even remember the last one who had.

Not that she'd ever really cared. She'd been too focused on her studies in high school. She'd managed her masters in genetic research by the time she was twenty-one—an incredible feat by any standards. She'd worked for Milestone Laboratories for the past year. They'd recruited her right out of university. One of her favorite professors had put a bug in Landon's ear. Of course she'd been the one who put the bug in her professor's ear. She'd needed a way into Milestone Labs. She'd had more than her future career on her mind. Since she'd completed her studies at the end of the winter semester, she'd gone right to work in the new year.

She'd gotten this job because she was highly qualified, not because of how she looked or how she dressed. Or even who she knew.

Okay, enough.

When they'd all taken a seat around the conference table, Dr. Landon explained his daily routine and Mr. Braddock made suggestions of when they could meet and the format for discussion.

Todd Thompson said nothing. He just sat there, careful not to look at Serena.

She didn't care. Not really. All that mattered to her was finding Molly safe.

Serena said another little silent prayer for Molly. She'd been missing for six weeks now. The baby could come at any time. Serena refused to believe she was dead. She had to be all right. They'd only just found each other. Fate couldn't be that cruel.

She thought back to her early life in one foster home after another. Not the first happy memory. When she'd reached sixteen she'd liberated herself, but the authorities had found her. But this time she'd ended up with a caring family. She'd finished high school and gone on to college with the support of that fine family. The years she'd spent with the Blakes had almost made up for the other sixteen years of her life. So much so, she'd taken their name when the elderly couple had offered to officially adopt her.

For a little while Serena had gotten a taste of what a real family was like. Her adoptive parents were both gone now; they'd died within six months of each other during her last year at university. It was as if one couldn't survive without the other. She wondered if she would ever know that kind of love. Probably not. She doubted it even existed anymore.

The Blakes had left everything they owned to her, ensuring that she wouldn't have to worry about the future, financially anyway.

Shortly after her adopted mother's death, Serena had found out what little there was to be known about her own biological family.

At first she hadn't cared. She'd been grieving her parents' deaths. She couldn't have cared less about who had donated the egg and the sperm. The Blakes had been her family. But then she'd stumbled across one pertinent detail. She had a sister.

A sister who'd been far more fortunate in those early years than Serena. Her first foster parents had been like the Blakes and had immediately adopted Molly.

Molly Ledbetter had grown up in Chicago with wealthy parents who had wanted nothing more than for their only child to be happy. Like the Blakes, the Ledbetters had been older, apparently having waited most of their adult lives for their own reproductive organs to make their goal of offspring happen. Though the Ledbetters were still alive, both were in nursing homes. Mr. Ledbetter suffered with advanced Alzheimer's with only rare lucid moments, while Mrs. Ledbetter had suffered a debilitating stroke that had left her unable to communicate in any way.

Basically, both Molly and Serena were alone.

Except for each other. Serena had set out to get to know her sister.

Eight months ago, after achieving a personal relationship with Molly and confirming that the woman was definitely her sister, Serena had told her. Molly had been thrilled, except for some reason, she hadn't wanted her husband to know.

It hadn't made sense to Serena, but she'd gone along with her newly found sister. Now she had no choice but to keep her secret to herself until she found Molly.

Serena couldn't say for sure what made her feel this way, but she was certain, absolutely certain, that Charles Landon had something to do with his wife's disappearance. Maybe it was all the extramarital affairs. Long before Serena had told Molly they were sisters, Molly had confided in her that Charles Landon had had many, many affairs. She'd never confronted him for fear of losing her marriage. She'd wanted her child to grow up in a safe, financially secure environment with both biological parents.

Serena had a feeling that despite Molly's good luck in landing a wonderful adoptive family the first go-around, somehow some part of her remembered the years before age four and those memories had planted fear deep in her heart. She couldn't risk losing the only family connection she had. Even if her husband was a bona fide bastard.

Serena understood that. Though she'd been only two when her biological parents had deserted her, and had no specific memories of them, she experienced an overpowering need to belong, to be a part of something. That need had driven her to find Molly, had prompted her to prod her professor into tossing out her name to Dr. Charles Landon himself.

Now, here she was all alone again. Only this time she was old enough, smart enough and strong enough to fight back. She wasn't a kid anymore.

Serena bit down on her lower lip to stop its trembling. Whatever Landon had done to Molly, he would pay…if she had to expose the bastard herself.

As mild-mannered and conservative as she had always been, she would not sit back and let him get away with this.

No way.

No one would get in her way. She let her gaze wander back to the man sitting beside her. This time he was looking at her and she had the overwhelming feeling that he knew exactly what she was thinking.

She sincerely hoped she had not already made a major mistake.

Chapter Five

Todd sat in the dark in his car. His gaze remained fixed on Serena Blake's town house across the street, but his attention was splintered.

Babysitting.

That was what his part in this assignment boiled down to.

Fury washed over him again. Even at Wellsly he'd gotten decent assignments. Not lead assignments, but that would have come in time…if he hadn't screwed up by narcing on the boss's daughter. How the hell was he supposed to have known she was the guy's daughter? Or that she was working undercover?

Todd banged his fist against the steering wheel. What the hell was he doing sitting here in the dark watching Landon's assistant?

Landon was the key to this investigation. He was the one whose wife was missing. He was the famous scientist. Todd was the one with the innate ability to charm folks. Why wasn't he working with Landon?

Because this was the Colby Agency and he was basically an inexperienced kid bucking for a job with the big dogs.

Braddock's remark about learning to play with the big boys flashed through his mind. Okay, maybe he didn't have ten years in the military and two in Homeland Security under his belt, but he could do this just as well as his big, badass mentor.

Todd blew out a heavy breath. Part of him recognized that he should be grateful for the opportunity. The Colby Agency didn't usually even consider guys like him. But it was hard to be appreciative when he was playing babysitter for some low-on-the-totem-pole assistant.

He shook his head, told himself to blow it off. He understood how these things worked. He had to prove himself and then he'd be in all the way. No point bellyaching about the situation. He knew the deal, just had to get right with it, that's all.

Turning the volume down low, he flipped on the radio and tuned in his favorite station. Might as well entertain himself. Hell, he'd be out here all night.

A rap on the glass right next to his head made him jump.

Todd whipped around.

Serena Blake stood outside his car door. He didn't

have to see her face. He'd recognize the ultraconservative sweater she wore anywhere.

Just then she whacked her knuckles across the glass again. How had she gotten out of the house without him seeing her?

Todd turned off the radio and powered down the window. "Yeah?"

She leaned down to put herself at his eye level. "Why are you sitting outside my house, Mr. Thompson?"

Well, hell. He supposed he could have taken a few precautions to be a little more anonymous. Maybe he hadn't given this girl enough credit.

"Do you usually scan for surveillance outside your home, Miss Blake?" What the hell was she doing running around outside at this time of night, anyway? It was almost midnight. Didn't she need her beauty sleep or something?

Her gaze narrowed. He couldn't tell if she was suspicious or pissed off.

"I'm calling Victoria Colby-Camp."

With that she straightened and stormed off. Well, at least he had his answer. She was ticked.

Todd barreled out of the car and went after her. "Whoa, now, wait a second. What's the problem?"

She stopped in the middle of the street and glared at him. With the aid of the street lamp he could see the fury on her face.

"Are you insane, Mr. Thompson?" She crossed her

arms over her chest and thrust out her chin. "I am not the suspect in this case! My—Dr. Landon is the one you should be watching. What in God's name are you doing outside my house?"

He could lie, but he had a gut feeling she wouldn't buy it.

"Maybe we should talk inside?" He glanced around the quiet neighborhood. Most of the houses were dark as were the cars parked along the street, but that didn't mean someone out here wasn't watching or listening.

"You are insane!" she snapped. "Do you think I would invite a strange man into my home at this time of night?"

He gestured to his car. "Then we can talk in my car."

She shot a disapproving glance at his car. "I don't think so."

He shrugged, disgusted. "All right, how about your car?"

For about ten seconds she just stood in the middle of the street trying to decide what she wanted from him.

It wasn't until that moment that he realized she was actually wearing pajamas. She'd pulled on the sweater instead of a robe. *And* she was barefoot. His gaze stalled on her small pale feet with their pink toenails.

"Okay, you can come inside, but only as far as the door."

That was better than nothing. "Fine."

She marched up to her front door and went inside.

Just inside the door she wheeled on him, forcing him to halt on the threshold.

"Why are you here?" she demanded.

Before he answered, he took a moment to assess her demeanor. The idea had seemed like the right thing to do at first, but half a minute into the visual evaluation he realized his mistake. Her pajamas were the lounge pants type. White with pink bunnies all over them. Whatever kind of top she wore was pink and the hem of it didn't quite reach her waist. A narrow strip of smooth skin was visible. She abruptly noticed where his gaze had stopped and wrapped the sweater back around herself.

When his gaze collided with hers once more, she was seething. Damn. He didn't need her calling Victoria.

Where the hell was that charm he was so famous for?

He decided that lying would be in his best interest.

"It's important that we ensure your safety at all times, Miss Blake." He said this in as serious a tone as he could muster with his attention slipping back down to survey those pink bunnies. Sweet. Real sweet. And cute. Miss Serena Blake was actually very cute out of that drab white lab coat. Her hair was mussed and her face was clean of makeup. She looked all of seventeen.

She blinked, taken aback by his half-truth. "You think I'm...I'm in danger."

Damn. He hated to scare her. "Maybe," he hedged.

She hugged herself a little tighter. "Oh. I didn't..."

She licked those full pink lips and he felt his pulse react. "Would you like some coffee, Mr. Thompson?"

As guilty as he felt for making her uncomfortable, at least he was off the hook. She wouldn't be calling Victoria to complain.

"Coffee would be good."

She gestured to her sofa. "Make yourself at home." She dragged in an uneven breath. "I'll…" She motioned vaguely toward the hall behind her. "It'll only take a minute."

He nodded but she'd already disappeared down the hall. Man, she was nervous. He looked around the room. Small but comfy. It wasn't exactly what he'd expected. The walls and furniture were that conservative beige he'd expected, but the splashes of color in the artwork and the throw pillows as well as the big old afghan gave the room life. He walked over to the small fireplace and perused the framed photographs on the mantel. Serena with an older couple. Her folks, he surmised. Both deceased, he remembered reading. Another of Serena dressed in her white lab coat with several other Milestone employees. A party of some sort.

It was the last photograph that really got his attention. Serena and Molly Landon. The missing wife of Dr. Charles Landon. The woman the police hadn't had luck in finding, suggesting that she might very well have grown tired of her life and split.

"Sugar or cream?"

He turned to find Serena settling a tray with two cups of coffee and a plate of cookies on the table between the sofa and the two chairs directly across from it.

When she straightened, she forgot to hold her sweater wrapped around her and he got a good look at the pink camisole that showed off that flat belly and was low-cut enough to give him a peek of cleavage.

"Black is fine." He licked his lips and remembered that this was his assignment, not a date.

She sat on the sofa and he took a chair across the table from her. He might be young and impulsive, but he wasn't stupid. This girl's sweet innocence was a colossal warning flag. His protective instincts were already on full alert.

With her coffee cradled in both hands, she turned those big brown eyes to his. "So, why do you think I might be in danger?"

What he couldn't say was that he had to rule out the possibility that she was a suspect on some level. He had to determine that her motivation for going after Landon was on the up-and-up. If Landon was up to no good or was involved in his wife's disappearance in any way, Serena's determination to prove it could certainly put her in jeopardy. That part he could say.

"If Landon gets wind that you have hired the Colby Agency, he's sure to be upset," Todd explained. He felt certain she understood this, but simply hadn't considered it fully.

She chewed her lower lip thoughtfully. Todd wet his own. She had nice lips. Full. Very sexy. The remembered feel of them against his palm made him sweat. Funny thing, he hadn't noticed at the time. He'd been sure he was caught poking around Landon's desk. Getting back into the chair where Landon had left him would have been impossible, since he hadn't had any warning until the door opened.

And she'd been dressed so conservatively. Skirt all the way to her knees. Low-heeled pumps. High-necked blouse and sweater and then that loose-fitting lab coat. What was it about that drab white lab coat that had made him ignore all those other little assets? Large, oval-shaped eyes. Silky hair that fell past her shoulders. Well, okay, the hair had been up. And those lips. Yeah, great lips.

"I suppose I knew that on some level," she said as she set her untouched coffee aside.

Todd sipped his, had to admit that she made a good cup of joe.

She shrugged, sending the ill-fitting sweater sliding off her shoulder and revealing more bare skin. "I guess I just wasn't thinking about myself."

"You mind if I take off my jacket?" Was it getting hot in here, or was it just him?

She blinked, frowned. "Do you always dress that way?"

Now he was the one taken aback. "What's wrong with the way I dress?" He sat his coffee on the tray and shouldered out of his jacket.

"I don't know. The jeans are…" She shrugged again. "I suppose they're typical for a guy like you."

A guy like him? What did that mean? She was a year younger than him, it wasn't as if they weren't from the same generation.

"And the shirt…" She assessed his shirt with his jacket off. "Why do you leave it untucked when you're wearing a jacket?"

She didn't like that his shirt was untucked? "Are you the fashion police or what?" Most women liked his look. But then, he had to remember, Serena Blake wasn't normal. She had, like, a gazillion IQ. He'd scanned the background data on her. She could be doing Landon's job if she really wanted to. Todd had thought that maybe she was too shy to step up to the plate, but maybe he'd been wrong. She didn't seem the least bit shy right now.

Her right foot had started to tap against the rug. He'd made her nervous. "No, I'm just saying…" She struggled for the right words; he cranked up the intensity in his gaze just for the fun of watching her squirm. "I guess I expected you to look more like Investigator Braddock."

Great. Now he didn't measure up visually. Was there anything else she didn't like about him?

"If we're being totally honest here," he said before he could stop himself, "you're not really what I expected, either."

Her hackles rose. He smiled at her gaping expression.

"And what did you...?" She huffed her frustration. "Just what did you expect?"

He shrugged nonchalantly and gave her tit for tat. "I don't know. Maybe thick glasses and a more harried demeanor."

Her eyes widened in outrage. "So you think I don't look the stereotypical visually challenged and utterly disorganized geek, is that a proper assessment?"

Oh, she was fired up now. "Actually, yes."

She stood abruptly. "I think you should go, Mr. Thompson."

There he went, getting on her bad side again. He pushed up from the comfy overstuffed chair. He actually dreaded climbing back into his car.

"I apologize if my bluntness offended you, Miss Blake, but you have to confess, you were a little frank yourself."

Where he grew up, turnabout was fair play.

She lifted her chin defiantly. He liked when she did that. She looked...cute, not quite so hoity-toity.

Damn, he'd really lost his grip here.

"And I...apologize if I offended you, Mr. Thompson." She crossed her arms over her chest and that snug little camisole that showed off the tempting shape of her small breasts. Small but very nice.

"Hey, no harm done. We're just getting to know each other. We'll be spending a lot of time together—I guess we might as well get used to each other."

She nodded. "You're right." She gestured to the chair he'd vacated. "Please, finish your coffee and have a cookie."

Just like a Girl Scout. No way this girl could be involved in anything underhanded. He didn't need to wonder about that a second longer. She could very well, however, be involved on some level that she didn't understand. And she might even be wrong about Landon. His wife could have chosen to leave her husband. Just because she hadn't mentioned it to Serena didn't mean it wasn't a viable possibility.

Todd settled back into the chair and reached for a cookie. "Tell me about your relationship with Mrs. Landon."

Serena reached for her coffee but she didn't drink, just held the warm mug in her hands as if she needed the warmth more than she needed the caffeine.

"We were friends. Good friends," she emphasized. "She would never have left of her own free will without telling me."

"What makes you so certain?"

She lifted one shoulder in an I-can't-explain gesture. "We were just close, that's all. I know she wouldn't go without telling me. I just know."

And there it was. Her first lie to him.

Todd knew all too well the signs to look for. The slight averting of her gaze. The tick in her otherwise smooth cheek. A nervous slide of her tongue over her lips. And the increase in her pulse rate. He didn't need to be touching her to feel the change; he saw the pulse at the base of her throat flutter a little faster.

For whatever reason, she'd just lied through her teeth.

But the last thing he wanted to do was to alienate her. To that end, he kept his conclusions to himself.

"How long had the two of you been close?"

She shifted in her seat. "I went over all this with Mrs. Colby-Camp." She met his eyes, but only briefly. "Is this really necessary?"

Todd leaned back in the chair and got more comfortable, his gaze never leaving her. Why would she lie? What was she hiding?

"It would be helpful for me to hear it from you."

She moistened her lips again and looked anywhere but at him. "All right." She cleared her throat. "We, ah, met at Milestone's New Year's Eve party. I'd just been hired and Molly was very nice to me. She took me around and introduced me to practically everyone."

According to what the Colby Agency had on Serena she'd gone to work for Milestone just over one year ago. That part of her story was accurate. "Why did Molly introduce you around? Molly wasn't an employee. Did she often get involved with her husband's work? You were hired as Landon's assistant, right?"

Serena nodded. Todd watched her throat work with the effort of swallowing. What was she hiding?

"I think maybe she wanted to ensure I knew who she

was. And that everyone knew that Delia Neely, my predecessor, was out."

Todd waited for her to continue. He didn't want to
push too hard. This appeared to be curiously sensitive
territory for her.

"I learned later that Landon had carried on an affair
with Delia and that Molly wanted to make sure I understood that Charles was her husband." Serena closed her
eyes. "When she'd introduced me to everyone who was
anyone, she dragged me off to the kitchen and warned
me that I'd better watch myself because she would definitely be watching. Then she laughed as if she'd suddenly realized that I represented no threat to her. We
became instant friends."

"Did you tell the police about this?" Todd knew she
hadn't, though he didn't know her reasons.

She shook her head. "They already thought she'd left
Landon on her own. I didn't want to give them any additional evidence to that end."

Todd studied her face. She looked pale and worried. Her eyes were glazed with emotion. One thing
was certain, she and Molly Landon had definitely
been close. Very close.

"You're that certain she didn't simply walk away."

This time Serena leveled her gaze on him and there
was no way to miss the resolve in her eyes. "I'm
positive that she would not walk away. Her marriage
was extremely important to her. She would never leave

him. No matter how many affairs he had. Family was her priority."

"There were others?" The Colby Agency report had concluded as much, but Landon was a cautious man. He took discreet to a new level.

Serena sighed wearily. "More than I probably even know about. He's always going out of town."

Todd braced for her reaction to his next question but he felt compelled to ask. "He never attempted to initiate a nonworking relationship with you?"

Fury streaked across her face, turning her cheeks a deep red. "No. Never."

He'd hit a nerve. "Did that bother you in any way? Make you feel inadequate?"

Apparently he'd just thought he'd seen her angry. This new outrage represented a zone he had no desire to encounter again anytime soon. The fury roared in her eyes and her fingers tightened on the cup. But it was the set of her mouth that told the real story. She could have bitten off his head and spit down his throat.

"Dr. Landon never approached me in any manner that was not work-related. Had he, I would have informed him I wasn't interested."

Todd's gaze tapered with the turn his hunch had just taken. He was on to something here. "But you wouldn't have quit? You wanted this job badly enough to stay no matter what, am I right?"

Her indecision as to what to say held her mute

for three beats. "Yes," she said sharply and without apology.

"Even though—" Todd leaned forward to pump up the intimidation factor "—you're overqualified for the position of assistant?"

"We all have to start somewhere, don't we?"

Well now, she had him there.

"I suppose we do," he allowed. Instead of relaxing in his chair once more, he braced his elbows on his widespread knees and kept his gaze steady on hers. "Have you applied for promotions since you started at Milestone?" He knew the answer to that one already, but he wanted to see her reaction.

Another lengthy hesitation. "No. I like my work. I have no desire to move from my department. Opportunities come along occasionally for promotion within a department."

"So you forgo the possibility of moving up the ladder more quickly to keep your position with Dr. Landon?" She'd said basically as much, except he wanted to hear her say the words. "He hasn't offered you a promotion?"

"Maybe you'd like a blanket, Mr. Thompson. These late spring nights can get a little chilly." She stood, an act of dismissal, without answering his question.

He pushed to his feet and reached for his jacket. "That would be nice, Miss Blake. I appreciate your concern for my welfare."

She spun on her heel and stamped off down the hall.

He moved to the door and waited for her. He thought about the photo of her and Molly Landon, both smiling as if the picture had been taken on the happiest day of their lives.

If Serena felt so strongly that Charles Landon had harmed his wife in some way, why was she so hell-bent on continuing to work with him?

What was she hiding?

If she, in fact, wanted so desperately to find Molly Landon, why didn't she come clean?

A blanket and pillow in her arms, Serena strode up to him and shoved the items at him without a word.

"Thank you, Miss Blake."

"No problem." Her manners wouldn't let her ignore him, but she hadn't gone so far as to say he was welcome.

He turned to the door, reached for the knob but hesitated. "You know, when a person goes missing, the only way to determine what actually happened is to get to the truth." He looked fully at her. "The whole truth, Miss Blake. That's the only way we'll learn what happened to your good friend."

Her expression hardened. "Good night, Mr. Thompson."

And that was that.

He wouldn't be getting any more out of her tonight.

Todd surveyed the street before hustling to his car. He slid behind the wheel and made himself comfortable with the blanket and pillow. He might not be able to do any real sleeping but at least he could relax. The pillow smelled like her. He wondered if it came from her bed. He held it to his face and inhaled deeply. Whatever the subtle perfume she wore, he liked it.

Liked her.

She was the kind of woman a guy could get into... way too fast. He recognized the danger. No way was he going there.

As appealing as she was, he also understood that she was lying to him. Hiding something pertinent to this case.

Maybe his babysitting job wasn't going to be so benign after all.

Just maybe Serena Blake was the key to learning what had really happened to Molly Landon.

Todd smiled and thought about checking in with Braddock, but he changed his mind. If he told Braddock what he suspected, he might decide that keeping an eye on Serena required a more experienced investigator. Todd wasn't about to let that happen.

If fate had smiled on him and put him in the position to break this case, he damn sure wasn't about to blow it.

He watched Serena's silhouette as she moved in front of her bedroom window. She tore off the sweater, tossed it to the floor then climbed into bed. Tomorrow his whole strategy was going to change. This was no longer a glorified babysitting job, in his opinion. Serena had information. Information he needed to connect the dots that would lead to the truth.

He'd noticed her naiveté on certain levels: he'd have to use that. He'd never met a lady he couldn't charm if he so chose. Three days tops and she would be spilling everything she knew to him while Braddock was still playing games with Landon.

Todd rubbed a hand over his chin. He'd have to proceed with caution, otherwise he'd scare her off. Serena Blake would require the old-fashioned kind of persuasion. Slow, easy, sweet talk and gentle urging.

He didn't have a problem with that.

In fact, he looked forward to the challenge.

Chapter Six

Serena held the pillow close to her chest and fought the tears. She would not...*would not* cry. Crying wouldn't help Molly. Crying wouldn't block out the truth.

She closed her eyes and summoned the pleasant memories from just a few months ago. Serena had been so thrilled when she'd found her sister. She felt certain Molly had been happy, as well, but she'd wanted to keep the information a secret from her husband.

Why?

Looking back now, and considering Todd Thompson's questions, Serena asked herself the hard questions. What had Molly been hiding?

Was she ashamed of the fact that she'd been adopted from a criminally negligent mother and her abusive boyfriends? Or was it something else? Something she couldn't bear to share with Serena?

What if she never knew? What if Molly was already dead?

Serena threw her pillow across the room and scrambled out of bed. She refused to believe that. No matter what anyone said, she would not give up hope. Molly was out there somewhere. And she was pregnant—with Serena's niece. She had to find her, had to help her. No matter the cost. If her savings weren't enough, she would mortgage her town house. She'd taken her inheritance and bought this place. She could borrow against it without any trouble.

But she needed some sort of clue. Some direction to go in. Even the police were stumped. They'd cleared Landon, and couldn't find any indication whatsoever that he'd had anything to do with Molly's disappearance. The police assumed that because Molly had made a large withdrawal shortly before her disappearance, she'd left on her own. They'd even looked into the possibility that she'd been involved in an affair. That maybe the child she carried wasn't Landon's and that was her reason for disappearing. But Serena was certain that wasn't the case.

Every instinct told Serena that this had something to do with Charles Landon. She just didn't know how or what. She had suspected for several months now that he'd promised his soul to the devil, so to speak, in an effort to achieve the necessary funding for his advanced stem cell research. He was still working to that end, focusing solely on that goal—one wouldn't know from his actions that his wife was missing. But Serena couldn't prove any of her accusations. Landon had left her totally out of that loop. Had Molly figured out he was into something unethical or illegal and confronted him? Why hadn't she told Serena?

They were sisters, after all.

She had to stop thinking about it. She'd never get to sleep otherwise and she had an early meeting. The Colby Agency was on the case now.

Without turning on the light, she peeked past the corner of the blinds. Between the meager moonlight and the dim glow from the street lamp she could just make out Thompson's beat-up old Volvo. The decade-old sedan looked every day of its age. Not at all like her sleek BMW. But then, she'd gotten a hefty inheritance. That was the only reason she'd been able to afford this place and a classy car. Her salary certainly wouldn't have allowed such luxuries.

She wondered about Todd Thompson. He was young. She hadn't gotten his date of birth when he'd flashed his license, but she recognized that he was very young. Twenty-two or three. She also suspected that he was new at the Colby Agency. Otherwise she doubted he would be assigned the lowly duty of watching her place. Landon was the important one in this case. She'd wager that Braddock was keeping an eye on Landon. Braddock had the experience. Victoria Colby-Camp wouldn't take any chances. Her agency's reputation was far too esteemed to take unnecessary risks.

Though Thompson was definitely a little rough around the edges, he was no fool. He'd sensed that she was lying to him or, at the very least, leaving things out. She had to give him credit. He might be new and was definitely young, but he was a quick study.

The idea that he'd asked whether or not Dr. Landon had ever made sexual overtures toward her infuriated her. Of course he hadn't. She didn't give off those come-on vibes. She'd heard the rumors about his previous assistant. She'd been all over him from the beginning. That she'd moved on so abruptly had facilitated Serena's needs, but given the appearance of having been caught. Molly hadn't ever mentioned confronting her, but it was possible she'd chosen not to speak of it.

As much as Serena loved her sister, she understood that there was a definite boundary in their relationship. At first she hadn't wanted to accept that some invisible wall stood between her and her sister, but she'd come to terms with it. They were close, very close. Closer than most sisters, in Serena's opinion. But there was that place they couldn't get past. Maybe Molly just couldn't talk about the way her husband had betrayed her. The wall that kept their relationship from going deeper seemed to involve her intimate connection with him.

Serena heaved a sigh. God, please don't let her be dead already. Let her be out there, safely tucked away for some unknown reason, waiting to be rescued.

Well, sleep was out of the question. She might as well get some work done.

Serena moved down the stairs as quietly as if she feared Thompson was somewhere nearby listening. She rolled her eyes. She had to put that man out of her mind.

Her town house wasn't that large. Two bedrooms and two baths upstairs. Living room, dining room turned office, kitchen and half bath downstairs. All she needed. More than she'd ever hoped for as a kid growing up in foster homes.

She went to her desk and sat in front of her desktop computer. She nudged the mouse to suspend the screen-saver, then clicked the necessary keys to get her to the report for this morning's briefing.

Serena studied her report. Milestone was nearing the end of its government resources. The line of cells purchased from the National Institutes of Health was almost exhausted. New clusters of cells would be needed for the research Charles Landon had in mind. That private funding he sought would put those cells within reach.

There was no law preventing the creation of new cell lines as long as no government funding was utilized. But Milestone Laboratories was ninety-nine percent government-funding dependent. That had to change for Landon's proposed research to go forward.

She was no fool. She could read between the lines. Others surely could, as well. Unless some other form of funding that she was unaware of came into play, in mere months all research would have to be suspended.

Considering that she noted no worry in either Landon or Miles, she felt confident that private arrangements had been made. Why not announce this news?

Serena arrowed down, perusing the report in spite of the fact that she knew the information by heart already. It was what she didn't know that worried her.

Surely an announcement of private funding was imminent. Did this change have anything to do with Molly's disappearance? And why wasn't Dr. Landon more concerned with his missing wife? Or his unborn child at the very least.

The first two or three weeks he'd been beside himself. Serena had almost felt sorry for him despite his numerous affairs of the past. But then, as soon as the police had ruled him out as a suspect and suggested that Molly had left on her own, Landon had turned his full attention back to work and that was where it had been since. He scarcely even mentioned his wife and child anymore.

It just didn't add up.

She supposed it could be a defensive mechanism. A way to protect his feelings and his ego. But she wasn't ready to give him that much slack. Maybe she should.

Deep in her heart she knew Molly would not just disappear. She had doctor appointments. She was pregnant. She couldn't risk neglecting medical care for the final weeks of her pregnancy. No one in their right mind would do something as foolish as that. She had to confess that the police had worked hard to find her, especially considering the pregnancy. What disappointed her was the fact that they had dismissed Landon so easily.

And maybe Landon was only guilty of being a selfish jerk. Hadn't he effectively shut out Arthur Miles in the past couple of years? Serena had heard the rumors. Milestone was started by Arthur Miles, but two years ago he'd run into financial trouble and had to sell a large portion of his stock. Somehow he'd failed to realize that Landon's quick move to buy had put him in the control seat with the most shares. If Miles held a grudge, he hid it well. He appeared content with sitting back and allowing Landon to hog the limelight.

Serena shut down her laptop and got up from her desk. She needed to sleep. She didn't want to think about any of this anymore.

She turned out the light and trudged back up the stairs. Vaguely she wondered if Todd Thompson had gotten to sleep with the aid of her pillow and blanket. What was the temperature outside? It hadn't felt that cold when she'd gone out there. But the temperature might have dropped. Before she could rein in her empathy she switched on the television in her bedroom and checked the weather station. Forty-nine degrees. Not so bad.

But he was tall. He wouldn't be able to stretch out in that car.

Cursing herself, she grabbed her sweater and stomped to the first floor. She unlocked and flung open the front door, left it that way while she marched down the walk and across the street.

This time she didn't go to the driver's side: she banged on the window on the passenger's side.

Abrupt movement inside the vehicle told her she'd roused him, if he'd been asleep.

The driver's-side door opened and his head and shoulders rose above the car on the opposite side. "What is it?"

He looked as if he'd just awakened and his hair was even more tousled than usual. And still he looked amazing. It was utterly ridiculous.

"Look, it's stupid for you to sleep out here. You can sleep on my couch."

He shoved his fingers through his disheveled hair and looked confused for a moment.

"It's not that complicated, Thompson. You can either continue to sleep cramped up out here or you can come inside. It's your choice."

Furious with herself for even asking, she did an about-face and stormed back to her house. She was an absolute idiot. She shouldn't have cared if he froze to death out here and it wasn't even close to freezing.

"Stupid," she muttered.

She no sooner cleared the threshold than the door slammed behind her. She spun around, startled to find Thompson right behind her. Her breath caught, giving away her surprise.

"Sorry."

Looking entirely unrepentant, he shuffled over to the sofa and collapsed.

"There's a bathroom down the hall," she snapped. "The second floor is off-limits."

"Thanks."

She almost groaned and forced herself to turn away. Upstairs she locked her bedroom door and climbed into bed. She lay there for a full thirty minutes with barely even a blink.

How could she sleep with a stranger downstairs?

She threw back the covers, got up and dragged her dressing table in front of the door.

"There."

That was better. If he tried to come through her door she'd have plenty of warning.

She climbed back into bed and lay there staring at the ceiling, or what she could see of it in the dark.

What felt like hours passed. She refused to look at the clock. When the heaviness of sleep settled on her, she relaxed and felt immensely grateful for the relief she knew would come.

Her eyes closed and images played through her groggy mind. Molly as a little girl only four years old.

Serena toddling, a mere two-year-old, alongside her. But it was only a dream. She had no memories from that time. Then another image pushed aside all others. Todd Thompson and his unorderly appearance. Tousled hair, untucked shirttail, that ancient leather jacket and those worn soft jeans. He was watching her…wanted to know her secrets.

But she couldn't let him see.

Molly had made her promise never to tell anyone. She couldn't let Molly down for any reason.

SERENA LISTENED TO every word Dr. Landon said in the briefing that morning. She watched his expression and his every gesture as carefully as possible. She couldn't understand why she didn't note any concern about the future of certain research studies. She'd been waiting for weeks to see some sort of reaction to the bottom line. At first she'd chalked up the oversight to Molly's disappearance. But she knew that wasn't the problem. He'd pretty much put the whole ordeal behind him.

The only time he brought up Molly and the baby anymore was when the newspaper or some television news channel ran a piece about the still-missing pregnant Molly Landon. Her case hadn't gotten nearly the coverage of similar cases of the past. Of course that was most likely because of the conclusions made by the local authorities and the FBI.

Serena studied Charles Landon. He was a relatively

handsome man. If one didn't know about his woman-
izing, one would likely consider him quite handsome.
But Serena knew him too well. He was a class-A jerk
with an ego to match his self-inflated image.

She wondered briefly where Todd Thompson had
gotten off to this morning. He'd been long gone when
she got up. He hadn't left a message, not that she'd expected him to.

She hadn't seen Mr. Braddock around, either. According to Landon's calendar, the two were having lunch
together at noon. Not in the cafeteria, either, as she and
Nolan did yesterday. Downtown at a ritzy restaurant.

The kind of place Landon used to take Molly in an
effort to impress his colleagues.

Serena clenched her jaw and held back the hate. She
couldn't let it eat at her like this. One way or another
she had to hang on to her professionalism until she
knew exactly what had happened to Molly. If Landon
got even a hint of her mutiny, he would fire her lickety-
split. She couldn't let that happen.

Thankfully the briefing ended and she gathered her
material to head back to her office. She could do with
a break from listening to his voice.

"Serena."

Speak of the devil. "Yes, sir?"

"I'd like to see you in my office." He glanced at the
Rolex Molly had gotten him for Christmas. "Say, in ten
minutes. Give me time to finish up here."

A stab of ice-cold fear went through Serena, but she managed an acknowledging nod. She wasn't exactly afraid of Landon. Not really. Not in the presence of so many colleagues, anyway. But the idea that he wanted to speak to her alone conjured up all kinds of other scary scenarios.

What if he wanted to fire her?

What if he'd figured out that she blamed him for Molly's disappearance?

Her heart pounding, Serena went straight to her office and put her report in the appropriate file and checked her messages. She took several deep breaths in an attempt to slow the thundering beneath her sternum.

The phone in her pocket vibrated. She jerked with a start, placing her hand to her chest to calm herself. She fished out the phone and pressed the talk button.

"Serena Blake."

"Good morning, Miss Blake."

Todd Thompson.

She'd recognize that rumpled voice anywhere. The sound and sexy quality exactly matched the man.

"What can I do for you, Mr. Thompson? I'm very busy this morning."

"I just wanted to make sure you were all right. I followed you to work this morning and you looked a little jumpy."

Her mouth gaped in astonishment. How dare he!

"I'm perfectly fine. I don't need you watching me,

Mr. Thompson." The very idea. Last night was one thing, but this was different. She was safe at work. There was always security in numbers.

"I was hoping you might be able to get the afternoon off so that we can do a little extra investigating."

She stilled, but her anticipation surged. Had he learned something that lent credence to her accusations? "I don't understand." She was almost afraid to hope.

"Dr. Landon said that you could assist me any way I needed you. I thought we'd take advantage of that offer and do some snooping."

That mounting anticipation started to thud against her temples. "Do you have new information?" God, that would be great. Every minute that Molly was unaccounted for lessened the likelihood of finding her safe and sound.

"Just meet me outside at half past noon if possible. We need to talk."

"Okay. I'll try."

He disconnected and Serena stared at her phone a long moment before slipping it back into her pocket. She'd been waiting for weeks to have someone on her side—to have help. She prayed it wouldn't be too little too late.

The intercom on her desk buzzed. "Serena, I'm waiting."

She jumped. "I'll be right there." She had to get hold of herself. Landon would surely suspect something if she continued to behave so out of sorts and jumpy.

She smoothed her hands over her jacket and cleared her throat. Landon was waiting. She had to get this over with.

Not bothering to knock since he was expecting her, Serena swiped her badge and opened the door to Landon's office. He looked up from his computer screen and motioned for her to take a seat.

Her back rigid, she settled into one of the upholstered chairs flanking his desk and waited for him to begin. She struggled to slow her galloping heart, but nothing did the trick.

Landon suddenly turned to her and reclined in his tufted leather chair. "I want to make a few things clear before we proceed further with this Sun Publishing business."

Her breath evaporated in her lungs. Was he suspicious? Did he know something wasn't right?

"I've looked into the offer and it's legitimate."

Her suddenly still heart stumbled back into a clumsy rhythm. "That's wonderful," she choked out, underscoring the statement with a wane smile.

Landon pursed his lips for a long moment before continuing. "My only concern is that the details will somehow wander off into the territory regarding my wife." His gaze bored straight into hers. "I don't want that to happen. This business with Molly is off-limits. Do not answer any questions where she is concerned. Do you understand me, Serena?"

"Yes, sir." She gritted her teeth to hold back what she wanted to say.

"I know how journalists can be. One or both will want to venture into that aspect of my life. I can handle Braddock, but I need to be sure you can stay out of trouble with Thompson."

"No problem, sir," she assured him, almost light-headed with anticipation now. "I won't talk about Molly. You don't have to worry."

Incredibly, Landon managed to look sad. "There's always the chance any outside interference could somehow damage the investigation the police are conducting. I can't take that risk."

Serena barely restrained the demand hovering at the back of her throat. *What damned investigation?* The police had made their conclusions. End of story.

"In any event," he said with a sigh of finality, "I don't want my personal life to get all tangled up with my work here. The past few weeks have been distracting enough. The media doesn't care how painful a subject is, their only concern is with selling papers or ratings."

For the first time since Molly went missing, Serena wondered if she had misjudged Landon. Was he really in pain? Had she so completely misinterpreted his feelings?

That just didn't seem possible.

"I understand, Dr. Landon," she assured him. "We all want Mrs. Landon and the baby back safe and sound. I won't do or say anything that will jeopardize that."

To her disbelief he smiled. Not the big, wide, toothy one he reserved for an audience of his colleagues, but a genuinely trusting one.

"I know I can trust you, Serena. You and Molly were friends. Of all the people here, I know how much you miss her."

Too flabbergasted to speak, Serena just sat there.

"I have a luncheon meeting with Mr. Braddock," he went on, moving out of sensitive territory. "I may not be back this afternoon."

She remembered the call from Thompson. "Mr. Thompson requested that I spend some time with him this afternoon. Is that all right with you, sir?" She braced for an outburst. Landon didn't want anything interfering with work. He wanted his employees focused and on the job.

"That's fine." He nodded. "Just remember what I said."

"Of course." She stood. "Is there anything else, Dr. Landon?"

He shook his head. "That's all."

When she would have turned away, he held up his hand as if he'd just remembered something. "Forward a copy of this morning's briefing notes to Arthur. He couldn't make the meeting."

"Yes, sir."

Serena left Landon's office far more confused than when she'd entered. At least she wasn't fired. But he had given her second thoughts about her investigation.

She couldn't back out.

What she'd witnessed just now could have been a big act designed for that very purpose. He knew her well enough to know what she wanted to hear.

She'd made a decision based on a series of events, not one moment in time. By the same token, she couldn't let one moment of sympathy change her mind.

She knew what she had to do.

Back in her office with the door closed, she forwarded a copy of the minutes one of the clerks had taken, along with hers as well as Landon's report to Dr. Miles. It was unusual for him to miss a briefing of this level, but it wasn't entirely unheard of. Right now she had enough on her mind worrying about Molly. Whatever was going on between Landon and Miles was not her problem.

For a second or two she considered whether she should call Thompson back, but then she opted to do so. How would he know whether to pick her up if she didn't call? She knew the reason for her hesitation. She was a sucker. All the way to the core. A part of her wanted to believe that Landon was telling the truth. That he hadn't had anything to do with his wife's disappearance. That he cared…that he hurt.

And maybe all those things were true. But there was only one way to find out for sure.

She checked her received call log on her cell and selected the number from which Thompson had called.

"Thompson."

"I can meet you at twelve-thirty. Will you be in your car?"

"Yeah. I'll park near your BMW."

"Okay."

"What's wrong?"

Her pulse skipped. Surely he couldn't tell from those few words that something was wrong. "Nothing. I'm fine."

"No, you're not. What happened?"

Oh, this man infuriated her. "Landon called me into his office."

"For what purpose?"

She hated the way he could ask those pointed questions in such a cold, unyielding tone.

"To tell me not to talk about Molly to you."

There, she'd said it.

Silence.

She stared at the phone, wondered if he would tell her that she'd made a mistake and that she should back off.

How could two minutes in the man's office have her feeling so uncertain?

"He's just protecting himself, Serena. Don't let him get to you."

"But what if he's telling the truth?" The ache of uncertainty tightened in her throat. "He said he missed her. That he didn't want to do anything that would jeopardize finding her." The burn of tears at the backs of her eyes made her all the more angry at herself. "What if I'm wrong, Thompson? What if I'm wrong?" She rested her head in her hand and let the tears rise over her lashes. As if she could have held them back. And why was she saying this out loud to one of the people she'd hired to prove she was right?

"Then there's only one way to find out." He exhaled, the sound somehow—stupidly—reassuring. "If Landon is telling the truth, we'll find he has nothing to hide. He won't be hurt by our investigation because we're going to be the epitome of discreet. You have my word on that."

He was right. If Landon was innocent, he had nothing to hide. Nothing she did would injure him.

"I'll see you later then." She pressed the disconnect button before he could respond. She didn't want to hear his voice, didn't want to think about how good it felt to have someone to lean on.

She didn't know Todd Thompson.

She didn't know anything.

Except that the Colby Agency was the very best in the business.

She had to hang on to that.

Chapter Seven

Todd showed his ID to the guard at the gate and was waved through without hesitation. The cover profile Victoria had selected provided instant VIP status with no glitches. Todd admired her instincts and boldness. He was definitely going to like working for Victoria.

The Milestone Laboratories facilities sprawled in front of him like the Pentagon. Tucked away amid more than a thousand acres of untouched forest land, and a mere twenty-five miles from Chicago's Loop, the facility employed approximately two thousand people, including hundreds of award-winning scientists and their assistants. Like Serena Blake.

Todd parked next to her black BMW. Nice car. Sleek but conservative in a sophisticated way—like the woman. Managing to land a position at Milestone was no small feat. Serena had done well for herself considering where she'd started. He'd read the background information on her twice.

Serena Blake had come into this world as Serena Horton. At the age of two she'd been abandoned by her mother. No father had been named on her birth certificate. From two until sixteen she'd bounced from foster home to foster home. The kid got into more trouble than you could stir with a stick. Not a happy story. At sixteen she'd cut and run, but the authorities had caught up with her a few days later. That was when Serena's luck changed.

A well-to-do older couple had taken her in and eventually adopted her. They set her up for life financially and gave her the opportunities most kids today took for granted. Serena hadn't taken a single day for granted and not once had she let her new parents down. She'd allowed her brilliance to shine through, graduated from high school a year early at the top of her class, then gone on to college and performed with the same amazing thirst for knowledge.

Milestone had recruited her straight from the university and was poised to pay her to continue her education toward a Ph.D. Dr. Landon had nominated her for the program just two weeks ago. Serena didn't even know yet. Braddock had learned this in his meeting with Landon yesterday. Landon claimed this program was the reason he'd passed her over for promotion.

That Charles Landon would carry on with his routine activities as if nothing had happened to his wife and unborn child seemed to indicate his innocence in any involvement with his wife's disappearance. But Todd knew that looks could be deceiving. Landon was practically a genius and he would understand exactly what he had to do to pull off his part, if any, in the crime.

On the other hand, his ability to move on also gave the appearance of indifference.

But if he had nothing to do with Molly Landon's abrupt disappearance, then where the hell was she? Serena was convinced she wouldn't have left of her own volition. Who had taken her? Why hadn't there been a ransom demand? The police suspected she'd simply taken off on her own. A rather large cash withdrawal made shortly before her disappearance seemed to point in that direction. According to the bank's security videotapes she had walked up to the teller all alone and appeared completely calm. There simply was no reason to believe she'd made the withdrawal under duress.

Her Land Rover was still unaccounted for, as well.

A very pregnant Molly Landon, the money and her vehicle had simply vanished. No one had seen or heard from her since. Not her obstetrician, not her husband, no one.

Todd cleared his head and sat up a little straighter as Serena Blake approached his car. She'd left her white lab coat behind. The navy skirt and jacket she wore covered every inch of her from knee to neck as usual. The matching low-heeled pumps added only an inch or so to her height.

"Sorry I'm late," she said without looking at him as she opened the door and lowered her fine-looking backside into the passenger seat. "I had to pull a report at the last minute for Dr. Landon." Her dark eyes met his. "Projections for the research he'd like to do if private funding becomes available."

"Advanced embryonic stem cell," Todd suggested.

She nodded. "I can't help wondering if Molly's disappearance has something to do with whatever he's up to. Enough private funding is crucial and very difficult to achieve. He can't afford for anything to go wrong. What if Molly had threatened him somehow?" She held his gaze a moment longer before looking away. "I know I'm reaching here. But the research is so controversial, it makes me wonder how far Landon would be willing to go to make it happen. He can't afford anything that makes him look bad."

He understood that she didn't want him to see the worry and desperation in her eyes. That was why she wouldn't look at him. Molly Landon meant a great deal to her. He wondered how the two women could have grown so close in the past fifteen months.

"Do you have any tangible reason for suspecting her disappearance could be related to his work? Did she indicate to you that she was upset or prepared to confront her husband in any way?" Maybe raise a ruckus about illicit affairs? He didn't have to say.

She shook her head. "No. She always pretended everything was fine. I don't have any real proof. I guess I'm grasping at straws. Whatever happened, it wasn't about money. At least not Landon's personal assets. The police turned his financial records inside out. He has plenty to take care of his personal needs. The only place where he needs money is for his research. And he knows that's coming. It's only a matter of time."

"What about the affairs?" Todd ventured carefully. That seemed the most likely theory to him.

"He told the police about his affairs," she said, disbelief heavy in her tone. "I was shocked. I couldn't believe he actually admitted any of it. Yet he gave them all the names except one." Her gaze connected with Todd's once more. "My predecessor."

Todd considered that news. "Why do you suppose he kept her name a secret?"

Serena shrugged. "Maybe to protect Milestone. Delia Neely was the only one who actually worked at Milestone. In fact, she stayed on even after I took her place. A handful of people, including Molly, knew what had been going on between Delia and Landon but no one had the nerve to talk about it. Everyone just acts like it didn't happen. But that affair could bring a mess of bad publicity down on Landon and Milestone. He needs that indiscretion kept quiet."

"Where is Delia Neely now?" Todd had understood that she'd left when Serena was hired.

"She resigned about six months ago, after working

in the bowels of research since I took her old job. The hands-on stuff. I don't know where she went after that."

"But she didn't come around Landon or you?" Todd's instincts had gone on point. He didn't like that he hadn't heard this before.

"Anything above level two was off-limits to her," Serena explained. "Her security clearance was downgraded. The whole incident was basically a demotion. But company policy ensures that employees maintain their benefits and salary level even in the event of a downgrade. The only way she would have lost any of that was to be fired."

Todd considered the information. "Still, a demotion is a demotion. Doesn't make sense that she'd stay after that kind of public humiliation."

"Maybe she needed the benefits. The health insurance is excellent and the salary is about the best an assistant can expect. She wouldn't have gotten any better if she'd gone somewhere else."

Todd turned the key in the ignition and started the engine. "Maybe."

"Where are we going?"

He glanced at the woman in the passenger seat. She wasn't particularly thrilled about going anywhere with him. He wasn't particularly thrilled about it, either…at least not about the keeping-an-eye-on-her part. But he'd figured out a way to make the best of that.

Victoria and Braddock had ordered him to stick close

to Serena. Stay on top of who she called, where she went, the whole nine yards. Initially he'd been seriously annoyed at being stuck babysitting, but he'd taken a bad situation and turned it around.

If Landon was involved in his wife's disappearance, which was the most likely scenario despite the absence of evidence, then there were aspects of his life that Todd and Serena could investigate. As his personal assistant, Serena knew a great deal about him professionally as well as personally. Plus, Todd had his suspicions about what Serena was keeping from him. For all he knew, her nomination for the prestigious work-study program could be a payoff for keeping quiet, but that didn't seem likely. Landon would have told her already if he'd hoped to gain her full allegiance with the offer.

And that theory definitely didn't jibe with her having contacted the Colby Agency. He stole another peek at her. Then again, maybe this whole setup was a ruse to further prove Landon's innocence.

Todd needed to know more. He needed to be as close as possible to Serena to get the truth. She seemed to want someone to save the day, and he knew how to play the part of hero and say all the right things to keep her distracted while he dug into an aspect his gut told him would tell the tale.

Serena was hiding something and Landon's last affair had been left off the list of truths he'd given the authorities. That was where Todd wanted to start—with the unknown. If the woman, Delia, didn't want to be dragged into Landon's current problem, there was a reason.

Maybe Landon and Delia were still involved.

If Landon was accustomed to extracurricular activities, Todd couldn't see him going cold turkey.

"How about some lunch?" he suggested.

His passenger looked startled at the suggestion. "I thought we were going to work on the case."

He grinned. "We are. But we have to eat." He kept one hand on the steering wheel as he maneuvered out of the gigantic Milestone Labs parking lot and patted his stomach with the other. "A guy's gotta eat."

Conversation lagged as he drove to the South Loop and merged onto Michigan Avenue. Chicago's Firehouse Restaurant was his favorite. The restored turn-of-the-century firehouse gave the restaurant amazing ambience. The food was great and the service top-notch.

A quiet booth in a half-empty dining room made for discreet discussion. Todd thanked the hostess and slid into the booth across from Serena.

"Have you been here before?" he asked.

"No." Her skeptical gaze settled on his. "What do you recommend?"

Ah, so he had himself a finicky eater. "How about a burger?

"I might just pass on the burger. Perhaps a salad."

What a shame. "Suit yourself."

The waiter arrived to take their orders and promised to return with their drinks as well as water.

"So tell me about Delia." No point beating around the bush.

Serena didn't answer immediately. Instead she relaxed into the fake leather of the booth and chewed on her lower lip.

"She was a few years older than me. Intelligent. Attractive. The typical blond beauty. Ambitious."

Serena sighed as she gathered her thoughts on the rest of what she wanted to say. "I only met her once for a brief overview of the files, but she seemed… nice. I don't know." She shrugged. "I feel like I'm being disloyal to Molly to say it, but she did. Delia seemed nice."

"Do you know how long she'd been working with Landon?" Todd couldn't help wondering when the affair began, and if it was purely physical or if the two had grown emotionally attached over time.

"Three years. I think Milestone was her first job, too."

Most scientists preferred younger assistants. That was nothing out of the ordinary. Maybe it was because the younger employees were more willing to do all the thankless jobs. Or because they were easier to mold. If they were female, the reasoning could very well have been about looks and the possibility of sexual favors.

Todd wanted to shake men like Landon. Women weren't playthings. As much as he enjoyed sex, he never went into it with any misunderstandings between him and his partner. The woman always knew it was about sex.

Ironic, he realized, that he'd only this morning decided to use some subtle seduction on his assignment. But this was different, wasn't it? This was work. The same rules didn't apply to getting the job done. This wasn't about personal gratification. It was about finding a missing woman. A pregnant one at that.

Guilt trickled through him, but he ignored it. This was his first assignment for the Colby Agency. He wasn't about to fail. No matter what he had to do to get the job done. This was a test…one he couldn't fail.

"Do you know where Delia Neely lives?"

"It's in my Palm Pilot." She dug around in her purse and produced the handheld electronic organizer. "Let's see." She entered the necessary data and nodded. "Yes, I have her address and her phone number. In case I needed to ask her about work," she clarified.

"But you never had to," he suggested. "You've never spoken to Delia outside Milestone."

"No." She frowned. Confusion flickered in her eyes. "Are you accusing me of something, Mr. Thompson?"

Just then their food arrived, saving him from having to answer without a little forethought.

But Serena Blake had no intention of letting the question go. "You didn't answer my question. Do you consider me a suspect of some sort in this case? I thought we had that all ironed out."

Todd placed both hands on the table on either side of his place setting. She glanced at his hands and he could almost see her heart start to drum in her chest. The move made her nervous. He considered her for seven or eight seconds before he answered. She didn't need to be too sure of herself. What she needed was to be worried about her standing with him and the Colby Agency. She needed to believe that finding the truth was not only important to Molly Landon but important to Serena Blake.

"I believe that you are sincerely worried about Molly Landon and that you are more than halfway convinced that her husband had something to do with her disappearance." He watched the relief claim her worried face. "But I also think you're harboring a secret or two that you haven't shared with me." A brick wall went up, shielding her emotions. "Whatever it is you aren't telling me edges that defining line in the sand a little closer to you. Suspect." He gestured to the left, then to the right. "Not a suspect. Right now, Miss Blake, it's a helluva narrow margin."

A glimmer of fury flamed above that brick wall she'd used to hide behind. "Think what you will, Mr. Thompson, but just remember, you work for me."

Oh, that was good.

"Yes, ma'am."

She was right, he did work for her. And that made him even more determined to make her come clean.

THEY DIDN'T HAVE FAR to go to find where Delia Neely lived. On 58th Street near Harper Avenue. She rented a two-room apartment over the garage of one of the stately mansions. But she wasn't home.

As they stood outside the door at the top of the exterior stairs, Serena used her cell phone to call the number she had listed as Delia's.

She frowned. "It's been disconnected."

Todd surveyed the upscale neighborhood and considered whether he wanted to risk adding breaking and entering to his score sheet. If Victoria found out, she would likely be very unhappy.

"Nobody's home!"

He turned and stared down at the woman who'd shouted the news up to them. Sixtyish. Stylishly dressed. The owner of the house. Too well-groomed and expensively dressed to be the hired help.

He gestured for Serena to precede him down the stairs. As he moved downward he said, "We're trying to find an old friend, Delia Neely. Does she still live here?" He seriously doubted it since her phone had been disconnected. Not to mention that finding her this quickly would have just been too easy.

"Delia moved out about six months ago," the woman said. "She didn't leave a forwarding address." The woman shielded her eyes from the sun as Todd and Serena came closer. "She left in a bit of a hurry."

"Really?"

"Yes," the woman went on, "she didn't give me a minute's notice, so I kept her deposit. She didn't even come or call back to complain. Most do."

Damn. "No forwarding address, you say?" He needed something to go on. "Did she give you the name and address of someone who would know her whereabouts when she filled out her application before moving in?" Most landlords required that sort of information for protecting themselves.

"She did, but the number's no good. I tried to call her to tell her she'd left a few items."

"What did she leave?" Serena asked. "Anything that might tell us where she went?"

The woman's suspicions roused.

"She actually owed us some money, as well," Todd improvised. "We were hoping to find her without having to take it to small claims court."

"I'm sure she intended to pay us back," Serena added, sounding wholly sincere.

Todd let that one slide since they needed this woman's cooperation. But he hoped this was no indication of how well she could lie. His storytelling didn't count. At least, that was what he told himself.

The woman shrugged. "She didn't leave anything important. Just a coat and a purse, but there was no money or relevant papers in it. A tube of lipstick and a business card."

"May we see the business card?" Anticipation kicked

in. The card would have the name and telephone number of someone she'd known in one capacity or another. This woman might not recognize the value but he did.

"The card was a dead end," she said, bursting his bubble as easily as if she'd jabbed him with a straight pin. "Some doctor." Her brow furrowed as she concentrated hard to remember the name. "Dr. Herbert Wright. Has an office downtown."

Todd felt Serena stiffen next to him. "Thank you, ma'am," he said. "We appreciate your help."

"If you run into her, tell her she should have given me notice and I would have given her the deposit back."

Todd waved in acknowledgment of the woman's comment then slid behind the wheel of his Volvo. He started the car and backed out of the driveway before turning to his passenger. "Did you recognize the doctor's name?"

Serena nodded. He frowned. She looked pale.

"Dr. Herbert Wright is Molly's obstetrician."

Todd's frown deepened. "Wait a minute. I read the report on Mrs. Landon. The obstetrician in the report was a Dr. Rice." He remembered the name clearly.

"That's the one Landon insisted she go to," Serena admitted. "She went a few times, but didn't like him, so she found another."

Todd knew that something was wrong with that picture. Did pregnant women often change obstetricians midterm?

"Landon can't know," Serena urged. "He would be extremely upset that she'd disobeyed him."

Well, well. The first of Miss Blake's secrets was revealed. He took a hard right and headed back to the South Loop.

Serena glanced around as if she didn't recognize the landscape. "Where are we going now?"

"To my side of the fifty yard line," he said flatly. He didn't like being lied to. Though he'd known she'd been keeping secrets, that didn't make him like it any better. If she wanted him to find the truth, she needed to come clean with him.

Her hands fidgeted with her seat belt. The shaky breath she exhaled backed up his assessment. She was afraid.

Good.

If he played the intimidation game well enough, seduction might not even be necessary. Not that he'd dreaded it or anything, but he recognized the risk. He was only human. Getting caught up in the moment could cost him, as well. Especially considering he was seriously attracted to Serena.

"I don't understand," she said softly as he braked for a red light.

"We're going to my place. That's what happens when you hit the fourth down without gaining enough yards. You lose the ball. It's my ball now."

She blinked in an attempt to hide the fear glittering in her eyes. "I don't play baseball, Mr. Thompson."

"Good thing," he said crisply, "since the analogy was in reference to football."

Man, who didn't know the difference between baseball and football?

Guilt pinged him again. Serena's life hadn't been a piece of cake. He doubted anyone in her early years had bothered to introduce her to sports, other than the kind learned on the streets. Once she landed with decent folks she'd been so focused on pulling her life together and making something of herself she'd probably been one of those bookworm types who didn't care for sports.

He had to remember that not everyone had been as fortunate as he was growing up.

Still, he wasn't such a pushover that he wouldn't use this little episode of tension to his advantage. She had more secrets. He needed to know what those were.

Pronto. Hence the trip to his place. His territory. A place where she wouldn't feel so at ease with her ability to handle the situation.

Any discomfort she experienced would just have to be chalked up to a sort of collateral damage.

"This is where you live?"

He parked at the curb in front of the Victorian-era house turned apartment building he called home.

Now that ticked him off. Just because he didn't live in a fancy town house on her side of town didn't mean anything.

"You got a problem with that?"

"No."

To his surprise, she smiled.

"It just reminds me of the frat houses I used to wish I could sneak into." She stared out at the place, which, now that she mentioned it, looked exactly like a college frat house.

"So why didn't you?" The question wasn't relevant to anything, but he wanted to know.

She laughed. He liked the sound. It was so spontaneous and incredibly sweet.

"Please, I would never have had the nerve. I spent my entire college life hiding in corners at the library and pretending I was invisible."

"Invisible?" he asked incredulously.

Her gaze bumped into his. "Pathetic, huh?"

A tendril of hair had slipped out of her meticulous do and draped along her cheek to curl up against her throat.

This was the Serena Blake he wanted to know. The innocent yet hopeful woman who just wanted someone to talk to and maybe to hang on to. And as much as he wanted to get to know her better, he was definitely not the guy for her. His full attention was on his future. Right now his life had to be about *him*. As selfish as that sounded, he recognized the pitfalls of a serious relationship. Those kinds of ties had to wait until his career and his future were more solid.

"Not pathetic at all," he said, offering an understanding smile. Miss Blake was too nice for her own good. "Sweet, that's what it is."

"I see." She turned her attention straight ahead and leaned back against the headrest, preventing him from seeing how his comment made her feel. But he'd heard her reaction in her voice. She hadn't liked his remark one bit.

Funny, he hadn't anticipated this. The girl with the super-duper IQ had secretly wanted to be like every other girl—noticed by boys.

"Sweet. You're right." She shifted her face back to him then, a new glint of determination in her eyes. "But I wasn't always so sweet, Mr. Thompson. There are things about me you won't ever know and couldn't begin to imagine."

She got out. Leaving him too stunned to reply.

Was that a warning…or an invitation?

Chapter Eight

Serena lagged behind as Todd Thompson climbed the stairs of the Victorian house that decades ago had been dissected into several apartments. Unlike the exterior, not much inside remained of the home's former glory. Despite the dim lighting, occasional glimpses of intricate molding and gleaming wood floors served as reminders of what had once been.

He stopped on the second-floor landing and waited for her to catch up.

"This is it."

He gestured to the red door on his right. Two more doors stood on the left, each designated with a single-digit number. Door number six sported a grapevine wreath embellished with silk flowers in spring colors and an equally colorful welcome mat, while door five offered a small plaque warning solicitors away. Thompson's door presented only one detail that spoke about his personality, an additional dead-bolt lock. The wooden staircase did a U-turn and continued upward to the third floor.

He unlocked the door, all three locks, and shoved it inward. After reaching inside to flip on a light, he backed against the wall and waited for her to enter ahead of him. "Make yourself at home."

Serena didn't hesitate. Part of her couldn't wait to get a closer look at who Todd Thompson was. The place looked neater than she'd expected. The shirt he'd worn yesterday lay, one sleeve inside out, across the arm of an upholstered chair. Newspapers and magazines cluttered the coffee table. A plaid sofa, flanked by tables and lamps, took up most of the space on one side of the room. A desk with two computers and a small entertainment center lined the opposite wall. Two upholstered chairs and an ottoman in coordinating colors completed the furnishings.

Beyond the living room was a small but efficient eat-in kitchen. Surprisingly, there were no dirty dishes on the counter or the table. He either didn't eat at home or cleaned up after himself unusually well for a bachelor under the age of thirty. And one who prided himself on looking unkempt.

She heard the click of the locks tumbling back into the secure position. "Do you have a cleaning lady?" The question kind of popped out of her mouth before she could stop it. Oh, well, after her admission in the car, why in the world would anything else that came out of her mouth surprise her?

"No." He glanced around his living room and quickly grabbed up his discarded shirt. One eyebrow arrowed upward with skepticism as his gaze settled on hers once more. "Do you think I need one?"

She shook her head. "Just curious."

He looked at once dubious of her response and yet somewhat amused. "Would you like something to drink? Water?" He looked thoughtful for a moment. "It's bottled and chilled."

"I'm fine, thank you."

"Okay." He tossed his shirt off the chair. "So, let's talk."

Serena took a seat in the closest chair while he plopped onto the sofa. Her mind was still reeling just a little with what they'd learned from Delia's landlady.

"I've thought about the idea that Delia was seeing Dr. Wright and there may be a logical explanation. Dr. Wright is a gynecologist as well as an obstetrician."

Todd didn't comment on her conclusion. Instead he asked, "What was Mrs. Landon's specific reason for changing doctors midstream, so to speak? That she didn't like him seems a little unspecific."

Serena remembered how angry Molly had been after her second visit to Dr. Rice. She hadn't liked him, she'd said. So she'd secretly switched to someone she preferred. "She said she didn't like his bedside manner. She found him intimidating. She liked Wright better. I got the impression she'd seen him before. Maybe for routine exams."

"I considered that possibility," he allowed.

"But we have to be sure. Why don't you call for an appointment? See if maybe you can be worked in this afternoon." He shrugged. "Make up an emergency of some sort. PMS or something."

She rolled her eyes and started to explain the acronym to him but why waste the time. When he didn't blink, she realized he was serious. "Me? Make an appointment with Dr. Wright?" How in the world would that provide any answers? "I'm certain you're familiar with doctor-patient privilege. He's not going to tell me anything about Molly or Delia." Though she was Molly's sister, no one could know that secret. She had to respect Molly's wishes.

"He won't have to tell you anything." He said this without so much as a flicker of uncertainty. "We'll get all the information we need from her file."

Okay, he'd definitely lost it now. "What're you talking about? They won't let us see someone else's file."

"When a patient is taken to an exam room," he countered, "their file is always slipped into that little pocket on the door, right?" He propped one ankle on his knee. "When the doctor moves to the next patient he takes the file and a moment to review before greeting the patient. Have you ever seen it done any other way?"

Serena threw up her hands. "Wait. I understand perfectly what you mean, but how is that going to help me get Delia's or Molly's file hung on my door?"

"It won't help us get Molly's, but say you're Delia Neely to ensure hers is handy."

A bark of laughter burst from her throat. "You're kidding, right? I can't say I'm Delia. Someone on staff may know her. We don't look anything alike. She was blond and...and thinner than me."

"Look." He sat forward and propped his elbows on his spread knees. "We can't risk using Molly Landon's name because of her high-profile case. We know Wright has seen her a number of times, not to mention her picture has been splashed all over the news. But we have a chance with Delia. She may have only been to Wright once or twice. According to her landlady, she disappeared months ago."

"She could be living somewhere else in Chicago," Serena argued. This was the craziest idea she'd ever heard. He had to be out of his mind to even think she would do something like this.

While she sat, staring agape at him, he fished out his cell phone and put in a call. To the Colby Agency, she supposed. He asked someone named Simon Ruhl to see if there was any current information available on a Delia Neely.

When he'd slid his phone back into his pocket he said, "Make the appointment. We can always cancel it."

She didn't like it, but if this move would help find Molly, she would try to be cooperative. A call to Information gave her the number she needed. Serena took a deep breath and entered it.

When the receptionist answered, Serena did what she

had to do. "Yes, my name is Delia Neely, and I'm a patient of Dr. Wright's. I'm having some trouble…and I wondered if maybe I could be worked into his schedule this afternoon."

The silence on the other end of the line had perspiration dampening Serena's palms. She'd never done this before. Not even as a belligerent teenager. What if the receptionist knew Delia and recognized that Serena's voice wasn't right?

"I'm sorry, Ms. Neely, but this office is closing." More of that awkward silence. "Perhaps you haven't heard, but Dr. Wright was murdered last night. When you've found another obstetrician, we'll be happy to forward your records."

The rest of what the woman said didn't register. Serena thanked her, the response autonomic, and dropped the phone back into its cradle.

Murdered.

Todd stared at her expectantly, but she couldn't pass along what she'd learned just yet.

Chicago was a thriving metropolis; murder happened. She saw it on the news more often than she cared to admit…but this felt different. Deep down inside where nothing but instinct and intuition functioned, she understood that this was somehow relevant to Molly's disappearance.

Maybe it was because Delia and Charles Landon had been lovers. Or maybe because Molly had hated

Delia so. But the idea that Delia had left her home of several years so abruptly and the fact that Dr. Wright had been murdered couldn't be mere coincidence.

Serena didn't believe in coincidences.

"Dr. Wright is—"

His cell phone interrupted her announcement. "Hold that thought," he said.

Serena sat, stunned, as Todd interacted with his caller in a series of one-word responses. Yeahs and uh-huhs. His facial expression didn't give anything away. She wondered if Simon Ruhl had checked up on Delia's whereabouts so quickly. She shouldn't be surprised. The Colby Agency would know all the tricks of the trade. They were the best, she reminded herself.

"Thanks."

She waited while he put his phone away, but considering what she'd just learned, her patience couldn't hold out. "What did you find out?"

"Delia Neely fell off the face of the earth six months ago. She didn't pay her final phone and utility charges. Her bank account balance hasn't changed. No charges since on her credit cards." He flared his hands. "She just vanished."

Impossible. "She was fine. I mean, she came to work that last day…in November, I think it was, and she seemed fine. She just didn't come back. Rumor was she called in and said she wouldn't be back."

Serena pushed to her feet. What did all this mean?

She rubbed at her forehead, tried to banish the ache that had started there. Was any of this related to Molly?

The affair made it seem so, but was she grasping at straws again?

"Is there any chance Delia Neely could be capable of kidnapping?"

The question caught her up short. Serena faced him and started to insist that wasn't possible, but was it?

"I..." She let go a weary breath. "I don't know. But if her bank account hasn't been touched, how can she afford to just disappear? Or take someone else with her? And for what purpose?" The only answer that appeared plausible considering no ransom demand had been made caused Serena to shudder.

"Could she have gotten some sort of payoff from Landon?"

That was a question she couldn't answer, couldn't even speculate about. Landon had money. That much went without saying. But would he allow himself to be blackmailed? He didn't seem like the type.

"I don't know." As much as she hated to admit she had no idea, it was the truth.

"Molly never said anything to you about Delia?"

He stood, watching her, analyzing her expression and body language. He knew she was holding certain things back, but she couldn't share any of that with him. He couldn't know that part...it was irrelevant to Molly's disappearance in any case. If she thought for one second that telling him would help Molly, she wouldn't hesitate.

"Never. She acted as if the affair never happened."

He didn't like that answer. "You didn't find that odd?"

Serena shrugged. "Maybe. She was very sensitive about her relationship with her husband. I suppose she could have been more upset than I knew. To be honest, the pregnancy seemed the only thing that mattered to her. The baby was all she talked about." Serena's chest ached at the idea that both Molly and the baby might be lost. She couldn't bear to lose anyone else.

He braced his hands on his hips and paced the room. "The coincidence that they're both missing and that they both used the same doctor feels off. I can't believe Landon would be stupid enough to pay Delia to off his wife. He'd have to know the police might discover the connection between him and Delia, considering the affair." He frowned. "But then the cops didn't look that hard, except he couldn't have known they wouldn't. Unless he has a friend on the force." He rubbed his jaw. "Still, I think for now our best bet is to follow up with Wright."

"Dr. Wright is dead," she blurted, that awful news reverberating in her mind. "The receptionist said he was murdered…last night."

That piercing blue gaze collided with hers. "Murdered?"

She nodded, unable to trust her voice. What did all this mean? Surely Delia wouldn't kill the doctor Molly had been seeing. That was crazy. The kind of stuff that happened in the movies or in novels. There were all kinds of other scenarios. Robbery, a relationship gone bad, professional competition. His death most likely had nothing to do with Molly or her disappearance. Or Delia, for that matter.

Todd fished out his phone again and put through another call to the Colby Agency. Five minutes later he got a call back. Serena had started to pace. She'd wrung her hands until they were numb from being squeezed.

When he ended the call, he gave her the details. "The cleaning crew found him in his car late last night. Two shots in the chest. No suspects yet. That's all Chicago P.D. was willing to give at this point."

Serena suddenly felt cold. No suspects. She refused to believe that Wright's murder was relevant to Molly's case. As suspicious as she was about the idea that both Molly and Delia had been patients of his…this just couldn't be related.

"Look."

Startled by the sound of his voice, she gasped at finding him standing so close. She hadn't realized he'd moved.

"Sorry. I didn't mean to startle you."

She pressed a hand to her throat. "It's okay. I guess I was just lost in my thoughts."

"I was going to suggest that if you don't have to get back, maybe we can go over the details once more. You know, start at the beginning."

Play the Lucky Hearts Game

and get...

2 FREE BOOKS
and a **FREE MYSTERY GIFT...**

yes! YOURS to KEEP!

I have scratched off the silver card. Please send me my *2 FREE BOOKS* and *FREE mystery GIFT*. I understand that I am under no obligation to purchase any books as explained on the back of this card.

Scratch Here!
then look below to see what your cards get you... 2 Free Books & a Free Mystery Gift!

382 HDL EFZW **182 HDL EFYM**

FIRST NAME   LAST NAME

ADDRESS

APT.#   CITY

STATE/PROV.   ZIP/POSTAL CODE   (HL-I-04/06)

Twenty-one gets you **2 FREE BOOKS** and a **FREE MYSTERY GIFT!**

Twenty gets you **2 FREE BOOKS!**

Nineteen gets you **1 FREE BOOK!**

TRY AGAIN!

The Harlequin Reader Service® — Here's how it works:

Accepting your 2 free books and mystery gift places you under no obligation to buy anything. You may keep the books and gift and return the shipping statement marked "cancel." If you do not cancel, about a month later we'll send you 6 additional books and bill you just $4.24 each in the U.S., or $4.99 each in Canada, plus 25¢ shipping & handling per book and applicable taxes if any.* That's the complete price and — compared to cover prices of $4.99 each in the U.S., and $5.99 each in Canada — it's quite a bargain! You may cancel at any time, but if you choose to continue, every month we'll send you 6 more books which you may either purchase at the discount price or return to us and cancel your subscription.

*Terms and prices subject to change without notice. Sales tax applicable in N.Y. Canadian residents will be charged applicable provincial taxes and GST. Credit or debit balances in a customer's account(s) may be offset by any other outstanding balance owed by or to the customer.

If offer card is missing write to: Harlequin Reader Service, 3010 Walden Ave., P.O. Box 1867, Buffalo NY 14240-1867

BUSINESS REPLY MAIL

FIRST-CLASS MAIL   PERMIT NO. 717-003   BUFFALO, NY

POSTAGE WILL BE PAID BY ADDRESSEE

HARLEQUIN READER SERVICE
3010 WALDEN AVE
PO BOX 1867
BUFFALO NY 14240-9952

NO POSTAGE
NECESSARY
IF MAILED
IN THE
UNITED STATES

Play the Lucky Hearts Game

and get...

2 FREE BOOKS
and a FREE MYSTERY GIFT...
yes! YOURS to KEEP!

I have scratched off the silver card. Please send me my *2 FREE BOOKS* and *FREE mystery GIFT*. I understand that I am under no obligation to purchase any books as explained on the back of this card.

Scratch Here!
then look below to see what your cards get you... 2 Free Books & a Free Mystery Gift!

382 HDL EFZW   **182 HDL EFYM**

FIRST NAME   LAST NAME

ADDRESS

APT.#   CITY

STATE/PROV.   ZIP/POSTAL CODE   (HL-I-04/06)

Twenty-one gets you
2 FREE BOOKS
and a **FREE MYSTERY GIFT!**

Twenty gets you
2 FREE BOOKS!

Nineteen gets you
1 FREE BOOK!

TRY AGAIN!

If offer card is missing write to: Harlequin Reader Service, 3010 Walden Ave., P.O. Box 1867, Buffalo NY 14240-1867

BUSINESS REPLY MAIL
FIRST-CLASS MAIL   PERMIT NO. 717-003   BUFFALO, NY

POSTAGE WILL BE PAID BY ADDRESSEE

HARLEQUIN READER SERVICE
3010 WALDEN AVE
PO BOX 1867
BUFFALO NY 14240-9952

NO POSTAGE
NECESSARY
IF MAILED
IN THE
UNITED STATES

She'd already done that twice. She didn't see the point, but maybe she was too close to the situation to be objective. "All right. I don't have to be back today. We can take all the time we need." She could scarcely believe Dr. Landon had been so lenient about allowing her to leave work. But then, this was about him as far as he knew. So, as usual, his motives were completely selfish.

"Good. How about some coffee?"

She nodded.

"This way to my bistro."

With a hand at the small of her back, he ushered her to his tiny kitchen. He dragged out one of the chairs at the table for two and motioned for her to sit. She obliged, still feeling a little unsteady from all the unnerving news.

Dr. Wright was dead.

Delia was missing…or at least unaccounted for.

Unable to focus her thoughts, she watched him scoop coffee grounds into the drip basket and then pour the water into the reservoir. When the smell of fresh coffee started to fill the room, he strode over to his desk and went through a couple of drawers.

He peeled off his leather jacket and left it hanging from the first chair he passed. With a spiral notebook and pen in his hand, he sauntered over to the table. He dropped the notebook and pen there and headed back to the counter and the coffeepot.

"Cream?"

"Yes, please."

With two mugs of steaming coffee in hand, he settled into the chair across from her. "Okay." He picked up the pen. "Let's talk about Charles Landon."

Serena went through the facts. Distinguished career. The major investor at Milestone, which when she really thought about it had to be a sticking point with Arthur Miles, who was the CEO if not the primary investor. Financial woes a few years back had forced Miles to sell a good portion of his company stock, she told Todd. Since she hadn't been around at the time she couldn't actually say that the move had come with any measure of tension, but she could speculate to that end considering the competitiveness she saw between the two men on a daily basis.

"And you never picked up on any rumors about his affairs, other than what you've already told me."

"No. Nothing except that there were several affairs, but I really didn't hear much about those until Molly…" She cleared her throat and stared into her empty coffee cup. "When she disappeared rumors were rampant." She met his gaze. "But Dr. Landon told the police about the affairs. I'm certain they questioned the women involved since Landon was cleared of suspicion."

"Molly never spoke of his infidelities."

Serena hadn't considered that fact strange until now. Had it simply been easier for her to pretend that the other women never happened?

"No, not really. She made comments, but they were

vague. The only way I knew for certain was through the rumors at work. But even my colleagues were tight-lipped about it. I didn't even hear about Delia for ages. I don't think I would have known what actually happened at all if Nolan hadn't told me."

"The mail clerk?"

She nodded. "He's Arthur Miles's nephew, and I guess he heard it through his uncle." Now that she thought about it, most of the rumors she had heard had come from Nolan. Did that make the information unreliable? His opinion would be colored by the influence of his relative and financial sponsor.

"The police haven't dug up anything on Landon that casts him in a bad light," Todd said. It wasn't a question. He was apparently relaying what the Colby Agency had learned.

"I can't say that I'm surprised," she admitted. "He's a stickler for the rules." Maybe that wasn't entirely true. But she didn't have any evidence to back up her suspicions.

"But…?" Todd suggested.

Good grief, he'd read her hesitation as if she'd said it out loud. "His patience has run thin more than once waiting for the private funding to move forward with his advanced stem cell research. I can't help wondering if he has done something or promised to do something illegal and maybe Molly found out." She heaved a disgusted breath. "That's probably not the case. It was the only extreme motivation I could think of."

"Considering the controversy surrounding that kind of research, I can see why you might reason along those lines."

Was he patronizing her? It was so difficult to read him. "There has to be some explanation for her disappearance. An expectant mother just doesn't walk away from her life for no reason." She closed her eyes a moment and grappled with the emotions that abruptly rattled her before meeting his gaze once more. "I tell myself that Landon wouldn't simply..." She moistened her lips and bit back the hurt. "That he wouldn't just kill her, especially since she was pregnant with his child. I mean, I work with this man every day. I can't believe he's a killer...but there doesn't appear to be any other explanation."

She braced her elbows on the table and massaged her temples. "I've tried to consider every angle. Maybe he promised something he couldn't deliver or ventured into illegal territory and Molly found out. They might have argued and things got out of control. Maybe he hurt her and didn't mean to...panicked and hid the body. Or maybe someone he owed something is holding her or—"

He reached across the table and took her right hand into his. "She could still be alive."

The softness of that husky voice...the sympathy she saw in his eyes damaged her defenses somehow and made her heart beat so much faster.

"But it's not likely," she admitted. She'd held that

possibility at bay about as long as she could. No one had seen or heard from Molly in six weeks. The chances that she was still alive grew slimmer every day. She knew the statistics, had watched similar cases play out in the news. Still, she couldn't bring herself to give up. She had to know. She had to try to find her…to learn the truth.

For the most part she'd been convinced Landon had done this…until today. When he'd told her that he didn't want to take any chances with hindering the investigation into finding Molly, Serena had seen the despair in his eyes. His desperation had been palpable.

Could anyone fake that kind of pain?

As much as she enjoyed the feel of Todd's strong hand around hers, her head throbbed with tension. She pulled free of his touch and rubbed at her temples.

"Do you have something for a headache?" She couldn't remember the last time she'd felt this kind of headache coming on. She'd suffered with migraines during her adolescent years, but she hadn't been hit by one in years. Damn, she didn't need this right now.

"Sure thing. Give me a minute."

She closed her eyes and focused on relaxing the band of muscles around her skull. So much tension. Not enough sleep. Prime precursors for a migraine.

A bottle of water as well as a bottle of over-the-counter painkillers appeared on the table in front of her.

"Thank you." She downed two of the pills and hoped they would do the trick.

"You need to relax."

His hands settled on her shoulders and she stiffened.

"I'm pretty good at this," he urged.

She shivered and closed her eyes. Told herself just to relax and enjoy.

"Very tense," he said as his hands began to knead her shoulders. "Just relax."

She couldn't do this. "I'm not sure—"

He leaned down close to her ear. "It's just a harmless shoulder rub, Serena. Relax."

The feel of his breath on her sensitive flesh combined with her own weariness made her cave. She did as he said, closed her eyes again and let the feel of his hands work their magic. The strength of his fingers as they squeezed and kneaded made her entire body weak with need. A moan vibrated across her lips. She didn't try to stop it. Even she wasn't that strong.

He touched her neck. She shivered. Felt her pulse quicken.

"You should wear your hair down," he murmured. Then those talented fingers trailed up her neck and threaded into her hair.

She wanted to protest but somehow the words wouldn't form on her tongue.

The pins holding her hair clattered to the table one by one. Her breath flew out of her lungs when his fingers moved more deeply into her hair, caressed her skull. Her head fell back, her neck limp with pleasure.

How could he do that?

Another of those satisfied sounds slipped past her lips. This felt so good.

Then he moved on to her temples, down her jaw and along her hairline where the skin was so responsive to touch that she had to bite her lip to keep from crying out. Her heart thundered. Her body felt too warm....

She didn't know where the brush came from but he was suddenly brushing her hair with soft, even strokes. It felt heavenly.

"Better?"

She might have survived without embarrassing herself if he hadn't uttered the solitary word so close to her ear. The feel of his lips against that ultrasensitive shell sent a stab of desire slicing through her. She gasped with the intensity of it. Her eyes flew open and only then did she realize how very close to a meltdown she was.

Scrambling out of the chair, she almost fell in her attempt to put some distance between them. "I should get back. I—"

If the deep sapphire of his eyes was any indication, she wasn't the only one affected by the turn the moment had taken. He blinked and the cloud of lust disappeared.

"There's something we need to do first."

Pull it together, Serena, she ordered. Finding Molly

was too important to let anything else get in the way, especially her own confused feelings.

"What?" Her voice came out a little more sharply than she'd intended, but she wasn't sorry. He'd had no business playing with her emotions that way. He had to have known what he was doing.

"We need Delia Neely's records from Dr. Wright's office."

"Are you insane?"

"The doctor is dead," he said unrepentantly. "Ms. Neely is—" he shrugged "—who knows where. I don't see how she would mind. Besides, what she doesn't know won't hurt her. All we need is a look. Sixty seconds, that's all."

"You're serious." They'd been through this routine before. How could the Colby Agency send her someone prepared to break the law?

"Dead serious," he returned with unabashed arrogance. "Think about it, Serena. If playing by the rules would give you the answers you wanted, the police would have found them. Whatever happened to your friend, it wasn't executed by the rules. We can either keep butting the same brick wall or we can go around it. The choice is yours."

He was right. Dammit. "I have to think." She turned away from him, struggled with that age-old problem: be a good girl and do this the right way or take a chance...do whatever it took to find her sister.

"The clock is ticking, Serena. Let's not waste time."

She wheeled on him. "All right. Let's do it."

A grin spread across his face. To her supreme irritation her heart fluttered.

"Now that's what I'm talking about."

Chapter Nine

Todd set his phone to vibrate. Braddock had called twice already. He would be mad, but Todd wasn't about to risk Braddock figuring out he was up to something. The man was entirely too perceptive. Todd definitely wasn't used to anyone being able to read him so well.

It wasn't as if what he was about to do was that bad. Wright was dead. Both patients, Molly Landon and Delia Neely, were missing in action. If one or both were in trouble, what he was about to do could possibly help.

Maybe the idea was slightly illegal, but sometimes walking that thin line was the only way.

He was rationalizing, he knew. But he couldn't stop now. He was on to something…he could feel it in his gut.

Braddock would blow a fuse, but Todd had no intention of ignoring where this lead might take him. Technically his orders were to pass along to Braddock anything he learned through Serena so that the more experienced investigator could follow up.

Except, how could he prove himself to Victoria if he waited around doing nothing but babysitting Serena?

Not that it was such a chore. He glanced at the woman next to him in the car. He thought about telling her that she should definitely wear her hair down all the time but he had an idea where that would lead. Straight to her telling him where to get off.

A ripple of lust went through him. He should never have started that massage. In the beginning his intentions had been honorable. He'd wanted to help. But the more he'd touched her and the more she'd responded to his touch…well, he'd worked up a hell of a physical condition. One that was way off limits when he was on the job.

"I must have been out of my mind to let you talk me into this," she muttered without glancing his way.

The sun had dropped below the treetops but its fading reach still provided enough of a glow for him to study her profile. She didn't like being involved with anything underhanded, which pretty much eliminated her, in his opinion, from any sort of suspect list.

She might not particularly like Landon, and no doubt considered him responsible for his missing wife, but she had no desire to harm him in any way. Serena Blake was genuinely concerned with helping the woman who was, or had been, her closest friend.

For the first time since he'd been assigned to this case he hoped like hell it wasn't too late to save Molly Landon and her unborn child. That goal had, of course, been in the back of his mind from the beginning, but now the missing woman was more than a detail in a case…she was real. Real because her fate would greatly affect the woman sitting in the encroaching gloom with him right now.

Todd leaned forward, watched a woman dressed in a nurse's uniform exit the clinic's side entrance. "That's the last one." The other three members of the staff had left nearly an hour ago. He'd done his research. He knew the names of every staff member as well as their work schedules.

"Oh, God."

Serena didn't want to do this. He should be ashamed of himself for pushing her into it.

"Look." He sighed, wanted to kick himself for going soft. This wasn't part of his plan. "You can stay in the car. This shouldn't take long."

"No way," she countered. "If you're going in, so am I."

He got the distinct impression that her insistence had something to do with distrust. Or maybe she simply couldn't resist a challenge, real or imagined.

"There's no reason for both of us to go in," he argued. *Other than,* a little voice reminded, *the fact that you are supposed to be keeping an eye on her.*

She grabbed him by the arm when he prepared to get out. "You're not going without me." Even in the near darkness he could see the determination glittering in her eyes.

"All right." His gaze dropped to her lips and he wondered how it would feel to kiss her…right now. A warning went off inside him. He was skating much too close to the thin ice. He had to back off. "Make sure you do exactly as I say. There might not be time to tell you twice."

"I can do that."

If she'd noticed him staring at her mouth, she didn't let on unless he counted the flicker of irritation that flared in her eyes.

Good. One of them needed to show some self-control.

Mentally kicking himself, Todd climbed out of the car. You'd think a guy with a psychology degree would see this kind of thing coming. But he hadn't. He'd assumed a certain level of immunity, just like in the past. He could do anything, fool anyone, without ever losing sight of his ultimate goal. What the hell had happened to all that objectivity? Where was the nonchalant guy who could walk into any situation and walk away un-scathed?

Not once in his life had he danced close enough to the flame to get burned. He'd always been too smart. Was his need to prove himself at the Colby Agency af-fecting his good judgment?

Serena met him at the front of the car. "How do you want to do this?"

Todd had already considered the clinic and the best route of entry. The last of the staff had left a few minutes ago and the cleaning crew would arrive soon. That was their ticket inside.

"First we wait."

She folded her arms over her chest and glared at him as if he'd suggested they climb back into the car and have a quick meeting of something other than their minds.

"We've been waiting. I thought the idea was to get inside after the last of the staff left for the day."

He adopted her stance. "And what do you propose we do about the security system?" Braddock would likely have a solution for that problem were he here. As if to punctuate the thought, Todd's cell vibrated.

"Oh. I hadn't thought of that."

He hadn't, either, until he'd noticed the sign declaring the property protected by a local and popular security company. But she didn't need to know that.

"So what do we do?" She surveyed the one-story clinic as if it were the White House, its boundaries near impenetrable.

"We wait for the cleaning crew to arrive. According to Chicago P.D.'s report, the cleaning lady found Dr. Wright about an hour after close of business." Todd looked at his watch. "If that's the usual routine, then we're ten minutes away from the crew's arrival."

"What if they're not coming tonight?" She glanced at the well-lit building once more. "What if they don't usually come until much later?"

"Then we'll just wait longer." He had to calm her

down. Panic and hysteria were two things they definitely didn't need right now. "But we have to get into place just in case."

The doctor's car had been towed to the forensics lab and though Todd felt certain the clinic had been gone over with a fine-tooth comb today, only the parking area would be considered the primary crime scene.

Todd's plan included waiting amid the shrubbery near the side entrance. He'd noticed when he sized up the situation that the rear exit was marked Emergency Exit Only, which meant most of the going and coming was done at the side entrance.

She didn't argue this time. Not even when he took her hand and started strolling along the sidewalk as if they were nothing more than a couple out for a breath of fresh air. They walked a block past the clinic and then doubled back. Unfortunately the weather had decided to stop cooperating and a cool drizzle started to fall.

Maybe it was the rain or the company Todd soon became aware they had, but Serena stayed close behind him as he weaved between the buildings that backed up to one another. The alley was wide, but between the trash cans, Dumpsters and the lack of efficient lighting, the going was nerve-racking. Who would have thought that with all the alleys in this city a whole community of homeless folks would have decided this particular one was the best location in town.

Various-size boxes had been confiscated for makeshift temporary housing. A foot popped out from a dis-integrating box they passed and Serena scooted closer to him. Todd held very still until the man had settled. He wasn't afraid of a physical altercation—he just didn't want to risk stirring up a ruckus.

He nodded to Serena and started toward their desti-nation once more. When they'd reached the end of the block beyond the rear entrance to Wright's clinic, he ushered her into the hiding place nature and lush land-scaping provided. The rain wasn't that bad, just enough to get damp.

"What if they see us?" Serena whispered as she at-tempted to see beyond the thick canopy of perennial greenery.

"As long as we keep still and quiet," he warned, "no one will notice us."

She didn't like it, but she shut up.

Todd watched the side entrance and the section of the parking area he could see from their hiding place. For about three minutes he felt confident he would get through this without incident, but then she shifted ever so slightly and the scent of her shampoo filled his nostrils.

The memory of how those silky strands had felt sliding through his fingers zinged him unmercifully. The urge to touch her…to trail his fingers along her smooth skin…expanded so quickly inside him that it was all he could do to keep his hands to himself.

"Here they are." She turned toward him abruptly and

even in the darkness somehow she sensed that he stared at her like a starving man. He felt her tremble.

"Yeah…." He moistened his lips. "Stay here." He moved in front of her before he could do or say anything else utterly stupid.

He shook it off and focused on the three people, two women and one man, chatting and gathering their supplies from the van they'd parked near the side entrance.

Todd retrieved the business card he would need from his interior jacket pocket and braced in preparation for his next move. When all three had moved to enter the building, first the two females, then the man, he eased from the concealing shrubbery.

As the door closed behind the group, he moved up next to it, caught the knob with one hand and slid the business card into place with the other. The door closed, but the card kept the latch from catching. He flattened against the side of the building and listened for any warning that his move had been noted. The footsteps and sounds of voices continued to diminish as they moved away from the entrance.

He motioned for Serena to join him. The building's exterior lighting provided sufficient illumination for her to see his intentions. She moved out of the bushes and hurried cautiously to where he waited.

Pulling her close to him, he murmured next to her ear, "Once we're inside, we'll need to find a place to hide near this entrance."

She pulled back and looked up at him, the worry in her eyes making his chest feel tight. "Can't we just look for the files and get out?"

He shook his head. "Too risky. We'll lay low until they're gone, then we'll have free run of the place."

"But how will we get out without tripping the alarm?" She moved her head side to side. "This isn't a good idea. We could be stuck in there all night, only to be caught tomorrow morning."

A smile tickled his lips. "Don't worry. I have a plan."

Serena wasn't sure she completely believed him, but she didn't have a lot of options here.

"Let's rock and roll."

Holding her breath, she moved up behind him as he eased open the door.

Any second now she expected someone to scream or for sirens to blare in the distance. She had to be out of her mind to do this.

If they could find Molly safe…it would all be worth it.

With that in mind, she followed the man she alternately disliked and lusted after into the clinic. She blinked at the bright fluorescent lighting. Thank God no one loitered in the corridor.

The chloroseptic smell was very nearly overpowering. Obviously the cleaning had started already.

Todd slowed the door as it shut behind him to ensure it made no sound, then he ushered her through the first door they encountered. Complete darkness folded in around them as the latch clicked, sealing them inside the tiny room. She didn't need any light to recognize their hiding place. A storage room. Her olfactory sense immediately recognized the varied scents of medical supplies. Even gauze had a particular smell if one paid attention.

Another click and the flame from a handheld lighter cut through the blackness. Todd surveyed the shelves lining the walls to get a handle on their surroundings.

"Supply room."

"Looks like," he agreed before relaxing his thumb, allowing the flame to die.

"I didn't know you smoked," she said, letting him hear her distaste.

"I don't. But the lighter comes in handy from time to time."

Okay, so he had a point there.

"How long do you think this will take?" she whispered since being overheard would be bad, really bad.

"Couple of hours tops."

She wished his optimism was contagious, but she was too nervous to feel anything but scared to death. What would they tell the police if they were caught?

Dr. Landon would definitely fire her for interfering with the investigation. What if her good intentions somehow made things worse for Molly?

Serena squeezed her eyes shut and blocked those kinds of possibilities. She couldn't bear to think that way. None of this was fair. Both she and Molly had been through enough in their lives. Maybe Molly had been a little luckier since she'd happened into a good family the first go-around, but God only knew what she'd suffered before that. Serena had only been two when her mother abandoned her, but Molly had been four. She might very well have vivid memories of that painful time.

If she were honest with herself Serena would admit that at times she'd sensed that Molly hid a number of bad memories. But she couldn't say that for sure. Molly was the epitome of an optimist. As soon as she'd found out she was having a girl all discussion of boy babies had ceased and she never looked back, despite having been determined that her first child had to be a boy.

She never complained about how late her husband had to work. Never fretted about anything. Molly Landon had lived the proverbial fairy-tale life. She loved her husband, loved her home, volunteered in the community when needed. She had the perfect life.

How could this happen?

It just wasn't fair.

Serena bit down hard on her lower lip. Who was she feeling sorry for here, Molly or herself?

Flashes from that awful past flickered like a bad movie across the screen of her mind. Every time she'd been moved to a new home, she'd felt hope. That maybe things would be different this time. That someone would really love her…that someone would care if she lived or died.

But it was always the same. The first mistake she'd made was the end of any hope at all. Yelling always signaled the end. Much yelling and sometimes the throwing of things, usually things she had managed to hang on to. Then the tension would escalate and she'd get slapped. The little slaps would eventually turn into shoves and full-fisted jabs at her body. Never her face. No one wanted to be accused of hitting a child. Abdominal bruises or the ones on her back could be explained by her clumsiness.

Clumsy, hardheaded Serena. She never listened and always got into trouble.

With the first hot, salty tear that slipped down her cheek, Serena wanted to scream. How could she let this happen? Especially now! She hadn't let herself wallow in self-pity like this in…in forever. She shuddered. Just cold, she told herself. Her clothes were a little damp.

But that was a lie.

As hard as she tried, a tiny sound issued from her throat. Not exactly a gasp, not exactly a whimper. Just one of those pathetic, helpless sounds that any other human within hearing range would recognize.

His hands wrapped around her shoulders as unerringly as if he could see perfectly in the dark.

She didn't want him to touch her…tried to pull away, but he was too strong.

He pulled her against his chest and wrapped strong arms around her. She told herself to resist but she just couldn't. She needed someone to hold her right now and he was all she had. He pressed his lips close to her ear and murmured, "It'll be all right."

How could he make a promise like that? He didn't know any more than she did what would happen...what may have already happened. That thought sent defeat twisting through her. He held her tighter, let the fingers of his right hand venture into her hair and cradle her head.

She didn't want to feel this, but there was no stopping the betrayal of her body.

Need quivered deep inside her...a need so long ignored she could scarcely bear the awakening.

The fingers of his left hand spread against the small of her back and her body instinctively understood. She melted against him. She heard his breath catch and the sound made her heart skip traitorously.

She clung to him, her arms wrapped around his powerful body as if letting go would surely mean the end of her existence. She wished she could reach up and touch his hair. She wanted to feel it in her hands but she didn't dare let go of him. Didn't dare do anything but let the sensations wash over her...over and over.

He held her that way on and on...just held her. She couldn't ignore the changes in his body, but somehow they felt secondary to the other respite he offered.

Somewhere beyond their cocoon the sound of a vacuum cleaner reminded her of reality and why they were in this dark supply closet.

He was the first to pull back, but not too far. He kept his arms draped loosely around her, pressed his forehead to hers. "You okay?"

His voice was like tattered silk dragging across her skin, smooth but with just enough roughness to pump up the friction, making her shiver.

"Yes. Thank you." She lifted her head, wished she could see his eyes. "I'm sorry I fell apart on you."

"No sweat."

His hands fell away and she felt suddenly cold, but one of them had to pull it back together. She couldn't blame it on the rain anymore since her damp clothes had dried. He moved to the door to listen. She took a moment to shore up her defenses a bit more firmly and took a step in that direction, as well.

The vacuuming had stopped and she could hear the crew talking and laughing. The anxiety she'd felt earlier that they might be trapped in here reemerged.

He'd said he had a plan.

She had to trust him.

His body tensed. Even though she wasn't touching him, she felt the change. And this tension had nothing to do with the hug they'd just shared.

The voices grew louder. They were close. Serena held her breath.

She heard the side entrance door whoosh to a close behind voices that started to fade.

Todd pushed the supply closet door open and bounded into the still lit corridor. Shielding her eyes, Serena followed. They'd waited in the dark so long her eyes were sluggish about adjusting.

Insistent beeps from the security system echoed from the keypad hanging by the exit.

They were going to be locked in here…with no way to deactivate the security system.

Todd stabbed a button and the noise ceased.

Serena stared at the readout, which read Cancelled. "How'd you do that?"

Incredible. How had he done that?

He pointed to the cancel button on the keypad and grinned. "You just have to cancel it before the selected mode kicks in."

She rolled her eyes and cursed herself for giving him far too much recognition.

"Which door would you suggest?"

The question snapped her back to attention. He was asking her for a recommendation?

She stared down the long corridor. Half a dozen doors flanked each side.

With a defiant lift of her chin she announced, "This way." She strode toward the center of the building to where she had decided the reception desk would be. An exit sign hung above the door that led into the lobby. Another door just beyond that provided access to where the clerical personnel signed in patients and pulled records.

Feeling triumphant, she grabbed the knob and gave it a twist.

The door was locked. Her victorious expression fell.

"I got it." He reached into his jacket pocket and pulled out two pairs of gloves. "But first things first." He tugged on a pair, offered the other to her. She did the same. Smart thinking. Fingerprints not belonging to authorized personnel found anywhere else in the building wouldn't be suspect. But in and around the files was a different matter.

He stepped in front of her, another card in his hand. This one a credit card.

With a twist or two of the knob and a couple slides of the plastic card, the door opened. Wearing a confident grin, he stepped back for her to enter the area authorized for clinic personnel only.

She rolled her eyes and walked past him. That was a cheap trick. Probably anyone could do it.

Like the door, the file cabinets were locked, as well.

They were going to get caught. "We should just give this up while we're ahead."

He held up a hand. "Not so fast."

She crossed her arms and watched as he pilfered through one desk drawer after the other. "It's not going to be that easy, Thompson. No one leaves their file keys just—"

At that precise moment he dangled a ring of keys in front of her.

As hard as it was, she kept all her comments about incompetence to herself. What was the point?

"I've got the Ls," he said, reaching for one of the drawers.

She couldn't hold his resourcefulness against him. "Here's the Ns."

They withdrew pink folders simultaneously.

Serena knew instantly that something was wrong. She snapped the folder open.

Empty.

"Looks like someone beat us to the draw."

Molly's folder was empty, as well.

"How could this happen?" Serena shook her head. "When I called this afternoon, wouldn't the woman with whom I spoke have mentioned this sort of thing?"

"She didn't know." Todd shoved the file back into its slot. "Whoever took the contents of these two files did it last night before—" he shot her a look "—or after he or she had killed Dr. Wright."

"Wait." She didn't want to believe this. Who would murder for a couple of files? Why would anyone see the contents as valuable? "You can't be certain. Maybe they're here somewhere?" She shrugged. "Or maybe there are other files missing."

"There's nothing preventing us from checking out your theory."

More than an hour later she learned another hard, cold fact about Molly's disappearance.

Someone wanted to hide information about her pregnancy. And that someone might very well be Delia Neely.

The only question was why.

Chapter Ten

Todd didn't dare even breathe as Victoria considered his penalty for failing to follow the rules. She'd ordered everyone else from her office, including Braddock, and now she stood behind her desk, her hands resting on the back of her elegant leather chair.

When he'd called Braddock two hours ago, he'd expected a meeting, but he hadn't anticipated a tribunal. He'd been ordered back to the Colby Agency, with his charge in tow. Braddock, Victoria and her two right-hand men, Ian Michaels and Simon Ruhl, had been waiting.

Things had gone downhill from there.

While Victoria's secretary, Mildred, entertained Serena, Todd had been interrogated unmercifully. But he could handle it. He'd been in the hot seat before. He had to admit, however, that the stakes were a little higher this time than the last.

"Do you understand the risk to this agency's reputation your actions may have precipitated?"

He swallowed, reminded himself that this was not a rhetorical question. "Yes, ma'am. I take full responsibility for my actions."

She lifted one eyebrow speculatively. "Admirable, Mr. Thompson, but hardly acceptable."

Maybe this wasn't going to be as simple as he had hoped.

"Mrs. Colby-Camp, you assigned me to watch Miss Blake," he offered. "In the course of my assignment I learned certain information that I felt compelled to check out."

Those dark eyes searched his and, to his surprise, she smiled. "Mr. Thompson, don't attempt to use your considerable charm on me. Better men have tried."

He blinked, reevaluated his position and opted to keep his mouth shut until she'd finished whatever she had to say. Clearly, he wasn't going to talk his way out of this one. At least not today.

"This agency works as a team, Mr. Thompson. We keep each other informed and no one goes off half-cocked. No one. If you discover intelligence that you believe impacts your case you share it with your colleagues, unless, of course, you're working alone, which you were not."

He nodded, felt a trickle of sweat slip down his back. "I understand."

Her analyzing gaze narrowed. "Do you really, Mr. Thompson?"

"Yes, ma'am. I should have called Braddock immediately so that he could assess what steps needed to be taken."

"Instead," she countered, "you chose to do this on your own, without proper backing and while ignoring the experience of your assigned colleague."

He started to offer another excuse, but that wasn't going to change her opinion.

"The bottom line," she went on, "is that you were less than satisfied with your assignment so you took it upon yourself to follow the first lead you discovered."

"Yes, ma'am, that's exactly what I did."

"Don't ever let it happen again, Mr. Thompson, or you will find yourself visiting job fairs again."

He pushed to his feet, determined to restate his case. "I'm certain Serena is holding back something relevant to Mrs. Landon. I can't be sure just what, but there's something more there. I need her to believe I'm in this with her…the whole 'us against the world' scenario."

She pretty much ignored his attempt at an excuse and stated for the record, "Certainly the fact that both her medical file and Ms. Neely's were missing may suggest a connection, but that alone isn't conclusive. We have no evidence that Charles Landon has continued his affair with Delia Neely."

"But you have to admit," Todd urged, unwilling to give up, "that Delia's abrupt disappearance and then the missing files is surely a lead that needs to be followed."

"Anything less would be unacceptable," she allowed. "But we have protocol, Mr. Thompson. You broke that important boundary. Without it we would not be where we are. Again, I warn you that we won't permit risks of this nature."

Victoria pressed her intercom button. "Mildred, send Mr. Braddock back in, please."

Time for more reprimands. He'd be lucky to get out of this with any of his hide intact.

A. J. Braddock strode into Victoria's office, his usual military bearing failing to displace the fury he apparently still felt at being left in the dark.

Victoria settled back into her chair and both Todd and Braddock followed her lead. Todd didn't have to look at his colleague to know he'd made a serious mistake going around him.

"Since you've studied this case more in-depth than anyone, A.J., what are your conclusions on how we should proceed?"

"Thank you for asking, Victoria." The older man shot Todd a pointed glare before laying out his game plan. "If I had to form a final conclusion on Landon at this point, I'd have to say that I don't have anything that would implicate him. If he's involved with his wife's disappearance, he's keeping it covered exceedingly well." He flared his hands in a noncommittal expression. "That said, I believe we need to prod our contacts at Chicago P.D. Considering the fact that Neely and both women's medical records are missing, our friends in blue may have details they don't realize are relevant."

Todd jumped in with both feet at the man's first hesitation. "Anything they discover regarding Wright's murder could be useful, as well."

Braddock acknowledged Todd's suggestion with a curt nod. "Any way we can shake that tree could prove useful to our case."

Never one to wait to be asked, Todd forged ahead with that line of thinking. "As I told you earlier," he reminded, "I believe that Serena Blake is keeping secrets pertinent to her relationship with Molly Landon. I think I can handle getting that information, but what I need is more information on her background as well as Molly Landon's."

"The background profile we provided," Victoria countered, "is as thorough as can be gotten on her life since the age of eighteen."

"That's my point," Todd explained. "I have a feeling this goes back further than that. I need to know more than the fact that she was adopted by the Blakes and handed her future on a silver platter. The same goes for the missing woman."

Victoria shifted her attention from him to Braddock. "How do you feel about this, A.J.? He is closer to Miss Blake than you—shall we loosen the reins to a degree?"

Braddock assessed Todd for a moment. An intimidation maneuver. The man already knew his answer before he bothered with the arrogant perusal.

"Only if he keeps me apprised of his every move," he qualified. "I'll stay on Landon and attempt to open up the communication lines a little more deeply with Chicago P.D."

"Excellent." Victoria appeared pleased, but that pleasant expression waned when she fixed her full attention back on Todd. "Bear in mind, Mr. Thompson, that Miss Blake is our client. I will not have you taking your persuasion tactics too far."

"I understand, ma'am."

"If Molly Landon is still alive, we must do everything we can to find her alive, but unnecessary collateral damage is unacceptable, Mr. Thompson. Don't forget that, not even for a moment."

With that warning ringing in his ears, Todd left Victoria's office. He had his reprieve. Another chance to prove himself.

And the opportunity to break this case.

"What did you find out?"

Serena had jumped to her feet the instant he exited Victoria's office.

The anticipation in her expression made him wish he had news of her friend's whereabouts. How could she look so damned innocent when he was certain she was keeping secrets from him?

He produced a smile for Mildred Parker. He already knew that this was one lady on whose good side he needed to stay. Then he took Serena by the arm and guided her toward reception and the elevators. He stabbed the call button and waited impatiently for an elevator to arrive.

"Where are we going?"

A chime announced the elevator's arrival and the doors instantly opened. New recruits Gabrielle Hanson and Michelle Robb breezed into the lobby. Todd smiled, his instincts immediately going on alert. Although they had all been hired as equals, he couldn't help considering these two women his immediate competition. Michelle said hello to Serena, then to Todd, but Gabrielle didn't bother. She rushed through the lobby, far too focused on her destination to bother with Todd or his guest. In his opinion, she was the one to watch. He considered the time, way past business hours. What were they doing here at this hour anyway? Research? Or an after-hours class on what *not* to do, using him as an example.

When they'd boarded the elevator and the doors had slid closed, Todd shifted back to the business at hand and considered what his next move should be. He and Serena needed to talk further. Whatever she was holding back could make the difference between cracking this case and wishful thinking. All he had to do was convince her to come clean with him. For that, having the home-field advantage wouldn't hurt.

"My place." He didn't make eye contact, already knew what he'd see there.

"Why are we going back to your place? I want to go home. I need to check my messages."

Dropping by her place wouldn't be a bad idea. If she and Molly Landon were that close, she could attempt to call her if the opportunity presented itself. That was an extreme reach but not outside the bounds of plausibility.

"We'll check your messages and then we'll go to my place," he offered.

"I'm not sure you understand, Mr. Thompson," she snapped. "You work for me, remember?"

He grappled for patience. Now why did she have to go and bring that up again? What did she want him to say? How could he do his job with her bossing him around?

"Yes, ma'am, I remember."

Serena resisted the urge to grind her teeth. Why was it every time she got angry with his highhandedness he pulled out that Southern charm?

She refused to look at him. She knew all too well what would happen. Getting caught up in his gorgeous exterior would only undermine her determination.

Work was on her agenda for tomorrow. She needed to be in her own home. A long, hot bath and clean clothes. She needed to unwind. To put the day's horrifying events behind her.

Molly's doctor was dead.

Serena shuddered.

Delia Neely was missing.

There had to be a connection. As certain as Serena had been that maybe Molly's disappearance was somehow related to Landon's work, that might not be the case.

She thought back to the few times she'd met Delia Neely. Could she be capable of kidnapping an expectant mother, or worse?

It seemed so unbelievable.

A new wave of fury washed over her. But even if Delia was responsible for all of this, that didn't let Charles Landon off the hook. He should never have cheated on his wife. If he'd kept his pants on, maybe this wouldn't have happened.

The elevator glided to a stop at the first-floor lobby level and Serena exited, Todd Thompson at her side. Security checked them off the after-hours log and Todd ushered her to his car. Her car was still back at the lab. She'd have no choice but to accept a ride to work from him tomorrow morning.

She leaned her head back against the headrest and closed her eyes. Sleep would help, but first she had to have that bath. The hot water would help her relax. Tension had been strumming through her for hours. The memory of how he'd held her in that supply room, chastely...almost. Though she'd felt the changes in his body that he couldn't deny, he never let the moment go beyond that point. He hadn't taken advantage of her moment of weakness. She appreciated that.

More than she should, maybe.

She didn't open her eyes again until he'd parked next to the curb in front of her town house. She hadn't left on any lights so the place looked dark as pitch. But she was glad to be here. Finally.

There were questions she wanted to ask but those would have to wait. Right now she needed some distance. A chance to catch her breath and shake off some of the silly notions loitering in her head.

Todd Thompson had a job to do. He was no fairy-tale romance hero. When the Colby Agency had done all it could to help her learn what had happened to Molly, he'd be out of her life. She couldn't let this get personal, had to maintain her perspective.

She dug in her purse for her keys as they climbed the steps to her door.

"Stay behind me."

Her head came up at his barked order. What on earth...

He pushed the door inward.

Her door was unlocked?

There was suddenly a gun in his hand.

He carried a gun?

She told herself not to be surprised. It wasn't unusual for private investigators to carry weapons...was it?

He stopped abruptly and she bumped into his broad back. When he continued to stand there without saying anything, she presumed that he was listening. She did the same.

Did he suspect whoever had broken into her house was still here?

Her heart thumped. She hadn't thought of that.

He shifted, moved his face close to hers. "Stay right behind me," he murmured. "I don't think there's anyone in here, but I don't want to take any chances."

She nodded, then muttered, "Okay," just in case he hadn't noticed.

Why would anyone break into her home? She had a TV and a DVD player, but no jewelry or cash. Undoubtedly her thief had left more than a little disappointed. She knew that later she would be angry that her home had been violated. But right now she just wanted to make sure it was safe to stay.

He didn't turn on the living-room light until they'd moved across the room, near the small hall that connected it to the kitchen. She blinked to adjust to the sudden brightness as the lamps on either side of the sofa illuminated.

"See anything out of place?"

She scanned the room and shook her head. "Looks just the way we left it." Including the blanket and pillow she'd given him last night, reminding her that he'd slept on her couch not so very long ago.

The kitchen and her office were clear. Thank God. By the time they topped the stairs together, her heart threatened to burst from her chest. The last place a person looked was always the place where trouble waited…at least in the movies.

She grabbed him by the shirt when he would have moved toward the guest bedroom. "Maybe we should call the police."

"Shh."

When he'd checked the guest room he turned on the light in the hall. "So far so good."

Enough. She couldn't stand the anticipation. She was ready for that bath and bed. Alone.

She stormed past him and flung open the door to her bedroom, simultaneously clicking on the overhead light.

It took several seconds for her mind to assimilate what her eyes saw.

Unlike the rest of the house, which was exactly as she'd left it that morning, her bedroom had been...ransacked. Totally destroyed.

"Oh, my."

He pushed past her and checked the closet then under the bed. When he stopped in the middle of the chaos, she felt her knees go abruptly weak.

Who would do this?

Wouldn't a thief have wanted to look for anything worth taking downstairs, as well?

"Whoa, there."

She hadn't realized she'd swayed until she felt his arms around her.

"Take a breath," he prompted. "It'll be okay. May not be as bad as it looks."

No, she thought, it was worse.

Someone had come into her home…touched her things.

He led her to her bed and ushered her onto the edge. "Stay right here while I check outside."

If he'd expected a response, he didn't get one. She couldn't manage verbal skills during the time it took for her eyes to take in the full extent of the situation.

Dresser and bureau drawers had been dragged out and their contents dumped. Her jewelry box, full of costume jewelry, sat upside down. Her closet looked as if it had exploded into the room.

She had to do something. She couldn't just sit here.

Summoning her courage, she pushed to her feet and started the insurmountable task of sorting through her belongings.

Putting things back into their proper place would be rather pointless if it wasn't for the need to determine if anything was missing. Maybe she should bag it all up and drag it down to the laundry room.

How could she wear anything a stranger had touched without laundering it first?

She couldn't.

"Let me help you."

Todd had returned. She didn't ask if he'd found anything. He'd likely tell her if he had. Right now she just wanted to make sure her stuff was all here.

He knelt next to her and helped her put the drawers back into place and then her things. She should have been embarrassed that he got a good look at her lingerie but she didn't have the emotion to spare right now.

When she could walk around the room without stepping on something, she felt a little better.

They tackled the closet next. She straightened her clothes on their hangers, then he hung them up. His help made things go a lot more quickly. Even though she didn't say so, she appreciated his being here.

"Missing anything?"

She shoved a handful of hair behind her ear and tried to think. Unless some article of clothing she couldn't readily think of was missing, all appeared to be here.

That made the whole situation even more bizarre than it already was. Who would care what kind of panties she wore?

"I don't think so."

"How about we walk through downstairs again just to be sure."

And then she knew.

Fear grabbed hold of her heart and squeezed like a vise.

The box.

She went through her room again. Checked the drawers, the closet, under the bed.

It wasn't here.

Panic welled inside her so fast she couldn't breathe. Couldn't think. Why would anyone take that box?

"Serena, what did they take?"

She stared up at him. Uncertain she could explain. "The only connection I had to my past."

The box. An old shoe box she'd decorated as a child. Inside it was the only picture she'd had of her and her sister *before*. She'd been maybe two, dressed in nothing but a diaper. Molly had been about four. She wore a little ruffled pink dress. At first glance one would have thought they were two perfectly normal children. But upon closer inspection you would see the marks on Serena's legs and the sad, tattered state of Molly's dress.

But it was all Serena had from that time.

A few other items from her childhood had been inside. The only four-leaf clover she'd ever found and the cut-out yearbook picture of the first boy she'd ever had a crush on. He hadn't known she existed, but she'd loved him desperately. The pink ribbon her father, the only father she'd ever known, Howard Blake, had tied in her hair for the father-daughter dance her sophomore year of high school. Serena had never worn a ribbon in her hair in her entire life. She'd started to argue but when she'd seen the emotion in his eyes, she couldn't say no.

Who would take those things?

"Come here."

Before she could comprehend his intent he'd taken her into his arms the same way he had in that dark supply room. The move confused her at first and then she realized she was crying.

She never cried so much.

As a kid she'd lost count of the number of times she'd cried before realizing that the tears never got her anywhere; then she'd stopped being so vulnerable. What was the point?

The emotional bouts she'd experienced the past few days were so unlike her…so difficult to endure.

She closed her eyes and inhaled deeply. Let herself sag against him. She felt so tired. So damned exhausted.

Nothing made sense anymore.

Charles Landon was suddenly acting like a caring husband.

Delia Neely had disappeared.

The missing files…

What did it all mean?

Surely none of that had anything to do with the sentimental mementos someone had taken from her house.

He pulled back far enough to look into her eyes. "Would you like coffee? Tea?"

She took a step back. She had to pull herself together again. She felt like Humpty Dumpty, in too many pieces this time to put back together.

"I just want a long, hot bath." She tried to smile but couldn't manage the feat. "I'll be fine. It wasn't…important. Just sentimental value." The idea that she'd lost the only picture of her and her sister together as children ripped at her heart.

He wiped a tear from her cheek and managed a smile that should have taken her breath. She really was in shock. "You take your time with the bath," he said softly. "I'll see what I can find in the kitchen for dinner."

She didn't remember saying yes, but he walked away so she must have.

When he'd closed the door, she searched her room again.

The box wasn't here.

She couldn't think about it anymore.

While the tub filled she rounded up her favorite pj's and clean underwear. She groaned as she considered that whoever had riffled through her drawers had just as likely touched this pair of underwear as not. She didn't care.

She was too tired.

After adding a few drops of bubble bath, she stripped off her clothes and slid into the deep, welcoming water. Heavenly.

She closed her eyes and relaxed, let the water do its work.

No one knew about the box or the picture.

No one but Molly.

Had she told her husband?

Had he told his lover?

Why in the world would anyone take that box?

It just didn't make sense.

Would it do any good for the police to search her home for strange fingerprints?

Would they even come, considering nothing of monetary value was missing?

She couldn't worry about that. What she had to do was to go downstairs and get some answers from Todd. He hadn't told her what had come out of the meeting with Victoria. Or what he thought they should do next.

It seemed as though she had more unanswered questions now than before she'd hired the Colby Agency.

If he was keeping anything from her...

There was only one way to find out: demand answers.

She rushed through the bathing ritual, dragged on her pj's and ran a brush through her damp hair.

Whatever Victoria had told him, Serena had a right to know. They needed to strategize about their next move.

Renewed bravado propping her emotions, she jerked the bathroom door open and marched out with the intention of going downstairs and demanding a powwow.

But that wouldn't be necessary. At least not the part about going downstairs.

Her on-again-off-again hero stood next to her bed with a tray in his hands. Whatever he'd thrown together for dinner, he'd brought it to her.

"I found vegetable soup. Hope that's okay."

He sat the tray, with its steaming bowl of soup, crackers, glass of milk and what looked like hot cocoa, on her bedside table.

"Let me know if I can get you anything else."

And then he strode back to the door, hesitated only long enough to say, "Good night," and was gone.

She just stood there, uncertain what to say or to do.

The tempting aroma of the soup finally penetrated her haze of confusion and she realized exactly what she had to do.

Eat. Get some sleep. And then, in the morning, when she was refreshed and rested, demand some answers.

In that order.

With her luck, it would never be that simple.

She would dream.

About him.

This plan to seek help from a professional had seemed so simple at first.

How had it gotten so complicated?

Chapter Eleven

Serena dropped her purse to the floor to keep her fingers from twisting repeatedly in the strap.

There was no reason for her to be so nervous.

She glanced around the studio apartment once more. It was just an apartment, not a lair. And yet, it felt exactly like that.

She'd overslept this morning so she'd had to rush to get ready in time to have that conversation with Todd she'd promised herself. To her utter dismay he'd insisted that the talk would have to wait until after they'd stopped by his place. Not that she could deny him a shower and a change of clothes, but it felt as if he were putting off her questions.

Maybe she'd imagined that part, but she wanted answers, and he'd didn't appear in any hurry to give them to her.

She couldn't sit here a second longer.

Pushing up from her chair, she decided she'd be

nosy. Why not? He'd certainly had a good look at her most private items. The memory of her undergarments tossed all around her room made her cringe.

And then she remembered the one thing the thief had taken. A wistful feeling went through her as her missing memory box bobbed to the surface of her scattered thoughts. She just couldn't imagine why anyone would take it.

Forcing her attention away from those painful feelings, she prowled along the bookcases lining part of the far wall. Lots of volumes on forensics and criminology. And literally dozens on psychology and the human psyche.

"Interesting." No wonder it felt as if he could read her every thought. If he'd read half these books, he probably could.

His desk was cluttered, as before, not that he'd been here to tidy it. He'd scribbled notes on two different pads. His penmanship was better than she'd expected. None of the notes he'd taken applied to her so she stopped reading. A coffee mug sporting the University of Alabama logo held pencils and pens. Definitely a Southern boy. She'd known the slight drawl was more than his attempt at cranking up the charm.

There was only one photograph. A small framed snapshot of Todd and an older couple. Considering the resemblance between him and the other man, she would guess these were his parents. She doubted the picture had been taken very long ago since Todd looked exactly as he did now. His hair seemed about the same length. She was pretty sure she recognized the shirt. Maybe he'd visited home recently.

Serena laughed at herself. She was definitely paying too much attention to this man.

The bathroom door opened and she quickly, guiltily, set the photograph back where she'd found it and turned to face her host. Her jaw practically hit the floor when he waltzed out of the bathroom wearing nothing but a towel. Water dripped from his wet hair and slid down his chest and back.

She should look away or say something to remind him that she was here, but she couldn't move…definitely couldn't speak.

He padded over to the bed and grabbed the clothes he'd selected. She could only imagine that he'd forgotten to take them into the bathroom with him. Otherwise he wouldn't be traipsing around in front of her half… half naked.

When he straightened and would have turned back to the bathroom, two things happened. He noticed she was standing there gawking at him and his towel sank even lower on his lean hips.

Her gaze should have been locked with his, but it wasn't. Her full attention had taken the same route as the towel.

"Sorry, left my clothes out here."

With monumental effort, her gaze made the journey

upward…over a ribbed abdomen and a sculpted chest, both gleaming with beaded water. An appealing sprinkle of body hair disrupted the incredible landscape of sleek skin stretched tautly over well-defined muscle.

"Five minutes and I'll be ready."

Finally her gaze collided with his and the full impact of her humiliation dawned on her. She'd spent no less than half a minute visually examining his torso. Judging by the expression on his face, she couldn't be sure if he was surprised or annoyed or…possibly intrigued.

Somehow she managed an up-and-down motion of her head. He held her gaze a beat or two longer before he pivoted and strode back into the bathroom.

She blinked, told herself to snap out of the trance she'd clearly slipped into.

She was an idiot. She knew and now so did he.

Maybe they didn't need to talk. Definitely not here. Neutral territory would be much safer. Her office. Anywhere but here. The whole place reeked of him. She could smell the soap he'd used and the shampoo clear across the room.

Keeping her attention on simple things, such as the plaid sofa instead of the rumpled bed, she resumed her seat in one of the matching upholstered chairs.

The roar of the hair-dryer signaled he would be ready soon. Or she hoped it did. She rounded up her purse and clutched it in her lap.

A strange vibrating sound made her jump. She

caught her breath and mentally grappled to identify the noise. Another pulsating throb tugged her gaze toward the dinette table. His cell phone scooted around on the Formica top as it buzzed again. With the hair-dryer still going, there was no way he could hear it.

Should she answer it?

No. Probably not. If it was the Colby Agency, a message would be left. If the caller was his girlfriend, Serena didn't want to know.

How dumb was that?

After four rattling buzzes, the phone fell silent once more. So did the hair-dryer. She sat stone-still and waited for him to emerge. This time he would be wearing clothes. Jeans, like he always wore, with a khaki-colored shirt this time. Same leather jacket and sneakers. She hadn't noticed until this morning that he wore sneakers. Not just any old sneakers, either, the big-name running shoes promoted by major athletes. Navy and black. Maybe the dark color was why she hadn't noticed.

Her head spun and she closed her eyes to regain her bearings. She should have had breakfast this morning. She hadn't had time, or she'd thought she hadn't.

The bathroom door opened and her gaze swung in that direction.

"How about some breakfast?" He patted his stomach. "I'm starved."

She glanced at the time on the digital readout of his

cable television receiver. There was still time, she supposed. Her stomach rumbled. She could eat. If he cooked she could question him about the meeting at the Colby Agency and his conclusions on where they should go from here.

Setting her purse aside, she got up so as to put them on even ground. "You cook, I'll ask the questions."

One side of his mouth quirked as if a grin had tried to make an appearance. "No problem. I'm pretty good at multitasking."

He forked his fingers through his hair, pushing it away from his face. The move called her attention there and she noticed that he'd shaved.

"Toast and scrambled eggs okay with you?"

"Sure."

When he'd gotten the process started, she asked, "What did you learn at the meeting last night? What were the conclusions reached?"

He looked thoughtful as he broke half a dozen eggs into the sizzling skillet. The man hadn't been kidding when he'd said he was starved.

"Landon is still the number one suspect," he said when he'd added a little milk, salt and pepper and started to stir the concoction. "But Delia Neely just moved into a tie with him." He looked directly at Serena then. "Are you certain there isn't more you can tell me about her? Molly didn't talk about her at all?"

She didn't have to think. "No and no. What little I

know, I heard by way of rumors. Molly never mentioned his affairs. I just assumed she knew because I would see the look in her eyes whenever she talked about him coming home late or going out of town on business. And she always got this distant look in her eyes, like she knew. Between that and the vague warning she'd given when we first met, I'm pretty sure she knew more than she talked about." Serena let the memories filter through her thoughts. "It was as if she had resigned herself to her fate of being a wife whose husband fooled around."

Todd deposited two slices of bread into the toaster. "Braddock's going to look into Delia's past a little more deeply. Maybe he can locate some next of kin."

It could have been Braddock who called a few minutes ago. "Your cell phone vibrated while you were… getting ready. I didn't answer it."

He scraped the eggs onto two plates. The piles were enormous. As he set the pan aside, the two slices of nicely toasted bread popped up. He placed them on one plate, then added two more to the toaster before taking the three steps necessary to reach the table to check his phone.

"Braddock." He glanced at her. "I should call him back."

She nodded. If the food got cold, it would just have to get cold. If there was news on Molly's case…

She mentally crossed her fingers and waited while he made the call. He made several one-word comments—yes, no and uh-huh—then ended the call.

He shoved the phone into the pocket of his jeans then went to the refrigerator for the orange juice. Her nerves jangled as she waited, but he knew she was waiting so she refused to ask. Damn him. He enjoyed being in control far too much.

As he filled two glasses he said, "Braddock nudged the agency's contacts at Chicago P.D. to see if they had anything new and if any mention of Wright's murder came into play. He got nothing." Todd set the juice aside and leveled his gaze on hers. "The routine background search found no next of kin on Delia. No recent activity on any of her accounts, bank or credit card. She appears to have dropped off the planet. But he'll keep digging."

"Has he learned anything from Dr. Landon yet?" Part of her still wanted to tie the whole situation to his work. The stem-cell frontier was so controversial. The race to learn what secrets the research held was ruthless. Achieving that funding was of extreme importance to Landon.

Todd carried the two plates to the table. She followed with the glasses of juice.

"Nothing," he said when they'd both taken their seats. "Every avenue he's discussed relative to his work has been both legal and widely accepted. He fully expects the private funding will be sufficient to accomplish all of Milestone's goals. He's certain he'll be one of the major pioneers."

And he would be, if all went as planned.

But none of that explained why his wife had abruptly gone missing. Or one of his former lovers.

"I want to believe him," Serena admitted as she picked at her eggs. "I want him to be the kind of husband Molly went on so about. I want this to have nothing to do with their marriage or the baby." Her eyes sought and found his. "But at the same time, for Molly's benefit, it needs to be about him. Otherwise, there's no reason why a ransom demand hasn't come. That scenario leaves only one conclusion, that Molly is dead, and I'm not ready to accept that."

"You're that certain she didn't just leave."

Serena nibbled her toast then washed it down with the orange juice. How could she make him see that the idea was both ludicrous and impossible? Molly would have done anything to keep her family together. That family unit was the most important thing in the world to her. There was absolutely no way she would do anything to damage it in any way. But she wasn't sure she could properly relay that certainty without telling him how she knew.

She and Molly were sisters. Serena knew.

Why didn't she just tell him?

Serena stared at her plate. Because Molly had begged her never to tell anyone. She was so afraid the truth would change how Charles Landon looked at her. She couldn't bear the idea of him seeing her as anyone other than the girl who'd grown up with a wealthy family... the perfect upbringing.

Serena carefully placed her fork on the edge of her plate and looked directly at Todd before answering. She let him see what she wanted him to see, sheer determination, absolute certainty. "There is no way she would have left. She loved him too much. Her marriage and the family they were creating were all that mattered to her. Everything else was secondary, even the affairs. She would never, ever leave him. Her whole life revolved around him and that baby."

He didn't let her off that easily. "How can you be so certain? You've only known her a little over a year. Maybe she didn't let you see the truth. How can you be sure she didn't lie to you? After all, Landon is your boss. Perhaps image was more important to her than you realized."

Anger flared before she could stop it. "She wouldn't lie to me. She did not leave her husband. No way. Not under any circumstances."

"All right. I get it."

His sudden about-face startled her. In an effort to cover her surprise, she scooped up a forkful of eggs and crammed them into her mouth.

"Let's go with your theory. Molly was taken against her will and is being held, or worse."

Serena's throat tightened and the eggs barely went down.

"Maybe Landon wanted to get rid of her, which seems out of character if he wanted the baby she was carrying," Todd offered.

"The only thing he loves more than his wife is his work," Serena countered.

"So if she had learned something or somehow was poised to injure his professional career, he may have wanted her out of the way."

"Right. I'm nearly certain that would be the only way."

"You do realize," Todd said, "that if that turns out to be the case, Molly and her baby are likely already dead."

Serena looked away, couldn't bear to maintain eye contact. He was right, she knew that. "And if that's the case," she said just as pointedly, her gaze going back to his, "I want him to pay."

"Then there's Delia Neely," Todd suggested. "She had or was having an affair with Landon. The only thing that stood in her way of having him all to herself was his wife and unborn child. That she abruptly dropped out of sight six months ago is suspicious in and of itself. But that doesn't mean she was planning a way to get rid of Molly."

"But she could have," Serena countered. Anticipation zinged her. That scenario suddenly felt like the most logical. It wasn't that she hadn't considered the possibility before, but she hadn't had enough details to give it credence.

"But what about Arthur Miles?" She hadn't really pondered his possible involvement. "Could he have done this to get back at Landon for gaining control? For hogging the limelight?"

"It's possible," Todd agreed. "We looked at that

aspect when we reviewed your case, but it seems unlikely since the takeover move happened more than two years ago. Why wait this long for vengeance? Plus," he added, "Landon is spearheading this funding drive. Miles needs him to ensure Milestone Labs stays at the forefront of this research."

Serena supposed he was right. "What do we do now?"

"Since Braddock is on top of Landon," he considered out loud, "why don't we focus on Delia?"

A surge of hope sent renewed anticipation through her veins. "I think that's an excellent idea."

"Eat up," he encouraged. "We have our work cut out for us."

Todd accompanied Serena to her office. He had no choice but to hang out there while she attended a morning briefing. He hadn't seen Braddock around. Landon had likely warned him that his morning would be occupied with meetings and Braddock should come in later.

Considering Delia Neely's known bank account had been inactive for six months, there had to be one that hadn't been discovered as yet. All they had to do was find it. Assuming she was alive.

Keith Devers in the research group at the Colby Agency was on top of that, but there was something Todd could do. It would be very useful if he could prove whether or not Milestone Laboratories was still in any way involved with her. It was a stretch since her employment had ended six months ago, but he had to check it out. So far Braddock hadn't found any ongoing connection between Landon and Delia.

But to do any looking here, Todd needed Serena.

Speak of the devil: she walked in.

"He got the funding." Her eyes looked wide with uncertainty or something on that order. "More than he'd asked for. He's ecstatic."

"That's good, right?" If Todd had Landon pegged right, getting the funding he wanted took the pressure off. And besides his affairs, was the only possible motivation for wanting rid of his wife.

Serena dropped onto the edge of her desk. "It changes everything, in my opinion." She shook her head. "If you'd only seen him. He was like a kid at Christmas." She choked out a laugh. "He even pulled me aside after the meeting and told me that he was thrilled. That the only thing missing now was Molly and the baby."

Now there was a guy with some extreme confidence or who was seriously not guilty.

"I have a plan."

Todd still wasn't sure how well this plan would work out, but considering what she'd just told him, it was about their only available lead right now. Her expectant expression made him ache to find some answers for her. The memory of how she'd looked at him this morning made him want to take her into his arms again. But he couldn't do that. He was supposed to be watching her… in case she was involved in Molly Landon's disappearance. But he knew better. This woman was innocent. In far more ways than he cared to consider.

"Is there any way to get into Milestone's accounting system to see if any payments have gone out to Delia Neely since her abrupt departure?"

Serena regarded his question with no small measure of skepticism. There was no way to get into the accounting system without proper clearance…unless…

"Maybe." She moistened her lips and asked herself if she could really do this. "Arthur's nephew, Nolan, is a hacker of sorts. He might be able to get in."

"A hacker?"

She nodded. "That's why he got thrown out of college. He changed his grades and a number of other students'. For a price," she added.

"What's he going to want in return?"

Serena couldn't tell if Todd was curious or if the idea ticked him off. Strange. "I don't know. He's always asking me out. A date maybe?"

The little rhythmic flexing and contracting that started in his tense jaw sent a flutter through her chest. Was he jealous? Or just being protective?

"See what you can get from him. I'll touch base with Braddock to see when he's coming in. Maybe he'll have some new information. You have your cell phone?"

She patted her lab coat pocket. "Yes."

"Call me the second you have something. I'll be here somewhere."

Now to find Nolan.

After asking around on two floors, Serena located him in the third-floor lounge.

"Hey, Nolan."

He looked up from his crossword puzzle. "I was just on my way to your floor."

His cart of undelivered mail sat next to the table.

"That's okay. I wasn't looking for my mail."

His face perked up. "Are we having lunch again?"

Okay, she had to do this right, had to make the effort worth the trouble for him.

"Actually." She eased down into the chair opposite him. "I was hoping we could go see that new movie we talked about the other day." She shrugged nonchalantly. "We could do dinner, as well, if you'd like."

That he practically drooled made her feel uneasy on one level but inordinately satisfied on another.

"Just name the time. I'm available whenever you say the word."

Guilt abruptly nagged at her. Leading him on this way was not a very nice thing to do. But she was desperate.

"How about Friday night?" If he helped her out, she would go out with him no matter what.

"You're on." He shoved the last bite of a doughnut into

his mouth. "I'll pick you up at six. We'll do the movie first. That okay?" he said between attempts to chew.

She nodded. "Sounds fine."

He suddenly leaned forward. "I guess you heard the news about Landon's funding?"

"Yes. That's amazing, don't you think?"

He looked less than impressed. "I'm not sure my uncle is so happy. He wanted to make that goal first."

Competition. Even in medical research, that was the name of the game.

"Do you ever hear anything from Delia Neely?" Even she felt taken aback by the sudden change in subject. But she had to get where she needed to be somehow and time was her enemy.

He looked confused but the confusion quickly morphed into a knowing expression. "I heard she still had a thing for Landon when she left."

"I heard the same thing," Serena fibbed. "I wonder why she left."

"My uncle says Landon fired her without actually *firing* her," he said with a quotation gesture, "to make his wife happy. Ironic that he ended up losing them both."

Serena let his last comment pass without argument. She needed him to believe he was the one in the know on the subject.

"Yeah, ironic," she agreed dutifully. Her gaze narrowed and she leaned across the table as he had earlier. "Do you think she's blackmailing him? Delia, I mean. What if he's still paying her even though she no longer works here?"

The light of excitement lit in his eyes. "My uncle would stroke out!"

She reclined in her chair once more. "Too bad we can't find out. Arthur might be very pleased with us if we uncovered some dirt." She made a scoffing sound. "I don't know about you, but I could use a promotion."

He rubbed his hand over his mouth, his expression distant. She prayed she hadn't said too much.

"There might be a way."

Adrenaline shot through her. "Really? How?"

He looked smug. "I've tapped into various systems around here before. In fact, I checked my salary against some of the other clerks—"

That he abruptly stopped talking told her he'd admitted more than he'd wanted to. "I wonder about mine," she said under her breath.

He relaxed. "Don't sweat it. You're doing way better than the other assistants."

A feeling of pride welled inside her. But she didn't have time for dwelling on the news. "Can you...I mean...would you want to check out the deal on Delia? I'm dying to know."

A grin split his face. "Why not? A little leverage is a good thing. We might need it sometime. Or sooner."

Less than ten minutes later they were huddled in Nolan's cramped cubicle in the mail room. Serena fisted her fingers to keep them still. She'd tugged at her skirt until she felt certain he'd noticed. For some stupid reason she'd picked the shortest one she owned this morning. Not that it was actually short by most standards, but it hit three inches above her knee, which was short for her. She'd even forgone her usual button-up blouse this morning and opted for a more feminine-looking sweater in a mint green that complemented her deeper green skirt nicely.

Not once in her life had she given what she wore that much thought. And he hadn't even noticed.

Todd, she meant.

Although she'd memorized most of his body, he'd barely glanced at her.

"Here we go."

Nolan dragged her attention back to the task at hand. He'd entered the accounting system and was now searching for, by way of Delia's social security number, when her last payment had gone out.

She shifted, more from the numbness setting in than her nervousness. Nolan had offered his chair but she'd declined. He would need it for doing what he was doing. So he'd turned his trash can upside down and presented it as a second seat. Her bottom wasn't handling the lack of cushioning too well.

"Aha."

Her gaze zeroed in on the results of his latest search.

"Oh, my God."

Once a month, a sum larger than Serena's monthly salary was processed to Delia Neely's social security number. How could he do that?

"Bastard," she muttered.

"Damn," Nolan breathed. "He is paying her. With Milestone funds. This is a new account number, too. See." He pointed to the screen. "These payments were initiated just six months ago."

Serena snapped out of her haze of fury. She had to be certain. "Is there a way to verify who authorized the payments?"

"Sure." His fingers flew over the keys. "Right there."

The series of numbers didn't mean anything to her. In fact, numbers was all the screen contained. The routing number for the bank and the account number. Another series of digits representing authorization. She should be writing this down. But how? She glanced at Nolan. His mouth hung open in something akin to astonishment.

"What's wrong?"

"This isn't possible."

She looked from him to the screen and back. "What isn't possible?"

He moved his head side to side. "This...this authorization number is my uncle's."

"What?" A surge of shock or disbelief pushed aside all other thought.

He tapped the screen above the authorization code.

"Those numbers mean my uncle authorized these payments."

"But…that can't be…" Serena stared at the numbers, wished she had a photographic memory.

"Nolan!"

Both of them jumped at the sound of his name being shouted from the other side of the mail room.

Serena knew that voice.

"It's my uncle." Nolan swore.

She nodded. "What do we do?" She needed those numbers.

"Let me back out of this system."

She had to do something. "Wait. Let me write this down…in case…we can't find it again."

He blinked but seemed to accept her explanation.

"Hurry!" he muttered.

She quickly wrote down the routing and account numbers and shoved the slip of paper into her pocket. She didn't bother with the authorization number. "Got it."

A few more flicks of the keys and the screen faded to his log-in page.

"Nolan! Where the hell are you?"

Arthur Miles was almost to the cubicle now….

"Damn," Nolan muttered.

Arthur would know they were up to something.

"Nolan," she said, uncertain she could do the only thing she felt might work.

He turned to her, worry scrunching his face. "Yeah?"

She licked her lips. "Kiss me."

Realization dawned in his expression. He grabbed her face with both hands and pulled her mouth to his. She refused to part her lips but that didn't keep him from kissing her hard, from delving his fingers into her hair.

"Nolan! What—"

They jumped apart. Serena's face went beet red all on its own.

"Good Lord." Arthur Miles, the single largest investor in Milestone Labs aside from Charles Landon, took a step back. "I apologize for the intrusion."

Nolan stood. "It's okay, Uncle Artie. Did you need something?"

Serena got to her feet, swayed slightly, tried to find a way to wipe her lips without either of the men noticing.

"I…" Arthur glanced at Serena but quickly shifted his attention back to his nephew. "Your aunt insists you come to dinner on Sunday night." He cleared his throat. "You may invite Miss Blake if you'd like."

"Cool." Nolan looked like the winner of the latest bachelorette competition. "You good with that?"

She managed a shaky nod.

The cell phone in Serena's pocket vibrated. "I should get back to my office. Dr. Landon may be looking for me."

Knowing she had to keep up the act, she stood on tiptoes and kissed Nolan on the cheek. "See you later." She smiled for Dr. Miles as he stepped aside.

Serena forced herself to walk, not run, to the elevator. Her phone kept vibrating but she couldn't answer it until she was back at her office.

In the elevator she wiped her mouth on her sleeve and shuddered. Nothing against Nolan, but he definitely wasn't her type. That she hadn't been kissed in ages only made the idea that her latest had come from him more depressing.

When the elevator stopped on her floor she hurried to her office, keeping her eyes straight ahead so no one would waylay her. She swiped her badge and pushed into her office.

Thank God.

"Where the hell have you been?"

Todd stood in front of her desk, his hands balled into fists at his sides.

"I—" Irritation kindled. "What's wrong with you?"

He reined in the anger in his eyes, but just barely. What the hell had happened?

"Molly Landon's father was found dead in his bed at the nursing home this morning. The authorities have been called in. Preliminary evidence indicates he was suffocated."

Denial slammed into her. She wanted to demand to know if he was sure...but that was ridiculous. Of course he was sure. And still what her ears had heard wouldn't line up with what her heart wanted to believe.

Molly's father was dead.

Murdered?

Like her doctor.

Dear God, who was next?

"What happened to your hair?"

His question was like a bucket of cold water in her face. "What?" Her hands went automatically to her head. Wisps of hair had fallen from her carefully arranged bun.

The memory of Nolan kissing her, burrowing his fingers in her hair slammed into her next.

"I—I got the information about payments to Delia."

That answer didn't appear to be the one he'd wanted.

Before either of them could say anything, the phone on her desk rang.

What now?

Chapter Twelve

Serena stood in the long line of supporters in the spotlight as a press conference focused on Dr. Landon and his funding announcement took place that afternoon at four.

Her smile felt nailed into place. Stiff and insincere. The one thing she could be sure of was that not a single hair on her head was out of place. Even now, humiliation steamed through her. She should have checked her hair before going back into her office. But she'd been too rattled. Almost getting caught by Dr. Miles and then having Todd Thompson call her cell phone looking for her had sent her emotions into a whirlwind.

She'd barely had time to come to terms with the news about Molly's father when she'd had to come to this press conference. In the intervening time Todd had confirmed that Molly's father's death was definitely a murder. Braddock had reached out to his contacts at Chicago P.D. The exact cause of death had been estimated as suffocation but the autopsy hadn't been completed as yet, so that could change.

Who would want to harm an old man with Alzheimer's? He rarely had a lucid day at this point. Serena couldn't help wondering if anyone had told his wife. Though she'd had a stroke three years ago and was unable to communicate, there was a chance she was aware of the goings-on around her. Would telling her be crueler than not telling her at all?

Molly wasn't here to make that decision.

There wasn't anyone.

Serena's gaze drifted to Charles Landon at the podium where he enthusiastically answered questions from the numerous representatives of Chicago's massive media machine.

How could this have happened? Molly was missing. Her doctor had been murdered and now…her father.

It was too much.

More than a dozen journalists and reporters shouted Landon's name in an attempt to earn the privilege of asking the next question. The whole scene felt surreal. Serena didn't want to be here…she wanted to go home and forget this day and last night.

Beyond her own troubling thoughts she heard Landon make his selection for the next question. She didn't recognize the reporter's name but his face seemed familiar. Maybe he represented one of the local television channels.

"Dr. Landon, we can all feel your enthusiasm. This is truly a step in the right direction for all of Milestone Laboratories." A round of applause followed the reporter's summation.

From the corner of her eye she could see Landon nodding and smiling, his whole face beaming with pride. Molly would want to be here for this. She would be so proud. Whatever made her husband happy, made her happy.

"With that in mind," the reporter continued, finally getting around to his question, "how do you suppose your wife would feel about this advanced research you'll be conducting? Was Mrs. Landon a supporter of your work?"

You could have heard a single intake of breath in the ensuing silence *if* anyone had been breathing.

Serena's gaze shifted to Dr. Landon. For several seconds she was certain he didn't intend to respond to the question, but then he did.

"Sir, my wife devoutly supports my work. She is my staunchest supporter, in fact."

Another round of applause followed Landon's smooth rebuttal. Serena imagined everyone in the room had taken a deep breath.

Everyone but her. She couldn't take her eyes off Landon long enough to remember to breathe.

He did love Molly. Whatever his marital crimes, he loved his wife and believed that she was still alive. That was the purpose of emphasizing *is* when the reporter had specifically used *was* in his reference to Molly.

She'd been wrong. She took in an unsteady breath. She'd spent all this time certain he was the one…and he couldn't be. This was the second or third time she'd seen the love for his wife in his eyes.

How could she have been so wrong?

But who then? Who would want to harm Molly?

Delia Neely's name zipped immediately to the top of the list. But why was Dr. Miles giving her money?

The epiphany came so fast and so furiously that she lost her breath all over again.

Dr. Landon's success in bringing in the needed funding put him on the forefront of this new frontier. Made him the center of attention. Where did that leave Dr. Miles?

In his colleague's shadow.

A step behind.

Nolan had said his uncle wasn't happy about Landon's achievement. Maybe Todd was wrong. Maybe the need for vengeance had been slowly smoldering.

There was the possibility that Dr. Miles and Delia Neely had conspired together to ruin Dr. Landon. What better way than to use his wife and his unborn child?

Serena's knees went weak and it was all she could do to stay vertical.

She sought Todd and Mr. Braddock in the crowd. Both men stood at the back of the fray. As soon as this press conference was over, she had to tell Todd what she'd concluded.

It was simple.

If they found Delia Neely, they would find Molly Landon.

Neither Delia nor Dr. Miles was a murderer.

Serena stilled. Felt herself go cold. Could she really be sure of that? Why else would Dr. Miles be giving money to Delia if she wasn't watching someone for him?

Blackmail money?

Did she know what he had done? Had she threatened to tell?

Serena didn't have any real evidence. All she had was supposition. Miles could insist that Delia continued to do freelance work for Milestone. And that wasn't impossible. But there were far too many coincidences for it to sit right with Serena.

Delia and Molly had used the same ob-gyn. Delia had carried on an affair with Molly's husband. She knew Molly's schedule. Probably knew everything about her.

Another stab of fear burrowed deep in Serena's chest.

Did she know about the connection between Serena and Molly? Had she somehow been listening in on their conversations?

That would explain what had happened to the memory box.

It might even explain Dr. Wright's murder.

But none of it explained away the murder of Molly's father, a helpless old man who scarcely remembered his own name most days.

Fury replaced the fear and pain Serena felt. She would find the truth. She wouldn't stop until she did.

SERENA DIDN'T TALK as Todd drove her home at five-thirty. The press conference had dragged on more than the allotted time. Then an impromptu celebration had prevented his getting Serena out of there for another hour.

He'd wanted to grab her by the arm and haul her out as soon as she'd come back from her rendezvous with that geek Nolan Fairbanks. She'd gotten the information on Delia Neely, but at what price? Serena had refused to say what had happened. But he could guess. Nolan had taken advantage of the situation. Had stolen a few kisses at the very least.

Dirt bag.

"Are you all right?" he asked as he pulled up alongside the curb in front of her town house.

She didn't look at him, just stared front and center as if she hadn't heard him. "No," she said wearily. "I'm definitely not all right."

He got out and rounded the hood to open her door. She let him. More uncharacteristic behavior.

Once they were inside, she came to life, threw her

purse down on the couch and turned on him. "It's Arthur Miles. He and Delia did this to Molly."

Todd held up his hands in a "whoa" gesture. "Let's not jump to conclusions just yet. We don't have any evidence that connects either of them to Molly's disappearance."

"What about the payments to Delia? Explain that." She bracketed her hands on her waist and dared him to come up with an answer.

"Delia Neely could be doing outside work for Milestone Labs. You don't know that she isn't."

From her crestfallen expression he knew she couldn't deny that possibility.

"There are just too many coincidences." She rubbed her eyes with the heels of her hands. She looked exhausted.

He wanted to reach out to her. To assure her he could make all this go away. But he wasn't so sure. They didn't have anything substantial yet.

She had a point, however, about the coincidences. "You're right."

The way she looked at him told him those two little words meant a great deal.

"That's why the Colby Agency is working overtime to trace the account number you gave me. By morning we should have the location of the bank Delia's using and, if we're lucky, the locations where she picks up cash. She could be using an ATM anywhere. But there's a possibility we can pinpoint how and where she's accessing the money."

Serena couldn't believe it. Finally, they were getting somewhere. "Tomorrow morning? We could have some information by then?"

He nodded. "It may take longer, but that's the goal."

A sigh of relief went out of her, making her legs want to give way beneath her for about the third time today. She dropped to the sofa and rested her head in her hands. Maybe this would all be over soon. Please, please, she prayed, let us find Molly alive and well. The baby could come anytime. They had to move quickly. No more delays. No more dead ends.

Molly's poor father. How could Arthur Miles or Delia Neely have hurt him?

It was all too much.

She'd held all those feelings deep inside her all day. But she couldn't hold them in a second longer. A sigh-sob tore out of her throat in spite of her best efforts to do this quietly.

"Hey."

She felt the sofa cushion shift and then the weight of Todd's strong arms going around her. She wanted to lean against him and cry until she'd cried out. But she couldn't. It would be a mistake. She'd already let him far too close. In a few days he would be gone and she'd be left behind with a broken heart.

No, thanks.

"We'll figure this out," he murmured in that velvety voice that was somehow rugged in spite of the soft way the sound moved past his lips.

"I don't want to talk right now," she managed to say between wiping her eyes and nose. "I don't even want to think."

He pressed his forehead to her temple. "Then we won't do either."

She told herself not to look at him. Not to be drawn in by that alluring feel of his breath on her skin. But she just couldn't help herself.

Her face mere centimeters from his, she held completely still and basked in the sensations crackling between them.

For the first time in her life she wanted to lose herself completely in her own selfish wants and needs. She didn't want to worry about tomorrow or any repercussions. She just wanted to touch him, to be touched by him.

He turned his head slightly…moved his lips a millimeter closer to hers. Heat roared through her. That tickling feeling deep in her belly made her yearn to close that marginal distance. But she didn't…she wanted this to last, to drag out the pleasure for as long as possible.

One tiny fraction at a time, his lips moved closer to hers until they just brushed. Her breath caught sharply and she couldn't bear the exquisite torture any longer.

Her lips parted slightly, issuing an invitation he accepted immediately. His mouth closed over hers and she lost herself in that same instant. The ebb and flow of heat and pleasurable tingles had her leaning closer, wanting her body aligned with his.

She could feel him moving, struggling with his jacket. She pushed it off his shoulders, heard it hit the floor. He leaned her back onto the sofa, let his weight settle down on her, setting her body on fire.

He pushed her skirt up, smoothed his hands over her thighs. She shivered. Moved her legs apart so that he could settle there. The feel of him nestled against her like that had her soaring toward climax. She made sounds of need, desperate moans and groans that seemed to urge him on.

One of his hands went beneath the hem of her sweater, flattened on her rib cage in a manner that was at once protective and possessive.

And then she did that thing she'd wanted to do for days. She plunged her fingers into his hair. Felt the silky strands between her fingers. She let her hands slip down to touch his face. The feel of that five-o'clock stubble on his jaw had her whimpering for something she couldn't name. She wanted to touch all of him…feel all of him deep inside her.

She wanted to be with him. Share all of herself, all that meant something to her, completely with him.

Gasping for more air, Todd pulled back from her

sweet lips. He had to catch his breath, had to slow this down. That she'd let him this close, opened herself to him, made him want to plunge ahead without thought. But he couldn't do that.

This wasn't just sex. There was no denying that glaring fact.

Her hips lifted and he felt sure his heart stopped with the rush of sensations that followed. The way she smelled…the way she tasted—he wanted to know all of her. To kiss her until she screamed his name and then he wanted to make love to her until she begged him to stop the delicious torture.

But that wouldn't be right.

"We should talk about this," he murmured between frantic gasps. Her mouth looked so full and lush. He desperately wanted to kiss her again…to lose himself completely.

"You're right," she said raggedly.

He pushed up to his knees and helped her to scoot up and move out from under him. He sat beside her and took a moment to catch his breath fully.

"I want to make love to you, Serena." He didn't want any question about that issue. He turned to look at her, needed her to see his true feelings in his eyes. "But I don't want this to be a mistake. If you don't want this the way I do, we should…" He cleared his throat and struggled for the right words. "We should think twice."

Damn, he almost sounded gallant.

But this wasn't gallantry. This was fear. For the first time in his life, he was scared to death of making a mistake.

He couldn't—wouldn't—risk hurting her.

"You're right."

He breathed a little easier then. He wanted her to understand.

"We should…" She seemed to have the same trouble with what she wanted to say. "We should take it slow. Know a little more about each other first."

Now there was a stellar idea.

Todd ran a hand through his hair, tried to get the memory of how her skin felt out of his mind. Her skirt was still hiked way up her thighs but he tried not to look.

"I haven't been completely honest with you, Todd."

The sound of his name on her lips was the first thing to penetrate the fog of lust around his brain. "You called me Todd."

She smiled shyly and his heart skipped a couple of beats. Then the rest of what she had said bored between his eyes.

"What haven't you been honest about?" Here it came. A bad, bad feeling swept over him. He'd known she was hiding something from him.

She wet her lips and want twisted in his gut.

"You know I was adopted when I was sixteen."

He nodded. "There were a lot of bad foster homes before that, right?" Her resigned expression was answer enough. His heart went out to her. Nobody should have to go through that.

"I don't really remember my biological parents," she went on. "But I had this picture." She got quiet for a moment. "It was in the box that was taken the other night. It was the only picture I had from back then."

He thought of his own happy childhood and he wished he could make the bad memories disappear for her.

She looked away from him then as if she couldn't bear to let him see what came next. "I wasn't alone in the picture. I had a sister two years older than me."

Several ideas collided at once in his mind. A sister two years older. The image of dark hair and eyes formed in his head. Only neither asset belonged to the woman next to him. Yet he'd seen the image before—in a Colby Agency file.

"Molly Landon, right?" he guessed, the realization rattling him.

She nodded. "Molly didn't want anyone to know. She wanted the world to believe her parents had died and that she'd always had this perfect family. The truth was too awful."

She didn't have to explain. He knew something about that awful truth. Her father hadn't even hung around long enough to have his name on the birth certificate—assuming her mother had even known who the father had been. As if that wasn't bad enough, her mother had neglected Serena, physically abused her or allowed her boyfriends to. Either way, her baby girl had ended up being taken away from her for a time. When the time was up, Mommy was nowhere to be found. Chances were Molly hadn't fared any better.

"You should have told me this before." He closed his eyes and considered the implications. The secret would only make her look guilty. The police would pound this information into the ground. They didn't have anything else to go on. This news would give them something to grab on to.

She smoothed the hair back from her face. "I couldn't. I promised her."

Fury lashed through him before he could stop it. The intensity forced him to his feet. "Dammit, Serena. Don't you realize that this information could impact how an investigation is carried out? With her adopted father's murder, this secret could lead to others. Others that could tell us what really happened."

She blinked, looked as shocked as if he'd slapped her. "I don't understand."

"Whoever took her could be someone from her past. Maybe her biological father or someone who knew him or her mother. The bottom line could be the money."

She shook her head. Pushed up to match his stance. "Wait. There hasn't been a ransom demand. That can't be right."

"Think about it, Serena. They could be waiting for the child to be born to up the stakes."

The horrified expression on her face told him she hadn't considered that possibility.

"I knew it. Dammit. What else have you been keeping from me?"

Maybe he shouldn't have pushed quite that far.

The horror he'd seen in her eyes moments before evolved into outrage.

"Nothing. That's it." The outrage abruptly drained from her face and pain took its place. "Oh, God."

"Look. I didn't mean that the way it sounded." Damn. He'd definitely gone too far.

"That's what this was all about." She looked at the sofa as if she saw something repugnant. "You seduced me to get me to break my promise." Her gaze lifted to his. "Get out."

"No." He held up his hands to slow the momentum. "This has nothing to with *that*."

She folded her arms over her chest in that gesture he'd come to recognize. "I said get out or I'll call the Colby Agency and demand a new investigator."

He couldn't let that happen. "I'll…be in my car."

He hesitated at the door, considered pleading his case from another angle.

But one backward glance told him the effort would be wasted. Unfortunately he'd been here before, a couple of times lately. He was definitely off his game.

"Good night."

He walked out and the lock tumblers rolled into place the instant the door closed.

"Stellar job, Thompson."

Problem was, yeah, he'd been here before, but he'd never been here with *her* before.

She made all the difference.

Chapter Thirteen

Todd's eyes cracked open about the same time dawn crept over the streets. He sat up and stretched in an attempt to loosen his stiff muscles. His shoulders and legs ached from the odd position he'd slept in.

His attention shifted to Serena's town house and he caught a glimpse of her moving past the window of her living room. She was up early. Or maybe she'd had a night like him—sleep had come only an hour or so before he'd awakened.

The way he'd lost control and let things get out of hand on her couch kept haunting him. That she'd assumed he'd only wanted to seduce information out of her had hit too close to home. It was true that when this thing started he'd been determined to do whatever was necessary to get what he needed. But luring her into having sex with him hadn't been on the agenda, especially after he'd gotten to know her.

She had definitely been hiding something, but he

would have found a way to get the truth out of her without resorting to seduction.

Wouldn't he?

A sick feeling turned over in his stomach. Could he really say that he wouldn't have?

He was one of the good guys, right?

The memory of how disappointed the people he'd gotten close to had been when they discovered that he wasn't who he'd claimed to be tightened like a band around his chest. No amount of apologizing had made up for the fact that he'd shined them on for nothing more than research.

He'd told himself that he would do it all over again if necessary to make the point.

Was that what he'd been doing here…making the point? Accomplishing the mission no matter the cost?

The hurt he'd seen on Serena's face flashed in his mind and he couldn't bear to think about it anymore.

He opened the car door and got out to stretch his legs. He paced the length of the car a couple of times to get his blood flowing. Wincing, he rolled one shoulder and then the other. Man, oh, man, sleeping behind the wheel was not nearly as comfortable as Serena's couch.

Too bad he'd screwed that up big-time.

His cell phone broke into musical notes and he fished it from his jacket pocket. He'd taken it off vibrate when he'd been banished to the car to ensure he didn't miss any calls.

"Thompson."

"Braddock here. I've got some locations for you."

That was fast. He'd expected some feedback today, but not quite this early. Good deal.

"In Chicago?"

"Believe it or not, yeah."

"Give me a minute." Todd leaned back into the Volvo and dug his city map out of the glove box. He grabbed a pen and used the roof of the car for a desktop. "Shoot."

Braddock ticked off the location of the main bank where the account was held then more than a dozen ATM locations from which it had been accessed.

"The only pattern I can see," Braddock noted, "are the five or six locations centered around a ten-block radius." He gave Todd the cross streets.

Todd studied the map. "Yeah, I see that. She could be holed up somewhere in that area."

"That's my thinking. I'll stay on Landon. Stop by the office and pick up a couple of photos, one of Molly Landon and one of Delia Neely. Cover that area as thoroughly and quickly as you can. See if anyone has seen either of them."

That was the direction he'd been considering as he studied the map. "What about Serena?" Todd didn't feel comfortable leaving her on her own. Not considering Dr. Wright and Molly Landon's adopted father, Howard Ledbetter, had both apparently been murdered.

"Take her with you. Don't let her out of your sight.

Have her call in sick. As it stands right now, it appears Landon's day is going to be filled with more press conferences and personal interviews."

"Will do."

Todd ended the call and tucked the phone back into his pocket. He turned to Serena's home. Might as well see if he could get a foot back in the door. He had a feeling that wasn't going to be easy.

Nor was talking her into going along with the plan Braddock had outlined.

What the heck. He'd always enjoyed a challenge.

SERENA TOOK HER COFFEE back up to her room to finish getting ready for work. She peeked past the blinds covering the window near her bed. Todd Thompson stood next to his car, his cell phone tucked between his shoulder and his ear and a map spread out on the top of the vehicle.

A frown nagged at her. What was he doing out there? Jerk.

She let the blind snap back into place. She didn't care what he did—she had no intention of interacting further with him. At least not on a personal level. She didn't want to risk setting back the investigation by requesting a different man on her case, but she didn't have to talk to him or…or anything.

Determined to get on with her morning, she walked to the dresser across the room and efficiently twisted then pinned her hair into place. That he liked it down flickered through her thoughts, but she banished the idea. What he liked was of no consequence to her.

Humiliation burned her cheeks when she considered how close to climaxing she'd come last night from nothing more than his kisses and the feel of his body against hers.

Pathetic.

When this was over she had to do something about her social life. She was too young to be celibate. She needed to get out once in a while. Socialize with people her own age. She should have started doing that long ago. Part of what held her back, she supposed, was the fact that she'd been younger than most everyone else she worked with.

Except Nolan.

She cringed at the recall that she'd promised to go out with him on Friday.

How would she ever bow out of that without hurting his feelings?

Her mind replayed that kiss and she shuddered. Then, before she could stop her naughty side, she compared the kiss she'd shared with Nolan to the ones with Todd.

No comparison.

Heat shimmered through her.

Damn him.

He'd made her become infatuated with him and she hated it!

She was supposed to be smarter than this. More logical.

Apparently she wasn't nearly as smart as she'd thought.

She stepped over to the full-length mirror and considered the rather plain-looking woman staring back at her. How could she even think that a guy as handsome and sexy as Todd Thompson would really be interested in her? He'd known she was holding out on him and he'd used her vulnerability to get the information out of her.

She was tall enough and reasonably thin. But there was nothing extraordinary or special about her at all.

The black skirt she'd chosen for today was, again, one of her less conservative ones. This one was almost to her knees but had a sort of sexy split in the back. The charcoal pullover looked nice, not sexy in any way, but nice.

Panty hose and shoes and she would be ready to go. She hesitated, considered her reflection again. Makeup had never been her thing…maybe a little lip gloss.

Serena rolled her eyes and turned away from the mirror. The longer she looked, the faster her self-confidence dwindled.

After searching half a dozen drawers she finally found a pair of panty hose. She breathed a sigh of relief and plopped onto the foot of the bed to pull them on. She knew it was old-fashioned but she just felt naked without her panty hose.

The chime of the doorbell made her jump. Her heart

bolted at the realization that it was likely Todd. And, to her dismay, her thumbnail went straight through her hose.

"Oh, damn." She heaved a disgusted breath. The mega run was at the calf, no way in the world to hide it.

She scanned her dresser and bureau drawers. She hadn't even bothered to push some of them back in. Stuff hung out in every direction.

What had happened to the order in her life?

Neat and organized had always been her best traits.

Further proof that she had no business getting involved with a man like Todd. His bad habits had rubbed off on her. The next thing she knew she'd be walking around with one side of her button-up blouse hanging out of her waistband. She gasped. And having sex someplace besides a bed.

The doorbell chimed again, propelling her into action. She peeled off the panty hose and threw them to the floor. Before she surrendered and went downstairs, she dug through a couple of drawers once more just to see if she'd overlooked another pair of hose.

Nothing.

She stepped into her shoes and did what she had to do.

Resigned herself to going to work half-naked.

Downstairs, Todd had apparently gotten impatient or worried and started to pound on the door.

For a moment she toyed with the idea of making him sweat a minute or two longer. But if he busted down her door, she'd just have to have it repaired.

She jerked the door open and it was all she could do not to laugh and cry simultaneously when she got a good look at him.

Alarm ruled his expression. Last night's five-o'clock shadow had turned into the morning-after stubble. Sleeping in the car had left his shirt slightly more wrinkled than usual. His hair was tousled in that appealing-as-all-get-out bed-head look. All in all, he looked like the sexiest man on the planet come to take her away from the humdrum of everyday life. Too bad she knew that wasn't the case.

Frustration roiled in her tummy. And since when had she spent so much time thinking about sex?

"You okay?"

She planted one hand on her hip. "Don't I look okay?"

He braced his broad shoulders against the door frame and that blue gaze slid down the length of her, lingered on her bare legs, making her shiver, then roved back up to her face. "You look great."

If she hadn't seen the approval in his eyes, she might have believed he was pulling her leg, no pun intended. But he was serious and that had her feeling all warm and tingly again.

But she was mad at him.

He'd used her attraction to him to get information out of her. Hadn't he?

Or had she been the one?

She couldn't remember—who kissed who?

Who started the whole thing?

Never mind. It didn't matter.

She was angry and no matter how amazing he looked or how much he flattered her, she wasn't going to let him off the hook.

"I need you to call in sick or something," he said as if he'd just given her an update on today's weather.

"What? I can't do that." She hadn't missed a day of work in her entire career. Never missed a day of college, either. Absolutely never. She couldn't call in sick unless she was bedridden or contagious.

He stepped inside, closed the door behind him. She couldn't help herself: she backed up a couple of steps. The disappointment on his face told her that the move had signaled just how she felt about him and last night.

Was she wrong to let him shoulder the brunt of the guilt for that momentary lapse in sanity?

"Delia Neely has been accessing the funds from Milestone via a number of ATMs. I have the locations. Several are centered around a particular location and Braddock thinks we should check it out. Flash Molly's and Delia's pictures to see if anyone has seen either one of them."

Serena's pulse quickened. "So Delia is still in town? She could be the one who took Molly?" All they had to do was to find Delia and follow her to wherever she was staying. And maybe they would find Molly.

"That's possible. But her payments from Arthur Miles and her abrupt departure from her last place of residence may not have anything to do with Molly. Landon could still be the one. But we need to follow this lead, to eliminate Delia as a suspect if nothing else."

Serena nodded. She understood. "I'll make that call."

AFTER STOPPING by the Colby Agency for the needed photos, Todd drove across town. Delia had used her debit card at two local markets in the area and one ATM, on more than one occasion.

There was every reason to believe she frequented this neighborhood for one reason or another. Maybe to visit a relative, maybe because she'd taken an apartment here.

"Where do we begin?"

Serena stared at the buildings along the street. No single-occupancy houses. Mostly apartment buildings and a few low-rent office buildings. Nothing to write home about.

"We'll start at the end of this block and work our way to the next cross street."

Her gaze bumped into his and he saw the uncertainty there. Not about what they were about to do, but about them, and last night. He hated that he'd let that happen.

"Should we split up, try to cover more territory that way?"

He shook his head. "No. I don't want you out of my sight."

However she felt about that she kept it carefully hidden, but she didn't argue.

They moved from building to building and asked anyone who would answer the door if they'd seen either of the women.

By noon they'd covered about half the area he'd outlined on the map. The remaining blocks were considerably less appealing visually and not exactly what one would call welcoming. Not a neighborhood where one would want to stroll after dark.

"This is going to take forever." She peered at the map in his hands. "We really should split up. I'll be fine. I have my cell phone. I can call you if I run into trouble."

He shook his head. "Forget it. We stay together."

She didn't like it, but she let it go at that.

Two hours later they hit pay dirt.

"Yeah, I know that one." The guy behind the counter tapped Delia Neely's picture. "She's got a room here." He picked up the picture and stared at it a bit longer.

"Are you sure it's her?" Todd didn't like the way the guy kept looking at the photo as if he wasn't really sure.

He tossed the picture back to Todd. "Yeah, it's her. The face seems a little different, but it's the same blond hair. The only thing is, I never seen her eyes. She's always wearing sunglasses."

Todd and Serena exchanged a look. Since Molly had dark hair like Serena, noticing the blond hair of Delia wouldn't be difficult. The eyes could have been the defining factor. Molly's were dark brown like Serena's.

Delia's were hazel, more green than brown. Not to mention Molly was very pregnant.

"Thanks." Todd considered his options and just how far the manager of this dump would be willing to go. The dilapidated motel rented by the hour as well as the day, which spoke volumes in itself. "Look, is the room across the hall from the blonde's available?"

The manager's gaze narrowed. "You some kinda cop?"

"No. Nothing like that." He looped his arm around Serena's shoulders. She stiffened but didn't resist. "She's an old friend of ours. We just want to surprise her, that's all. We do this kind of thing all the time." He shrugged one shoulder. "You know, play games."

Todd let the innuendo hang in the air.

The manager's face split into a grin. "Yeah, I know what you mean." He reached behind him and grabbed a key. "That'll be fifty bucks."

Todd selected a one hundred dollar bill from his wallet and placed it on the counter. "I want to be sure our little surprise stays a surprise."

The manager grabbed the bill. "You got it, pal."

Todd curled his fingers around the key and gave the guy a wink. "If it works out the way I hope, I'll leave another in the morning."

The manager snickered. "How about I ring your room when she comes through? This is the only way in or out except for the emergency exits, which don't open from the outside."

Todd gave him a nod and then ushered Serena toward the stairs. She didn't ask any questions until he'd reached their room on the fourth floor.

"Are we just going to wait?" she whispered with a covert glance at the door across the hall.

Todd considered the door, as well, then unlocked their own. When they were inside with the door closed he said, "I want to see if she returns alone. Maybe follow her when she leaves again. If she's involved with Molly's disappearance, we have to know the location of the hiding place or who she's working with."

"What if Molly's right across the hall? All tied up or drugged?"

He sympathized with her anticipation. She wanted to find her friend—her sister. She wanted Molly to be safe and for life to go back to the way it used to be. He wished he could save her all the heartache that was likely to come. Even if Molly was fine, things would never be the same again. Kidnap victims, especially those who were held long-term, didn't just go on as if the nightmare had never happened. There were side effects.

"If she's not and we break in anyway, we could jeopardize the location. Delia may have the room bugged. She might receive a warning if whatever security she has in place is breached. Remember, if Landon or Miles is in on this, they have the kind of money that would afford all the high-tech gadgets."

Her brow furrowed in confusion. "I just can't get right with the idea that Miles is in on Molly's abduction."

"He's the one paying Delia, right?"

She nodded but didn't look convinced.

"Remember, this could be about bringing Landon down. Miles could be jealous of his recent strides in stem cell research."

The sound of squeaking bed springs from the room above them interrupted whatever she'd intended to say next.

Their gazes lifted to the dingy, cracked ceiling.

The intensity of the sound increased. And then came the chorus. A woman's cries of pleasure. A man's responding groans.

Serena looked away, folded her arms over her chest and scooted even closer to the door as if preparing for escape.

Todd considered taking off his jacket. It was a little warm in here. He glanced at the air-conditioning unit on the other side of the room. It would make too much noise and he needed to be able to hear anyone coming in the hall. He couldn't be one hundred percent sure he could trust the sleazy manager.

So he just stood there, sweat breaking on his skin, as the noise from upstairs reached a crescendo.

The woman started to squeal even more enthusiastically, then came, "Oh! Oh! Oh! You're a god! A master!" Followed by extreme grunting and inaudible mumbling by the man.

Todd tried his level best not to look at Serena, but he couldn't help himself.

She rolled her eyes. "Please. Like any guy who would be caught dead here could be called a god."

Serena realized what she'd said as soon as the words were out of her mouth. Todd looked puzzled for about half a second then he just looked the other way.

Well, hell, she hadn't meant to be rude. Surely he understood how she'd intended her comment.

"I didn't mean you," she felt compelled to say. "I was referring to the usual clientele." She tugged at the neck of her sweater. Was it hot in here?

"That's okay, I know what you meant."

Funny thing was, he didn't sound as though he understood.

"Men." She huffed and braced against the door to shift her weight from her feet. "You're all such babies. Any sort of criticism about your manhood, real or imagined," she added with a pointed look at him, "just devastates you."

"When did *my* manhood enter the discussion? I thought we were talking about him?" He gestured to the ceiling.

Serena waved a hand back and forth as if to erase his comment. "Forget it."

Was he touchy today or what?

"I wasn't the one who got all emotional after a simple kiss," he quipped.

Her mouth gaped. How dare he bring up her moment

of emotional vulnerability! "I thought I could confide in you." What a total jerk! "You took advantage of the situation."

He leaned toward her, his own fury streaking across his face, making her heart beat faster. "And then you got all annoyed because I questioned you about it."

She scoffed. "I got all annoyed? Please, you were the one grilling me like a brand-new prosecutor on his first hot case."

"Keep your voice down," he whispered fiercely. "I'm trying to help you find Molly."

She'd had it with him. "I'm going over there."

He grabbed her by the wrist. "No, you're not!"

Just then both parties overhead started to scream with orgasm.

Serena glared at Todd, who'd jerked her closer to make sure she didn't escape him. "Let me go."

"Just calm down," he rasped.

For maybe three seconds she thought about slapping his face. And then she did the absolute last thing she could have imagined even if she'd lived a million years.

She grabbed him by the ears and pulled his mouth down to hers. She kissed him hard. Didn't let go even after he clearly surrendered.

He kissed her back, plunged his tongue into her mouth in an act of possession. She moaned, shivered from head to toe. She'd dreamed about this all night. Hadn't been able to sleep for thinking of him.

His hands were under her sweater…on her breasts. Heat erupted every place he touched. But it wasn't enough.

She trailed her hands down his chest and to the closure of his jeans. She wanted to touch him there, wanted to feel him in her hands. Her fingers fumbled with the button and then the fly. He shuddered deliciously, emboldening her. Her movements more frantic with each passing moment, she shoved his jeans and underwear down his hips, felt him thump against her. She cried out, found him with her needy fingers and stroked, encircled him. He felt so smooth…so hot. How had she lived this long and not touched a man this way? She wasn't a virgin, but there had only been two lovers for her and both those times had been over in an instant with little or no foreplay.

He growled like a wild animal, hiked her skirt up to her hips and ripped off her panties. And then he grabbed her by the bottom and lifted her off her feet. She wrapped her legs around his waist.

He pressed her back more firmly against the door, or maybe it was just his added weight, but she loved the feel of him so close. His mouth hadn't left hers…he kissed her over and over. He nibbled at her lips, made her ache to taste more of him.

His fingers traced her intimately and she gasped, struggled to stay still. She wanted to buck into his touch, to beg him for more. He guided his tip to her and plunged inside in one forceful stroke. Her breath left her…her heart seemed to stop.

"Look at me," he murmured between ragged gasps for air.

Panting as if she'd run ten miles, she lifted her gaze to his and felt her heart melt like a pat of butter in a frying pan. She loved the way he looked, loved the disheveled way he dressed, the earthy way he smelled.

"You are so beautiful," he whispered. "I..." He swallowed hard. "I..."

She pressed her fingers to his lips. "Don't talk." As much as she loved his voice, she didn't want to talk... didn't want to be sweet little Serena. She wanted to be wicked. She wanted to let that side of her that she never showed anyone bloom with all the wickedness she could muster.

He grinned sheepishly and then he moved, just an inch or so...the slightest shift of his hips and she started to come undone.

She'd didn't last long...he didn't, either.

They were both too desperate for each other....

And she melted a little more...relished her very first orgasm.

Chapter Fourteen

Todd didn't want to move…it felt right to be like this with Serena. He brushed his lips across her cheek. She shivered, the sensation rippling all the way through her body. He'd never realized how something as simple as that could affect him….

"I'm…" She moistened her lips. "I'm not sure what to say."

He smiled, couldn't help himself. There was that innocence peeking out again. She tried to pretend that she was this strictly professional woman who never let her hair down, but she was incredibly hot. He liked that he'd been able to tear down those defenses of hers.

"You don't have to say anything." Another smile tickled his lips. "Except maybe 'you're a god' if you've a mind to."

A smile flirted with her lips. "I've never done anything like this before. I liked it…a lot."

"I know." He did—that she'd never done it before, that is.

Across the room the old rotary-type phone jangled.

His gaze met Serena's. As much as he regretted having to do this…he withdrew and settled her on her feet. She headed for the bathroom while he pulled himself together in time to snatch up the receiver before the third ring.

"She's on her way up."

"Alone?"

"Yep."

Todd dropped the receiver back into the cradle and moved into position by the door. He withdrew his weapon and hoped he wouldn't need it.

"Is she here?"

He glanced at Serena. Her hair had fallen loose around her face, making her look even younger and so sweet he could hardly drag his attention back to business.

Keeping an eye on the peephole, he braced himself as a figure came into view. Dark glasses. Blond.

He pulled back. "Check it out."

For one second Serena froze. What if Delia had already done the unthinkable? Maybe that was why she received payments from Arthur Miles.

Holding her breath, she peered through the security peephole in the door just in time to see a blonde with dark glasses reach the door across the hall. The woman fumbled with the key before she managed to get the door unlocked. Once the door was open, she disappeared inside and slammed it behind her.

"Is it her?"

Serena turned back to Todd. "Maybe. I couldn't see her face very well for the glasses."

"I have to make a call. Keep an eye on the door."

Serena did as he said while he made his call. He informed someone, probably Braddock, of their location and the situation.

The door across the hall opened and the blonde rushed out, moving out of visual range before Serena could get a decent fix on her.

"She's leaving!" Serena whispered as loudly as she dared.

Todd was next to her before the words stopped echoing in the silence of the room. He took a look and swore. Serena's eyes widened. She hadn't heard him use that language before.

"I'm going after her." He reached for the knob.

"Wait!" She grabbed his arm. "What am I supposed to do?"

"Stay here," he ordered.

Before she could argue, he was gone.

She stood there, stunned that he'd actually left her. Not that she was afraid. But she should be going after Delia with him.

She couldn't just stand here. Summoning her courage, she opened her door and stared at the one across the hall. If Molly was in there…

Before she could change her mind, Serena walked straight over to the other door and turned the knob.

Locked. Dammit.

She pushed against it, but that didn't get her anywhere.

Biting her bottom lip, she considered her options. She could stand here like a helpless dummy or she could do something.

Without a second thought she dashed back into the room where she and Todd had made love and snatched her purse from the bed. She dug through it until she found a credit card and then strode back to the door across the hall. Her heart galloped like a racehorse on the final stretch to the finish line.

If Todd could do it, so could she.

She inserted the credit card into the crack between the door and the frame and started to slide and jiggle it while she twisted the doorknob.

Just when she started to give up, something gave way. The knob twisted and the door moved inward.

Victory soared through her.

She glanced toward the far end of the hall at the stairs and the elevator. No sign of Todd or Delia.

"Okay." She was going in.

TODD REACHED the first floor just as the elevator doors closed.

"Damn!"

A whistle called his attention to the manager's desk. The manager hitched a thumb toward the front entrance.

Todd rushed out of the lobby, ground to a stop on the sidewalk and looked both ways. A glimpse of blond hair flying around the corner of the building and into the alley on the right had him tearing out in that direction.

He slid to a stop at the corner and risked a look. She hadn't stopped, was still running.

He rushed after her, pushed harder. He couldn't let her get away.

If he found out that bastard at the desk had double-crossed him he would kick his butt all the way to hell and back.

Todd reached out...could almost touch her...there...

His fingers curled around her shoulder and he yanked her back. They both lost their balance and went down. She fought like a wildcat. He wrestled her onto her back, saw the gun in her hand that hadn't been there before. He deflected her aim. She screamed but the weapon didn't discharge. He slammed her arm against the pavement until the weapon flew out of her hand.

He pinned her right hand with his knee and ripped off the dark glasses.

Shock radiated through him. "What the hell?"

SERENA LOOKED in the bathroom and under the bed.

Nothing.

Her hopes plummeted.

She had been praying so hard that Molly would be here. That she would be safe.

She sat back on her heels and closed her eyes. It just wasn't fair. Molly had been through enough. She didn't deserve any more hurt in her life.

Heaving a weary sigh, she stood, glanced around the room once more, then did a double take. Something red on the closet door pulled her in that direction. It looked as if fingers dipped in red paint had clawed at the knob and bumped into the white-painted door.

As she neared it, she realized it wasn't paint.

It was blood. She touched it.

Still damp...blood.

Oh, no. Please, no.

Her heart bumping against her sternum, her fingers curled around the knob and she gave it a turn. She pulled it open and the first thing her eyes landed on was a swollen belly. And blood...so much blood.

"Oh, no!"

Serena dropped to her knees and leaned into the closet. Tears streamed down her cheeks and somehow she forced herself to look at Molly's face....

She blinked...not Molly.

Horror rocked through her.

Delia Neely's horror-filled eyes stared at her, un-moving, unblinking.

A gaping wound had split her throat like a heinous grin. A river of blood spilled from the wound.

Her hands shaking, Serena reached out...touched Delia's arm.

Serena gasped. Her skin was still warm.

She fell backward. Scrambled up onto all fours. Whoever had killed her...the blonde...had done so only moments ago. Her body wasn't cold yet; blood still poured from her.

The baby.

Serena's gaze fell to the woman's swollen belly.

"Oh, my God."

She rushed over to the phone and stabbed the number for the front desk. When the manager answered, she yelled, "We need an ambulance! A woman is bleeding to death up here!"

Serena slammed the phone onto its cradle and rushed back to the closet.

She had to get her out of here, had to try to stop the bleeding. She couldn't reach her in there without...

Forcing herself to breathe and ignoring the light-headed feelings, she grabbed hold of Delia's bent knees and pulled her out of the closet.

Serena jumped to her feet and stumbled to the bath-room for towels. She raced back to Delia and dropped onto her knees. She placed a hand towel against her throat and applied as much pressure as she dared.

It didn't help.

There was nothing she could do. Delia was dying or dead already. Her pupils were fixed. Not good.

Serena looked down at the woman's belly. What about the baby? The baby might still be alive.

How could she tell? She placed her hands on the rounded flesh and tried to hold her breath to slow her pounding heart.

In her peripheral vision she saw something shiny on the closet floor.

The knife.

Serena shuddered and shifted her attention back to Delia. What did she do? Wait for help…

She glanced at the window and hoped the ambulance would get here soon.

But what if it didn't?

Todd bolted through the open door. "You okay? Man alive!"

Serena didn't bother answering. She tried different ways to slow the blood, but it just wouldn't stop. It soaked through the towels.

"Help isn't going to get here on time." Serena closed her eyes. She started to shake. She had to do something.

Todd put his hands on the woman's belly. His breath hitched. "The baby moved."

Panic closed Serena's throat. "What do we do?"

His gaze fixed on hers. "Did you study anatomy?"

She shook her head, then nodded. "It was a while ago. But I had a course…."

Could she do this?

If they didn't do something, the baby would die.

She gazed toward the window once more…still no ambulance. Then she looked at Todd. "Hand me that knife." She pointed to the closet.

For a second or two their gazes held, then he scrambled over to the knife. He wiped it clean on his shirt and handed it to her. It didn't matter that it was in all likelihood the murder weapon…they had no choice.

It needed to be sterile…but she couldn't worry about that right now. Delia was dead. The baby would die, too. Whatever Delia's sins, this baby deserved a chance at life.

"All right," she said, more to herself than to Todd.

All she had to do was take it slow and stay shallow. And pray.

SERENA STOOD outside the hospital room, her gaze glued to the patient in the bed beyond the viewing window. She'd cried until she'd felt empty emotionally.

The sounds around her made her shudder. People moaning and crying out for help.

The psychiatric ward of the hospital.

Landon was in a conference with a team of the best psychiatrists in the city.

The blonde who'd run from the hotel room had been Molly.

Serena closed her eyes and shook her head. How could this be right?

Molly had killed Delia.

Not with the gun she'd been carrying: it had jammed. Ballistics, however, showed that it was the same gun used to kill Dr. Wright.

They didn't have all the details yet, but the best they could piece together between Molly's ramblings and the original obstetrician she'd gone to was that Molly had lost her baby. Her uterus had been damaged as a child, the result of abuse by her father and possibly even her adopted father since she kept ranting about him and how he hadn't deserved to live. Apparently Molly had been the one to sneak into the nursing home and suffocate him.

Shortly after she'd lost the baby she'd discovered that Delia Neely was pregnant. Thinking that the baby the other woman carried was her husband's child, Molly abducted Delia with the intention of killing her once the baby was born. Then Molly would pass the baby off as her own and claim that Delia had been the one to do the kidnapping and that she'd had to kill her to escape. The knife she'd used to kill Delia had been purchased in case of complications during the imminent birth. All sorts of home birthing guides had been found in the room.

The police had found a pint container of lighter fluid

hidden in the toilet tank. Todd concluded that when the time came, Molly had intended to burn the room, including Delia's body, in an effort to cover the evidence of the woman having recently given birth.

She'd thought of almost everything.

Except her only sister's determination to save her.

Serena just hadn't known she would be saving Molly from herself. The sleazebag manager at the motel had told her that some old friends had come looking for her. Molly had flipped and cut her losses…literally. The picture, or what was left of it, from Serena's memory box had been found in that sleazy hotel room, as well, torn into a dozen pieces.

"Hey."

Serena looked up and Todd was there. The smile was automatic. Barely twenty-four hours had passed since the two of them had entered that rundown motel. So much had happened. Not enough time to think about…what had taken place between them.

Her heart warmed at his nearness. She'd fallen so hard for him.

And now their time together was over.

"Hey," she said back.

"The baby's doing fine. Child Services came in to take a statement. The police contacted Arthur Miles and he admitted the baby was his. He and Delia had begun an affair shortly after Landon ended things with her. Miles had loved the idea that Landon knew. It was his way of getting back at him, but it backfired. Delia got pregnant and Miles had no choice but to support her or have her spill her guts."

Serena experienced a chill. It wasn't that Child Services didn't do a lot of good. They did. But she couldn't help remembering her early life...and that of her sister. Could they stand back and let that little girl's life hang in the balance like that?

"What'll happen to the baby now?" Her voice sounded stark after the long hours of just standing here looking in at her sister.

"Miles wants nothing to do with her."

"Do you think..." Serena turned her face up to Todd's. "That maybe they would let me adopt her? She deserves a good home."

He looked thoughtful for a moment before answering. "Your chances might be better if you could assure them that the baby girl would have a father to keep her in line." A grin tilted one side of his mouth. "I know just the guy for the job."

"I...don't know what to say." Her heart skipped at least two beats. Was he proposing? "Maybe we should clarify the terms of your offer."

He shrugged one of those broad shoulders. "I don't know—that might take some time."

Serena looked in on her sister one last time, then she took the hand of the man she loved. "I asked for a few days off. I don't have anything but time just now."

The fellowship for her Ph.D. was the only good news she'd had in a while. Dr. Landon had given her the news just before she'd had to tell him about Molly. He hadn't realized Serena had come to his office for that…she'd felt so guilty for believing he'd hurt Molly in some way. She also understood now that the only reason he'd passed her over for promotion was so that she would be free to accept the fellowship. She'd also learned that Landon's numerous affairs were a result of his wife pushing him away. Their intimate life had been so tense he'd feared touching her. That was the main reason he'd worried the police were right about Molly leaving him. Getting pregnant had seemed her only goal in their marriage.

All those worries were behind Serena now. She had to move on. And moving on with Todd was the one thing she wanted to do more than anything else in this world.

"The hospital'll call you if they need you." He tugged her toward him. "Let's get out of here."

As they walked toward the elevator, she asked, "You don't have to stop in at the Colby Agency?"

He shook his head and pressed a kiss to her temple. "Braddock's taking care of the report."

"I like Braddock," Serena said, suddenly more thankful than ever for Todd's partner.

Todd pulled her into the elevator with him. "Me, too." He enveloped her in his arms. "But I like you a lot better."

His mouth lowered to hers as the elevator doors slid closed.

Maybe the past hadn't been everything she'd hoped for…but the future was looking a whole lot brighter.

VICTORIA COLBY-CAMP set aside the final report on the Blake/Landon case. Not a happy ending, but at least the child's life had been spared. Thank God for Serena's and Todd's quick thinking. The ambulance would have been too late to save the baby.

A light rap on the door pulled Victoria's attention away from the troubling thoughts.

"Victoria?" Nicole Reed-Michaels waited in the doorway.

"Nicole, come in. I was just about to call you." Gabrielle and Michelle had completed their final evening session on the Agency's computer systems. Training Todd Thompson would take place when he returned to work. All staff members were required to know the system.

Victoria noticed that Nicole looked a bit distressed and she hoped that the children weren't ill. "Is everything all right?"

"I'm not sure."

The response was completely unlike Nicole. "Explain, please."

"It's Gabrielle."

One of the new recruits. Victoria reached for a file on her desk. She'd already spoken with Ian and Simon. She felt confident that Gabrielle was ready for her first assignment. The young lady had spirit.

"She's missing."

Missing? "She was here yesterday," Victoria countered.

Anger flashed in Nicole's eyes. "Yes, she was. Yesterday was the day she received access to the secure server to complete the final phase of her training."

Victoria suffered a tremor of tension, but she didn't react until she heard the rest.

"She called in sick today."

"And you have reason to believe that is not the case?"

"This morning we discovered a breach. An unauthorized file was downloaded from the secure server."

"Have you initiated security protocol?" Victoria steeled herself for the worst: the possibility that Gabrielle had been employed by an unethical competitor. But nothing could have adequately prepared her for what was to come.

"Yes. At first I was perplexed because she only downloaded one file. A single file," Nicole emphasized. "That's the only thing she took."

Victoria felt a moment of bewilderment, as well. "Which file?"

Nicole wet her lips and swallowed, the effort visible. "The file on Trevor Sloan. As you know, that file contained information regarding *Angel*."

Victoria stilled. "There's more." Not a question. She could feel the coming storm.

Nicole nodded. "When the breach was brought to my attention I reviewed Gabrielle's file in an attempt to determine if perhaps she was a mole contracted by a competitor."

But that wasn't the case. The other shoe was about to drop.

"Gabrielle Hanson fabricated her time at Texas A&M. She was actually doing time in prison for assault with a deadly weapon."

Victoria shook her head. That didn't make sense. "How could she have flown under our radar like that?" The Colby Agency research department employed the very top in their fields. They weren't prone to mistakes.

"She faked everything. Her name isn't even Hanson. It's Jordan. She borrowed someone else's identity, all the way down to the fingerprints."

"So I have to assume that Miss Jordan has some vendetta against either Angel, who is dead, or Sloan, who won't appreciate his seclusion being interrupted," Victoria considered. She would have to call Sloan immediately to warn him of the breach.

"It gets worse."

A new finger of tension prodded Victoria's spine. "Go on."

"According to Gabrielle Jordan's birth certificate, her father was Gabriel DiCassi."

Angel.

Ice slid through Victoria's veins.

"Victoria—" Nicole leaned forward "—we may be looking at a long-awaited case of vengeance here."

"Find her," Victoria ordered. "I want A.J. on her tail now."

"Let me take care of this," Nicole insisted. "I'm the one who recruited her. I can find her."

Victoria moved her head side to side. "The decision to hire Gabrielle was made by committee. End of discussion. A. J. Braddock will take this one. You'll have your hands full with securing our systems more fully." Victoria reached for the phone. "You bring A.J. up to speed and I'll warn Sloan."

Nicole looked as if she might argue the point, but she obeyed Victoria's order.

Victoria held on to the receiver a moment before she entered the number she knew by heart. Whatever Gabrielle was up to…she didn't have all the facts. And, if vengeance was on her mind, she had no idea who she was dealing with.

Trevor Sloan didn't play games…he played for keeps.

The last person who threatened his family had paid the ultimate price.

* * * * *

Look for RAW TALENT,
the next installment in the
COLBY AGENCY: NEW RECRUITS
miniseries, coming next month
from Debra Webb and Harlequin Intrigue.

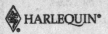

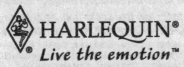

If you enjoyed what you just read,
then we've got an offer you can't resist!

Take 2 bestselling
love stories FREE!

Plus get a FREE surprise gift!

BITS AND PIECES

At first glance, everything appeared normal. The two familiar motorcycle helmets—one black and one white—were in their accustomed places atop the filing cabinet. Beside it, Kenny sprawled in one of the chairs.

Sprawled . . . his jaw sagged, his eyes glazed. Mouth open, he stared at her unseeingly.

"But what—?" Tamsin sidestepped him, staring at a crimson rivulet, leaking from beneath the black crash helmet. Something pale and white as the underbelly of a fish swam behind its smoke visor.

"No . . ." Tamsin whispered. "No!" She forced herself to look again—more closely—at the black crash helmet.

From inside it, two pale lifeless eyes stared back at her. For the first and only time in her life, Tamsin heard herself screaming.

Bantam Crime Line Books offer the finest in classic and
modern British murder mysteries
Ask your bookseller for the books you have missed

Agatha Christie

DEATH ON THE NILE
A HOLIDAY FOR MURDER
THE MOUSETRAP AND
  OTHER PLAYS
THE MYSTERIOUS AFFAIR
  AT STYLES
POIROT INVESTIGATES
POSTERN OF FATE
THE SECRET ADVERSARY
THE SEVEN DIALS MYSTERY
SLEEPING MURDER

Dorothy Simpson

LAST SEEN ALIVE
THE NIGHT SHE DIED
PUPPET FOR A CORPSE
SIX FEET UNDER
CLOSE HER EYES
ELEMENT OF DOUBT
DEAD ON ARRIVAL

Elizabeth George

A GREAT DELIVERANCE
PAYMENT IN BLOOD

Colin Dexter

LAST BUS TO WOODSTOCK
THE RIDDLE OF THE THIRD
  MILE
THE SILENT WORLD OF
  NICHOLAS QUINN
SERVICE OF ALL THE DEAD
THE DEAD OF JERICHO
THE SECRET OF ANNEXE 3
LAST SEEN WEARING

Michael Dibdin

RATKING

Liza Cody

HEAD CASE

John Greenwood

THE MIND OF MR. MOSLEY
THE MISSING MR. MOSLEY
MOSLEY BY MOONLIGHT
MURDER, MR. MOSLEY
MISTS OVER MOSLEY
WHAT, ME, MR. MOSLEY?

Ruth Rendell

A DARK-ADAPTED EYE
  (writing as Barbara Vine)
A FATAL INVERSION
  (writing as Barbara Vine)

Marian Babson

DEATH IN FASHION
REEL MURDER
MURDER, MURDER
  LITTLE STAR
MURDER ON A MYSTERY
  TOUR
MURDER SAILS AT MIDNIGHT

Dorothy Cannell

THE WIDOWS CLUB
DOWN THE GARDEN PATH
coming soon: MUM'S THE
  WORD

Antonia Fraser

JEMIMA SHORE'S FIRST CASE
YOUR ROYAL HOSTAGE
OXFORD BLOOD
A SPLASH OF RED
QUIET AS A NUN
coming soon:
COOL REPENTANCE
THE WILD ISLAND

DEATH IN FASHION

Marian Babson

BANTAM BOOKS
NEW YORK · TORONTO · LONDON · SYDNEY · AUCKLAND

This edition contains the complete text
of the original hardcover edition.
NOT ONE WORD HAS BEEN OMITTED.

DEATH IN FASHION
A Bantam Book / published by arrangement with
Walker & Company

PRINTING HISTORY
Walker edition published April 1986
Bantam edition / December 1987
2 printings through February 1990

ISBN 0-553-18507-1

Published simultaneously in the United States and Canada

PRINTED IN THE UNITED STATES OF AMERICA

O   11 10 9 8 7 6 5 4 3 2

DEATH IN FASHION

Chapter 1

"Hell!" said the Duchess. "Those bastards have delivered the wrong flowers!" She pushed the tinted aviator glasses to the top of her head and narrowed her astonishing violet eyes to check the colours again. She shuddered in agony.

"Kenny, love—" Her gaze swept to the teenage despatch rider who was perched on a frail gold-painted bamboo chair, his white helmet on the filing cabinet beside him. "Kenny, love—take these wretched weeds back to those bleeding imbeciles and tell them we're putting on a fashion show—not a frigging funeral!"

"Yeth, your Grathe," Kenny said. Humiliatingly, he could feel himself going scarlet as he realized that his lisp had slipped out of control again. And he was lying, too, because he was going to do no such thing. Well, not in *those* words. And, to look at her, you'd think butter wouldn't melt in her mouth. You'd never dream she'd even *heard* language like that. It just went to show . . .

"Come along, Kenny, don't stand there dreaming. Skates on! Finger out! We haven't got all day, you know."

"Yessss, your Grayssss." It hadn't come out right this time either. The sibilants whistled through the reception area.

"Stop hissing at me—" the violet eyes flashed fire—"and get your bike!"

"Right!" With a firm decisive movement, Kenny swept the helmet from the top of the white-painted flower-besprigged filing cabinet and buckled it on.

"God!" Medora, Duchess of Farthingale shuddered. "You look like something from outer space in that thing! You all do. Where's Nikko?"

1

"He's picking up some leather supplies at Wagon Train," answered Tamsin, whose Executive Assistant duties included acting as despatcher, coordinator, general dogsbody and den mother. "He ought to be back in about twenty minutes."

"That's what I was afraid of," the Duchess sighed. "It's up to you, Kenny." She hung the floral wreath on one arm and thrust the huge spray into the other. "Come back with the goods!"

"Right!" He sketched a salute, despite his encumbrances. This was more like it. *It's up to you, Kenny. Come back with the goods!* That was something to tell Mum when she asked tonight, as she always did, "What did Her Grace have to say to you today, Kenny?"

Two whole—flattering—sentences that didn't need censoring. It was the best day he'd had since he started this job.

With a modified swagger, a close imitation of Nikko's—and about the only thing Nikko did he'd ever want to imitate—Kenny stalked through the outer waiting-room, ignoring the giggles and remarks of the waiting models. Just because he looked like a walking floral display. What did they know? Look at them!

A pack of drabs! All their phoney glamour secreted in the multi-tiered make-up boxes they carried. Just looking at those naked, curiously raw faces was enough to turn a man's stomach. Just think of all the blokes staring at their painted faces in magazines and fancying them. Little did they know!

Go home with one of them and it would be like the old Music Hall joke about the bridegroom who watched his bride remove her make-up, her wig, her teeth and her glass eye and place them in the bureau drawer. When asked if he wasn't coming to bed, he replied, "I'm coming as soon as I can decide whether I should sleep in the bed or the bureau drawer!"

The lordly sneer carried him through the anteroom, down the stairs and into the street. The high-pitched giggles faded away, the mocking faces receded.

Not Sunny, of course. She wasn't like that. She

looked at you when she was talking to you and she saw *you*. Not just a mirror to reflect herself—rather, her own image of herself.

Sunny was real—and she admitted the reality of everyone she talked with. She was going to be a top model—and soon. The goodness of her shone out of her photographs. It wouldn't be long before the public recognized it and paid tribute to it.

There was nothing he wouldn't do for her. Him— and a million other red-blooded males.

Kenny stamped on the starter and, *vroom-vroom*, his motorcycle roared into life. If only there was something he *could* do for her . . .

Say . . . say she was crossing a street one day. In a hurry, not noticing the lights had changed against her, just as some berk in a sports car jumped the light. She could see the car hurtling toward her . . . and she froze. Not that it would make any difference. There was no way she could move fast enough to escape. Nothing could save her now.

Nothing? . . . *Vroom-vroom* . . . Kenny had seen the danger. Fearlessly, against all the odds, he raced his motor, urging his trusty mount forward at top speed—a speed he had never attained before—threading the needle through the lines of traffic, the racing automobiles.

Vroom-vroom . . . he bore down upon her, just a split-second ahead of the rampaging sports car with its drunken driver, and swept her up—one-armed—across his handlebars while, with a final burst of speed, they zoomed to safety!

"Oh, Kenny, Kenny . . ." Later, she reposed in his arms, still trembling at her narrow escape. "Oh, Kenny, you saved my life! I'm still alive—thanks to you. Oh, Kenny, how can I ever thank you?"

"Just keep on living," he answered nobly. "Saving your precious life was the best day's work I ever did—the best I ever will do. Your beautiful smile is the only reward I shall ever seek."

"Oh, Kenny," she sighed. Her slender white hands reached up to stroke his face. "Kenny, I was lost—but you have given my life back to me. I can never repay you. There is no gift great enough for me to vouchsafe you!"

"I ask nothing!" He captured her hands, kissed her dainty fingertips. "The fact that you are here to grace this world for years to come is sufficient reward for me."

"Oh, Kenny, Kenny . . ." She pulled her hands free and caressed his face wildly, passionately. "Kenny, have you ever thought about growing a moustache?"

Chapter 2

Press Release:

DECEMO DESIGNERS
LONDON FASHION WEEK
Arrivederci Roma . . . farewell Florence . . . even Paris is passé.

 The brightest, the greatest, the best designers in the world are all here in London! And the eyes—and the pocketbooks!—of the world are assembling here now for the legendary London Fashion Week. Not since the Swinging Sixties have our own homegrown designers ridden the crest of such a wave of international enthusiasm.

 New York looks to us for inspiration. Seventh Avenue waits with bated breath—

"Oh hell!" The Duchess hurled down her pen. "I can't pour out any more of this crap! Take over, Tamsin. Just puke it up along those lines. You know what these bastards expect."

"Sure." Tamsin rolled a fresh sheet of paper into her typewriter. Wincing only slightly, she transferred the Duchess's purple prose to the top of the page and carried on. She'd learned to shlock it up with the best—or worst—of them.

> Brightest star in the new firmament is the brilliant Decemo, of Decemo Designers, whose revolutionary concept is: Total Apparel—Total Appeal!
> From hat to shoes, Decemo dresses you with the flair and imagination that has made him a byword in—

Even Tamsin was stopped by that one. She couldn't really, in a Press Release paid for by her employer, specify the circles in which he was a byword—or what that word was.

Chapter 3

"The way *I* see it—" the high dominating voice overrode the other piercing voice—"a hat would *kill* this dress—simply *kill* it! It's *pour le sport*, after all."

"But we agreed hats were to be the major theme this season." Mad Hattie, the Hatter, was true to her name. Madder than ever, she was going down fighting.

"A major theme, dear. Not *the* major theme." Decemo adjusted the drape of the garment on the docile model who was standing in frozen boredom, having heard it all before and expecting nothing better than to hear it all again.

"That wasn't what you told me when I signed that contract!" Hattie's spiked hair bristled with fury. "If I'd known—"

"Hush, dear. Dirty linen—"

"That's not all that's dirty around here!"

"All right, Reba—" Decemo gave the model a dismissive slap on the flank, rather as one would send a horse back to the stable after dismounting. "Run along and tell Mme. Arlette to tack down those tucks and press them, then let me have another look at it."

Reba glided from the room

"A turban—" Hattie pressed her claim. "A small turban would be the *making* of that sports dress."

"Too, too Forties, dear. I know we're into nostalgia, but where will it all end? If I let you get away with that, the next step will be pineapples, bananas, and the whole Carmen Miranda fruitbowl on the turban. I'm only thinking of your own good, dear. Your reputation—such as it is."

"My reputation is a hell of a lot better than yours!"

"Temper, temper, dear. You'd better get yourself under control before the American buyers arrive. They expect stiff upper lips over here. This isn't Paris, you know."

"I've had an offer from Paris," Hattie said abruptly.

"Haven't we all? But you? Poor dears, they've lost all sense of direction. They're getting desperate. Just remember which side of the Channel your bread is buttered on—not to mention your contract."

"As soon as these showings end, I'm going to get the best damned lawyer in town and go over that contract with a fine-tooth comb—"

"It won't do you any good, dear. That contract was drawn up by the *worst* lawyer in town—and it's watertight."

The intercom buzzer sounded and Decemo flipped the switch. "Yes, Tamsin?"

"Nikko is back. Do you want the leather accessories now?"

"What kept him? I've been waiting for *hours*. Have him bring them in—and then send Reba back."

"I hope he's brought a couple of skins," Hattie said. "I want to try some leather hats—"

Reba and Nikko arrived simultaneously. Nikko was carrying two large boxes.

"Over there, dear. Then take the garment bag on

the back of the door and get it over to the *Daily Record*. They're doing a feature for Fashion Week—last bloody minute, of course. It always is. Sunny is there already, waiting—"

"*I* could have done that," Reba said suddenly.

"Done what?" Decemo looked at her blankly.

"Modelled that feature. You always send Sunny out on these assignments. You never give me a chance."

"Oh no, not that!" Decemo sighed theatrically. "Not insurrection in the ranks! I've told you before, dear. Sunny is building up into a *name*. We'll get more publicity with her as lead model—"

"*I* could be a name," Reba said stubbornly, "if you'd use me for the publicity instead of her. I'd never have signed that contract if I'd realized 'in-house model' meant I'd never get out of the house. Sunny was lucky— Jake wouldn't let you have an exclusive on her."

"Anything else?" Nikko paused in the doorway, garment bag over his arm.

"Yes. Wait at the *Daily Record* until they've finished the photo session and bring that dress straight back. Don't let them hang on to it. We need it for the showing this afternoon. They promised me they'd only keep it about an hour."

"Right." Nikko opened the door and turned to leave.

"And stop at the butcher's on the way back," Decemo ordered. "I want a nice plump capon. I'm doing Poulet Decemo for the dinner party."

Chapter 4

"Bloody decimated chicken again," Nikko complained, passing Tamsin's desk.

"Tough," Tamsin commiserated mechanically.

"Probably that, too!" The door slammed behind him and Nikko was gone.

"Tamsin, have you finished that bloody copy yet?" The Duchess whirled through *en route* to the studio from the showroom. "We need a hundred photocopied for this afternoon. And send Kenny for sandwiches—I'm bloody starving!"

"As soon as he gets back from the florist's. Good morning—" Tamsin picked up the telephone on the first ring. "Decemo Designers . . . Oh, good morning, Ms Warner—?" She raised a questioning eyebrow to the Duchess.

"Christ, no!" the Duchess snapped and disappeared.

"I'm sorry, Ms Warner, she isn't here just now, but you'll see her at the Opening. This afternoon at three. You got your ticket? Good . . . good . . . yes, I'll look forward to meeting you, too." Tamsin replaced the receiver, still smiling mechanically.

"All right, Tamsin—" The Duchess reappeared briefly in the doorway. "Herd the cows in!"

Correctly interpreting this, Tamsin opened the door of the ante-room and surveyed the assembled models. "Would you come this way, please?" She led them into the studio which, for this week, would double as the dressing-room. Drawing-boards and worktables had been shoved back against the walls. The room was currently dominated by the free-standing racks crowded with the garments to be shown.

The quartet of models twittered into the room, staring around avidly, but their predatory eyes were foiled by the shrouded racks. White cotton sheeting hid the garments completely so that there was no chance of anyone spying out preferred colours or styles and laying claim to them. The twittering changed to a mutter of discontent. Stealthy hands stretched out to twitch at the concealing cloth.

"All right, girls!" the Duchess ordered briskly. "This is a dress rehearsal. We have forty-two complete outfits to be shown. That means you each have seven and you'll have to move at top speed back here to make your changes in the time allowed and keep the show moving smoothly. Now, will you each stand by the appropriate rack as I call your name—" She consulted a list in her hand.

"Gloria . . . Rack One. Jackie . . . Rack Two. Suzanne . . . Rack Three, and Carla . . . Rack Four. Now, if you'll just remove the protective covering, we'll have a dry run at getting you in and out of the outfits quickly. Lillian will act as dresser for Gloria and Jackie; Hattie will dress Suzanne and Carla . . ."

"What about the other two racks?" Gloria eyed them jealously. "The A and B racks?"

"Our own house models have those. Sunny will be modeling Rack A and Reba will show Rack B. Mme. Arlette will dress them."

"EEeekkk!" It was a scream of anguish from Carla. She had unveiled her rack and was staring in horror at one of the dresses revealed. "I can't wear that poison green colour! I can't! I look terrible in it!"

Tamsin groaned under her breath. The narration for the fashion parade had already been written and the pacing of the models as carefully calculated as a countdown to a rocket launch. They couldn't change any of it now.

"I can't . . ." Carla wailed. "Besides, green is unlucky. Everyone knows that."

A dangerous gleam in the Duchess's eyes gave warning of how unlucky green was really going to be if Carla kept on making a fuss, but she said mildly. "Oh, that *is* a shame. Look, we haven't time to do anything about it now. Just try it on for the rehearsal and we'll sort something out later."

"Well . . ." Sulkily, Carla allowed herself to be persuaded. "Only because we're pressed for time—but I don't like it!"

Tamsin admired the finesse with which they both avoided the true reason Carla had no choice but to capitulate: she was the Size 20 model chosen to display their

new Let Them Eat Cake range and no other dresses
would fit her. Nothing else could possibly be sorted out
in time—and they both knew it.

"Don't touch that rack!" the Duchess snapped as
Gloria, taking advantage of Carla's tantrum, tried to peek
beneath the sheet concealing Rack A.

"I was only looking," Gloria pouted.

"Well, don't! It's nothing to do with you! Lillian, get
her into her first outfit—and see that she minds her own
business!"

Mme. Arlette cleared her throat warningly and met
Tamsin's eyes. The Duchess's good behaviour was beginning to crack and it could not be allowed to. If the models walked out in a fury, it was too late to replace them.
The Duchess could not talk to the hired help the way she
talked to the permanent employees.

"Oh, this will look lovely on you, with your colour-
ing." Quickly Lillian slid the first dress off the hanger
and shook it enticingly before Gloria's eyes. "You're
going to be a hard act to follow in *this* little number—if I
do say so myself."

"Mmm . . ." Gloria slid an appraising eye over the
rest of the rack before expertly shucking off her street-
wear and reaching for the dress. "You designed this, did
you?"

"I never said that?" Lillian paled and involuntarily
looked over her shoulder guiltily.

"You didn't have to. Do you think we don't know?"
Casually Gloria stepped into the dress. "These big designers are all the same. They catch you babies as you
graduate from design schools, sign you up for coolie
wages and pick your brains until your contract runs out.
Or until you get smart and walk out on them—which-
ever comes first. Don't just stand there—zip me up, will
you?"

"My friend—" Obediently, Lillian zipped up the
dress. "She went to work for Zoom Lens and her salary is
even worse than mine."

"Not by much, I'll bet." Gloria stepped over to the
full-length looking-glass and surveyed herself critically.

"So far, so good. Hurry up with the rest of it, will you?"

"Yes, here—" Lillian shook leather sandals and a body purse out of one box, then scrabbled in another for the matching hat.

"*Not* like that!" Hattie screamed in anguish. Abandoning Carla, she dashed over, snatched the hat off Gloria's head and replaced it at a rakish tilt. "*That's* the way to wear it!"

"You've ruined my hair-do!" Gloria shrieked, recoiling.

"Come back here and finish these buttons!" Carla snapped at Hattie. "I can't possibly reach them."

"Your Grace—" The temporary receptionist (normally it was part of Tamsin's job) appeared in the doorway, looking distraught. "The flowers are here. *The proper* flowers."

"Tamsin, see to them," the Duchess ordered.

Gratefully, Tamsin smiled and made her escape from the confusion, which was inevitably destined to get worse. This was her second Collection, so she had had some idea of what to expect. She had warned her flatmates that she would be unavailable for any socializing, put her boyfriends on Hold, and reminded her parents that she loved them but was going to be lost to them for the next fortnight or so.

"And don't forget to send Kenny for—those items!" the Duchess called after her.

Tamsin nodded mutely. She had learned that one did not bandy words like "sandwiches" around in front of models with impunity. At worst, they tended to insist on their share—after which they did not fit their garments so perfectly. At best, it led to exhaustive monologues on the subject of their current diets. The less they had their attention drawn to food, the better.

Kenny was nowhere in sight, but the reception area was ablaze with bright fragrant blossoms.

"That's better," Tamsin said.

"Here we are—" A cheerful elderly woman bustled in carrying a trough of tulips and ferns. "That's the last one. Where do you want it all?"

"In the showroom—" Tamsin opened the door. "A basket at each side of the stage, the spray at the end of the catwalk, the rest in the corners. Here, I'll help—" She caught up one of the baskets.

"It does seem strange to be bringing flowers *to* Covent Garden." The woman followed in her wake, carrying the distinctive spray destined to mark the end of the catwalk for those models who would not wear glasses and had lost their contact lenses.

"Well, *that's* more like it!" The Duchess parted the stage curtains and advanced down the catwalk. "What on earth possessed you to send over those ghastly weeds?"

"Weeds?" The florist drew herself up. "We haven't sent anything over. I've brought them myself. I've been at Nine Elms since dawn, matching the flowers to those swatches you gave me. If you've had any weeds, you didn't get them from us!"

They glared at each other. The Duchess opened her mouth to speak and Tamsin trembled at what might come out. The florist looked quite capable of snatching up her flowers and departing in a huff, leaving them with a bare showroom.

"Tamsin! Tamsin!" A voice called above the thunder of footsteps rushing up the stairs. Kenny burst into the room, a wreath still hung over one arm. Tamsin wondered if he had ridden through the traffic like that, with the spray of flowers lashed to his despatch box. "Tamsin, they won't—" He looked up, saw the Duchess and bobbed his head, nearly his knee. "Oh, I'm sorry. I didn't know you were in here your Grace."

"For God's sake, stop curtseying!" The Duchess's venom was fortunately diverted to Kenny, where it could do no harm.

"Sorry, your Graysss."

"And stop—" She noticed the wreath for the first time. "What are you doing with that monstrosity?"

"They won't take it back, your—I mean, they said it's nothing to do with them. They never saw it before."

"Certainly not," the florist said indignantly. "That thing didn't come from us. We'd never have done something like that for a fashion show. Why, that's a funeral wreath."

"Funeral—!" The Duchess took a deep breath and blistered the air briefly.

"Did you call?" Mme. Arlette peeked through the curtains.

"No—get back! Forget it!"

"We are ready to commence. Do you wish to read out the commentary as the models appear?"

"No—not yet! Wait a minute—" The Duchess looked around frantically as the curtains parted. "Drop that!" she snarled at Kenny. "If the girls see it, there'll be merry hell to pay! This is someone's rotten joke to upset us."

"Oooh . . ." Obediently Kenny let the wreath fall to the floor. "Who'd do a thing like that?"

"We'll find out later," the Duchess promised grimly. "Meanwhile—" She lifted the skirting concealing the catwalk supports and kicked at the wreath. "Get that under here until the rehearsal is over—"

"We have here—" Mme. Arlette announced— "Costume Number One . . ."

Reba posed between the parted curtains, twirled, and began a slow advance toward them.

"Tamsin—" the Duchess dropped the skirting. "Smuggle that away afterwards—and get rid of it. Don't let anyone see you. If you get caught, I'll have your guts for garters!"

"Are we going to have music for the rehearsal?" Reba stopped midway and looked down at them.

"Go back! Go back!" the Duchess snapped. "We're not ready for you yet. We—" she improvised hastily— "we haven't finished the seating yet."

Chapter 5

"It's beautiful, all right," Sunny confided, swaying under the massed weight of the thousands of bugle beads handsewn on to the glittering creation, "but I wouldn't like to wear it for very long." She paused, considering. "I wouldn't like to try sitting down in it, either," she added.

"Any woman who can afford to buy that dress deserves a few little problems the rest of us don't have." The photographer and his assistant were both in jeans.

"It *is* a bit over the top." The Fashion Editor was dressed in a model Sunny recognized as being from Forbidden Fruit's Autumn Show. Sold at a knockdown price, no doubt, to keep the goodwill of the *Daily Record*. "It's aimed at the American market, of course."

"I think there's something for everyone this season." Sunny spoke cautiously; she had already learned the dangers of saying anything too quotable in front of the Press. Even remarks that were quite innocent in themselves could be twisted alarmingly to produce an unintended effect. Later apologies and disclaimers were never quite convincing—everybody always claimed to have been misquoted.

"Bend the knee a little more, head higher . . . and don't forget to smile. We don't want to make it look like wearing the dress is a *chore*, do we?"

Sunny knew better than to rise to that one. She had probably said too much as it was. She shouldn't have mentioned how heavy the dress was. Or the bit about sitting down.

"The dress is called Indigo Charisma," she said innocently. That ought to be safe enough. She'd forgotten momentarily just where she was. There were so many outside assignments these days; Jake seemed to be lining up one after another. She was spending all her time rushing from one photo session to the next. She was getting overtired, but what could you do? As Jake said, you had to ride the crest of the wave when it was rolling your way.

And Jake was right; the wave had started to roll when she met him. She could have blushed like Kenny to think about how dumb she had been when she was just starting out. She was lucky—so lucky—that she had met Jake at that media party and that he had thought her worth taking in hand, that he had fallen in love with her. Not many girls—especially not many models—had that kind of luck. No wonder Reba was mad with jealousy.

Just look at the way he had renegotiated that stupid contract she had signed with Decemo before she knew any better. Jake had fixed it so that she could now do outside work. Of course, it still wasn't good enough to satisfy Jake but, as he had said, they had both still been learning. Soon Jake was going to approach Decemo again and get even better terms. Then Reba really would go wild.

So would the other girls. Sunny knew that jealousy was really at the bottom of some of the remarks they made about Jake being an "operator". Naturally, he was a bit of a one, as he himself said, being a Jack-of-all Media-Trades gave him a lot of contacts—and advantages. Now that he was free-lancing, he could devote more time to managing her career, as well as his own.

Maybe too much time at the moment. When he got back from the States—He should be back now. She pushed the thought away. When he got back, perhaps she could suggest they take a holiday. The West Indies, perhaps, where they could lie on a beach and just look at the rolling waves instead of trying to ride them. All this riding was really quite exhausting.

Still, it was good to know that she was going to be "at home" for the next solid week. Working nowhere else than Decemo Designers would make a nice restful change. There was only one possible fly in the ointment. More of a snake than a fly, actually . . .

She bent her knee, lifted her head and parted her lips in the radiant ecstatic smile able to convince millions of consumers that such ecstasy could be theirs—if only they would buy the advertised product.

"Very nice, darlin'," the snake spoke. "But hurry it up, can't you? His nibs will have kittens if I don't get that dress back inside the hour."

"Oh God!" The photographer straightened in exasperation. "You made her jump. That shot's ruined."

"Sorry," Sunny apologized. "Let's try it again."

"We'll have to." He dropped back to his crouch, darting a poisonous glance at Nikko. "And you—do you think you could mind your own business this time?"

"Keeping his nibs happy *is* my business." Nikko spoke with quiet menace. "He wants that dress inside an hour and he'll have it inside an hour—if I have to tear it off her back while you're still poncing around with your lights and camera angles."

He'd enjoy that. Sunny repressed a shudder. Nikko gave her the creeps—the absolute *creeps*. Those beady little eyes always watching her, so unblinking they might be lidless, like a snake's. Even when he was nowhere in sight, she could always tell when he had arrived and was studying her from some dark corner; she could *feel* his gaze slithering over her. This time, she did shudder.

"Oh, is that so?" the photographer straightened up again, meeting Nikko's challenge. "We'll see about that. Get me the Great Decemo!" he snapped to his assistant.

She scurried to the telephone and dialled wildly while Nikko and the photographer engaged in a staring match.

Sunny tried not to look at either of them. No good was going to come of this clash of male egos. It never did. Whatever the outcome, someone was bound to lose— and would for ever bear a grudge against anyone who had witnessed his loss of face.

"I'd like—" she began, but stopped abruptly, realizing her predicament. She could not waltz off to the loo in this little creation. No one would believe her. It had

taken two people to shoehorn her into it—it might take
three to prise her out. She was firmly encased in the
shimmering spectacular gown which was assuming all
the endearing qualities of a strait-jacket. She was trapped.

Sunny closed her eyes and tried to pretend that she
had drifted off into a doze. Some models could sleep
standing up; she had watched and envied them. Reba
was able to go off into a trance for hours while Decemo
fussed about, draping and redraping fabric around her
motionless body.

She couldn't close her ears, though.

"*You* may fancy the rough trade, mate," the photographer was snarling into the phone. "But they cut no ice
with me. So call off your bully-boy or I'll see that you
never get a mention in this paper again!"

"Really, his behaviour was *quite* uncalled for." The
Fashion Editor took the phone and cooed into it severely. "The session was going very well. It might possibly run over by half an hour or so—but surely it can't
mean that much to you. If it does, of course, I'll be quite
happy to cancel the feature entirely. The Complex have
been longing to get some publicity from us. I can quite
easily substitute something from their Collection—" She
paused and smiled.

"He wants to speak to you—" She held out the receiver to Nikko.

Throwing her a look of blistering hatred, Nikko took
the phone. He listened silently, obviously unwilling to
give them the satisfaction of hearing any explanation or
apologies from him, but the tenor of the squeaks and
shrieks issuing from the other end of the line was un-
mistakable and the tips of his ears grew red.

Finally he slammed down the receiver in a fury.

"And you can wait downstairs." The photographer
rubbed salt in the wound. "We'll send the dress down
when we've finished with it."

Just before he slammed the door, Nikko turned and
Sunny caught the full force of the promise of vengeance
in his eyes.

* * *

"It's shaping up . . ." The Duchess ran an expert eye over the rows of gilt bamboo chairs set out on either side of the catwalk. "We'll seat Irene Warner there, Mitzi Kayce there—and the reporter from *Women's Wear Daily* between them. It's a rotten trick to play on the poor bitch, but it may stop them from killing each other."

"Why don't you just seat them on opposite sides of the catwalk?" Tamsin asked.

"Don't be silly. They'd be so busy trying to see what the other was noting down that they wouldn't pay any attention to the show."

"I suppose we couldn't have invited them on different days?"

"We could have. We also could weight our entire collection with paving stones and drop it off Tower Bridge into the Thames."

"Oh!"

"That's right." The Duchess nodded. "They're that important—and that difficult. Each one owns a chain of specialty shops which dominates her area. Warner has an East Coast chain, Kayce has a West Coast chain. They each have plans to move into the other's territory. Once a year, they carry their private war to Europe and battle over the Collections. As though we didn't have enough troubles of our own, we have to spend extra time kowtowing to them and trying to make sure we don't favour one over the other—but that they each get special treatment."

"I see." Although it was Tamsin's second Collection, she was beginning to realize how fortunate she had been that the rival buyers had not been at the first one. "That's why they get seats in the front row." Only the first three rows were reserved for the most influential buyers, journalists and private customers, everyone else had to scramble for the unreserved seats.

"That—" the Duchess smiled grimly—"is one of the reasons. The other is that neither of the distinguished ladies is above doing a few quick sketches and taking them to a tame manufacturer in the States to be copied.

This way, we get to keep an eye on them while they're keeping an eye on each other."

"Isn't that illegal?"

"Also immoral, and very fattening—to their purses. I wouldn't go so far as to call the little bitches out-and-out pirates, but I'd be the last to deny that they'd be quite at home with black eye-patches and parrots on their shoulders."

"There's so much to worry about." Tamsin frowned. "To think I was once so unworldly that I thought all we had to do was get the Collection together, show it and start taking orders for it. I never dreamed there could be so many other problems."

"You're young yet." The Duchess patted her on the head. "But don't worry, I guarantee you'll age about thirty years over the next week. The worst is yet to come." She glanced at her watch.

"We have three hours to lift-off." The Duchess surveyed the room critically. "Flowers . . . okay. Music tapes . . . in place and ready for switch-on. Stage curtains . . . working. Chairs . . . all set out. I think everything is ready here. Let's start the rehearsal." She took out a stop watch, adjusted it and raised her voice.

"Is everyone set back there?"

"*We've* been ready for ages," an aggrieved voice called from behind the curtains. "But Sunny isn't here yet."

"Never mind, we'll start without her and reckon in the timings for her appearances. Tamsin—"

Tamsin switched on the tape and the music swirled through the showroom, beginning softly, then rising in a rapid crescendo. The curtains parted and Reba glided on to the stage. She paused for maximum effect, then advanced down the catwalk.

Cocking a snook at tradition, the show was beginning with the wedding dress, a promise that the Decemo Collection would begin where other, lesser, collections left off.

Reba reached the end of the catwalk and, with a kick-turn that was sure to bring a round of applause

("Only the English can really handle a train—it's in their blood or something") she retraced her languid steps to hesitate once again between the parted curtains.

Casually, almost absently, she ran her hands down her ribcage from bust to waist, unobtrusively detaching Velcro fastenings to free her from the long skirt and train and stand revealed in a day-length hemline that turned the wedding dress into a stunning cocktail dress that could be worn anywhere—as the Duchess's commentary observed.

Jauntily then, to the rhythm of unheard applause, Reba traversed the catwalk once again, paused to toss her bridal bouquet atop the crumpled mound of white chiffon and lace, and exited through the shimmering curtains.

"And now—" The Duchess allowed a couple of beats to pass before taking up the commentary again. "Decemo introduces his 'Let Them Eat Cake' range for the luscious and lovely larger lady—"

Carla materialized in the gap between the curtains, her arms outspread, posing with a new authority and assurance. It had obviously dawned upon her that she had a better role to play in this showing than she usually had.

"Carla . . . wrapped in magnolia magic . . ." Smoothly the Duchess uttered words she had vowed would choke her, as Carla paraded down the catwalk, hips swinging to emphasize the layered-petal effect of the short skirt. Regaining the stage, she affected surprise at noticing the froth of discarded long skirt and train. With a wink of pure mischief to the audience, she swept it up around her waist and fastened it to the concealed Velcro pads beneath her top tier of petals.

She posed for a moment while someone behind the curtain hastily arranged the veil on her head and thrust the bride's bouquet into her hands, then moved forward, traversing the catwalk again as the Luscious Lovely Bride.

"Marvellous Carla," the Duchess called encouragingly. "You'll get a great round of applause on that. Now, don't forget—when you throw the bride's bouquet, pitch it right down front here. For the rest of the show-ings, it won't matter where you toss it, but this afternoon we'll let Mitzi and Irene fight over it. I suppose—" she turned to Tamsin—"we have a standing order for two bouquets a day for the rest of the week?"

"They'll be delivered fresh every morning," Tamsin assured her. "The florist promised faithfully and she won't forget—it's a quite a big order."

"And expensive," the Duchess grumbled. "Still, it will be good PR. The old tarts adore getting something for nothing—and the more unlikely, the better. A bridal bouquet is just the ticket. It will have them scrambling in the aisles. Pity we can't throw in the man, as well. That would really make our name."

"But is that the sort of name we want, dear?" Decemo appeared on stage. "We're supposed to be ped-dling *fashion*."

"Quiet!" The Duchess narrowed her eyes at him. "Or I might ask Nikko if he'd oblige."

"He might agree," Decemo smirked, "but he'd never be able to deliver."

"I wouldn't bet on that," the Duchess muttered. "That Hire Boy would plug a pig if the price was right."

"*What?* What was that?" Decemo advanced to the edge of the stage and glared down threateningly.

"You heard," the Duchess said. "Now let's stop ars-ing around and get on with the rehearsal. Time's getting short," Kenny could feel the blush spreading from his neck to his hairline, but it was good to know somebody else had Nikko's number. He couldn't wait to get home and tell Mum. But . . . how could he put it?"

"*I wouldn't trust that there Nikko*—" Yes, that was better. More ladylike. And something Mum had often said herself. She'd be delighted to know the Duchess agreed with her. "*Myself, I wouldn't trust him no farther than I could throw him.*" Yes, that was regal, almost. And it wasn't really lying—it was just saying what the Duch-ess had said, only in nicer words. The gist of it was all there.

"Kenny! What the hell are you skulking in the cor-

ner for?" the Duchess suddenly demanded. Unfairly. He
wasn't in any corner—he was right there in the doorway,
plain to be seen.

"Yes—what are you doing there?" Even more unfairly, Decemo joined the attack. "Where's Nikko?"

"I don't know," Kenny said. "I've only brought the
sandwiches, haven't I? Do you want them in here?"

"Hell, no!" the Duchess snapped. "And don't say
that word out loud. If the models hear, they'll want
some—and they can't afford it. One more lettuce leaf
into any of them and they'll never fit the dresses. Take
them away, like a good boy, and hide them outside until
we're ready for them."

"Yeth, your Grathe." The tips of his ears scorching
again, Kenny turned to go and collided with someone
who had appeared in the doorway behind him.

"*There* you are!" Decemo snapped. "Where have
you been? What took you so long?"

"Yeah . . . uh . . . sorry about that—" Nikko shouldered Kenny aside and moved into the room. "Couldn't
be helped. I'm afraid there's been a bit of an accident."

Chapter 6

"Accident?" Decemo leapt from the stage. "What
sort of accident? You—you're not hurt?"

"Nah, I'm all right."

"If this showing is a success," Decemo promised,
with a sigh of relief, "we'll get you a proper car. You
shouldn't be taking chances on one of those frightful
motorcycles. They're death-traps."

"It wasn't that kind of accident," Nikko said uneasily, as though suspecting Decemo's relief would not
last long. "Nobody came within an ace of touching me.
Too bad about—" He shrugged and held out his arms.

A garment bag lay across them, limp as a recently-dead body. Black blurred tyre marks across it added to the illusion. Another victim of a fatal road accident.

"What's that?" Decemo shrieked. "What's happened?"

"I couldn't help it," Nikko said. "Honest, guv, it wasn't my fault. I was rushing to get it back here to you and it fell off the back of my cycle in Fleet Street. The berk behind me ran right over it before I even knew I'd lost it. Both wheels, before he could stop. You know what the traffic's like down there."

"No! No! Not Indigo Charisma!" Decemo snatched the garment bag from him. In the silence, the others were conscious of faint unsettling noises from the depths of the bag.

"You can't have—Not even *you* would—" Decemo carried the garment bag tenderly to the catwalk and laid it out full length.

"It wasn't *my* fault," Nikko protested. "It was that nerd behind me. He should've stopped as soon as he saw it fall off my despatch box. He was going too fast—no control." Nikko gave Kenny a filthy look and added pointedly, "He was still carrying L-plates."

Ignoring him, Decemo gently worked the zipper open. He seemed to be hitting frequent obstructions. Drawn by the commotion, the others crowded out of the dressing-room and on to the stage where they watched breathlessly. Those on the showroom floor edged nearer—but not too near—dreading the inevitable.

"There—" Decemo reached the end of the zipper and hesitated, as though steeling himself for the final revelation. The long wide tongue of the garment bag lay limp against its contents.

With a deep breath, Decemo grasped the tip of the tongue and flipped it back.

At first glance, everything looked all right. Decemo's hands were shaking visibly as he reached in and lifted out the glittering dress—the pride of his collection.

Slowly it emerged, deceptively intact at first. Then,

as it shook free of the garment bag, there was a casade of glass splinters. They struck the floor and rebounded to cling to shoes, stockings and trouser legs. A shimmering layer of broken bugle beads remained in the bag.

"Ruined! It's ruined!" Decemo held his ravaged creation out at arm's length while they all assessed the damage. The vibration of his voice sent another shower of splinters to the floor. From a swath the width of a tyre mark across both front and back, shards clung to the material only by the thread still holding them.

"It took weeks to sew on those thousands of beads—weeks!" Mme. Arlette slipped from the catwalk to the floor and stooped to pick up the hem of the dress Decemo still held suspended by its shoulder-straps. A fresh cascade of splintered glass tinkled to the floor. She looked as though she might cry.

Kenny blinked in sympathy. He hadn't been working here long, but he was learning. He knew that there was no way that dress could be repaired in time for the Opening. Maybe not at all. Caitlin sometimes seemed to work miracles, but this might be beyond her. Thank heavens it wasn't his machine that it had slipped off of—or that had run over it.

For a brief moment, his sympathy extended even to Nikko. He glanced to him, intending to exchange a brief nod of camaraderie—and froze as he caught the expression on Nikko's face.

Nikko was gloating.

It hadn't been an accident. He had deliberately crushed the fragile dress.

Almost immediately the expression was gone, wiped away and replaced by one of concern. But Kenny had seen it and now he knew the truth of the situation, even if no one else did.

"*You*—" Decemo whirled at Nikko. "You did this deliberately? You *filth!*"

"Naw—it was an accident." Nikko shrugged. "An accident. 'Strewth."

"Don't lie! Don't even speak to me! Look at what you've done! Look at it!" Decemo twitched the dress

from Mme. Arlette's hands and shook it in front of Nikko.
Another glittering shower plunged to the floor. Decemo
took a step forward and glass crunched under his feet.

"It was the berk behind me." Nikko backed away.
"He didn't stop in time. Honest—"

"You don't know the meaning of that word!" Decemo
suddenly gave a mirthless bark of laughter. "There are
plenty of things you don't know. You think you've ruined
the show as well as the dress with your petty little revenge, don't you? Well, you haven't. I don't tell you everything. I'm not finished yet!"

"Yeah? Good for you." Nikko's words were all right,
but his tone was ugly. A dangerous gleam had appeared
in his eyes when Decemo said *"I don't tell you everything."*

"Get out!" Decemo snapped. "I'll deal with you
later!"

"All right, settle down!" the Duchess called out to
the twittering models. "Let's get on with the rehearsal.
We've wasted enough time."

Immediately Sunny heard the news—and there was
no shortage of tellers—she recognized it as Nikko's revenge for having been put in his place at the newspaper
office. A vicious, wanton revenge—the destruction of all
that innocent beauty, just because his pride had been hurt.

He'd had it coming. *Brought it on himself,* as her
Gran would say. It was just too bad that the sort of people
who did that always blamed everyone else for their
downfall.

She shivered. Nikko didn't just blame Decemo for
his humiliation. In some twisted way, he extended the
blame on everyone who had witnessed it. The people at
the newspaper were safe enough; he wouldn't be able to
get at them. But she was here under the same roof with
him for the next week. Trapped and vulnerable. She
would have to be on her guard against all the dirty tricks
he might ever have heard of—or be able to think up on
his own.

Ground glass in the cold cream—that was a classic,

wasn't it? More in the theatre than in a model's dress-
ingroom—they seldom had one all to themselves. She
would be surrounded at all times—and there was safety
in numbers. Just the same . . . there was plenty of splintered glass around here just now.

"Take a deep breath—" Hattie directed briskly—
"and hold it."

"I am holding it," Carla groaned as the zipper struggled up over her too-generous ribcage. "All these designers skimp-cut their material. That's the trouble."

"If you think the designers skimp-cut," Hattie said,
"what do you think about manufacturers?"

"Don't get me started on *them!*" Carla snarled.
"Hanging's too good for them!"

"Nobody hangs any more." Reba had a literal mind.
"Parliament abolished capital punishment decades ago."

"More's the pity—*ouch!* Be careful, can't you?"
Carla glared at Hattie. "Hanging would do some people a
world of good."

"You needn't blame me," Hattie said, "just because
you're bulging out over the zipper. I saw you sneaking
two eclairs with your cup of black coffee."

"Girls! Girls!" Mme. Arlette called them to order.
"It's too late for tantrums. We have five minutes!"

With small shrieks of dismay, they accelerated their
preparations. "Where's my bracelet? . . . My shoes?"
Panicstricken voices shrilled, all talking at once. "Who
took my scarf?"

Outside, beyond the velvet curtains, the music
throbbed hypnotically and other voices could be heard,
raised in greeting as members of the audience hailed
each other across the showroom.

"It's filling up out there," Gloria reported, peeking
between the curtains. "Looks like standing room only."

"Come back here," Lillian ordered. "Your hemline
isn't right yet. You can't go out there like that."

"I wasn't going out," Gloria pouted, returning to
stand quietly while Lillian bent to the errant hem. "I was
only looking."

"That's what they all say," Mme. Arlette pointed out. The ripple of laughter released some of the tension in the room.

"All set back here?" The Duchess appeared behind them, giving rise to several startled screams. Like a general reviewing the troops, she stared at each model in turn, not missing a single wrinkle or loose thread.

"Hell," she sighed. "You'll have to do."

She might have been more gracious about it, Sunny thought. It was strange the way everybody assumed model girls had no feelings. The way some people treated them, it was easy to see that they really did consider the models just animated clothes racks, something to hang the garments on, but otherwise negligible. Probably that sort of treatment was the reason some of the models were given to fits of temperament. If one screamed, others had to acknowledge her presence.

"Kenny—" With the Duchess, at least, you had to admit that she showed no favourtism. She was just as rude to the boys as the girls. "Where the hell are you? Stop skulking in corners and collect all the chairs you can find in here. We need them outside."

"I told you it was standing room only," Gloria said.

"Those vultures in Fleet Street—" The Duchess met Mme. Arlette's raised eyebrows as Kenny snatched away the chair she had been using. "Some of them saw the accident with the dress and spread the word. They're swarming outside—hoping the show's been ruined."

"It has not." Mme. Arlette permitted herself a small tight smile. "In this particular case, we were prepared for . . . contingencies."

"And a damned good thing, too!" The Duchess gave her an answering secret smile.

Sunny wondered if there was any truth in the rumour that the Duches was financing Decemo Designers. A not-so-silent partnership would explain the depth of her involvement, which seemed to go far beyond the usual role of fashion show commentator.

"Still—" Mme. Arlette was talking over her head to

the Duchess, automatically buttoning and smoothing
Sunny's dress—"it is, perhaps, unfortunate that there
were so many witnesses to the . . . accident."

"I wouldn't put it past the little sod to have sent out
a photo-call for it!"

"Yes . . ." Mme. Arlette shrugged. "Most unfortunate. In the past, there have been other *petits amis*, but
never one who has intruded so. It is better when business and pleasure do not mix."

"With any luck," the Duchess said, "we'll soon have
seen the last of this one."

"Surely, in this life, one makes one's own luck—?"

"Give or take a consonant, I couldn't agree more."
Again their eyes met in mutual understanding. "We'll
have to see what we can do about it. I don't think Decemo is quite competent to order his own affairs in this
instance."

"He is, possibly, more besotted than is wise—"

Sunny couldn't help it, she sneezed. Both older
women reacted as though a statue had suddenly come to
life. It was unfair. If they chose to hold a conversation
right in front of her, she couldn't help hearing. What was
she supposed to do—stand here with her hands over her
ears?

"All right, Kenny—" The Duchess turned away
abruptly. "Got all the chairs? Set them out along the
wall, then grab a bottle of champagne and start circulating—top everyone up."

Kenny nodded, struggling with too many chairs left
him breathless. Wooden legs bristling in every direction
from under his arms, he moved crabwise toward the side
door.

"Let me—" Sunny moved forward and opened it for
him, glad to get away for a moment.

"Th-th-thank you." Kenny appeared overcome by
this normal courtesy. He had been having a rough time
of it around here lately. He went pink, but beamed.
"Thank you, Thunny."

Oh dear. That sent him pinker than ever. Poor
Kenny.

"That's all right," Sunny said quickly, as though she hadn't noticed. Was a lisp something a person outgrew, like spots? She hoped so. It did bother poor Kenny dreadfully.

The Duchess and Mme. Arlette exchanged a final nod, then the Duchess mounted the steps to the stage and stepped through the curtains.

A momentary hush fell over the auditorium, then a rustle of expectancy. The music hesitated, then changed into the lilting overture. There were several incredulous gasps as some members of the audience recognized the lead-in to the "Wedding March."

The curtains parted to the half-way mark, the music slipped into the familiar beat. Reba stepped forward and the show was on.

It was all going along perfectly. Tamsin recklessly splashed more champagne into every glass in sight. Now and again, she spared a split-second to cock an eye at the catwalk. Primarily, though, her job was to keep a close watch on the audience and make sure they were happy. That wasn't hard.

They were ecstatic. As expected, they had recognized the challenge thrown down by opening with a wedding gown. The expectancy was electric now.

Tamsin made her way along the front row, trying to be unobtrusive as she topped up glasses. She needn't have worried, she might have been invisible. Everyone was watching breathlessly. Carla was starting her first lap on the catwalk now, white-petalled skirt swaying provocatively.

The journalists in mid-row had all set their glasses on the floor and were scribbling frantically in notebooks. As Tamsin bent to fill their glasses, her old talent for reading upside down again stood her in good stead. It had been useful in school, it was invaluable in real life.

"MAJOR DESIGNER MAKES A MAJOR STATE-MENT . . . ????" The question marks evidently did not refer to the heading, but to the fashion editor's query to herself as to whether Decemo could bring it off or whether the rest of the collection would fizzle out after this dazzling start.

Mitzi Kayce nodded a perfunctory acknowledgement as her glass was refilled but did not take her gaze from the catwalk. Irene Warner did not even notice fresh liquid bubbling into her glass. Already small excited marks in some private code were apparent on their programmes.

Carla was stepping into the discarded skirt now, bending backwards for a moment while unseen hands placed the wedding veil on her head. She caught up the wedding bouquet and started for the catwalk again.

As the Duchess had predicted, the wave of applause drowned out any commentary. None was needed.

"TO HELL WITH CALORIES—GLAMOUR OVERCOMES ALL!" Tamsin caught back a smile at the overheated prose, but it was just the sort of response they had hoped for. The show had just started and already there was no doubt that they held the audience in the palms of their hands.

Remembering Carla's instructions about the bouquet, Tamsin hurriedly moved clear of the first row. She didn't want to be caught in the scramble when the bouquet was thrown.

She was just in time. Already Carla had pivoted for the return trip along the catwalk. Tamsin leaned against the wall and decided against a mental bet as to which rapacious lady might snatch the bouquet for herself. They were too evenly matched. It was anybody's guess.

Carla reached the stage, twirled again, raised the bouquet to her face and inhaled deeply, then held it away from her at arm's length. Slowly, tantalizingly, she swung it out towards the audience.

"One . . . Two . . ." Several eager hopefuls in the back rows surged to their feet, hands outstretched.

"Three!" Neatly and economically, Carla dropped the bouquet into the front row, as instructed.

There was instantaneous bedlam. Both buyers dived for it, so did the journalists. The bouquet bounced off too-eager hands and fell to the floor. Their frantic grappling sent it skidding under the skirting of the catwalk.

Dignity forgotten, both buyers scrabbled for it on their hands and knees, as anxious to score a point off the other as to possess the bouquet.

"I've got it! I've got it!" Mitzi screamed.

"No, I've got it!" Irene cried gleefully.

Behind them, the audience laughed and applauded, craning their necks to discern which one really was the victor.

"I've got it!"

"*I've* got it!"

Both still uttering crows of triumph, they backed out from under the catwalk, clinging to their prize.

It was not until they straightened up and looked down that they saw that they were each holding tight to one side of a funeral wreath.

Chapter 7

"*Oooh . . . oooh . . . oooh—*" Mitzi wailed. A purple ribbon, which had been concealed somewhere in the framework of the wreath, shook loose and unrolled, draping across her wrist like an unwanted bracelet, flaunting gilt initials: *R.I.P.*

"*Oooh—waaa—*" Mitzi gave way to full-fledged hysterics.

"Oh my God!" Irene Warner went ashen, staring at the ribbon as though it were a snake poised to strike next at her. She swallowed visibly, obviously fighting down her own hysteria.

"I forgot!" Tamsin was frozen with horror. The Duchess had kicked that wreath under the catwalk *pro tem* and told her to get rid of it later. But so much had been going on that she had forgotten its existence. And now it had been unearthed at the worst possible moment. "I forgot all about it!"

"*What is it?*" . . . "*What's happening?*" The audience in the back rows and on the other side of the catwalk were on their feet, leaning forward. In another moment the whole auditorium would be in an uproar. And it was all her fault.

"Here—" Abruptly, Kenny thrust his serving bottle of champagne into her hands and dashed forward. He pushed his way through the front row spectators, who were crowding round, and snatched the wreath from the nerveless fingers of the two buyers. The way behind him was blocked, so he vaulted to the stage and disappeared behind the curtains, panting but triumphant.

"*Aaaah—yeeeow—*" Mitzi screamed.

"For heaven's sake—!" Irene looked at her with all the distaste of the East Coast Establishment for the excesses of the West Coast. "Get a grip on yourself, woman!"

"Water—" Someone shouted advice from farther down the row. "Get her a glass of water."

"Throw it over her—" someone else suggested enthusiastically.

"No, no—she's hysterical." The diagnosis came from a voice at the back. "She needs more than that. You'll have to slap her face."

Irene's eyes lit up. It was obviously an opportunity she had dreamed of for years. Before anyone could move to stop her, she swung back her arm in a roundhouse swing and delivered a *Smack* that resounded through the room.

Mitzi's eyes rolled up, she buckled at the knees and sagged to the floor.

"Fight! Fight" Someone screamed.

"No contest!" Someone more realistic answered.

The newspaper reporters at the back knocked over chairs in their rush from the room and toward the nearest telephone.

"WARNER K.O.s KAYCE . . ." Tamsin heard one

of them joyfully rehearsing her copy as she ran. *"The longstanding rivalry between these two major buyers exploded into honest-to-God fisticuffs today at the Decemo Collection as tempers flared and nerves exploded when both buyers dived for the bride's bouquet. . . ."*

"Let me through—Please, let me through—" Decemo tried to battle his way through from the aisle.

"Stand back—Give her air—" The Duchess leaped down from the podium and lied valiantly. "She's fainted!"

"The winnah!" A laughing spectator grasped Irene's hand and waved it in the air. "The winnah—and still champion!"

"Bend her over and put her head between her knees." Decemo, thoroughly confused, was going along with the official story—likely or not.

"*Ooooh* . . ." Mitzi swam back to consciousness, not surprisingly, in an evil mood. "I'm going to sue!" She took a deep breath and looked round menacingly, trying to focus. "I'm gonna sue every God-damned one of you for every penny you're worth!"

"Now, now, dear—" Decemo grabbed her by the back of her neck and swept her head forward, bending her double, ignoring her squawks of protest.

"Get them out of here—" The Duchess pulled Irene Warner free of her supporters and gripping her firmly around the waist, hurried her toward the stage door. "Get them out of here! And—for God's sake—put them in separate rooms!"

"I'm sorry! I'm so terribly sorry—" Tamsin was close to tears. "I *meant* to pull that wreath out from under the catwalk and get rid of it. But so much kept happening— and I forgot. I'm *so* sorry—"

"Never mind that now." The Duchess glanced at the wreath with cold distaste. "Not a great deal of harm has been done—thanks to Kenny. Not one in fifty of them will remember what triggered the hysterics. That was good work, Kenny."

"Thank you, your Grace." Kenny glowed. Wait till Mum heard this!

"Here—" The Duchess caught up a bottle of champagne and bestowed it on him. "Take this home with you. A token of our appreciation. There'll be a little bonus later."

"Ooh, your Grathe!" Kenny felt his ears go red again. Mum would never open it—well, maybe at Christmas. And afterward she'd probably have the bottle bronzed to stand on the mantel beside his bronzed baby shoes. "Thank you!"

"And get rid of that thing now!" the Duchess ordered. "Better tear it to pieces first. A few of those newspaper bitches are bound to remember it and I wouldn't put it past them to go nosing through the rubbish bins to try to retrieve it. We don't want a photograph of a funeral wreath superimposed over our Collection."

"I'll do it, your Grace." Kenny repossessed the wreath and began wrenching at it, prolonging his moment of glory.

"That's right—" Hattie moved over to join Kenny, snatching viciously at the purple ribbon. "It's bad enough now, with all of them waiting to see if we're going to parade a patched-up dress and try to pass it off as an inspired creation." The ribbon ripped free and she clawed off the offending gilt letters, twisting them into shapeless gilt rolls.

"We mustn't keep them waiting much longer."

No one had been surprised at the declaration of an intermission. With so many fashion journalists out telephoning their news desks, it was only to be expected. The writers on more comfortable deadlines had settled back to enjoy the renewed lashings of champagne and bitchiness. Such glorious scandal seldom took place right before their eyes. Even if they couldn't use it in their copy, they could dine out on it for months to come. They might grow restive eventually, but not for a while yet.

"I'll see if Decemo's ready." Grateful for something to do, Tamsin crossed the studio and tapped on the door of Decemo's private office. He had Mitzi Kayce in there, attempting to smooth her ruffled feathers. Heaven knew what it must have cost him by this time to placate her—if placated she was.

Irene Warner had been ensconced in the Duchess's small domain, the Publicity Office, with Sunny to dance attendance on her. She seemed quite happy and in a state of some euphoria at having achieved an ambition she had never thought possible. Everyone had spent some time in assuring her that a slap in the face was a well-known antidote to hysteria and it was not her fault that Mitzi Kayce had turned out to have a glass jaw.

The problem was going to be convincing Mitzi of that fact.

"Yes, she's doing very well." Decemo had come to the door in response to Tamsin's knock. He spoke a little too heartily, glancing nervously over his shoulder. "I'm sure she's ready to resume her seat for the rest of the showing."

"I don't suppose—" The Duchess spoke without any real hope. "I don't suppose she could be persuaded to walk back into the showroom arm-in-arm with Irene? Just to demonstrate that there are no hard feelings?"

"Over my dead body!" Mitzi, swaying, appeared in the doorway behind Decemo. "I've got plenty of hard feelings. And I've got that bitch dead to rights! She assaulted me without provocation. You saw it. You're all witnesses. My lawyers will be in touch with you."

"Perhaps you'd rather go back to your hotel?" The Duchess still had no great hope.

"And leave *her* with a clear field?"

"We could arrange a private showing later. . . ."

Across the room, the other door trembled ominously.

"Forget it." Mitzi shoved Decemo aside and swayed forward. It was obvious that the hospitality had been as lavish in his office as it was outside during the enforced intermission.

"We will ask *Vogue*, on the other side of the catwalk, to exchange seats with Irene," Decemo suggested quickly. "That will be the best solution. It will cause talk, but—" He shrugged.

There was no way they were going to be able to avoid talk. It was not necessarily a bad thing. With every house in London showing, anything that attracted attention was not to be despised. Someone had once ruled that there was no such thing as bad publicity—as long as they spelled your name right.

"I don't even want to be in the same *room* with that bitch!" Mitzi snapped.

"You never did, dear," Decemo muttered under his breath.

"Are we—?" The door of the Publicity Office opened and Sunny popped her head out. She took in the scene quickly. "No, I guess we aren't." She ducked back out of sight and the door shut firmly.

"Here—" Nikko slid through the curtains. "You lot going to hang around in here much longer? If you don't start up again soon, that lot out there are going to be too sloshed to see the dresses."

"The show must go on," Gloria said with a nervous giggle.

"That's right." The Duchess took a firm grip on Mitzi's arm. "Just come along," she coaxed. "You want to take your seat for the rest of the showing, don't you? And afterwards—" she added hastily, as Mitzi began pulling away—"we can have a quiet drink and discuss things. There's a very special dress I'm sure would be perfect for you. If you like it, we can reserve it for you at the end of the showings."

"Is that so?" Mitzi's eyes gleamed. "I'd heard your best creation was destroyed earlier today."

"A lot of people heard that rumour." The Duchess levelled a deadly look at Nikko. "However, it isn't quite true. Come and see."

Oh, great! Kenny chortled to himself, running down the stairs. It had been real great. Super! Terrific! That look! The expression on Nikko's face when the big model stepped out on the catwalk wearing the dress he thought he'd ruined.

Serve him right, the berk! He'd been furious that he hadn't spoiled the showing. Furious.

They'd outsmarted him, that was the truth of it. Nikko had never guessed that there had been two versions of the dress. Naturally, Sunny would have been called upon for the photographs. But, for real life, Decemo had made a duplicate for his 'Let Them Eat Cake' range. And it had gone over even better than it would have done if Sunny had been modelling it. Not surprising, when you came to think about it. More than a few of the fashion writers in the audience had a weight problem. It had flattered and encouraged them to see a real glamour creation on a large model. The applause had been thunderous.

Oops, careful! Kenny slowed his steps, abruptly mindful that the champagne shouldn't be shaken up too much. Not that it really mattered; it would have plenty of time to settle down before Mum could bring herself to open it. She wouldn't half be thrilled, though. A present from the Duchess! She'd save it till Christmas, at least.

Maybe even until his twenty-first birthday. Wouldn't that be exciting? They'd drink a toast to the Duchess and he'd be able to remember—he'd always remember—the look in her eyes and the softness in her voice when she bestowed the cham—

"Hello, young Kenny!" Nikko stepped out of the shadows into his path. Nikko, still furious and dangerous as a snake coiled to strike. "In a good mood, are we?"

"Hello, Nikko." Kenny went to sidestep him, instinctively trying to shelter the champagne bottle under his jacket.

"What you got there?" Nikko snatched the bottle away from him. "Been tea-leafing, have you?"

"It's mine!" Kenny tried to repossess the bottle, but Nikko held it out of his reach. "The Duchess gave it to me."

"Ooh-er! Aren't we moving in high society circles,

then? Think I'd believe that? Pull the other one, there's bells on it!"

"You give that back!" Kenny leaped for it and missed. "Stop shaking it about!"

"Oh-ho, you think you know that much, do you?" In spite, Nikko shook the bottle furiously. "Well, let me tell you, Young Kenny, you're still wet behind the ears. And in a few other places, too—"

"It's mine!" Kenny blinked back the betraying tears of rage—nothing else—but they'd be taken in the wrong way if he let them escape. "Give it to me!"

"You want it?" Nikko laughed nastily. "Then suppose you ask *me* for it. Nicely mind you, because what *I* say goes. *My* word is what counts around here."

"You?" Kenny could not let that pass. "You're just another messenger. You're no better than what I am!"

"Don't you believe it! I'm next to the man in charge—and it won't be long before I'm in charge myself. I've got the paper that says so. Let me give you a tip, young Kenny—not that it's ever likely to be of any use to you." He was juggling with the bottle now, tossing it from one hand to the other. "Get them when they're hot—they'll promise anything, sign anything, then."

"You be careful!" Kenny caught his breath as Nikko nearly dropped the bottle. He snatched for it again. "You give me that! It's mine!"

"You want it?" Nikko caught it by the base, shaking it again. "All right, then, I'll give it to you—"

"No! Stop! Don't—"

A final shake . . . SMASH! The fragile neck of the bottle shattered as Nikko slammed it against the edge of the building. The champagne sprayed out of the bottle. Nikko aimed the spray at Kenny.

"You want it! You've got it!"

"Stop it!" Kenny put up his hands to protect his eyes. Fizz and foam splashed over him, dripping off his helmet, running down his leather jacket. "Don't—"

But it was too late. It was already done. Mum would never see the gracious gift from the Duchess. She'd never even hear about it. He couldn't bring her an empty broken bottle. And it wouldn't be the same to buy another.

His little triumph was gone—spoiled, ruined. He'd never even be able to think about it again without remembering the subsequent humiliation. Nikko had spoiled everything.

"I'll kill you!" Kenny sobbed. "Someday I'll kill you!"

Chapter 8

Sunny decided that she didn't really like herself very much. She was not a nice person. If she had been a really nice person—or even had the courage of her convictions—she wouldn't have remained hidden in the recessed doorway, she'd have stepped out boldly and stopped Nikko from bullying poor Kenny.

But she'd been afraid. Nikko was already nursing a grudge against her because of what had happened this morning. She did not want to give him any additional cause for grievance. So she had stayed sheltered and silent, despising herself for it, and watched Nikko work off his bad temper on Kenny.

She was a rotten coward. Even now that Nikko had leaped on to his motorcycle and roared off laughing, she could not bring herself to step forward and say something comforting to Kenny. For one thing, there was nothing to say; for another, it might make it even worse for Kenny to know that she had witnessed the scene.

Now Kenny was stumbling toward the doorway, ineffectually dabbing at his leather jacket with a handkerchief. Of course, he'd want to get to the washroom and clean himself up before he went home. The most

tactful thing she could do right now was get out of the
way. She pressed back against the door until it swung
inward. She slipped inside and melted into the shadows.

Upstairs, the Duchess turned away from the half-
open window and met Mme. Arlette's steady gaze.

"Is it possible?" she asked. "Nikko is just bluffing—
boasting—isn't he? Decemo wouldn't be such a fool?"

"Wouldn't he?" Mme. Arlette shrugged. "When the
madness first seizes him, anything is possible. No gift is
too great. There was a friend—just before you joined us.
He was rather a pleasant boy, but one with strange fancies. He wished for a solid silver breastplate studded
with semiprecious stones to wear to a masquerade party.
Decemo indulged him—in that and in many other expensive fancies." She sighed. "A pity he did not last
longer. His desires begin to seem quite modest."

"No wonder the firm needed a fresh injection of capital," the Duchess said grimly. "I trust Decemo realizes
that the money is for the firm and not his to use as he
pleases."

"Unfortunately," Mme. Arlette said, "he can dispose
as he wishes with any or all of his shares in the actual
business."

"And even more unfortunately—" the Duchess was
sunk in gloom—"the repercussions can affect us all."

"Do not despair, Medora. There is reason to hope
that the madness will soon pass. And then he is excellent
at retrieving what seems to be an impossible situation.
That breastplate, for example, provided cuff links, earrings and bracelets for the staff and favoured clients to
mark the opening of the next Collection."

"I'm not sure we'll be able to wait for this thing to
run its course. Nikko is getting more destructive and disruptive by the minute."

"That is true. What, then, do you suggest?"

"Something," the Duchess said quietly, "is going to
have to be done about Nikko."

*   *   *

There was so much to be done. Tamsin helped carry the armloads of clothes to the back room for the quick brushing and touching up with the steam iron that would restore their pristine freshness for tomorrow's showings.

When the telephone rang, her arms were full and Hattie darted to answer it. The person at the other end of the line had hardly begun to speak when Hattie started tapping her foot impatiently.

On her return trip through reception, Tamsin noted with amusement that Hattie's foot was still tapping, even though she was cooing agreement and delight into the telephone; her face was thunderous. Nor did it clear when the conversation terminated.

"Typical!" Hattie slammed down the receiver. "Absolutely typical! God, how I hate the media!"

"What's the matter?"

"That rotten rag—the *Record!* They couldn't do everything at once, could they? It might not be disruptive enough! *Now* they want to do a feature on our sandals and leather jewellery. *Now*—like for tomorrow's editions. Just because they've thought up a cute headline: THONGS FOR THE MEMORY—" She broke off, making retching noises.

"You agreed, of course? Tamsin asked anxiously. Two features in a row in the *Record* was the sort of publicity that couldn't be bought.

"Oh, sure." Hattie laughed. "I'm not *that* crazy. I said we'd send the stuff over tonight and they promised faithfully they'd be finished with it in time for someone to collect it in the morning. *Not* Nikko!"

"I should think not," Tamsin agreed. "Kenny will have to go. Is he still around?"

"I think he and Nikko have left for the night. I wish I could."

"Never mind, it will soon be over. All we have to do is last out the week. Then we can all collapse quietly. I can drop off the leatherwear on my way home. . . ." Tamsin hesitated. "Unless you'd like to."

"Why should I like to?"

"Because," Tamsin said cautiously, "I thought you might deliver the goods wearing your craziest hat—and perhaps they might decide that they'd like to do a feature on hats, too. If not this week, then some time in the future."

"Oh. . . ." Hattie cocked her head to one side and reflected. The idea of personal publicity was new to her.

Tamsin waited, realizing that what she had just suggested was tantamount to mutiny. Decemo did not encourage any of the team to get ideas above their station. He advocated a low profile for everyone but himself.

"I'll do it!" Hattie decided.

"Good!" Tamsin picked up a piece of chalk and turned to the noticeboard behind the desk. "And I'll leave a message for Kenny to make the pick-up first thing in the morning."

The blackboard was in the centre of the cork board covering the wall from desk-height to ceiling. It was surrounded by pinned-up sketches, swatches of material, publicity shots, advertisements torn out of magazines and various notes. Normally adequate for their needs, the blackboard was far too small this week for all the communication necessary and was already filled with scribbled messages. Tamsin studied them critically.

A few of the messages were already obsolete. Check Bonnard's Windows could go; those interested had already been to view the magnificent window display Bonnard's had given Decemo Designers. Some other messages were totally obscure, perhaps they had meant something to someone once; others were unreadable. And who had written Up the Revolution?

They could all go. Tamsin spit inelegantly on an ill-favoured swatch, of a material so detestable that it had been immediately designated as a cleaning cloth, and cleared the slate of all messages, leaving it glowing a dull black.

Kenny—She chalked up the message for morning while Hattie deliberated aloud.

"Moonflash? Delayed Reaction?" All her hats had names, which annoyed Decemo intensely. Only special

gowns should have names. He considered it pretentious
to have names for hats and said so. Of course, this merely
drove Hattie to fresh excesses. "Cold On King's Road—?"

"Moonflash," Tamsin voted firmly. The dark silver
and blue creation that looked like a moving thun-
derstorm set off Hattie's multicoloured spiked hair-do
dramatically and was wild enough to attract any photographer's awed attention.

"You really think so?" Hattie was willing to be convinced.

"I'm sure."

That settled that. Hattie darted off; Tamsin began
the round of empty offices and workrooms, turning off
lights. The duty fell to the last to leave of an evening.

Was she really the last? How strange that a building
could empty so completely in such a short time. The
Duchess had been the first to leave, rushing off with Decemo to make the obligatory appearances at the series of
cocktail parties and receptions being held all over town
to mark the opening of another Fashion Week. Mme.
Arlette and Lillian had been the next to go, anxious to
slip into some of the evening showings and check on the
opposition.

When the cat's away. . . . Below, the front door
slammed, telling her that Hattie had now departed. To
be fair, everyone had been working overtime for weeks to
get everything ready for this week. They were entitled to
get out and have some fun at the festivities. She had an
invitation herself for one of the Galas tomorrow night.

It was as well she'd volunteered to be the first on
the rota for late-night duties this week. It gave her a bit
of time to recover from the day. Tamsin shuddered. Perhaps, given enough time, she could forget that the scene
this afternoon had been her fault. If only she had remembered to get rid of that wreath—

No, not entirely her fault. It was because of the
wreath. Who had sent it? Decemo was not the most popular couturier in London and the possibilities were endless. Any number of rival designers, unhappy customers,
perhaps even disgruntled members of the staff, might

have wanted to do something to upset the House and the Showing.

They had succeeded beyond their wildest dreams. Or had they? The "fight" between Irene and Mitzi would become legendary, but would the cause be remembered? Their enmity was too long-standing and well-known, anything might have set it off. Who would remember what after a certain passage of time?

A week was supposed to be a long time in politics; a day could be even longer in the fashion world.

Thank heavens this day had ended. Tamsin swung the dimmer switch to leave a subdued light in the reception area so that the cleaners wouldn't walk into complete darkness. It would be nice if they returned the compliment once in a while, instead of leaving lights lit all over the offices in their wake.

On her way down the stairs, she hesitated, frowning. *Had* she heard a faint sound just then? But she had just gone through every room and they had all been empty. At least, no one had been in sight. One didn't check closets and corners nor, for that matter, look behind the racks of shrouded garments.

Furthermore, one wasn't going to turn back and do so now. Tamsin continued firmly on her way. Perhaps a swatch or sketch had dropped to the floor from the noticeboard. It could not possibly be someone lurking in the darkness, waiting to spring out and destroy the Collection as soon as the coast was clear.

She was through for the day, there was no need for her imagination to work overtime.

Tamsin hurried down the narrow dark street towards the oasis of light that was the wine bar on the corner. Once round the corner, the vista opened out before her. A bright full moon illuminated the great Covent Market building and the portico of St. Paul's, Covent Garden, the actors' church, giving it the appearance of a stage setting, as once it had been. Eliza Doolittle might make her entrance at any moment, with her basket of flowers.

More likely these days, the enterprising young actress in Eliza's costume who purveyed nosegays to appreciative tourists. The night was mild and fragrant with the full glory of spring and the buskers, auditioned and licensed by the Local Authority, cavorted in their appointed places, drawing the laughing spectators. The tables spread outside wine bars and pubs were full, music rang out from a group of buskers at one end of the market, reverberating beneath the glass roof, adding to the gaiety and life of the market.

For a moment, Tamsin envied them. All these carefree people—the ultimate consumers—to whom fashion was simply a matter of which trend they preferred and whether they could afford it. Even then, it was probable that the lure of the second-hand clothing stall and the jumble sale would win out over the high-priced original designs being launched down every catwalk in London this week.

And why not? Fun fashion was for the kids—who started their own fads. Serious fashion was for export.

Export or Die. . . . The old slogan of some half-forgotten Export Drive leaped into her mind and she shuddered despite the clemency of the night. Surely it would never come to that.

In the morning, Tamsin found Decemo Designers still standing. It proved that her qualms of the night before had just been some sort of delayed-reaction Opening Day Nerves. Everyone was cheerful and happy; nothing dire had happened to any of the creations.

UP THE REVOLUTION had been re-chalked on the blackboard. The message for Kenny had been erased.

"It worked!" Hattie sidled up to her and spoke in a conspiratorial murmur. She was wearing Moonflash, jeans and sweatshirt proclaiming NEVER MIND WHAT I LOOK LIKE—READ MY MESSAGE. The sweatshirt was several sizes too large for her and one Tamsin had never seen before. It raised an interesting question as to where Hattie might have spent the night.

"It worked," Hattie said again. "He's definitely interested. Oh, Tamsin, thanks."

"That's fine." Tamsin frowned absently at the blackboard. "Has Kenny made the pick-up already, then?"

"Oh no—" Hattie followed her gaze. "I erased that myself. It isn't necessary. Pete's going to return the things personally and take a look around. I *told* you he was interested."

"Good. And did you—?" Tamsin waved her hands toward UP THE REVOLUTION.

"No." Hattie was uninterested. "That was there when I came in. I don't know who did it." She didn't care, either.

"*Good* morning—" Sunny called out blithely, dashing past them, slightly late as usual, but still displaying the disposition that had won her her name.

Immediately on her heels came the florist with the two bridal bouquets and a trug of replacement blossoms for any flowers in the display that might have faded and wilted since yesterday. Tomorrow the entire display would be replaced.

The telephone began ringing and Tamsin moved to answer it. The blank notepad on the desk told her that the Duchess had not arrived yet. If she had, it would have been covered with notes, instructions, telephone numbers and names—leftover gleanings from the night before, some of which the Duchess would not be able to account for by midmorning.

While she was still trying to fob off the importunate caller, who seemed to feel that their lives would be incomplete without delivery of twenty gross of boxes of carbon paper a month, the Duchess entered with an armload of newspapers.

"Post-mortems in the studio—starting immediately!" she called as she went past. "Bring your notebook!"

"Look—" Tamsin tried once more to cut off the telephone salesman. "We're just not interested. We don't use *one* box of carbon paper a year. We're just not that sort of operation."

"Then what did you fill in the coupon for?" The voice was aggrieved. "Wasting our time like this—"

"What coupon?" But there was a sharp click and then a buzzing sound. He had hung up.

With a mental shrug, Tamsin picked up her notebook and hurried after the Duchess.

The newspapers were spread out over the big worktable under the windows, heedless of the smudging printers' ink. There was already a long dark streak on the soft beige heavy silk of the Duchess's jacket, of which she was oblivious. All her attention was concentrated on the fashion coverage. She whirled the pages of every paper, hurling to the floor all such irrelevant pages as contained reports of minor items such as war, famine and pestilence. The front pages were the first to go and soon she stood ankle-deep in crumpled newsprint. The post-mortem was in full cry.

"*Look*—just *look* at the cut of that jacket!" Decemo sneered over a competitor's work. "It could fit a camel— too bad he's put it on a boy."

"I don't fancy his shorts, either," Hattie said. "If you ask me, diamanté zippers are vulgar."

"What do you expect, dear? Rumour has it that he started out designing for strip shows in Soho. It shows, doesn't it? Perhaps he can capture the pop star market— something like that with a matching sequinned truss should go a treat."

"Personally—" Lillian was studying a full-page spread in a different paper—"I think it's time holes were *out*."

"So we've noticed, dear. If you get much more buttoned-up, we're going to have to trade you to Brooks Brothers."

"Hell!" The Duchess hurled a page into the air, had second thoughts and caught it before it had time to settle to the floor. "We've made the gossip column in the *Record* and the sod has located us in Seven Dials instead of Covent Garden!"

"Can we sue?" Decemo's nostrils flared, scenting battle.

"Not worth it—but we'll damned well demand an apology!" The Duchess riffled more pages impatiently. "God, how I hate Statements!"

"It does no harm, however—" Mme. Arlette was pleating a rich brocade in peacock colours—"to be considered to be making one." She had shown no interest in the newspapers. Her attention was already turning toward the next collection.

Of them all, only Reba noticed that Sunny had retreated into a corner and was frowning over her picture in the *Daily Record* fashion spread. Reba sauntered across and looked over Sunny's shoulder.

"You must have been a bit tired," she said sympathetically. "Those bags under your eyes don't usually show."

"I haven't been sleeping well," Sunny admitted. "I'll be glad when this week is over."

"Boyfriend still in the States?" If some of the sympathy had left Reba's voice, Sunny didn't notice.

"He promised me he'd be back in time for the showings. I was sure he would, he's usually so good about things like that. I expected to find him in the house when I got home last night, but. . . ." She sighed. "He hasn't even telephoned." She found herself raising her voice against a commotion in the distance. "It's not like Jake."

"WHAT?" Reba shouted. Outside, a siren whooped hysterically, drowning out all sound, all thought.

"IT'S NOT LIKE—" the room was abruptly silent—"Jake."

"Fire engines—" Hattie and Lillian had opened one of the windows and were leaning out. "They've stopped right outside!"

"They're coming in," Lillian shrieked. "In *here!*"

Footsteps thundered on the stairs, across the outer office. The door quivered and sprang open. Large men dashed into the studio, their enormous hip-boots and big yellow helmets made them look about seven feet tall. Some of them carried axes. They looked around expectantly.

"All right," one of them said. "Where's the fire?"

Chapter 9

The Duchess was the first to put a name on it. A milder, yet more sinister name than she usually put to anything.

"Harassment!"

The firemen had gone. Decemo's apologies and protestations of innocence had been accepted, but someone had definitely put in an emergency call and given this address.

"Harassment! That's all we bloody well need!"

The evidence was mounting and could no longer be denied: the funeral wreath, now the Fire Department, even the persistent carbon paper salesman who claimed that someone had filled out and mailed in his coupon. And don't forget the destruction of the elaborate beaded dress—never forget Indigo Charisma. . . .

"Well, don't look at me!" Nikko had raced up the stairs immediately behind the firemen. "I didn't have nothing to do with it."

"Didn't you?" the Duchess asked dangerously.

"No—" He turned to Hattie and Lillian, arms outspread. "Would I do a thing like that?"

"Yes!" the designers chorused.

"Well, I didn't! Straight!" He turned back to the Duchess in injured innocence. "You want to look for someone who's got a grudge against this place. Not me." He slanted a sly look towards Decemo. "I've got a vested interest in it, haven't I? I want us to have a big success."

"See that you remember that," the Duchess said. "This is business—big business. Stop interfering with it!"

"Let's not waste any more time on this." Decemo was pale. "We have too much to do today."

49

* * *

At a conservative estimate, five thousand buyers—mostly foreign—and three hundred international fashion journalists were in London to view the British Collections. Not all of them would find their way to the studios of Decemo Designers, but a good proportion would. And they would be in a buying mood.

They had started out last week in Milan, next week they would be in Paris. London, sandwiched neatly in the middle of the international junket, reaped the benefits. After the elegant and expensive Milan Collections and before the equally expensive but increasingly grotesque Paris shows, London represented an oasis of bright, affordable fashion with the bonus of street credibility. An additional bonus was the bliss of being able to speak the language and arrange deals without interpreters. Or, in the case of English-speaking principals, the unease of wondering whether you both understood the same thing. In London, they could relax and enjoy it all, while knowing that they were also doing their duty in the heart of the international fashion world.

Collectively, they would hand out orders worth more than four million pounds.

Decemo Designers intended to get their share of the orders. On the Opening Day, they had had the single inaugural show in the afternoon, knowing that all the Opening Night parties would absorb the buyers in the evening. From today onwards, they would present two showings a day, one in the afternoon and one in the early evening.

Everyone would be working at full stretch, showing, charming, selling. Fashion was Britain's fourth largest industry, its fifth largest export. It was big business, growing bigger every day, now that the halcyon days of the Swinging Sixties seemed renascent, with the world focusing on London designers once again.

Make no mistake about it, no matter how demanding, how fractious, or how frivolous these buyers might seem, they were here to spend their money—and there must be no impediment placed in their way.

* * *

"Oh God!" the Duchess moaned. "Not a bed made, not a pot emptied—and the Fleet's in!" She snatched up the pages of her commentary and dashed into the showroom to take her place on the podium for the afternoon showing.

"Considering the hangover she must have—" Decemo watched her as she went—"she's holding up very well." he sighed. "Far better than I—but then, she hasn't all my worries and responsibilities."

Especially worries, Tamsin thought. Nikko had been making himself more obnoxious than usual all morning; he had obviously come off second-best in whatever fight there had been the night before. The ruined dress had been sent to the East End workrooms for restoration and it was clear that the subject was never to be referred to again.

However, there was no time to brood. Several buyers had arrived late and had to be seated even though the show was in progress. The soundtrack blasted from the showroom with the opening of the door. It would not be surprising if everyone had constant headaches, the hospitality was just a convenient scapegoat.

Tamsin found herself looking forward to evening when she could return to her quiet flat, lean back in a hot bath and forget all the cares of the day. But there were hours to go before that could happen. Meanwhile, there was the endless clamour.

"Tamsin—" Mme. Arlette stood in the doorway. "I cannot think how it can have happened, but we are out of pins. Please send Kenny to get a large supply—all sizes. And quickly! We are in desperate need!"

"Tamsin—help!" Sunny dashed past, still in costume, on a quick detour from the catwalk. "Can you ring the house and see if Jake's come back yet? I haven't heard a word from him—and I'm so worried!"

"Tamsin—book a table at *C'est Chérie* for dinner at eight. There'll be four of us."

"Tamsin—would you?" . . . "Tamsin—could you?" . . . "Tamsin, please—"

All this and the telephone, too. Tamsin listened to the bell ringing in Sunny's empty house, reluctant to put down the phone because it would then spring into a malevolent life of its own. She hung on patiently, maintaining the illusion that she was making an urgent call and that there was hope of an answer. It was the first moment she'd been able to sit down in hours.

The afternoon showing had just ended and the audience was streaming out of the showroom. Defensively, Tamsin gripped the receiver tighter and began making squiggles on the notepad in front of her, carefully avoiding all eyes trying to meet her own. It had begun raining and she had no intention of being landed with the impossible task of trying to round up taxis for dozens of importunate foreigners.

Ring-ring . . . ring-ring . . . Tamsin held the receiver firmly against her ear so that no telltale sound could leak out and made another wild series of squiggles. To the uninitiated, they would resemble shorthand. Even the initiated would be confused, those who understood Pitman's thinking that she was using Gregg's and those—mostly American—who might have learned Gregg, assuming that it was Pitman's because it was well-known that Pitman was the English system. Those few who understood both would either assume that she had invented her own system or consider it *infra dig* to let it be known that they had once been on such a lowly level that they could interpret such pothooks.

Unfortunate, perhaps, that one had to stoop to subterfuge but in any job it was necessary to work out certain protective time- and energy-saving tricks in order not to be driven right down into the ground.

In fashion, perhaps more than in most businesses. Too many rampaging temperaments demanding attention and partisanship could erode lesser egos to the point of nervous breakdown. It wasn't going to happen to her.

The ringing stopped abruptly. For a moment, Tamsin thought someone had answered the phone. Then she saw the familiar blood-red-tipped fingernails resting on the cradle, cutting her off.

"Stop arsing around!" the Duchess snapped. "We've got too much to do before the next show. What are you playing at, anyway?"

"I was making a call for Sunny," Tamsin said. "Her boyfriend hasn't come back yet. She's growing frantic—"

The telephone began to ring. Instinctively, the Duchess drew back her hand and the call came through on the receiver Tamsin still held pressed to her ear.

". . . *Record*. . . . We'd like a quote about the fire. Was anyone hurt? Any damage done? Are you planning a Fire Sale?"

"Fire? We've had no fire," Tamsin said blankly. "I don't know what you're talking about."

"You can play it that way if you like, but we have pictures of the fire engines in front of your place. Plus an eyewitness who saw them. You'd do better to give us something reasonable we can print—"

"Photographs—" Suddenly it fell into place. Hattie's conquest, who hadn't appeared—throwing Hattie into a filthy mood. But the leather goods had been returned as promised. They had found the box in the ante-room. He must have delivered them at the same time as the fire engines arrived. No photographer worth his salt would let a picture opportunity like that go by for the mere sake of seeing a girl again. Nor would he have waited to discover what was happening once he had ascertained that there were going to be no thrilling pictures of smoke and flames and people leaping from the upper stories. He must have rushed back to the paper to develop his pictures and hand the story on to the news desk for the follow-up.

"What is it?" The Duchess tugged impatiently at the phone and Tamsin surrendered it gladly. She watched as the Duchess began asking questions and her face changed with the replies. One could follow the ripple of calculations across her face: was it better to admit harassment or just play dumb?

"Sorry," the Duchess decided coolly, "it was only a false alarm. Not worth your wasting space on, I'm afraid. The firemen were here, but someone had given them the wrong address. Perhaps," she added maliciously, "they wanted Seven Dials—this is Covent Garden. . . . That's quite all right—I quite understand. . . ."

Throughout her conversation, she was smiling, nodding and mouthing messages to the buyers flocking toward the exit. At the same time, she managed to discourage those who showed signs of lingering for conversation after her call was completed.

There was a long silence and Tamsin suddenly recognized her own tactic. The journalist at the other end had rung off, but the Duchess was still clinging to the receiver, murmuring a pretence of conversation while the room cleared.

Finally only one buyer still loitered, optimistically hoping for the Duchess to finish her call, but the Duchess was equal to her.

"No, I'm afraid I simply can't allow that!" She swung about, facing the wall, her back stiff with indignation. "First of all, you must understand—No, don't interrupt me—"

With a shrug of resignation, the buyer gave up and slipped out quietly. The Duchess turned back to Tamsin when she heard the door close.

"Thank heavens for that," she said. "I thought the silly cow had taken root!"

"Don't hang up," Tamsin warned quickly. "It will only start ringing again."

"You may be right." The Duchess set the receiver down on the desk beside the phone. "We won't tempt fate for a while longer, anyway. We could do with some peace and quiet before they begin arriving for the next showing."

They had approximately forty-five seconds of peace and quiet before the agonized screams tore through the silence.

Chapter 10

"The make-up room!" The Duchess pinpointed the source of the screams and sprinted for it, Tamsin close on her heels.

"Sunny! That's Sunny screaming!" Kenny came racing up from behind. In his anxiety, he nearly elbowed the Duchess aside. He caught himself just in time.

Together, they dashed through the dressing-room and reached the door of the small office that was currently being used as the make-up room.

"*Now* what?" the Duchess pushed her way through the crowd gathered in the doorway. Mme. Arlette was standing over Sunny, who was huddled on a chair in front of the mirror, her screams giving way to heart-rending sobs.

"What is it?" The Duchess addressed the question to Mme. Arlette. "What's happened here?"

"I do not know." Mme. Arlette gave a Gallic shrug. "She will not speak. She only screams and cries."

"We can hear that," the Duchess said grimly. "Come on, let's try to get some sense out of her."

"Sunny! Come, Sunny—" Mme. Arlette grasped Sunny's shoulders and pulled her upright. "You must tell us what is wrong before we can help you."

"My face!" Sunny screamed. "My face!" Her hands covered it. Her voice rose in a desperate wail. "My face!"

"What's the matter with it?" The Duchess tried to pull her hands away. "Let me see."

"No! No—I'm afraid! There was glass—ground glass—in my cold cream. I didn't see it! I was in a hurry. I—I rubbed it all over my face before I felt—" Sunny lost all coherence again and sobbed wildly.

"Ground glass." The Duchess was not the only one to turn pale.

"*I've* used that jar of cold cream," Carla said. "We all have. We borrow each other's things all the time. It—it could have happened to any of us!"

A ripple of horror went through the models. A couple of them looked longingly towards the exit; it would not take much more to stampede them through it.

"Let me see that—" The Duchess picked up the jar of cold cream and squinted into it. "There does seem—" She glanced anxiously at Sunny. "There does seem to be . . . foreign matter . . . mixed into the cream."

"Please, Sunny," Mme. Arlette coaxed. "Please, let us see what damage has been done. Only then can we begin to help you."

"Shall I phone for an ambulance?" Tamsin asked.

"I'll take her on my bike," Kenny said. "She won't have any waiting and we'll get there faster."

"Please, Sunny—" Mme. Arlette eased the hands away from the ravaged face while Sunny renewed her sobs.

"That's it. Let us see—Good girl—"

Exhausted by the struggle and the storm of her own emotions, Sunny allowed her hands to be gradually prised away. She kept her eyes tightly closed and, in the last instant, as her hands fell away, she twisted her body so that her back would be to the mirror on the dressing-table.

"There we are—" Mme. Arlette cupped Sunny's chin gently and turned her face towards the light. "Now, let us see—"

"There's no blood," the Duchess said critically. "She must have stopped rubbing instinctively when she first felt the grit."

"None at all," Mme. Arlette confirmed. She frowned and bent closer. "You can open your eyes now, Sunny. Your face is unharmed."

"It can't be—" Sunny's eyelids flew open and she squeezed them shut again instantly. "I *didn't* stop. I—I was upset. I was thinking about something else. I scrubbed and scrubbed—I *must* have drawn blood . . . scarred myself. . . ."

"You're all right," Tamsin said. "Honestly you are, you—you've had a lucky escape." *This time*. This was more than harassment, this was an attempt on a model's livelihood, if not her life. Tamsin suddenly remembered the unidentified sounds she had heard as she was leaving the building last night. Had that been someone creeping through the studio on their way to sabotage the cold cream?

The harrassment campaign was growing deadlier. Where would it end?

"I don't understand." Sunny turned slowly, seeking the reassurance of the mirror. "I *must* be—"

"You're all right," Kenny said softly. "You're . . . you're beautiful."

"I don't understand it, either," the Duchess said slowly. Glittering granules of crystal stood out in the cold cream smeared on Sunny's face. Yet she was unharmed.

"Let me see that!" Mme. Arlette reached out and took the jar of doctored cold cream from the Duchess. She sniffed at it suspiciously, then bent to study Sunny's face again.

"*Mon Dieu!* Can it be—?" She suddenly flicked a fingertip across Sunny's cheek and carried it to her tongue. "It is!" She began to laugh. "It is *salt!* Table salt! *Mon Dieu!*—I have not seen such a thing in years. In decades. I had almost forgotten!"

"Seen what?" the Duchess asked impatiently. "What are you talking about?"

Sunny stared into the mirror, tracing the lineaments of her face with a fingertip. Some of the crystals adhered to her finger. She stared at them wonderingly. Then cautiously . . . very cautiously . . . she transferred them to the tip of her tongue. Little by little, she began to relax.

"It *is* salt," she breathed thankfully. "It's not ground glass, at all. It's only salt."

"And very good for you," Mme. Arlette assured her.

"There was a time when that was all that any of us used. Now that I think of it, I believe it was better than the commercial preparations we have today."

"What—?"

"It was just after the war, you understand. I had married my English soldier had returned to London with him. I became a model—fashion has always been what I know best. But there was the rationing . . . the shortages . . . the austerity . . . the lack of everything one wanted and needed. Yet there was still the desperate yearning for glamour and life that would not be denied.

"So few cosmetics, as we know them now, were available to us. There were far more important things to import. So, we improvised. Oh, how we improvised!

"We removed what make-up we had with liquid paraffin. Black boot polish was used for mascara and—yes— to conceal the grey hairs in darker heads. We used fine oatmeal mixed with warm water for a face pack. And salt. Salt instead of toothpaste to brush our teeth. Salt mixed into cold cream and smoothed over the face with gentle circular movements was the best treatment ever devised for removing the dry flaky skin. They use special creams for it these days, call them exfoliating cream, and charge excessively. Also washing grains, to me they are much the same."

"Salt. . . ." Sunny's face glowed back at her from the mirror as she tissued off the cream and grainy harmless crystals. She had been given a reprieve. She was not to be scarred for life, her career ruined, her future in tatters. "It's only salt. . . ."

"Yes." The Duchess and Mme. Arlette exchanged glances. The panic was averted . . . this time. But someone had mixed the salt into the cold cream and placed it in the make-up room where the models would dip into it.

"Hey—!" There was a shout from the outer office. "Hey—where is everybody? Anybody home?"

"Jake!" Sunny gasped. She leaped from her chair and rushed towards the sound of the voice.

They collided in the doorway, the tall dark man with

a flight bag swinging from his shoulder and the lithe blonde girl who flung herself into his arms and clung as though she was never going to let go again.

"Hey, sweetheart—take it easy! What's the matter?"

"Nothing, Jake," Sunny said breathlessly. "Everything is fine. Now that you're back, nothing will ever go wrong again!"

"Nikko did it." Sunny had no doubt at all. "He's got it in for me."

"Has he?" Jake's jaw tightened. "Then we'll have to do something about Nikko, won't we?"

That was the most marvellous thing about Jake. He believed her. He realized she knew what she was talking about and he was prepared to act on her word alone. He was blissfully, unequivocally on *her* side.

She settled back into the cushions with a happy sigh. The little terrace house seemed like home again, now that he was back. They were drinking duty-free bourbon and listening to the tapes of the latest New York shows he had brought back with him. He moved back and forth between the living-room and the kitchen where he was grilling steaks and making salad. Jake loved to cook and she didn't, so he had long ago taken over the kitchen. Delicious smells were curling out from it.

"Feeling better now?" Jake refilled her glass.

"Lots. I—I'm sorry I was so silly." Now that it was over, Sunny was embarrassed at the way she had behaved. Over-reacted. It wasn't like her to have hysterics. "I—I was so frightened."

"You were entitled to be." Jake's face was grim. "If your face had been destroyed—"

"Don't!" Sunny shuddered and took a long swallow of her drink. "All of my life went rushing before my eyes—including the life I haven't lived yet."

"Steady, sweetheart." He knelt beside her. "The bad things didn't happen. And from now on, all the good things are going to come true. I wasn't going to show you this until later. But wait—"

Just as she was leaning forward into his arms, he got up and dashed away. She heard the locks of his suitcase click. Another surprise, another treat, for her.

That was something else wonderful about him. He brought colour and excitement with him. Life was more exhilarating when he was around. It wasn't just the presents—it was the thought behind them, the caring, the love.

"Here—" He was back, pushing a video cassette into the television attachment and adjusting it. "Just watch this. This is where we're going next!"

The screen sprang into a flamboyant dazzle of colours; shimmering and swirling scarves suddenly dropped one by one against a black background to spell out the name of one of New York's leading designers.

The picture dissolved into a long shot of a catwalk, the music surged, the lens zoomed in—and the show was on. Models burst through the curtains and danced down the catwalk.

"Oh, Jake!" Sunny caught her breath. "It's fantastic!"

"Sure it is. That's why they're all doing it now. The major designers are turning out their own videos and putting them into the department stores along with their clothes. The customers can watch the show, then go straight to the racks and pick up the garment they want. And we're going to do it, too. We'll let Decemo see this in the morning. He'll go for it. I know he will. I've got a film crew all lined up. They're freelance, usually do commercials. Their boss is one of the top photographers in town—he's moonlighting on this until he gets on a solid enough footing to be able to kick his regular job. They're dead keen on it. I went straight to their studio from the airport, that's why I was a bit late getting home."

"More than a bit. I expected you two days ago." She tried not to feel upset about it, but if Jake had been here, Nikko would not have dared to pull such a trick. It was only because he thought she was unprotected . . . vulnerable. . . .

"Sorry, but it's all in a good cause. I've been laying a lot of groundwork in New York. I couldn't get away when

I planned. Anyway—" He gave her the smile that always melted her—"I'm here now."

"Yes. . . ." Sunny watched the models parade across the small screen, her foot began tapping in time to the music. "Jake, do you really think Decemo will agree?"

"When he sees that video, he'll be wild to turn out one of his own. It will take him about thirty seconds to convince himself that it was all his own idea."

"I didn't mean that. I meant . . . about the other?"

"He'll agree." Jake's face was dark. "He can't keep you tied to that rotten contract. If he tries, we'll get the best lawyer in town."

"Decemo's got an awfully good lawyer."

"So, our lawyer can beat his lawyer. Don't worry. It may not even come to that. This video will be good for you. It will give you the chance to move in front of the camera; you'll learn a lot about filming. It will be useful practice. It will help us to get you where you're going."

"Tell me again," Sunny said, a child pleading for a bedtime story. "Please—" She closed her eyes.

"You're great," he said. "You know it yourself. You're too good to be stuck in one place. You're wasted as a house model. You should be moving into the big time . . . Paris . . . New York . . . flying to top assignments all around the world. And not just modelling. That's just the start."

"I could see it all happening, just the way you've always said." A tear slid from beneath her eyelid. "All the while my face was scratching and burning—and I was afraid it was all over before it even started."

"You can dance, you can sing, you can act. You can move up to work in films and the theatre. Lots of models have done it. Look at Lauren Hutton, Twiggy, Margaux Hemingway, Lorraine Chase . . . you can be right up there with them. We'll build you. We'll keep slotting you into as many outside assignments as we can get. We'll have a new portfolio taken. We'll feature you on the video. By the time Decemo notices what's happening, you'll be too big for him to hold on to. There'll be too much of a scandal if he tries."

"He'll try." Sunny opened her eyes. "He'll have to. Don't you see? If one of us manages to break her contract, the others will all try it. His whole empire will crumble if he loses us. He can't afford to let us go."

"Then—" Jake snapped off the set and watched the picture dwindle down to a dot and disappear. "Then we'll have to . . . persuade him."

Chapter 11

So, *vroom-vroom*, Nikko goes speeding down the Ring Road. There were traffic lights ahead, with a juggernaut lorry waiting on the cross street. The green flicked off, the yellow came on. The light was changing, but Nikko wouldn't care about that. He'd be sure he could make it. He always shot the lights. But the driver of the juggernaut was a foreigner, pig-headed, behind schedule—and he did have the right of way. He got the green signal, Nikko got the red. The juggernaut pulled out from the cross street, faster than he ought, faster than you might think a juggernaut could start up. But Nikko didn't stop—never had any intention of stopping. He was going to leap past under the juggernaut's nose and—
Splat!

No, it was too quick that way. He didn't have time to suffer, to know what a right berk he'd made of himself. Try something else. . . .

Say . . . they were alone at night in the office. Except for Sunny. She'd stayed behind to do something or other . . . Kenny let his mind slide over the details. Anyway . . . he was tidying up some papers, checking his calls for morning. Nikko had disappeared. Then Sunny screamed. Screamed the way she did yesterday. Only there weren't all those people to rush to help her now. Only Kenny and Nikko.

Kenny took the stairs three at a time, wondering where Nikko was. He burst into the room and saw that Nikko was the reason Sunny was screaming. He was standing over her, twisting her arm behind her back, pawing at her. . . .

Kenny leaped at him, tearing him away from Sunny, who fell to the floor sobbing helplessly. They fought, crashing around the room overturning chairs, sending tables flying. A lamp overturned—there was always a lamp—with a shower of sparks. The sparks fell on some soft filmy material and it blazed up.

"Fire!" Sunny screamed. "Fire! Oh, Kenny, save me!"

With a herculean effort, Kenny broke free of Nikko's bearhug, escaped the fingers clawing for his eyes, and delivered one mighty punch that sent Nikko reeling toward the window.

He fell through it, breaking the glass and hanging over the sill, half in and half out. But the air rushing into the room fanned the flames and they roared out of control.

"Kenny, help!" Sunny sobbed.

"Kenny! Here, mate—give us a hand!" Nikko was close to crying, too.

But there was time to save only one of them. Sunny or Nikko. No contest. And nobody could ever blame him because, of course, Sunny had to come first. . . .

Kenny frowned. No . . . that wasn't too satisfactory. Not personal enough. Not a proper revenge.

Say . . . say . . . he went down to Nikko's motorcycle when there was nobody around. There was plenty you could do to sabotage a machine. Just a couple of strategic nuts loosened . . . a wheel bent slightly out of true. True . . . it could all come true. If he only had the nerve. All he had to do. . . .

Kenny gave a sudden shudder of fear . . . of excitement . . . of anticipation? It was suddenly all too real. Too possible. It could be made to happen. Justice could be served.

No! His mind flinched away. No! He could never do

a thing like that! He stifled the niggling little ideas, denying the realization that they would come back to tempt him again and again.

Say—He tried desperately to drown them out. *Say* . . . something else. *Say* . . . they got a letter-bomb delivered here at Decemo Designers. . . .

He could see it now; a big bulky envelope with something funny about the look of it. Strange printing straggling across the front of it and the suggestion of wires inside.

"Now what could this be?" Tamsin wondered, staring at it dubiously.

"I wouldn't open it, if I was you." Kenny advised. "I don't like the look of it. I think you ought to call the police."

"You would!" Nikko jeered. "Scared of your own shadow, aren't you? Here—give it to me! *I'll* open—"

Boom!

Yes, that was a lot better. But still too quick and easy for him. Now, *say*. . . .

"Kenny!" Tamsin called for the third time. Kenny was a million miles away—and not anywhere pleasant, to judge from the way he was frowning and grinding his teeth. "KENNY!"

"Oh! Sorry, Tamsin." He leaped to his feet, looking guilty. "What is it?"

"Take this over to Bluebeard's Boutique—" She handed him a parcel. "And these are okayed drawings and copy—" she added a large flat envelope—"to go back to the advertising agency. You'd better deliver them first. They want to use them for an ad in the Sundays."

"Right." Kenny took his crash helmet from the top of the filing cabinet and snapped it on. "Don't worry. It's as good as done."

"I'm sure it is." Tamsin couldn't help smiling. Kenny was such a good boy, so good-hearted and willing, but like a little boy, never quite sure of himself and swaggering to disguise the fact.

He clattered down the stairs, narrowly averting a

collision with the postman, who had just arrived. Tamsin accepted the bulky packet of letters, held together with a rubber band, and returned the postman's cheery greeting.

Junk mail, mostly. One for Decemo . . . swatches from one of their regular suppliers . . . the Duchess . . . more junk mail. Rapidly Tamsin sorted through the post, ending with a large pile of junk mail. Inevitable at this time of the year. They were sending out plenty of advertising themselves to their own customers, it was not surprising that a great deal should be coming back to them from firms they did business with. It was a classic case of large fleas, smaller fleas, and so on *ad infinitum*.

Tamsin carried Decemo's mail through to his office. He had not arrived yet, nor had any of the models. In the workroom, Lillian laboured over the ironing board while Mme. Arlette inspected every garment with critical eyes, often taking infinitesimal stitches in seams that looked all right to anyone less observant.

The door to the make-up room stood open and Hattie could be seen leaning into the mirror, touching up the red portion of her locks with a fresh application of mercuro-chrome, so much cheaper than the spray colours produced commercially for that purpose. Every generation discovered its own economies and improvisations. Surely Mme. Arlette must approve.

"Tamsin—" Mme. Arlette had other things on her mind. She glanced with dissatisfaction at the two letters she had received. "Has there been no word from—" she lowered her voice—"Caitlin?"

"Not so far." Instinctively Tamsin lowered her own voice, although only the designers were in earshot and Caitlin's existence was no secret to them. Most designers had their own outworkers who executed the designs created in the studios. In private homes, rural cottages and council flats all over the country, special workers sewed on beads and sequins, made lace, knitted, hand-embroidered designs and generally did the donkey work for the big names who took the final credit. Depending on the extent of the paranoia of the designer who employed

them, some of them never even saw the finished costume until it appeared in newspapers and magazines.
They were each simply given their own bits to work on:
the sleeves, the bodices, the skirts, which were then collected from them—or posted in from the farthest-flung
outworkers—and assembled into the complete garment
by someone else, under the designer's supervision. The
names and addresses of each designer's stable of outworkers were jealously guarded, lest rival designers
swoop on them and carry them off to work under their
banner.

"I do not like it. We should have had word from her
by now. She is being temperamental again." Mme.
Arlette sighed deeply. "See if you can raise her on the
telephone."

"Right away," Tamsin said, without much hope. Although Decemo had had a telephone installed at his own
expense in Caitlin's flat and paid the bills for it, he could
not force her to use it—or answer it—if she was not in
the mood. Locked in a wheelchair as she was, she had
perhaps more excuse for temperament than some of the
other people in the fashion world.

As she had expected, the bell just kept ringing at
the other end of the line. After a few minutes, she replaced the receiver, lifted it again, and dialled the East
End workrooms—sometimes called the factory, but
never, never called the sweat-shop—which Caitlin supervised.

Once again, there was no answer. If Caitlin was
there, she was not answering the telephone, and the
bevy of little Indian girls she supervised were bright
when it came to sewing—brilliant, some of them—but
their grasp of English was as fragile as their fluttering
saris. Basically incurious, they would not dream of attempting to cope with whatever problems were represented by the ringing phone. They would have already
learned from Caitlin's responses, whenever she answered, that the telephone brought nothing but demands for impossible delivery dates, complaints about
work in progress, unreasonable requests, impertinent in-

quiries. Nothing good ever came of answering the telephone. They would continue sewing, laughing and chattering amongst themselves, ignoring the summons of the bell.

They were cheap labour because the language barrier kept them from realizing the extent of their exploitation. The same language barrier also meant that they were sometimes unsatisfactory when anything more than the rudimentary skills was demanded of them.

"It's no use." Mme. Arlette appeared beside Tamsin, conceding defeat. "I'll have to go over there myself. Order me a taxi."

The taxi was more easily obtained. By the time Mme. Arlette had shrugged herself into her coat and given interim instructions to Lillian, the taxi was waiting for her.

"It is probably no use at all," Mme. Arlette said. "If the news were good, she would have told us. Nevertheless, it never does any harm to make a sudden unscheduled appearance."

"Keeps them on their toes," Tamsin agreed. It also upset them for the rest of the day, but that was a small price to pay for the surge of work that resulted. The damaged dress had been sent over there for urgent restoration. After the initial burst of hysteria following upon delivery of the glorious Indigo Charisma, which had been the pride of the workrooms, there had been silence. It was to be hoped that all the girls were labouring madly on it.

"One can only hope—" Mme. Arlette threw a final despairing glance at the grey clouds outside the window—"that it does not also rain!"

Tamsin knew exactly what she meant. The East End workrooms were at the end of a long and very narrow cul-de-sac. An alley, really. Only a motorcycle could navigate it with ease. Once in it, no larger vehicle could turn around. Taxi-drivers took one look and decanted their passengers at the entrance to the alley, leaving them to finish their journey on foot. It was in a still unreconstructed part of the East End, with deserted half-destroyed warehouses looming on both sides of the alley, giving rise to uneasy fears about muggers at worst and rats at best. To trudge the length of that endless narrow strip in a deluge would be a nightmare.

"Tamsin—" The Duchess had arrived. "Send Kenny for some sandwiches, we're having a working lunch with some buyers. They'll be arriving any minute. Have him go to that place where they do the fancy ones.'

"Kenny's just gone out on two deliveries. He can't possibly get back in time."

"Here I am!" Nikko stood in the doorway, grinning broadly. He swaggered over to the filing cabinet and deposited his black helmet on top of it. "Won't I do?"

"That's the trouble," the Duchess snapped. "You'd do anything!"

"Too right!" He wriggled his hips at her with deliberate insolence. "Go on, try me."

"Where's Decemo?" The Duchess was not amused. In fact, she was moving toward what was known privately amongst the staff as her Off-With-Their-Heads mood.

"Ah, well, good question." Nikko seemed determined to provoke. "Ought to be here by now, oughtn't he? Slacking off, our boy. Other interests and all that." He smirked.

"This week," the Dutchess said coldly, "there *are* no other interests. The export buyers have first call on our time."

Something in her tone made Tamsin more certain that the rumour about the Duchess providing financing for Decemo Designers was true. Only that could explain her constant presence and intense personal involvement in the operation.

"Ah, well—" Did Nikko know it, too? He shifted uneasily, obviously prepared to backtrack. "His nibs said it was an important meeting. With Sunny and her boyfriend. Back from the States with all sorts of artsy-fartsy ideas, Jake is. Wants us to do a videotape for the American market. Decemo likes the idea. They're setting it up now. He'll tell you all about it when he gets here."

"*If* he gets here—" The Duchess's glare was glacial. "And he had better. He knows how important it is. You don't keep Seventh Avenue waiting."

For the first two days, the buyers had swanned around town "just looking", comparing one Collection with another, then taking their handouts, programmes and notes back to their hotels and doing some close figuring. Now they were on their rounds for the second time—and this time they were serious. Now they were going to get down to some concentrated bargaining—and buying.

"He'll be along," Nikko said. "Probably."

"He'd better be! After you've brought the sandwiches, find him and tell him to get here in time or I'll chew his balls off!"

"What makes you think he's got any?"

"I won't argue the point," the Duchess said icily. "You've been in a better position than I to know the truth of the matter."

Chapter 12

"I'll kill the sodding bastard!" the Duchess raged. "I'll strangle him with my bare hands!"

"What's the matter?" Tamsin stared blankly at the tray of succulent sandwiches which seemed to be the cause of all the fury. Nikko had deposited them on the desk and rushed off, not waiting for any reaction. Why should there be any? They looked all right to her. As ordered, Nikko had fetched them from the expensive shop some distance away. Beneath the cling-film were mounds of neatly-trimmed triangles overflowing with thick juicy fillings, oozing lettuce and mayonnaise. To tell the truth, they made her mouth water. Why was the Duchess looking as though she had just swallowed a spoonful of powdered alum?

"Look at them! *Look* at them!" The Duchess shook with fury. "He knows perfectly well that at least three of the buyers are Orthodox Jews—and every damned one of those sandwiches contains bacon, ham or prawns. He's done it deliberately! I'll murder him. No jury on earth would convict me!"

"Oh dear!" Tamsin began to grasp the enormity of the problem. She ought to have suspected something when Nikko had slammed the tray down on her desk and rushed off so quickly, but she had merely thought that he was trying to avoid being sent out for the coffee and pastries to accompany the sandwiches.

"Get rid of them!" the Duchess ordered. The buyers were beginning to arrive. "Send them into the studio and let Mme. Arlette and the girls have them. Take a couple of the girls and go down to the wine bar on the corner and get a selection of salad plates. Hurry!"

One more catastrophe narrowly averted. Perhaps something useful might eventually come of it. Even Decemo was beginning to look thoughtful as the Duchess detailed the complaints against his favourite, but he rallied quickly.

"Nikko is just high-spirited," he defended. "He doesn't mean any harm. He just likes his little jokes."

"That little joke could have cost us three of our biggest orders," the Duchess pointed out.

"But it didn't. It didn't do any harm at all."

"Only because we caught it in time."

"I'll speak to him," Decemo promised blithely. "I'll speak to him severely."

"See that you do." The Duchess was quite severe herself.

"Oh, I will, I will. Now—scolding over?" He gave her his most winsome smile. "Then let me tell you the *riveting* news! We're going into film."

"*Are* we?"

"Yes. Jake is setting it up. He's found the most marvellous little freelance film crew and he's bringing them over to start filming this afternoon's showing. They'll probably want a few chairs cleared away to give them room—" The winsome smile had disappeared and there was a calculating glint in his eyes. "If we can shoot the models while they're working anyway, we ought to be able to save on any extra fees."

"They're more likely to shoot you—down in flames," the Duchess warned. "Those girls come from an agency—they have some muscle behind them. You can't treat them the way you treat your own people. You'll have to pay them a thumping extra fee."

"Mmm. . . ." The calculator behind his eyes flickered rapidly; one almost expected to see a final total register in the glittering orbs. "Well, actually, we don't need them all, do we? Sunny and Reba are house models. The only outside model we really need is Carla— because of her size."

"Keep going, you're getting there."

"Mmmm . . . yes. In that case, we'd probably do as well in the long run, if we filmed at night with our own girls—and Carla. On film it wouldn't matter how long the costume changes took. It wouldn't show."

"And we wouldn't need to do away with any seating." That was the Duchess's chief concern. "We can't spare one chair. We have them standing against the walls, as it is."

"My most spectacular success to date." Decemo took all the credit.

"Yours—and a few other people's," the Duchess reminded him. "You'd do well to share out the laurels. Or you might find yourself without any designers for next season."

"Nonsense! They'd never be able to break their contracts!" His face shadowed suddenly, as though he might have remembered some unnoticed loophole. "Never," he said firmly, but seemed to be reassuring himself rather than anyone else.

"You should be more careful," the Duchess said. "You're reaching the point where adverse publicity might be as damaging as losing your bright young things. If any of them decided to tell their trouble to one of the scandal sheets, you could be pilloried."

"They're lucky to have jobs at all in this financial climate!" Decemo dismissed her qualms. "And they know it. If they went around complaining publicly, they might not find it so easy to get another job. Certainly not with a top designer. No one likes troublemakers."

"I've tried to talk sense to you." The Duchess sighed. "On your head be it."

"It will be, duckie, it will be," he assured her.

The afternoon showing was moving towards its close. The music had gone uptempo and louder. The audience was gratifyingly appreciative. They were smaller fry now, buyers for independent shops, journalist from lesser publications, students from art colleges. Nevertheless, their money and praise was as welcome as anyone's. It was already evident that both would be forthcoming.

In the reception area, Tamsin was coping with yet another telephone call from an importunate salesman and wondering when the new temp would arrive to relieve her. (The last one had left in high dudgeon after learning that the only perk was free coffee and not exclusive gowns at knockdown prices.)

Across from her, Nikko and Kenny were sitting on their chairs—only Nikko could sprawl on an upright chair—their crash helmets on top of the white flower-decorated filing cabinet, awaiting their next assignments. Nikko had a lazy grin on his face as he listened to her trying to fend off the caller.

He was responsible, she was sure of it. Damn him! She would not give him the satisfaction of seeing how annoyed she was. She tried to keep her face impassive as the salesman swore that her firm had sent in a form requesting full information on their new computer. He was incensed that she would not now agree a date for a representative to call and demonstrate it.

"We are *not* interested," she said firmly. "We never

have been. We never will be. I'm afraid you have been
the victim of a hoax—and so have we. I'm sorry you've
been troubled—"

She winced as the receiver at the other end of the
line slammed down, imperilling her eardrums.

"Don't look at me," Nikko said immediately. "I know
what you're thinking, but it isn't so. I had nothing to do
with it."

"Prove it," Tamsin said coldly.

"Can't, can I? That's why they've done it. They knew
I'd get the blame."

"Who are *they*?"

"Oh no." He shook his head at her. "I can't prove
that, either—"

"How very convenient."

"No, wait—" As intended, he was stung. "I'll find
out. I'm working on it."

"Don't strain yourself."

"You know, you shouldn't talk to me like that. It isn't
smart. You don't know the half of what goes on around
here. I could tell you a thing or two—"

"No doubt." Tamsin recognized the echoes of the
Duchess at her most glacial in her own tones and decided she could do worse. "However, there are certain
things I'd rather not know."

"Right!" Nikko was looking distinctly beleaguered.
Seeing this, Kenny had cheered up immoderately. "Have
it your own way. You'll be sorry. It's your funeral."

"Planning to send a wreath?" Tamsin quelled him
with the reminder that all had not been forgiven and forgotten, at least, not by everybody.

A burst of applause from the showroom indicated
the end of the fashion parade. The doors were flung open
and the half-dozen or so who were always the first to
leave sprinted for the stairs, frowning portentously at
their watches, letting the onlookers know that they had
far more important appointments awaiting them.

Gradually, the less pretentious began streaming
out, laughing, talking to each other, deploring the inev-

itable lack of taxis. Several nodded to Tamsin in a congratulatory way, admitting they had enjoyed the showing and approved the fashions.

The stragglers were still clustered around the catwalk, chatting with the Duchess and Decemo, who were at their most gracious. Some of these casual conversations would eventually harden into firm export orders.

The models milled about in the dressing-room, awaiting any summons to change back into a requested costume and display it for close inspection when it would be thoroughly examined and discussed. Quite often, minor changes to be effected by the designer were enough to clinch the sale. It behoved everyone to be at their most flexible.

Serious discussions were still continuing in the shoproom when Decemo appeared at Tamsin's desk.

"Has anyone arrived yet?" he asked.

Involuntarily Tamsin's gaze slid towards Nikko.

"Anyone important, I mean. Jake . . . and the camera crew."

Nikko's eyes hardened. One more grudge chalked up against the old firm. They'd be lucky if they didn't get a hearse at the door, next.

"Not yet," Tamsin said. She tried not to look at the affronted Nikko. Or at Kenny, who was so obviously enjoying Nikko's discomfiture. "Are they late?"

"Not really." Decemo checked his wristwatch mechanically. "No time was specified, but they should have been here by now."

"I'll let you know as soon as they arrive," Tamsin offered, hoping Decemo could take the hint and depart. Nikko looked as though he might be building up to a scene and there were still a lot of buyers around.

"Thank you, Tamsin." Without another glance in the direction of the messengers, Decemo went back to the showroom.

Tamsin tactfully did not hear Nikko's remark as the door closed behind Decemo. Kenny snickered.

"What are you laughing at?" Nikko demanded dangerously. "You don't know you're born yet, you stupid little nerd!"

Kenny sobered abruptly.

Tamsin tried frantically to think of an errand for one or both of them. Preferably sending them in opposite directions, before Kenny decided that he ought to vindicate his precarious manhood and the situation got out of hand.

"Kenny—" she began.

The clatter of footsteps on the stairs cut her off. Jake led the way into reception, followed by three men, two of them wrestling with camera and lighting equipment, the third encumbered by nothing more than a light-meter hung round his neck.

"Where's Sunny?" Jake asked.

"Still on duty in the showroom," Tamsin said. "No, please—" she added as he started forward. "You can't go in there yet. They're very busy." She pushed the buzzer under her desk to alert Decemo.

"Here!" Nikko lurched to his feet to loom menacingly over the man with the light-meter. "What are *you* doing here?"

"I'm going to work here now," the man said. "Won't that be cosy, lover-boy?"

"You're not! I'll see to that!" Nikko dived for the showroom.

"Hold it!" Jake ordered. "This has nothing to do with you. You're not in charge here. I've made these arrangements with Decemo's backing. So you can just shut up and sit down!"

"A lot you know—" Nikko blustered. "I've got more say than you think—"

"What's going on here?" Decemo appeared in the doorway, radiating fury.

"Your lad is getting above himself again," the photographer said. "Seems to think he can tell you what to do. Can he?"

"Nikko—" Decemo swept him with a look of icy contempt—"I've told you before. *I* run the business—

you run the errands. There's a pick-up at the workrooms.
Suppose you see to that!"

"Right! Right!" Nikko glared at Decemo. "I'll see to
that, all right. Then I'll see to a few other things! Don't
think you're going to get away with this!" He stormed
out.

"Sorry about this," Decemo sighed. "It's such a
fraught week, anyway. All our nerves are on edge."

"He's not picking up Indigo Charisma, is he?" Tamsin asked nervously. "I thought it would be safer—I
mean, better—to let Kenny handle that pick-up."

"Quite right. We wouldn't want anything to . . .
happen, again." Decemo nodded approval of her forethought. "No, it's nothing but a bundle of scrap material
to bring back here. Mme. Arlette wishes to experiment
with patchwork for next season. By all means, send
Kenny for Indigo Charisma. Nikko is a dear boy, but impetuous. We won't let him get his hands on it again."

While Kenny preened, Decemo turned to Jake.
"This is the film unit? They understand they mustn't disturb any seating arrangements until after the evening
showing?"

"This is Pete, our director and cameraman—" Jake
indicated the man with the light-meter—and the fast lip.
Tamsin smiled and nodded in her turn, making a mental
note that it would be necessary to keep him well apart
from Nikko. The other two names went by unnoticed as
she worried.

"We just want to get a look at the place where we'll
be shooting." Pete told Decemo. "Take a few light-readings, decide the best spot for the camera, leave a bit of
equipment in the corner—"

"You can't leave equipment in the showroom!" Decemo was aghast. "Tamsin will find you a place to store it
where it will be out of everyone's way. And any seating
you disturb will have to be replaced before you leave. We
must keep everything in readiness for the showings."

"There isn't much space anywhere this week," Tamsin said doubtfully. "Perhaps there's room in the broom
closet." She led the way into the dressing-room, glancing

inside first to make sure the girls were more or less dressed, preferably more.

Since Decemo hadn't yet given them the bad news about their chances of appearing on film, there was a flutter of excitement among the models as the ciné equipment passed through their midst.

Don't get your hopes up, Tamsin felt like warning, but that would have been too indiscreet.

"Oh!" Hattie turned and saw Pete. Her sudden deep rich blush was as red as her mercurochromed locks. "Oh. . . ." Almost visibly, she decided to play it casually. "Hello . . ." she turned back to her block and felt.

"Look—" He walked over to her. "I'm sorry I'm a little late—"

"Only by a couple of days." She savaged a piece of veiling and draped it over the felt. "Don't let it worry you—I wasn't holding my breath."

"Look—it's still on," he said. "Everything we talked about—and I mean everything."

"Really? I couldn't care less." She became very busy with feathers and brilliants. Her colour had receded and she was now paler than normal.

He shrugged and returned to the others. "You win some . . . you lose some," he muttered.

Unfortunately, Tamsin thought, the main loser was likely to be Decemo Designers. Along with everything else, they were now going to have a cameraman on the premises who was actively at odds with two of the staff.

Chapter 13

Only Sunny welcomed Pete as a friend. But Sunny welcomed everyone as a friend until proven otherwise— and sometimes long after that.

It was as well she had someone to be friends with

because, after Decemo had explained the situation to the other models, none of them were speaking to her.

"How cheap can you get?" They were speaking *at* her, instead. Most unfairly. It wasn't her fault. Just because Jake had set it up. How were they to know that Decemo would decide to cut out the other models?

"Hang around here and you'll find out!" There was a nasty ripping sound as Gloria tore off her dress and hurled it to the floor. She trod on it as she stepped forward to retrieve her own dress from the rack. If she were not in the mood she was in, it might have been an accident.

"No, thanks!" Suzanne followed suit. A button skittered across the floor. "I'll never work in this dump again! If they try to book me for next season, I'll bloody well refuse. They can't treat us like that!"

The last showing had ended and the camera crew were setting up in the emptied showroom. Muted sounds carried through the curtains to the dressing-room, driving the models to fresh fury. Chairs scraped the floor and clattered as they were removed and stacked. Voices called out instructions and information as cameras and lighting equipment were moved into place. All the preparations for filming—and they weren't going to be part of it!

"It's monstrous!" Jackie fumed. "I've got a good mind to—"

"If you ruin any of the dresses, you will never be invited to model here again!" Mme. Arlette had entered silently and stood frowning at the dresses on the floor.

"Who wants to come back?" But the rebellious mutter came ventriloquilly. Second thoughts were already setting in. It was all right to posture, but Decemo was becoming one of the hottest names in the fashion industry. They could not afford to refuse such a booking.

"I don't see why you're complaining." Carla was complacent. "We were only booked for the showings. Anything else is just gravy."

"It's all right for—*you*." Rancour still simmered. "Just because no one else can fit your dresses—"

"Who'd want to?"

"Girls! Girls!" Mme. Arlette called them to order. "There is no need for all this. The decision is not yet final. Tonight is only the start of the filming. We shall have to see how it progresses. It is quite possible that you may all be asked to do your share of the fashion parade."

"In a pig's eye!" Reba murmured serenely to Sunny.

She had forgotten. Reba was still talking to her. But you always tended to forget Reba. She was so often standing around in what appeared to be a mindless trance that it was sometimes hard to think of her as one of the living models at all. One of the plastic mannequins, yes. Until she opened her big mouth—usually at the most awkward moment.

"Shh!" Sunny winced. "Mme. Arlette is just getting them calmed down. Don't start them off again."

"Silly little cows!" Reba shrugged and moved away. She drifted over to the window and looked down at the narrow street below. She froze into immobility, her eyes glazed over, she was off into one of her trances again. At least, it kept her mouth shut.

Mme. Arlette was quietly gathering up the dresses from the floor and examining them for necessary repairs. Her face was grim but she did not jeopardize the precarious peace by making any further comment. Only those who knew her might suspect that some sort of retribution would be meted out at a future date.

"You're lucky—" Carla called to her departing colleagues. "At least you can go out and have a good time now—or go home and catch up on your beauty sleep. We'll probably be working till all hours."

The last one out slammed the door. Violently.

"They'll be all right tomorrow." Carla excused her friends. "Once they've adjusted to the idea that they're not going to get in on the new act, they'll be all right."

"Of course, they will," Sunny said comfortingly. "Anyway, it's me they're mad at. They aren't going to take it out on you. You needn't worry."

"I'm not." Carla glanced at her watch with a compla-

cent smile. "I've got nothing to worry about. I'm on overtime now."

Just the same, it was not so easy. Sunny had never
imagined that filming was so . . . well . . . boring. They
seemed to stand around for ever waiting for the lights to
be adjusted and then readjusted. It was all right for
Reba, who could slip into her famous impersonation of
an inanimate object, but she was almost ready to scream.
Even Carla was beginning to twitch.

"All right," Pete shouted. "Let's try it again."

With weary sighs all round—except for Reba, of
course—they launched themselves down the catwalk
again. It was hard to project the desired vivacity and enthusiasm on the umpteenth try. Sunny was conscious
that a blister might be forming on her heel; she longed to
get out of these rotten shoes. Lord help the customer
who bought a pair! Carla had surreptitiously gathered a
handful of bead-encrusted material in each hand and was
lifting it, trying to ease the weight of the dress.

Only Reba seemed unconcerned by anything.
When her cue music started, she sailed through the curtains on exactly the same foot, with exactly the same
smile on her face, at exactly the same pace.

"The creature's not human," Carla muttered. "She's
a robot. If you stuck a knife in her, she'd bleed springs
and cogwheels."

"I don't know how she does it," Sunny agreed. "I'm
so exhausted I could cry. Maybe she *is* a robot. That
would explain a lot of things."

Reba was half way down the catwalk, it was time for
Carla to burst through the curtains, looking as though
she were on her way to a sensational party and couldn't
wait to get there. Unfortunately, she looked more as
though she was going to sag to her knees and collapse.

"Can't we step a little livelier there?" Pete criticized. "This is supposed to be a *moving* picture, you
know."

"We're awfully tired." Sunny made her own entrance and looked towards Jake pleadingly. "We've been

doing this for hours—and we'd already put in a full day."

"Reba isn't complaining." There were moments when Jake believed more in fanning rivalries than in giving comfort. "Are you, Reba?"

"I'm all right," Reba said. "I could go on all night."

"Why shouldn't you be all right? You don't have to wear the heaviest dresses," Carla pointed out. "This dress weighs like a suit of armour."

"It certainly does." Sunny backed her innocently. "The one I had weighed a ton—and there's so much more of yours."

Too late, she realized that it was not the most tactful remark she could have made.

Someone snickered loudly. When Sunny turned indignantly, she found Nikko's face carefully blank.

"Do we have to have all these people around?" Again, she sought Jake's support.

"Yeah—" Pete's glance toward Nikko was meaningful. "I could do with a few less people around here, myself."

"Did I say anything? Did I do anything?" Nikko spread wide his hands in appeal. "I'm just hanging around here in case I might be useful. Because I want to do my share in building up the business. *I'm* not racking up overtime—"

Kenny cringed. He tried to avoid the eyes he felt sure were looking at him accusingly. *He'd* have been quite happy to go home at his usual time, but the Duchess had taken him aside. Him. Medora, Duchess of Farthingale, had asked a personal favour of him. He could not let her down.

"Kenny," she'd said. "I can't be here tonight. I have a prior engagement I can't escape. Promise me you'll stay here until everyone has left. Indigo Charisma is nearly ready. I want you to be the one to collect it. I don't want Nikko anywhere near it again. I wouldn't put it past him to pour petrol over it and set it alight. Caitlin has her instructions, she's to ring up and ask for you personally as soon as it's ready. It might not even be tonight but—" she levelled her large violet eyes at him—"but I want you here, just in case. Will you do that for me?"

"Oh, yeth . . . yess . . . yeth." He'd have promised her anything when she looked at him like that. "I'll never fail you, your Grathe—Graysss. . . ."

"Well, don't look at us." Hattie took exception on behalf of the designers. "Lillian and I have to help with the changes. Don't think—" she carefully refrained from looking at Pete—"we're here because we want to be. We're on duty, that's all. Of course, if the girls would *rather* struggle in and out of the dresses by themselves. . . ."

Mme. Arlette stood to one side, arms folded, disdaining to join the fray.

"I've finished my work," Tamsin admitted guiltily. She had only stayed on to see what filming was like. She had absolutely no excuse for remaining. It was sheer nosiness, that's all. "I—I can leave now."

"I didn't mean you," Pete said.

"We all know who you meant," Nikko said. He challenged Decemo directly. "What about it? You running the shop—or is he?"

"I am." Decemo looked from Nikko to Pete and the scales barely quivered. "Perhaps it's time everyone went home. We're all overtired."

"I'm not," Reba said.

"Most of us are overtired," Decemo corrected.

"You're a good girl, Reba." Jake spoke with the warm approval which usually belonged to Sunny alone. Sunny felt a strange twinge of alarm.

"Let's go home now, Jake." Sunny tired to pull his attention, his approval, back to herself. "Decemo says we can."

"Sure, sure." But his gaze still lingered speculatively on Reba. "You go and change."

"Shall I?" Sunny turned uncertainly to Decemo.

"Oh yes, yes, yes!" he snapped. "We never really expected to be able to film the whole show in one evening, anyway."

"I've got the colour lab on standby," Pete said. "We'll drop the film off now and tomorrow night we'll be able to see the rushes. We did pretty well tonight. We may have as much as two minutes."

"Two minutes!" Carla was horrified. "We've been here for hours!"

"These kind of films aren't shot," Pete explained. "They're spliced together. We'll run the rushes and choose the best shots out of all the takes. The whole thing will only run five or six minutes altogether. Shoppers haven't got all day to stand around in department stores, you know."

"And I've been nagging my agency to get me some TV ads," Carla said bitterly. "No more." She turned to Hattie. "Come and get me out of this . . . creation."

"Mmm, yes," Decemo watched with dissatisfaction as the models left. "I'll chase Caitlin when I get home. They *must* have Indigo Charisma ready for Sunny in time to be included in this video. Carla is all very well, but. . . ." He shrugged.

Kenny suppressed a yawn and began to think hopefully about the meal Mum would be keeping warm for him in the oven. He had not been quite so bored as the others, but it had been a long day. Also, although he hesitated to admit it to himself, he felt a bit cheated. He had kept his pledge to the Duchess by remaining until the last minute, but there had been no rush call for his services.

There had been no dramatic ride through the dark streets to collect Indigo Charisma from the workrooms. The fabulous dress was still undergoing repairs—or ought to be. He wouldn't put it past Caitlin and her workers to have packed it in and gone home for the night, even though they knew how important it was.

For a moment he toyed with a new fantasy: "Fear not, your Grace. I wouldn't admit this ordinarily, but I'm a dab hand at beadwork. When I was a little boy, my Mum taught me. . . ."

No, even in fantasy, he couldn't imagine his large awkward fingers picking up the tiny beads and threading them on the slender needle. Try again. . . .

Say . . . he offered to bring the dress home to his Mum. "My mother, your Grace, will be able to fix up that there dress in no time at all. No trouble following the design, either. She's an expert needlewoman." He'd fold the dress carefully into his despatch box and roar through the night. He'd walk into the house, toss it casually to his mum and she'd say. . . .

She'd say—"*What the bleedin' 'ell do you think you're about?*"

The fantasy crumpled abruptly upon the rocks of a personality too strong to fit into the script.

All right . . . go back to the real thing. What was really going to happen: the fearless dash through heavy traffic to the East End workrooms after the call came. Roaring down the narrow alleyway, pulling up short in front of the door. Then all the pretty twittering little Indian girls in their fluttering saris watching with proper awe and respect as he stalked through the workrooms, doffing his helmet, to collect the pride of the collection from Caitlin's office. . . .

"Spending the night, Kenny?" Tamsin snapped off the overhead lights, leaving only the dim nightlight.

"Oh!" Kenny blinked. "Has everyone gone?"

"We're the last," Tamsin assured him. "Come on, let's go. Your're asleep on your feet—and so am I." She yawned. "I'll be glad when this week is over."

Chapter 14

The message was chalked on the blackboard in block capitals when Tamsin arrived next morning:

KENNY
COLLECT I.C. FROM CAITLIN. SOONEST.

So, it was ready at last. She gave a sigh of relief and went through to the Publicity Office. She was not particularly surprised to find no hot coffee ready and waiting. True, the first one to arrive in the morning was supposed to start the big pot of coffee that simmered all day, but it seldom worked out that way. In theory, the receptionist should do it but, with the procession of temps they had had lately, that had gone by the board. In practice, it was usually left to Tamsin to clean out the dregs of yesterday's coffee and start the day's supply perking.

Apart from the message on the blackboard, there was no indication that anyone else had been in. Hattie and Lillian usually made a perfunctory appearance before dashing out to the bakery for a doughnut or Danish for breakfast, but this morning there was not even a scarf tossed over a chair or one of the sketchpads which usually marked their passage and promised their return.

Tamsin lifted out the filter of soggy grounds, carefully wrapped it in a discarded newspaper and deposited it in the empty wastebasket. Then she carried the business portion of the machine into the washroom to clean and fill it.

The place was still deserted when she returned. Of course, on such a grey and misty morning, she could not blame the designers if they lingered in the warm fragrant bakery until they decided someone else would have started the coffee going. Probably Lillian—or more likely Hattie—would come dashing back at any moment, clutching the familiar grease-stained bag and clamouring for her first cup of the day.

She'd just have to wait. Tamsin slotted in a fresh filter, measured coffee into it, set it in place and switched on the machine. It would take about ten minutes until it finished its little performance and there was a pot of coffee available.

Serve them right. Eventually, people might learn that the first one to arrive meant the first one.

The roar of a motorcycle below cut off her mental fuming. Kenny? She glanced out of the window to verify the fact. Yes, Kenny, thank heavens. The last thing in the world they wanted was to entrust the precious gown to

Nikko again. She went out into reception to meet Kenny as he came up the stairs.

He bounded up the stairs two at a time, whistling. He raised a hand in greeting, but his eyes automatically sought the blackboard—and brightened.

"It's ready, then," he said.

"Waiting for you to pick it up. Better get started before Nikko comes along. You wouldn't want him to beat you to it."

"Right away." He was back down the stairs without having taken off his helmet.

The point about Nikko was a good one. Tamsin picked up the despised swatch and wiped the message off the blackboard. Now Nikko would never know. It was safer that way. Otherwise, if Nikko came in and saw the message, he might try to race to the workrooms ahead of Kenny and gain possession of the garment. To annoy everyone, if for no worse reason.

Tamsin studied the blackboard critically, then moistened the swatch and went over it again. Now it gleamed greyblack, no residue of a message showing. That was better.

More footsteps on the stairs. She turned to face an unknown female who appeared to have wandered into the wrong building. "Yes?" she inquired.

"Good morning. I'm your new temp," the female announced.

"Oh, not again!" Tamsin cried in exasperation. "What happened to the one who was here yesterday afternoon?"

"Oh, she got a chance to join an overland trek to India. You couldn't expect her to give up an opportunity like that, could you? I've got her time sheet for you to sign. This my desk?"

"I suppose so," Tamsin sighed. "Where are you off to next week?"

"Corsica, probably. Only it may be the week after next. And it might be the Greek Islands." She sat down and pulled out her knitting. "Any special instructions, or is it just the usual?"

"What's the usual?" Tamsin asked faintly.

"Oh, answer the telephone, make the coffee, sort the post. You know."

"We *do* expect a few letters typed." If anyone got time to dictate any, but she wasn't going to let the girl get off to a completely wrong start. "Basically, you're taking over the lesser part of my job while I'm otherwise occupied this week."

In truth, the reception duties were becoming less and less Tamsin's responsibility and there was talk of trying to find a permanent receptionist. One—this being Decemo Designers—who could double as a model when the workload required it.

"Perhaps you'd like to start with typing out these notes." Tamsin handed over a sheaf of scribbled comments Decemo had made during last night's filming. "If you have any trouble with the handwriting, you can ask me."

"Sure." The girl frowned at her knitting. "Just as soon as I start work. I haven't signed in yet, you know. I got here too early. I gave myself plenty of time leaving home in case I had trouble finding the place. It's not nine o'clock yet."

Surprised, Tamsin checked her watch to discover that it was true. Only quarter to nine. Much earlier than she had thought. She was conscious of a faint sense of unease. Why had she thought it was later? Too overtired to sleep well last night, she had given up and arisen early and arrived here . . . when? About fifteen or twenty minutes past eight, it must have been.

Yet there had been a message waiting on the blackboard, denoting that someone had been here ahead of her. That must have been why she thought it was later. Because it was awfully early for a message to have come through from the workrooms. They didn't start work until eight-thirty there. Of course, Caitlin might have worked all night putting the finishing touches to Indigo Charisma herself. She took pride in her work and knew how important the dress was.

That must have been what happened. Satisfied,

Tamsin nodded to herself and went to inspect the show-room to make sure that all evidence of last night's filming had been cleared away.

Sure enough, it was as she had suspected. The cam-era and lighting equipment had been stowed away, but the chairs had not been replaced. Tamsin quickly made up the missing rows, by which time the coffee was bub-bling merrily in the other room.

She returned to the coffee-making machine, moved the first brewing over to the electric ring to keep it hot, then cleaned and refilled the machine to set a second pot brewing. A constant supply of hot coffee was more neces-sary than ever this week with the steady stream of buyers and journalists flowing through the studio.

"Tamsin—you're here already!" Hattie raced into the room, scattering belongings, and hurled herself into a chair where she sat gasping for breath. "I don't know how you do it! I was sure I'd be first in today."

'Even the temp was ahead of you,' Tamsin said wick-edly. 'You'll have to get up earlier.'

"Not bloody likely!" Hattie ruffled her hair, belatedly remembered that she shouldn't and began twisting it into spikes again. "The only reason I joined Decemo Designers was because the hours were ten to six."

"That's what I like about it, too."

"Except for London Bloody Fashion Week, when we get all these jet-lagged berks likely to show up at six A.M. because it's only midnight back in good old God-knows-where. And we're supposed to be here to humour them."

"It isn't quite that bad—" Tamsin broke off as Mme. Arlette appeared in the doorway. Automatically she poured a cup of coffee—black, no sugar—and held it out encouragingly to her.

"*Mon Dieu!* It is the crack of dawn!" Mme. Arlette crossed the room, navigating so far as could be seen by the scent of the beckoning coffee rather than any visual boundaries.

"Just three more days," Tamsin said cheerfully.

"Then they're all off to Paris and it's the French's problem." Too late, she remembered that Mme. Arlette *was* French and it was her problem here and now.

"*Aaah, merci!*" Mme. Arlette possessed herself of the coffee and took a deep revivifying swallow. Fortunately, she had not noticed Tamsin's gaffe. She shuddered and drank again.

"This nature of ours," she complained, "is not suited to the daybreak hours. Artistes should not have to rise at dawn."

"So we were just saying." Tamsin brought coffee to Hattie and poured a cup for herself. She set out a cup in readiness for Lillian, who must surely be returning with her snack bar nibbles at any moment, and sat down to relax while she could. The day would swing into action soon enough. From the ante-room came the comforting rattle of a typewriter, indicating that the temp had decided to start her day.

"If I were awake enough," Mme. Arlette said reflectively, "I would enjoy this part of the day. It is pleasant to sit down with friends and colleagues before the rush begins."

"And before the boss gets in," Hattie agreed. "I notice *he* isn't killing himself to get here early—no matter what week it is."

"I do not mind that so much," Mme. Arlette said. "But I think he should not show so much favouritism to—his favourite. It is bad for morale that Nikko should not arrive until well after the others. He is, after all, a mere despatch-rider. I have mentioned this to Decemo before."

"Never mind," Tamsin said. "Kenny's been in—and he's gone to collect Indigo Charisma. It can go back into the showings today."

"So soon?" Mme. Arlette looked at her watch. "Is the factory, too, beginning earlier this week?"

"Pardon me—" There was a perfunctory tap at the open door and the temp entered. "Do I smell coffee?"

"Come in," Tamsin said guiltily. "I meant to tell you. We keep a pot going all day. Help yourself."

"Great, but first I'd like to use the loo. If you don't mind telling me where it is."

"Oh, sorry. I forgot."

"Everyone forgets," the girl sighed. "That's the main thing I hate about temping. People will tell you everything except where to find the loo."

Tamsin led her to the small bright washroom and toilet. "This is the one we use. The men use the one out front, just before you get to the reception area.

"So I noticed. It makes a change. I was in a place once where every loo except for the one on the ground floor was for the men. I suppose they thought a woman's time wasn't worth as much as theirs, so it didn't matter if we had to go all the way down to the ground floor, no matter where we were working. Of course, it was against the building code—him an architect, too. Still," she shrugged, "he was paying for it." The girl walked into the washroom and closed the door behind her.

Glad to escape, Tamsin went back to the others, conscious of the sound of a motorcycle stopping outside. Kenny must have made record time, the traffic could not have been too heavy.

"Aaah," Mme. Arlette set down her empty cup. "He is back." She turned towards the door expectantly. "I wonder how good a job they have made of it."

"Magnificent, I should expect," Tamsin said, "knowing Caitlin. We probably won't even be able to tell where the beads were resewn." She refilled the coffee cups, this time including one for Kenny.

"Oh, ta—" The temp returned just in time to take up the cup, assuming it was hers. She helped herself to cream and sugar, sipped appreciatively, then looked around to join in any general conversation or gossip.

Almost visibly, they closed ranks against her. It was nothing personal but, any second now, Kenny was going to walk into the studio bearing the dress for inspection. They had kept the problem within bounds so far; no outsider should be around to carry tales at this crucial point.

"I think I hear the telephone ringing." Tamsin threw her a cue.

THERE'S NO MYSTERY TO THIS OFFER!

It's free! There's no obligation! No purchase necessary!
Enter the world of mystery *Classics* with *The Agatha Christie Mystery Collection* as your guide!

HERE'S WHAT YOU GET:

1. **FREE!** The New Bedside, Bathtub and Armchair Companion to Agatha Christie is yours to keep — *free*. The story of Agatha Christie's works and life — her plot outlines, stories on her filmed and staged works, but never whodunit! It normally sells for $12.95 but its yours to keep — *free and without obligation!*

2. **FREE PREVIEW!** Agatha Christie, the most popular novelist *ever*, with more than 500,000,000 copies of her books in print — now *you* can sample FREE for 15 days AND THEN THERE WERE NONE — in a special collector's edition. Read and enjoy this "classic" for 15 days — if you decide you don't want it — simply return it and owe nothing.

3. **EXCLUSIVE VALUE!** *The Agatha Christie Mystery Collection* offers you exclusive value that can't be matched. This special collector's edition:

• Is not available in bookstores anywhere.
• Each book is bound in rich, Sussex blue, with densely padded bindings, exquisite to the touch.
• Simulated leather covers are set off with distinctive gold embossing.

And best of all you pay only $11.95 (plus shipping and handling) for each luxurious volume.

4. **NO OBLIGATION!** Remember there is no obligation. Sample AND THEN THERE WERE NONE *free* for 15 days — return it and owe nothing. You keep your free copy of the fascinating Agatha Christie Companion book regardless. If you keep AND THEN THERE WERE NONE, pay just $11.95 plus shipping and handling and start your *Agatha Christie Mystery Collection*. Sample a different Agatha Christie novel, about once a month — always with 15 days to preview — always with the right to cancel anytime.

Take a trip into the "World of Mystery" today! Stamp your passport — complete, detach and mail your free-offer card.

FREE – Fascinating Agatha Christie Companion Book – a $12.95 value!

FREE – Preview of AND THEN THERE WERE NONE

No obligation! No purchase necessary!

ENTER THE WORLD OF MYSTERY!

YES! Please send me AND THEN THERE WERE NONE for a 15-day free examination and enter my subscription to *The Agatha Christie Mystery Collection*. If I keep AND THEN THERE WERE NONE, I will pay just $11.95 plus postage and handling and receive one additional volume about once a month on a fully-returnable 15-day free-examination basis. There is no minimum number of volumes to buy, and I may cancel my subscription at any time. My Free BEDSIDE COMPANION is mine to keep no matter what I decide.

20172

PLACE PASSPORT STAMP HERE!

LA45

NAME

ADDRESS   APT. NO.

CITY   STATE   ZIP

Here's your passport to the Agatha Christie "World of Mystery"

• It's free! • No obligation! • Exclusive value!

"Okay, I can take a hint." The temp drew herself up. "I know when I'm not—"

Fortunately, just them, the telephone did ring. Tamsin smiled innocently.

Giving her a suspicious look, the temp turned on her heel and left. The telephone stopped ringing almost immediately.

They sipped their coffee in companionable silence for a while . . . too long a while.

"But what is keeping Kenny?" Mme. Arlette frowned toward the empty doorway.

"Perhaps it wasn't him," Hattie said. "Perhaps it was Nikko."

"At *this* early hour?" Mme. Arlette gave a grimace of disbelief. "Even so, he has had time to get here. He is not slow to claim his coffee, that one."

"I'll go see what's happening." Tamsin said resignedly. It was unlikely that Kenny had been so smitten by the charms of the new temp that he had forgotten his duty; there must be some other reasonable answer. Possibly the telephone call had been for him—a sudden notification of the illness of his mother, or something.

"I suppose so—" the temp was saying into the telephone, her back turned to the entrance. "I can stick it for a couple of days, anyway, but—" She saw Tamsin and broke off abruptly.

A private conversation with the Agency, Tamsin surmised grimly. From the rapid turnover, it was apparent that Decemo Designers was not rated as a plum assignment in the temp world. She sent the girl a false smile and turned to check the rest of the reception area.

At first glance, everything appeared normal. The two familiar crash helmets—one black and one white— were in their accustomed places atop the white-painted flower-besprigged filing cabinet. Beside it, Kenny sprawled in one of the chairs.

Sprawled . . . his jaw sagged, his eyes glazed. Mouth open, he stared at her unseeingly.

"Kenny—?"

He did not respond.

Blast! She became aware of a thin crimson rivulet trickling down the front of the filing cabinet. *Hattie's spilled her rotten mercurochrome. We'll never get it off if it dries.* Automatically she started forward to try to wipe it off the white paint.

"No!" Kenny lurched to his feet. "No! Don't!" He moved between her and the filing cabinet. He seemed to be trying to block her view.

"But what—?" She sidestepped him, staring at the crimson rivulet, tracing it back to its source. It was leaking from beneath the black crash helmet. Something pale and white as the underbelly of a fish swam behind its smoked visor.

"Kenny—" Her mind blanked out, refusing to accept the evidence of her eyes. "Kenny, where's Nikko?"

He shook his head. His hands waved wildly. He seemed to be indicating the top of the filing cabinet. Then he suddenly thrust her to one side and stumbled into the men's washroom. Sounds of violent retching followed.

"No . . ." Tamsin whispered. "No!" She forced herself to look again—more closely—at the black crash helmet.

From inside it, two pale lifeless eyes stared back at her.

For the first and only time in her life, Tamsin heard herself screaming.

Chapter 15

Bedlam . . . pandemonium . . . hysteria . . . Sunny walked right into it. She halted just inside the door, unable to believe that she could have come to the right place. She must have taken a wrong turning somewhere,

entered the wrong doorway. This was never Decemo Designers!

Yet she recognized Tamsin—almost recognized her.
It was a Tamsin she had never seen before—and never
wanted to see again. This quivering, shrieking wreck
bore little resemblance to the cool coordinator who kept
the place running smoothly.

Hattie was howling in a corner. That was not so surprising. All the designers were temperamental, their
temperament just took different forms.

Some unknown female was also screaming her head
off, but to little avail. No one was going to worry about
her.

Mme. Arlette moved among them, distributing
slaps to the face with fine abandon. She greeted Sunny
with relief.

"Sunny—come help! It is too much, this. Sudden
mass hysteria! Get cold water. Throw it in their faces.
The strain has been too much. First—I cannot believe
it!—Tamsin cracked. And now they have all given way.
We must restore them before the buyers arrive."

"I'll drink to that!" Jake, immediately behind Sunny,
strode forward to take over. She watched him gratefully.
Jake always knew what to do.

"You—" Jake rounded on the unknown female.
"Who are you and what are you doing here?"

"I'm the temp," she wailed. "And I'm doing
nothing. I'm leaving!" She snatched up her wrap and her
knitting and fled.

"Well, that's reduced the decibels by one-third,"
Jake said philosophically.

"You shouldn't have let her go." Faced with a practicality, Tamsin began to recover. "The police will probably want to talk to her."

"The police?" Jake took an involuntary step backwards. "What have they got to do with this?"

"They—They—" Tamsin gave a long shuddering sob
and started for the telephone. "They'll have to know. I'll
have to call them."

"Wait a minute—" Jake caught her outstretched hand just as she was about to pick up the receiver. "What is all this? Let's talk this over. Why should we involve—?"

"Yes," Mme. Arlette backed him. "What is the matter, Tamsin. Why this hysteria? Why the police? Is it . . . more serious harassment?"

"It can't be," Jake said. "I mean—so early in the morning?"

"I'm sorry, Tamsin." Kenny stumbled out from the washroom. "I'm all right now." He still looked quite green around the gills. "I didn't mean to push you."

"What's the matter with you?" Jake asked suspiciously. "What have you been up to?"

"I'm sorry, Tamsin." Kenny ignored Jake. "I'm awfully sorry. I shouldn't have brought it here but—but I didn't know what to do with it. I picked it up—and then I couldn't put it down again because—because it would be like throwing him back into the gutter—"

"What's the matter with him?" Jake demanded of Tamsin. "What's he talking about?"

Tamsin just closed her eyes and shook her head—it was sweeping over her again. It was bad enough to realize it—she could not explain it.

Neither could Kenny. His face had gone blank again, his gaze turned inward, watching the nightmare replay. The mist had been patchy as he roared through the ever-more-deserted streets, past derelict warehouses, towards the isolated work-rooms. It had seemed spooky, even then. He had never really liked the place, he admitted that to himself now. Then, suddenly, the mist had become so thick that he had slowed instinctively as he approached the entrance of the long narrow alley. It looked more like the mouth of some dark cave than ever, with a black shape like a sentinel beast guarding the cave. When he'd blinked and edged closer, the shape had turned into a black helmet lying in a dark viscous pool. He'd dismounted and gone to investigate. People shouldn't leave expensive helmets lying around—and it had looked vaguely like Nikko's helmet, although it couldn't be. . . .

It couldn't be . . . it couldn't be. . . . Like the mist, his recollections became patchy. He'd picked it up. . . . *Hello, Nikko, what you doing here?* . . . He couldn't put it down again. . . . *Better come back with me.* . . . The despatch box—that was better than the gutter, wasn't it? . . .

"I'm sorry, Tamsin, I didn't think—" He spoke loudly—as though words could drive out the images. "I'll talk to the police. I should have called them myself. I didn't think. I—I just—" He broke off, swallowing hard.

There were more footsteps on the stairs, then Reba and Lillian strolled into the room. They stopped short, just inside the door, caught by the strange atmosphere.

"I know I'm late," Lillian said, "but you don't have to be like *that* about it."

"*I'm* not late," Reba said grandly. "Models don't have to get here until work has started. But—" She wrinkled her flawless forehead in puzzlement. "But what is everybody doing out here? And what's the matter with Hattie?"

"That's what I want to know," Jake said grimly. "If anybody could bother to tell me."

The telephone rang abruptly. Jake grabbed the receiver before Tamsin could get in. Loud ululating noises issued from it.

"Hello—Hello—I can't hear you. There's too much noise on the line. Can you speak up? . . . Oh, hello, Caitlin. What? Wait a minute—" He struck the receiver with the palm of his hand several times. The high eerie wailing did not diminish.

"It's no use. Let's hang up and try for a better line—"

A rattle of words at the other end of the line stayed his hand.

"What? Take it easy, Caitlin. I can't understand what you're saying. Try it again—louder and slower. It sounded—" he grinned. "It sounded as though you said 'headless body'—"

"*Jake!*" Sunny whispered. She plucked at his elbow. She had followed Tamsin's gaze at the words "headless body" and seen what Tamsin was looking at. She wanted to scream, but her vocal cords seemed paralysed. All that would come out was this faint bleat. *"Jake!"*

"You did? Oh, come on now, Caitlin. Fun is fun, but it's too early in the morning for games. What did you really call to say?"

"Jake . . . Jake!" Sunny pointed to the top of the filing cabinet.

"Give me the telephone!" Mme. Arlette snatched it from his suddenly nerveless grasp. She, too, was looking at the filing cabinet. Her jaw tightened. "Yes, Caitlin, I am listening. You have the police there, yes? . . . Yes . . . I agree." She listened in silence for a moment.

"Yes, Caitlin, I fear you are correct. It *is* Nikko. No . . . no, there can be no mistake about it. You see, we have the head here."

Lillian began to scream. Reba slipped gracefully to the floor in a ladylike faint.

"Oh my God!" Another practicality occurred to Tamsin. One she did not feel competent to deal with.

"Who's going to break the news to Decemo?"

The police had come and gone. They had come from the East End because the death had occurred in their bailiwick and it was therefore their responsibility to follow through on it. They left, taking the head with them to be reunited with its torso.

They also took Kenny. For questioning.

Helping with inquiries. The official phrase, with its grim undertone of putative guilt, was repeated at intervals. It was obviously intended to be soothing. The police had appeared to be sympathetic to Kenny's babbled claim that he couldn't remember what had happened. That he hadn't really seen anything—except the head, lying just outside the entrance to the alleyway. He'd thought at first it was Nikko's helmet, fallen off somehow, and had stopped to retrieve it, thinking he'd joke with Nikko about being careless when he returned it. Only . . . only . . . it had been awfully heavy when he picked it up . . . and found Nikko's head still in it.

Kenny, embarrassed, had had to retreat to the washroom again before he could go away with the police to help with further inquiries. He was only seventeen and clearly in a state of shock.

For that matter, so was everyone. Without a great deal of encouragement from the police, who felt *they* should be asking the questions, the staff had managed to piece together some of the story. There had been a thin steel cable stretched across the alleyway at throat height for someone on a motorcycle and all but invisible in the grey early morning mist. Nikko, going at his usual daredevil speed, had never had a chance.

The initial hysteria over, second-stage shock had set in. Everyone had moved back into the studio. No one wanted to sit at the reception desk, staring at that filing cabinet, even though Jake, using language the Duchess might have envied, had swabbed it down with wet paper towels after the police had finished with it.

After that, he had taken a good look at them all and dashed out, returning shortly with a bottle of brandy.

"Jake is a tower of strength," Sunny said fondly, as he departed on his errand of mercy.

"Yes," Mme. Arlette had agreed and immediately telephoned the Duchess again. This time she got through.

They were still sipping their first glass of brandy when the Duchess arrived.

"What the sodding hell is going on here?"

As the Duchess glared at them, Hattie and Lillian suddenly felt restored enough to drift back to their drawing boards, although they still kept a firm grip on their glasses.

"Medora—" Mme. Arlette came forward, discarding formality. "The situation is extremely grave."

"It certainly is!" the Duchess snapped. "The first showing is coming up and, from the looks of it, our two house models are going to be reeling down the catwalk. We'll be lucky if they don't fall off into the customers' laps."

"I am *not* drunk!" Stung, Sunny set down her glass.

"Neither am I," Reba said haughtily. "But I wouldn't

care if I was," To underline this, she took another sip.

"You'd be drinking, too," Hattie said. "If you'd seen what we've seen."

"All right." The Duchess softened her tone. "I've heard about it. It was terrible for you. So was the cause—a steel wire stretched across the alley. A nasty way to go." With a faraway look in her eyes, she shuddered.

"And an even nastier sight for someone to come upon," Mme. Arlette pointed out. "I fear both Kenny and Caitlin will have bad dreams for many nights ahead. As will the rest of us. I think it would be wise to replace that filing cabinet."

"We'll do that," the Duchess said. "But I can't understand what Nikko was doing at the workrooms at that hour. He's never been up with the lark before."

"There was a message on the blackboard when I got here—and I was early," Tamsin answered. "It said Indigo Charisma was ready and Kenny was to go and pick it up. Nikko must have got here before any of us, seen the message—and rushed off to collect the dress."

"Not quite before anyone," the Duchess said. "Who was here first? Who wrote the message on the blackboard?"

There was silence.

"The little man who wasn't there, eh?" The Duchess nodded grimly. "All right, we'll try again—and I'll promise the culprit immunity from a scolding for being so careless as to chalk up the message where anyone could see it. I'll agree that it was most unlikely that Nikko would ever have been here so early. You couldn't have known. Now, who wrote the message? Any takers?"

Silence again. Then: "It wasn't on the board when I got in," Hattie said. "And I was the first, after Tamsin— and the temp."

"I erased it," Tamsin admitted. "So that Nikko shouldn't see it and try to race Kenny to the workrooms. But it was on the board when I arrived."

"All right," the Duchess said. "We'll let it go for the moment. Undoubtedly, the police will have something more to say about it. By the way, I don't suppose they let slip just what kind of wire it was?"

"Does it matter?" Mme. Arlette sounded weary. "There are so many kinds of wire, so readily available. It could have come from a grand piano, or it could have been the sort of wire one uses to hang pictures. A child could have found some and improvised a trap, not realizing how deadly it could be. A delinquent could have stolen a reel of thin cable from a construction site and decided to have some—some *fun!* Vandals, maniacs—" Her voice broke. "There is no shortage of people who might do this sort of thing. We are living in a strange and violent age."

"You think it could be part of the harassment campaign?" the Duchess suggested softly.

"Oh, now wait a minute," Jake protested. "I know you people have been having a rough time, but be reasonable. Who'd go that far? After all, those incidents were really more like practical jokes."

"It might not have been intended to be fatal," Tamsin said. "The message was for Kenny. He's more careful than Nikko. He wouldn't have turned the corner at such speed. He could have seen it and stopped in time."

"Kenny . . ." the Duchess said thoughtfully. "I suppose he has no enemies—that we know of?"

"Only Nikko," Sunny said, then looked surprised at herself. Jake squeezed her arm warningly.

"No . . ." the Duchess decided regretfully. "He wouldn't have fallen into his own trap. Not Nikko."

"What about the . . . jokes?" Jake asked. "Are you going to tell the police about them? You haven't so far. But . . . when they come back? . . ."

"A good question." The Duchess and Mme. Arlette crossed glances.

"Jake makes an excellent point," Mme. Arlette said. "It is better not to launder our soiled linen in the public eye. Now that Nikko is dead, it is unlikely that we will have any more trouble. We have always known the source of our problems."

"Mmm," the Duchess said. "Just the same, I'd like to learn more about the whole . . . accident."

"Caitlin might be able to tell us more," Mme. Arlette said. "It was she who notified us that they had . . . discovered the body there."

"Caitlin. . . ." The Duchess looked thoughtful. "She never did get along with Nikko, did she?"

"Did anyone?" Mme. Arlette gave her Gallic shrug.

"He was impossible," the Duchess agreed. "Nevertheless, his demise—and the manner of it—may present difficulties."

"Surely not insurmountable?" Mme. Arlette murmured.

"Not for *us*. . . ."

They met each other's eyes and looked away again quickly.

"Fortunately—" Mme. Arlette glanced toward the young designers—"the work on the new collection is progressing well."

"And this one looks like being a great success. Decemo can coast along on the sheer momentum for a while. Any publicity needn't necessarily be a bad thing."

The rumour *was* true, Tamsin realized, listening to them. The Duchess *did* have a substantial investment in Decemo Designers. The businesslike, almost conspiratorial, discussion confirmed it.

The telephone rang in the outer office. Tamsin started for it. The Duchess put out a hand, halting her.

"Let the temp get it," she said.

"The temp has left," Tamsin said.

"Again?" The Duchess rolled her eyes heavenward. "No stamina, those silly cows."

"One *did* come in this morning—" Tamsin apologized for the defection. "But she left after we found the—Found Nikko." In all fairness, she added, "You can hardly blame her."

"No, I suppose not," the Duchess said absently. "Well, ring up and order another one. On second thought, perhaps you might try a different agency. We may be blackballed at the usual one."

Once the temp had made her report, they probably would be. Agencies put up with a lot in the interests of the high earnings their employees reaped, but there were limits. When the police descended to question the girl—as they undoubtedly would—and long unpaid-for hours were wasted, that limit would undoubtedly be reached.

The telephone continued to ring.

"Oh, all right." The Duchess released her abruptly. "Answer the damned thing!"

Trying to pretend that the filing cabinet and its grim memories were not there, Tamsin flung herself at the reception desk and picked up the receiver. Instinctively she whirled to face the wall—anything to put the filing cabinet out of sight. But the blank blackboard brought another overriding memory. She scarcely heard, at first, the voice at the other end of the line insisting that she had filled in a coupon asking for full details of their special offer of a built-in double oven with free full set of—

"No!" she screamed into the mouthpiece. "No, no, no! It's a hoax! We never filled out your rotten coupon! We're not interested! We have enough problems . . . enough problems!" She slammed down the receiver, fighting back tears.

"More harassment!" The Duchess appeared behind her. "Did you get the name of the place? Ring them back quickly and tell them to send us the coupon. We'll match up the handwriting. All we need is that bit of proof—and then I'll tear the little bastard limb from bloody—" She broke off aghast, abruptly realizing what she was saying.

"It is all right." Mme. Arlette patted her shoulder. "There will be no more of this. Perhaps once or twice, from coupons already in the post—a fleabite. It is over . . . now."

Chapter 16

"My darlings—" Decemo stood before them, rallying his troops. "I know how you must feel—and you know how I must be feeling—" He swayed dramatically, a willow wand in the teeth of a hurricane. From somewhere, he had unearthed a black silk suit, black shirt and deep purple four-in-hand tie.

Widow's weeds, Tamsin thought irreverently. Yet they suited him. The dead-white mask of his face was expressionless, but his voice quavered and halted before resuming—

"The Show Must Go On! Our poor dear Nikko would have wanted it to."

Beside her, the Duchess barely repressed a snort. What poor dear Nikko would really have wanted was for Decemo, in a paroxysm of grief, to set fire to the premises and then commit suttee on the blazing pyre.

"And so, my darlings—"

Outside, in the showroom, the buzz of anticipation rose to a frantic pitch. There had been a Stop Press item in the early editions, but the grapevine had been faster and far more efficient. Full details were still lacking, but enough of the foreground had been sketched in to give the general idea. There was standing room only out there as everyone hoped that they might somehow get some inside information.

"I would rather it had not been a *succès de scandale,*" Mme. Arlette murmured caustically.

"And so, my darlings—"

The models, dressed and poised to hit the catwalk, rustled expectantly.

"I want you to go out there and make Nikko proud of

us! I know that, somewhere, he's watching and cheering us on. He wouldn't want us to—to destroy ourselves with grief." Decemo pulled out a black-bordered linen handkerchief and mopped at his forehead, discretely touched the corners of his eyes.

"We may be *distrait*, we may be inconsolable—but we must be triumphant. For *his* sake. And so, I ask it of you, my darlings, and I know you will not fail me—go out there and make Nikko proud of us!"

He collapsed into a chair, his handkerchief hiding his face. The curtains parted and the fashion parade commenced.

"Pardon me for being so confused," Jake muttered to Tamsin, "but is he asking the girls just to sail out and saunter down a catwalk—or to charge out there and fight, fight, fight for Old Notre Dame?"

"Shhh!" It was a legitimate comment, but Tamsin was concerned. Decemo was not usually so camp. Was it the measure of his grief or was he indulging in a little posturing?

Behind the handkerchief, Decemo was stirring again. Tamsin moved quickly to distance herself from the irreverent Jake just before Decemo stood and, still clutching his handkerchief, came over to join her.

"Was it all right, do you think?" he asked anxiously.

"Inspiring," she said, since that had obviously been intended.

"Oh, good." He folded the black-bordered handkerchief neatly and tucked it into a pocket where it would be readily available. "One didn't want to go over the top—but some natural emotion must be allowed to show through. Otherwise, people might think that one was *unfeeling*."

"I'm sure no one would ever think that."

They were standing at the foot of the steps leading up to the stage. The girls moved past uneasily, almost genuflecting in tribute.

"One hopes not—" He pulled out the handkerchief again, touched it discreetly to the corner of one eye, then dabbed at his forehead. A fine mist of white powder momentarily obscured his expression. "One tires—but the shock . . . the shock. . . ." Suddenly he looked older, years beyond his chronological age. "It's all so— The shock. . . ."

"Why don't you sit down?" Tamsin guided him back to his chair. "Jake had some brandy here earlier. I'll see if I can find it."

"Dear girl, you're so kind." With a sigh, Decemo leaned back and closed his eyes. "I must gather my forces. I must appear on my accustomed cue. My public expects it. The show must go on . . . go on. . . ."

He had recovered enough, however, to stand by the doorway at the end of the showing and accept the kudos and the veiled expressions of sympathy.

"Thank you . . . thank you." The black-bordered handkerchief was much in evidence. "So kind of you. . . . Yes, yes . . . a great loss. Such a brilliant, promising talent—" The fact that Nikko had merely been a messenger-boy had already become somehow obscured in the mists of legend.

"You poor dear. So brave—" Irene Warner leaned forward to brush his cheek with her lips. "You mustn't look back, you must look to the future. You've outdone yourself with this Collection—and I'll be placing the most substantial order yet."

They were all placing their orders. They had not quite the face to view the Collection more than once without doing so. And, for some of them, this was the third visit. Drawn by the hint of scandal, the *frisson* of horror, they counted the cost of an order a small price to pay for a story they would dine out on for months to come. In truth, most of them would have returned to place firm orders anyway. The Collection was brilliant, their customers would mob the fashion departments as soon as it went on sale.

The fact that each order would be accompanied by a video cassette was an undiscovered bonus as yet. If—

"We *are* going on with the filming, aren't we?" Carla had asked anxiously.

"So far as I know," Tamsin said. "It has all been arranged and I don't think Decemo could back out now, even if he wanted to." And if he did, Jake would have something to say about it. He would not stand by and let his pet project be scuttled.

"That's good," Carla sighed with relief. "We ought to get along a lot faster tonight—without Nikko mucking things up."

"I didn't realize he was upsetting you."

"Upsetting *me!* Didn't you see what he was doing last night? Every time no one was watching him, he was nudging the lights out of place with his foot. That was why they had so much troule and had to keep adjusting them."

"No wonder the photographer wanted him out of the place. He must have suspected it, but couldn't prove it."

"I caught Nikko at it once, but I was afraid to say anything. He frightened me." Carla shuddered. "I can't say I'm sorry he's gone. Life will be a lot smoother without him."

"Yes," Tamsin admitted. "It will, but I shouldn't make a comment like that in front of Decemo."

"As if I would! He's taking it awfully well, isn't he? It can't have sunk in yet."

"He'll be all right as long as he keeps busy—and has an audience. It will be different when he's alone."

"Poor devil." Carla glanced around uneasily. "I suppose we all ought to go to the funeral. Whenever it is."

"I don't know much about these things," Tamsin said. "But I think it will be a while before the police release the body. They're still asking questions. They're supposed to be bringing Kenny back here later and then they've said they want to talk to the rest of us again. The Duchess got them to agree to wait until the afternoon showing is over."

"I'm surprised they'd bother so much. All these motorcycles are just accidents looking for a place to happen. It only surprises me that more of them don't get killed."

"Nikko always did take dreadful chances," Tamsin admitted. "Decemo was always on at him about it. But he couldn't have foreseen vandals.

The Duchess spent every moment of free time between showings on the telephone. She had sent her solicitor to the police station to provide moral support, if nothing else, for Kenny and Caitlin, then made a series of calls to influential friends who might be able to bring some sort of pressure to bear on the police. She had had a hectic afternoon.

For once, the strain showed in her face as she turned away from the telephone. She looked almost haggard and there were dark shadows under her eyes.

"More coffee, Medora?" Mme. Arlette moved forward to place a fresh cupful on her deck.

"No, thank you." The Duchess pushed it away. "I've had too much already. Any more caffeine and I'll never sleep tonight. I may not sleep, anyway. Where's Tamsin?"

"Yes?" Tamsin materialized at her side, notebook at the ready.

"Any news?"

"Kenny isn't back yet," Tamsin reported. "Caitlin is still helping with inquiries, too. I managed to reach the workrooms forelady at home, but she has hardly any English. I got about ten words out of her—none of them any use—and then she started wailing."

"Par for the bloody course," the Duchess sighed. She dropped her tinted glasses over her eyes and switched on an automatic smile as the first of the audience arrived for the evening showing. "Let me know as soon as any of them turn up."

"Yes, of course." The Duchess wasn't the only one who wanted full details of the accident. There were more journalists than buyers crowding in for the next show. Tamsin moved to block their way as some of the more enterprising tried to go behind the scenes, rather than into the showroom.

"Tamsin, I've just heard. Is it true?" Mitzi Kayce

pushed aside a couple of hopeful fashion writers to confront Tamsin eagerly.

"What have you heard?" Tamsin was cautious, mindful of listening ears. "Er, come inside for a minute." She
drew Mitzi into the dressing-room and shut the door
firmly behind them before Mitzi could yodel out whatever indiscretion was coming next. So far, the newspapers hadn't learned about the gruesome discovery on
the filing cabinet—but Mitzi might well have heard
something. She was the sort who was always first with
the news—the most scandalous news.

"Nikko—he's really dead?"

"Yes." Tamsin shuddered. "There's no doubt about
it."

"And Decemo is prostrate?"

"Not noticeably, I hope, dear." Decemo appeared
behind them. "One tries to carry on. There'll be time for
all that later. Right now, the show must go on. And you'll
want to get to your seat, won't you, dear, so that you
won't miss any of it?"

"Oh, but I've seen it before—"

"Not properly. Hurry, now, we're ready to begin—"
Expertly he manoeuvred her out of the dressing-room
and into the showroom. The music had already started.

Above the music was the sound of some sort of commotion from the reception area. Tamsin hurried out before it could disturb the audience.

"I can't sign for anything—" A wild-eyed receptionist, who had been on duty all of three hours, confronted a large belligerent man in overalls. "I'm not
authorized, I'm only the temp. Besides, it can't be right!
This is a fashion house."

"Right? Of course, it's right. This is the address—" a
grubby finger stabbed at an invoice—"isn't it?"

"What's the matter here?" Tamsin asked crisply.

"She won't sign my delivery note." The man was aggrieved. "Here—can you sign for it?"

"Sign for what?"

"What you ordered. I've got a ton of gravel in the
lorry down below. Where do you want it?"

Chapter 17

"This persecution cannot go on for much longer," Mme. Arlette said. "These are the things that he had already set in motion. Now that he is dead, they will soon stop."

"I refuse to listen to any more of this!" Decemo rose to his feet. "I cannot believe that my poor dear Nikko had anything to do with this hideous spite campaign. He—He always had my interests at heart. He wouldn't disrupt the studio during the most important week of the year. He'd know how bad it might be for business."

"I am sorry—" Mme. Arlette did not apologize for her suspicion, but for voicing it. "I should not have said such a thing. It is possible that he is innocent." She did not sound convinced. "Time will tell."

"Yes, it will," Decemo said coldly. "You'll see. This isn't like Nikko, at all. And now, I'm going to lie down and rest until the film unit gets here. I'm quite, quite exhausted!" He swept out.

"I hate to admit it," the Duchess said thoughtfully, "but he may have a point there. It would have been more like Nikko to have ordered a ton of manure."

The familiar scenes of London sped past in a blur, looking strangely distorted seen from the back seat of a police car. Holborn Viaduct was just stone balustrades and railing, the monumental bronze Victorian figures too far above the level of his restricted vision to be seen. Holborn Circus . . . High Holborn . . . the reverse of the journey he had taken this morning on the way to the factory; the journey Nikko must have taken before they

both made their nightmare return journey together . . .
or partly together.

Kenny shook his head again, even though he had
discovered hours ago that it was useless. He could not
dislodge the images imprinted on his brain. They would
be there until his dying day. Maybe longer. Maybe he'd
never escape them . . . in this life or the next.

"You all right back there?" The policeman not driving turned his head to check. The police had tried to be
kind. They had even sent out for something to eat . . .
not that he could. That was another worry, would he ever
be able to eat again? At the mere thought of food, his
stomach quaked.

"We're all right," Caitlin said, then muffled a squeal
as the car took a sharp turn. She slid along the seat and
clutched at Kenny for support.

He put his arm around her to steady her, barely
aware that he did so. Her wheelchair was folded up and
stowed in the boot. She was more subdued than he had
ever seen her. Of course, she'd taken her share of the
shock, more than her share. No girl should ever have had
to look at a thing like that. His arm tightened protec-
tively around her.

Say . . . he fought desperately to ward off reality as
they wound through the streets of Covent Garden. *Say*
. . . he'd been earlier this morning . . . got there before
Nikko . . . seen the message on the blackboard and gone
off on that errand. . . .

*Then he'd have been the one lying in that alley in two
pieces instead of Nikko!* Reality slapped him in the face.

No! No! . . . Say . . . say he wouldn't have been
travelling so fast. *Say* . . . he'd had to slow down so's he
wouldn't hit a stray puppy that had dashed out into the
road just before he got to the turning. Then he'd have
been able to stop when the sunlight—the sun would
have broken through the clouds suddenly—when the
sunlight glinted on that wire stretched across the alley.
He wouldn't have come to any harm then. And Nikko
. . . Nikko would still be alive.

But he wasn't. Reality struck again. For the first time in his life, Kenny's daydreams were failing him.

And the reality was crueller and more vicious than anything he had ever tried to escape before.

KENNY . . . the message on the blackboard had been headed *Kenny.* They meant *him,* they'd wanted *him.* Someone had intended that it was he who ought to have gone charging off and smashing into that deadly trap.

It was *him* they'd wanted torn to pieces.

But why? What had he ever done to anybody that they should want to kill him? What? . . . Why? . . .

He'd seen the question lurking behind the eyes of the policemen as they'd questioned him. Sometimes politely, sometimes menacingly, they'd gone over the questions, hour after hour. After a while he'd caught the rhythm and been able to answer the questions behind the question, the ones they didn't quite ask.

No, there was no reason. No sane reason . . . he didn't want to think beyond that. He wasn't connected with crime in any way. He wasn't racing dope supplies across the city to fill orders telephoned to pushers. He wasn't acting as a lookout for thieves. He wasn't privy to any specialized dangerous knowledge. He wasn't working with gangsters, spies or muggers. He was just what he seemed to be: a seventeen-year-old in his first job with his first motorcycle. He was no danger to anyone; no threat. Who'd want to kill him?

There was no reason . . . no sane reason . . .

"Here we are—" The police car drew to a halt in front of Decemo Designers. Kenny stared blankly at the familiar entrance.

"All right, son." The paternal copper was becoming more annoying than any of the others. The familiarity grated on Kenny's nerves. "Here we are. If you'll just get out, I'll take care of the little lady, son."

Don't call me son! But he couldn't say it. There was no point in antagonizing the police. Not over a silly thing like that.

Caitlin threw him a plaintive glance. They were two

of a kind, from the same sort of background. The police weren't exactly their enemy, but they weren't friends, either. They were a neutral force which could veer— quite capriciously—in either direction.

"You take care of her chair—" Kenny slid out of the car and reached for Caitlin. He was inexpert, but she was helping as much as she could. He straightened up triumphantly, holding her in his arms. She was lighter than he had expected. He could carry her up the stairs easily.

"I'll take care of Caitlin, myself."

To everyone's relief, Decemo received the police with dignified reserve. The police, in their turn, seemed neither censorious nor surprised. Their questions were clear and concise. The same could not be said for the answers they received.

No one would possibly want to kill KENNY! Everyone was firm about that.

And Nikko?

Well. . . . The police began to get the message.

"Of course, the message was addressed to Kenny," Tamsin told them. "But anyone would have known that, if Nikko had seen it first, he'd have rushed over to collect the dress . . . just to be irritating."

It was unfortunate that she had erased the message. They had only her word—and Kenny's—that it had ever existed. And that it had said what they claimed it said.

"I blame myself," Decemo told them, a shade too emphatically. (They looked in danger of believing him.) "It was a silly little *spat*—that was all it was. I should never have let him rush out of the house in anger. Otherwise, he'd have arrived at the normal hour with me. . . ."

"Nikko was . . . impetuous," Mme. Arlette let them know. "He was . . . interested in all aspects of the work here. Yes, he would have thought nothing of hurrying over to make the pick-up, no matter who was assigned to do so. He was . . . most impetuous." Let them make what they would of that.

"Nikko?" Medora, Duchess of Farthingale, cleared her throat and spoke thoughtfully, her large violet eyes wide with disbelief. "I suppose it's possible, but . . . I find it very hard to think of Nikko as . . . a victim. Surely it must have been an accident, a freak accident. Children—vandals—you ought to catch them before they start derailing trains. You're wasting your time here. The only crime you'll ever unearth around here is character assassination."

The police were patient and persistent. They had really expected no better on the early rounds of inquiries. East End or West End, people closed ranks when their own circles were threatened by outsiders.

It was as well they had such patience. Already the novelty of their presence was wearing off and the designers, irreverent by nature, were reverting to type. Even they remained guarded, however.

"Honestly," Lillian claimed, "I haven't been paying that much attention. You don't know what it's like, launching a Collection. King Kong could walk into the showroom and all I'd think would be: do we have enough material to run up anything in his size?"

"You don't imagine we get a chance to notice what's going on, do you?" Hattie complained. "They've been working us double all week. Along with everything else, we've had to dress the models for the showings. And, let me tell you, that's no picnic. You wouldn't believe how awkward they can be."

"The other models?" Tamsin frowned. "They've gone home for the day. They aren't included in the filming—only Carla. But they wouldn't know anything. They've only been hired for this week, brought in from outside, an agency. Only Reba and Sunny are house models—and they're too busy to talk right now. Not that they'd know anything, anyway."

The police insisted.

"Wait a minute—" Tamsin had a brainwave. "I think Reba might be free. You can talk to her." That ought to convince them that the models were too thick to know if it was raining outside, let alone anything of importance.

In the showroom, however, the camera crew were already at work. Pete, busy taking readings from the light-meter hanging from the leather cord around his neck, was quite ready to stop and talk for a moment.

"Nikko dead? That's the best news I've heard all week. It should happen to a few more in this business. What happened? Did he get shot by a jealous lover?"

He sobered at being told what had happened. "Nasty, very nasty. Say—" he snapped his fingers— "that's an old Indian trick, isn't it? You'd better check out the girls at the factory. See if any of them have Thuggee boyfriends or relatives."

"My girls had nothing to do with it!" From the corner where she had been sitting in her wheelchair watching the filming, Caitlin flew to the defence of her brood. "They're all good, honest, respectable girls. Just because they don't speak English, you can't blame this on them!"

"I'm not saying they're not good girls, but you don't know what even good girls get up to these days. One of them might have been playing around and her husband or boyfriend was out for revenge. It's possible."

"It's nonsense. . . ." But Caitlin's voice wavered, a thoughtful look came into her eyes. She was obviously mentally running through the roster of her girls and trying to recall what she knew of their private circumstances. It *was* just possible.

The police were looking thoughtful, too. An interpreter had already interviewed most of the factory girls, but had the right questions been asked?

Kenny had moved his chair from the reception area into the studio. No one blamed him. They wouldn't have wanted to sit alone out there beside the filing cabinet, either. Although they were too busy to fraternize, they all sent him friendly smiles and the occasional odd word. Basically, they just wanted to rush through tonight's filming and get away from the place.

Kenny sat silently, in a trance he might have borrowed from Reba. His mind veered between the overactive and the total blank. He had argued himself to a standstill. No one could have wanted to kill him . . . but

Nikko was dead in his place . . . doing his job. If it was an honest mistake, why hadn't someone admitted writing that message on the blackboard? Everyone denied it. Some were even swinging round to suggesting that he and Tamsin had imagined it or—

The ice-cold hand touched his suddenly. He leaped to his feet, prepared to defend himself. He looked around wildly.

"I'm sorry, I didn't mean to startle you." Caitlin looked up at him.

"No. No—I'm sorry." That was why he hadn't heard any footsteps approaching, the rubber-tyred wheels were soundless. He sat down again, to get closer to her level. "Are you all right?"

"Just tired. I . . . I thought I'd like to leave now. . . ." She gave him an imploring look and he knew the favour she didn't like to ask.

"Sure, right. I'm through here myself now. They're going to be packing up soon. Nobody's going to work too late tonight. They won't need me for anything." He walked beside her as she wheeled herself out to the reception area, realizing that she wanted—and must be allowed—to do as much as possible for herself. She stopped, with a sigh, at the top of the stairs.

"Right," he said. "I'll carry you down and sit you on the bottom step, then come back for the chair, right?"

"That's fine," she said. "Then, if you can just find me a taxi, I'll be all right."

"You sure?" At the foot of the stairs, he was strangely reluctant to put her down. "Look—have you had anything to eat today? I mean, when the coppers brought in those sandwiches, did you eat any?"

"No," she said, "Did you?"

"I couldn't, either," he said. "Wait here a minute—" Forgetting that she could do nothing else, he raced back to the top of the stairs and returned with her chair.

"Look—" he said, "it's no good us going without food. No sense making ourselves ill. I could fancy a bite now and I reckon you could, too. Why don't we roam around the market, watch the buskers, then stop in somewhere and get a bite to eat? I—I'm in no hurry to get home tonight, are you?"

"No . . . no, I'm afraid we've both got some nightmares waiting for us when we get to sleep. I'm no hurry to meet them."

Covent Garden Market still bustled, no longer clamorous with vendors of fruit and vegetables, but with tourists and trendies. Now one of the liveliest places in Longon, filled with bright shops, pubs, street theatre, boutiques and restaurants, it had become the gathering place for those who worked in the neighbourhood and the Mecca of suburbanites. When the British Theatre Museum opened there soon, it would attract more tourists than ever. It was a splendid place to have a snack before the theatre or a more leisurely meal and an evening's entertainment.

Best of all, for tonight's expedition, was the fact of so many eating places at street level within the Market itself, tables and chair spilling out into the centre of the enclosed precinct. It meant that Caitlin's chair could be wheeled straight up to a table and parked without attracting attention or fuss.

"This is so nice, Kenny—what a super idea of yours!" Caitlin beamed across the table at him.

"It is nice, isn't it?" The new helmet and gauntlets he had been saving up for receded into insignificance. He looked around as appreciatively as Caitlin. What a difference it made to be sitting at a table with a girl of your own, part of the crowd. He wondered if she'd like to do it again some time. There was no reason why she had to be stuck away up in that old factory—not now that he knew how easy it was to carry her up and down stairs. She was one of the designers, she ought to come to the studio more often.

He wished he hadn't thought of the factory—it brought back so many other thoughts. Quickly he looked around to try to dispel the grim memories. One of the cockatoo hair-dos at a nearby table caught his attention, it looked familiar.

"There's Hattie," he said, "over there—with Pete."

"And very cosy, too." Caitlin giggled wickedly. "Isn't that interesting."

"Yeah . . . yeah, I heard something about that." Overheard was more like it, but it was suddenly important to give an impression of being more in the know than he was. "She was pretty mad at him yesterday, looks like they've made up."

"And then some. They couldn't get much closer together—in a public place."

"Quite a few familiar faces here tonight." It made him sound like a regular. "There's one of the foreign buyers—"

"Where? She twisted round eagerly. "Which one?"

"Over there—The American with the suntan. She's from California. Mitzi something." He would never forget Mitzi, but perhaps that was a story he shouldn't tell. Funny, though, about that funeral wreath. . . .

"Mitzi Kayce! She's bought a lot of my designs for her chain. She's coming this way—"

She was, but stopped before she reached them. She halted at Hattie's table, glaring down at Hattie and Pete.

"Oh-oh!" Kenny recognized the signs. The lady was working up to another scene. He watched, glad that he was at a safe distance.

It began quietly, but clearly acrimoniously. Pete seemed to be on the defensive. Gradually, voices rose until Kenny could hear what they were saying. The whole arcade could hear.

". . . wondered where the hell you'd disappeared to!" Mitzi shrieked. "I might have known I'd find you with some little slut. You never change!"

"Shh . . ." Pete cringed. "People are—"

"How dare you call me names?" Hattie rose in righteous wrath. "Who do you think you are?"

"You know who I am! What you don't know is who *he* is!"

"He's the best cameraman in London!"

The Manager appeared in the doorway of the restaurant and began moving purposefully across the pavement.

"That's what *he* says! And has the son-of-a-bitch also told you that he's my ex-husband?"

"Come on—" Pete got to his feet, light-meter swinging with the violence of his movement. "Let's get out of here."

"Oh no you don't!" Mitzi grabbed the strap of the light-meter, pulling him forward across the table. "Not until you write me a cheque for all that back alimony—"

"Please, madam—" The Manager had reached them.

"You keep out of this!" She shook off his restraining hand. "This is the first time in years I've caught up with the little bastard—" She jerked at the strap. "And I'm not—"

"You leave Pete alone!" Hattie tugged at the strap, trying to get it away from her.

"So it's like that, is it?" Mitzi jeered. "Well, I wish you joy of him—which is more than I ever got. But first—"

In response to a quiet signal, a burly waiter moved to the Manager's side. Their eyes met, communing silently, then they enclosed Mitzi in an expert pincers movement, freed Pete's strap, and moved her toward the exit.

"It's all right," the Manager assured interested spectators. "Madam is a little overtired, that's all."

"And don't forget emotional," Hattie muttered.

Someone was scribbling frantically at a nearby table. Gossip columnists and their tipsters frequented the Market, too.

"You really see life Up West here, don't you?" Caitlin said wistfully.

"You ought to come more often," Kenny said. "It's not good for you to be stuck away at that old factory—"

Immediately he wished he'd kept quiet. They'd been having a lovely time, now a shadow was between them again—and it wasn't just the waiter bringing their meal.

"Yes," Caitlin agreed sadly. "It keeps coming back when you don't expect it, doesn't it?"

"Yes," he admitted.

"Kenny, I've been thinking. What that man—that Pete—said couldn't be true. Even if someone wanted to kill one of my girls, they wouldn't try to do it that way. It wouldn't work. The girls all walk down the alley to the factory. They'd have seen the cable stretched across the road and just ducked under it. No one would have been hurt—or even taken it as a warning. They'd have just thought it was one more mysterious custom we had. Or maybe something the Council had got up to."

"It—" His throat tightened; this was the unthinkable. "It might have been meant for you."

"No, Kenny, that wouldn't have worked, either. If I'd just been going along in the chair, as I do on fine days, I'd have seen it and avoided it. Besides, I wouldn't have been going fast enough for it to do any harm. And if it had been a rainy day, I'd have been in the invalid car, and the wire would have slid right over the roof. It couldn't possibly have been meant for any of us." Her hand was warm as she placed it over his. "I'm sorry, Kenny."

"Yeah." He didn't know whether her sympathy was because he was feeling so downcast, or because somebody wanted to murder him.

Either way, he could do without it.

Chapter 18

Sunny was unusually silent that morning, not that Jake was paying any attention. Jake was in a world of his own, so deeply preoccupied that he had even burnt the toast without noticing it.

Sunny ate it anyway. Toast was the least of her worries right now. She looked across the breakfast table despairingly, hoping for reassurance, but Jake had propped the morning paper up between them. She knew very well he wasn't reading it—he hadn't turned a page in ten minutes. She knew what he was thinking about—*who* he was thinking about.

Reba.

She shuddered.

"Someone just walked over my grave," she said.

"Have another cup of coffee." He was uninterested. He didn't care. Not any longer. He didn't even look up.

Sunny pushed away her cup.

No response.

She leaned back in her chair and looked around the kitchen as though she might be seeing it for the last time. As though she were saying goodbye to it.

Goodbye to the stainless steel sink with disposal unit Jake had insisted on having installed before they moved in. Goodbye to the built-in double oven she had given Jake for their first Christmas, paid for with her fee for that outside modelling job for *Glamour Woman*. Goodbye to the silly little souvenir egg-timer Jake had brought back from New York two trips ago, shaped like the World Trade Building towers, with the sandglass balanced between them. Goodbye—her gaze roved towards the doorway—

Goodbye to the long lovely lounge with its wall-to-wall carpeting and all the antiques they had bought together. A good investment, Jake had said, in case things didn't always go well in the future—

She sniffed.

"You're not starting a cold?" That was all he cared. If she had a bad cold, she couldn't work.

"No—" *I'm starting a scream. Can't you see? Don't you care?*

Goodbye, sweet little terrace house where we've been so happy. Where *I've* been so happy. Goodbye to the dreams of the future, to all the exciting plans, to—

She sniffed again.

He picked up the newspaper, shook it out and

turned a page. She might not have been there at all. Perhaps, in his mind, he had left her already.

For Reba.

Silly, stupid, mindless Reba. Reba the trance queen, who could repeat the same actions endlessly without tiring, without ever changing them. Reba the robot. No—be fair. There was more to it than that.

Reba photographed like a dream. It had shown clearly in the rushes. That blank vapid smile came out on the screen like the Mona Lisa's. That expressionless face had seemed deep and mysterious, changing subtly as shadows played across it. Each tiny movement of the muscles beneath her skin had been magnified and enhanced, turning her from an ordinary pretty model into a raving beauty.

By contrast, Sunny had looked like a gawky teenager, still shadowed by puppy fat, not quite out of the awkward age.

"When—" Sunny had asked later—"when did you take all those pictures of Reba? The close-ups?

"Oh—" Jake had been elaborately casual—"we were fooling around for a bit after you and Carla left. Reba wasn't tired, so she helped us try some different lighting effects."

"I see." She had seen everything—including the handwriting on the wall. Oh, she'd known that there'd be other girls coming along, pushing and crowding, trying to snatch the fame, the money, the assignments away from those above them. She just hadn't expected it so soon. She was only nineteen. She'd reckoned on another year or two getting to the top and then ten years or so of staying there—with Jake behind her.

Reba had always envied her Jake.

From little remarks Reba had let drop, Sunny knew that she believed she could get ahead faster and better if she had a smart manager behind her. If she had someone like Jake. If she had Jake himself.

Sunny hadn't slept well last night. She had dark circles under her eyes—not that it would matter on the catwalk. It probably wouldn't matter in the filming, either. It was obvious that they were going to concentrate on Reba.

The video cassette that was supposed to be her practice swing at the great film and television world was going to be Reba's triumph instead.

It wasn't fair! There had never been any problem in her photo sessions. Why should movement make so much difference? She could learn—she'd have to learn—but they were all in so much of a hurry. Jake might not be willing to wait for her to learn a new technique. Not when he had Reba standing by and perfect to start work without delay.

Reba was tireless and ambitious. Better yet, from Jake's point of view, Reba was malleable. She wouldn't complain, wouldn't assert herself, wouldn't fight for her rights. She would bend herself entirely to Jake's will.

And that was what Jake had always found lacking in Sunny. He had never really been happy about her independent streak. After the first few unsuccessful attempts to erode it, he had bowed to the inevitable and allowed her to set her own pace.

If he had Reba, Reba would do the bowing.

"Jake—"

"Hmmm?" He rustled the paper, reluctant to set it aside, although he must have memorized that page by now.

"Jake—" She hated herself for questioning, for testing him, but she had to know. "Jake, we're going to finish filming the cassette tonight, aren't we?"

"Probably. Tonight or tomorrow night. What difference does it make?"

"I was just wondering—It's coming along all right, isn't it?"

"Fine. Just fine." He did not look at her.

"Caitlin promised me we'd have Indigo Charisma for the first showing this afternoon. That means we'll be able to include it in the filming tonight."

"Yes—" He seemed uneasy. She feared what might be coming. She and Reba were the same size.

"Jake, would you do me a favour? Please?"

"What is it?" He was not going to commit himself.

"Tonight . . . when I'm wearing Indigo Charisma—don't let Pete film it."

"What?" He threw the paper to one side. At last she had his full attention. "Are you crazy? Decemo would go mad! That's his grand finale. He doesn't want to leave it just to Carla. You've *got* to model it!"

"I intend to." She concealed a small smile of triumph. He had said it. *She* had to model the gown. "I mean, I don't want Pete on the camera. I don't think he does it well enough. That dress is too much for him. Even when he did the shots for the *Record*, they didn't turn out as well as they ought to have done. Did *you* honestly think so? Let one of the other men do the filming tonight. Please. . . ."

He frowned. She could see his mind working. But it was true. The *Daily Record* spread wasn't half as good as it should have been. The video work was appalling.

It couldn't be her. She'd photographed beautifully in every other assignment she'd ever had. She'd never had these terrible results with any other photographer. For all his posing and his flaunting of his stupid little light-meter, Pete couldn't be much good.

It couldn't be her. It had to be Pete.

"Please—" She was close to pleading. "Please, Jake, let someone else work the camera tonight."

"We'll see," he said.

The natives were getting restless. Tamsin's parents had been on the telephone this morning, before she left the flat, urging her to come home/be careful/quit that job at once/and an endless permutation of those requests. They had done everything but forbid her to speak to any strange people—which was just as well, there were a lot of strange people in the fashion world. She had broken away finally by promising to go home for the weekend as soon as London Fashion Week had ended. She managed not to promise anything else.

Tamsin's flatmates had been waiting to pounce when she got home last night, with demands for all the gory details, their appetites whetted by varying press reports. In order to maintain minimum diplomatic relations with them (she could not face hunting for a new flatshare right now), she had had to answer their questions and discourage their speculations. It had made for a long night.

Then her parents, first thing in the morning. . . .

It had made her late for work, of course. Even the Duchess was there ahead of her.

"Good afternoon," Decemo said pointedly, as she walked in. His injured air said that if *he* could be here early, with all his tribulations, the least the staff could do was get here on time.

Tamsin nodded coldly, her attitude proclaiming that if a little leeway couldn't be allowed in view of all the disruption, then he knew what he could do about it.

"Tamsin—" The Duchess fortunately cut off this silent acrimony with a call to duty. "Tamsin, do you know anything about—" she consulted a scrap of paper in her hand—"about some sketches someone promised to one of the Japanese buyers?"

"I think Lillian was handling that. Ask her—"

"She isn't here," Decemo said in martyred tones. "She came in, collected some sketches and swatches and went off again. I thought you'd sent her over to the factory to—" he hesitated, then continued firmly—"to collect Indigo Charisma."

"No one is going to collect it," the Duchess said quickly. "Caitlin decided she'll flag down a taxi and send it over that way. It seemed more tactful than asking Kenny to go for it. But I don't know where Lillian went—" She opted for the bright side. "Perhaps she's taking care of the Japanese—"

"She should be here!" Decemo snapped. "She has to be back to dress Gloria and Jackie for the first showing. She should be here now."

"If she isn't back in time," the Duchess said, "Tamsin will have to dress them."

"I can't—" Tamsin was swept by a form of stage fright. "I've never dressed any models. I wouldn't know how."

"Don't be silly," the Duchess said. "There's no great art about it. You'll get the hang of it in no time."

"Don't fret" Decemo threw her a word of cheer. "Lillian may be back in time. If she isn't you'll find Gloria and Jackie very helpful They'll tell you what you need to do."

"It's easy," Hattie encouraged, as Decemo and the Duchess swept off for a luncheon appointment with an American wholesaler who wished to discuss the possibility of a range of bed linen and bath towels to be designed by Decemo. "Just watch what I do. Basically, it's just getting zippers and buttons undone and having the dress all ready for the model to step into, then zipping and buttoning when she's inside. You won't have any trouble."

"Not if Lillian gets back in time to take over." Tamsin clung to a hope that was fading fast.

"Don't count on Lillian." Hattie gave her a lopsided smile. "I'm not telling Decemo, but I happen to know she's gone on a job interview. She's not going to hurry back."

"Lillian?" It was silly to feel as though she were being left behind on a sinking ship.

"Didn't you hear Decemo say she'd taken sketches and samples with her? He isn't putting two and two together right now—but he'll get the message soon enough. I'm lining up some interviews myself next week."

"But where will Decemo Designers be without you both?"

"Don't be daft." Hattie was patronizing. "Don't you know half the designs are done by Mme. Arlette and Caitlin, anyway? And Decemo. He'll just sign up a couple more innocents from the art colleges' new graduates and carry on. Don't worry about him—he'll land on his feet like a cat."

"But your contracts—"

"Oh, those—" Hattie was unconcerned. "I don't think we'll have any problem now. Not after all this trouble. No one will blame us for wanting to get away—and

Decemo won't be able to make us stay, contract or no contract. Murder cancels everything."

"Murder?" Tamsin gasped, then wondered how she could sound so incredulous, so naive.

Because, of course, that had been the unspoken suspicion looming behind the police inquiries, lurking around all the corners no one cared to investigate too closely.

That steel cable had not suddenly stretched itself across the alleyway of its own volition. Someone had put it there.

Chapter 19

"Mind what you're doing, can't you?" Gloria snapped. "Your hands are like ice!"

"Sorry—" Tamsin tried to fumble buttons through buttonholes without touching bare flesh—of which, there seemed to be an awful lot. If Gloria wasn't careful, she'd be eligible for the 'Let Them Eat Cake' range before too many seasons passed.

"You should have learned better by *now*," Gloria complained.

Perhaps she should. It was the evening showing and Lillian still had not returned. It was possible that she was not going to come back at all.

For reasons best known to himself, Pete had arrived early and was in huddled consultation with Hattie whenever she could snatch a moment—and sometimes when she couldn't—from dressing Suzanne and Carla. His presence was yet another unsettling influence. Carla didn't need to worry and Suzanne had the advantage of being right there to be changed.

It was her own two who were fractious. Obviously feeling that it was their chance to scale another rung on the ladder, they were using every excuse to raise their voices, to flounce about, to do anything that might attract Pete's attention.

It didn't make it any easier to get them in and out of their costumes. The show was running late, several musical cues had been missed and the Duchess's commentary was fraying at the edges as she laboured to cover the holes in the show left by the non-appearance on schedule of the models.

"And now—" the Duchess said, from the other side of the curtains. Her voice rose dangerously. "And *now*—"

Decemo appeared on the stage steps, beckoning frantically; but Gloria was still using delaying tactics.

"You've misbuttoned somewhere," she accused. "Just *look* at that wrinkle. I can't go out there like this."

"I haven't." Tamsin was struggling to get Gloria's discarded dress back on its hanger and unzip the gown Suzanne would be rushing back to change into. "You're slumping, that's the trouble. Stand up straight and it will be all right."

"What *are* you doing here?" Decemo hurried over, glaring at them both. "You're taking far too long with these changes."

"Nothing." Gloria drew herself up, the wrinkle disappeared. "If you *will* use untrained dressers, what do you expect?" She sailed off just as Suzanne arrived, already unzipped, but not—Tamsin was certain—from any desire to be helpful.

"It's not my fault," Tamsin told Decemo. Behind Suzanne's back, she rolled her eyes meaningfully from the model to the photographer.

"Oh, I see." Decemo caught on immediately. He was well versed in the machinations of models. "What's he doing here, anyway?"

"I don't know, but I wish he'd go away. We'd move along a lot faster."

"Leave it to me," Decemo said. He went over to Pete. Tamsin heard him say, "I'd like to talk to you."

"That makes two hearts that beat as one," Pete said. "I've been wanting to have a little talk with you."

"In my office—" Decemo deftly removed him from the scene.

After that, things began to get back to normal. Apart from a tendency to sulk, Gloria and Suzanne speeded up their changes. Decemo had closed his door firmly, so languishing glances availed them nothing.

"Watch what you're doing!" They continued to work off their bad temper on Tamsin but, with the end in sight, she was able to take it.

Just three more changes . . . two more changes . . . then the final change. They were spitting with fury at being deprived of their prey.

"You're the worst dresser I've ever had!" Suzanne hurled her dress to the floor and stood, splendid in anger, wearing only flesh-coloured briefs. She glanced hopefully towards the closed office door.

"I could have made the changes quicker on my own!" Gloria, not to be outdone, also stripped off. The door remained closed.

Mme. Arlette smiled innocently and opened a window. A chill damp breeze swept through the room.

"Eeek!" they screamed and shivered. "Shut that window! It's freezing!"

"Not if you have some clothes on," Hattie said. "The rest of us are perfectly comfortable."

"You're rotten! Rotten! You're all rotten!" Close to tears, Gloria threw on her clothes. Silently, but no less quickly, Suzanne did the same.

But they lingered, joined now by Jackie, and still the door did not open. Matters were not helped when the other two film men arrived and began clearing away the chairs and setting up the lighting in the showroom.

By now, Mme. Arlette had disappeared into the Publicity Office and Tamsin eyed the curtained stage wistfully, hoping for reinforcements. The Duchess would clear them out quickly enough.

Meanwhile, Gloria had made eye contact with one of the crew as he carried some reflectors from the broom closet. She had obviously written off the two in the bush and was about to concentrate on the bird in hand.

He, it appeared, was willing. He slowed his steps and gave her a cheeky wink. "Where've you been, then?" he remarked. "You on tonight, are you?"

"No—" Gloria pouted. "They don't want me."

"Barmy, then, they must be. Why wouldn't they want you?"

"She's too expensive," Tamsin said pointedly.

"Oh-ah." He got a thoughtful look on his face and moved away. Point taken.

"Now look what you've done!" Gloria was enraged.

"Cheer up." Tamsin arranged the last dress on its hanger and pulled the shrouding dustsheet over the rack. Too bad she couldn't also pull one over Gloria, like hooding a parrot's cage, and shut her up. "Lillian ought to be back on duty tomorrow and you won't have to put up with me anymore."

"I hope so!" In her fury, Gloria actually took a couple of steps toward the door before realizing her mistake. She halted, prepared to dig in her heels. "You're impossible!"

So are you! Tamsin bit back the reply. It would do no good to get into an argument; it would only give Gloria an excuse for prolonging her departure. Tamsin turned away.

She heard the door open behind her and hoped that Gloria was leaving, but did not turn around. She realized her mistake when the hand fell on her shoulder.

"Where is he?" Mitzi Kayce whirled Tamsin round to face her. "Where is the frigging son-of-a-bitch? I know he's here. Where is he hiding?"

"Who?" Tamsin asked blankly. Over Mitzi's shoulder, she could see the models brighten in expectation of a scene. She also saw Hattie move quietly to the door of Decemo's office, open it and slip inside.

"You know damned well who! Don't give me that! He's here sniffing after that little bitch—" Mitzi raised her head and stared around suspiciously. "Where is she?"

"Who?" Tamsin asked again, although she had a pretty good idea by this time.

"Mitzi, dear—" Decemo emerged from his office,

opening the door just wide enough to slide through and closing it quickly behind him. "What *is* the matter? We can hear you all over the place." Without waiting for an answer, he turned his fire upon the models. "And what are you still doing here? The showings are over. You aren't required until tomorrow." He flapped his hands at them. "*Scat!*"

"Can't we stay and watch the filming?" Gloria protested.

"No, you can't! We haven't time for any nonsense."

"We wouldn't get in the way," Suzanne promised. "We'd just stand quietly in a corner—"

"And put the others off their stroke. Oh no you won't!" Decemo made shooing motions again. "Go away now, like good girls. We'll let you see the video after it's finished."

That wasn't what they cared about, at all. They glanced at each other indecisively, still not ready to give up.

"What's going on here?" The Duchess appeared and swept them with a searching look. "There's no point in your hanging about," she said. "You should have gone home an hour ago. Run along now."

The force of her personality carried them before her as she herded them out of the studio, across reception and down the stairs. She returned to the studio and seemed surprised to find Mitzi Kayce still there.

"Oh no! You don't get rid of *me* that easily," Mitzi said. "I'm staying until I get what I want."

"What *do* you want?"

"I want to talk to my ex-husband. Here and now. I'm not leaving until I do!"

"Your ex-husband?" The Duchess sent Decemo a puzzled glance.

"Not me, dear—" He raised his hands in a protestation of innocence. "I promise!"

"Your photographer—I know he's working here!"

"Pete?" The Duchess's eyes sought Decemo's. Some unspoken message seemed to pass between them.

"He isn't here," Decemo said quickly. "He left ages ago. He won't be coming back. Not tonight."

"I don't believe you," Mitzi said flatly.

"It's true," Sunny said. "Jake is bringing someone else in to do the filming tonight."

Sunny was not a good liar. Truth shone out of her eyes and her voice had the ring of sincerity. She was radiant. Jake had kept his promise. That must have been what Decemo had taken Pete into the private office to tell him. He was not wanted tonight. They were going to use another photographer—one who would take proper pictures of her. Pete had then left, as Decemo said, while she was on stage.

Even Mitzi was eventually convinced. Pete had left and was not coming back. She would have to look for him elsewhere. Tamsin helpfully supplied the address of the *Daily Record*. Why should Decemo Designers have all the fun?

Decemo watched from the window until Mitzi's taxi drove away, then turned to applaud Sunny.

"You were brilliant, dear, brilliant!" he said. "I didn't know you had it in you. You almost convinced me. That ciné camera is turning you into a real little actress."

"I don't underst—" But Decemo had crossed the room swiftly to throw open the door of his office.

"You can come out now," he called. "The coast is clear. She's gone!"

Hattie and Pete walked out into the studio. Both were tight-lipped. Hattie looked pale and strained, as though they might have been quarrelling.

Pete! Pete was still here, wearing his light-meter like a chain of office. Sunny stared at him in consternation.

"Thanks," he told her. "You were great. The old cow would have hung around all night, if it hadn't been for you. Come on, let's get started now. We've wasted enough time already."

"Started—?" Sunny followed him into the showroom. "But—haven't you seen Jake? Hasn't he talked to you?"

"Jake? Haven't seen him all day." Pete marched over to the camera and began to take light-readings.

"But—" Sunny turned wildly to Decemo. "Surely Jake said something to you? He promised me he would."

"I haven't seen him either." Decemo said. "He ought to be here soon. He can tell me all about it then."

"But—" Sunny stood there, stricken.

"Move it!" Pete shouted at her. "We've already got you in that outfit. Get backstage and change—and make it snappy!" He was snarling at her—and Jake wasn't here to protect her.

"I'm all ready, Pete," Reba said.

Reba!

Sunny knew now that Jake had lied to her. He had never had any intention of replacing Pete behind the camera. He wasn't here tonight because he didn't want to face her accusing looks when she discovered that.

He didn't care any more. He had Reba instead. Pete was in on it, too. Look at the way the three of them had sneaked back here the first night and taken all that extra footage of Reba. The wind was blowing in that direction even then—and she had been too stupid to notice it.

Sunny stumbled back to the dressing-room. Through a haze of misery, she was dimly aware that Mme. Arlette was shoe-horning her into Indigo Charisma. At least Reba wasn't going to get to wear that.

Not unless they sneaked back again tonight after everyone else had left and shot more film with Reba wearing it then.

Something tugged at a corner of Sunny's mind, but she was too engulfed in her own misery to pay attention. Relentlessly, she twisted the knife in her own heart.

Reba. Jake and Reba. Even the camera and Reba.

They said, if you wanted to be a top model or film star, the camera had to love you.

She had never had any problems before. The camera had loved her, flattered her . . . until Pete got behind it.

Pete. The rot had set in with him. Now he was even

shouting at her. She swallowed against the lump rising in her throat, feeling desolate and forlorn.

Just a short time ago, she had been on top of the world, with everything going for her. Now it was all over.

The camera didn't love her any more. . . . Jake didn't love her any more.

They loved Reba instead.

Chapter 20

It was a gloriously bright and shining morning, which made it all the more exasperating that the cleaners had left every light in the building on all night again. Tamsin went round the offices, turning off the lights. Her irritation grew as she approached the showroom and saw from the glare that not only the ordinary lights had been left on, but the special film lighting equipment was still blazing away.

It was bad enough that the film unit hadn't bothered to tidy away their equipment last night; it was intolerable that the cleaners should have switched on those lights. They had no business touching them at all.

Unless—With her hand on the doorknob, she hesitated. Unless they were still filming in there. Could they have worked through the night in an effort to finish the video? Certainly Decemo would have agreed to anything that might speed up the process and overtime was overtime, whether it was divided into two lots on consecutive nights or all crammed into one marathon session. The hours would amount to the same—and so would the bill.

With this in mind, she knocked on the door and waited. She received no invitation to enter.

As she hesitated, the sheer emptiness of the building closed around her. She had already been through the other rooms and knew that no one was in them. The coffee-making machine was off, the inch of coffee still in the pot was dark and cold. No sound at all came from the showroom. No one was in there; the crew had simply departed last night—or early this morning—without bothering to turn off their lights and tidy up. They had probably found and finished the remains of Jake's brandy.

She pushed open the door and went in.

The blinding glare struck her like a physical bow. The heat generated by the lights had turned the room—large as it was—into a hothouse.

Instinctively she stumbled towards the lights, one hand shielding her eyes against them. Turning them off was the first priority; the second was to open a window.

She had almost reached them when she tripped and nearly fell, catching herself just in time. She looked down at the soft obstruction that had nearly sent her flying.

This time she managed not to scream.

She must be getting hardened to it. But his head . . . his head. Once again, it was the head that was the nightmare. This one was still attached to the body but. . . .

The eyes protruded, so did the tongue, swollen and purple. Flesh puffed out on both sides of something narrow embedded in his neck, garotting him.

Pete . . . at least, it had been.

She backed out of the room quickly, forgetting any intention of turning off the lights. She lost her grip on the door and it slammed behind her.

"Excuse me," she said automatically. As though what remained in the room could have heard. How silly. She caught back a giggle. Imagine apologizing to . . . to *that*.

The giggle fought to escape and she knew that she must not let it. If she began to laugh, she would not be able to stop. And it was no laughing matter. There were things she must do, people she must notify.

Offhand, she couldn't remember one of them. In a

daze, she wandered through to the Publicity Office and began making coffee. The others would be arriving soon and they would want their cups of coffee.

They would need them. So did she.

Against all expectations, Kenny had slept well; if there had been dreams, he did not remember them. Mum had made him one of her great fry-ups—eggs, bacon, sausage, tomato, mushrooms and fried bread—for breakfast. The traffic hadn't been too heavy and he'd been able to go fast enough to let him hope that his nerve was returning and he'd get back to normal speed soon.

He hadn't even been daydreaming. He had been giving serious consideration to what a lovely name Caitlin was. No treacherous s's in it at all.

He parked his motorcycle in its accustomed place outside Decemo Designers and went up the stairs without a qualm. The memory of Caitlin nestling in his arms as he carried her up and down those stairs had obliterated the nightmare fragments of that other time when he had carried the black helmet with its grim contents.

The blackboard was blank, he was relieved to observe. He avoided looking at the filing cabinet and went straight through to his new post in the studio. He hung his helmet over the back of his chair and frowned.

There was a strange noise coming from the Publicity Office. There was also an overpowering smell of coffee. Maybe something was going wrong with the coffee-machine.

Kenny sauntered over to check, at first glance, it seemed that all was well. Tamsin was taking care of it. Then he looked more closely.

Tamsin was standing over the coffee-pot, mechanically spooning coffee into the filter. But the filter was full—overflowing. The grains of coffee were sliding down the sides of the pot to sear and scorch as they struck the glowing red electric coils. That was the source of rich dark aroma permeating the atmosphere.

The strange noises were emanating from Tamsin

herself. Soft, choking, bubbling, hiccoughing sounds she seemed unable to control.

"Tamsin—" Kenny approached cautiously. "Tamsin, are you all right?"

"Good morning, Kenny." Tamsin smiled brightly. "I was just making the coffee." She frowned judiciously at the overflowing filter and carefully added another spoonful.

"Yeah, yeah, I can see that." Kenny surreptitiously switched off the machine. "Here—" He took the tin of coffee from her hand and she let it go without noticing.

"Why don't you sit down for a minute?" He led her gently round the desk and eased her into a chair. "I'll finish doing that for you."

"How very kind of you." She was polite, social—and he had the feeling that she didn't know he was there at all. Until she suddenly burst out, "Oh, Kenny, Kenny, I'm so glad you're here!"

"Yeah, well. . . ." There was one thing about having gone through deep shock himself. He could now recognize the symptoms in others. "What's the matter, then?"

"Matter?" The bright social look shuttered her face. She was off again. "I don't know. I—I—" She frowned absently. "There was something—But I can't quite remember—"

"Yeah, well, don't worry about it," he said quickly. "Just let me get this coffee ready. A nice cup will do you good."

He spooned coffee from the filter back into the cannister. While doing so, he looked around searchingly. Nothing to upset anyone in here. He ran a mental check over his path from the front door, up the stairs, through reception—he hadn't been able to keep from taking a quick sideways glance at the filing cabinet, so he knew there was nothing there. The studio was okay. So what was it, then—just some sort of delayed reaction?

"Tamsin—" A sudden terrible fear struck him. "Tamsin—there's nothing wrong at the factory, is there? Caitlin . . . Caitlin's all right?"

"Caitlin?" Tamsin looked at him as though she had never heard the name before. "Why shouldn't she be all right?" An uneasy frown rippled across her brow.

"Caitlin?" She clutched at Kenny's arm frantically, sending coffee spilling all over the floor. "Oh my God! Kenny, has something happened to Caitlin?"

"I don't know. I was asking you." He could feel a fine perspiration breaking out all over him. Funny, that, when he had such cold chills at the same time. "Don't you know?"

"Know what?" Tamsin had released him, now she was making little squiggles on a desk pad. "Kenny, what *are* you talking about?"

"Here—" With great relief, Kenny became aware of footsteps outside. "Someone's coming." He would welcome anyone.

"Good morning, Tamsin . . . Kenny." Mme. Arlette appeared in the doorway, wrinkling her nose against the coffee-scented clouds of smoke.

"Good morning," Tamsin said brightly. "We're just making the coffee."

"That's right," Kenny said. He had never been so glad to see Mme. Arlette in his life. He'd always been just a bit in awe of her, her being sort of starchy and exotic both. But she was a woman and ought to be able to deal with this. It was getting beyond him.

"Tamsin—" He rolled his eyes towards her in a frantic signal. "I don't think Tamsin's feeling very well."

"No?" Mme. Arlette moved closer to inspect Tamsin.

"I'm perfectly all right," Tamsin said coldly. "It's just that—" She frowned again. "That—there's something I have to tell you. But I can't quite remember—"

Kenny had lowered the mound of coffee in the filter to a reasonable level and now he concentrated on the rest of the operation, certain that Tamsin was in capable hands. He switched on the machine and looked up to see Mme. Arlette frowning in concern.

"How long has she been like this?" Mme. Arlette asked him.

"I came in and found her that way. She was standing

here pouring coffee into the filter and it was going all over the place. That's why it smells so."

Tamsin appeared unaware that they were discussing her. She had gone back to making squiggles.

"I do not like this—"

"Can't say I'm crazy about it, myself." Just a few days ago he would never have dreamed of answering like that. Now neither of them noticed.

"The others will be arriving at any moment—" Mme. Arlette looked at her watch. "Possibly Medora—"

Someone came running up the stairs. That would be one of the designers. No one else was ever in that much of a hurry.

"Here comes Hattie now," Kenny said. "Or maybe Lillian."

"Oh, yes—" Tamsin broke clearly in a curiously toneless voice. "I remember what I wanted to say: Whatever you do, don't let Hattie look in the showroom."

Kenny and Mme. Arlette met each other's eyes and spontaneously dashed for the showroom. They threw open the door and stood blinking against the glare of the lights. It took a moment for their eyes to adjust and focus.

"*Oh mon Dieu!*" Mme. Arlette swayed against Kenny. "*Mon Dieu!*"

Kenny gulped and swallowed hard against a rising tide of eggs, bacon, sausage, tomato, mushrooms and fried bread, all of which seemed to be trying to bale out of his stomach at the same time.

It was immediately obvious that there was nothing they could do. They had arrived far too late to be of any help. They retreated hastily and closed the door behind them.

"That's right," Tamsin approved. "You mustn't let Hattie see."

Kenny found that Mme. Arlette was still leaning weakly against him. He supported her over to a chair, then looked around for one for himself. He wasn't feeling so well, either.

"Of course—" Tamsin announced in ringing tones, as though the thought had just occurred to her. "Of course you'll have to let the police look."

Chapter 21

The police looked long and exhaustively. They brought in their experts, they measured, searched, questioned—and questioned again. This time there could be no doubt. This could not be some sort of misadventure to be blamed on children, vandals, yobbos or malevolent maniacs passing by.

This was incontrovertibly murder.

Inevitably, it raised questions harking back to the earlier, now thoroughly questionable "accident". It was unlikely that there might be two independent deaths in suspicious circumstances connected with the same firm. The probability was that they were linked, which meant that the current case could then be handed over to the East End precinct in which the first death had occurred. It would be their responsibility to follow through on the whole case.

The police eventually left to liaise with their East End colleagues, leaving chaos behind them. And despair.

"*Look* at that!" Decemo recoiled from the explicit outline chalked on the floor of the showroom. "How can we let anyone see that? Someone *do* something!"

Sunny felt sick, absolutely sick. Because they had been putting away the cameras when she went home last night. Now the cameras were back in place and the lights had been on all night. She knew what that meant. Just as she had suspected, they had sneaked back and gone on filming after she was out of the way.

With Reba.

And Jake hadn't come home at all last night.

Oh, he'd telephoned, with some phoney excuse she didn't believe for a minute. Something about taking the film to the laboratory and standing over them so that they'd process it quicker. She'd pretended to believe him. What else could she do? Even though, in her heart, she knew he was lying.

Now, he'd have to admit the truth. The police would be able to check his story and prove it false. Better to tell them where he'd really been.

With Reba.

Unless he decided on quite another lie. Unless he decided to tell the police that he had gone home, as usual—depending on her to back his story.

Because—The thing that had been bothering Sunny suddenly crystallized. Because, if he admitted they'd sneaked back to do extra filming last night, he'd also have to admit that it wasn't the first time, that they had done the same thing the first night. That would mean admitting that he had been in a position to chalk that message on the blackboard—the message that had sent Nikko racing to a death-trap.

But it had been meant for Kenny. Why would Jake have wanted to kill Kenny?

Oh, sure, Kenny had a crush on her. Everyone knew that. But she wasn't the only one. Kenny was at the age and stage where he had a bit of a crush on every reasonable female. You don't kill a kid for that. It just didn't make sense.

Especially when Jake didn't want her any more himself. Of course, that first night, he wouldn't have known that. They hadn't seen the rushes yet and discovered the way Reba radiated magic when filmed with a ciné-camera.

The magic she lacked.

But she had only lacked it since Pete was behind the camera. With him out of the way and a new cameraman on the job—

Sunny realized uneasily that she had a very good motive for murdering Pete herself.

Did anyone else realize it?

* * *

Tamsin closed her notebook with a sigh of relief. The Duchess had just dictated several quite unnecessary letters, but they had done the trick. She was feeling a lot better now. The plunge into routine had helped to swing the world back to normal for her.

As normal as a day like this could possibly be. The police had gone. The bod—Pete—had gone. It had been necessary to cancel the three o'clock showing because the police were still busy in the showroom. The six o'clock showing was going to go ahead as scheduled. Most of the people who had tried to attend the early showing would return for the late one—if only to find out what had been going on.

Meanwhile, there was a great deal of work to be done. To their credit, everyone was buckling down to it.

Kenny, acting off his own bat, had unearthed a bucket and mop from the broom closet and was in the showroom struggling to remove the chalked outline from the floor. He was not very expert with a mop, but he was trying hard.

Hattie had refused an offer to dispense with her services for the rest of the day and was working away in the studio. Not surprisingly, her creativity was at a low ebb, so she was doggedly blocking out basic shapes to use later. She was stunned and resentful at what she felt was a personal blow from Fate. She wasn't pretending that she considered Pete the great love of her life, but she had expected a longer romance than this.

It had not helped that the police had removed her experimental strips of leather for forensic tests. Hattie had left the strips soaking in a bowl of water overnight, preparatory to stretching, shaping and plaiting them for hat trimmings.

Someone else had found a deadlier use for one of them.

Again, more from the line of questioning than from any direct admission, the police had revealed the manner of Pete's demise.

He had not been strangled by the leather strap of

his own light-meter, as had at first appeared to be the case. Someone had knocked him unconscious, then strangled—or partially strangled (the results of the autopsy might eventually determine which)—him with one of the wet leather strips. They had then left the strip around his neck to complete the strangulation as it dried out and contracted under the blazing hot lights.

"Tamsin—" Kenny slipped almost furtively out of the showroom, looking over his shoulder. "Tamsin, can you come here for a minute?" He seemed quite agitated. "*She's* in there!"

"Who is?" The Duchess looked up sharply.

"That Kaythee woman!" He took a deep breath and shook his head, annoyed at himself. "That Mitzi Kayce—" he enunciated carefully.

"Bloody hell!" The Duchess leaped to her feet. "What's she doing here? How did she get in?" She moved toward the showroom, keeping any hint of urgency out of her pace. The outside models were arriving now and clustering together at the far end of the studio, as though for the protection numbers were supposed to provide. They must not have any excuse for hysteria, there was still the evening showing to get through.

Kenny opened the showroom door and they slipped into the auditorium quickly, then halted. Mitzi Kayce was standing with bowed head, staring down at the fading chalk outline on the floor.

"Mitzi, my dear, I'm so sorry." The Duchess approached reverently. Pete had, after all, been Mitzi's husband at one time. There might still be some residue of affection that had brought her here to mourn. Unfortunately, she could not be permitted to indulge her grief in a place which would be needed very shortly for the next showing.

"That's okay." Mitzi's voice was muffled.

"Is there anything I can do?"

"No, I was just standing here . . . thinking." Mitzi raised her head, something glinted in her eyes.

"We understand," the Duchess said soothingly. "Believe me, if there *is* anything—"

"I was just wondering—" The glint of Mitzi's eyes hardened into speculation. "The son-of-a-bitch always was bone-lazy. I wonder if he ever got around to changing his will?"

By about five-thirty, Tamsin began to realize that something was desperately wrong.

They had expected the large influx of buyers because of combining the two showings; they had resigned themselves to an invasion of journalists; they were not surprised by the appearance of a fringe audience of suppliers, student designers, even a few outworkers.

But who were all these other people?

They were crowding up the stairs, spilling into Reception, pushing each other and shouting encouragements and insults back and forth.

Their accents ranged from Mayfair to Liverpool, taking in all the less salubrious places in between. Their clothes were ripped, holed and safety-pinned. Their hair-dos ranged from shaven stubble through Mohican to Hattie hair-clones. They were never potential customers.

"HATTIE!" Tamsin's voice rose, almost to a scream. "*Hattie!*"

"What's the matter?" Hattie materialized behind her.

"Hattie—" Tamsin turned to her in relief, "Hattie, your friends are here." She indicated the swarming mob.

"No friends of mine." Hattie took one look and disowned them. "I've never seen them before in my life."

"But—"

"What are they doing here?" Hattie moved forward, as indignant as Tamsin herself. "They're off their territory."

"Gate-crashers!" Tamsin tried to repel them, to block the doorway at the head of the stairs, but there were too many of them. They pushed past, buffetting her, knocking her out of their way.

"Here—stop!" Hattie tried to close the door against them. She hadn't a chance. Like Tamsin, she was hurled to one side.

"What's going on here?"

Reinforcements at last. The Duchess, Decemo and Kenny were there, making an impenetrable wedge in the doorway. The invaders began piling up on the bottleneck of the stairwell.

"What's going on here?" the Duchess demanded again.

"It's all right, missis," someone called. "We've got tickets." Squares of white cardboard were flourished in the hands of those at the top of the stairs.

"Tickets? What sort of tickets?" Decemo snatched at one. "Let me see that!" He squinted at it unbelievingly. "What *is* all this?"

"For the big show," the ticket's owner said. "For Indigo Charisma. They're appearing here tonight, aren't they?"

"*It* is," Decemo said coldly, giving rise to an assortment of cheers and catcalls.

"Just what do you imagine—" the Duchess raised her voice, speaking over the hubbub—"Indigo Charisma to be?"

"Newest Pop Group, innit?" . . . "Bigger than Culture Club!" . . . "Here before their new American tour." . . . "Getting a gold record next week" . . . The answers volleyed at her.

"It's a dress?" Decemo tried to shout them down. "It's not a Group—it's an evening gown!"

"Naw—you got it wrong!" They would not be persuaded. "It's a sneak preview of their new act. Read the ticket."

"Where did you get these? The Duchess had taken the white square from Decemo and was examining it with distaste. Over her shoulder, Tamsin could read the printed message:

Free Admission—Decemo Designers
6 p.m.—Come Early—for
Last Public Appearance in Britain of
Indigo Charisma
Prior to Coast-to-Coast American Concert Tour

"Where did you get these tickets?" the Duchess demanded.

"Some fella was giving them out all over the Market today. What's the matter? Aren't they any good?"

"So it hasn't stopped—" Decemo went pale. "It's still going on!"

"Today . . ." the Duchess said slowly. "Then it wasn't Nikko, after all."

Chapter 22

"Look, it could have been a lot worse," Jake was impartially trying to convince both Sunny and Reba. "We finished filming the video last night. I took the film over to the colour lab myself. I was there all night while they developed it—and it's sensational! All that needs doing now is the cutting. And we don't need Pete for that."

Jake wasn't really unfeeling, Sunny assured herself. He'd been as shocked and upset as the rest of them when he heard about Pete. It was just that he seemed able to bounce back faster than any of them.

Even Reba was looking vaguely askance at Jake's glib dismissal of a human life. Pete might not have been a general favourite, but he had been here and alive only yesterday. Maybe it was beginning to filter through to Reba that Jake was a little too adaptable. No one likes to think that they could be considered quite such a disposable commodity.

Sunny had had her taste of it through the dark lonely hours of last night. She would never view Jake in quite the same light again.

"I suppose we won't be able to show the rushes tonight—" Happily unaware of this, he continued making his plans. "But maybe some time tomorrow. We'll choose the best shots, then it's just a technician's job, splicing them together. No problem."

Sunny waited.

"So you girls don't have a thing to worry about," he summed up. "You're going to be all right. I'll look after you—" He cast a sudden uneasy glance at Sunny as he added, "Both of you."

She'd known it was coming. He'd been building up to it for days now. Perhaps she ought to be grateful that he was still willing to take care of her, now that he had Reba. Or perhaps he was planning bigger things—his own agency. A whole stable of models. They were just the beginning.

She had always known that Jake was ambitious, but she'd thought he'd been ambitious for her.

"Sunny—" Mme. Arlette had returned from a short consultation with the Duchess in the showroom and was holding out the next dress for her to step into.

Everyone was too ambitious around here. It was like a drug in the atmosphere.

"All right, Sunny." Mme. Arlette gave her a gentle push to start her forward. "No time for dreaming. There's your cue."

Sunny made the mistake of looking back as she mounted the steps to the stage.

Jake was smiling at Reba.

As she looked ahead, things weren't much better. All through the show, it had been disturbing to observe the weird mixture of types in the audience. Of course everyone knew the reason for all the strangers—those faked tickets someone had distributed. Although most of the pop fans had gone away grumbling, some had waved their tickets and insisted on their rights. Any free show would do—even a fashion show. It had been easier to admit the contentious ones and hope for the best.

So far, all had been well, but they were coming up to the moment they had been dreading. Some reaction from the cheated fans was inevitable.

"And now," the Duchess announced as first Carla,

then Sunny, stepped on stage and advanced to the catwalk, "we have the substance and shadow. . . ." (Carla had bitterly resented the addition of that line to the script. Sunny wasn't very happy at being called a shadow herself.)

"The substance and shadow of . . . Indigo Charisma!"

"Go on, then—" The shout came from the back of the auditorium. "Sing something!"

A programme whizzed past their heads. Then another. And another. They were at the very end of the catwalk and had just turned. It was a long way back—with all the missiles flying about them.

"Give us a song!" The howl rose from several throats around the room.

Sunny kept moving automatically, her eyes fixed on the haven of the stage, her mind on the sanctuary of the dressing-room—and Jake. She had never had to deal with hecklers before. She had occasionally watched buskers in Covent Garden coping with such a situation and had admired their assurance, some of them even turned the whole thing into a joke. But now it was happening to her—and it wasn't funny.

"Keep moving," Carla muttered in her ear as she faltered. "Just keep moving . . ."

Easier said than done. Someone rolled a glass across the catwalk at Sunny's feet. She stumbled and nearly fell.

"She can't dance either!" someone gibed.

"Go on, then, sing us a song!" The howl was taken up again. "Sing! . . . Bring on the Group!"

"All right, you bastards." Carla halted abruptly. "You want a song?" She took a deep breath, inflating her lungs. The beaded bodice shimmered awesomely, taking the strain.

"*AAAaaaa*—" Carla let rip with the cry of the Valkyries. It filled the room and reverberated back from the farthest walls. It drowned out the taped music, it silenced the hecklers, it stunned Sunny. She thought her eardrums might never recover.

The cry carried them back to the stage, still ringing out over all lesser sounds. Even the Duchess had broken off the fashion commentary, recognizing her inability to compete.

All in one breath and it was not exhausted yet. Carla pushed Sunny through the curtains and remained facing the audience, magnificently defiant as the cry died away.

"Blimey!" someone whispered into the silence. Then the applause burst out. It turned into a standing ovation; some of the erstwhile hecklers were the first to leap to their feet.

Carla dipped in a prima donna's bow and vanished through the curtains.

"My dear!" Decemo rushed forward to clasp her hands. "*What* are you doing here? Covent Garden, yes— but you belong in the Opera House, not on the catwalk!"

"Give me time," Carla said. "That's where I'm heading. The modelling is paying for the voice lessons."

"That was pretty sensational," Jake came up to her, elbowing Sunny aside. "Do you have a manager?"

Beyond the curtains, they could hear the excited buzz of voices, the rustle of programmes, the scraping of chairs, the sounds of an audience departing after another successful showing.

"No, I'm sorry—" They heard the Duchess's voice raised. "You can't go back there."

"Oh, please. We just want her autograph—" The curtains quivered and parted. Two of the pop fans advanced upon Carla, the Duchess in pursuit.

"Please—" They extended their counterfeit tickets to her. "Would you sign these for us?"

"Oh . . . well. . . ." Carla blushed and took the squares of cardboard, looking around vaguely. "Has anyone a pen?"

"Jake will have," Sunny said. Jake always had things like that, he was usually more than ready to offer them. But he had turned away and was deep in conversation with Reba, his back to them.

"Jake," she called, but he paid no attention. "Jake—" She raised her voice. "Lend Carla your pen."

Without turning around, he pulled it from a pocket and held it out to her. It didn't do him any good.

"Oi!" The autograph hunters were staring at him, pointing at him. "That's the bloke that was giving out those tickets!"

"All right," Jake said. "So I provided a wider audience than usual. Sue me!"

"It may come to that," the Duchess said coldly.

"What I *do* not understand—What I shall *never* understand, Jake, dear—" Decemo spoke in tones of sweet reasonableness; the measure of his agitation showed in the flash of his dressmaker's shears as he slashed at the *toile* draping Reba. "What is the *reason* for this monstrous betrayal? What did you think you were *doing*? What sort of *statement* were you making—?" Snip, snip, slash.

"If you hated the *name*—if you thought Indigo Charisma sounded like a—a Pop Group—" slash, slash, snip—"then why didn't you take me aside and mention it privately? Why this—this public humiliation?"

It was just as well, Tamsin thought, that Reba hadn't an ounce of imagination. She stood there placidly as Decemo worked off his rage and indignation, taking it out on the *toile*. The razor-sharp shears sliced and slashed at the thin white muslin shrouding her flawless figure. One slip—and it wouldn't be so flawless. If Reba had had any nerves at all, or even a rudimentary sense of self-protection, she would have fled from the studio screaming. Reba had missed her calling—rather, her calling had missed her. Had she been born a few decades earlier, she would have made an invaluable foil in a Music Hall knife-throwing act.

"He didn't mean it—" Sunny tried desperately to defend her idol . . . her clay-footed idol . . . her former idol. Why did the old loyalties still remain? Why were they still able to tear you apart, even when—especially when—you knew they were no longer reciprocal?

They were gathered in the studio, the nucleus of Decemo Designers. Kenny, still looking faintly bewildered, had been pressed into service to guard the door in case Jake tried to escape before the kangaroo court had finished their proceedings. Hattie and Lillian watched from a corner. Mme. Arlette, Foreman of the Jury, stood beside Tamsin, considering her verdict. The Duchess and Decemo were conducting the prosecution. Only Sunny—perhaps against her better judgment, was acting for the defense.

"Jake couldn't know it was the wrong time for a publicity stunt," Sunny pleaded. "He wasn't here all day. He didn't know what had happened to Pete. I wasn't able to reach him to tell him—" She broke off remembering her efforts to contact him during the day.

"Strange as it may seem," the Duchess drawled, "I'm not particularly concerned with what he was doing today. We know all about that. What I'd like to know is what he was doing on all those other days."

"Other days?" Decemo's shears clipped a shoulder-strap from the *toile*, their tips dangerously close to Reba's ear. Reba didn't even blink.

"The other days when we've had trouble," the Duchess clarified. "The day someone sent the funeral wreath . . . and the Fire Brigade. All those coupons filled in with our names—not to mention the salt in the cold cream."

"No!" Sunny gasped, remembering how terrified she had been. "No! Jake wouldn't have done a thing like that to me!"

"Wouldn't he?" The Duchess levelled an accusing gaze at Jake. "Wouldn't you? . . . Didn't you?"

Decemo lowered his shears, *toile* forgotten, waiting for Jake's answer.

"I was in the States—" Jake looked to Sunny. "You know that."

"Were you?" the Duchess asked. "Remember, the police will be able to check the airport records."

"Now, wait a minute," Jake said. "We don't want to involve the police in this."

He had said much the same thing once before, Tamsin recalled. When she had said she was going to telephone for the police; before he had realized it was for quite another reason. He had assumed she was going to report the harassment and that quick defensiveness had sprung into play. He had wanted to stop her.

"He *did* do it." Tamsin was certain now. "I thought I heard a noise in here just as I left that night. Next day, there was the cold cream incident."

"No—" Sunny whispered. "Not the cold cream! Jake—"

"Don't be a baby," he snapped. "It didn't hurt you any!"

"He came back from the States on schedule," the Duchess said. "He simply didn't go home. He was too busy organizing all his little games. Then he showed up here, pretending that he had just arrived, which gave him an alibi for all the things he couldn't have done because he was out of the country. He had a duplicate key to the front door—most of us have. We're far too casual with keys around here."

"But why?" Decemo seemed unable to take in the enormity of it. "Why?"

"Why not?" Jake looked at him with dislike. "Shake up the old place a bit. Shake loose your grip on Sunny's contract, too. If enough things started going wrong, if the business began to look as though it were in trouble, you couldn't hold her to it. You couldn't hold any of them."

"*You!*" Decemo began shaking uncontrollably. "*You* were responsible for Nikko's death!"

"Wait a minute," Jake protested in alarm. "You can't blame that on me. The other things—the practical jokes—okay, I admit them. But I had nothing to do with Nikko's death."

"Oh yes you did! You were responsible. Letting us all think—*making* us all think—that he was behind the harassments, the spite—"

"I can't help what you thought."

"You *meant* us to blame Nikko! Don't deny it!"

"Have it your way," Jake shrugged. "I'll admit the thought did cross my mind."

"Nikko—forgive me! I should have had more faith in you!" Decemo closed his eyes, swaying. "I was a fool! I was manipulated! But I shall avenge you—"

He leaped for Jake, shears drawn back to stab to the heart.

"No!" Sunny screamed. She threw herself in front of Jake.

Sunny! Kenny sprang forward in automatic reflex. He was still bewildered but, whatever was happening, it mustn't be allowed to happen to Sunny.

He hurled himself on Decemo and brought him down before the shears struck flesh. Decemo continued to fight, but now Jake joined the fray. While they grappled wildly, the Duchess crouched and took possession of the dressmaker's shears. That evened the odds and they were able to bring Decemo under control.

"I suppose," Tamsin said, "I'd better call the police again."

"Of course, it was on the cards that he might kill Nikko eventually," the Duchess said later. "Believing him responsible for the spite campaign simply precipitated the event."

"How ironic," Mme. Arlette said, "that he who had exacted so many impossible contracts was persuaded to sign one himself. Truly, love is blind."

"And Nikko had begun throwing his weight around recently. It was getting quite noticeable."

"He was becoming an embarrassment." Mme. Arlette nodded thoughtfully. "Had we been less trusting, it might have occurred to us that Decemo himself could have returned to the studio that night and chalked the message on the blackboard. Then, how easy to engineer a quarrel in the morning and ensure that Nikko would fling himself out of the house in a vile mood. Naturally, believing that he owned part of the business, nothing would keep him away at such an important time. He would arrive, discover the message and—for whatever reason of his own—race to collect the dress before Kenny could.

"Meanwhile, Decemo had gone straight to the workrooms to set the trap—"

Tamsin stifled a yawn. The others had left after the police had finished and dismissed them. The Duchess and Mme. Arlette, however, were tarrying like a couple of bridge partners replaying an unsatisfactory hand. She was here because the Duchess was still dictating notes for tomorrow.

"Diminished responsibility," the Duchess said. "It's a good plea. Balance of the mind disturbed, and all that."

"Unfortunate about the photographer," Mme. Arlette said. "That he should have done the extra filming and thus been here to see Decemo leaving the message on the blackboard."

"Even more unfortunate that he should have decided to try a spot of blackmail." The Duchess shrugged. "What can you do about people with no sense of self-preservation?"

"But Decemo Designers will continue—" Mme. Arlette looked thoughtful. "Although perhaps not under the same name."

"Perhaps not," the Duchess agreed. "We can still manage. Then, after things settle down. . . . Broadmoor or Dartmoor, they'll probably let him have a sketchpad—even if they keep the scissors away from him."

"Meanwhile, we must concentrate on preparing the Autumn Collection. There is much to be done. We must bring Caitlin into the studio. We can no longer afford to waste her in the workrooms."

"I want Kenny inside, too," the Duchess said. "He's too valuable to be a messenger. I won't have him risking his neck on that motorcycle. We'll start training him for sales or publicity." She looked thoughtful. "The girls said they'd be here first thing in the morning. They're all rallying round. We have a good team, Arlette."

"The best, Medora—and they need to be. They will be tested to the utmost over the next few months. We can and we will present an Autumn Collection—but it will be hell getting everything ready in time."

"Absolute hell!" said the Duchess happily.

THE END

ABOUT THE AUTHOR

MARIAN BABSON is the author of over twenty-five mysteries. She lives in England.

The following
is a preview of
THE STALKING LAMB
by Marian Babson
to be published by Bantam
in March, 1990

They let her sit by the window now. Encouraged it, in fact. As they encouraged her in her needlework, exclaiming over it, admiring it, urging her to finish the pattern, although her hands were still too awkward to manage the frame properly and the blunt needle kept slipping out of the grasp of the strange puffy pink sausages which were her fingers. It was occupational therapy, and that was good in their lexicon. It conveyed to them that she was responding, taking an interest in something again, coming back to life.

They were wrong. It was just something to do while she was waiting. Waiting for the pattern to be finished. But they didn't know she knew that. They thought she believed them when they told her Aaron was dead.

Something moved in the mews below. She turned her head swiftly to focus on what had been a mere flicker at the corner of her eye. A yellow door had opened and closed quickly in the house at the end. No one had gone in or out. Perhaps the occupant had been starting out and had gone back to collect something she had forgotten. It didn't matter. A false alarm. That was all it was this time.

Her attention didn't return to her needlework, it stayed in the mews. So peaceful and charming down there, a little Georgian cul-de-sac where time might have stood still through the centuries. It hadn't, of course. There were electric lights and television aerials down there, the ringing of a telephone heard through an open window.

She liked to study the life in the mews, though. It made her feel like a scientist watching some strange species. Or an anthropologist taking mental notes on a totally alien way of life.

At other times, she liked to dream, projecting herself back into the distant past. The very distant past. It was her only escape. The recent past was a nightmare, the present unbearable. She had no future.

The yellow door opened again and the Yellow Lady hesitated in the doorway, obviously giving final orders to a sullen Scandinavian au pair who sulked in the shadows, radiating a monumental Nordic gloom. Evidently there had been another contest of wills but, as was only to be expected, the Yellow Lady had won. It was surprising how much one learned about the lives going on in the mews by just observing from the window.

Now the Yellow Lady stepped out into the mews, drawing on beige suède gloves, picking her way carefully over the cobblestones in her beige suède shoes, the folds of her blonde mink coat rippling about her as she walked. She wasn't really yellow, of course, more of an all-over beige or fawn, the improbable beige-blonde of her hair just a few shades brighter than her skin, which was wrinkled and sallow, with a colour that might be the result of jaundice or the closest an English skin could return to its natural shading after too many years of a constant tropic sun. The blonde mink was almost always in evidence, too—further proof of too much of a lifetime spent in the tropics, of blood thinned beyond the power of an English sun to warm it again.

Now the Yellow Lady was walking down the mews, on her way to what? A bridge party? An art exhibition? Luncheon with friends? The theatre? Something warm and live and glamorous, surely. She was such an imperious, splendid old lady you couldn't imagine her life except in terms of exquisite civilization.

The thought came unbidden: *Belle might have grown into an old lady such as that—had she been allowed to live.*

Don't think about that! Shut it out! Wall it off! Think about anything but that!

There was another mink in the mews—a black diamond. And a full length chinchilla. Also worn by imperious old ladies, who enveloped themselves in them as ancient knights had donned armour as protection against a hostile world.

She liked to watch the old ladies pass by. This was an expensive area of town, and they were not the sad defeated old ladies of poverty. These were the indomitable ones, who had loved well and married wisely. Who had lived through two wars, through bombing and fire, who had survived because they had the will to survive.

This was an expensive area of town. Who was paying the bill for them at this private nursing home? The police? The court? No one answered when she asked that question.

A room to herself—she knew enough to know that that wasn't guaranteed under the National Health Scheme. Yet there had been no bills forthcoming for her signature, now that she might be able to scrawl one again. Ginny could not have signed—Ginny might never be able to sign for anything again.

She hoped they weren't sending the bills home to Harriet. Their elder sister—and guardian—had problems enough of her own and no access to the Trust Fund set up for her two younger sisters. Furthermore, Harriet and Martin had enough hospital bills of their own to face. After two miscarriages, Harriet was now grimly enduring months of total bedrest, trying to ensure that her present pregnancy successfully reached full term and produced a healthy child.

There was nothing anyone could do for herself, it was too late. It was only a question of time now.

But Ginny. Poor Ginny, who was lying in another room in this vast expensive place. From which the reports on her progress—her non-progress, rather—were issued. Poor little Ginny, more a prisoner than any of them, trapped in the immovable hulk of her own body, unable to speak, unable to move. Could she still think? Remember? Did she have nightmares, too, and wake unable to scream?

Don't think about that, either!

Was that someone at the door? She stiffened expectantly, then relaxed as nothing happened. No. No, it was all right. No one was going to intrude.

They meant well. They were very kind, even though the kindness had a tingle of guilt about it, and a touch of vindication. *See,* they seemed always to be saying, *we are not like the people you have had such an unfortunate experience with. You just met the wrong people. Everyone here isn't like that. You must believe that, you must. If you want to get better.*

They meant so well, but they were so helpless—and so inept. As inept as she had been when she first landed. As gauche, as trusting, and as naïve. How could they be otherwise? They were the fortunate ones. Life hadn't taught them what it had taught her. They still believed what they were saying.

The Yellow Lady paused in her progress along the mews almost directly under the window, to speak to the young man working in the back garden of the nursing home. A pleasant young man, there every day (the best-tended back garden in London) who occasionally looked directly up at the window and grinned. He even waved sometimes—when no one was watching—uniting them in a momentary conspiracy. She knew, and he knew she knew. The grin, the wave, admitted it. Unlike the others, he seemed to disdain pretence, to realize that the shock, the horror, had not unhinged her, nor even incapacitated her mental processes. Beneath the surface apathy, she was still alive, still aware. She might try to disguise it, even from herself, but he knew.

The Yellow Lady glanced upwards briefly, just a glimpse of intense blue before the golden eyelids were lowered again. What had she been told? Certainly not the truth. The dwellers in the mews must not know—must not be disturbed, must be allowed to function in their normal ways, like some placid deep sea denizens, drifting along unmindful of the sharks slicing silently through their unheeding midst.

The girl drew back from the window, beyond the range of prying eyes. The sudden reflex action was so swift, almost violent, that it set the wooden tapestry stand rocking on its floor base. She stretched out her awkward hands to catch it as it tilted and threatened to fall.

She stared at the emerging picture unseeingly for a moment, the Gainsborough picture of a country family, the wife sitting on a bench under summer trees, the husband standing, gun swung negligently under his arm, hunting dog at his feet. Another world, another time, a long time ago, remaining only on canvas and in flakes of paint, pages of books, fragments of materials in museums, heirloom jewellery, handcrafted furniture. Safely over and done with, beyond the reach of living memory.

That was why she had let them persuade her to work on it. It was so safe, so remote—and so large. She would never finish it, but they didn't know that.

"Most people do the figures first, dear." She had begun by painstakingly filling in the background, ignoring the hinting words, the suggesting tone. *"Of course, you want to begin to get your fingers nimble again before you start on the people. You want to warm up on the background before you tackle the figures. So sensible of you, dear."* She had let them make their own deductions, invent their own excuses. They could interpret her thought processes any way they liked. It was nothing to her. She continued to work on the background: there was an expanse of sky, of grass, of trees, of distance. It would all take time, lots of time. She might not have enough time to get to the people. That was fine, even though they were remote eighteenth-century people, caught on a distant summer's day, who could pose no possible threat. She didn't want anything to do with people any more.

But . . . although the frame had stopped rocking, she was

still holding it. Now she looked at the picture closely, not concentrating on one small square at a time as she did when working on it. *The background was finished.* The people, too, were finished.

How long had she been here? Shock swept over her. *How long had they kept her cooped up in this luxurious prison? What would be their excuses if she demanded an explanation?* "Under observation"? "Detained at the Queen's pleasure"? "Protective custody"?

How much longer would they keep her here?

It didn't matter. Carefully, she rummaged through the basket of silks in her lap, electing an off-white shade, measuring a manageable length and biting it off. She was supposed to call the nurse for the scissors, but seldom bothered. (Silly of them not to let her keep the sewing scissors. If she wanted to open a vein, she had the needles. It might be more difficult but, with enough determination, it could be done.)

The dog. She stabbed with the thread at the eye of the needle. There was still the dog to do. Her clumsy blunted fingers would not respond to the commands of her eyes and brain. The thread buckled against the needle, sliding away, refusing to thread through. She bit her lips grimly, fighting the obdurate thread, the inflexible needle. Suddenly, they capitulated, meeting and melding. She exhaled a deep breath that sounded almost like a sob. It was all right. She could do the dog.

And . . . when the dog was done? There was someone, wasn't there, who had unravelled each day's work as she finished it? Had the doctor, the nurses, noticed how far along she was? Would it be possible for her to unpick some of the background? Penelope—that was it—Penelope waiting for Ulysses.

Waiting for Aaron.

She knotted the end of the thread and inserted the needle painstakingly into the pattern. As she pulled it through the canvas, the needle slipped from her numb fingers to fall into space, swinging there at the end of the thread. She retrieved it before it fell away from the thread to the floor, and took another careful stitch. Then another.

When she looked out into the mews again, the Yellow Lady had gone. The gardener was still directly beneath the window, coaxing the long narrow strip of garden towards some improbable perfection. Already, a herbery had been created in the time since she had begun sitting by the window and the plants now sprouted leafy fronds, heedless of the advancing winter. She wondered when—if ever—he worked in the spacious area at the front of the nursing home. Or had they come to some arrangement about that? She hoped the nursing home appreciated their luck. It seemed they had drawn a policeman with a genuine feeling for a garden. It was to be hoped that they would find someone clever enough to keep it up—afterwards.

Could anyone suspect the real truth?

She moved back from the window, not that it would make any difference. Aaron would know where she was, right down to the very room. He would know, too, how many police were guarding her—or trying to. Probably, it would just amuse him.

She was the bait in the trap. Tethered here by the window, while they all waited. The stake-out.

The Judas goat, who led the unsuspecting lambs into the slaughterhouse. The only one to emerge unscathed at the other side. Until the very end.

Now she was being used as the Judas goat to draw Aaron himself into the abattoir. In a way, something in her admitted the justice, the fittingness, of it.

Wasn't that the way Aaron had used her?

The sun had come out as the ship sailed into Southampton Water.

"England is putting on her smiling face for you," Belle said. "I'm *so* glad."

Belle could get away with remarks like that. Amy and Ginny had exchanged amused, appreciative grins, and then turned back to the rail. In the distance, still far enough away to seem totally unreal, a toytown coast slid past them. Houses perched on miniature cliffs, tiny automobiles moved along white threads that must be roads, or perhaps highways. Occasionally, matchstick figures lifted an arm in greeting as the flagship sailed by.

It seemed impossible that a full-sized country could lie beyond those Lilliputian approaches; that, by nightfall, they would be in a city, in the centre of one of the world's great capitals.

A sensation of total unreality—of desolation, almost—swept over Amy. Surely, it couldn't be the beginning of home-sickness—not on her first trip away from home? She glanced at Ginny again and saw that Ginny felt it, too. Unnerved, she looked around at the others crowding the rail.

The clicking of cameras, the cacophony of voices, betrayed the uneasiness of people trying to impose their own image on events around them. An image they increasingly felt was dwindling as an alien unknown shore drew near to engulf them.

It cheered her slightly to realize that the others felt the same way. Most of them. There were some who stood quietly smiling, watching the coastal panorama with a peaceful satisfaction. It wasn't alien to them, it was home.

Belle was one of these. She turned from the rail with a proprietary air. "How do you like it?" she asked.

They consulted each other's eyes, and Ginny spoke. "It looks awfully small," she said.

"It is." Belle's laugh bubbled up. She was on her own territory, now it was her turn to laugh at the mistakes, the small gaucheries. "You're looking at the Isle of Wight." She waved a hand towards the landfall looming up on the far side of the ship. "That's England over there."

The flat was in a huge Victorian conglomerate on the Knightsbridge/Kensington borders. If they were not so tired from the excitement of landing and the journey, they would have been overawed. As it was, they stood in the lobby, weighed down by their luggage, and surveyed it all with a detachment that passed for keeping their cool.

"Over here—" Belle led them past a leather-covered hall porter's chair and into an elaborate ironwork cage which must be the elevator.

"We're on the fourth floor—" Belle pushed the button.

"Wait a minute," Ginny said. "The doors aren't shut tight." She tugged at them.

"That's all right," Belle said. "Actually they needn't be shut at all. The lift will still work."

"Isn't that awfully dangerous?" Ginny asked. "An elevator shouldn't move while the doors are open—and the doors shouldn't be able to open when the elevator's moving."

"You Americans are so safety-conscious." Belle was amused. "It's all right if you're careful—why, my cousins and I used to play with it on rainy days. Mind you, we were careful not to let Gran'mère catch us. And, anyway, over here it's called a lift."

"I don't know—" Ginny refused to be diverted. "I still think it's awfully dangerous."

"This is nothing," Belle assured her. "Wait until we have our week in Paris and you see some of those *ascenseurs*—they're really hair-raising."

"This is bad enough for me, thanks." Ginny watched dubiously as the lift, slowly but inexorably, moved upwards and jarred to a halt.

"Here we are," Belle said, opening the door. "Home!"

They'd known, in a vague way, that Belle came from

money—but not how much. Reflected as dark enchanted shadows in the depths of the great gilt-framed pierglass above the console-table, they watched Belle sweep across the hall, making the place her own.

"Oh, good, there's post—no, mail—no—we're in *my* country now." Belle laughed, sweeping up the handful of letters waiting in the footed silver salver beside an exquisite silver candelabrum on the console-table. Antique silver, with the glow that only generations of polishing and cherishing could give—rather like Belle herself.

"Two for you." Belle passed the red-white-and-blue airmail envelopes to Ginny. "One for Amy—and the rest, I'm afraid, for me." The rest seemed to be mostly local. Only two were airmail and Belle tossed them down to spill carelessly across the shining surface of the console. "I'll read them later," she said, tearing open one of the local letters.

Belle swept them down the corridor with her and flung open double doors near the end. Champagne in an ice bucket. A roaring fire. A cold collation.

"Darling Sybilla!" Belle said. "I must ring up and thank her instantly. You'll be all right—?" Halfway out of the room, she turned. "You're not starving, or anything, I mean? Do start, if you like. I'll only be a minute. I'll ring her from my room." Barely waiting for their assurances that they could manage by themselves for a few minutes, she left them.

"Well, well, well," Ginny said, unbuttoning her raincoat. "Where's Jeeves, do you think? Wasn't it a bit remiss of him not to have greeted Our Miss Belle at the door?"

"He's probably up in York at the manor house, taking care of darling Gran'mère Sybilla." Amy slipped into Ginny's mood and grinned at her. "After all, Our Miss Belle will be going up there first thing in the morning. His place is up there. He's too good to waste on a couple of visiting school friends. At the same time—" she took another look around—"whoever has been taking care of things here hasn't done too badly by us."

"I'll say they haven't." Ginny began a slow perambulation of the room, coming back in front of the fire and shrugging out of her coat. "This is what it means, isn't it?" she asked.

"This is what it really means. You and I have always known what it is to have enough money, but this is the difference between enough money and real wealth." Ginny stared reflectively at the farther wall. "It's having a Lely, not because it's a Lely or a good investment, but because it's a picture of dear old great-great-great-great-somebody-or-other, and Lely just happened to be the fashionable one to go to at the time she wanted her portrait painted."

"This is the difference," Amy agreed, longing to pick up at least one of the china figures parading along the mantelpiece and see if they really did have the Chelsea red anchor on them—probably bought while still warm from the kiln. She didn't quite dare, however. Belle would be back at any moment, and she didn't want to be caught acting like a crass American tourist.

She turned to Ginny, looking for the familiar and the reassuring, but Ginny was looking back at her with a strange and unfamiliar expression—as though she were straining to see something that was not quite there. Then, catching her eye, Ginny shrugged and laughed.

"I just had the oddest feeling for a minute," Ginny said. "You know—sort of, 'See Naples and die'; see London—and—"

"She hasn't changed a bit!" Belle burst back into the room. "I don't know why I should have expected her to. Except that, when one has been away for two years, and so many things seem to have happened, it seems as though every*thing* and every*one* must be different."

"That's just because you've been living so much," Ginny said. "Your grandmother won't change because she's done all her living, she's set in her mould now. You're still fluid."

"You make me sound like a sloppy jelly!" Belle shuddered, then laughed again. "You're right about Gran'mère's having lived—though I'm not sure you ought to put it in the past tense—'

"You mean, 'There's like in the old girl yet'?" Amy felt she had to make some contribution to the conversation, perhaps to shake off the uneasy feeling that would not leave her—or to keep the others from noticing it.

"And then some! Gran'mère's indestructible, you know. If a Japanese prison camp couldn't finish her—and she was no spring chicken then—nothing could! I'm not sure anything about her would surprise me. Not even if she suddenly sprang a fourth husband on us all!"

"You're bragging again," Ginny said, but her grin was tolerant. They'd brag, too, if they possessed a forebear like that. Their grandmothers had been pleasant, placid women who played bridge, watched television, enjoyed morning coffee klatches. All very well, but you had to admit it, ordinary.

The exploits of Gran'mère Sybilla had become almost legendary in their circle. They loved hearing about her, marvelled that she could have turned out a late offspring as dull and colourless as Belle's mother, but secretly bet that Belle would turn into something special before too many more years went past. Greatness often skipped a generation, didn't it?

"Oh, I *wish* you'd change your minds and come up to York with me," Belle said. "Why don't you? Gran'mère would love to have you—it wouldn't be any trouble at all. Come and get the train with me in the morning. *Do!*"

Briefly tempted, Amy and Ginny exchanged glances again and tacitly decided to stand by their original decision. Legends, like conflagrations, were best viewed from a distance.

There was a quick rap before the door opened. Amy didn't look up from her needlework. *Aaron wouldn't bother to knock.*

Someone slipped inside and closed the door quickly. She still didn't look up.

"You're a fine one, I must say." Little Nurse Jellicoe sounded almost aggrieved. "Do you know you're the only patient in this whole place who never looks up when anyone comes into the room?"

She looked down into the mews, empty, deserted. The window was only open a few inches, despite the soft mildness of the early autumn afternoon. *Aaron would not come in through the door—he'd use the window.*

"They call them patients." Nurse Jellicoe was advancing into the room, coming within her restricted area of vision. Carefully, she took another stitch in the dog's tail—the dog which should have been white, but was emerging as a silvery-grey ghost hound. She must have chosen just the wrong shade of silk.

"Patients," Nurse Jellicoe repeated, coming closer. "*Impa*tients, is more like it. You're the only one the word *patient* could apply to. The others are all champing at the bit to get out of here and be gone. Don't you ever want to get away?"

She looked up then, meeting Nurse Jellicoe's worried grey eyes calmly. "No," she said truthfully.

"Oh, come now." By this time, Nurse Jellicoe ought to be used to receiving the wrong answers, but she continued advancing towards the window warily, as though there might be booby traps concealed beneath the smooth shiny linoleum. "And what about your sister? Aren't you going to ask me how she is today?"

"You'll tell me anyway." That was the truth, too.

"Well," Nurse Jellicoe admitted it with a shrug. "There's no change. She's just the same, neither better nor worse."

How much worse could you get? Only dead, that was all. For Ginny, lively, vital Ginny, that might be preferable.

"You ought to go up and visit her," Nurse Jellicoe prodded. "All this time, and you haven't been to see her once."

"Has she asked for me?"

"She can't talk," Nurse Jellicoe said, "I've told you that. Can't . . . or won't. If you went up, we might find out which."

She turned away. By rights, Ginny ought never to want to see her again. She would not inflict herself on Ginny when Ginny was helpless to protest.

"An awful business . . ." Nurse Jellicoe trawled the line automatically, although she must know by this time that it would bring no response, no rush of girlish confidence. "Well . . ." with another shrug, she abandoned it. "I've just dodged in for a minute—Matron's doing the rounds with the obstetrician."

The mews was deserted now. The gardener had abandoned his post in favour of an early lunch (or could he keep watch on the mews from wherever he ate?) and only the solitary mechanic still wrestled stubbornly with the innards of his ancient automobile. Movement again caught her eye—the yellow door opening once more. This time, the sullen au pair stalked into the mews, slamming the yellow door behind her in a defiant gesture that lost something of its defiance when one knew that the mistress of the house was not within.

Strange, that the Yellow Lady would put up with such a moody unfriendly creature. You wouldn't expect it of her somehow. You'd think she'd like to surround herself with laughing happy people, you'd think—

She pulled herself up short. She had no right to form an opinion of anyone—least of all from just occasional glimpses. Perhaps the au pair was a very good worker and not so sullen as she appeared. Perhaps the Yellow Lady didn't notice servants enough to know what their temperament was.

She couldn't say. She had forfeited all right to ever decide anything about anyone, ever again. *She had no judgment.*